William Peoples

Peoples' Pocket Stair Builder

and Carpenters' Hand Book

William Peoples

Peoples' Pocket Stair Builder
and Carpenters' Hand Book

ISBN/EAN: 9783337381196

Printed in Europe, USA, Canada, Australia, Japan

Cover: Foto ©Andreas Hilbeck / pixelio.de

More available books at **www.hansebooks.com**

PEOPLES'
POCKET STAIR BUILDER

—AND—

Carpenters' Hand Book.

CONTAINING FIFTY-ONE PLATES, AND OVER FIVE HUNDRED FIGURES, WITH A FULL DESCRIPTION FOR EVERY FIGURE.

—EMBRACING—

Carpenters' and Stair-Builders' Geometry, Problems, Conic Sections, Cylindric Sections, as applied in the construction of the Wreath part of Hand-rail. Rules for the Measurement of Surfaces. The Construction of Ladders, Box Stairs, Dog-legged, Open Newel, Cylinder, Circular and Elliptical Staircases.

ROOFING—Hip, Valley, and Jack Rafters. Purlins, Splayed Work, and Bevels for the same. Transverse Strength of Joist and Beams, and easy formulas for their safe load.

ALSO,

Excavators, Stone and Brick Masons, Plasterers and Carpenters' Memoranda; with a variety of miscellaneous information, useful in the practice of the Architect and Builder; together with a Glossary of Architectural Terms, and General Index.

BY WILLIAM PEOPLES.

DAVID WILLIAMS COMPANY, Publishers, 232-238 William St., NEW YORK.

PREFACE.

For some years it has been the aim of the author to prepare a small book for the young stair builder, carpenter and joiner, as a handy reference, that would be to them what Haswell and Trautwine are to the engineer. Having now worked at the trade of carpentry and stair-building 43 years, the author is free to say from experience, that a little book of this kind for the pocket is a much needed acquisition for the benefit of the apprentice and journeyman as well.

So much has been said on the subject that it is next to impossible to be wholly original, and no claim of that nature is preferred. It is simply an arrangement of ideas, gleaned from the various work of authorities, and modified by the author's practice, embodied in book form.

If this little volume should lead the student of carpentry and stair-building to study the subject carefully, and be induced to practice the same with pleasure and profit to himself, the author will be satisfied that his efforts have not been in vain.

The young man should provide himself with a drawing board, say 24″ by 36″ and ¾″ thick, with two battens across the back to keep the board true; joint the same square and straight, and to a parallel width. Provide a set of draughting instruments, T square about 3′ long, and two triangles, one 45° and the other 60°, a dozen thumb tacks, a 6-H pencil and rubber. Use India ink for inking. The instruments can all be bought separately, and if the young man cannot afford to purchase a full set of good tools, then buy one at a time, for one good tool is worth more than a chest full of bad ones.

The apprentice should study these plates one at a time, by drawing each figure to a larger scale, either quarter, half or full size; let all leisure time be applied in this way, and if persevered in, the success of the young man is as sure as the sun shines or the earth moves.

Peter Nicholson's schooling was very limited (only three years) ending at twelve, and yet by persevering industry he mastered the higher branches of mathematics, and produced the "Carpenters Guide," that was for half a century the carpenters and joiners palladium. Then let not the young man get discouraged, but apply his mind and his heart to his trade, studying the same in all its branches, first the rudiments or first principles, then the higher branches: if so, he cannot fail of attaining the highest skill, and demanding the best wages.

Mind, there is no royal road to this end; all spare time from his regular duties should be applied at the draught-board and his books, while serving his apprenticeship. What is true of Mr. Nicholson is also true of hundreds of other self-made men; and yet at, or near the end of the nineteenth century, when many are running to and fro and knowledge is being increased, when mechanics and professions are opening their store houses of knowledge and scattering it to the four winds, through the press and other avenues the young man of to-day has a comparatively easy task over those who have gone before.

The author recommends the study of the prismatic solid in connection with his drawing, as the best means to gain a thorough knowledge of hand-railing; for in the solid the reason for every line may be more easily understood. The use of the trammel is also recommended to trace the curves of face-mould for all platform and level landing cylinders up to 24″ diameter and all over that diameter and for winders, where the mould is increased in length, the bisection of the chord and use of ordinates is found to be the most simple and convenient method to find the trace of the mould. This, the author believes, is the first time this method has been recommended in a general way.

Proving the angle of tangents on the face-mould is also recommended; for if the parallelogram be incorrect on the diagonal or chord, the joints of wreath piece will be incorrect, and the result a bad piece of work.

The manner of taking the dimensions in the building and trimming the well, together with instructions in laying out the stairs and preparing them at the bench ready to put up, is explained, so that the young man with a little study and practice may soon learn to do the work. Also the method of taking the lengths of straight rail, from the stairs, when stepped up, and jointing and dressing the rail at the bench ready to be set up in the building, is shown and recommended as the best and most economical.

The carpenter and joiner will find some useful information in framing hip and valley rafters and bevels for the same, and also a method to find the bevels for any kind of splayed work; also formulas for the strength of joist and their safe load.

A brief history of stair building is also added, together with a list of nearly all the different authors that have written on the subject in our language, which the author believes will be interesting to the stair-builder.

A glossary of terms and an index is also added to make the book complete.

THE AUTHOR.

CONTENTS.

COMPRISING IN ALL THE DIFFERENT PLATES, 516 FIGURES.

History of Stair Building.

As our country is comparatively new, being now 1892, only four hundred years since its discovery by Christopher Columbus, [1492.] Therefore, for a more extended knowledge of the art, we must study the earlier history of architecture among the Egyptians, Chaldeans, Assyrians, Persians, Greeks, Romans, French, German and English nations.

EGYPTIANS. Some of the pyramids were erected 3500 to 3000 B. C.; the chambers inside were accessible by means of narrow inclined passages. Stairs do not appear to have ever been used in the pyramids, unless perhaps, in some opened recently; but in the tombs of the same date flights of steps are always found.[1]

CHALDEANS. Their temples were sometimes built with off-sets, forming a terrace every story, and reached by flights of steps or inclined planes from one story to the next, as in the case of the Tower of Babel, erected 2247 B. C., which is described in one of the mosaics at St. Marks,[2] Venice, showing inclined boards for obtaining access to scaffolding, instead of ladders.[3] Herodotus[4] says, "numbers of houses were three and four stories high.

ASSYRIANS. Owing to the scarcity of stone, sun-dried brick were used for walls, and probably wood for roofing and interior finish—hence their buildings have long since disappeared, the ruins scarcely being visible. The ruins of the largest royal palace at Nineveh, erected by Sennacherib about 704 B. C., show the remains of an inclined plane, ten feet wide; close by is also seen, the ruins of an inclined terraced temple.

PERSIANS. The ruins of Persipolis, the ancient capitol of Persia, show the palaces to be reached by the grandest double-flight of platform stairs in the world.[5] The steps leading to the first terrace are 25′ 7″ wide; the rise is 4″ high by 14″ in the tread;[6] there are fifty-five rises unconcealed on one side of the platform, and forty-eight to the landing; from four to six steps being cut from a single block of marble. A second double-flight leads to the next terrace; steps 16′ long, 3″ rise and 14″ tread, having thirty-two steps to each flight; ten to fourteen steps being cut from a single block.[7] The sides of the steps are walled up and decorated with sculptures, representing processions bringing tribute to the King. These palaces formed one of the most imposing groups of buildings ever erected, and is said to have been partially burned by Alexander the Great, after his conquest of Persia 330 B. C.

---

1. N. Clifford Ricker, Professor of Architecture, in the Illinois University.
2. Erected 976—1071 A. D.
3. Marwick's History of Stair Cases.
4. Flourished 484—408 B. C.
5. Encyclopædia Britannica.
6. Gwilt's Dictionary of Architecture.
7. Stuart's Dictionary of Architecture.

JERUSALEM. Solomon's Temple was erected 1011—1004 B. C. Ezekiel B. C. 774, in his description of the temple locates nine flights of steps. This temple was destroyed by the Chaldeans under Nebuchadnezzar, B. C. 588. We read that when the Queen of Sheba saw "the ascent by which Solomon went up to the house of the Lord. there was no more spirit in her." Among the ruins of these more eastern nations, nothing is more remarkable than these great flights of steps. The builders of those days among the Jews, Chaldeans and Persians so far as we know, were the only people who really understood the value of this feature. The Egyptians seem wholly to have neglected it, and the Greeks to have cared little about it, but was not so at Nineveh and Persipolis,[8] for from the indistinct traces left, the stairs must have been one of the most important parts of the design.

MEXICO. The Pyramids of Mexico resemble those of Assyria. being terraced and having inclined planes. The Pyramid of Papantla was seven stories high, with five flights of steps leading to the cell, which formerly existed on the top.[9] This prehistoric structure was built of stone. Baked brick was mostly used in the building of these pyramids. See Prescott's Conquest of Mexico.

GREECE. In the Ancient Doric Temple of Concord, at Agrigentum, Island of Sicily, [when erected unknown] a flight of forty-one steps[10] leads to the roof from near the entrance; they are close, being constructed in the thickness of the wall. Similar stairs are said to be found in the temple of Jupiter at Olympia, erected about 435 B. C.

The Syracuse Theatre, erected 480—406 B. C., had eight radiating flights of steps.

The Temple of Jupiter at Aizana, has a grand flight of outside steps 98′ 6″ wide, erected about 146 B. C.

ROME. The ancient Romans borrowed largely from the Greeks and Etruscans; the temples and theatres of the Greeks served as models, from which they improved and built up their capitol. Vitruvius,[11] however, makes no mention of stairs as being an important adjunct of the dwelling house; if the stair case had been of much consideration, he would have most likely described them. He gives the numbers 3, 4 and 5 for a right angle triangle, and suggests the hypothenuse of the same as a good proportion for the inclination of a flight of stairs. Rule. divide the whole height into three equal parts, and take five of those parts for the length of the inclination.

The stairs in the Pantheon[12] are triangular on plan, so were they in the Baths of Caracalla.[13] In the Baths of Diocletian[14] the stairs were built between walls, in the same manner as we build box stairs between plastered partitions. It is said that 40,000 Christians were compelled to erect this structure to appease the wrath of this Roman tyrant.

The summit of the historic column of Trajan[15] is reached by a winding staircase, containing 185 steps; they are carved out of solid blocks of marble twelve feet in length, and five feet thick.

---

8.   James Ferguson's History of Architecture, Vol. 1; Page 192.
9.   N. Clifford Ricker.
10. Joseph Gwilt's Encyclopædia of Architecture.
11. Architect, he flourished under Augustus Cæsar, B. C. 15; he wrote the earliest special treatise on architecture extant.
12. Erected probably 26 B. C.
13. Finished about 217 A. D,
14. Erected about 302 A. D.
15. Erected 114 A. D.

The country house at Pompeii has steps with a rise of twelve inches.[16] The Romans, also the Greeks, prided in wide outside steps at the main entrance of their temples.

The magnificent temple of the Sun God at Baalbec,[17] has a flight of outside steps 164 feet wide between the buttresses.

Of the thirty odd different kinds of artisans, advertised for by Constantine the Great, for the building of Constantinople,[18] it appears "stair hands"[19] were required. The towers and minarets of the Mahometan Mosques, had winding inclined planes, and winding stairs to reach the upper stories; sometimes the stairs were built winding around the outside, at other times they were built in the thickness of the walls.

ITALY. In this beautiful land of art, during the middle ages from 1000 to 1500 A. D., the main stair cases were often constructed on the outside of their buildings, the climate being more favorable than in the more northern countries.

In court yards they were often built alongside of the wall, and supported on pillars and rampant arches, sometimes they were protected with a raking roof, supported by columns, set on pedestals at regular intervals, and balustraded between the pedestals; these outside steps were often treated very artistically for dwellings, public buildings and palaces, as they led to the principal floor; sometimes they were double, starting from opposite sides, and landing on a spacious platform at the main entrance to the building; this treatment offered a good chance for architectural display. Marble was mostly used in the construction of these stairs. Previous to 1500 A. D., very little importance was attached to the inside stairs; they were commonly built in the thickness of the walls.

The Campanile or Leaning Tower, at Pisa,[20] is circular on plan; the external diameter is 53 feet, and the height is 183 feet; the walls are 13 feet thick, and the stairway is built in their thickness, so were the stairs in the beautiful Campanile,[21] near the Florence Cathedral.[22]

The open newel staircase is of Italian origin, and was the invention of Nicola of Pisa,[23] 1205—1278; the idea was afterwards utilized and improved by the renaissance architects of Italy, from the beginning of the sixteenth century.

In the Belvedere of Pope Julius II, 1503—1518, an inclined plane or turn-pike stair case of five revolutions leads to the upper story; the stairs, or inclined plane was carried on continuous cylindric vaulting, and is supported on the side next the well by eight columns in each tier.[24] The architect, Andrew Palladio, 1518—1580, improved the art of stair-casing during his day.[25]

---

16. Stuart's Dictionary.
17. Erected it is supposed by Antoniuus Pius 138—161 A. D.
18. Founded about 328 A. D.
19. See London Building News, 1890.
20. Built 1174 A. D.
21. Erected at the beginning of the Fourteenth Century.
22. The Campanile in the Piazza of St. Marks, Venice; the height to the loggia is about 177 feet, and is reached by a ramp or inclined plane, making thirty-six rounds; the foundation was laid in 888 A. D.
23. A noted Architect of Pisa.
24. Marwick's History and Construction of Stair-cases.
25. He says 'stair-cases will be commendable if they are clear, ample and commodious to ascend; inviting, as it were, people to go up. They will be clear if they have a bright and equally diffuse light; they will be sufficiently ample if they do not seem scanty and narrow to the size and quality of the fabric. But they should never be less than four feet in width, that two persons may pass each other. They will be convenient with respect to the whole building if the arches under them can be used for domestic purposes; and with respect to persons, if their ascent is not too steep and difficult, to avoid which, the steps should be twice as broad as high."

Many circular and elliptical stair-cases were constructed throughout Italy, of a stately and monumental character. The Farnese Palace stairs is 73′ by 28′; that in Carlo Mademo's Mattei Palace, with its marble walls and rich stucco ceilings, 65′ by 49′; that in Ferdinando Fugo's Palace Corsine 72′ by 45′; while those in the workhouse at Genoa, and in the stupendous unfinished Royal Palace at Caserta, Naples, are no less than 115′ by 63′, and 163′ by 85′ respectively. Scamozzi,[26] 1552—1616, mentions a double winding staircase made by Pietro del Boyo and John Cossin so contrived that two persons, one ascending and the other descending, should never meet. This style of a stair-case was common through France in Mediæval times. A patent was taken out in our own country for this kind of a staircase, by W. J. Keim, New York, 1868.

The well of the staircase in the Palace Braschi, by C. Morelli,[27] is quadrangular, 46′ by 34′, having straight flights of the open newel style, similar to those of to-day. The steps are ten feet long each in one piece, supported by the walls at one end, and resting on rampant arches, springing from columns at the outer strings; the columns are sixteen in number, and of red, oriental granite; they stand on pedestals, which receive a broad railing and heavy baluster, which, together with the steps, are of white marble.

The wall side is decorated with pilasters opposite each column and a half balustrade corresponding to the outer railing; arches spring from the columns to the pilasters across the soffit of the stairs, forming domical vaulting which is divided into panels, and enriched with beautiful frescoes. The spandrels of the arches are paneled and ornamented with carvings; niches are formed in the walls for the display of statuary. This design of Morelli's is one of the most beautiful staircases in Rome. A fine illustration of two stages of this stair case may be seen in Marwick's History of Staircases.

FRANCE. During the first century A. D., the stairs in France were constructed similar to those of Italy, Outside steps were sometimes built at right angles to the building, at other times parallel to the same resting on arches, supported by piers; sometimes they were roofed over to protect them from the rain. During the first centuries the tower stairs were built in the thickness of the walls.

The French were partial to the winding stairs, they are to be found in most of their buildings throughout the country, from about 1000 to 1500 A. D. On account of so many towers, mostly square or circular on plan, the winding staircase suited best, and also they required less room in their construction. They, like the Italians first built the well for the staircase square, circular or octagonal on the plan; later on for their public buildings, the oblong well was occupied with the open newel staircase, having straight flights and quarter pace landings.

After 1540 A. D., the French Renaissance style became more classical and dignified. The leading French architects traveled extensively in Italy, from which they gathered ideas and improved on them to suit their taste and country. The churches, chateaus and palaces are monuments of their genius and skill as architects and builders.

---

26. Stuart's Dictionary of Architecture. Scamozzi is said to be the inventor of the two-foot joint rule, also the angular Ionic Volute.
27. Flourished 1780 A. D.

The Chateau at Chateaudun,[28] is chiefly noted for its magnificent stone winding staircase, one of the finest ever constructed.[29] The well is partly square and partly octagonal on plan; the steps wind around a solid newel built of stone; the steps are built in the newel and walls at the ends, each tread is a solid stone, rectangular in section throughout, giving to the soffit the same appearance as above; the tread and rise is without nosing and scotia,[30] as was the custom in Mediaeval times. The shaft of the newel is deeply cut away, to form a bold projecting half hand-rail and string, which winds spirally around the newel; the space between the rail and projecting base or string remains plain; at the junction of the steps, with the newel on the underside, another set of mouldings project from the newel, forming a cornice; the shaft between the rail and cornice is ornamental, with slender columns and panels between the columns; the panels are elaborately enriched with carved arabesques. On the wall side, engaged columns fill each angle, extending from the steps and floors to a projecting cornice, that fills the angle made by the steps and walls; at the upper end the newel is finished with a cap, from which spring arched semicircular groins, to connect the columns in the angles on the wall sides, this vaulting gives support to the roof, and distributes the weight of the roof and vaulting, partly on the newel and partly on the walls, and gives to the whole a beautiful and appropriate finish.

Many beautiful staircases of the Renaissance period may be found throughout France, erected after the beginning of the sixteenth century.

In the Chateau Chambord,[31] a double staircase is erected, the well is thirty feet in diameter; the stairs wind around a hollow newel ten feet in diameter, which ends at the terrace level; a smaller stairs is built in this hollow newel extending beyond the terrace, where it is terminated by an elegant circular arcade crowned by a circular tower, this being beautifully decorated with classical columns and flying buttresses. These double staircases were common throughout France, they were built of wood and also of stone. Owing to the large size of newel required in this kind of stairs, to obtain a fair width of tread at the narrow ends, a third winding stairs was sometimes constructed inside the newel; at other times the space is divided into rooms, and at other times it is used as a well. The French and Germans[32] often made their steps and rise from solid oak timber, quartering the log, and turning the heart side up; this made a solid and noiseless staircase. Some of these wooden stairs, built during the middle ages, are still to be seen in some of the old turrets throughout that country.

Two wooden staircases in the Holy Chapel in Paris, are probably the oldest in existence, being constructed in the thirteenth century.[33]

ENGLAND. In England the transition began in the reign of Henry VIII, 1509—1547, from the Norman conquest 1066, up to and during part of his reign, close, or blind newel stairs walled

---

28. A fine illustration of two stages of this staircase may be seen in the American Architect and Building News; of September 17, 1881. Erected about 1498--1515 A. D.

29. N. Clifford Ricker.

30. Parker's Glossary of Architecture.

31. Founded 1526 A. D.

32. The Stadhaus at Leyden, Holland, has a fine outside stairs built at the beginning of the seventeenth century. See illustration in the American Architect, for March 27th, 1886.

33. Marwick's History of Staircases.

up on the sides, and arched over in the form of a tunnel was the prevailing style; at the angles heavy piers projected from the walls, finished with base, and cap from which spring groins; the piers were low, and took the form of newels.

In the reign of Queen Elizabeth 1558—1603, the open newel staircase became more studied; the blind straight flights between walls were modified so as to admit light above the hand-rail, and in place of balusters the space was close and sometimes plastered under the rail. This gave place to a more ornamental construction, broad short flights, with elaborate and heavy carved newels at the angles, supporting vases, baskets of flowers, miniature statues, columns, lions or griffins. In this reign the newels formed one of the chief decorative and constructive elements of the design. The hand-rails were broad and massive; under the rail was filled in with fancy cut scroll work, or heavy turned balusters set on a close string, which was paneled and ornamented with bold carved work, and finished on the lower edge with hanging scroll, terminating at the newels in the form of pendants.

This and the succeeding reigns of James I, 1603—1625, also Charles I reign 1625—1649, the balustrade and newel occupied at no other period a position of such conspicuous importance.

The decorative feature of the Elizabethan staircase arrived in this reign at its zenith, and the best period had passed; after this the style had bcome more debased.

Style, like history, repeats itself; at the present and near the close of the nineteenth century, we are copying after the style of Elizabeth in our staircases, with short flights, close outer strings around a quadangular well hole, with massive and elaborate carved newels, sometimes extending to the ceiling, and finished with arches; at other times the newel is surmounted with statuary of some antique design.

Serious objections are urged against this style of staircasing— too many quirks and projections for catching and harboring the dust, and the expense to renovate and keep them in a good sanitary condition; indeed, after a few years in use, it is impossible to avoid the disease-breeding accumulations. For this reason this style of staircase should be avoided in domestic architecture. The open string, and return nosings, with circular turns in the angles in place of newels, and finished with turned balusters and a continuous hand-rail, gives a more cheerful aspect to the hall, with less expense and better health to the occupants.

This style of open string and continuous hand-rail was a great improvement over the old ramp and knee hand-rail and square well hole. In England, about the beginning of the eighteenth century, the solid newel for winding stairs, gave place to the open circular well hole, with rail and balusters, thus admitting light and air, and a better sanitary condition of the building.

The first lines published for constructing a continuous hand-rail, over a circular well hole containing winders, was by HALFPENNY, of London, 1725. The method is very much mystified[3][4] but shows an effort.

The ingenious MR. FRANCIS PRICE, was the next in 1735. He gives a method to draw the straight ramp and knee, also a wreathed ramp and knee over a quarter circle on plan; also a falling mould for squaring the wreath part; also a method to find the length of long and short balusters under the wreath rail, laid off from the center line of rail on the stretchout. He also gives a

31. See Peter Nicholson's Dictionary of Architecture, by Lomax. Page 76.

method for building up the rail, by glueing blocks to suit the falling line of the rail; he also gave lines for the construction of the scroll, and showed how to ease off an angle, by the intersection of lines; he made use of ordinates to find the contour of raking mouldings.

MR. LANGLEY, 1738, was the next. He shows the face-mould for the quadrant to be one-fourth of the ellipsis, having the joints of face-mould on the major and minor axis of the ellipsis, and of course the plank would be canted only one way, without any spring; this would require very thick plank to form the wreath rail over winders, spaced equally around the well hole. He made use of ordinates in the construction of the face-mould.

MR. WILLIAM SALMON, 1748, was the next author. He follows Mr. Price, and gives the lines for a face-mould over winders around a circular well hole, without springing the plank. He mentions for the first time a custom among workmen, the method of glueing up the rail with thin strips over a drum made to the concave diameter of rail, when enough strips were thus laminated for the breadth of the rail, and the glue had perfectly dried, the twist was taken from the drum and afterwards moulded to the required shape, and set up all in one piece over the winders.[35]

MR. ABRAHAM SWAN, 1750 came next, and was followed by MR. WILLIAM PAINE, 1774. In the "Practical Builder" he draws the face-mould for the turnout wreath-piece at the scroll, in the same way as shown by Mr. Swan; he used ordinates at right angles to the hypothenuse of pitchboard. At this time he gave two methods how to obtain a backing for a hip rafter, either straight or curved. Later on, he issued the "Builder," illustrating various kinds of stairs, and the manner of drawing face-mould for the same, by using ordinates. For winders, in a semicircular staircase, having straight steps above and below, he shows the face-mould drawn so as to make the wreath for the semicircle all in one piece; the transverse axis of the face mould being plumb over the chord of semicircle; the face edge of the plank would coincide with the diameter of the semicircle, and the joints connecting the straight part would be spliced joints, for the plank would be canted only the one way; hence very thick stuff would be required to avoid kinks in the twist part of the rail. Like his predecessors, he discovered the wreath-piece to be a portion of a cylindric section, and the curve of face-mould to be elliptical; but what portion of the ellipsis required for each correct face-mould remained a mystery.

MR. PETER NICHOLSON,[36] in 1792 published for the first time his "Carpenters Guide," and subsequent editions down to 1835. He cleared away some of the mist connected with the construction of the face-mould; he discovered how to draw the elliptic curve through three points, which he termed resting

---

35. In our country MR. ASHER BENJAMIN, 1792, superintended the erection of a circular staircase in the State House, at Hartford, Connecticut. The rail was glued up of strips one-eighth of an inch thick, which was claimed to be the first geometrical rail, over a circular well hole, constructed in this country.

36. MR. PETER NICHOLSON was a native of North Britain; he was born on the 20th of July, 1765, in the Parish of Preston Kirk, in the County of East Lothian; at a very early age he evinced a strong mechanical genius, and also a turn for drawing whatever presented itself to him, whether of animated nature or otherwise; three years instruction was the most he ever had at a country school, which he left at the age of twelve. Although his scholastic instructions were very limited, he was bent on inquiry, and that decidedly of a mathe-

points; one point at each end, and the other *at, or near the center*
of mould; [not certain as to the exact location.] This new
method determined that portion of the ellipsis for the face-mould,
over a quarter circle, to contain the minor axis, and hence, the
mould was wider at each end than at some intermediate point,
which was equal to the true width of the rail; this required the
plank to be canted two ways, and was termed the "springing" of
the plank. In all former authors the narrow part of face-mould
was always at one of the joints, for a quarter circle on plan,
and the plank was canted but one way.

Not being certain as to the exact location of the center resting
point, left the system in doubt and made the subject an abstruse
and difficult task for the learner, and also for the more practical
man; the cutting plane, or plane of plank would sometimes be
correct, at other times wide of the mark.

In 1849 MR. JEAKES published his orthogonal system of
hand-railing. MR. ASHPITEL published a work on hand-railing
in 1851. In 1853, MR. JOSEPH GALPIN and MR. LANGLEY
BANKS published a treatise on stair-casing, in which the systems
practiced by several stair builders of London were published. We
will notice the systems of Messrs. Clark, Foster, Weston and
Perry.

MR. WILLIAM CLARK'S method to find the face-mould, was
on the orthogonal or square cut principle; he makes use of a
parallel mould, cuts the joints square to the tangents, and finds
the joint bevels in the same manner as Mr. Riddle in 1855. Mr.
Clark illustrates his principle with card board.

MR. FOSTER also shows a face-mould on the orthogonal
system, the mould being parallel in width.

MR. WESTON'S method in some particulars is similar to Mr.
R. Riddell's in his 1855 and 1859 editions. He shows the development of tangents in elevation from the ground plan; he finds
the angle of tangents for the face-mould correctly, and also the
joint bevels from the tangents in elevation; he makes the joints
at right angles to the tangents; he takes a point from the diagonal
on plan, for the center of all face-moulds[37] at the angle of

---

matical nature. At the age of twelve he assisted his father in his
business, but did not relish the occupation of a stone mason, and at
the end of a year he was bound to serve for four years as an apprentice to a cabinet maker, in the neighboring village of Linton. During
his apprenticeship, young Nicholson employed every leisure moment
in improving his mind. He studied algebra assiduously, from day-
light in the summer mornings till six, when he went to work, as well
as in the evenings when his labors were over. After serving to the
full extent of his time, he went to Edinburgh and worked at his trade,
and studied the higher branches of mathematics.

At the age of twenty, he came to London, where his uncle named
Hastil, carried on an extensive business as a builder; here he still
pursued his mathematical studies together with drawing; soon his
fame spread among his fellow workman, who, anxious to improve
themselves, solicited to become his pupils; he opened a school with
about ten, the fame of his teaching soon brought an influx of pupils.
This gave Mr. Nicholson more leisure, which he devoted to the invention and arrangement of an original treatise on carpentry and
joinery, which was published under the title of "Carpenters New
Guide," in 1792. He also published several works on architecture
and the higher branches of mathematics. He commenced his
Architectural Dictionary in 1810, and finished the same in 1819."

Abstract from the Memoirs of Peter Nicholson by John Bowen.

---

37. This point taken from the diagonal on ground plan and
applying the same to the diagonal on the cutting plane for the
center of rail is correct only when both tangents are of the same
length. This same principle was published some time ago in the
"American Builder," by MR. LANGSTAFF.

tangents on the cutting plane through which he finds the trace of the center line of his face-mould, by using a pliable strip, from his center line he draws the concave and convex curves of mould to a parallel width.

Mr. W. E. PERRY's method differs a little from that of Mr. Weston's; he finds the angle of tangents for the face-mould from the tangents and chord in elevation; he also finds the directing ordinate and joint bevels from the tangents in elevation; he finds the center line of rail on the face-mould correctly by the use of ordinates, drawn from the tangents in elevation in the same way as Mr. JOHN JONES describes in his 1888 edition of hand-railing. Mr. Perry makes use of a parallel face-mould.[38]

NEWLAND's "Carpenters and Joiners Assistant," 1860—Mr. Newland's treatment of the cylindric section for hand-railing, is similar to that of Mr. Nicholson.

In 1864, Mr. JOSHUA JEAYS published his second edition "The Orthogonal System of Hand-railing," in it there is a great deal of original matter.

In 1871. Mr. GEORGE WALTON published his "New Treatise and Practical Guide to Stair-casing and Hand-railing," the principle is the same as published by Mr. Riddle, in the 1859 edition. He shows the tangents in elevation developed from plan; he finds the angle of tangents and directing ordinate, also the joint bevels from the tangents in elevation; he describes the trace of face-mould with the trammel.

In 1878, Mr. WILLIAM TWISS published his block system of hand-railing. He finds the parallelogram on the cutting plane direct from the tangents in elevation, and recommends the trammel to give the perfect trace of face-mould; the joint bevels he finds either from the block, cut to the rake of the tangents, or from the tangents in elevation.

In 1882, Mr. FRANK O. CRESWELL, published a small work on hand-railing and stair-casing; the principle is similar to Mr. Riddle's 1859 edition of the elements of hand-railing; he finds the angle of tangents, directing ordinate, and joint bevels from chord and tangents in elevation, developed from plan. The trace of face-mould he finds with the trammel.

The same year, 1882, Mr. GEORGE COLLINGS published his "Practical Treatise on Hand-railing." He finds the parallelogram on the cutting plane, from the chord in elevation, and the hypothenuse of joint bevels from the parallelogram on the cutting plane; the trace of face-mould he draws with the trammel; the position or location of the major and minor axis, he determines by the trammel and rod in nearly the same way as shown at Fig. 10 Plate 1.

In our own country, Mr. ASHER BENJAMIN, in 1831, published his lines for the construction of the face-mould, similar to that of Mr. Nicholson.

In 1838, Mr. MINARD LAFEVRE issued a book of lines for the stair builder, they were similar to Mr. Nicholson's.

In 1840, Mr. JOHN HALL published a work on Hand-railing. He claimed an improvement in the formation of the face-mould, by the use of the Ellipsograph, of which he claimed to be the inventor. The principle is to draw the ground plan of rail on

---

38. The four last authors show the face-mould drawn to a parallel width, equal to the true width of rail, from a center line; this does not give a correct face-mould for the cylindric section on the cutting plane. Had Mr. Perry made the concave and convex sides of his face-mould concentric elliptic curves, his system would have been without fault; his center line on the mould is the correct elliptic curve.

the draught board, then at the center of well hole erect a vertical shaft, say one inch in diameter, and one or more feet long, from which extends an arm, made to slide and turn on the shaft, the arm to have a pencil fixed near the end, and over from the center of shaft equal to the radius for the concave and also for the convex sides of rail. Now elevate the material from which the face-mould is to be made, over the ground plan to the required inclination of wreath piece ; then move the arm, and the pencil will describe the elliptic curve of face-mould correctly if the material has the correct inclination. He also improved Mr. Nicholson's system.

The next was Mr. SIMON DE GRAFF, 1845. He made use of the ordinates, but claimed the invention for making the wreath for the semicircle in three pieces. This work of Mr. Simon De Graff, was the last book published exclusively on stair building, on the Nicholson system, in our country.

After Mr. Peter Nicholson issued his 1835 edition of the "Carpenter's Guide," the ingenious Mr. PETER ESTERBROOK, stair builder, of New York, was led to investigate the subject of hand-railing more scientifically, as to the uncertain location of the center resting point of Mr. Nicholson. He claims to have made the discovery of the tangent system, thereby locating the correct resting point, which gives the true inclination to the tangents, from which the cutting plane or plane of plank is determined as we have it to-day; In 1859, in company with Mr. J. H. Monckton, they issued a work on stair building.

In the meantime other works had appeared and gave to the world the benefit of the tangent system. In 1848, Mr. R. A. CUPPER, in Ohio, issued his first book "The New Practical Stair Builder's Guide," and later, 1851, his "Universal Stair Builder." These two books simplified the theory of stair building. The principle being correct, it gave the American stair builder a much easier task than he formerly had.

Mr. Cupper claimed the discovery of the tangent system, and thereby the correct resting points; also to be the inventor of the tangent box, of which he gave several plates, clearly illustrating the principle of the tangent system, whereby the stair builder could see at a glance the whole principle, as Mr. Reynolds says, in a "nut shell." He determined the correct position of the transverse axis and the parallelogram for the face-mould on the cutting plane; and describes the method of cutting the crooks out and making the joints square to the face of plank; the use of either the plumb bevel or the two joint bevels, for squaring the wreath piece; the drawing of the face-mould; either with a string trammel or by ordinates: in fact he prepared the way so plain for those having the practice, to simplify and make the subject still plainer for others to follow.

In 1849 Mr. REYNOLDS issued his valuable little treatise and supplement for the stair builders library..

In 1850, Mr. DAVID GAW, stair builder, of Pittsburgh, Pa., partially prepared a work on the subject, but owing to a fatal accident the work was never completed. He found the parallel-ogram or angle of tangents for the face-mould, direct from the chord line in elevation, and described the face-mould with the trammel.

In 1850, the ingenious Mr. RIDDLE issued his "Scientific Stair Builder," in which he determined the parallelogram or angle of tangent on the face-mould, from the transverse axis on the cutting plane. He gave a greater variety of stair plans, explained and made plainer the government of the tangents, showed how the joint bevels may be obtained from the parallelogram on the cutting plane, and the general application of the trammel to the construction of the face-mould, for all wreath pieces that are circular on plan.

In 1855, he issued his second edition of the "Scientific Stair Builder," in which he described the parallelogram or angle of tangents, and the seat of trammel, direct from the inclination of the tangents in elevation. He also described the underside of rail for the straight part, drawn through the center of baluster, for the correct height of wreath rail in the cylinder.

In 1858 and 1860, he published the second and third edition of his "Elements of Hand-railing." He described the tangents, treads, and rises in the elevation as spread out, or developed from tangents on plan. This was a decided improvement, for it gave the stair builder greater control over the inclination of tangents, and allowed the length of the odd balusters to be measured from the elevation. Mr. Riddle also published eight or ten other books for the benefit of the stair builder, and also for the carpenter and joiner. He died March 12th, 1882, at his home in Philadelphia, Pa , loved and respected by all, age 74 years.

In 1855, Mr. J. R. PERRY, of New York, issued a work on stair building; followed in the same year by MESSRS. MILWAIN and YOUNG. They found the angle of tangents direct from the chord line, and used a parallel mould.

In the following year, 1856, MESSRS. VAUGHN and GLENN published a small work on the subject. They used the parallel mould.

In 1856, Patrick O'Neil, of Richmond, Va., published a book for the stair builder, on the tangent box system, much the same as described by Mr. Cupper, in his first book.

MESSRS. EASTERBROOK and MONCKTON, in 1859, issued "The American Stair Builder." They described two ways to find the angle on tangents on the cutting plane; one from the transverse axis on the cutting plane, and the other from the tangents in elevation.[39] In the former, the trammel or rod is used to describe the curves of face-mould; and in the latter, a pliable strip is recommended in tracing the curves of mould.

JOHN THOMAS, in 1863, published a book on stair building. The principle is similar to that published by Milwain and Young, and also by Mr. Langstaff. The angle of tangents is eased off by the intersection of lines for the trace of face-mould.

In 1869, A. RUSSELL, of Memphis. Tenn., published a very good but brief work on hand-railing. He described the parallelogram or angle of tangents for face-mould, from the chord line in elevation, and used the trammel to trace the curves of mould; he found the joint bevels from the parallelogram on the cutting plane.

In 1858, Mr. C. E. LOTH issued a very good book on stair building, in which is found a great deal of interesting matter on the subject. He finds the angle of tangents from the transverse axis on the cutting plane, and the trace of mould through points determined by ordinates.

In 1872, also in 1888, Mr. JAMES H. MONCKTON published two works on the subject; in the former he described the angle of tangents from the diagonal of the parallelogram instead of the chord, as others have done. He also described the curves of

---

39. This method of finding the angle of tangents was published by MR. R. G. HATFIELD, in his "American House Carpenter," he says it was invented by a Mr. Kells, an eminent stair builder of N. Y. City.

face-mould with the trammel. In the latter work he finds the angle of tangents from the chord, and the trace of face-mould by ordinates drawn from the tangents and a flexible strip.

In 1873, MR. WILLIAM FORBES published a work on hand-railing, called the "Sectonian System." This method is similar to the tangent box system; he makes use of a parallel mould.

In 1874, MR. J. R. REAVES, of Hamilton, Canada, issued a work on stair building. He finds the parallelogram for the face-mould direct from the tangents in elevation, and the curves of mould by the trammel, similar to Mr. Riddle in his 1855 edition.

In 1875, MR. L. D. GOULD added his book to the stair builder's list. In it there are some original ideas. He finds the axis on the cutting plane from the chord and diagonal on plan, and the angle of tangents from the axis on the cutting plane. He makes use of the string, to trace the curves of face mould, similar to Mr. Riddle, in some of his later works.

In 1880, MR. R. J. SHERRATT published his book on hand-railing. He finds the angle of tangents from the transverse axis on the cutting plane, and the trace of mould with a string.

In 1884, MR. F. T. HODGSON published a treatise on stair building, the title of which is "Stair Building Made Easy." Another publication by an "OLD STAIR BUILDER," appeared in 1883, entitled "A New System of Hand-railing." The system is similar to Mr. Weston and W. E. Perry's, and later Mr. Jones.

In 1889, MR. J. V. SECOR issued a work on Hand-railing. He finds the parallelogram for the face-mould direct from the chord in elevation, and the bevels from the parallelogram on the cutting plane. All the above works are not without some merit to the diligent inquirer after a thorough knowledge in the art of stair building.

PLATE I.

Figure 1. A *point* has position but not magnitude, as at *A*. Since a true point has no size, a line has no breadth. A line is the path of a point in motion, but as we make lines they of course have breadth. Lines are termed right, or straight lines, curved, or mixed.

Fig. 2. *BC* shows a *straight line*, having length and breadth, but no thickness; is composed of points, and if straight is the shortest distance between any two given points.

Fig. 3. Shows *parallel lines*, which may be straight as *DE* and *FG*, or curved as *HXI* and *JXK*, Fig. 5; and if prolonged they would be equally distant from each other throughout their extension.

Fig. 4. A *curved line LMN*, is one that does not lie in a straight line between its extremities, it may be regular or irregular as *OPR*, Fig. 8.

Fig. 5. *Parallel curved lines*, *HXI* and *JXK*, are such, provided they are everywhere the same distance apart; if they are circles they will be concentric.

Fig. 6. Shows a *mixed or compound line*, *STVW*, being part straight and part curved.

Fig. 7. A *zigzag line*, *AB*, is composed of a series of straight lines as the Chevron Moulding in the Norman Architecture.

Fig. 8. An *irregular or mixed curve*, as *OPR*, is used in landscape gardening.

Fig. 9. *Converging lines*, *CD* and *EF*, if prolonged will converge at *O*; they are also called *oblique lines*.

Fig. 10. *Horizontal line*, *AB*, indicates a level or horizontal line, and is at right angles to a plumb line. The surface of water at rest is always horizontal. *Perpendicular line*, *CD*, is perpendicular to *AB*; any line may be said to be perpendicular to a right line.[1] when the angle is a *right angle*, or an angle of 90 degrees as *BCD*.[2]

Fig. 11. *Acute angle;* an angle that is less than a right angle, as *ABC*.

Fig. 12. *Obtuse angle;* an angle that is greater than a right angle, as *ABC*.

Fig. 13. *Curvilinear angle.* The angle *GHJ*, formed by the intersection of curved lines. And when the angle is formed by straight and curved lines they are termed *mixtilinear angles*, as *KLM*.

---

1. A right line, is a straight line.
2. In describing an angle, the middle letter denotes the angle.

Fig. 14. *Diagonal line;* is a line joining two opposite angles, from corner to corner, as **AB**.

SUPERFICIES.

A surface has length and breadth, but no thickness, for instance: a shadow gives a good representation, its length and breadth can be measured, but not its depth. A solid has length, breadth and thickness.

A Plane Figure, is a portion of a plane enclosed on all sides with lines; when the lines are straight, the figure is termed a *polygon* or *rectilineal figure.* Polygons have different names, according to the number of their sides, and means a many angled or sided figure.

A Polygon of three sides, is a *triangle;* of four, a *quadrilateral;*[3] of five, a *pentagon;* of six, a *hexagon;* of seven, a *heptagon;* of eight, an *octagon;* of nine, a *nonagon;* of ten, a *decagon;* of twelve, a *dodecagon.*

A *Regular Polygon,* is a polygon whose sides and angles are equal, each to each, and its perimeter is the sum of the bounding lines.

A *Parallelogram,* is a quadrilateral which has its opposite sides parallel. There are four kinds, the *square, rectangle, rhombus* and *rhomboid.*

Fig. 15. A square has its four sides equal, and all the angles are right angles, as at **A, B, C, D.** The enclosed angles at **E, F, G, H,** are termed *internal angles;* at **A, B, C** and **D,** they are termed *external angles.*

RULE.—To find the area, square one of the sides. *Example:* 16 0″×16 0″=256 feet. *Ans.*

Fig. 16. A *rectangle,* is a parallelogram whose angles are right angles, and the opposite sides only are of equal length, as **ABCD.**

RULE.—To find the superficial area, multiply the length, 23′ 0″ by the breadth, 16′ 0″. *Example:* 23′ 0″×16′ 0″=368 feet. *Ans.*

Fig. 17. A *rhombus* **ABCD,** is a parallelogram, having all four sides equal in length, but only the opposite angles equal. This figure is sometimes termed *lozenge,*

RULE.—To find the area, multiply the side, 16′ 0″ by the altitude EA, 14′ 0″. *Example:* 16′ 0″×14′ 0″=224 feet. *Ans.*

Fig. 18. A *rhomboid,* is a parallelogram having both opposite sides and opposite angles equal; or two of whose sides are greater than the other two.

RULE.—To find the area, multiply the length, 18′ 0″ by the altitude AE. 16′ 6″. *Example:* 18′ 0″×16′ 6″=297 feet. *Ans.*

A *triangle,* is a polygon bounded by three straight lines, containing three angles. There are four kinds, the *right angle triangle,* the *equilateral,* the *scalene,* and the *isosceles triangle.*

Fig. 19. A right angle triangle, **ABC,** has one right angle and two acute angles; the side **AB,** opposite the right angle is termed the *hypothenuse,* the side **AC,** the *base,* and the other side **CB,** the *perpendicular.* Fig. 19 is known among builders as the 6, 8 and 10 triangle, for squaring the foundation walls of buildings.

RULE.—To find the area, multiply the length of the base, 6′ 0″ by one-half the perpendicular, 8′ 0″÷2=4 feet. *Example:* 6′ 0″×4′ 0″=24 feet. *Ans.* This rule answers for all triangles, for a triangle is one-half a parallelogram, having the same base and altitude.

---

3. Quadrilateral, is a plane surface inclosed by four right lines. There are three classes of quadrilaterals; namely, *trapezoids, trapeziums* and *Parallelograms.*

4. The altitude of a parallelogram is the distance between its opposite sides; of a trapezoid, it is the distance between its parallel sides; of a triangle, it is the distance from any vertix to the side opposite, or to that side prolonged as *CD,* Fig. 22.

RULE.—To find the length of hypothenuse *AB*, when the base *AC* and the perpendicular *BC*, are given. Add together the squares of the base, and perpendicular, and the square root of the sum will be the length of the hypothenuse. *Example:* $6^2 + 8^2 = \sqrt{100} = 10$ feet. *Ans.*

This rule is valuable to carpenters and builders, when estimating; for finding the length of valleys and hips, also the length of braces, and figuring for the strains in the same. Every young man should study well this problem.

To find the length of base or perpendicular, when the hypothenuse, and either one of the other sides are given.

RULE.—From the square of the hypothenuse, subtract the square of the side that is known, and the square root of the remainder will be the length of the unknown side. *Example:* $10^2' - 8^2' = \sqrt{36} = 6$ feet. *Ans.*

Fig. 20. An *equilateral triangle.* The three sides, *AB*, *BC* and *CA*, and the three angles at *A*, *B* and *C*, are equal, and are equal in area to one-sixth of a hexagon whose sides are the same, and the given side *BC*, is equal to the radius of a circumscribed circle. The cooper to find the radius of a barrel head, sets the dividers so as to step around in the groove just six times.

RULE.—To find the area multiply the length of the base *BC*, 16′ 0″ by half its altitude *EA*, 13.49 feet. Thus, $16' \ 0'' \times 12'.92' = 107.92$ feet. superficial. *Ans.*

Fig. 21. An *Isosceles Triangle.* *ABC* has two sides equal, and all the angles are acute.

RULE.—To find the area, multiply the base, *BC*, [15′ 0″] by half the altitude, *EA*, [20′ 0″] thus; $15' \ 0'' \times \frac{20' \ 0''}{2} = 15' \ 0'$ feet. *Ans.*

Fig. 22. A *Scalene Triangle.* *ABC* has one obtuse and two acute angles, the angle *BCA* being obtuse, its altitude, *AD*, is found by prolonging the base line *BC* to *D*. The area is found in the same manner as at the preceding—by multiplying the base by half its altitude.

Fig. 23. A *Trapezoid.* *ABCD,* is a quadrilateral which has two of its sides parallel to each other, as *AB* and *CD.*

RULE.—To find the area, multiply the sum of the parallel sides, *AB*, [20′ 0″] and *CD*, [26′ 0″] by the altitude, *EG*, [10′ 0″], and half the product will be the area. *Example:* $26' \ 0'' \ 20' \ 0'' = 46' \times 14' \ 0'' = \frac{644}{2} = 322$ feet. *Ans.*

Fig. 24. A *Trapezium.* *ABCD* is a quadrilateral which has no two of its sides parallel to each other.

RULE.—To find the area, multiply the diagonal, *CB*, [26′ 0″] by the sum of the two perpendiculars, *AF*, [18′ 0″] and *DH*, [6′ 0″], falling upon it from the opposite angles, and half the product will be the area. *Example:* $18' \ 0'' + 6' \ 0'' \times 26' \ 0'' = \frac{624}{2} = 312$ feet. *Ans.*

PLATE 2.

THE CIRCLE.

Fig. 1. *A circle, ABCD,* is a plane figure bounded by one line which is termed the *circumference,* and is equal to 360 degrees, and it is such that all straight lines from a certain point within the figure called the *center,* to the circumference, are equal to one another, and the space within the whole circumference is termed the circle.

The *diameter* of a circle is a straight line drawn through the center at **O**, and terminated by the circumference at **AC**, dividing the circle into two semi-circles.   The *radius* of a circle equals half the diameter; the span of the dividers, when describing the boundary of any circle is termed the radius, as **OC**.   When more than one line radiates from the center to the circumference they are termed the *radii*, as **OM**, and **ON**.

RULE.—To find the area of a circle. Square the diameter **AC**, (20' 0"), and multiply by the decimal .7854. *Example*: 20' 0" × 20' 0" × .7854 = 346.36 square feet. *Ans.*

The diameter being given, how to find the circumference.

RULE.—Multiply the diameter by the constant, 3.1416. *Example*: 20' 0" × 3.1416 = 62.8320 feet. *Ans.*

A *tangent*, to a circle, is a straight line, which touches the circumference but does not intersect it how far soever the line be produced, as **EF**.   An *arc* is part of a circumference.

Fig. 2. A *semicircle*, **ABC**, is the figure contained by a diameter and that part of the circumference cut off by the diameter **AC**, and is equal to 180 degrees.

Fig. 3. A *quadrant of a circle*, is the half of a semicircle bounded by the arc **ABC**, and the two radii, **OA** and **OC**, and is equal to 90 degrees.

Fig. 4. A *chord* is a straight line joining any two points in a circumference, but not passing through the center, as **CE**. A *segment* is that portion of the circle contained between the chord **AB** and the arc **ACB**. **CD** is the *versed sine*. How to find the diameter of a circle when the chord and the versed sine are given. Let the chord **AB** equal 36' 0" and the versed sine **CD** equal 6' 0".

RULE.—Divide the square of half the chord by the versed sine; to this product add the length of the versed sine, and the result will be the length of the diameter of the circle, of which the arc of the circle is a part. *Example*: 36 ÷ 18 × 18 = 324 ÷ 54 = 6 + 60 ft. *Ans.* The radius will equal the half of 60' or 30 feet.

Fig. 5 shows two concentric circles, **AB** being the outer diameter, 20' 0", and **CD** the inner diameter, 16' 0".

RULE.—To find the area of the space included between the circumference of the concentric circles. Multiply the sum of the two diameters by their difference, and this product again by the decimal .7854. *Example*: 16 + 20 = 36 + .7854 = 113.00, area required.

Fig. 6. **ABCD** shows the *convex*, or outside; and **EFGH** shows the *concave*, or inside of a curved surface.

PROBLEMS.

Fig. 1. *To bisect a given line.* Let **AB** be the given straight line, from the points **A** and **B** as centers, with any distance greater than half **AB**, describe arcs cutting each other at **C** and **D**. Draw the line **CD**, and the point **E**, where it cuts **AB**, will be the middle of the line required. **CD** will also be perpendicular to the given straight line **AB**; and the angles will all be right angles.

Fig. 2. *From a given point outside of a given straight line, to let fall a perpendicular to the given straight line.* Let **A** be the given point, and **BC** the given straight line. With any radius greater than **AH**, describe arcs from the center **A**, cutting **BC** at **D** and **E**. Again, with any radius greater than half **DE**, draw arcs from **D** and **E**, intersecting at **F**. Join **FA**, cutting **DE** at **H**; then **HA** will be perpendicular to **BC**, and passing through the given point **A**, as required.

Fig. 3. *To set up a perpendicular at the end of a given line, AB.* From *A* and *B* describe arcs of equal radius intersecting in *D*, then with the same radius draw the semicircle from *B* through *A* to *C;* draw *BD* produced to intersect the semicircle at *C.* Join *CA*, then *CA* is the perpendicular required.

Fig. 4. *Another method.* Let *AB* be the given line, and *A* the point to erect the perpendicular. With equal radii from *A* and *B*, draw arcs cutting at *C;* through *BC* draw the straight line produced to *D*, make *CD* equal *BC.* Join *DA*, then *DA* is the perpendicular required.

Fig. 5. *Another method to erect a perpendicular near the end of a given straight line.* Let *AB* be the given straight line, take any point as *C*, and any radius greater than *AC*, and describe arcs at *D* and *E;* then take another point *F*, and describe arcs intersecting at *D* and *E.* Join *D* and *E*, then the line *DE* will be the perpendicular required.

Fig. 6. *To erect a perpendicular from a given point D, on a given curved line ABC.* From the point *D*, describe arcs with equal radius, cutting the given curved line at *E* and *F;* again, with equal radius describe arcs from the points *E* and *F*, intersecting at *K.* Join *KD*, then the line *KD* will be perpendicular or normal to the given curved line *ABC.*

Fig. 7. *To erect a perpendicular to a given curved line ABC, from a point J, outside the given line.* With any radius greater than the distance from *J* to the given line, draw the arc cutting the curved line in *K* and *L;* also draw arcs with equal radius from *K* and *L*, intersecting at *M.* Join *MJ*, cutting the curved line in *P*, then *JP* will be the perpendicular required.

Fig. 8. *Three points ABC, out of a straight line being given, to find the center of a circle so that the three points may be in the circumference of the circle.* From *C* and *B*, with equal radius, draw arcs, cutting at 2 and 3. Also from *A* and *B*, with equal radius, draw arcs, cutting at 4 and 5. Join 4 and 5 produced, also join 2 and 3 produced, intersecting at *D;* then *D* is the center to sweep through the three points *ABC*, as required.

Fig. 9. *The span AB, and height CD, of a segment being given, to find the center E, to draw the curve ADB.* With any radius greater than half *AB*, draw arcs from the points *A* and *B*, intersecting each other in 2 and 3. Again, with any radius draw arcs from the points *A* and *D*, intersecting each other in 5 and 4; join 5 and 4 produced, join 2 and 3 produced, intersecting at *E;* then *E* is the center to sweep the arc through *ADB.*

Fig. 10. *Another method. The span AB, and height CD, being given.* With any radius greater than *AC*, and with *A* and *B* for centers, draw arcs intersecting at *E;* join *ED*, draw the chord at *AD.* With the points *A* and *B* for centers, draw the arc 2-3, also 4-5 indefinite. Make 4-5 equal 2-3; join *A5*, prolonged to intersect *DE* at *H*, for the center required.

Fig. 11. *Another method. The chord or span AB, and height CD, being given, to sweep the arc ADB, without finding a center.* In very flat arches, and wide span, or when the radius is very long, this method may serve a good purpose.

3

At *A* and *B* tack a 10d wire nail, then take two strips five inches wide, and a few inches longer than the span, let them be jointed straight on one edge; now place one strip to line *AD*, and the other strip to line *DB*, have the jointed edge against the nails, cross and nail them together at *D;* see that the strips are close to the two nails, then near the end tack on a brace. Now hold a pencil in the angle at *D*, and move the triangle against the nails, and the pencil will describe the curve required.

Fig. 12. *A circle ABC, and a tangent DE, to the circle being given. to find the point of contact.* Take any point in the tangent *DE*, as 2 ; draw 2 *F* bisect 2 *F* at *H*, and with the radius *HF*, describe the semicircle 2 *KF*, cutting the tangent and circle in *K*, then *K* is the point of contact required.

Fig. 13. *The arc of a circle ABC, and the tangent LD, being given, to find the point of contact, the center of the circle being unknown.* From any point as *D* on the tangent, draw any line cutting the arc as *DFE;* bisect *DE* in *O*, then with *OE* for a radius, draw the semicircle *EHD*. At *F* erect a perpendicular to *ED*, cutting the semicircle in *K*, then with *D* as a center, and *DK* for a radius draw the arc *KL*, cutting the given arc in *L* for the point of contact as required.

Fig. 14. *To draw a tangent to a given circle ABC, that shall pass through a given point A.* From the center *O*, draw *OA* through the point *A*, draw *EF* perpendicular to *OA;* then *EF* is the tangent required.

Fig. 15. *A triangle ABC, being given to draw a circle that will be tangent to three given sides.* Bisect[6] the angles at *A*, *B*, *C*, and the intersection at *O* will give the center of the circle required.

PLATE 3.

PROBLEMS.

Fig. 1. *To bisect a given angle ABC.* With any radius, and *B* as a center, describe arc cutting *AB* and *BC* in *D* and *E;* again, with *D* and *E* as centers, describe arcs intersecting in *F;* join *BF*, then the angle *FBA*, is equal to the angle *FBC*.

Figs. 2 and 3. *To transfer an angle B, A, C, Fig. 3. equal to a given angle 3, 2, 4, Fig. 3.* With any radius, and 2 as a center, draw the arc 3, 4 ; then with the same radius, and *A* as a center, draw the arc *BC;* make *BC* equal 3, 4 ; join *AC*, then the angle *CAB* will equal the angle 3, 2, 4, required.

Fig. 4. *From a given straight line AB to construct a square.* With *A* and *B* as centers, and *AB* for a radius, describe arcs intersecting at *C* and prolonged; again, with *A* and *C* as centers, and equal radius, draw arcs intersecting at *E;* join *EB*, cutting the arc *ADC* in *D;* then with *CD* for a radius, and *C* as a center, draw the arc intersecting at *F* and *H;* join *AF*, *FH* and *HB*, completing the square required.

Fig. 5. *On a given side AB, to construct a regular Hexagon.* From the points *A* and *B* as centers, and *AB* for a radius, describe arcs cutting each other in *C;* and from the point *C*, with

---

6.   To bisect a given angle see Fig. 1, Plate 3.

the distance *AB*, describe the circle *AFB*; then with the distance *AB*, step around the circumference the points *B, D, E, F, G*; join *BD, DE, EF*, &c., for the hexagon required.

Fig. 6. *On a given line AB, to describe a regular polygon of any required number of sides.* With *AB* as a radius, and *A* as a center, describe the semicircle *BCD*, prolong *AB* to *D*.

If a heptagon (seven sides) be required. Divide the semicircle into seven equal parts as 1, 2, 3, 4, 5, 6, *B;* from the center *A*, draw lines through the divisions 6, 5, 4, 3, &c , prolonged, always omitting the last two divisions; with *BA* for a radius, describe arcs from *B* to *C*, and *C* to *E*, *E* to *F*, and from *H* to *G* and *G* to *F;* join *BC, CE, EF, FG. HA* and *GH*, and the heptagon is complete.

Any regular polygon may be drawn in this way, the semicircle being divided off equal to the number of sides required in the polygon. The young man will find this a good problem for practice in accurate drawing.

Fig. 7. *To construct a regular polygon, having eight sides, (octagon) from a given right line AB.* Prolong *AB* to *C* and *D;* make *AD* and *BC* each equal *AB;* draw the semicircles *A 2 D* and *B 3 C;* draw arcs with equal radius from the points *D, A, B, C*, intersecting at *E* and *F;* draw *E*2 and *F*3 perpendicular to *DC*, bisecting the semicircles at 2 and 3 ; join 2 *A* and 3 *B* prolonged; make *AH* and *BJ* each equal *AB;* draw *AK* and *BL* indefinite, and perpendicular to *AB;* draw *HN* and *JM* each parallel with *AK*, and equal in length to *AB*. From *N* and *M*, with radius equal to *AB*. draw arcs cutting the perpendicular lines in *K* and *L;* join *NK, KL* and *LM*, and the octagon is complete.

Fig. 8. *A square ABCD, being given to form an octagon, or find the distance from the edge B to set a gauge.* Draw the diagonals *AD* and *BC*, intersecting at *O*, with *AO* for a radius, and *A* as a center; draw the arc *OH*, then *BH* is the required distance from the edge to set the gauge; draw arcs through the center *O*, from the four corners *A, B, C, D*, to intersect the sides of the square at 1, 2, 3, 4, 5, 6, 7. Join *H*2, 3 4, 5 6, and 7 1, and we have the octagon required.

A regular polygon of any number of sides may be easily constructed, by first drawing a circle, and dividing the circumference into the number of parts required for the sides, and then joining the divisions.

Fig. 9. *To divide a given line AB, into any number of equal parts.* Let *AB* be the given line; at *A* draw any line indefinite, as *AC*, and at any convenient angle to *AB;* set off towards *C* the number of equal divisions the given line is required to be divided, as 1, 2, 3, 4, 5, 6; join 6*B*, draw 5 7, 4 8, 3 9, 2 10, and 1 11, parallel with 6*B*, then the given line *AB* will be divided proportionately into the number of spaces required.

Fig. 10. *Shows the same principle applied to diminishing or increasing the length of a bracket.* Let *AB* be the length (10″) of the given bracket divided into any number of parts, as 1, 1, 1, &c.; draw *AC* equal to the depth of the bracket; draw 1 2, 1 2, &c., perpendicular to *AB*, cutting the curve in *C*, 2, 2, &c.; make *AD* at any convenient angle to *AB;* make *AD* equal the length of the diminished or increased bracket, in this case diminished to 7¼″, join *BD*. From 1, 1, 1, &c., draw line parallel with *BD*, intersecting *AD* in 3, 3, 3, &c.; draw lines indefinite, and perpendicular to AD, from the points A, 3, 3, &c.; make AC, 3 4, &c., equal AC, 1 2, &c., respectively; then trace the curve through the points 4, 4, 4, &c., for the diminished bracket required.

Fig. 11. *To divide a given line AB, or a board into any number of equal divisions.* Let AB indicate a board 10″ wide, and let it be required to divide the same into twenty-one equal parts. Now 21 half-inches equal 10½″; take the rule or steel square, place it diagonally across the board to 10½ inches as indicated at DC, mark the divisions every half-inch, as 1, 2, 3, 4, &c., draw lines parallel with DK, cutting the given line AB, into twenty-one equal parts as required.

Or suppose it be required to divide the same board into twelve equal parts, then place the square diagonally across as HJ, measuring 12 inches; then every inch will be a division on the diagonal line JH, and lines drawn parallel with DK through the divisions, will divide AB equally as required.

This problem is very useful to draughtsmen and mechanics, being a very ready method of dividing any line into a given number of equal parts.

Fig. 12. *Two straight lines AB and BC, meeting at any angle as ABC, how to connect them with a curve by intersecting lines.* Make BD and BE each equal, divide BD into any number of equal parts, as 1, 2, 3, 4, 5, 6; divide BE into the same number of parts, connect $1D$, $1E$, 2–5, &c., as shown, and through the intersections trace the easing required.

The stair-builder sometimes makes use of this problem to ease off the angle on wall strings formed by the level base and raking string; the distance BD or BE is usually taken at two-thirds of a tread, this is optional with the workman as a matter of taste.

Fig. 13. *Shows the easing to be an elliptical curve, the distance BD being less than BE.* Divide BD into any number of equal parts, say 8, divide BF into the same number of equal parts 1, 2, 3, 4, 5, 6, 7, 8, &c.; join $1D$, $1C$, 2 7, 3 6, &c., and trace the curve as before; this easing is used where the treads are increased in width at the starting of a straight flight of stairs, or in winders.

Fig. 14. *Shows how to find the development or "stretchout" of a given semicircle ABC, or any portion of a semicircle.* Draw DE indefinite and parallel with AC, and tangent to the curve at B; then with AC for a radius, and A and C for centers, draw arcs intersecting at F; join FA and FC prolonged, intersecting DE at D and E; then the length of the straight line DE is equal to the circumference of the semicircle ABC nearly. Any division of the semicircle may now be found from the stretchout. Make BH equal 4¾ inches; join FH, intersecting the semicircle in J, then the distance from B to J, on the curve, will equal 4¾ inches; in like manner any number of divisions may be found. The distance BD or BE, equals the stretchout of the quadrant AJB. If the stretchout of the quadrant only be required, then with OC for a radius, and the points O and C for centers, draw arcs intersecting at L; draw LC prolonged to E, then BE is the development of the curve from B to C.

PLATE 4.

THE CONE.

Fig. 1. *Exhibits a "right cone," and is defined as being generated by the revolution of a right angle triangle around one of its sides, that forms the right angle, and is termed a "circular cone."* A line from the apex *B*, to the center *A*, is termed its *"axis."* In "oblique" cones, the axis is inclining to the plane of base *CD*, at an angle other than a right angle. A *"truncated"* cone, is the lower part of a cone cut by a plane parallel to its base.

Conic Sections. Four curves, called conic sections, may be found by cutting the right cone in different directions. If the cone be cut by a plane parallel to its base, as *EF*, the section is a *"circle ;"* if the plane cut the cone from side to side, as *GH*, and at any angle other than a right angle to its axis, the section is an *"ellipse,"* as shown projected at Fig. 3 ; if the cutting plane be parallel to one side of the cone, as the line *JK*, the section will be a *"parabola,"* as shown projected at Fig. 4 ; again, if the cutting plane be parallel to the axis *AB*, as *LM*, then the section will be a *"hyperbola,"* as shown projected at Fig. 5.

To find the superficial area of the slanting side of a right cone:

RULE.—Multiply the diameter by the constant 3.1416, and that product by one-half the slant height for the superficial area. *Example:* Required the superficial area of the slanting sides of a right cone, the diameter at the base equals 16′ 0″, and the slant height equals 25.3′. Thus, 16′ 0″×3.1416=50.26′, equals 50.26′ for the circumference. Then, 50.26′×25.3′=635.8′, equals 635.8 square feet. *Ans.*

$$\frac{}{2}$$

To compute the cubic feet of a right cone:

RULE.—Multiply the square of the diameter by the decimal .7854 ; then multiply that sum by the perpendicular height, and take one-third of the product for the area required. *Example:* Required the area in cubic feet of a right cone, the diameter at the base is 16′ 0″, and the perpendicular height equals 24′ 0″. Thus, 16′×16′=256×.7854 = 201.062 square feet for the superficial area of the base. Then, 201.062 ×24′ 0″=4825.488÷½=1608.496 equals 1608.4969 cubic feet for the area required.

Fig. 2. Shows the base of the cone ; the shaded part marked *B*, indicates the base of the parabola, and the shaded part marked *C*, indicates the base of the hyperbola.

Fig. 3. Shows the ellipse projected from the plane *GH*,: Fig. 1. How to locate the minor axis and trace the curve. Return to Fig. 1, bisect *GH* at *N*, through *N*, and parallel to the base *CD*; draw *EF*, cutting the axis *AB* at *O*, with *O* as a center and *OF* for a radius; draw the arc cutting the perpendicular from *N* at *P*; then *NP* is the semi minor axis sought.

Make *GH* equal *GH*, Fig. 1; make *NP* and *NC* equal *NP*, Fig. 1: draw the rectilineal parallelogram *GHAB*, divide *HA* into four equal parts, as 1, 2, 3 ; also divide *NH* into four equal parts, as 4, 5. 6. From the focus *P*. draw the intersecting lines *P*1, *P*2, *P*3 ; from the focus *C*, draw lines through the points 4, 5, 6, to intersect at 7, 8, 9, for the one-fourth of the ellipse. Now draw the ordinates 8-10. 9.11 parallel to the minor axis *CP*; divide *GN* to equal *NH*; now transfer the distance on ordinates 6-8, 5-9 to the opposite sides, using the transverse axis *GH* for a base line, then trace the elliptic curve through the points, for the ellipse required.

Fig. 4. *Shows the curve of a Parabola projected from the plane JK, Fig. 1.* Make *DE* equal to *DE*, Fig. 2 ; bisect *DE* at *K*, draw *KJ* perpendicular to *DE*. and equal to *KJ*, Fig. 1; draw the rectilineal parallelogram *DFGE*, divide *KE* into four equal parts as 1, 2, 3 ; divide *EG* into four equal parts, as 4, 5, 6; connect *J* 6, *J* 5 and *J* 4 ; from the points 1, 2, 3, draw lines parallel to *KJ* to intersect the lines from the focus *J*, at 7, 8 and 9. Now divide the opposite side in the same manner, and trace the parabolic curve through the points *E*, 7, 8, 9, *J*, 10, 11, 12, *D*.

Fig. 5. *Shows the curve of a Hyperbola, projected from the plane LM, Fig. 1.* Make *FG* equal to *FG*. Fig. 2 ; bisect *FG* at *M*, draw *ML* perpendicular to *FG* and equal to *ML*. Fig. 1 ; draw the rectilineal parallelogram *FBAG* ; divide *MG* into four equal parts, as 1, 2, 3, divide *GA* into four equal parts, as 4, 5, 6 ; connect *L* 6, *L* 5 and *L* 4. Prolong the side of cone *DB*, Fig. 1 to intersect *ML* prolonged at *R*. Now prolong *ML*, Fig. 5, to equal *MR*, Fig. 1 ; at *R* draw *R* 1, *R*2 and *R*3, intersecting *L*4, *L*5 and *L*6 at 7, 8 and 9 ; divide the opposite side in the same manner, and trace the Hyperbolic curve through the points *G*, 7, 8, 9, L, 10, 11, 12, and *F*.

Fig. 6. *Shows how to draw a pattern for the turner, to turn a circular moulding for a given moulding, and have them member on a given miter.* A shows the given moulding, and *BC* shows the given miter; draw lines from the different members on moulding to intersect the miter *BC* at 1, 2, 3, 4, 5. From the center *O* draw arcs from the points 1, 2, 3, &c., on the miter, to intersect the radial line *OD;* then transfer the ordinates on the given moulding to Fig. 7, as 6-7, drawn at right angles to *DO;* then trace the contour of moulding to be turned, through the points, for the pattern required. If the circular moulding is turned to the exact pattern of the given moulding, then the miter will be curved, as shown at Fig. 8.

At *AB* and *C,* Fig. 8, is shown the intersection; now draw the curve through the three points, as described for Fig. 8, Plate 2, for the miter.

Fig. 9. *Shows Graphically how to find approximately the number of feet of wreath rail in a winding stair case when estimating.*

The diameter of well hole is 4′ 0″, and the height of story is 12′ 0″, having 24 risers in one revolution.

RULE.—To the square of the height add the square of three times the diameter of well hole, and extract the square root for the hippothenuse, or length of wreath rail approximately.

EXAMPLE.— 12′×12′=144+[4′ 0″×3=12′0″×12′ 0″=144′] 144+144=$\sqrt{288}$= 17′ 0″ for the length of the wreath rail approximately.

For the correct measurements, first find the exact circumference, then proceed as before.

RULE.—To find the circumference, multiply the diameter by the constant 3.1416.

EXAMPLE.—4′ 0″×3.1416=12.5664; equals 12.5664 for the circumference of well hole. Then proceed as above. 12×12=144+12.566×12.566= $\sqrt{301,904356}$=17.35 feet; which equals 17.35 feet for the exact length of weath rail at the cylinder line.

If the ground plan be elliptical, then find the circumference by the rule for the ellipse, and proceed as above.

PLATE 5.

THE ELLIPSE.

PLATE 5. *Shows the Ellipse,* **AB**, Fig., 1 is the *Transverse Axis,* and is commonly termed the *Major Axis,* for short.

The *Conjugate Axis* is the short axis, as **CD**, Fig. 1, bisecting the Major Axis at right angles and terminated by the curve; it is termed for short the *Minor Axis. Foci,* are two points found on the major axis as *J* and *K,* Fig. 2, from which to draw the circumference with a string; the two points together are termed the *Foci;* singly, one is termed *Focus.*

Vectors are the two lines that radiate from any point in the circumference to each of the foci as *DJ* and *DK,* or *LJ* and *LK,* Fig. 2. It is a known property of the ellipse, that the sum of the two vectors is equal to the transverse diameter.

Center. The center of the ellipse is at the intersection of the axis, as at *F,* Fig. 1.

Vertix. Is the extremity of the axis, as at the mixed angles at *ABC* and *D,* Fig. 1.

Normal. The axis *AB* and *CD* are always normal to the curve at their *Vertices.* To find a line normal to the curve at any intermediate point, bisect the vectors at the circumference, as shown by the line 1 2, Fig. 8, which is normal to the curve at the point *H.*

In this way the mason finds the joints for the arch stones in elliptical arches at any point desired.

Tangent. Any line at right angles to the normal at the point of contact with the curve will be tangent to the curve at that point, as the line 3 4, Fig. 8.

Semi-ellipse. Both the axis divide the ellipse into two parts, as *ADBA,* or *CBDC,* either are termed semi-ellipsis; the area is the same in either case.

Elliptical Quadrants. The same axis divides the ellipse into four equal parts, termed elliptical quadrants, all having the same area, as *CFBHC,* Fig. 1.

RULE.*—*To find the circumference of an ellipsis, the major and minor axis being known.* Multiply half the sum of the two diameters by 3,1416, and the product will be the circumference nearly.

EXAMPLE.—The major axis, Fig. 1, equals 14' 0", and the minor axis equals 10' 6". required the circumference: $14.0 + 10'.5 = \frac{24.5}{2} = 12.25' \times 3.1416 = 38,484$ feet, answer.

RULE —To find the area of *an Ellipse.* Multiply the major axis by the minor axis and the product again by the decimal .7854, and the result will be the area.

EXAMPLE.—14' 0"×'10.5×.7854=115.453 square feet, answer.

Fig. 1. *Shows how to draw the ellipse with a trammel, the major axis AB, and minor axis CD, being given.* Pivot the trammel in the center at *F,* with the arms centered on the axis lines *AB* and *CD.*

Make the distance from pencil to minor pin equal the semi-minor axis *CF',* and the distance from pencil to major pin to equal the semimajor axis *AF';* now place the pins in the grooves, and trace the curve through the points *ACBD,* for the ellipsis required.

The trammel is the most practical tool for the Stair builder to trace the curves of the face mould, especially for platform cylinders, say up to 24 inches diameter; the elliptic curve can be more correctly traced with the trammel than in any other way, the curve being absolutely correct.

---

*Bonnycastle's Mensuration.

The Stair builder should not consider his kit complete unless provided with a trammel. For platform cylinders up to the size above mentioned, the arms of the trammel need not be longer than 7 inches each, and the rod not over 20 inches long, and ¼″ square, having at the end a head drilled out to admit a pencil, and a set screw, to secure the pencil in place; also, two movable heads, with set screws and pins, the pins may be one-sixteenth in diameter, to fit neatly into the grooves of the trammel; these two heads are fit so as to slide easily on the rod, they are ¼″ by ¾″ square, and the set screws should be on the opposite side from the pins, for convenience, when setting them.

The first pin from the pencil is termed the *minor pin*; the other is termed the *major pin*.

At Fig. 1, the trammel is shown having four arms; for the Stair builders' use, only three arms are required, made ¼″ thick and ½″ wide, with grooves at right angles and a scant eighth of an inch deep, and a strong sixteenth wide, so that the pins may slide freely in the grooves; have at the center, on the underside, a small point for a pivot for centering the trammel.

This instrument should be made of brass. After using the tool for a short time, the Stair builder would not be without it. The author has used the trammel on platform cylinders for the last forty years. For winders and large curves the ordinate as herein set forth is found to be the most convenient for economy in drawing a correct face mould.

Fig. 2. *A rectilineal parallelogram, 1, 2, 3, 4, being given, to find the major and minor axis, also the foci, and draw the ellipsis with a string, so that the curve will be tangent to the parallelogram at the points A, B, C and D.*

Bisect 1 3 and 2 4 at *A* and *B*, also bisect 1 2 and 3 4 at *C* and *D*, join *A B* and *C D*, forming right angles at the center *F;* then *AB* will be the major axis and *CD* the minor axis required. With the semimajor axis *AF* for a radius, and *D* as a center, draw the arc intersecting the major axis *AB* at *J* and *K;* then the points *J* and *K* will be the foci required.

Now fasten a pin in each focus *J* and *K*, pass a thread around the pins, wrapping the two ends twice around the one pin, and holding the ends under the thumb of the left hand, then with a pencil nicked slightly near the point, stretch the thread until the point *D* is reached; now trace the curve through the points *DBCA* for the ellipsis required.

Fig. 3. *Around a given rectangle, ABCD, to describe an ellipsis.*

Bisect *AC* and *BD* at *E* and *F*, join *E* and *F* and produced; bisect *AB* and *CD* at *H* and *J*. Join *HJ*, intersecting *EF* at the center *O*. Make *HK* equal *HB*, join *KA*, cutting *EF* at *M*. Then *AK* will equal the semimajor axis, and *AM* the semiminor axis. Make *ON* and *OP* each equal *KA*. Let *OR* and *OS* each equal *AM;* now trace the elliptic curve through the points *ABCD*, as required.

Fig. 4. *An Ellipsis, ABCD, having been given, and the position of the major and minor axis is unknown, to find their position.*

Draw any two parallel lines cutting the ellipse, as *AC* and *BD*. Bisect *AC* and *BD* at 1 and 2. Join 1 2 produced to intersect the ellipse at *E* and *F;* bisect *EF* at 3; then the point at 3 will be the center of the ellipse. With any radius less than the semimajor axis, and 3, for a center, draw the arc cutting the ellipse at *H* and *J*, join *HJ;* through the center 3, draw the minor axis *KL*, parallel with *HJ*. Bisect *HJ* at 4, join 4 3 and produced, cutting the ellipse at *M* and *N*, for the major axis, as required.

Fig. 5. *To draw an ellipse or oval, ABCD, with the dividers, the major axis AC being given.*

Let *AC* be the major axis, divide the same into four equal parts, as *A* 3, 3 2, 2 1, 1 *C*. Make the two middle parts equal the diagonal of the square 1–6, 3–7; prolong the sides of the square at 1 and 3 indefinite; then with 3 as a center, and 3 *A* for radius, draw the arc *FAE*. Also from the center 1, draw the arc *HCJ*, then with 7, as a center and 7 *H* for a radius, draw the arc *HBF*. In like manner, from the center 6, trace the opposite side *EDJ*, and the ellipse or oval is complete.

Fig. 6. *An Ellipse shown by the dotted line 2, 3, 4, 5, being given; to draw other lines that will be parallel to the given ellipse; 2 4 is the major axis, and 3 5 the minor axis.*

Draw equal arcs on each side of the given ellipse to the required width, then trace the curves so as to tangent the arcs, for the parallel lines required as *ABCD*, for the convex curve; and *JEHF* for the concave curve. If a pattern be required, trace either of the outer curves, then use a gauge for the parallel width.

Fig. 7. *An Ellipse ABCD being given; to draw another ellipse EFGH, through a given point F, that shall be proportional to the given ellipse.*

Let *ABCD* be the given ellipse, *AC* the major axis and *BD* the minor axis, and *O* the center, and *FH* the minor axis for the proportional ellipse. Join *AB*, from *F*, and parallel to the dotted line *AB*, draw the proportional line *FE*. Make *OG* equal *OE*, for the major axis. Now trace the elliptic curve through the points *EFGH*, which will be proportional to the given ellipse, as required.

If any line, or lines, be drawn radiating from the center *O* to the circumference of the given ellipse, as *O* 2, *O* 3, or *O* 4; the width of any concentric or proportional ellipse may be established at any of these points by the use of the proportional lines. Say draw *A* 2, then draw *E* 5 parallel to *A* 2, now 5 is the point through which the proportional ellipse will cut on the radial line *O* 2. In the same way draw other proportional lines, as 2 *D*, *D* 3, and 3 *C*, &c., parallel to which draw 5 *H*, *H* 6, and 6 *G*; then trace the elliptic curve and it will be found to pass through the points 5, *H*, 6, &c. These proportional lines are sometimes found useful when drawing the face-mould.

Fig. 8. *To draw a line perpendicular, or normal to the curve of a given Ellipse; also to find a tangent to the same curve.*

Let *ACBD* be the given ellipse; and the point *H* be selected for the line normal to the curve; find the foci *E* and *F*, draw the vectors *EH*, and *FH* produced; bisect the angle formed at *H*, and draw the normal line 1 2, which will be perpendicular to the curve of the ellipse at the point *H*, as required.

At the point *H*, and at right angles to 1 2, draw the line 3 4; then 3 4 will be tangent to the ellipse at the point *H*. Another way, to find a tangent to the curve: Let the vectors converge at the point *J* and prolong indefinitely. Bisect the angle in *K*, join *KJ*, then the line *KJ* will be tangent to the ellipse, and the point of contact will be at *J*.

Fig. 9. *A Semiellipse ABC, being given to find a tangent to the curve at any point without the foci.*

Let *AB* be the major axis, and *O* the center, and *OC* the semiminor axis produced to *H*. Draw the quadrant and radii *OD* and *CF*; perpendicular to *OF* draw *FH*; draw *FJ* parallel with *OB*, join *HJ* and produced, for the tangent required, the point of contact is at *J*; the tangent *KL* is found in the same way, *K* being the point of tangency.

If the curve of the ellipse is not given, the point of tangency may be found by taking the radius *OA*, and *O* for a center, draw the arc cutting *OD*, produced in *M*, from *M* draw the perpendicular cutting *KD* in *K*, then the point *K* will be the point of contact.

Fig. 10. *The radius of any Quarter Circle, and its accompanying Rhomboidal parallelogram ABCD, being given; how to trace the curve of an Ellipse with a trammel through the points A and C, so that AB and BC shall be tangent to the curve at the points A and C; and at the same time locate the position of the major and minor axis, the length of the major axis, and position of both major and minor axis being unknown.*

Pivot the trammel in the point *D*; set from pencil to minor pin the distance equal to the radius *DL*, of quarter circle, (which is always equal to the length of the semi-minor axis of its accompanying ellipse). Place the pencil in the point *C*, and the minor pin in the groove at *F*, and the major pin in the groove at *H*; now slightly fasten the major pin, and move the rod to the point *A*, holding the trammel firmly. If the pencil reaches beyond the point *A*, slide the major pin closer to the minor pin, and fasten again, also move the trammel a little, and try again, until the pencil will pass through the point *AC*. Then fasten securely the major pin, and trace the elliptic curve *KCAJ*, as required.

The position of the trammel now gives the direction of the major axis *JK*, also the minor axis *DL*, and the pencil describes the elliptic curve. *FC* equals the length of semi-minor axis, and *HC* equals the length of semi-major axis, and the sides *AB* and *BC* of the Rhomboid are tangent to the curve at the points *A* and *C*, as required.

Fig. 11. *This problem is the same as the preceding for the center ellipse, and is intended that proportional lines A L, L 3, 3C, CK, and their parallels, may be drawn, giving the width of concentric ellipses at the points A, L, 3 C, and K.*

The radius of any circle, as has been stated, always equals the semi-minor axis of any accompanying ellipse. Then *DL* equals the length of the semi-minor axis : and *A* is another fixed point at the end of the parallelogram ; *C*, at the opposite end, is another fixed point, that the curve has to pass through; on the diagonal line *DB* another point, 3, may be established ; the method to establish this point is shown at Fig. 4, Plate 24 ; also Fig. 2, Plate 32. Now join *LA, L 3, 3 C, CK.* Make *L 2, L 2,* each equal half the thickness of the cylindric section. Draw 2 4 parallel with *AL*, also 2 5, 5 6, 6 7, parallel with the center proportionals, intersecting the radials *DB, DC, DK* and *DA.* At these intersections the points are given through which the curves will pass, a pliable strip may be used to trace the curve through the points, instead of the trammel.

A line that will be normal to the curve at the point *A* is drawn at right angles to the tangent *AB* as *PS*.

At *C* an indefinite amount of straight wood may be added parallel to *BC* prolonged from the points 6, 6.

Fig. 12. *Shows how the Ellipse may be drawn with a straight-edge, and a pliable strip.*

Let *AB* indicate the major axis, and *CD* the length of the minor axis, and *O* the center of the ellipse required ; let *EF* indicate the straight-edge. Make a nick at *H* ; make *HJ* equal *OC* ; let *HK* equal *OA* ; now move the rod at intervals, keeping the points *J* and *K* directly over the axis lines, and marking points at the nick *H*, as 2, 3, &c., then trace the elliptic curve through the points, using a pliable strip.*

* Mr. Russell has applied this method to describing the elliptic curves of the face-mould.

PLATE 6.

THE SCROLL.

Exhibits how to draw the Scroll.

Fig. 1. [Scale, 3″ equal 1 foot.] *Shows how to draw the Scroll by quadrants.*

Let **AB** indicate the full width of scroll from out to out. Divide **AB** into eight equal parts; bisect **AB** at **C**, drop half a space to **D**; perpendicular to **AB** draw **DF**, equal to a whole space; bisect **DF** at **O**; with **O** as a center, and **OD** as a radius, draw the semicircle from **D** to **F**. Make **AE** equal a space, draw the diagonal **EB** intersecting the semicircle at **H**, draw **FH** and **DH** indefinite. From **F**, and at right angles to **FD**, draw **FJ**, and at right angles to **FJ** draw **JK**, and at right angles to **JK** draw **KL**, &c., establishing the points **D, F, J, K, L** and **M**, from which to draw the scroll by quadrants.

With **D** for a center, and **DB** as a radius, draw the curve to intersect **DF** prolonged at **N**; again, with **F** for a center, and **FN** as a radius, draw the curve to intersect **FJ** prolonged at **E**. Proceed in like manner to draw the other quarter circles **P, Q, R** and **S**. Make **BT** equal the width of rail, and draw the inside curves in like manner. Draw the shank **BV** at right angles to **BA**.

It will be observed that any number of revolutions may be drawn in this way; the shank may be drawn at either of the quadrants. From **S** around to **E** is termed one revolution, and from **E** around to **B**, is half a revolution. Draw the eye of scroll from the center **H**.

Fig. 2. [Scale, half size.] *Shows how to find the centers from which to draw the Scroll, drawn half size, and agrees with Fig. 1. the lettering being the same.*

Fig. 3. [Scale, ¾″=1 foot.] *Shows the width of Scroll AB, divided into seven equal parts. The centers from which to draw the quadrants, are found precisely the same way as at Fig. 1.*

Fig. 4. [¾″ scale.] *Shows the curtail step,* and is drawn from the same centers as Fig. 3; **B** is the Block, and is cut out to the shape, from a thick piece of very dry stuff, the depth of the rise less the thickness of step. **R** is the rise, which is shouldered at **W**; **V** is the veneer, and is reduced at **W** to a scant eighth of an inch, and is still further reduced tapering towards the end at **K**, to a sixteenth of an inch. A kerf at **K**, is shown for the veneer to enter. Folding wedges are shown at **W**, to be entered from both sides at the same time, to strain the veneer to place evenly; **S** shows the outer string, and the concave side of block is shown veneered to match the string. This may not be necessary, unless the outer string be of some fancy wood; **N** shows the nosings of steps.

Let it be observed, that by dividing the width of scroll into a greater, or less, number of spaces, the revolutions will be closer together, or open, as the case may be.

The line **EB** will pass through the center **H**, and the two lines **FK** and **DJ** will form right angles at **H**.

Fig. 5. [Scale, 1½″=1 foot.] *Exhibits a reciprocal Scroll, drawn by segments.*

Draw **AB** and **CD** to form the four right angles at **O**; divide each right angle into four equal parts, and draw the radial lines through the center *O* indefinite. Draw the eye of scroll at *O*; from the verge of eye, draw the chord 2 3 at right angles to *O* 2; from the point 3 draw the chord 3 4 at right angles to *O* 3; from the point 4 draw the chord 4 5 at right angles to *O* 4. Proceed in this way on each radial line, until a sufficient number of revolutions are laid off. Then connect the points 2 3, 3 4, 4 5, &c., by segments, in this manner. With *O* 31 for a radius, and 31 for a center, draw arc at *F*, with the same radius and point 32 for a center, draw arc intersecting at *F*. Then, with *F* for a center, draw the arc from 31 to 32. Again, with *O* 30 for a radius, and point 30 for a center, draw arc at *H*, with the same radius and point 31 for a center, draw arc intersecting at *H*, then, with *H* for a center, draw the arch from 30 to 31.

In like manner find point *J*, and others, from which to complete the spiral line for the convex curve of pattern. Draw the concave side *DLN*, also the center line *MP*, parallel to the convex curve. The straight, or wreath rail, may connect the scroll at any point in the curve, at right angles to the radius of any segment.

This scroll has a beautiful effect at the starting of a winding flight of stairs; a ground plan made for winders to conform to this mixed curve, the result will be a very graceful twist.

Figs. 6, 7 and 8. [Scale, one-half full size.] *Shows how to find the contour of a Moulded Cap, from a given section of rail, so the turner may turn the cap to suit the profile of rail.*

Fig. 6. *Shows a section of Hand-rail* $3\frac{3}{4}'' \times 2\frac{1}{4}''$.
Draw the parallelogram *ABCD*, for the half section of rail. Divide *BC* into any number of parts, as 1, 2, 3, 4, &c.; draw *BA* indefinite; anywhere on *BA* prolonged, say *O*, Fig. 7. Draw *OE* at right angles to *OB*, and equal to the radius of newel cap, say 4″. Then with *OE* for a radius, and *O* as a center, draw the circumference of cap, intersecting *OA* at *F*; make *FG* equal to half width of rail *BC*; prolong *CD* to intersect the circumference of cap at *H*, connect *GH* for one side of miter. Parallel with *GB*, and from the points 1, 2, 3, &c., draw lines cutting the contour of rail section at 0, 0, 0, and to intersect the miter *GH* at 1, 2, 3, &c.

Fig. 7. *Shows the Miter into the Cap, Fig. 8.*
From the center *O*, carry the points 1, 2, 3, &c., on *GH* to *KE*, Fig. 8. Make *EQ* equal *AB*, for the thickness of cap. Now, transfer 1 0, 2 0, 3 0, also *P* 0, *N* 0, &c., from Fig. 6 to corresponding lines, Fig. 8, then through the points *K*, 0, 0, 0 and *L*, Fig. 8, trace the contour of moulding required for the cap. The pattern may be made similar to that at Fig. 7, Plate 4, which should be two or three inches long for hand hold. If this pattern be neatly made, and in the hands of a good, practical turner, the cap will member at the miter with the common moulding.

PLATE 7.

THE FACE-MOULD.

The eight following plates are intended as lessons for the young man to draw the face-mould, and make models for a wreath-piece. The triangular system herein set forth is believed by the author to be the most economical method for the construction of face-moulds over ground plans of large diameter, or over winders. The half size of rail will suit best, for the models; pine, or some soft wood, may be used for practice. If the drawing is made one-quarter full size, then "soap"* may be used, which may be cut out with the knife; this last method will do for studying the application of bevels, and the sliding of the mould; but does not increase the skill of the young man in the use of his tools; to be a good Stair-builder, he must be expert in working with the drawing-knife and spoke-shave, in which there is a great sleight.

Plate 7. [Scale, 1½″=1′.] *Exhibits the construction of the Face-mould for a Wreath-piece of a Hand-rail, to stand over a quarter circle on plan, the radius for the center line being 15″. The Wreath-piece to contain a full easing, hence one tangent will be inclining, and the other horizontal; the rail to be 3″ wide by 4½″ deep.*

As the wreath-piece is to contain a full easing over a ground plan of one-quarter circle, the face-mould will be one-quarter of an ellipse, the axis of which will form the joints of the wreath-piece.   Also one bevel only will be required, that at the joint on the major axis, which will be at the wide end of mould; the square will be applied at the joint on the narrow end of face-mould, which will be on the minor axis.

Fig. 1. *Shows the ground plan of the Quarter Circle.*
Draw **OA** and **OB** at right angles, with **OA** [15″] for a radius, draw the dotted line **ASB** for the center of rail. Make **A 2, A 3** each equal half the width of the rail [1½″]. Draw the width of rail, 2 4 and 3 6, for the cylindric section on plan. Draw the tangents **AD** and **BD** perpendicular to the radial lines **OA** and **OB**, and we have the square parallelogram **OABD** on plan. Draw the chord **AB**, bisect **AB** at **C**; bisect **CB** and **CA** at **E** and **F**; bisect **AF** at **G** ; in this case the tangent **AD** will be the director of ordinates, because the wreath-piece is to have a full easing. Parallel with the director **AD**, draw ordinates from the points **GFC** and **E** to intersect the concave, convex, and center lines at the points 2, 4 and 3.

Fig. 2. *Shows the development and elevation of Tangents from plan.*
Let **XX** indicate a base line. Make **HD** and **DA** equal the tangents **BD** and **DA** on plan, Fig. 1; draw **AE, DF** and **HG**, perpendicular to **XX**. Assume **HB** to be the height the wreath-piece is required to raise; connect **BD**, for the length of tangent in elevation, that will stand over tangent **BD** on plan, Fig. 1; the other tangent, **AD**, is horizontal for a wreath-piece having a full easing, and its length remains the same as on plan [15″].
Make **HJ** equal the chord **AB**, on plan, Fig. 1, parallel with the perpendicular **DF**, draw the half width of rail, cutting the tangent **DB** at 2 ; then **D 2** will be the increased width for half the mould at the wide end.
Bevel. In this case but one bevel is required, and that is found as shown in the angle at **B**.

Fig. 3. *Exhibits the Face-mould.*
Draw the right angle **BDA** indefinite ; make **DB** equal tangent **DB**, Fig. 2.   Let **DA** equal tangent **DA** on plan, Fig. 1. Parallel with tangents **DB** and **DA**, draw **AO** and **BO**, and we have the rectilineal parallelogram **OADB** on the cutting plane, or plane of plank, that will stand over the square parallelogram **OADB** on plan, Fig. 1.
· *Proof.* The chord **AB** and diagonal **DO**, must each equal **BJ**, Fig. 2.   Draw the chord **AB** ; bisect **AB** at **C** ; bisect **BC** and **CA** at **E** and **F** ; bisect **AF** at **G**.   Now, in this case, the

---

*Recommended by Mr. Collins, in the *Encyclopedia of Architecture.*

tangent *AD* becomes the director; draw ordinates from the points *G, F, C* and *E*, indefinite, and parallel to the director *AD;* make *A* 4; *G,* 2, 3, 4; *C,* 2, 3, 4; *B* 4; *B* 6, &c., each equal corresponding-ing points on plan, Fig. 1.

Make *A* 7 and *A* 8 each equal *D* 2 in elevation, Fig. 2 ; now trace the curves for the center, concave and convex sides of mould, through the points as shown, using a flexible strip. If a trammel or rod be preferred, *O* is the center for the trammel and the semi-minor axis *OB* and semi-major axis *OA* are given.

For long face-moulds the use of ordinates in this way will be found more convenient, as the work can be done in less space, and any number of points in the elliptic curve can be established correct enough for practice.

The trammel, however, gives the elliptic curve for face-moulds absolutely correct, for all wreath-pieces, standing over a ground plan, that is a portion of a true circle.

The rod may be used instead of a trammel, as shown at Fig. 2, Plate 4.

The section at *M* shows the bevel applied from the face of crook, through the center of plank ; the dotted line indicates a gauge line determining the center of plank, and is applied the same at both joints so as to have the wreath-piece taken from the center of plank. Now, make a "Block Pattern" of thin stuff to the size required for the rail; in this case, 3"×4½", as indicated at *M* and *N;* have a line, 2 3, drawn through the center, and a small screw filed off to a point placed in the center *O,* so that a light tap with the hammer will hold the pattern in place.

The pattern is centered at the intersection *O,* made by the gauge line, and the tangent *AD,* that is squared over the joint, through which the bevel found in the angle at *B,* Fig. 2, is applied ; and the line 3 2, on the block pattern is made to agree with the bevel line; then scribe around the pattern for the section of rail on the joint. At section *N* the try square is applied through the center of crook, from the face of plank ; the block pattern is centered at the intersection, and is governed by the square ; the shaded parts show the amount of over wood that has to be removed in the formation of the wreath-piece.

Fig. 4. *Exhibits an isometrical view of the plan, elevation and center line of Face-mould, on the cutting plane OADH.*

The plan of tangents *OABD* agrees with those at Fig. 1 ; *BH* is the height ; *BA* the chord on plan, and *HA* the chord in elevation. The dotted line *AJB* indicates the center line of rail on plan, and *AJH* the center line on the cutting plane.

The chord *AB* on plan, is bisected at the points *E, C, F, G,* in manner as described at Fig. 1 ; the ordinates, 3 *G,* 3 *F,* &c. are made parallel to *AD.* From the points *E, C, F, G,* perpendiculars are drawn, cutting the chord *HA* in elevation, and dividing *HA* proportionately with the chord *BA,* on plan. Ordinates are again drawn ; this time from the chord *HA,* in elevation, parallel with *DA;* the points in the ordinates on the horizontal plane are transferred to corresponding ordinates on the cutting plane, using the chords *AB* and *AH* as a base.

The curve traced through the points *H,* 3, 3, *A,* shows the center line of rail on the cutting plane, and indicates the dotted line on the center of face-mould, Fig. 3. The student will see through this more readily by the study of blocks or prismatic solids ; dress up a block five or six inches long, say 2" square, cut it to the bevel shown at *B,* Fig. 2, across its two opposite sides, the other two sides will be square to the face ; then by dividing it across the angles, as *ABHA* on the chord lines, into two triangular prisms, he will see at once the whole system in a "nutshell."

Fig. 5. *Shows the manner of cutting out the crook from the plank; then applying the bevels, and sliding the moulds.*

One may be able to draw a correct face-mould, and yet fail in applying the bevels and sliding the mould. The shaded part at sections *M* and *N*, Fig. 3, show the width at the joints required for the wreath-piece to square; at *N*, $\frac{3}{8}''$ on the concave and $\frac{1}{8}''$ on the convex side, is enough wood to allow. In this case, observe the wide end of mould about equals the width of shaded section at *M*, but at *N* the section is a little wider than the mould, to allow for dressing down. Now lay the pattern on the plank, mark the convex side, then shift the mould at the narrow end to the required width shown by the section, and mark the concave side of mould; also at the joints allow $\frac{1}{2}''$ for jointing, then cut out square through the plank. The band saw is the best tool for this work; now dress off the upper side of crook true, and out of wind, this must be carefully done for the face-mould, and bevels may all be correctly drawn, and if the crook be not true on its face, the work will not prove satisfactory. Now, mark the tangents on both sides of the face-mould, directly opposite to each other. Do this on all face-moulds. The heavy lines, 2 3, 4 5, show the joints of crook for the wreath piece; place the mould on the crook keeping it in the center of the stuff on its face. Now carefully mark the joints 2 3 and 4 5, and also mark the tangents shown by the heavy lines *AD* and *BD;* see while doing this the mould does not shift; now lift the pattern and complete the marking of the tangents on the face of crook, then square and cut the joints 2 3 and 4 5, dress the joints, square to the face of crook, and also square to the tangents, by applying the stock to the joint and the blade along the tangent; then carry the tangents across the joints, square to the face of crook as shown by the heavy lines, through the center of sections at *M* and *N;* then mark the tangents *AD* and *BD* on the other side directly opposite and square to the joints. Now set a gauge to the half thickness of plank, and center the crook as shown by the dotted lines on sections *M* and *N;* then at *M* apply the bevel found in the angle at *B*, Fig. 2, from the face of crook, through the intersection made by the gauge line.

Next apply the block pattern square to the line made from the bevel, mark around the same for the section of rail; proceed in the same manner at section *N*, using the try square instead of a bevel. Now let it be observed the center line at section *M*, made by the bevel, intersects the face of crook at 6; then square across on the upper side of crook parallel with *AD* the line 6 *D;* on the under side of crook, the point 7 extends beyond the face of crook in this case, and the tangent cannot be marked on the crook.

At section *N* the square is shown applied, and the tangent *C H*, on the face-mould will rest over the tangent *BD*, on the crook; and the tangent 6 *F* on the face-mould will rest over the tangent 6 *D* on the crook.

The light solid lines 8, 10, and 9, 16, 11, show the face-mould applied to the face of crook. Observe it is shifted from *A* to 6 at the lower end, and the same distance from *B* to *C*, at the upper end, on the upper side of crook; and on the under side of crook, the dotted lines 12, 13, 14 and 16, *D* 15, show the face-mould has shifted from *B* to *E* at the upper end, and from *A* to 7 at the lower end. As we cannot mark the tangent on the crook at 7, on the under side, slide the mould on the crook until the center line made by the bevel shown at section *M*, Fig 6, will line with the tangent on the mould shown at 7, keeping the joint on mould even with the joint on crook, and also the tangent on the mould at the narrow end must lie over the tangent *BD*, on the crook. Observe now the face-mould on the upper side of crook has shifted from *B* to *C*, at the narrow end, while the mould shown by the dotted line has shifted from *B* to *E* on the lower side. Note also the joint at the wide end of mould is on line with the joint of crook; the joint therefore answers for a slide line when sliding the mould, this is always the case when the plank is canted only one way, as in this case. Now scribe around the mould on the upper side of crook, on the convex side, S *FH* 10, and also for a short distance at 5, on the concave side, the balance of mould leaves the crook.

On the under side, scribe around the mould on the concave side 12, 13 and 14, and for a short distance at 15, on the convex side, the balance of mould on the convex side leaves the crook. Observe the scribe lines at 14 and 15, do not extend to the joint 4 5; they may be carried to the joint leaving a small amount on each side of the block pattern to be dressed off when the adjoining wreath piece is connected. Also note the curve of face mould on the upper side of crook, at joint *B*, cuts the joint to one side of the block pattern as shown by the dotted lines at *a* and *b*. Do not be alarmed at this seeming disagreement, for the block pattern does not give the correct contour or outline of the squared section of rail for a joint within the wreath, when the plane of joint is oblique to the axis of cylinder, as at joint *B*, it being at right angles to the inclination of tangent *BD*. For this reason all wreaths that have their joints oblique to the axis of cylinder should be worked off to the bevels, leaving some over wood at the joints to be taken off when they are bolted together. When the wreaths are separated it will be seen that the sides of the section are concave on the concave side, and convex on the convex side of rail; this curve is elliptical and tangents the block pattern at the center of rail, as shown by the dotted lines at section *N*, Fig, 6.

The joint at *A* is different, it being a plumb joint. the tangent *AD* being level, consequently the joint will be parallel to the axis of cylinder, and the block pattern gives the true contour of the squared section of rail.

All joints that are made square to inclining tangents are oblique to the axis of cylinder. If the joint at *B* was joined to straight rail, then the contour of the squared section of rail would be curved at the upper side down to the center of joint, and straight from that to the lower side, the curve forming a tangent to the side of block pattern at the center of rail. The straight part belongs to the straight part of rail and terminates at the spring of cylinder, as shown by the dotted line *JK*, Fig. 6. The triangular piece at *J* shows the straight part. Suppose the joint at *B* to be plumb, or a splice joint on the line *JK*, Fig. 6, instead of a butt joint, then it will be seen that the two sides of the squared section of rail would be straight and parallel to each other, and the plane of the joint would be parallel to the axis of the cylinder; then the wreath piece would cover exactly one-quarter of the circle. This being a butt joint, it will be observed the triangular piece between *K* and *B*, Fig. 6, is cut away, and must be supplied by the adjoining wreath-piece, which makes up for the seeming disagreement at 4 and 5, Fig. 5. In the same way the triangular piece at *J* makes up for the lower side of the adjoining wreath-piece.

For this reason, a joint connecting a wreath-piece with the straight rail should never be made at the spring line, but add on some straight wood, at least what the mould would slide, as *BC*, Fig. 5. For wreaths on winders connecting ramps, the distance

BC or *A* 6, Fig. 5, will be enough straight wood to add for shank; but for wreath-pieces on platforms, or level landings, 6″ straight wood for shanks is a fair allowance, to ease off the straight rail, into the wreath part ; and should be measured in and priced as wreath rail, as the labor on this part of wreath-piece is equal to that of any other part.

Fig. 6. *Shows the concave side of crook* turned up, having the concave side worked off to the bevel and square, and the face-mould *SS* shifted on the upper and lower side so that the center of mould agrees with the center line 6 7, made from the bevel through the center of crook.

Two face-moulds are shown here but only one is required ; it will be observed that by tacking the face-mould on the upper side of crook, the edge 9, 16, 11 Fig. 5, will serve for a guide to work off the concave side of wreath-piece to the required bevel.

The scribe line 12, 13, 14, Fig. 5, on the opposite side of crook serves as a guide to shape the wreath piece for the lower side. For the convex side of wreath piece, if the face-mould be tacked on to the lower side of crook, the edge of pattern will give the line for the convex side of wreath piece ; the scribe line 8, *F. H,* Fig. 5, gives the curve of mould on the upper side of crook.

The surplus wood should be removed from the concave side first, then the best way is to gauge for the convex side, using the "Cupper gauge," shown at Figs. 13 and 14, Plate 21. After the wreath piece is shaped to the bevel on the concave and convex sides, then use a pliable strip to form the twist of wreath as shown at 2, 3, *B. Falling-moulds,* made of paste board or tin, to the required depth of rail, were made in former days, to obtain the falling line of the wreath piece ; now a thin strip ½″ wide and one-sixteenth thick, is bent around the convex and also on the concave side of wreath piece and the twist line traced agreeably to the eye, the thin strip is easily adjusted so as to avoid any kinks or abrupt places. Next take off the surplus wood from the top side of wreath piece first ; when dressed off, to please the eye and touch; gauge for the lower side.

Remember when dressing off the wreath piece use the tools so as to conform to the pitch of wreath piece as *JK,* Fig. 6 ; this direction is very easy found at any time by marking the end of mould on the crook, as 15, 14, Fig. 5 ; then a line from 14, through 5, Fig. 6, gives the direction for the tool ; pencil lines parallel to 5 14, may be drawn with a parallel ruler from end to end of the wreath piece as a guide for the tools. A large gouge and mallet are about the best tools to rough down the surplus wood, then use the drawing-knife, cylinder-plane and spoke-shave to dress off to the concave arris of the face-mould ; also use a short straight-edge to rest on the arris of mould and the scribe line on the crook, in the direction of *JK,* Fig. 6, as a guide to true up the concave side of wreath piece.

PLATE 8.

Plate 8. *Exhibits how to draw the face-mould for a quarter circle for a wreath-piece having an intermediate easing ; the tangents will be different in their inclination, hence two bevels will be required.*

Fig. 1. *Shows the plan of the quarter circle.* Draw *OA* and *OB* indefinite, and at right angles. From the center *O* draw the quarter circle *ASB* to the radius of 15″; draw the tangents *AD* and *BD* square to the radial lines *OB* and *OA;* on each side of *A*, set off the half width of rail [1½″] as *A* 2 and *A* 4; from the center *O* draw the concave side of rail 2, 2, 2, and also the convex side 4, 4, 4, thus completing the cylindric section 2, 2, 2, and 4, 4, 4, on plan. Draw the chord *AB;* bisect the chord at *C;* bisect *CB* and *CA* at *E* and *F;* bisect *AF* at *G*.

Fig. 2. *Exhibits the development and elevation of tangents from the plan,* Fig. 1. Let *XX* indicate a base line. Make *BD* and *DA*, equal the tangents *BD* and *DA* on plan Fig. 1; perpendicular to *XX*, draw *BC, DE* and *AF.* Assume *BC* to be the height the wreath piece has to raise; from *C* and square to *CB*, draw *CE* prolonged. Also assume the inclination of the lower tangent to cut *DE* at *G*, draw *CG* prolonged to intersect *XX* at *H*, draw the tangent *AG* to intersect *BC* at *J*. From *D*, and square to *CH*, draw *Dk;* from *E*, and perpendicular to *AJ*, draw *EL*. Make *CM* equal the chord *AB* on plan, Fig. 1. Parallel with *DE*, draw the half width of rail, cutting the tangents *AG* and *CG* at 2 and 3 respectively.

Bevels. Let *PN* indicate a line drawn parallel with *XX;* draw *PQ* square to *XX*, and equal to the radius *OA*, Fig. 1. Make *PS* equal *DK*, and *PR* equal *EL;* draw *QR* and *QS*, and in the angle *PSQ*, is found the bevel for the joint of wreath-piece at the narrow end of face-mould, and in the angle *PRQ* is found the bevel for the joint at the wide end of mould.*

Fig. 3. *Exhibits the face-mould.* Make the tangent *BD* equal *CG*, Fig. 2; with *B* as a center, and *MB*, Fig. 2, for a radius, draw arc at *A;* again, with *D* as a center, and *GA*, Fig. 2, for a radius, draw arc intersecting at *A*, connect *DA;* parallel with *DA* and *DB*, draw *BO* and *AO*, for the parallelogram *AODB*, on the cutting plane, that will agree when in position, with the square parallelogram *OADB* on plan Fig. 1.

Proof. The diagonal *OD* must equal the distance *MJ*, Fig. 2; if so, the parallelogram is correct. Make *BH* equal *GH*, Fig. 2; draw *HO* for the direction of minor axis ; make *A* 2 and *A* 4 each equal *G* 3, Fig. 2; make *B* 2 and *B* 4 each equal *G* 2, Fig. 2, draw the chord *AB;* bisect *AB* at *C;* bisect *CA* and *CB* at *F* and *E;* bisect *AF* at *G;* from the points *A, G, F, C, E* and *B* draw ordinates indefinite and parallel with the director *HO*. On plan, Fig. 1, make *BH* equal *DH*, Fig. 2, join *HO* for the directing ordinate ; from the points *A, G, F, C, E* and *B* draw ordinates parallel to *HO*, cutting the concave, center and convex sides of rail in the points 2, 3, 4. Now transfer the points in the ordinates Fig. 1, to the corresponding ordinates Fig. 3, using the chords as base lines, then trace the curves through the points.

Make the joints at *A* and *B* square to the tangents *AD* and *BD*. The sections at *M*, show the joint centered by the dotted line, and the tangent line is squared over the joint intersecting the gauge line ; the bevel at *R*, Fig. 2, is applied through the intersection, from the face of crook.

---

*When the tangents happen to be nearly the same length, the difference in width of the face-mould at the joints will be slight; then apply the steepest bevel to the joint that has the radial line the greatest distance from the minor axis. In that case the minor axis should always be drawn on the mould whenever practicable. Another sure way is to apply the steepest bevel to the joint that is made from the shortest tangent; this rule applies to all face-moulds for wreath pieces that are circular on plan.

Observe the bevel as applied will raise the joint at ***B*** up. The section at ***N*** shows the tangent squared across the joint, and the same gauge as applied at ***M*** gives the intersection through which the bevel found in the angle at ***S***, Fig. 2, is applied. Observe the bevel is applied the opposite from that at ***M***, and will cross * the tangents, and thus pitch the joint at ***A*** down. The shaded parts at ***M*** and ***N*** show the width to saw out the crook at the joints. To find the amount of over wood required at ***K*** on the normal line ***GK***, to saw out the crook; take ***F***, Fig. 1, as a center and ***FC***, Fig. 3, for a radius; draw arc cutting the diagonal ***OD*** at ***f***, join ***fF***; draw the half depth of rail, [2¼″] parallel with ***Ff***, cutting ***DO*** at ***b***; from ***b*** and square to ***Ff***, draw ***bJ***. From ***J*** draw a line parallel to ***OD***, cutting the concave curve of rail at ***h***; from ***h*** and at right angles to ***OD***, draw ***hc***; then from ***c*** to the concave curve is the amount of over wood required on the concave side of mould at the normal line or point ***K***, Fig. 3. On the convex side only enough over wood to clean off the saw marks, say ⅛″, is all that is required, but the amount increases gradually towards the ends, to the amount shown by the shaded parts, at sections ***M*** and ***N***.

Fig. 4. *Exhibits an isometrical view of the ground plan, elevation, governing ordinate, and the center line of rail on the cutting plane.* It is not intended for a working drawing, but simply to show from the triangular prisms the construction of lines, to find the cutting plane and the direction of the governing ordinate on the horizontal and cutting planes.

The learner will find it a great advantage to cut blocks to the inclination of tangents, when drawing his face-moulds, and from them he will discern more clearly the reason for this or that line. This is termed Stereotomy, or the study of the Science of Solids. The stone cutters are noted for this study, as one expert in the business can tell at once if what he requires is in a particular solid.

OABD shows the ground plan as described at Fig. 1, and indicates the end of two triangular blocks forming a square and is supposed to be a horizontal plane: ***ASB*** shows the center line of rail on plan; ***AB***, the chord; ***DG***, on edge of solid equals, the height ***DG***, Fig. 2; ***OO***, on the opposite corner of solid equals ***G E***, Fig. 2; ***BP*** indicates another corner of the solid, and equals the whole height as shown at ***BC***, Fig. 2; draw ***AO***, and ***AG***, connect ***PG*** and ***AO***, also ***PO*** for the parallelogram ***AGPO*** on the cutting plane, which indicates the parallelogram for the face-mould, Fig. 3. Now to find the directing ordinate on the horizontal plane, prolong ***BD*** indefinite, prolong ***PG*** to intersect ***BD*** prolonged, at ***Q***, join ***QA***, for the *director* sought; this line is termed the "intersecting line," by some; the "level" or "horizontal line," by others; the direction of the minor axis is always parallel with this line. If the other side ***BO*** of solid were prolonged same as ***BD***, and ***PO***, also prolonged to intersect ***BO***, then if a line be drawn from the inter-

---

*The term "cross" or "crossing the tangents," means that the bevels are applied to the opposite sides of tangents at the joints. Observe at joint *A*, section *M*, the bevel points to the right of the tangent *AD*. Let the eye follow the tangents around to joint *B*, and the sharp angle of bevel is seen to point to the opposite side of tangents at section *N*, thus crossing the tangents. This will be the case with all wreath pieces having two bevels, when the curve on plan is a quarter circle or more than a quarter circle; it is only when the plan is less than a quarter circle that the bevels do not cross; and then only when the minor axis is not in the mould.

section to the point **Q**, the line would pass through the point **A**, thus showing the line **QA** to result from the intersection of the two inclinations with the horizontal plane. If the learner would dowel on the triangular prisms **DQAG** to the side of the solid **D GA**, and do the same at the adjoining side **AOO**, then cut them to the inclination of the cutting plane, he will then see that all lines drawn parallel to the director **QA**, both on the horizontal and cutting plane, are of the same length, those on the cutting plane being parallel to those on the horizontal plane and all parallel to the director **QA**. This makes a fine study for the student in stair-building.

Make **BH** on the horizontal plane equal **DQ**; join **HO** for the director within the parallelogram **OADB**, on the horizontal plane. For the director on the cutting plane **AGPO**, make **PJ** equal **GQ**, join **JO** for the director on the cutting plane. It will be observed that the director **HO** on the horizontal plane, and also the director **JO** on the cutting plane, are both the same length, and parallel with the director **QA**. By drawing them within the parallelogram it saves room on the drawing board; **QD** is represented in the elevation by **DH**; and **QG** by **HG**, in elevation Fig. 2. The director **JO** on the cutting plane is the direction of the minor axis. If a line through **O** be drawn at right angles to **JO**, it would be the direction of the major axis; **OK** equals the radius **OA**, Fig. 1, for the center line of rail, and is the semi-minor axis of the elliptic curve, for the center line of rail.

AB is the chord line on the horizontal plane; **AP** is the chord line on the cutting plane, and represents **BM**, Fig. 2; the chord on the horizontal plane is first spaced off then the chord on the cutting plane is divided off proportionately with the chord on plan, as shown by the perpendicular lines **CC, EE**, &c.

For large face-moulds less room is required and time saved in their construction by the use of ordinates in this way, as shown in the triangular prism **ABD** on plan, and **APG** on the cutting plane. Bisect the chord **AB** on plan at **C**; bisect **CB** and **CA** at **E** and **F**, draw **F 3**, **C 3** and **E 3** parallel with the director **O H**; from **F, C** and **E**, on the chord **AB**, erect perpendiculars to intersect the chord **AP** at **FC** and **E** on the cutting plane; thus dividing the chord **AP** in elevation proportionately with the chord **AB** on plan. From the points **F, C** and **E** on the chord **AP**, draw ordinates parallel with the director **OJ**; then transfer the points **F 3**, **C 3**, from the ordinates on the horizontal plane to the corresponding ordinates on the cutting plane, and trace the elliptic curve through the points **A 3**, **3 P**, using a pliable strip.

The bevel shown at the angle **G** is taken from the angle **AG D**, Fig. 2, and the bevel shown at **O** is taken from the angle **GC B** Fig. 2. The student can test the correctness of joint bevels before applying them to the crooks by squaring up a piece 2″x 2″x6″ long, and cutting the same to the inclination that the tangents in elevation make with the perpendiculars as shown; then by applying the bevels at **M** and **N**, square to the inclination, will prove their correctness; this does not require much time, and will be a satisfaction to the beginner to know he is right as he proceeds with his work.

Fig. 5. *Shows the manner of sliding the mould.* The heavy curved line indicates the crook as sawed out from the plank, the dotted lines at the ends show ½″ over wood to make the joints. The face of crook must be carefully taken out of wind; then place the face-mould in the center of crook, mark the joints, also transfer the tangents from the face-mould to the crook;

also mark the normal line *LP*. Now lift the mould and finish the marking of tangents *AD* and *BD*, and the normal line *LP* on the face of crook. Cut and dress the joints square to the face, and also square to the tangents ; now carry the tangents across the joints square to the face of crook as shown by the heavy lines 2 3, at sections *M* and *N*. Then turn the crook over and mark the tangents on the opposite side square to the joints.

Now set a gauge to the half thickness of crook and mark both joints alike, as shown by the dotted line *OO*, drawn parallel with the face of crook. The bevels are shown applied at sections *M* and *N*, through the intersection made by the gauge line. The block pattern is then applied at right angles to the center line 6 7, made from the bevels. Observe the bevels are applied so as to cross the tangents, and also that they cut the upper side at 6, and the lower side of crook at 7. Now *A* 4 and *B* 4, on the upper side of crook, equals 2 6, at sections *M* and *N;* and *A* 5 and *B* 5, on the lower side of crook, equals 7 3, at sections *M* and *N*.

From 4 and 5, draw 4 *D* and 5 *D* parallel to tangents *AD* and *BD;* this should be carefully done as these lines 4 *D* and 5 *D* are to guide the face-mould. Now apply the face-mould so that the tangents 8 *D* and 9 *D* on the mould will agree with the tangent 4 *D* on the upper side of crook. Two holes are seen in the mould to aid in arranging the mould over the tangents on the crook correctly. If the mould be exact over the tangents, then the joints on the mould will be parallel with the joints on the crook.

When the tangents on the mould agree with the tangents on the crook, scribe around that portion of the mould that rests on the crook, then transfer the minor axis *GK* from the mould to the crook on the upper side. Now apply the mould to the opposite side of crook, sliding the same until the tangents 12 *D* and 10 *G* on the mould agree with the tangent 5 *D* on the crook, then scribe around the pattern and mark the minor axis as before.

At *H* the thickness of crook is turned up showing the pattern applied to both sides, and the point *KK* gives the direction to hold the tools when removing the surplus wood from the concave side of the wreath piece; the sections *M* and *N* show the over wood removed from the concave side and ready to gauge for the convex side, or if preferred, tack the mould on the crook and use the arris of the mould for a guide where the scribe line runs out, and work off the surplus wood to the distance the mould will allow, then shift the mould to the opposite side and treat in the same manner at the opposite end of crook.

At the minor axis, and for some distance beyond on either side, the mould will be in the way and must be removed, then work to the scribe line and use the judgment as to how much or little to take off. After the learner has squared up a few twists he will not need to tack on the face-mould for a guide. The more practical man will not be troubled in this way, but proceed at once to take off the surplus wood, guided by the scribe line on the crook together with the eye and judgment, and in this way detect any abrupt places in the curve. Then by elevating the crook into its natural position by standing one end on the floor while the other is lifted until the bevels will appear plumb, and by sighting down and around the curves, he will detect any abruptness. After the sides of wreath piece have been formed, then bend a thin strip around the concave and also on the convex side of large twists, and mark the twist lines of the wreath piece, keeping the section of rail at the minor axis *LP,* in the center of crook, for here at the minor axis, the bevels blend, and the section of rail as shown by the block pattern, is at right angles or square to the face of

crook ; and the center of rail is in the center of crook, as shown at
Q; QS and QT being equal to the depth of rail [$4\frac{1}{2}''$].

Observe the curved sides of wreath piece as shown by the
dotted lines at sections M and N, tangent the block pattern at the
center. This is mentioned merely to warn the learner not to
work down close to the block pattern at the joints, when the
joints are made in the circular part of wreath piece, but leave
some wood so that when the adjoining wreath piece is bolted on,
they both can be dressed off together, holding the tools perpendicular to the ground plan. If straight wood be added on at
either or both joints, let it be not less than what the mould slides,
4 9 or 5 12 ; then the block pattern will give the true contour of
rail section.

Comparing Fig. 5 with Fig. 5, plate 7, it will be observed that
the face-mould has shifted past the joints A and B at both ends,
while that at Fig. 5, Plate 7, the joint at A shows the pattern has
shifted on the line of joint. The reason of this is, because in the
former case, both tangents in elevation Fig. 2, are shown inclining, and the mould is shifted in two directions, while in the latter
case, one tangent is inclining and the other is level, and the
mould is shifted in one direction.

PLATE 9.

Plate 9. [Scale $1\frac{1}{2}''=1$ foot]. *Exhibits the construction
of the face-mould for a wreath piece over a quarter circle,
when the tangents are both the same inclination. Hence the
wreath piece will have no casing, and only one bevel will be
required for both joints ; the width of rail equals 3'' by 4½''
deep.*

Fig. 1. *Shows the plan.* Draw OA and OB at right
angles and of indefinite length. Make OA equal the radius
for the center line of rail. From the center O, draw the center
line of rail ASB, make A 2 and A 3 each equal the half width
of rail ; draw the concave and convex sides of rail 2 T 2 and 3 H
3. Perpendicular to the radial lines OA and OB, draw the tangents AC and BC; draw the diagonal line OC.

Observe when the tangents on plan are of equal length, and
both the same inclination in elevation, the diagonal OC always
becomes the director. This face-mould is very simple to draw
and could be laid off on the plan, to avoid a net work of lines,
make a separate drawing for the face-mould.

Draw the chord AB, bisect the same at D; bisect AD and
DB at E and F; bisect AE and FB at G and H. From the
points A, G, E, D, F, H and B, draw ordinates parallel to the
director OC, cutting the concave, center and convex sides of rail,
at 2, 3 and 4.

Fig. 2. *Exhibits the development and elevation of tangents.* Let XX indicate the edge of drawing board ; make BC
and CA equal the tangents BC and CA on plan, Fig. 1. At
right angles to XX draw the perpendiculars AD, CE and BF;
assume BG to be the height that the wreath piece is required to
raise. Connect AG, cutting the perpendicular CE at H. From
C and square to AH, draw Cj; make Bk equal the chord BA,
Fig. 1 ; parallel with CH, draw the half width of rail, cutting A
H at 2.

Bevels. In this case both tangents have the same inclination. As a result only one bevel will be required for both joints. The dotted line *LM* indicates a gauge line parallel with *XX*. Make *MP* equal *CJ*, draw *MN* at right angles to *XX*, and equal to the radius *OB*, Fig. 1; draw *NP* produced to the edge of board for convenience when adjusting the bevel, as shown..

Fig. 3. *Exhibits the face-mould.* Draw *AC* equal to the tangent *AH* in elevation; with *A* for a center, and *KG*, in elevation, for a radius, draw arc at *G*; again with *C* for a center, and *CA* as a radius, draw arcs intersecting at *G*, connect *CG*. Parallel with *CA* and *CG*, draw *GO* and *AO* for the parallelogram *OACG*, on the cutting plane; draw the diagonal *OC* for the director.

Proof. The diagonal *OC* must equal the diagonal *OC* on plan Fig. 1; if so the parallelogram is correct.

This is very important, that the tangents have the correct direction, for the joints are made square to the tangents, therefore be careful to give the tangents the right angle at *C*, for they control the joints.

Draw the chord *AG*; bisect *AG* at *D*; bisect *DA* and *DG* at *E* and *F*; bisect *AE* and *FG* at *J* and *H*. From *A*, *J*, *E*, *F*, *H* and *G*, draw ordinates, indefinite and parallel with the director *OC*. Now transfer the points 2, 3, 4, &c. on the ordinates on plan, Fig. 1, to the corresponding ordinates on face-mould. Make *A* 5 and *A* 6, also *G* 7 and *G* 8, each equal *H* 2, in elevation, Fig, 2. Now trace the curve through the points 5, 2, 7, &c., for the concave, and through the points 6, 4, 8, &c., for the convex side of face-mould using a pliable strip. Make the joints at *A* and *G* square to the tangents *AC* and *GC*; the sections at *M* and *N* represent the joints at *A* and *G*; the tangents, after being transferred from the mould to the face side of crook. They are then squared over the joints as shown at *M* and *N*; the dotted lines indicate gauge lines for centering the plank. The bevel found in the angle at *P*, Fig. 2, is applied through the center, then the block pattern is applied square to the line made from the bevel, as shown.

Observe the bevel at *M* as applied will pitch the joint at *G* up, and the bevel as applied at section *N* will pitch the joint at *A* down.

The shaded parts show the amount of over wood at the joints that has to be removed, and also the width required at the joints to saw out the crook a sufficient width and thickness to contain the twist of wreath piece. At the points 2, 4, on the director, the section of rail is square to the face of crook. Hence, at that point the bevels blend, and the width of face-mould is equal to the true width of rail. At that point, enough over wood on the convex side to dress off the saw marks, is all that is required, but on the concave side, owing to the curvature of rail section, more or less is required to saw out the crook; for a deep rail and a small cylinder the increased width will be greater, as the depth of rail decreases, and the diameter of cylinder increases, the amount of over wood at the normal line decreases. In most cases, half inch will be sufficient on the concave side.

Fig. 4. *Exhibits an isometrical view of the solid to agree with the plan Fig. 1 and elevation, Fig. 2; and is intended, not as a working drawing, but to lead the student in hand-railing to study the prismatic solid, for in that the learner will see the reason why, for every line sooner than by any other method.*

The plan or end of solid is represented by the parallelogram *OACB*. From the center *O*, draw the center line of rail *ASB*; make *BG* equal the height *BG*, Fig. 2; let *CH* and *OO* equal the height *CH*, Fig. 2, connect *HA* and *OA*, also connect *GO* and *GH*; for the parallelogram *OAHG* on the cutting plane, standing over the horizontal plane *OACB* as shown.

The diagonal *OC* is the director on the horizontal plane which bisects the chord *AB* at *D*; bisect *AD* and *DB* at *E* and *F*. From *E* and *F* draw ordinates parallel with the director *DC*, to intersect the center line *ASB* at 3 *S* and 3. The chord *AG* on the cutting plane, stands directly over the chord on the horizontal plane *OACB*, as shown.

Bisect the chord *AG*, on the cutting plane *OAHG*; at *J*, bisect *JA* and *JG* at *K* and *L*; draw the diagonal *OH* for the director on the cutting plane.

From *K* and *L* draw ordinates indefinite; now transfer the points 3, *S*, 3, from the ordinates on the horizontal plane to the corresponding ordinates on the cutting plane at 4, 4, 4; then trace the elliptic curve through the points *A*, 4, 4, 4, *G*, for the center line of rail.

If a bevel as shown at *M* be applied square to the inclination *AO*, both on the side of solid and over the cutting plane, it will be found to agree with the bevel found at *P*, Fig. 2, and may be used by the beginner to prove the bevels found in the usual way before applying.

The sides of the block are marked for cutting with the bevel, taken from the angle *AHC*, Fig. 2, and is applied as shown at *H*, Fig. 4, on all four sides.

Fig. 5. *Exhibits the sliding of the mould to conform to the bevels in the formation of the wreath-piece.* The heavy curved line indicates the crook as sawed from the plank. The face of crook must be carefully dressed out of wind, where there is steam, this is quickly done on a hand jointer; then if the face-mould be made of wood test the correctness of joints by applying the stock of square to the joint and the blade to the tangent. If correct, place the face-mould in the center of crook and tack a brad at each end to prevent the mould from shifting; then mark the joints, also mark the position of tangents *AD* and *BD* on the crook from the mould, also the normal line 4 2, then lift the mould and complete the marking of tangents and the normal.

Now cut and dress off the joints square to the face of crook, and also square to the tangents, then carry the tangents across the joints square to the face of crook as shown by the lines 2 3, at sections *M* and *N*; also mark the tangents *AD* and *BD* on the opposite side of crook square to the joints.

Then center the plank with the gauge as shown by the dotted lines intersecting the lines 2 3, at *hh*; then through the intersection apply the bevel at *M* and the reverse way at section *N*, so as to have the bevels cross the tangents.

Apply the block pattern square to the line 6 7, made from the bevel, showing the twist of wreath-piece in the rough crook; now make *AC* and *BE* on the upper side of crook, equal 2 6, on the section; draw *CD* and *ED* parallel to *AD* and *BD*, repeat the same on the lower side of crook; *HD* and *FD* is parallel to *AD* and *BD*.

Now slide the face-mould so as to agree with the tangents on the crook; tangents *ad* and *bd* on the mould must lie over tangents *CD* and *ED* on the crook; when in the right position tack a brad at each end to hold the mould in place, then scribe around that portion of mould that lies over the crook including the joint. Also mark the minor axis 5 8, on the upper side of crook; repeat this operation on the lower side as shown by the dotted lines.

It will be seen now from the position of the two moulds and the bevels, the formation of the wreath rail in the crook, a line from 10 on the lower side of crook, to 8 on the upper side, gives the direction to hold the tools when taking the surplus wood from the concave side of wreath-piece.

At sections *M* and *N* the over wood is shown removed from the concave side. As the joints are made at the spring lines to connect other wreath-pieces, it will be observed the block pattern does not give the correct outline of the sides of rail section as shown by the dotted curved lines; but if the joint were to connect with straight rail at the upper end, then the block pattern will give the correct outline for the lower half of rail section, while the upper half would be curved. And also at joint *A* the upper half would be straight and the lower half curved; for this reason when the wreath-piece has to connect an easement or straight rail, there should be straight wood added on for shank equal to *Eb* or *Ca*, the distance that the mould slides from the joint; the shaded part indicates the face side of crook.

PLATE 10.

Plate 10. [Scale, 1½″ 1′]. *Exhibits the construction of the face-mould for a wreath-piece having a full easing, when the segment on plan is less than a quarter circle; in this case the angle of tangents on plan will be obtuse.*

Fig. 1. *Shows the plan.* Let *OA, OB* be the radii; [15″] draw the tangents *AC* and *BC* at right angle to the radii, creating the obtuse angle at *C*, draw *AR* and *BR* parallel with the tangents *BC* and *AC*, forming the (Rhombus) parallelogram *RACB* on plan. Draw the center, concave and convex sides of rail from the center *O*; prolong the tangent *BC* indefinite. From *A* and square to *BC* prolonged, draw *AE* for the base of bevels.

Fig. 2. *Exhibits the development of tangents in elevation from plan.* Draw *XX* for a base line. Make *BC* and *CA* equal *BC, CA* on plan, Fig. 1, draw perpendiculars at *A, C* and *B* from the base line *XX*.

Now as the wreath-piece is to have a full easing, one of the tangents must be level or horizontal, and the other inclining. We will allow tangent *AC* to be level, and hence becomes the directing ordinate and tangent *CB* will be inclining.

Let it be observed also that when the cylindric section on plan is less than a quarter circle and a full easement is required, as in this case, then two bevels will be required.

Assume *DB* to be the height the wreath-piece is required to raise, draw *DC* prolonged. Make *CE* equal *CE*, Fig. 1. Make *BG* equal the chord *BA*, on plan. Make *BJ* equal the diagonal *RC*, Fig. 1; draw *EK* square to *DC*.

Bevels. Return to plan, Fig. 1. As the tangents on plan, Fig. 1, are both the same length, the bevels for the two joints will have one base, *AE*, Fig. 1. Make *EF* equal *EK*, Fig 2. Let *EH*, Fig. 1, equal the height *BD*, Fig. 2. Join *FA* and *HA*, for the bevels as shown. Parallel with *BH*, draw the half width of rail [1¼″] cutting the hypothenuse of bevels at *L* and *M*.

The full width of rail is drawn on ground plan, for the purpose of using ordinates in tracing the face-mould.   Draw the chord AB on plan.   Bisect AB at G; bisect GB and GA at J and K; bisect KA at N.   From the points N, K, G, J and B, draw ordinates parallel to the director AC, cutting the concave, center and convex lines of rail, at 2, 3, 4, &c.

Fig. 3.   *Exhibits the Face-mould.**   Make DC equal DC, Fig. 2.   With D as a center and DG, Fig. 2, for a radius, draw arc at A; with C as a center and tangent AC, Fig. 1, for a radius, draw arc intersecting at A, connect AC.   Parallel with CA and CD, draw DB and AB, creating the [Rhomboid] parallelogram $BACD$, on the cutting plane, or plane of plank.

Proof.   The diagonal BC must equal JD, Fig. 2, if so, the angle of tangents at C is correct.

Draw the chord AD.   Bisect AD at G; bisect GD and GA at J and K; bisect KA at M.   From the points M, K, G, J and D, draw ordinates indefinite and parallel with the director AC. Now, from the ordinates on plan, Fig. 1, transfer the points 2, 3 and 4, to corresponding ordinates on face-mould, Fig. 3, using the chord lines as a base.

Make joints at A and D square to the tangents AC and DC. Make A 5 and A 6 each equal HL, Fig. 1; also make D 7 and D 8 equal FM, Fig. 1; then trace the curve through the points 5, 2, 7, for the concave side, and through the points 6, 4, 8, for the convex side of face-mould, using a flexible strip.

The section at P shows the tangent AC squared over the joint; the dotted line indicates a gauge line for centering the plank, and the bevel taken from the angle at H. Fig. 1, is applied from the face of crook, through the intersection at P for the center of rail; then the block pattern is applied square to the bevel, giving the squared section of rail on the joints.

The section at R repeats the operation; the bevel is taken from the angle at F, Fig. 1, and applied from the upper or face side of crook.   Note the bevels in this case, do not cross the tangents; let the eye start at A and follow the tangents around to D; it will be seen the bevels both point to the right of the tangents.

The reason the bevels do not cross is because the minor axis is not in the face-mould but away beyond to the right.   To economize room we have made use of the ordinates, but if the trammel or rod be preferred, then from A draw a line indefinite and at right angles with tangent AC; then prolong the diagonal CB to intersect the line from A at O.   Now OA will be the length of the semi-major axis for the center line of rail.   And at right angles to OA will give the direction of the semi-minor axis, which is always equal to the radius of the circle on plan; draw the radial line OD indefinite; from the points 7 and 8, draw lines parallel to tangent CD, cutting OD at 9 and 10, for the point of tangency or the connection of the straight with the curved part; 9 and 10 are the points through which the elliptic curve will pass. †

---

* When proceeding to draw the face-mould, always take the longest tangent with the dividers first; this will be found the most correct and economical way.

† Let it be observed that for all cylindric sections on plan *less* or *greater* than a quarter circle, the increased width of mould at the ends may be laid off from the joint bevels, but not correct, only when the joint is parallel to the axis of the cylindric section, as at joint A or when the tangent is level as AC; the accompanying bevel is shown at H, Fig. 1, and applied at section P Fig. 3.   But not correct when the tangent is inclining, as CD, in elevation.   The points 7 and 8 at joint D, Fig. 3, are not the correct points through which the elliptic curve will pass.   The point 8 will be outside the curve, and the point 7 will be inside the curve.   The points 9 and 10 on the radial line OD are the correct points.   See Fig. 3, Plate 11.

Fig. 4. *Exhibits an isometrical projection of the Prismatic Solid.*

The rhombus *ACBR* shows the plan, and agrees with the parallelogram *RACB*, on plan, Fig. 1, and indicates the end of a block resting on a horizontal plane ; *BD* shows the height, connect *DC*. *DS* is parallel with *AC* and *SA* is parallel with *CD*, thus indicating the rhomboid on the cutting plane or plane of plank. The diagonal *CR* is prolonged equal to *CO* on plan, Fig. 1, from which the center line of rail *ANB* is drawn; *CBD*, *SRA* and *BDSR* show three sides of the prism ; *AB* is the chord line on plan, and *AD* shows the chord on the cutting plane ; the shaded part *ABD* shows the block to be divided on the chord plane, thus separating the prism into two triangular prisms.

Bisect the chord *AB* on the horizontal plane at *G;* bisect *GA* and *GB* at *K* and *J;* bisect *KA* at *M*. From *M*, *K*, *G* and *J* draw ordinates parallel to the director *AC*, to intersect the center line *ANB* at 3, 3, 3, 3. Now draw perpendiculars on the chord plane, dividing the chord *AD* on the cutting plane proportionately with the chord on the horizontal plane at the points 2, 2, 2, 2 ; draw the ordinates 2 4, 2, 4, &c., parallel with the director *AC*, and equal to *M* 3, *K* 3, &c.; then trace the elliptic curve through the points *D*, 4, 4, 4, 4, *A*, using a pliable strip. To find the center of the ellipse, prolong the diagonal *CS* to intersect a perpendicular line from *O* at *P;* then *PA* indicates the direction, and also the semi-major axis. From *P* and square to *PA*, gives the direction of the minor axis.

The student in stair-building should take great interest in the study of these solids.

Let him first prepare the solid to agree with the parallelogram *ACBR*, on plan, and 5″ or 6″ long; divide it on the chord plane *ADB*, then dowel them together, and cut to the required pitch. If he adds the sections *ARO* and *BRO*, forming the trapezium *ACBO*, and cutting them all off to the cutting plane, he will have the length of the semi-major axis, *AP* and the radial line *DP*, for the point of contact, and by adding another triangular piece, *BQO* [*Q* is not shown], and cutting it off to the same plane, he will have the length of the semi-minor axis *PT*, which is plumb over *OQ* on the horizontal plane, and is always equal to the radius of the circle. If the student will apply his mind to the study of these solids, he will soon master the most intricate problems in hand-railing.

Fig. 5. *Shows the application of the Face-mould to the Crook.*

The heavy line shows the crook as sawed out from the plank. After the crook is taken carefully out of wind on the face side, apply the face-mould in the center ; mark the joints at *A* and *D,* also the tangents *AC* and *DC*. Now lift the mould, and finish marking the tangents, which should be carefully transferred from the face-mould to the crook, as shown by the heavy lines *AC* and *DC*. Next, line the joints *A* and *D*, cut and dress them square to the face of crook, and the tangents ; then square the tangents across the joints as shown by the lines 2 3, at sections *P* and *R*. Now, center the plank with the gauge, and through the intersection made by the gauge, apply the bevel 6 7. Then set the block pattern square to the line 6 7, and scribe around the pattern showing the twist of wreath-piece at the joints. Now the distance, 2 6 and 3 7, is what the mould has to slide at the joints, to carry the lines of twist correctly from end to end of the crook. At joint A, let AB, on the upper side of crook equal 2 6, at section P; and AE, on the lower side of crook equal 3 7, at section P. Then parallel with tangent AC, draw BC on the upper side of crook; and parallel with AC, on the lower side of crook, draw EC.

It will be observed that EC cannot be drawn on the crook, but the mould is shifted down so that the tangent ac on the face-mould will agree with the center line 6 7, as shown at section P.

At joint D make DH, on the upper side of crook, equal 2 6, at section R; and DF, on the lower side of crook, equal 3 7, at section R. Now, parallel with DC, on the upper side of crook, draw HC; and parallel with tangent DC, on the lower side of crook, draw FC. The tangents are now marked on the crook, ready to apply the mould, which must lay over these lines, having the tangents ac and dc to agree with the tangents BC and HC, on the upper side of crook ; and tangents EC and FC, for the lower side of crook, in this case, the sliding of the mould will be easily done, for the line of joint A is the line of the major axis of the ellipse, and thus becomes a slide line for the joint of face-mould, if correctly made.

If the face-mould is made from wood, it is well always to test the correctness of the joints before making the joint on the crook, by applying the stock of the try-square to the joint and the blade of square to the tangent, on the mould.

The face-mould as shown is shifted so that the tangents ac and dc agree with the tangents BC and HC, on the upper side of crook, and while in this position scribe around the convex side of mould. In the same manner slide the mould on the lower side of crook until the tangents ac and cd will agree with the tangents EC and FC, then scribe around the concave side of mould.

The dotted lines at section R show the sides of rail section curved, while at section P the block pattern gives the true profile of rail section, because the tangent AC is level, and the joint is square to the tangent ; hence the plane of joint is parallel to the axis of the cylinder. The joint at D is oblique to the axis of cylinder, because the joint is made square to the tangent DC, which is inclining.

It will be noticed at J and K, on section P, that there is a great saving of material in cutting out the crook square to the face of plank. This want at J prevents the profile of mould on its concave side being transferred to the face of crook, by tacking the mould to the crook in its proper position, the lower arris of mould as shown supplies this want, for the upper side of crook. On the lower side, we have the scribe line complete for the concave side. After working off the surplus wood from the concave side of wreath-piece, then use the Cupper gauge, and gauge the wreath-piece to a parallel width ; then dress off to the gauge line; the bevel at joint A gives the direction to guide the tools, or a line from the edge mould through the center of plank at joint D, will give the direction.

For the twist line, use a pliable strip and apply it to the top side of wreath-piece on the concave, and also on the convex sides, to agree with the block pattern at the joints. After tracing carefully the twist line, remove the surplus wood from the upper side of wreath-piece, then gauge for the depth.

While gauging for the depth the gauge will help to detect any abrupt places in squaring the upper side of wreath-piece, especially when there is a want of wood on the arris of wreath-piece as is often the case. If there be several wreath-pieces, ramps or easements connected, bolt them all together before applying the thin strip for the falling line of rail.

PLATE II.

Plate 11. [Scale, 1½″=1′]. *Exhibits the construction of the face-mould for a wreath-piece having an intermediate casing, when the cylindric section on plan is less than a quarter circle.*

Fig. 1. *Shows the cylindric section, the radius* **OA**, *for the center line equals 14″.*

From the center **O** draw the center line of rail **ASB**. As ordinates will be used, draw the full width of rail, dividing equally on each side of the center line.

From **A** and **B** draw the tangents **AC** and **BC** perpendicular to the radial lines **OA** and **OB**. Parallel with **CA** and **CB** draw **BL** and **AL**, forming the parallelogram **LACB** on plan. Prolong tangent **BC** indefinite. From **A**, and at right angles to **BC**, draw **AD**, the seat line for bevels.

Fig. 2. *Exhibits the development of tangents from plan Fig. 1. As this wreath-piece is to have an intermediate casing, both tangents will be inclining, but each will be different in their inclination. And also two joint bevels will be required.*

Let **XX** indicate the edge of drawing board, and **BC**, **CA** equal the tangents **BC** and **CA** on plan, Fig. 1; from which erect perpendiculars to **XX**, as shown.

Assume **CD** to be the height that the tangent **AC** on plan, has to raise. Draw **AD** prolonged to intersect the perpendicular from **B** at **F**. Again assume **BE** to be the height of both tangents, draw **ED** prolonged to intersect the base line **XX** at **G**.

From **E**, and parallel to **XX**, draw **EH**, cutting the perpendiculars from **A** and **C** at **H** and **J**; make **CK** and **JL** each equal **CD** on plan, Fig. 1. From **K**, and perpendicular to **DG**, draw **KM**. From **L**, and square to **AF**, draw **LN**. Make **EP** equal the diagonal **CL** on plan. Let **EQ** equal the chord **AB** on plan, Fig. 1.

Bevels. Returning to the plan, make **DF** equal **MK**, Fig. 2, and **DH** on plan, equal **LN**, Fig. 2; draw **FA** and **HA** for the bevels required, as shown.

Parallel with **BH** draw the half width of rail [1½″], cutting the bevels at **Y** and **X**.

As the face-mould in this case is traced by the use of ordinates, first find their direction on plan, Fig. 1.

Make **BJ** equal **CG**, Fig. 2; draw **JL** for the director; join **AB** for the chord. Bisect the chord **AB** at **Q**; bisect **QA** and **QB** at **M** and **N**; bisect **AM** at **P**. From **A, P, M, Q, N** and **B** draw ordinates parallel with the director **LJ** to cut the concave, center and convex sides of rail at the points 2, 3, 4, &c.

Fig. 3. *Exhibits the face-mould.*

Make **EDG** equal **EDG**, Fig. 2, with **E** as a center, and **BQ** Fig. 2, for a radius. Draw arc at **A**, then with **D** for a center, and **DA**, Fig. 2, as a radius, draw arc intersecting at **A**. Join **DA**. Parallel with **DA** and **DE**, draw **EL** and **AL**, establishing the parallelogram **LEDA** on the plane of plank, which will agree with the parallelogram **LACB**, Fig. 1, when in position.

Proof. The diagonal **LD** must equal the distance **PF**, Fig. 2, join **GA** for the director. Draw the joints at **A** and **E** square to the tangents *AD* and *ED;* draw the chord *AE.* Bisect *AE* at *G;* bisect *AG* and *BG* at *M* and *N;* bisect *AM* at *P.* From *A, P, M, G, N* and *E,* Draw ordinates indefinite, and parallel to the director *AG.*

Now transfer points 2, 3 and 4, on the ordinates, Fig. 1, to corresponding ordinate on the face-mould as shown, using the chords for base lines. Make *A* 5 and *A* 6 each equal *HX,* Fig. 1, make *E* 7 and *E* 8 each equal *FY,* Fig. 1. Now trace through the points for the concave, center and convex curves of face-mould. Remember the points 5 and 6, at joint *A,* and 7 and 8, at joint *E,* are not quite correct, and would not do to set the rod or trammel by, but are near enough for the practical man, when using a strip. If the point of tangency, or the connection of straight with the curved part is required, then return to plan, Fig. 1. Prolong the chord at *A,* also the ordinate 4 *A,* and draw an ordinate from the joint at 6. Now with *P* for a center, and *AP,* Fig. 3, as a radius, draw arc cutting the ordinate at 5; draw *P* 5 prolonged, to intersect the ordinate from 6 at 7. Return to Fig. 3, and make *A* 1 equal 7 5, Fig. 1, and 1 9 equal 6 9. Fig. 1, draw 9 10 through *A,* for the points of contact for joint *A.* The points for joint *E* may be found in the same way.

If the center *O* be required, so as to trace the face-mould with the trammel or rod.

Then return to Fig. 2. Make *EV* equal the diagonal *OC,* Fig. 1. From *V* erect the perpendicular to intersect *FP* prolonged, at *Y.* Now prolong the diagonal *DL,* Fig. 3, to equal *YF,* Fig. 2, at *O.* From *O,* and parallel with the director *AG,* draw *OB,* equal to the radius *OB,* Fig. 1, for the semi-minor axis; and a line at right angles to *OB,* through *O,* will be the direction of the major axis. Draw the radial lines *OA* and *OE* indefinite; from the points 7 8 and 6 9, on the joints, draw lines parallel to the tangents, to intersect the radial lines at *a* 8, and 9, 10 for the points of tangency, through which the elliptic curve will pass.* The mould may now be drawn with the trammel or straight-edge, without the use of ordinates. The section at *W* shows the bevel found in the angle at *H,* Fig. 1, applied from the face side of crook; and the section at *R* shows the bevel found in the angle at *F,* Fig. 1, applied through the center made by the intersection of the gauge line with the tangent *EH,* that is squared over the joint; the bevel line governs the block pattern. The shaded part shows the surplus wood that has to be removed to form the twist of wreath-rail, and also the width at the joint, to saw out the crook.

Fig. 4. *Exhibits an isometrical view of the prismatic solid to show the student the combination of lines in perspective, and the parallelogram on the cutting plane in position over the parallelogram on the horizontal plane.*

The rhombus *ACBL* indicates the horizontal section of solid and agrees with the parallelogram *LACB,* on plan, Fig. 1. *ASB* shows the center line; *AB,* the chord on plan; *CD,* the height of lower tangent, and *BE,* the height of both tangents; connect *ED* and *DA.* Parallel with *DE* and *DA* draw *AL* and *EL,* for the parallelogram *ADEL* on the cutting plane, which agrees with the parallelogram *ACBL* on the horizontal plane. Prolong the horizontal line *BC* indefinite; prolong *ED* to intersect *BC* prolonged, at *G,* establishing the point *G;* connect *GA* for the director.

---

* These correct points for the trammel are more clearly explained at Fig. 3, Plate 12.

Bisect the chord *AB* and draw the ordinates parallel with the director, to intersect the curve *ASB*, as shown. From the chord on plan, erect perpendiculars to intersect the chord on the cutting plane, from which draw ordinates parallel with the director *AG;* then transfer the points in the circle on the horizontal plane to corresponding ordinates on the cutting plane, using the chords for base lines, as shown.

To save room on the drawing board, *VL* may be drawn for the director within the parallelogram by making *EV* equal *DG.*

By applying the bevel to the sides of the solid, and over on the cutting plane, keeping it square to the inclination of the tangents as shown at *F* and *H*, will give the correct bevels for their respective joints.

Fig. 5. *Shows how to slide the mould.*

The heavy line indicates the crook as sawed out from the rough plank. The dotted lines parallel with joints *A* and *E*, shows the over wood required in making the joints. First dress the face side of crook carefully out of wind, then center the face-mould on the crook and carefully mark the joints and position of the tangents. Now lift the mould and finish marking the tangents *AD* and *ED* on the face of crook; then square the joints from the face. Cut and dress them square to the tangents *AD* and *ED*, and also to the face of crook, carry the tangents across the joints square to the face, as shown by the line 2 3, at sections *Q* and *R;* also mark the tangents *AD* and *ED* on the opposite side of crook square to the joints.

Now center the thickness of crook with a gauge as shown by the dotted lines at sections *Q* and *R.* Through the intersection at 4, 4, apply the bevel, intersecting the upper surface of crook at 6, and the lower side at 7 ; then apply the block pattern square to the line 6 7, given by the bevel, and trace the profile of the squared section of rail on the joint, showing the twist of the wreath-piece at the joints.

Now 2 6 is the distance at the joints the face-mould has to shift on the upper surface of crook, and 3 7 the distance on the lower side of crook; then where they intersect the upper and lower sides of crook, as *B* and *C*, at joint *A;* and *F* and *G* at joint *E;* then parallel with tangents *AD* and *ED*, draw *BD* and *FD* for the upper side of crook, and for the lower side of crook draw *CD* and *GD*, parallel to *AD* and *ED.*

Then slide the mould so that the tangents *ad* and *ed* on the mould, will coincide exactly with the tangents *BD* and *FD* on the crook ; when the mould is in its correct position, the joints on the face-mould will be parallel with the joints on the crook. When the mould is in the correct position, fasten to the crook and scribe around the mould, and also the joint at *a,* so that when placing the mould on again, to work off the surplus wood, the mould may be easily adjusted.

Now arrange the mould on the lower side of crook in the same manner, as the tangents *ad* and *ed* on the face-mould will agree with the tangents *CD* and *GD*, on the crook ; then scribe around the mould and the joint at *e.* The face-mould is shown on the lower side of crook by the dotted lines, and on the upper side of crook by the light solid lines. When scribing the outline on the crook, the minor axis should be transferred also to the crook, on both sides which will give a plumb line for a guide to direct the tools and also to center the rail, when tracing the falling line of wreath-piece ; *MN* shows the minor axis through the center of crook, 5 8 on top, and 9 10 on the lower side of crook.

At *P* and *S* the surplus wood is shown removed from the concave side of wreath-piece, and ready to gauge for the convex side. Between the two face-moulds at 6 and 7, is shown the cylindric section minus the triangles at *J* and *L*.

The profile of the squared section of the rail at the joints *A* and *E* will be curved as shown by the dotted lines at sections *Q* and *R,* if they connect other wreath-pieces.

PLATE 12.

[Scale, 1½″=1′.] *Exhibits the construction of the face-mould for a wreath-piece without an easing, when the cylindrical section on plan is less than a quarter circle.*

Fig. 1. *Shows the cylindrical section less than a quarter circle.*

The radius *OB* equals 15″. Draw the center line *ASR;* draw the radii *OA* and *OB;* draw the tangents *AC* and *BC* perpendicular to the radii ; set off on each side of the center line the half width of rail, and draw the concave and convex sides. Parallel with tangents *CA* and *CB,* draw *BL* and *AL,* and we have the parallelogram *LACB,* on plan.

Prolong the tangent *BC* to the left. From *A,* and at right angles to *BC* prolonged, draw *AD,* the seat of bevel.

Fig. 2. *Shows the development and elevation of tangents for a wreath-piece without an easing, the two tangents must have the same inclination, and only one bevel will be required for both joints.*

Let **XX** indicate the edge of drawing board. Make *BC* and *CA* each equal tangents *BC* and *CA,* on plan. Fig. 1. From *AC* and *B* erect perpendiculars to **XX**. Assume *BD* to be the *height* required for the wreath-piece to raise, draw the inclination *AD,* cutting the perpendicular from *C* at *E.* Make *BF* equal the chord *AB,* on plan, Fig. 1. Make *CH* equal *CD,* on plan, Fig. 1. From *H,* and perpendicular to *AE,* draw *HJ.*

Bevel. At Fig. 1. make *DE* equal *JH,* Fig. 2, connect *EA;* parallel with *EB,* draw the half width of rail, cutting *EA* at *F.* Draw the chord *AB,* and diagonal *CL,* bisecting *AB* at *G;* bisect *AG* and *GB* at *J* and *H.* From *A, J, H* and *B,* draw ordinates to intersect the concave, center and convex curves of the cylindric section at 2, 3, 4, &c.

Fig. 3. *Exhibits the Face-mould.* Make *DE* equal the tangent *DE,* in elevation, Fig. 2; with *D* for a center, and *DF,* Fig. 2. for a radius, draw arc at *A;* again, with *E* as a center, and *ED* for a radius, draw arc intersecting at *A.* Join *AE;* parallel with *EA* and *ED,* draw *DL* and *AL,* for the parallelogram *LDEA,* that will agree with the parallelogram *LBCA,* on plan, Fig. 1.

Proof. The diagonal *EL* must agree with the diagonal *CL* on plan, Fig. 1. Make joints at *A* and *D* square to the tangents *AE* and *DE;* make *A* 2 and *A* 3, also *D* 4 and *D* 5, each equal *EF,* Fig. 1; prolong *EL* to *O,* equal to the diagonal. *CO,* Fig. 1. Draw the radial lines *OA* and *OD* prolonged. From points 2 and 3, also 4 and 5, draw lines parallel to the tangents *AE* and *BE,* to intersect the radial lines at the points *a, b* and *d, h,* for the points of contact.

As we will use ordinates, to locate points in the curves, draw chord **AD**, intersecting the diagonal at **G**.   Bisect **GA** and **GD** at **J** and **H**.   From the points **A, J, H** and **D,** draw ordinates parallel with the director **EL** indefinite.*

Now transfer the points on ordinates, Fig. 1, to corresponding ordinates on face-mould, using the chords as base lines; then trace the curves through the points 2, 3 and 4, for the inside, center and outside of face-mould, using a flexible strip.

If a trammel or rod be preferred to trace the elliptic curve of face-mould, then pivot the trammel at **O** with the arms at right angles to the semi-minor axis O 3, as shown ; set from pencil to minor pin on the rod, the distance O 2, for the concave side of mould, then place the pencil in point **a,** and drop the pins in the grooves, and fasten the major pin ; then trace the curve through the points **a,** 3, **d.**   For the convex side set from pencil to minor pin, the distance O 4, then place the pencil in **b;** drop the pins in the grooves, and fasten the major pin, and sweep the convex curve.

The radial lines **OA** and **OD** give the points of contact or connection of straight with the circular part.

The sections **M** and **N** show the tangents carried over the joints, square from the face of crook ; the dotted lines indicate the thickness of plank centered with a gauge. The bevel is applied from the face of plank through the intersection, and the block pattern is shown applied square to the bevel for the twist of rail at the joints ; the shaded part indicates the width at the joints to saw out the crooks, and is shown by the dotted lines 5, 7, 9, 6, 8, 10, at the face-mould.

At the normal line 7 8, $\frac{1}{8}''$ on the convex side, and $\frac{3}{8}''$ on the concave, is all the over wood that will be required to saw out the crook at that point, as the section of rail at this point is always square to the face of plank, and the width of face-mould at this point is always equal to the true width of rail.

When marking out the crooks, lay down the face-mould on the plank, set off on each side of the joint the amount that the crook has to be wider than the face-mould, as **A** 6, **A** 5, and **D** 9, **D** 10.   At the minor axis set off 4 7 to equal $\frac{1}{4}''$, and 2 8 to equal $\frac{3}{8}''$.   Now shift the mould from 3 to 5, and the point 1 move to 7, so that the mould will cut the point 7 ; after marking the plank from 5 to 7, proceed in the same manner to mark from 9 to 7 ; repeat the operation for the concave side from 10 to 8 and 6 to 8, allowing $\frac{1}{2}''$ surplus wood to make the joints at **A** and **B,** as shown.

This method saves making an extra mould to saw out the crook which is unnecessary.

Fig. 4.   *Shows an isometrical perspective of the solid, and the cutting plane AEDL, in position over the horizontal plane, ACBL.*

ACBL indicates the end of block resting on a horizontal plane and agrees with the parallelogram **ACBL** on plan, Fig. 1 ; **CE** is the height of the lower tangent, and **BD** indicates the whole height of both tangents.   Join **DE** and **AE;** draw **DL** and **AL** parallel with **EA** and **ED.**   This is done with the bevel set to the angle **ADB,** Fig. 2.   Now cut the block to these lines, and we have the parallelogram **DLAE** to indicate the parallelogram laid down at Fig. 3, on the face-mould.   Now prolong **BC**

---

* Whenever the tangents are both the same inclination, and the same length in elevation, the diagonal becomes the director, and is normal to the curve, and on it, the minor axis is set off.

Indefinite. Prolong DE to intersect BC prolonged, at G, join GA for the director of ordinates. It will be observed now that if the diagonal EL be drawn, it will be parallel with the director GA, because the dotted line EG is equal to DE. This is always the case when both tangents are equal on plan and in elevation, then the diagonal LE is always the director and the minor axis.

From A and square to BG draw $AH;$ this indicates the seat for the bevel shown at AD, Fig. 1. From H and square to EG draw $HJ;$ this indicates the height for the bevel as shown at HJ, Fig. 2. JA indicates the hypothenuse of bevel at EA, Fig. 1. The same bevel is found direct from the block as shown at K, by applying the bevel square to the inclination, both from the side of block and from the cutting plane.

The chord lines AB, on the horizontal plane, and AD, on the cutting plane, in this case come over each other, so that the perpendiculars connecting the bisections are not shown as at Fig. 4, Plate 11.

To show the point for trammel, prolong the diagonal CL to O, then dowel on the triangular blocks ALO and BLO, and cut them off to the cutting plane $DLAE$. We will then have the trapezium $DEAN$, shown correctly at $DEAO$, Fig. 3. The point N answers to the point O, Fig. 3, and is the center for the trammel, which is always set at right angles to N 3, the semi-minor axis, which is equal to the radius O 2.

Fig. 5. *Shows the manner of shifting the face-mould on the crook.*

The heavy lines show the crook as sawed out from the rough plank, having the joints A and D cut and dressed. The dotted lines at the joints show the ½″ of over wood cut away. The shaded part indicates the upper surface of crook.

First dress off the upper side of crook carefully out of wind; place the face-mould in the center of crook; mark the joints A and B, also the tangents and minor axis PQ on the upper side. Now lift the mould and complete marking the tangents AE and DE, on the upper side of crook. Now square, cut and dress the joints carefully, by applying the stock of square to the joints and the blade to agree with the tangents.

After the jointing is done, carry the tangents across the joints square to face of crook, as shown by the line 2 3, at sections M and $N;$ and also square the tangents from the joints on the opposite side of crook. Next center the joints at 4 with a gauge, as shown alike at both joints by the dotted line. Through the intersection at 4, apply the bevel 6 7, reversing them as shown at sections M and N.

Apply the block pattern square to the line 6 7, for the squared section of rail on the joints, showing the twist of wreath-piece.

Now 2 6 is the distance the mould has to shift on the upper surface of crook at each joint, and 3 7 is the distance on the lower side. Then make AB and DH equal 2 6 for the upper side of crook, and AK, also DJ equal 3 7 for the lower side of crook.

Now draw BE and HE parallel with AE and DE; also draw tangents KE and JE parallel to AE and DE on the lower side of crook.

Then shift the face-mould so that tangents ac and de will lay over the tangents BE and HE, on the upper side of crook; when the mould is in the correct position, fasten with two tacks, and scribe around the part of mould that lays on the crook, and also at the joint. Mark the minor axis 5 8 on the upper side of crook. Now shift the mould to the under side of crook, with the tangents *ae* and *de* to agree with the tangents *KE* and *JE*, as shown. Now mark around the edge of mould and the joint that remains on the crook; also mark the minor axis 9 10 for the direction to hold the tools when removing the surplus wood from the concave and convex sides of wreath-piece.

The sections at *M* and *N* show the over wood at *R* and *S*, removed from the concave and convex sides of wreath-piece, showing the cylindric section containing the wreath-piece, with the least possible waste of material.

By tacking the mould to the crook the arris of face-mould will be a guide to dress off to the bevels where the crook is cut away, as shown at *XX*, &c.

By squaring across the wreath-piece at *P* and *Q*, and the squared lines intersected by the gauge, as shown at 4, will give the center of rail to regulate the falling line of wreath-piece, and by drawing a line from 10 on the lower side, to 8 on the upper side of crook, will give the direction to hold the tools when removing the surplus wood from the concave side of wreath-piece; in like manner 9 5 gives the direction on the convex side.

For the twist or falling line of wreath-piece, use a thin, flexible strip, bending it around the wreath-piece, being guided at the joints by the corners of block pattern, and the depth of rail laid off at the crossing of the minor axis; the eye and judgment must guide the strip between the joints and minor axis.

The tangents being both inclining, and the joints both made at the spring of cylindric section, the straight lines as marked from the block pattern at sections *M* and *N*, will not be the correct contour of rail section, but will be curved as shown by the curved dotted lines; for this reason the surplus wood at the joints on the concave side, should not all be removed, but left full so that when the adjoining wreath-piece is bolted on, they both can be dressed down neat to the required curve made by the face-mould. The surplus wood may all be removed from the convex side, as the block pattern on that side allows a surplus to be taken off after the two wreath-pieces are bolted together.

PLATE 13.

Plate 13. [Scale, ¾″=1 foot]. *Exhibits the construction of the face-mould for a wreath-piece, where the cylindric section on plan is greater than a quarter circle.*

In this case the angle of tangents on plan will be acute. Three kinds of face-moulds are here shown. Classified thus: A face-mould for a wreath-piece containing a full casing; one without an casing, and the other with an intermediate casing. We will first show how to draw the face-mould for a wreath-piece having a full casement.

Fig. 1. *The shaded part shows the cylindric section on plan.*

The radius *OA*, *OC*, for the center line of rail equals 13″; the width of rail 2 3, equals 4″. At right angles to the radii *OA* and *OC*, draw the tangents *AB* and *CB*. From *A*, and perpendicular to tangent *CB*, draw *A* 7. for the seat of bevels. Draw the chord *AC*, also the diagonal *BO*, cutting the chord at *J*.

Fig. 2. *Exhibits the elevation of tangents.*

Let *XX* indicate a base line. Make *CB* and *BA* equal tangents *CB* and *BA*, Fig. 1; perpendicular to *XX*, draw *CD*, *BG*

and *AL;* assume *CD* to be the height that the wreath-piece has
to raise; as the wreath-piece has to have a full easing. then one
tangent will be horizontal and the other tangent will incline
the whole height.

Then draw *BD* for the inclination of tangent *CB*, on plan,
tangent *AB* will be level. Make *CH* equal the diagonal *BO* on
plan, Fig. 1; make *CF* equal the chord *AC* on plan, Fig. 1,
Make *CE* equal *BJ*, Fig. 1; let *B* 7 equal *B* 7, Fig. 1. From
7, and square to *BD* draw 7 8. Bisect the height *CD* at *N;*
draw *NE* produced, to intersect the perpendicular from *H* at *K*.

Bevels. Returning to plan, Fig. 1, make 7 8 equal 7 8,
Fig. 2, and 7 *D* equal *CD*, Fig. 2. Join *A* 8 and *AD* for the
bevels at 8 and *D*.

Fig. 3. *Exhibits the face-mould.*
Make *CB* equal *BD*, Fig. 2. With *C* as a center, and *FD*,
Fig. 2, for a radius, draw arc at *A*; again, with *B* as a center.
and tangent *AB*, Fig. 1, for a radius, draw arc intersecting at *A*;
Join *BA*. Perpendicular to *BA* draw *AE* indefinite: draw the
chord *AC*. Bisect *AC* at *D;* draw *BD* prolonged. to intersect
AE at *O*. Join *OC* and we have the trapezium *ABCO*, on the
cutting plane, or plane of plank, that will agree when in position, with the trapezium, or qudarilateral *ABCO* on plan, Fig. 1.

Proof. The diagonal *BD* and *BO* must agree with *NE* and
NK, Fig. 2. if so, the angle of trapezium at *B* is correct.

From *O*, and square to *AE*, draw *OX* equal to the radius
OA, Fig. 1. Then *OA* will be the semi-major axis, and *OX*
will be the semi-minor axis of the elliptic curve.

Make *X* 2, *X* 3, each equal the half width of rail. [2″].
Make joint at *C* square to tangent *B C*, the major axis gives the
joint at *A*. Join *X C* and *X A;* from points 2 and 3, draw the
proportional lines parallel to *X A* and *X C* to intersect the radial
lines at 10, 5 and 9, 8 through which to draw the elliptic curves
of face mould. Now center the trammel at *O*, square to the minor
axis *O X*. Then take the rod and set from the pencil to the
minor pin, the distance *O X*. [The minor pin is now fastened,
and the major pin is loose.] Now place the pencil at *A*, and drop
the pins in the groove, and fasten the major pin at the point *O*.
Then trace the curve for the center line of rail through the points
A X C. For the concave side of face mould, set from pencil to
minor pin, the distance *O* 2. Now place the pencil at 5 and drop
the pins in the groove, and fasten the major pin at the point *O*,
then trace the concave side of face mould through the points
5, 2, 9.*

For the convex side of face mould, set from the pencil to
minor pin, the distance *O* 3, on the minor axis; then place the
pencil at 10 and drop the pins in the groove, and fasten the major
pin at *O*. Now trace the curve through the points 10, 3, 8, completing the face-mould. If a trammel is not at hand, or the
inclination of tangents be steep, requiring a large trammel, then
draw the two right angles at *O*, to indicate the seat of trammel,
and use a rod, and find points in the elliptical curve as shown at
figure 12, plate 5. In this case the semi-major and semi-minor
axis are given. The distance 9 6, on the rod equals the semi-

---

*If the elliptical curve should cut the joint at *C*, making the distance *C* 4, greater than *C* 12, do not conclude the work wrong, for this
is natural. The difference is greater in face moulds over winders that
are steep, the variation regulates itself when the wreath piece is
worked off to the plumb bevels, showing the vertical sides of rail section at the joints to be concave and convex.

minor axis O 2, and the distance 9 7 equals the semi-major axis
OA, for the concave side of mould.   Now move the rod at intervals, keeping the points 6 and 7, over the right angles as shown,
and make points at the end of the rod, through which trace the
elliptic curve, using a pliable strip.

Repeat the operation for the center and convex curves of face-
mould; *OA* and *OX* are the semi-major and minor axis for the
center line, and *O* 10 and *O* 3, are the semi-major and minor axis
for the convex curve of face-mould.   For long and steep face-
moulds, the system of ordinates as before described, will be found
the most convenient and economical.

At sections *L* and *N* the tangents are shown squared across
the joints. The dotted line indicates a gauge line. The bevel in the
angle at *D*, Fig. 1, is applied at section *L*, from the face of
crook, through the intersection made by the gauge.*

The block pattern is applied square to the line made from the
bevel.   At section *N*, the bevel found in the angle at 8, Fig. 1, is
applied from the face of crook through the center of section; the
block pattern is then applied at right angles to the bevel, thus
showing the twist of wreath-piece in the crook.   The shaded parts
show the amount of wood required at the joints to saw out the
crook; at the normal line 3 2, less wood is required, as shown at
Fig. 3, Plate 12.

Fig. 4 *shows the plan of a cylindric section greater than a
quarter circle.   How to construct the face-mould for a wreath-
piece without an easing.   The shaded part shows the cylindric
section on plan.*

Let *OA* and *OC* indicate the radii.   With *OA* as a radius,
draw the center line *AXC*; draw the tangents *AB* and *CB* perpendicular to *OA* and *OC*.   From *A*, and square to tangent *BC*,
draw *A* 7, for the seat of bevel.   Draw the chord *AC* and the
diagonal *BO*.

Fig. 5.   *Exhibits the development and elevation of tangents.*

Let *XX* indicate a base line.   Make *CB* and *BA* equal tangents *CB* and *BA* on plan, Fig. 4.   Perpendicular to *XX*, draw
CD, *BM* and *AL*.   Now as this face-mould is for a wreath-
piece without an easing, consequently both tangents will have
the same inclination, and but one bevel will be required for both
joints.   Make *CD* equal the whole height the wreath-piece has
to raise.   Join *AD*, cutting *BM* at *E*.   Make *CF* equal the
chord *AC*, Fig. 4.   Let *B* 7 equal *B* 7, Fig. 4; from 7, and perpendicular to *AD*, draw 7 *G*.

Bevels.   Returning to Fig. 4, make 7 *D* equal *FG*, Fig. 5.
Join *DA*, and in the angle at *D* is found the bevel for both
joints.

Fig. 6.   *Exhibits the face-mould.*
Make *CB* equal *DE*, Fig. 5.   With *C* as a center, and *FD*
Fig. 5, for a radius, draw arc at *A*; again, with *B* as a center,
and *AG*, Fig. 5, for a radius, draw arc intersecting at *A*.   Join
BA.   Draw the chord *AC*.   Bisect *AC* at *D*.   Draw the diagonal
BD prolonged, to equal *BO* on the plan, Fig. 4, as at *O*.

---

*The correctness of bevels may be proved thus, with *C* as a center
and the hypothenuse of bevel as *AD*, Fig. 1, for a radius, the curve
must tangent *AB*, as shown at *H*.   For the other bevel, *AJ* must equal
A 8, Fig. 1.

Draw the radial lines *AO* and *CO* and we have the trapezium *OABC* on the cutting plane, that will agree when in position, with the trapezium *OABC* on plan, Fig. 4.

Proof. The diagonal *BD* must equal *BP* on plan, Fig. 4. As both tangents have the same inclination, and are both the same length, then the diagonal *OB* becomes the director. Make *OX* equal *OX*, Fig. 4 for the semi-minor axis; make *X* 2 and *X* 3 each equal the half width of rail [2″]. Join *XC* and *XA*. From 2 and 3 draw the proportional lines parallel to *XA* and *XC*, cutting the radial lines *OA* and *OC* at 1 6 and 6 9, for the points through which the elliptic curve will pass. Make joints at *A* and *C* at right angles to the tangents *BA* and *BC*.

Now pivot the trammel at *O* with the axis at right angles to the minor axis *OX;* then set the minor pin from pencil to equal *O* 2 for the concave side of face-mould. Now place the pencil in the point at 6, and drop the pins in the grooves, and fasten the major pin ; then trace the curve through the points 6 2, 6 for the concave side of face-mould. For the center line, set from pencil to minor pin the distance *OX;* place the pencil in the point at *C* and drop the minor pin in the groove, then slide the major pin until it drops into the groove, then fasten the pin and trace the center line of face-mould.

For the convex side, set from pencil to minor pin the distance *O* 3 on the minor axis; then place the pencil in the point at 9, and drop the pins into the grooves ; then fasten the major pin and trace the convex curve of face-mould through the points 1, 3, 9. Sections *L* and *N* show the bevel found in the angle at *D*, Fig. 4, applied through the center of joints. The block pattern is applied square to the bevel, and shows the twist of wreath-piece at the joints. For all wreath-pieces greater than a quarter circle, a bevel will be required at both joints, and they will always cross the tangents, because there will always be a point in the face-mould that will be equal to the true width of rail, which is termed the normal line.

Fig. 7. Exhibits the ground plan of a cylindric section greater than a quarter circle. How to construct the face-mould for a wreath-piece, having an intermediate casing.

With *OA* for a radius, draw the center line of rail *AXC*. The shaded part shows the true width of rail on plan. Perpendicular to the radii *OA* and *OC*, draw the tangents *AB* and *CB*. Draw the chord *AC* and the diagonal *BO*, cutting the chord at *P*. From *A*, and square to tangent *BC*, draw *A* 7.

Fig. 8 shows the development and elevation of tangent from plan Fig. 7.

Let *XX* indicate a base line. Make *CB* and *BA* equal the tangents *CB* and *BA*, Fig. 7; perpendicular to *XX*, draw *CD*, *BM* and *AL*, indefinite. Now for a wreath-piece having an intermediate casing, both tangents must be inclining, but one must have a greater inclination than the other. Let *BG* be the height that the lower tangent has to raise, and *CD* the whole height of both tangents. Join *AG* and *GD* for the increased length of tangents in elevation; prolong tangent *AG*, to cut, the perpendicular *CD* at *E;* also prolong tangent *DG* to intersect the base line *XX* at *H*. Make *CF* equal *AC*, Fig. 7. Let *CP* and *CJ* equal *BP* and *BO* on plan, Fig. 7; also make *B* 7 and *MN* each equal *B* 7 on plan, Fig. 7. From 7 and square to *HD*, draw 7 8, and from *N* and square to *AE*, draw *N* 9. Bisect *ED* at *R*. Make *CS* equal *ER*. From *S* through *P* draw a line to intersect the perpendicular from *J* at *K*.

Bevels. *As both tangents in this case have different inclinations, two bevels will be required.*

Return to plan, Fig. 7, and prolong tangent *CB* indefinite. Make 7 8 equal 7 8 in elevation, Fig 8; also make 7 9 equal *N* 9 in elevation, Fig. 8. Join 8 *A* and 9 *A* for the bevels required, as shown in the angles at 8 and 9 on plan, Fig. 7.

Fig. 9. *Exhibits the face-mould.*

Make *CBN* equal *DGH*, Fig. 8; then with *C* as a center and *DF*, Fig. 8, for a radius, draw arc at *A*; again, with *B* as a center, and tangent *AG*, for a radius, draw arc intersecting at *A*. join *BA*, draw the chord *AC*; bisect *AC* at *D*; draw *BD* indefinite.

Proof. If the diagonal *BD* equal *PS*, Fig. 8, then the angle of tangents is correct. Make *BO* equal *KS*, Fig. 8; draw the radial lines *OA* and *OC*, indefinite; join *AN* for the director; from the center *O*, draw *OX*, indefinite, and parallel to director *AN*. Make *OX* equal the radius *OA*, Fig. 7, for the semi-minor axis; through *O*, and at right angles to *OX*, draw 6 6 for the direction of the major axis.

Make joints at *A* and *C* perpendicular to the tangents *AB* and *CB*; make *X* 2 and *X* 3 each equal the true width of rail. Connect *XA* and *XC*. From 2 and 3 draw the proportional lines parallel to *XA* and *XC* to intersect *OA* and *OC* prolonged, at 7 7 and 8 8, for the correct points through which the elliptic curve will pass.

The points 8 8 and 7 7 on the radial lines, are the points of tangency, or the connecting points of the straight with the circular part.

To trace the face-mould with a trammel, pivot the trammel in *O*, with the arms resting on 6 6. For the convex side of mould; set from pencil to minor-pin the distance *O* 3, then place the pencil in the point at 8, drop the minor-pin in the groove at 6, and slide the major-pin until it drops in the groove at 9, then fasten the major-pin, and trace the elliptic curve through the points 7, 3, 8; repeat the operation for the center and concave side of face-mould.

If room be a consideration then use the ordinates for any of of these moulds, by drawing the ordinates parallel to the director *AN*, using the chords as base lines as directed in former plates. At sections *L* and *N* the tangents are shown squared across the joints, and the plank is centered as indicated, by the dotted gauge lines, and the bevel found in the angle at 9, Fig. 7, is applied at the joint *A*, and the bevel found in the angle at 8, Fig. 7, is applied at joint *C*. The block pattern is then applied at right angles to the lines made from the bevels and gives the twist of wreath-piece at the joints as shown. Observe the bevels as applied; cross the tangents, because the minor axis, *O* 3, is in the mould. At the points 2 and 3, the bevels blend and the section of rail at that point is square to the face of crook. The sliding of the mould has been explained and applies the same here.

Observe the bevel at section *L* is applied, so as to throw the joint at *C* up, and the bevel at section *N* is applied so as to throw the joint at A down, corresponding to the tangents *AG* and *GD* in elevation.

PLATE 14.

Plate 14. [Scale, ¾″=1 foot]. *Exhibits the construction of a face-mould for a wreath-piece over a cylindric section, that is elliptic on plan, said section being less than a quarter of an ellipse.*

Figs. 1, 2 and 3. *Shows how to construct the face-mould for a wreath-piece without an casing.*

The plan of the twist part of rail being less than a quarter of an ellipse. Draw the center line *ASB* of the ellipse, also draw joints at *A* and *B* normal to the curve.* At right angles to the joints, draw the tangents *AC* and *BC;* parallel to *AC* and *BC* draw *AO* and *BO* for the parallelogram *OACB* on plan. Parallel to the center line *ASB* set off the width of rail, draw the chord *AB;* prolong tangent *BC* indefinite, from *A* and square to *BC* draw *AD*

Fig. 2. *Exhibits the development and elevation of tangents from plan, Fig. 1.*

Let *XX* indicate a base line. Make *BC* and *CA* equal tangents *BC* and *CA* on plan, Fig. 1; perpendicular to *XX* draw *BD* and *CE* indefinite. Assume *BD* to be the whole height the wreath-piece has to raise, connect *AD*, cutting *CE* at *H*, for the inclination of tangents.

Make *CJ* equal *CD*, Fig. 1; make *DG* equal twice *CH;* let *BF* equal *OC*, Fig. 1, make *BK* equal the chord *BA*, Fig. 1; from *J*, and perpendicular to *AD*, draw *JL*.

Bevels. As both tangents have the same inclination, only one bevel will be required. Return to Fig. 1, make *DN* equal *J L*, Fig. 2, join *NA* for the bevel at *N*. Parallel to *BN* draw the half width of rail to cut the hypothenuse *NA* at *Q*

Fig. 3. *Exhibits the face-mould.*

Make *BC* equal *DH*, Fig. 2; with *B* as a center and *DK*, Fig. 2, for a radius, draw arc at *A;* again, with *C* as a center, and tangent *AH* in elevation, Fig. 2, for a radius, draw arc intersecting at *A;* join *CA*. Parallel to *AC* and *BC*, draw *BO* and *AO* for the parallelogram *OACB*, on the cutting plane, that when in position will agree with the parallelogram *OACB*, on plan, Fig. 1.

Proof. The diagonal *CO*, must equal the distance *FG*, Fig. 2. If so, the angle of tangents at *C*, must be correct. Draw the chord *AB*, bisect *AB* at *D;* bisect *BD* and *AD* at *E* and *F*. Make *BH* equal *AH*, Fig. 2; join *HO* for the director. From the points *A, E, D, F* and *B*, on the chord line, draw ordinates indefinite and parallel to *HO*.

Return to plan, Fig. 1; bisect the chord *AB* at *J;* bisect *AJ* and *BJ* at *E* and *F;* make *BH* equal *CA* in elevation, Fig. 2, connect *HO* for the director on plan. From the points *A, E, J, F* and *B*, draw ordinates parallel to the director *HO* to cut the concave, center and convex curves at 2, 3 and 4. Returning to Fig. 3.

Make joints at *A* and *B* at right angles to the tangents *AC* and *BC*. Let *A* 5 and *A* 6, also *B* 7 and *B* 8, each equal *NQ*,

---

*To draw a line normal to the elliptic curve at any point in the curve. see Fig. 8, Plate 5.

Fig. 1. Now transfer the points 2, 3 and 4, from the ordinates on plan, Fig. 1, to corresponding ordinates on face-mould : then trace the concave side of face-mould through the points 7, 3, 5; and the convex side through the points 8, 4, 6, using a pliable strip.

The sections at *P* and *R* show the tangents carried across the joints square to the face of crook; the joint is centered with the gauge and the bevel found in the angle at *N*, Fig. 1. is shown applied through the center of both sections so as to pitch the joint at *A* down, and the joint at *R*, up.

The block pattern is then applied square to the line made from the bevel, showing the twist of rail section at the joints; the shaded part shows the width required at the joints to saw out the crook in the rough, and also the amount of surplus wood to be removed in squaring up the wreath-piece.

Fig's. 4, 5 and 6. *Exhibits the construction of face-mould when the wreath-piece has an intermediate easing, the plan being the same as at Fig. 1.*

Fig 4. *Shows the plan.*

The joints at *A* and *B* are drawn normal to the center elliptic curve *ASB;* and the tangents *AC* and *BC* are at right angles to the joints. Draw *AO* and *BO* parallel to tangents *AC* and *BC;* from *B* and at right angles to tangent *AC* prolonged, draw *BT;* from *A*, and perpendicular to tangent *BC* prolonged, draw *AV,* connect *AB* for the chord. Bisect *AB* at *D;* bisect *AD* and *B D* at *E* and *F;* bisect *AE* at *H.*

Fig. 5. *Shows the development and elevation of tangents from the plan, Fig. 4.*

Let *XX* be a base line; make *BC* and *CA* equal tangents *BC* and *CA*, Fig. 4. Perpendicular to *XX*, draw *BD* and *CE.*

As the wreath-piece is to contain an intermediate easing, the tangents will have different inclinations. We will assume *CH* to be the height that the tangent *AC* on plan has to raise, and *BD* as the height that both tangents are required to raise.

Draw tangent *DH*, prolonged to intersect *XX* at *J;* draw the tangent *AH* prolonged. Make *CV* equal *CV*, Fig. 4; also make *ET* equal *CT* on plan. fig. 4: from *V* and square to tangent *DH* prolonged, draw *VK;* from *T* and at right angles to tangent *AH* prolonged, draw *TM.*

Make *BQ* equal the diagonal *CO* on plan, Fig. 4; let *BS* equal the chord *AB*, Fig. 4; make *DN* equal twice the height *HC*.

Bevels. As both tangents have different inclinations two bevels will be required. Make *VP*, Fig. 4, equal *VK*, in elevation, Fig. 5. Join *PA;* parallel with *PB* draw the half width of rail [2″] to cut the hypothenuse of bevel at 5. The angle at *P* gives the bevel as shown. For the other bevel, make *BR*, Fig. 5, equal *BT*, Fig. 4; let *BU* equal *TM;* join *UR*, and the angle at *U* gives the bevel. Parallel to *BD* draw the half width of rail [2″] to cut the hypothenuse of bevel at 6.

Fig. 6. *Exhibits the face-mould.*

Make *BC* equal tangent *DH* in elevation, Fig. 5. With *B* as a center, and *DS*, Fig. 5, for a radius, draw arc at *A;* again, with *C* as a center, and tangent *AH*, Fig. 5, for a radius, draw arc intersecting at *A;* join *CA;* parallel to tangent *AC* and *BC* draw *BO* and *AO*, establishing the parallelogram *OACB* on the cutting plane, that will, when in position, agree with the parallelogram *OACB* on plan, Fig. 4.

Proof. The diagonal *OC* must equal the distance *QN*, Fig. 5. Draw the chord *AB*. Bisect *AB* at *D;* bisect *AD* and *BD* at *E* and *F;* bisect *AE* at *H*. Make *BL* equal *JH*, Fig. 5; join *LO* for the director on the face-mould. From the points *A, H, E, D, F* and *B* draw ordinates indefinite and parallel to the director *LO*.

Make joints at *A* and *B* square to the tangents *AC* and *BC;* let *A* 6 and *A* 7 each equal *U* 6, Fig. 5; make *B* 5 and *B* 8 each equal *P* 5, Fig. 4. Now transfer the points 2, 3 and 4 from the ordinates on plan, Fig. 4, to corresponding ordinates on the face-mould as shown, using the chords for base lines; at section *M* the bevel found in the angle at *U*, Fig. 5, is applied, and at section *N*, the bevel found in the angle at *P*, Fig. 4, is applied in the usual way.

Observe the bevels cross the tangents because there is a point in the mould that is narrower than at either of the joints.

Figs. 7, 8 and 9. *Are introduced to show a face-mould having both tangents inclining, and at the same time, the bevels will not cross the tangents.*

This never happens only when the cylindric section on plan is less than a quarter circle, or a quarter of an ellipsis, for then the angle of tangents is obtuse; there are five different face-moulds for the obtuse plan as follows:

FIRST. A face-mould having one tangent level, the other inclining, requiring two bevels, that in no case cross the tangents in their application, such as the ordinary newel wreath, or for startings and landings where one of the tangents is horizontal, as shown at Fig. 3, Plate 10.

SECOND. When both tangents are inclining and different in their inclination, requiring two bevels, which in their application, do not cross the tangents, as at Fig. 9.

⟩ THIRD. When both tangents are inclining and different in their inclination, but requiring only one bevel, the square being applied at the opposite joint, as at Fig. 12.

FOURTH. When both tangents are inclining and different in their inclination, requiring two bevels, but crossing the tangents, as shown at Fig. 6.

FIFTH. Having both tangents inclining and of the same inclination, requiring only one bevel for both joints, and crossing the tangents in their application, as shown at Fig. 3.

Fig. 7. *Shows the plan of tangents and repeats Fig. 1.*

The joints at *A* and *B* are drawn normal to the curve; the tangents *AC* and *BC* are drawn square to the joints; *AO* and *BO* are parallel to *BC* and *AC*, creating the parallelogram *AOCB* on plan. From *A* and at right angles to tangent *BC* prolonged, draw *AD;* from *B* and square to tangent *AC* prolonged, draw *BF*.

Fig. 8. *Exhibits the development and elevation of tangents.*

Let *XX* indicate a base line; make *BC* and *CA* equal the tangents *BC* and *CA*, Fig. 7. At right angles to *XX*, draw the perpendiculars *BD* and *CF*, indefinite; assume *CH* to be the height for the lower tangent and *BD*, the height for both tangents; draw the tangent *AH*, prolonged indefinite; draw the tangent *DH* prolonged to intersect the base line *XX* at 2. Make *CJ* equal *CD* on plan, Fig. 7; make *FG* equal *CF* on plan, Fig. 7; let *BK* equal the chord *AB* on plan, Fig. 7, and *BL* equal the diagonal *CO* on plan, Fig. 7. Make *DM* equal twice the hight of *CH*, join *LM* for the length of diagonal on the face-mould, connect *DK* for the length of chord on the face-mould. From *J* and square to tangent *DH* prolonged, draw *JN*; also from *G* and square to tangent *AH* prolonged, draw *GP*.

Return to plan, Fig. 7, make *BL* equal *C* 2 in elevation Fig. 8, connect *LO* for the director on plan. Bisect the chord *AB* at *Q*; bisect *AQ* and *BQ* at *R* and *S*; bisect *AR* at *T*.

From the points *A*, *T*, *R*, *Q*, *S*, and *B*, draw ordinates parallel to the director *OL*, to cut the concave, center and convex curves of rail at 2, 3 and 4.

Bevels. Make *DH* on plan, Fig. 7, equal *JN* in elevation Fig. 8; join *AH* for the hypothenuse of bevel. Make *FJ* equal *GP*, Fig. 8; join *JB* for the hypothenuse of bevel at the wide end of mould.

Parallel to tangent *CB*, draw the half width of rail [2″] to cut *HA* at 5; parallel to tangent *AC*, draw the half width of rail to cut *JB* at 7.

Fig. 9. *Exhibits the face-mould.*

Make *BC* equal tangent *DH* in elevation Fig. 8; with *B* as a center and *DK*, Fig. 8, for a radius, draw arc at *A*; again, with *C* as a center and tangent *AH*, for a radius, draw arc intersecting at *A*; join *CA*, parallel to *AC* and *BC*, draw *BO* and *AO* for the parallelogram *OACB* on the cutting plane, or plane of plank that will agree when elevated into position with the parallelogram *OACB* on plan, Fig. 7.

Proof. The diagonal *OC* must agree with the length of *LM*, Fig. 8. If so, the angle of tangents at *C* is correct.

Make *BD* equal *H* 2, Fig. 8, connect *DO* for the director on the face-mould; draw the chord *AB*. Bisect *AB* at *Q*; bisect *AQ* and *BQ* at *R* and *S*; bisect *AR* at *T*. From the points *A*, *T*, *R*, *Q*, *S* and *B*, draw ordinates indefinite; make joints at *A* and *B* square to the tangents *AC* and *BC*; let *A* 7 and *A* 8 each equal *J* 7, Fig. 7; also make *B* 5 and *B* 6 each equal *H* 5, Fig. 8. Now transfer points 2, 3 and 4 from the ordinates on plan, Fig. 7, to corresponding ordinates on the face-mould as shown; then trace the curve through the points 8, 4, 6, for the convex side, and through the points 7, 2, 5, for the concave side of face-mould.

The sections at *M* and *N* show the bevels applied in the usual way; observe they do not cross the tangents, because the long tangent *DH*, in elevation, intersects the horizontal line *XX*, between the point *J* and the center perpendicular from *C*. This will be explained at Fig. 11.

Fig's. 10, 11 and 12. *Exhibits a plan of tangents that repeats Fig. 1. To show the construction of a face-mould on the dividing line between one in which the bevels cross the tangents in their application, and a face-mould in which the bevels do not cross the tangents.*

Fig. 10. *Shows the plan.*

The joints *A* and *B* are made normal to the curve, and the tangents *AC* and *BC* are drawn at right angles to the joints; parallel to *AC* and *BC* draw *BO* and *AO* for the parallelogram *OACB*. At right angles to tangent *BC* prolonged, draw *AD*; also from *B* and at right angles to tangent *AC* prolonged, draw *BF*.

Fig. 11. *Shows the development and elevation of tangents.*

Let *XX* indicate a base line; make *BC* and *CA* equal the tangents *BC* and *CA*, Fig. 10. From *XX* erect the perpendic-

ulars *BD* and *CD;* assume *CF* to be the height that tangent *AC*
on plan is required to raise; make *CJ* equal *CD*, Fig. 10. Connect *JF*, and prolonged to intersect the perpendicular *BD* at *D;*
then *BD* is the whole height of wreath-piece, from center to center of rail, and *AF* and *FD* are the increased length of tangents
AC and *BC* on plan Fig. 10. At right angles to *BD* draw *DE;*
make *EH* equal *CF*, Fig. 10; from *H*, and at right angles to
AF, prolonged, draw *HK;* make *BL* equal the diagonal *OC*.
Fig. 10; make *BM* equal the chord *BA* on plan, Fig. 10; let *DN*
equal twice *FC*.

Return to plan, Fig. 10. In this case *DA* becomes the
director on plan; draw the chord *AB*. Bisect *AB* at *Q;* bisect
AQ and *BQ* at *R* and *S;* bisect *AR* at *T;* from the points *T*,
R, Q and *S*, draw ordinates parallel to the director *AD*, to intersect the concave, center and convex curves of rail at 2, 3 and 4.

In this case only one bevel will be required, because the tangent *DF* in elevation, Fig. 11, when prolonged, intersects the
base line *XX*, at the point *J*, and the point *J* coincides with the
point *D*, Fig. 10, which is square from the point *A* to the tangent
BC, Fig. 10; and *DA* then becomes the director, and is parallel
in this case with the joint at *B*.

Observe in elevation, Fig. 11, when the tangent *DF* is prolonged to the base line *XX;* if it intersects the base line between
the points *J* and *C*, as shown at *C*2, Fig. 8, in all such cases, two
bevels will be required, but they will not cross the tangents in their
application. But if the inclination of tangent *DF* should intersect the base line to the left of the point *J*, then there will be two
bevels required, and also they will always cross the tangents as
shown at Fig. 5, where tangent *DH* produced intersects the base
line *XX* at *J* to the left of the point *V*. Let it be remembered
from this that the point *J*, is the dividing point in the application
of the bevels, as to either, they cross the tangent, or they do not.

Let the student bear this in mind, for it is difficult sometimes
to know which way to apply the bevels; this only happens when
the tangents on plan are obtuse at the angle *C;* when the tangents
on plan are acute, bear in mind that the bevels will always cross the
tangents in their application.

When the tangents on plan form a right angle, the bevels will cross
the tangents on all wreath-pieces where both tangents are inclining,
and where one tangent is level, and the other inclining, the square
will apply to the joint made on the inclining tangent.

Bevel. Prolong *BO*, Fig. 10 indefinite; make *BM* equal
HK in elevation, Fig. 11; join *FM* for the bevel at *M;* parallel
with *BM* draw the half width of rail [2″] to cut *MF* at 9.

Fig. 12. *Exhibits the face-mould.*

Make *BC* equal *DF*, Fig. 11; with *B* as a center, and the
distance *DM*, Fig. 11, for a radius, draw arc at *A;* again with *C*
as a center, and tangent *AF*, Fig. 11, for a radius, draw arc intersecting at *A*. Connect *AC;* parallel to *AC* and *BC*, draw *BO* and
AO, creating the parallelogram *OACB* on the cutting plane, that
will coincide with the parallelogram *OACB* on plan when elevated
into position. Make joints at *A* and *B* perpendicular to the tangents *AC* and *BC;* draw the chord *AB*. Bisect *AB* at *Q;*
bisect *AQ* and *BQ* at *R* and *S;* bisect *AR* at *T*. Make *BD*
equal *JF* in elevation, Fig. 11; join *DO;* then *DO* becomes the
director, which is at right angles to tangent *BC*. From the points
A, T, R, Q and *S*, draw ordinates indefinite and parallel to the
director, then transfer the points 2, 3 and 4 on the ordinates on
plan, Fig. 10, to corresponding ordinates on face-mould as shown.

Make *B* 7 and *B* 8 each equal *B* 7 and *B* 8 on plan, Fig. 10; let *A* 5 and *A* 6 each equal *M* 9, Fig. 10; now through the points 5, 2, 7 trace the concave curve, and through the points 6, 4, 8 trace the curve for the convex side of face-mould.

The section at *N* shows the bevel found in the angle at *M*. Fig. 10, applied in the usual way; at section *M* the square is applied from the face of crook as shown.

If it be required to find the point of tangency, prolong *DA*, Fig. 10. With *T* as a center, and *TA*, Fig. 12, for a radius, intersect *DA* at *K*; draw *TK* prolonged, draw 6 *P* parallel to *DK*. Make *AP*, Fig. 12, equal *KP*, Fig. 10; draw *PL* parallel to *OD* and equal to *L* 6, Fig. 10; draw *LA* prolonged, make *AV* equal *AL*, then *L* and *V* are the points of tangency.

PLATE 15.

Plate 15. [Scale ¾″—1 foot.] *Shows how to place the risers and balusters in platform and quarter-pace cylinders. When winders in a semi-circle are to be used, Fig's. 15 and 16 shows how the treads may be graduated in width at the narrow ends so as to form a graceful curve connecting the wreath part of string.*

Fig. 1. *Shows a 6″-cylinder.*

The tread is to be 9″; the radius *OF* equals 3″; with *O* for a center and *OF* [3″] for a radius, draw the semi-circle *BFC*; draw *BA* and *CD* to indicate the straight part of outer string connecting the circular part. With *F* as a center and *FO* for a radius, draw arc intersecting at *H*; through *F* and *H* draw a line to intersect *DC* prolonged, and also *CB* prolonged, at *J* and *K*; then *K* is the focus and the distance *JC* is the stretchout of the curve from *F* to *C*. Now make from *J* to the face of No. 16 rise to equal half a tread 4½″; and from face of No. 16 to face of No. 17 rise, to equal 9″; opposite Nos. 16 and 17 rise, draw the face of No. 15 and 14 rise, thus locating the face of risers in a 6″ cylinder.

Observe the face of Nos. 14 and 17 rise are 8½″ from the joint of cylinder on the straight part of string; this must be carefully noted when proceeding to construct the face-mould, so that the correct height of wreath-piece may be established.

Fig's. 2 to 4. *Shows a 7″, 8″ and 9″ cylinder.*

The location of risers are found in the same manner as at Fig. 1, the lettering being the same. Observe at Fig. 2 the face of No. 13 and 15 rise are opposite and equal 8″ from the spring of cylinder; at Fig. 3 the face of risers is 7½″ from the spring of cylinder; at Fig. 4 the tread is 10″, and the face of Nos. 13 and 16 risers is 8″ from the joint of cylinder.

Fig. 5. *Shows a cylinder 10″ in diameter.*

The stretchout *CJ* for the quarter circle and location of risers, repeats Fig. 1, the treads are 10″. Make *JL* equal half a tread [5″] for the face of No. 18 rise and 10″ more to the face of No. 19 rise; draw the face of No. 16 and 17 rise directly opposite; now locate the position of short baluster on No. 16 and 19 treads and space off the intermediate balusters; then draw the face of Nos. 17 and 18 rise to intersect the cylinder and to suit the balusters; No. 17 rise may continue straight into the cylinder, but No. 18 rise should be curved so that the nosing may return without too much peak at the miter.

The face of No. 16 and 19 rise are 7″ from the joint or spring of cylinder.

Fig. 6. *Exhibits a 12″ cylinder.*

The treads are shown 10″; the stretchout *CJ* for the quarter circle is found in the same manner as at Fig. 1.   Only in this case observe the stretchout is for the center line of rail instead of the string line.

By locating the risers around the string line in the cylinder gives the true inclination on the string line, thus allowing the veneer to be straight; having no casing in case the cylinder be veneered; by spacing off the regular treads on the center line of rail, the veneer for the face of cylinder will have an easing above and also below, connecting the circular part with the straight ; this gives to the wreath part of rail more inclination, and thereby helps the appearance of the rail.

The cylinder is 12″ in diameter, and if 2″x2″ balusters be required the center line of rail will equal 13½″ diameter, or a radius of 6¾″.   Here the face of Nos. 13 and 16 rise are opposite, and 4¼″ from the joint or spring of cylinder.

Now locate the short baluster on No. 13 and 16, treads and space off the intermediate balusters around the cylinder, then curve No. 14 and 15 rise, to suit the balusters at *M* and *N*.

The intersection of No. 14 rise is made opposite that at *N*; the rise No. 14 is termed a "concave rise," and No. 15 rise is termed is a "convex rise."

Fig. 7. *Shows the treads laid off on the center line of rail for a cylinder 14″ in diameter.*

The dotted line shows the center line of baluster, and is struck with a radius of 7¾″; the tread is 10″, *JC* is the stretchout for the quarter circle *PNF*.   Make *JL* equal half a tread [5″] for the face of No. 16 rise, and to No. 17 rise to equal 10″; draw No. 15 and 14 rise opposite.   Now take *LC* as a radius, and the verge of baluster at *N* for a center, draw arc to intersect *BC* prolonged at *P*; then *PN* will equal the radius of curve; find point on the opposite side in same manner for No. 15 rise; the face of No. 14 and 17 rise are 2¾″ from the spring of cylinder.

Fig. 8. *Shows the treads laid off in the cylinder on the center line of rail in the same manner as at Fig. 7; the face of No. 12 and 15 rise are shown 1″ from the spring of cylinder; this cylinder is 16″ in diameter.*

Fig. 9. *Exhibits the manner of locating the treads on the center line of rail for a cylinder of 20″ diameter.*

The balusters being 2″x2″; then the radius for the center line of rail will equal 10¾″; the treads are 11″.   With *O* as a center and *OB*, 10¾″ for a radius, draw the center line of rail *BFC*; the solid line indicates the face of cylinder.   Draw the diameter *BOC* indefinite, perpendicular to *BC* draw *OF*, also *BA* and *CD* indefinite; with *F* as a center and *FO* for a radius, draw arc intersecting the center line of rail at *H*, through *H* and *F*, draw a line to intersect *CB* and *DC* prolonged at *K* and *J*.   Then the point *K* is the focus and *JC* is the stretchout for the quarter circle *CNF*; set off from *J* to *L* half a tread [5½″] to the face of No. 16 rise; from that set off No. 17 and 18 riser as shown, draw the face of Nos. 13, 14 and 15 rise opposite.

Now locate the short balusters on Nos. 13 and 18 tread, and space off the intervening balusters to suit; then with the side of baluster at *N* as a center, and *LR* for a radius, draw arc to intersect *BC* prolonged at *P*.   With *P* as a center, draw arc from *L* through **N** to intersect the cylinder line for the convex rise; repeat the operation for the concave rise from the point **M** on the opposite side.   The face of No. 13 and 18 rise are shown 10″ from the spring of cylinder.

Fig. 10. *Shows how to place the risers in a quarter cylinder so that the wreath-piece may be constructed with the least expense.*

Draw the right angle **OA** and **OC**.   The radius **OX** for the cylinder line equals 6″, the balusters being 2″x2″, then the radius **OA** for the center line of rail, will equal ¾″ more, or 6¾″.

The solid line shows the string line, and the dotted line indicates the center of baluster, which is the center of rail.

Draw the tangents **AB** and **CB**, forming the right angle at **B**; from **B** set off half a tread [5″] each way on the tangents for the face of No. 12 and 13 rise; set off No. 11 and 14 rise, to equal a tread [10″] as shown; observe the face of No. 11 and 14 rise, both cut the front string 8¼″ from the spring of cylinder on either side.

Now locate the short baluster on No. 11 and 14 treads, and space off the intervening balusters around the cylinder, then curve No. 12 rise to suit the baluster; No. 13 rise in this case may run in straight or may be curved also, as the stair-builder may desire.

Fig. 11. *Shows a quarter cylinder of 8″ radius, the solid line being the face of string, and the dotted line indicates the center line of rail.*

The radius **OA** equals 8¾″; **AB** and **BC** show the tangents forming a right angle at **B**.   For want of room, the face of No. 14 rise is placed at the point **B**; then from **B** set off on the tangents a full tread either way, as No. 13 and 15 rise; draw them in to intersect the outer strings, and at right angles to the same. Now space off the balusters in the cylinder and curve No. 14 rise to suit the baluster; take a tread [10″], for a radius, and say at **D** as a center, draw arc at **P**; then **P** for a center, draw the curve for No. 14 rise; the face of Nos. 13 and 15 rise is 1¼″ from the joint of quarter cylinder.

Fig. 12. *Shows a quarter cylinder, the radius being 10″.*

If 2″x2″ balusters be used, then the radius for the center line of rail will equal 10¾″, as shown by the dotted line.   Draw the tangents **AB** and **BC**, forming a right angle at **B**; the spacing of the treads in the upper flight of stairs locates No. 16 rise on the tangent **BC**, two [2″] inches from the angle at **B**; the regular tread being 10″, then the face of No. 15 rise, from the angle at **B** on the tangent **AB**, must equal 8″, or the difference between **BD** and the regular tread which equals [10—2=8] eight inches.

Set off No. 14 and 17 rise to equal 10″ each; the face of No. 14 rise cuts the string 1″ from the spring line.   Mark the position of No. 1 and 6 baluster; then space the intervening balusters Nos. 2, 3, 4 and 5 equally, and draw the face of No. 15 and 16 rise into the cylinder to suit the balusters.   The face of No. 15 rise continues straight into the cylinder, and the face of No. 16 rise requires to be curved.   With the regular tread [10″] for a radius and a point at the verge of No. 4 baluster at **F**, draw arc cutting No. 17 rise at **H**, from **H** draw the curve tangent to No. 16 rise to intersect the face of cylinder.   The curving of the risers is discretionary with the workman; the curve may be more or less; they should be drawn, however, so that they will miter with the return nosings without too much peak at the point of miter. The above quarter cylinders we have first decided on the radius of curve, this need not be the rule; for the position of risers may be first decided upon, then afterward the radius of quarter circle as described at Fig. 13.

Fig. 13. *Shows how to place the risers in a quarter turn, so that one wreath will be required, and from the least possible thickness of stuff.*

Draw **BA** and **BC** at right angles and of indefinite length; from **B** set off half a tread 4½″ on the line **BA** and **BC** for the place of No. 12 and 13 rise; then make No. 11 and 14 rise equal a regular tread 9″ as shown. Draw the face of No. 11 and 14 rise at right angles to **BA** and **BC.**

Now decide upon the radius of quarter cylinder, say 10″, and the balusters being 2″x2″, which will make the radius for the center line of rail equal 10¾″. Then make **BD** and **BF** each equal 10¾″; draw **DO** and **FO** at right angles to **BC** and **BA**; with **O** as a center, draw the curve from **D** to **F** for the center line of rail. The solid line shows the face of cylinder the radius of which is ¾″ less or 10″. The face of No. 11 and 14 rise are 2½″ from the spring of cylinder. Mark the center of No. 1 and 6 baluster, then space off the intervening balusters 2, 3, 4 and 5, equally on the center line of rail and curve No. 12 and 13 rise to suit the balusters as explained at Fig. 12.

Fig. 14. *Exhibits how to place the risers in a quarter circle, so that two wreath-pieces may be required, and that they may be worked from the plank with the least possible thickness of stuff.*

Draw the right angle **OA** and **OB** indefinite; make **OA** equal the radius [12″¾] for the center line of rail, draw the center line of rail **ACB;** the solid line shows the face of cylinder, the radius of which is ¾″ less or 12″. Bisect the center line of rail **ACB** at **C**, draw **OC;** at right angles to **OC** draw the tangent **CD** and **CF;** also draw tangents **AF** and **BD** at right angles to the radial lines **BO** and **AO.** Prolong **DB** and **FA** for the direction of straight string.

The width of tread is 11″; then set off from **C** on the tangents half a tread [5½″] each way for the face of No. 14 and 15 risers; again set off a regular tread [11″] each way for the face of No. 13 and 16 risers; draw the face of No. 13 and 14 rise at right angles to the face of string as shown; observe the risers cut the face string 6″ from the spring of quarter circle on each side. Now locate No. 1 and 7 baluster, and space the intermediate balusters 2, 3, 4, 5 and 6, equally; then curve No. 14 and 15 risers to suit the balusters as shown.

Some stair-builders prefer to place the risers in this way in a quarter circle, and making the wreath in two pieces, to relieve the casing on the lower edge of the quarter cylinder, particularly when the balusters are over 2″ in diameter; by placing the risers as shown at Fig. 14, less abruptness is encountered at the joining of the cylinder with the straight string.

Fig. 15. *Shows how to lay off a veneer when there are winders in the cylinder.*

The plan of cylinder is 13″ in diameter. How to place the winders so as to form an agreeable casing above and below at the connection of the straight with the circular part of outer string.*

---

*This method of graduating the steps around the cylinder does not govern the pitch of rail. The stair-builder has to raise the inclination of tangents to make the height of rail agreeable for those passing up or down; this graduating of the steps is to form a pleasing easing, connecting the straight string with the cylinder.

AB equals the diameter 13″, *AC* and *BD* indicates the straight string; with *A* and *B* for centers, and *AB* as a radius, draw arcs intersecting at *F*; parallel with *AB* draw *HJ* indefinite, so as to tangent the curve at *L*. From *F* and through points *B* and *A* draw lines to intersect the tangent line at *H* and *J*; then *JH* is the stretchout for the semi-circle *ALB*.

Fig. 16. *Shows the elevation of risers and manner of raduating the width of winders at the narrow end.*

At right angles to *HJ* draw *JG* equal to the height of six risers, more or less, as the case may be. Join *GH*. At *H* place the pitchboard and draw the inclination *HK*, also place the pitchboard at *G* and draw the true inclination *GM* for the straight string; bisect the angles at *H* and *G*, draw the curves 2, 3 and *QXR* at will, the workman using his judgment as to the amount of curve that will suit best. Now draw Nos. 12, 13, 14, 15, 16, 17, and 18 treads to intersect the mixed line *K* 2, 3, *Q, X, R*, and *M*. From the intersections draw the riser lines parallel to *JG* to intersect the stretchout *HJ* at 5, 6, 7, 8 and 9, from which draw lines to the focus *F*, intersecting the cylinder line at *a, b, c, d* and *e* for the location of the face of risers graduating them on plan, Fig. 15, agreeable to the curve in elevation Fig. 16 as shown. The face of No. 12 and 18 rise is 3″ from the spring of cylinder; No. 11 and 18 treads are each 9″ wide, No. 10 and 19 treads are the regular width 11″. Now locate the center of short baluster. on No. 11 and 19 treads and space of the intervening balusters on the center line of rail, shown by the dotted line *C7D*, the face of risers may be shifted a little to suit the balusters as shown at *a* and *d*, also No. 18 rise is shifted ½″ to suit the baluster. From the internal angle of rise and tread, Fig. 16; set off the width of string and draw the lower edge of string to please the eye as shown by the dotted line *YXO*; the veneer should be laid off with lead pencil so as not to abraid the surface of veneer that would, when bending the veneer over a drum, cause fracture; neither should the veneer be notched out for the treads and risers until the cylinder is taken from the drum; *XX* shows the length of staves in the rough.

These cylinders may be constructed in different ways; there is more economy in the use of staves; good glue and very dry material should be used; for painted work use soft pine for staves. For hard wood finish, the veneered cylinder makes the best and most finished work, but the expense is greater. For the thickness of veneer see letter press for Plate 28.

PLATE 16.

Plate 16. [Scale, ¾″=1 foot]. *Exhibits the construction of a face-mould for a wreath-piece landing on the level; also starting from the level to rake, the tangents on plan being either at right angles, acute or obtuse. Also shows how to place the risers in the cylinder at the starting or landing, so as to make one face-mould answer for both wreath-pieces.*

Figs. 1, 2, 3 and 4. *Shows the plan, elevation and face-moulds for a wreath landing on the level.*

The tread is 9″ by 8″ rise. The face of No. 16 rise is 3″ from the spring of cylinder, and hence the face of No. 17 rise must be in the cylinder 6″; the balusters are 2″ diameter, and

5

the rail double moulded, 3″ wide and 4″ deep; the cylinder is 10½″ in diameter, then the radius for the center line of rail will equal $\left\{\dfrac{10\frac{1}{2}}{2}=5\frac{1}{4}''\div\frac{3}{4}=6''\right\}$ six inches [6″]. Then with 6″ as a radius, and O for a center, draw the semi-circle ACE; enclose the semi-circle with the rectilineal parallelogram $ABDE$; draw OC perpendicular to AE, and we have the tangents AB, BC, CD and DE on plan; draw the chord AC; prolong tangent BA and DE to the left for the direction of straight rail.

Fig. 2. *Exhibits the development and elevation of tangents.*

Let XX indicate the edge of drawing board; make AB, BC, CD and DE equal tangents AB, BC, CD and DE on plan, Fig. 1; from the points A, B, C, D and E draw perpendiculars to XX indefinite.

Now elevate Nos. 15, 16 and 17 treads and risers, keeping the face of No. 16 rise 3″ from the spring line at A; through the center of baluster OO draw the under side of rail; parallel with OO draw the center of rail,* cutting the perpendiculars at H and J. From the floor line set up 4″ to under side of rail, and half the depth of rail more [2″] to the center of level rail; parallel to XX draw the center of level rail, cutting the perpendiculars at K and L. Draw LJ prolonged to M, and cutting the perpendicular from C at N; through N, and parallel to XX, draw WR, cutting the perpendiculars at P and Q; prolong HJ to intersect WR at G; parallel to XX draw HS, cutting BP at T; then NS is the height for the lower wreath-piece, and RK is the *height* for the upper wreath-piece; prolong HS to E, then EL will be the whole height. Make HU equal the chord AC, Fig. 1; from T, and at right angles to tangent NJ prolonged, draw TV; from P, and at right angles to tangent HJ prolonged, draw $P2$; parallel to BP draw the half width of rail [1¼″], cutting the tangents at 3 and 4 for the increased width of mould on the radial lines; make Ry equal the chord AC, Fig. 1.

Bevels. Make ab parallel to XX; at right angles to XX draw dh equal to the radius OC, Fig. 1; make d 7 equal TV; and d 6 equal $P2$, also make d 5 equal the *height* RK; draw h 7, h 6 and h 5 prolonged to XX.

Fig. 3. *Exhibits the face-mould.*

Let AB equal HJ, Fig. 2; with A as a center, and WU, Fig. 2, for a radius, draw arc at C; again, with B as a center, and NJ, Fig. 2, for a radius, draw arc intersecting at C. Join BC. Parallel to AB and CB, draw the radial lines CO and AO for the parallelogram $ABCO$ on the cutting plane that will coincide with the parallelogram $ABCO$ on plan when in position.

Proof. The diagonal BO must equal MU, Fig. 2, if so, the angle of tangents at B is correct. Prolong tangent BA 6″ to F; make joints at F and C at right angles to tangents BA and BC. Make AD equal JG, Fig. 2; draw DO for the direction of minor axis; make C 2 and C 3 each equal J 4, Fig. 2, also make A 4,

---

*Let it be observed right here that for all wreaths starting from the level to rake, or those from the rake to a level, and also turn outs at the newel, and wreaths on winders; also platform wreaths, when it is required to find the length of odd balusters. In all such cases the center line of rail must be drawn in this way to obtain the correct height for each wreath-piece. For platform wreaths, when the length of odd balusters is not required, the center line of rail may be drawn at once from the external angle of step and rise, for the inclination of tangents and height of wreath-piece as shown at Fig. 2, Plate 20.

A 5, each equal *J* 3, Fig. 2. Let *O* 8 equal the radius *OC*, Fig. 1, for the length of semi-minor axis; make 8 6 and 8 7 each equal the half width of rail [1¼″].

Parallel with *AF* draw 5 10 and 4 9 for the shank of mould. Now pivot the trammel in *O* with the arms at right angles to *O* 8; then set from pencil to minor-pin the distance *O* 7, place the pencil in the point at 3, drop the pins in the grooves, and fasten the major-pin; then trace the curve for the convex side of mould through the points 5, 7, 3: again, set from pencil to minor-pin the distance *O* 6, place the pencil in the point at 2, and drop the pins in the grooves, then fasten the major-pin and trace the curve through the points 4, 6, 2, for the concave side of face-mould; proceed in like manner to trace the center line.

The section at *M* shows the bevel found in the angle at 7, Fig. 2, applied from the face of crook so as to pitch the joint at *F* down: the section at *N* shows the bevel found in the angle at 6, Fig. 2, applied so as to pitch the joint at *C* up; the block pattern shows the section of rail when squared up, the shaded parts indicate the surplus wood that has to be removed in the formation of wreath-piece.

Fig. 4. *Shows the face-mould for the wreath-piece on the level.*

Draw the right angle *EDC*, make *DC* equal *NL*, Fig. 2. make *DE* equal *ED* on plan, Fig. 1. Parallel with *DE* and *DC* draw *CO* and *EO* for the parallelogram *OCDE* on the cutting plane, or plane of plank.

Proof. The chord *EC* and also the diagonal *OD* in this case must equal *KY*, Fig. 2; prolong tangent *DE* to *F* 6″. Make joint at *F* square to *DF*; make *C* 2 and *C* 3 each equal the half width of rail [1¼″]; let *E* 4 and *E* 5 each equal *J* 3, Fig. 2. Parallel to *EF* draw 4 6 and 5 7, for the shank of mould; as the difference between the semi-minor axis *OC* and the semi-major axis *OE* is so little, the compasses will suit best to draw the concave and convex curves as shown. The section at *M* shows the bevel found in the angle at 5, Fig. 2, applied so as to pitch the joint at *C* down; the section at *N* shows the square applied allowing the shank *FE* to have a horizontal position. The block pattern is applied at right angles to the line made from the bevel showing the twist of rail in the crook at the joint.

Figs. 5 and 6. *Show how to place the risers in the cylinder for a wreath, starting from the level, so as to make the face-moulds drawn for Fig. 1 answer for Fig. 5.*

Fig. 5. *Shows the plan.*

The tangents *AB*, *BC*, *CD* and *DE*, enclosing the semi-circle *ACE*, coincide with plan, Fig. 1. Prolong tangents *BA* and *DE* to the right, for the direction of straight rail; the radius *OC* for the center line of rail equals 6″.

Fig. 6. *Shows the elevation and development of tangents, and also the treads and risers.*

Let *XX* indicate the edge of drawing board; make *AB*, *BC*, *CD* and *DE* equal tangents *AB*, *BC*, *CD* and *DE* on plan, Fig. 5. From *A*, *B*, *C*, *D* and *E* erect perpendiculars to *XX* indefinite; let *XX* also indicate the floor line; from the floor line set up 4″ to the under side of rail, and the half depth of rail [2″] additional, making 6″ from the floor to the center of rail as shown on the left. Parallel with *XX* draw the center of rail cutting the perpendiculars in *F*, *G*, *H*, *J* and *K*; make *KL* equal *EL*, Fig. 2, for the whole height that both wreath-pieces have to raise.

Now through the point **L** draw the inclination for the center of rail, cutting the perpendicular from **B** at **M**; join **MG**, cutting the perpendicular from **C** at **N**; from **N** and parallel to **XX** draw **NS**; parallel to the center line of rail **ML** produced, draw the under side of rail **PQ**. From **XX** on the floor line set up the height of No. 1 and No. 2 rise; draw No. 2 tread at right angles to **AL**, cutting the under side of rail at **O**, then **O** is the center of baluster, and if the baluster is 2″x2″, then the face of No. 2 rise will be 1″ to the left, making the face of rise 2¼″ from the spring line **AL** of cylinder, as shown.

Now return to plan, Fig. 5; make the face of No. 2 rise 2¼″ from the spring line **AE**; set off to No. 1 rise to equal a tread [9″].

Mark the center of baluster on No. 2 tread, from that space off the balusters in the cylinder; then draw the convex rise to suit as shown.

It will be observed now that the height **LS**, Fig. 6, agrees with the height **NS**, Fig. 2, and the height **NH**, Fig. 6, agrees with the height **KR**, Fig. 2, hence one set of face-moulds and bevels will answer for both wreaths, starting and landing.

Figs. 7, 8 and 9. *Exhibits the plan, elevation and face-mould for a wreath-piece, starting from the level to a rake, the angle of tangents on plan being obtuse. Hence the circle on plan is less than a quarter circle. The regular tread is 10″ and rise 7″, the balusters are 2″×2″ and the rail is 4″ wide by 2½″ deep. How to place the risers in the cylinder so that the wreath-piece will raise on the level to the proper height for the long balusters.*

Fig. 7. *Exhibits the plan.*
AB, BC shows the tangents. Prolong tangents **BA** and **BC** for the direction of straight rail. From **A** and **C** draw dotted lines at right angles to the tangents **BA** and **BC** intersecting at **O**; parallel with tangents **BA** and **BC** draw **CD** and **AD** for the parallelogram **ABCD** on plan. From **A** and at right angles to **CB** produced, draw **AF**; from the center **O** draw the center line of rail from **A** to **C**.

Fig. 8. *Exhibits the development and elevation of tangents from which to find the face-mould and position of No. 2 rise on plan, Fig. 7.*
Let **XX** indicate the edge of board, and also the line of floor. Make **CB, BA** equal tangents **CB** and **BA** on plan, Fig 7; from the points **CBA** erect perpendiculars to **XX** indefinite; from **XX** set up half a rise [3½″] to the underside of rail, and 1¼″ additional or 4¾″ to the center of rail at **D**; from **D** and parallel to **XX** draw **DE** through **E**, draw the true inclination of the center line of rail indefinite, cutting the perpendicular from **C** at **H**; parallel to **EH** prolonged, draw the underside of rail; from **XX** set up the height of No. 1 rise 7″; parallel to **XX** draw No. 1 tread, intersecting the underside of rail at **O**. Then **O** is the center of baluster; as the balusters are 2″x2″, then the face of No. 1 rise will be one inch [1″] to the left of **O**, or 2½″ in the cylinder, and as the treads are 10″ the face of No. 2 rise will be 7½″ from the spring line of cylinder as shown.

Thus establishing the location of risers so as to give the proper height to the wreath-piece as required; from **H** and parallel to **XX**, draw **HJ**, cutting the perpendicular from **B** at **K**; then **EK** is the height that the wreath-piece has to raise.

Make **EL** equal **BF**, Fig. 7, from **L** and at right angles to **HE** prolonged, draw **LM**; make **JN** equal the chord **AC**, Fig. 7

Let *JP* equal the diagonal *BD*, Fig. 7; prolong *JH* and make *JQ* equal *BO* on plan, Fig. 7; through *D* and *P* draw a line to intersect the perpendicular from *Q* at *R*.

Bevels. Draw the gauge line *ST* parallel to *XX*; at right angles to *XX*, draw *VW* equal to *AF*. Fig. 7. Make *V* 4 equal *LM*, Fig. 8, let *V* 5 equal the *height* *EK* in e'evation, Fig. 8: draw *W* 4 and *W* 5 prolonged to *XX*, parallel to *ST*. draw the half width [2″] of rail, cutting the hypothenuse of bevels at 6 and 7.

Fig. 9. *Exhibits the face-mould.*

Make *AB* equal *EH*, Fig. 8; with *A* as a center and *DN*, Fig. 8, for a radius, draw arc at *C*; again, with *B* for a center and tangent *AB*, Fig. 7, for a radius, draw arc intersecting at *C*. Join *BC*. Parallel to *AB* and *BC*, draw *CD* and *AD* for the parallelogram *ABCD* on the cutting plane or plane of plank.

Proof. The diagonal *BD* must agree with *DP*, Fig. 8. If so, the angle of tangents at *B* is correct.

Prolong tangent *BA*, 6″ to *F*; also prolong the level tangent *BC*, 6″ to *H*; make joints at *F* and *H* at right angles to the tangents as shown; from *C* and at right angles to tangent *BC*, draw *CJ* indefinite; prolong the diagonal *BD* to intersect *CJ* at *O*; draw the radial line *AO* for the point of tangency, or the intersection of straight shank with the curved part of face-mould; for proof that the intersection at *O* is correct, the diagonal *OB* must equal *DR*, Fig. 8. Make *F* 2 and *F* 3 each equal 4–6, Fig. 8; also make *C* 4 and *C* 5 each equal 5–7, Fig. 8; parallel with *FB*, draw 3–9 and 2–8; parallel with *CH* draw 5–7 and 4–6; at right angles to *OC* draw *OK* equal to the radius *OA*, Fig. 7. Make *K* 10 and *K* 11 each equal the half width of rail [2″]; now *OC* is the semi-major axis and *OK* the semi-minor axis. Instead of a trammel use a straight edge to find the elliptic curves of this face-mould. Draw the two right angles at *O* to indicate the arms of trammel; for the concave side of mould take the straight edge and mark from the end at 8 to *L*, the distance *O* 10, for the minor notch; again mark the major notch at *P* equal to *O* 4; now move the rod at intervals, keeping the two notches on the right angle lines, then marking points at the end of rod, through which draw the curves, using a flexible strip; proceed in like manner to draw the center and convex curves of mould. Points on the diagonal *OB* may be found, giving three points in the curve through which to draw the curves, and thus dispensing with the trammel. To find the points return to Fig. 8: make *QY* equal to the radius *OA*, Fig. 7: parallel to *JD* draw *YF*, parallel to *YF* draw the half width of rail [2″] intersecting *DR* at *G*. At Fig 9 make *BS* equal *DF*, Fig. 8; let *S* 12 and *S* 13 each equal *FG*, Fig. 8. giving the three points required.*

Observe bevels as applied at sections *M* and *N* makes the wreath-piece answer for a landing on the level, instead for a starting off the level as shown on plan, Fig. 7; by turning the wreath-piece upside down, when squared up before moulding, it will then answer for plan, Fig. 7. The bevel applied at section *M* is found in the angle at 5, Fig. 8; and the bevel at section *N* is found in the angle at 4, Fig. 8. Observe they do not cross the tangents in their application.

---

*The correct width for any face-mould on the diagonal line was first given by Mr. J. H. Moncktou. then by Mr. Secor. The above method will suit for small-face moulds, but for long moulds more points in the curve are required as a guide for the flexible strip.

Figs. 10 and 11. *Shows how to place the risers in the cylinder so as to make the face-mould for the plan, Fig. 7, answer for a landing.*

Fig. 10. *Shows the plan.*

The radius for the center line of rail, the tangents, and angle of tangents, coincides with those of Fig. 7; CB and BA are the tangents; OA is the radius for the center line of rail, the dotted line indicates the string line.

Fig. 11. *Exhibits the elevation and development of tangents, and also the landing, tread and rise.*

Let XX indicate the edge of drawing board; make CB and BA equal tangents CB and BA, Fig. 10; from the points C, B, A, draw perpendiculars to XX indefinite; anywhere on the perpendicular from B place the rise of pitchboard, and draw the true inclination for the center of rail as DFH. Parallel to DFH draw the under side of rail; parallel to XX draw DJ prolonged, for the center of level rail; now make JK to equal $4\frac{3}{4}''$ for the floor line to agree with AD, Fig. 8. Through K, and parallel to XX, draw the floor line intersecting the under side of rail at O; then O is the center of baluster; the baluster being $2''$ in diameter set off 1 inch more to the face of rise marked No. 15; draw No. 15 rise at right angles to XX, and set off No. 14 tread and rise, thus locating the face of No. 14 rise $8\frac{3}{4}''$ from the spring line of cylinder. As the treads are $10''$ then the face of No. 15 rise will be in the cylinder $1\frac{1}{4}''$ from the spring line. $[10''-8\frac{3}{4}''=1\frac{1}{4}'']$.

Observe the height LF equals the height KE, for Fig. 8. Now return to plan, Fig. 10, and make the face of No. 14 rise $8\frac{3}{4}''$ from the spring line OC; thus arranging the risers in the cylinder on plan so that the face-mould, Fig. 9, will also suit for the landing wreath-piece.

Figs. 12, 13 and 14. *Shows the plan, elevation and face-mould for a wreath-piece, starting from the level to the rake, the angle of tangents on plan being acute; the curve on plan being greater than a quarter circle.*

The regular tread is $10''$, the rise $7''$, balusters $2''$ in diameter, and the rail $4''$ wide by $2\frac{1}{2}''$ deep.

How to place the risers in the cylinder so that the wreath-piece will raise the proper height on the level, for the long balusters, and at the same time be worked from the least possible thickness of plank.

Fig. 12. *Shows the plan.*

AB, BC are the tangents; at right angles to the tangents, draw AO and CO; from the center O describe the center line of rail from A to C; prolong the tangents for the direction of straight rail. Draw the chord AC, from C and at right angles to AB draw CD.

Fig. 13. *Exhibits the development and elevation of tangents, and also the treads and risers.*

Let XX indicate the edge of drawing board and also the line of floor. Make AB, BC equal tangents AB, BC on plan, Fig. 12; draw perpendiculars to XX from the points A, B, C indefinite; from XX set up half a rise to the underside of level rail and $1\frac{1}{4}''$ additional to the center of rail at D; parallel with XX draw DF; through F draw the true inclination of the center line of rail, cutting the perpendicular from A at H; parallel with FH produced, draw the underside of rail. Now on AH set up the height of No. 1 and 2 risers; parallel with XX draw No. 1 and 2 treads, cutting the under side of rail at *O, O* for the center of baluster, as the balusters are 2″, then the face of No. 1 and 2 rise will be 1″ to the right, or the face of No. 2 rise will be 4½″ from the spring line *AH;* and as the treads are 10″ the face of No. 1 rise will be 5½″ in the cylinder.

Now return to plan, Fig. 12; make the face of No. 2 rise 4½″ from the spring line; set off the face of No. 1 and 3 rise and draw them at right angles to *BA* prolonged; locate the balusters at No 2 tread and space them off around the cylinder, and curve No. 1 rise to suit the baluster. Returning to Fig. 13 draw *HJ* parallel to *XX*, cutting the perpendicular from *B* at *K,* then *FK* is the *height* the wreath-piece is required to raise; bisect *DJ* at *P.* Make *JL* equal *HB* on plan, Fig. 12; let *JM* equal the chord *AC*, Fig. 12; draw *PL* prolonged to intersect the perpendicular from *R* at *N.*

Make *FQ* equal *DB*, Fig. 12; from *Q* and at right angles to *HF* produced, draw *QS.**

Bevels. Parallel with *XX* draw *TV;* draw *TW* perpendicular to *XX*, and equal to *DC*, Fig. 12; make *T* 4 equal *SQ*, Fig. 13, make *T* 5 equal the height *FK*, Fig. 13. Draw *W* 4 and *W* 5 produced to *XX* for the inclination of bevels. Parallel with *TV* draw the half width of rail, cutting the hypothenuse of bevels at 6 and 7.

Fig. 14. *Exhibits the construction of face-mould.*

Make *AB* equal *HF*, Fig. 13, with *A* as a center, and *DM*, Fig. 13, for a radius, draw arc at *C;* again, with *B* as a center, and the tangent *CB* on plan, Fig. 12, for a radius, draw arc intersecting at *C*, draw *BC*, draw the chord *AC*, bisect *AC* at *H*, draw the diagonal *BH* prolonged.

From *C* draw a perpendicular to tangent *BC*, and intersecting *BH* produced at *O;* draw the radial line *OA* for the trapezium *OABC* on the cutting plane, that will agree, when in position, with the parallelogram *OABC* on plan, Fig. 12.

Proof. The diagonal *BHO* must equal *PLN*, Fig. 13. Prolong tangent *BA* 6″ to *J* for shank; also prolong *BC* to *L*, 2″, for straight wood to help the easing at the connection of straight rail. Make joints at *J* and *L* at right angles to the tangents. Let *C* 2 and *C* 3 each equal 5 7, Fig. 13; make *J* 4 and *J* 5, each equal 4 6, Fig. 13. Draw the semi-minor axis *OP* indefinite, and at right angles to *OC*, make *OP* equal the radius *OA*, Fig. 12.

Let *P* 10 and *P* 11 each equal the half width of rail [2″] parallel with *JB* draw 4–6 and 5–7; also parallel to *LB* draw 3–9 and 2–8; now place the trammel in the point at *O* with the arms on the semi-major axis *OC.* Set from the pencil to minor pin on the rod the distance *O* 11, then place the pencil in the point 3, drop the pins in the grooves and fasten the major pin; now trace the convex curve through the points 7, 11, 3. Repeat the operation for the center and concave curves of face-mould.

The section at *M* shows the bevel found in the angle at 4. Fig. 13, and the bevel applied at section *N* is shown in the angle at 5, Fig. 13.

***

*The point Q should be opposite the point *D*, Fig. 12, or to the left of the perpendicular *BK*, as shown at Fig. 2, Plate 13; the results however are the same either way, for a mould of this kind having a full easement.

Figs. 15 and 16. *Shows the plan and elevation of a cylinder landing to accompany Figs. 12 and 13, which is for a starting. How to place the risers so that one face-mould will answer for both wreath-pieces.*

Fig. 15. *Shows the plan.*
OC is the radius, *CB* and *BA* are the tangents.

Fig. 16. *Shows the development and elevation of tangents and the treads and risers.*

Let *XX* indicate a base line; make *AB* and *BC* equal tangents *AB, BC,* Fig. 15. From the points *A, B, C* erect perpendiculars to *XX* indefinite; parallel to *XX* draw *DF,* from *F* draw the true inclination of the center line of rail, cutting the perpendicular from *A* at *H;* parallel to *FH* produced, draw the underside of rail shown by the dotted line. Make *DK* equal *FB,* Fig. 13; [4¾''] from *K* and parallel to *XX,* draw the floor line, cutting the underside of rail at *O,* then *O* is in the center of baluster, the baluster is 2'', then the face of landing rise, No. 15, will be 1'' to the right of *O.* Now set off No. 14 tread and rise which locates the face of No. 14 rise 5¾'' from the spring line *AH* of the cylinder.

Parallel to *XX* draw *HJ;* it will be observed that the *height JF* is equal to the *height KF,* Fig. 13, and.that they both are the same height [4¾''] from the floor line to the center of rail.

Now return to plan, Fig. 15, draw the face of No. 14 rise 5¾'' from the spring line *OA,* then as the regular tread is 10'', the face of No. 15 rise will be in the cylinder 4¼''; now space off the balusters from No. 14 rise around the cylinder, then curve No. 15 rise to suit the baluster as shown.

PLATE 17.

Plate 17. [Scale ¾''=1 foot.] *Exhibits the construction of a face-mould, for a quarter cylinder having flyers above and below the quarter pace. Also the face-mould for a wreath-piece starting from a newel, the cylinder being less than a quarter circle on plan.*

Figs. 1, 2 and 3. *Shows the plan, elevation and face-mould.*

For a quarter circle, tread is 10'' and rise 7'', the balusters are 2''x2'' and rail 4''x2½''.

Fig. 1. *Shows plan similar to Fig. 10, Plate 15; the risers are placed in the quarter cylinder so the wreath-piece may be worked out in one piece, and may have the same inclination on the line of tangents as the straight part of rail.*

The radius *OA* for the center line of rail equals 6¾'', draw the radii *OA* and *OC* at right angles; parallel to *OA* and *OC* draw the tangents *CB* and *AB,* forming the square parallelogram *OABC* on plan; prolong tangents *BA* and *BC* for the direction of straight rail, the face of No. 12 and 13 rise is 5'' from the angle at *B;* No. 11 and 14 rise is spaced off a regular tread 10'', locating the face of No, 11 and 14 rise 8¼'' from the spring of cylinder at *A* and *C.**

Often the stair builder has to furnish rails to order from the country. In all such cases he must know the diameter of cylinder, height of rise, width of tread, the location of risers at the cylinder, if at the spring, or out from the same, size of balusters, also rail; if the rail is on the right or left ascending the stairs.

Fig. 2. *Shows the elevation and development of tangents, also the treads and risers from plan.*

Let **XX** indicate the edge of drawing board. Make **AB** and **BC** equal tangents **AB** and **BC** on plan, Fig. 1; from the points **A, B** and **C** draw lines perpendicular to **XX** indefinite: now elevate the treads and risers, keeping the face of No. 11 and 14 rise 8¼″ from the spring lines **A** and **C**; draw the true inclination of rail from the external angle of No. 11 and 13 tread and rise, cutting the perpendiculars at **D, E** and **F**. Parallel with **XX** draw **DH,** cutting the perpendicular from **B** at **J**; then **HF** is the *height* the wreath-piece has to raise; from **J** and at right angles to **DE** draw **JK**; make **HL** equal the chord **AC** on plan, Fig. 1. Parallel with **BE** draw the half width of rail [2″], cutting the inclination of rail at **N**.

Bevels. As both tangents have the same inclination only one bevel will be required. Parallel to **XX** draw **PQ**; at right angles to **XX** draw **QR** equal to the radius **OC**, Fig. 1; make **QS** equal **JK**, draw **RS** prolonged to **XX**.

Fig. 3. *Shows the face-mould.*
Let **AB** equal **ED** in elevation, Fig. 2; with **A** as a center and the distance **LF**, Fig. 2, for a radius, draw arc at **C**; again, with **B** as a center and **AB** for a radius draw arc intersecting at **C**; draw **BC**; parallel to tangent **BA** and **BC**, draw the radial lines **CO** and **AO** for the parallelogram **OABC** on the cutting plane.

Proof. The diagonal **BO** must equal the diagonal **BO** on plan, Fig 1.
Prolong tangents **BA** and **BC** 6″ to **D** and **E** for the length of shank; make joints at **D** and **E** at right angles to **BD** and **BE**. Draw the diagonal **BO** for the direction of minor axis; draw **FH** indefinite through **O** and at right angles to **OB** for the direction of major axis.

Make **OJ** equal the radius **OC**, Fig. 1, for the length of semi-minor axis; let **J** 6 and **J** 7 each equal the half width of rail [2″]; make **A** 2 and **A** 3 also **C** 4 and **C** 5 each equal **EN**, Fig. 2. Parallel with **BE** and **BD** draw 5–9 and 4–8, also 3–11 and 2–10 for the width of shank. Now pivot the trammel at **O** with the arms on the axis **FH**, then set from pencil to minor-pin on the rod, the distance **O** 6, for the concave side of mould; now place the pencil in the point at 4, drop the pins in the grooves and fasten the major-pin, then trace the curve for the concave side of mould through the points 2, 6, 4. Repeat the operation for the center and convex curves of mould.

The sections of crook at **M** and **N** show the bevel found in the angle at **S**, Fig. 2, applied from the face of crook; the block pattern is applied at right angles to the line made from the bevel, giving the section of rail and twist of wreath-piece at the joints.

Figs. 4, 5 and 6. *Shows the construction of face-mould for a quarter cylinder on plan corresponding to Fig. 12, Plate 15, where the learner is instructed how to place the risers in the cylinder.*

Fig. 4. *Shows the plan.*
The face of No. 14 rise is located 7″ from the spring of cylinder and the face of No. 17 rise is placed 1¼″ from the spring of cylinder; the radius for the center line of rail equals 10¾″.

The tangents **AB** and **CB** are at right angles to the radial lines **OA** and **OC**, forming the square parallelogram **OABC**, on plan.

Fig. 5. *Shows the development and elevation of tangents, also the treads and risers.*

Let *XX* indicate the edge of drawing board; make *AB* and *BC* equal the tangents *AB* and *BC* on plan, Fig. 4; from the points *A, B* and *C* draw perpendiculars to *XX* indefinite; now elevate the risers and treads, keeping the face of No. 14 rise 7″ from the spring line at *A*, and the face of No. 17 rise 1¼″ to the right of the spring line at *C*; from the external angle of No. 14 rise, draw the true inclination of the rail, cutting the perpendiculars at *D, E* and *F;* from *D*, and parallel to *XX*, draw *DH*, cutting *BE* at *J;* then *HF* equals the *height* the wreath-piece is required to raise; from *J*, and at right angles to *DE*, draw *JK;* parallel with *BE* draw the half width of rail [2″] cutting the inclination of rail at *N;* make *HL* equal the chord *AC*, Fig. 4.

Bevels. Draw *PQ* parallel to *XX;* at right angles to *XX* draw *PR* equal to the radius *OC*, Fig. 4; make *P* 5 equal *JK*, draw *R* 5 prolonged to *XX* for the bevel as shown.

Fig. 6. *Shows the face-mould.*
Make *AB* equal *DE*, Fig. 5; with *A* as a center, and *LF*, Fig. 5, for a radius, draw arc at *C;* again, with *B* as a center, and *BA* for a radius, draw arc intersecting at *C*, join *BC;* parallel to tangent *BC* and *BA*, draw the radial lines *OA* and *OC*, and we have the parallelogram *OABC* on the cutting plane, that when in position, will agree with the parallelogram *OABC* on plan, Fig. 4.

Proof. The diagonal *BO* must agree with the diagonal *BO* on plan, Fig. 4, if so, the angle of tangents at *B* is correct.

Prolong tangents *BA* and *BC* to *D* and *E* 6″ for straight wood on shank; make joints at *D* and *E* at right angles to *BD* and *BE;* draw the diagonal *BO* for the direction of minor axis. Make *OJ* equal the radius *OC*, Fig. 4; let *J* 6 and *J* 7 each equal the half width of rail [2″]; let *A* 2 and *A* 3, also *C* 4 and *C* 5, each equal *EN*, Fig. 5. Parallel to *BD* and *BE* draw 2 10 and 3 11, also 5 9 and 4 8, for the width of shank.

If it be preferred to find the several points in the elliptic curve and use a pliable strip in tracing the curves, then return to plan, Fig. 4; draw the true width of rail [4″] from the center *O* equally on each side of the center line. Draw the director *OB* and the chord *AC*, forming the angle at *V;* bisect *AV* and *CV* at *T* and *W;* from the points *A, T, V, W* and *C* draw ordinates parallel to the director *OB*, cutting the convex, center and concave curves of rail at *a, d, h,* &c. Now return to Fig. 6; draw the diagonal *OB* and the chord *AC*, forming the angle at *V;* bisect *AV* and *CV* at *W* and *T*. From the points *A, T, W* and *C* draw ordinates indefinite and parallel to the director *BO;* now transfer the points on the ordinates from plan, Fig. 4 to corresponding ordinates on face-mould, using the chord *AC* as a base line, then trace the curve through the points as shown, using a flexible strip.

The sections at *M* and *N* show the bevel found in the angle at 5, Fig. 5, applied through the center of plank, so as to pitch the joint at *E* up, and the joint at *D* down.

Figs. 7, 8, 9 and 10. *Shows how to construct the face-mould for a quarter cylinder having two wreath-pieces; the student is shown how to place the risers in the cylinder at Fig. 14, Plate 15.*

Fig. 7. *Shows the plan.*

Draw **OA** and **OB** to equal 12¾″ and forming the right angle at **O**; from the center **O** draw the center line of rail **ACB**; bisect the curve **ACB** at **C**; draw the radial line **CO**; at right angles to the radial lines **CO, AO** and **BO**. draw lines tangent to the curve and intersecting at **D** and **F**, for the length of tangents **AF, FC, CD** and **DB** on plan.

Draw the tangents **FA** and **DB** prolonged, for the direction of straight rail; from **C**, and at right angles to tangent **AF** prolonged draw **CH** parallel to tangents **CD** and **BD**, draw **BL** and **CL** for the parallelogram **LCBD** on plan. Now from **C** on the line of tangents **CF, FA** and **CD, BD**, set off half a tread each way, then a whole tread more, thus locating the face of No. 13 and 16 risers 6″ from the spring line of cylinder.

Fig. 8. *Shows the development and elevation of tangents, also the treads and risers.*

Let **XX** indicate the edge of drawing board. Make **AF, FC, CD** and **DB** equal the tangents **AF FC, CD** and **DB**, Fig. 7. From the points **A, F, C, D** and **B** draw perpendiculars to **XX** indefinite; elevate the treads and risers, keeping the face of No. 13 and 16 rise 6″ from the spring lines **A** and **B**; from the external angles of No. 13 and 16 rise, draw the inclination of rail, cutting the perpendiculars at **H, J, K, L** and **M**; from **H** and parallel to **XX**, draw **HN**, cutting **FJ** at **P**; then **KN** is the *height* the wreath-piece has to raise from **A** to **C** on plan, Fig. 7. From **K** and parallel to **XX**, draw **KQ**, cutting the perpendicular from **F** at **R**; make **RS** equal **FH**, Fig. 7; from **S** and at right angles to **HK**, draw **SV**; make **HT** equal the chord **BC** on plan, Fig 7.

Bevels. As the tangents all have the same inclination, only one bevel will be required for all joints.

Draw **ab** parallel with **XX**; perpendicular to **XX** draw **df** equal to **HC**, Fig. 7. Make **dh** equal **SV**, Fig. 8; draw **fh** prolonged to **m**; parallel with **XX** draw the half width of rail cutting **mf** at **y**.

Fig. 9. *Shows the face-mould, the trammel or straight edge being used to draw the elliptic curves.*

Make **AF** equal **HJ** in elevation, Fig. 8; with **A** as a center, and **TQ**, Fig. 8, for a radius, draw arc at **C**; again with **F** as a center and **FA** for a radius, draw arc intersecting at **C**. Join **FC** parallel with **FC** and **FA**, draw **AL** and **CL** for the parallelogram **LAFC** on the cutting plane.

Proof. The diagonal **LF** must equal the diagonal **LD**, Fig. 7. If so, the angle at **F** is correct.

Prolong the diagonal **FL** to **O** equal to **DO**, Fig. 7, draw the radial lines **OC** and **OA**. Make **OP** equal the radius **OA** on plan, Fig. 7; prolong tangent **FA**, 6″ to **T** for length of shank; make joints at **T** and **C** at right angles to **FT** and **FC**. Let **C** 2, and **C** 3, also **T** 4 and **T** 5 equal **ym**, Fig. 8; from 4 and 5 draw lines parallel to **TA**, intersecting the radial line **OA** produced at 7 and 6; let **P** 8 and **P** 9 each equal the half width of rail [2″]. Now pivot the trammel in the point at **O** with the arms at right angles to **OP**; for the convex curve, set from pencil to minor-pin on rod, the distance **O** 9, [14¾″], then place the pencil in the point at 7. and shift the major-pin until both drop into the grooves, then fasten the major-pin and trace the curve through the points 7, 9, 3, for the convex curve of mould; proceed in like manner to trace the concave curve through the points 6, 8, 2, for which set the minor-pin to **O** 8, or 10¾″ for the semi-minor axis, and proceed as above.

The sections *M* and *N* show the bevels applied from the face of crook through the center of plank, so as to pitch the shank down, and the center joint up.

Fig. 10. Shows the face-mould drawn by the use of ordinates; less space being required than by the trammel; in many cases the ordinates are to be preferred, as in large sweeps where the room required for the trammel is limited; it will be seen in this way any number of ordinates can be used.

On plan, Fig. 7, set off the half width of rail [2''] on each side of the center line of rail *ACB*. Draw *Cy* indefinite; draw the chord *BC* prolonged; perpendicular to *BC* as a center, and *TQ*, Fig. 8, for a radius, draw arc cutting *Cy* at 2; draw *B* 2 prolonged; draw any number of ordinates parallel with the director *LD* to cut the curves of rail, and also the chord *BC* on plan, and prolonged to intersect *B* 2 at 3, 4, 5 and 6, &c.

Fig. 10. *Shows the face-mould.*

The parallelogram *LCDB* is laid off in the same manner as at Fig. 9, and need not be repeated.

Prolong tangent *DB*, 6'' to *T*; make joints at *T* and *C* at right angles to *DT* and *DC*; draw the chord *BC* prolonged, make *BC* equal *B* 2, Fig. 7. Now transfer the spaces 6 5, 5 4, 4 2 and 2 3, on plan, Fig. 7, to the chord *BC*, Fig. 10, now draw ordinates through the points 3, *B*, 4, 5. 6, 5, 4, *C* and 3, parallel to the director *DL* indefinite; then transfer points on the ordinates on plan, Fig. 7. to corresponding ordinates on face-mould, using the chords *BC* as a base line; now through the points trace the curves for the face-mould.

The sections at *M* and *N* show the bevels applied reverse to those at Fig. 9; at section *N* the bevel is applied so as to pitch the shank up, and at *M* the bevel is shown applied so as to pitch the joint at *C* down.

Figs. 11, 12 and 13. *Shows the elevation, ground plan and face-mould for a "turnout" starting from a newel, the post is 8''×8'', balusters 2''×2'', rail 4''×2½'', the rise and tread is 7''×10''.*

Fig. 11. *Shows the elevation.*

Begin by elevating two or three risers and treads from the base line *XX*, as No. 1, 2 and 3 rise. From the top of No. 1 step set up to the underside of rail the difference [5''] that the newel post is longer than a short baluster and 1¼'' more, making 6¼'' from the top of No. 1 step to the center of rail as shown. At this height draw the center of level rail *DH* parallel with *XX*; from the face of No. 2 and 3 rise set off the center of short baluster *OO*, through *OO*, draw the inclination of the underside of rail; parallel with *OO* draw the center of inclining rail to intersect the center of level rail at *F*; from *F* let fall the perpendicular intersecting the base line *XX* at *B*.

Now commence the plan, Fig. 12. Draw *YT* indefinite, to indicate the center line of rail or center of baluster on plan. Set off No. 1, 2, 3 rise and the point *B* to correspond with Fig. 11. Set the center of newel at *H* on line with the face of No. 1 rise, and in this case let the side of newel be on line with the center of baluster, and as the newel is 8'' in diameter, the center of newel will be out 4'' from the center of baluster. For small halls this is the usual way to locate the newel when a turnout wreath-piece is required; the newel may be set on an angle, or square with the rise, or may be set further out or in, as the stairbuilder may desire; the location is a matter of taste and convenience; the principle in getting the face-mould is the same.

From the center of newel at **H** draw **HB**, draw the verge of cap cutting **HB** at 2; from 2 set off the half width of rail [2″] to the point of miter at **A**; make **BC** equal **BA** for the tangents on plan. From the points **A** and **C** draw the radial lines at right angles to the tangents **AB** and **CB**; from the converging point (not shown on plan) draw the curves of rail on plan. The face of No. 3 rise is 5½″ from the spring of cylinder; draw **AO** and **CO** parallel with the tangents **BC** and **BA** for the parallelogram **OABC** on plan; from **A** and square to **YT** draw **AD**.

Now return to elevation. Fig. 11, make **BA** and **BC** each equal tangents **BA** and **BC** on plan. Fig. 12, from the points **A** and **C**, draw perpendiculars to **XX**, cutting the center of level rail at **D** and the inclining rail at **G**; prolong **DF** to intersect **CG** at **H**, then **HG** is the *height* the wreath-piece is required to raise in the curve. Make **HJ** equal the chord **AC**, Fig. 12; let **HK** equal the diagonal **BO**, Fig. 12. Make **FL** equal **BD** on plan, Fig. 12; from **L** and at right angles to **GF** prolonged, draw **LM**.

Bevels. Draw **nP** parallel to **XX**; draw **Pq** perpendicular to **XX** and equal to **AD**, Fig. 12; make **pr** equal to **LM**, Fig. 11, also make **ps** equal the height **HG**, Fig. 11, draw **qr** and **qs** prolonged to edge of board for convenience when setting the bevels. Parallel with **np** draw the half width of rail [2″], cutting **rq** at 3, and also **sq** at 4.

Fig. 13. *Shows the face-mould.*

Let **CB** equal **FG** in elevation, Fig. 11. With **C** as a center and **JG**, Fig. 11, for a radius, draw arc at **A**; again, with **B** as a center and tangent **BA**, Fig. 12, for a radius, draw arc intersecting at **A**, join **BA**; draw **AO** and **CO** parallel with tangents **BC** and **BA** for the parallelogram **OABC** on the cutting plane.

Proof. The diagonal **OB** must equal the distance **KG**, Fig. 11. If so, the angle of tangents at **B** is correct.

Prolong tangent **BC**, 7″ to **D** for length of shank, make joints at **A** and **D** at right angles to **AB** and **BD**; make **A** 2 and **A** 3 each equal **S** 4, Fig. 11, make **D** 4 and **D** 5 each equal **r** 3, Fig. 11: prolong the joint line at **A** indefinite, also prolong the diagonal **BO** to intersect the joint line at **L**, from **L**, through **C**, draw the radial line for the point of tangency or connection of straight with the circular part. From the points 4 and 5, draw lines parallel with **BD** to cut the radial line **LC** produced at 6 and 7; now connect the points 2, 6 and 3, 7 with the curves as shown, using a flexible strip, being careful to draw the curves to tangent the straight part at points 6 and 7; also see that the curves connect the joint **A** about square to the joint. The curves may be drawn with the trammel centered at **L**, with the arms resting on the semi-major axis **LA**; but to use the trammel in this case would be too unhandy and attended with too much loss of time. Face-moulds of this kind the practical stairbuilder can draw the curves by using a pliable strip thinned down at one end.

The sections of crook at **M** and **N** show the bevels applied from the face of plank; the bevel found in the angle at **S**, Fig. 11, is shown applied at section **M** and the bevel shown at the angle **r**, Fig. 11, is applied at section **N**. Observe they do not cross the tangents in their application.

Fig. 14. *Shows the same face-mould drawn with less lines, but not so correct as shown at Fig. 13.*

To find the angle of tangents at **B** lay down the steel square and draw the right angle **ASD** indefinite; make **SB**, **BC** and **CD** equal **MF**, **FG** and **GV**, Fig. 11. With **B** as a center and tangent *AB*, Fig. 12, for a radius, draw arc intersecting *SA* at *A*, connect *BA*, thus establishing the angle of tangents at *B*.

Proof. The distance *AC* must equal *JG*, Fig. 11. Make joints at *A* and *D* at right angles to *BA* and *BD*; let *A* 2 and *A* 3 each equal *S* 4, Fig. 11, also let *D* 4 and *D* 5 equal *r* 3, Fig. 11; from 4 and 5 draw lines indefinite, and parallel to *SD*; now draw the concave and convex curves of mould, using a pliable strip tapered at one end. Connect *A* 4 on plan, Fig. 12, for the miter on plan; make 2 6 equal 3 4, Fig. 12, draw *A* 6 for the miter on face-mould.

Any face-mould may be drawn in this way, if the stairbuilder prefers; by increasing the number of lines a third point in the curve may be found on the diagonal *OB* prolonged, Fig. 13, to which we will refer at another time.

The bevels as applied at sections *M* and *N* are the same and applied in like manner as those shown at Fig. 13.

At Fig. 14, if the points of tangency, or connection of the straight with the circular part is required, then draw the proportional line *AC*; from 2 and 3 and parallel to *AC*, draw lines to intersect the parallel lines from 4 and 5 at 6 and 7; then the points at 6 and 7 show the connection of the straight with the circular part without extending the long lines as at Fig. 13.

PLATE 18.

Fig. 1. *Exhibits the plan of a half pace winding "dog-legged" stair-case. Hall 5.3″ wide, the center of rail being the center of hall, and so of all succeeding flights composing the staircase.*

The rail starts at the first newel and terminates at the second, and from second to the newel at the landing finishing with a ramp and knee against the newel; if instead of winders there be a platform, then the first length would intersect the lower edge of outer string on the return flight, miter and finish down the lower edge of string and the triangular space filled with balusters of odd lengths or ornamental panel work. On account of room winders occupy the half pace in this case instead of a platform. The newel at the winders is placed in the center of hall 2′ 7½″ from wall to center of post. The space is divided off on the semi-circle into six winders; the risers and tread part of steps should be housed into the post, also the nosings that join the post at right angles to its face.

The manner of getting out winders for this kind of stairs is explained at Plate 20.

Fig. 2. *Shows plan of quarter pace winding stairs of 13 risers.*

The flyers to the winders is open on one side and the flyers above the winders is closed between partitions; in the quarter pace four winders are used divided off equally on the quarter circle. The corner is allowed to be cased up so as to receive the risers and steps at the narrow end. The flyers or straight steps, Nos. 1, 2, 3, 9, 10, 11, 12 and 13 are housed into wall strings on the right and left hand side. The first three steps are sided up on the right with narrow flooring and cut off hand-rail high and capped, the siding is ploughed into the post ½″. In first-class houses No. 4 and 9 steps may be diminished at *A*, so as to increase the width of winders at the narrow ends, the corner may be rounded and the string carried around, and the steps and risers housed into the string, thus taking away the sharp angle of the winders at the narrow ends, and giving a better finish to the string and wall rail, if used.

Fig. 3. *Shows plan of a quarter pace box stairs containing 12 risers.*

[Scale ¼″=1 foot]. The stairs are planned so as to admit light at the quarter pace, a window should not be neglected in these close stairs, either on the side, or as a skylight in the roof, for both light and ventilation. The construction is the same as explained for Fig. 1, Plate 19.

Fig. 4. *Shows plan of an outside steps at the front door.* [Scale ⅜″=1 foot].

The height at a point 3′ 3″ from the building to the level with the top of the front door sill equals 3′ 9½″, which being divided into seven equal parts, will allow 6½″ for the height of each rise; and as we are not limited to the run, we may use Blondel's formula for the relative width of tread to the height of rise.

$\overline{Rule.}$ From the constant 24″ take twice the height of rise, [24″−6½″×2=11″], for the tread, equals 11″ for the breadth of tread; this gives an easy grade to the steps, 6½″ rise, by 11″ tread. The breadth of steps from wall to outer edge of nosing is 3′ 5″, the landing should drop down one rise below the door sill, then there will be 6 risers as shown to the platform. A stone at *B* is bedded in the pavement to start the first rise off, sometimes the first step is of stone, which is better, as the wood work is kept higher off the ground.

Fig. 5. *Shows the elevation.*

The steps are of white pine, 1½″ thick, the nosings are returned on the front string over plain brackets; the balusters are shown dovetailed into the steps; the newel post is shown anchored into the stone, having an "upset" bolt leaded into the stone, and extended up into the post with a nut at the end as shown at *A*.

For the full width of steps, take the tread 11″ plus the projection of nosing [1½″] equals 12½″, plus ⅜″ for tongue into the rise at the internal angle, equals, [11″+1½″+⅜″=12⅞″] for the full width of steps 12⅞″.

For all outside steps, each step should have a wash of ¼″ in every 12″, so as to allow the water to run off; this is not too much, for the step is liable to turn up at the nosing, and the middle of step to become dished and hold the water after a rain; the reason that the steps become caped, arises from the dampness underneath, and for this reason the steps and risers should have a heavy coat of paint on the underside, before fixing in place, so as to prevent the wood from taking the moisture.

Then after the pitchboard is made in the usual way 6½″ by 11″; take off on the tread side of pitchboard ¼″ at the right angle and nothing at the point, this will give each tread the required wash, and reduce the rise to 5¾″ by 11″ on the cut out of "horse" or string.

How to take the lengths of rail so as to cut and make all joints at the bench. Plumb down the face of No· 2 and No. 6 rise on the face of string as 2 *B* and 6 *C*, then the distance *BC*, [4′.3½″] taken parallel with the lower edge of string, is the length for the inclining rail; then measure from the face of landing rise, [No. 6] to the center of baluster on the corner [5′.2″] then take the distance *HJ* on plan, from center of baluster to wall.

Having the lengths of rail, how to make the easing patterns, and mark the points B and C, on the patterns, so that the rail will be the required height at the newel, and also on the level, and cut all joints at the bench.

First with the pitchboard lay off a few steps and risers as 1, 2 and 3, from the edge of a board, say 12″ wide; draw the under side of rail through the center of baluster *kk*; parallel to *kk* draw *nn* for the center of rail. Now make *ma* equal half a rise, [3¼″] and draw the under side of rail *ap*; then transfer the angle *apk* to the board from which the pattern is to be made, and ease off the angle with the easing pattern for the under side of rail; now gauge for the width of pattern; then lay the pattern down on the drawing so the lines *kp* and *ap* will agree with same lines on the pattern; then mark the face of No. 6 rise across the pattern to intersect the center line *nn* at *r*.

For the easement at the newel, decide upon the length of short baluster from top of steps to the under side of rail at the center of baluster, say, 1′.11″. Also decide upon how much higher the newel is than a short baluster measuring from the top of step to the under side of rail, say 5″. Then make *FS* equal 5″, and draw the dotted line *ts* at right angles to the rise; then transfer the angle *tsk* to the board from which the pattern is to be made, and ease the angle to suit; then dress off to the curve, and gauge to the width required for the depth of rail; now lay the pattern over the drawing to the lines *ts* and *sk* so that they will agree with same lines on pattern, then mark the face of No. 2 rise cutting the center line *nn* at *x*; also mark the line of newel post. Then the distance *xr* equals the distance *BC* on the string, and is equal to the length to cut the straight rail on the rake, less the straight wood on the patterns, as shown on rail in elevation.

Now the post is to be 5″ longer than a short baluster [1′. 11″] equals [1′. 11″+5″ = 2′. 4″] from the top of step to underside of rail 2′. 4″, or from the top of stone to underside of rail 6½″ more, or 3′. 0½″.

Lines are shown converging at *H*, from which the curve of easement may be drawn.

Fig. 6. *Shows plan of an outside cellar flight of stairs under a store-room.* [Scale ¼″ = 1 foot].

The opening is 4′. 0″ wide, and the run for the steps is 4′. 6″. The height from cellar floor to level with the top of stone sill at pavement is 6′. 3″.

Fig. 7. *Shows the elevation.*

The height 6′. 3″ being divided into nine risers [6.′ 3″ × 12″ = 75 ÷ 9 = 8 ³⁄₁₆ full] equals 8³⁄₁₆″ full for the height of rise, the run being divided by 9. [4′. 6″ × 12″ = 54 ÷ 9 = 6″] equals 6″ for each tread.

Right here let it be observed we have divided the run into the same number of parts as the height for the risers, and not made the space for the treads one less as in other cases, for this reason, if we had taken the whole space and made the division one less then the horse and skid piece *B* would have extended out beyond the wall at *A* too far.

The steps should be made from 2″ oak, housed into oak horses and well spiked together and made, measuring between the strings about 12″ narrower than the width of opening. This allows 6″ on each side for the skids *BB*, which project above the edge of steps so that in sliding heavy boxes down they will protect the steps. These skids are spiked to the horses and also into a timber placed between the horse and the wall; *D. D, D.* shows the housings. The horse is 12″ wide.

The opening to the pavement is closed with iron doors resting on a heavy iron bar shown at *F*. These doors, after folding down on this bar, are locked by two other iron doors folding in a vertical position, and are held in place by the bar shown at *H*.

Fig. 8. *Shows the elevation of a step-ladder used to get into the "cock-loft," or "blind-garret," and also for an exit to the roof in case of fire, or any repairs that may be needed.*

The height from floor to underside of rafters is 11'. 0''; the run is 4'. 0''; the height to garret floor is 9' 0''. The whole height we will divide into eleven risers at 12'' each, that will allow No. 9 tread to come level with the attic joist. The whole run equals 4'. 0'', or 48''. The tread at the top of ladder is 9½'' wide, which will leave 4'. 0'' minus 9½'' equals 3'. 2½'', which being divided into eleven parts equals 3½'' for each tread, and also 3½'' more for the foot of ladder at *A*; also the sides of ladder should be at least 1¼'' thick and 8'' wide.

In this case it will not be necessary to make a pitchboard take the steel square and with 12'' on the blade and 3½'' on the tongue, draw the tread *DF* from the tongue; and the rise *FJ* from the blade, continue the line *DF* to *H*, and with the compasses take the hypotheuuse *DJ*, and space off eleven spaces on the edge of horse *AX* as *J* 2, 2 3. Then place the two horses together and transfer the divisions; then set the bevel to the angle *JDH*, and with it lay off the steps, also their thickness and gain in the horses ½''. At two or three intervals tenon the step through the horses and glue and wedge the tenons *F* and *K*. The ladder may be 26'' wide. At *L* a trap door is shown leading into the garret and the scuttle *M* in the roof; the door in the roof should be carefully covered with tin and the curb around raised above the roof with flashings carried up and turned over the upper edge of curb; also the tinning on the door extended down to the roof to answer for cap flashing; if the tinning be done in this way there will be no leaking; two hooks and steeples are required to fasten and keep the door in place. At *C* is shown a light railing for hand-holt.

For outside steps, sap wood should not be used, a sound knot is to be preferred; if the heart side be turned down the step will wear longer for exposed work; if inside then the heart side will be more durable, but is more difficult to work smooth than the side nearest to the bark. Oak is to be preferred for outside steps; white pine is better than yellow pine; all outside steps should be constructed so as to admit a free circulation of air, and painted underneath as well as above to protect them from the dampness. The following is a very good proportion for the thickness to length of steps.

Steps 3'. 0'' long, 1⅛'' thick.   Steps 6'. 0'' long, 1½'' thick.
Steps 3'. 6'' long, 1 3-16'' thick.   Steps 6'. 6'' long, 1⅝'' thick.
Steps 4'. 0'' long, 1¼'' thick.   Steps 7'. 0'' long, 1¾'' thick.
Steps 4'. 6'' long, 1 5-16'' thick.   Steps 7'. 6'' long, 1⅞'' thick.
Steps 5'. 0'' long, 1⅜'' thick.   Steps 8'. 0'' long, 2'' thick.
Steps 5'. 6'' long. 1 7-16'' thick.

PLATE 19.

Plate 19. [Scale, ¼''=1 foot]. *Shows various plans of close or box stairs, built either between two walls or a wall on the one side and lined up on the other with flooring. In first-class box stairs a wall rail is secured to the wall by "hold-fasts," and is allowed to project clear of the wall not less than one and a half [1½''] inches.*

Fig. 1. *Shows the plan of a flight of box stairs having a straight run of 16 risers, landing on a level with the floor in the next story.   How to proceed and construct the same.*

First take the height of story from top to top of joist, [10′.2″] as shown in elevation, Fig. 2; then the width of opening, [3′.0″], then the horizontal distance from the face of first rise to plumb with the last rise.   [11′.3″].

Having taken the measures, then proceed to lay off the risers. Provide a story rod made from pine 1½″ square, and 12 or 16 feet long, dressed up square, and for convenience, mark off one side into feet and number the same; have the rod kept in a rack for this special purpose.

Now set off on the rod the height of story,* Fig. 2, equal to 10′, 2″, then with a large pair of dividers, space off the height into 16 parts, which will equal 7⅝″ each, and are termed the "risers"; the number of full steps will always be one less; therefore in this case there will be 15 full steps required.

Now the horizontal distance including the landing equals 14′, 3″.   We must allow for the quarter pace at the landing at least 3′, 0″, leaving for the run the horizontal distance 11′, 3″. which equals 135″ to be divided into 15 equal parts.   [135÷15″ =9″] equals 9″ for each division termed the "tread"; if including the projecting nosing, each division is then termed the "step."

Now we have the pitch or cut out on horse 7⅝ rise by 9″ tread.   The next will be to make a pitchboard, have the grain to run parallel with the hypothenuse or long side; see that it is exact to the rise on the rod as shown at **A** in elevation, also to the tread as shown at **B** on plan, Fig. 1; if there are several flights of stairs to the same pitch then make the pitchboard from some hard wood. Two wall strings will be required, the one on the left ascending will require an easing at the starting and also at the landing, the string on the right will not require any easing, as the room will not admit of any.

Now select the planks for the wall strings about 12″ wide; allow the external angle **C** of rise and tread to extend down from the top edge of string from 3″ to 4″, then the breadth of pitchboard more, say to the internal angle of tread and rise marked **D**; through the point marked **D**, run a gauge line 2 2 from the edge of string; then take the pitchboard and turn the hypothenuse or long side down on a flat surface, and with a well pointed knife-blade mark the extreme points of pitchboard, (see Fig. 7, Plate 20) take the space thus marked off, with a large pair of dividers carefully; and step off on the gauge line the required number of risers and treads.   Then apply the pitchboard as at *H*, with the long edge of board to the gauge line, and with a knife blade mark the rise and tread as indicated in elevation. After all the risers and treads have been marked off apply the Housing pattern and mark the housings for the rise, tread and wedge-room† with the pencil.   Now with a square mark all the internal angles of risers and treads out on the edge of string as at 3, 3, 3; then turn the face side of No. 2 string down on No. 1 and transfer the divisions.   Carry the points over to the gauge line that has already been run on No. 2 board and apply the pitchboard and housing pattern as before; both strings will now agree.

---

*The stair-builder's height of story is from top to top of floors; the carpenter's height of story is in the clear from floor to ceiling.

†The wedges are usually ⅝ at the thick end and tapered to a ¼″ at the thin end in a distance of 10″.   For all lengths the taper should be the same.

Glue on at 4 the triangular piece to form the easing at the lower end. Measure up from the floor line the height of base [7″], draw lines with pencil parallel with the floor line as shown. Then take the easing pattern, Fig. 3, and apply the shank *CD*, to the upper edge of string and tangent the level line 4 5, in elevation, and draw the full easing as shown. Do the same at the lower end, clean off the surplus wood and kerf in at each end ½″; so as to make a clean joint at the joining of the base. *The rule for height of base, including the moulding relative to the height of story* is one inch for every foot high the story is in the clear.

The easing pattern shown at Fig. 3 is drawn ¾″ to the foot. the arc *ABC* has for its radius 19″, and is made from ½″ stuff. For all full easements starting and landing, the stair-builder will find this pattern very useful.

Housing in the Wall String. Where the stair-builder has steam power, there is nothing to equal Mr. Parry's Router for gaining in the wall strings. Much time is saved over the old method, for with its use, the gauge line nor any laying out with the pitchboard is required on the wall string to be housed, all that is necessary to be done is to set the dividers to the hypothenuse of pitchboard, and mark the divisions 3, 3, 3, &c., along the edge of string, then each division serves as a guide to shift the string on the machine.

If the work is to be done by hand labor, the speediest way is to bore two or three holes in each tread and rise at the external angle *C,* in elevation. Then mortice and clean out to the required depth, and cut down to the depth of housing with a "back-saw," having a guide fastened to each side of the saw to gauge the depth of the housing; then clean out with a chisel, or a "hand-router," that is sold in most of the hardware stores for that purpose.*

Stairs of this description having a straight run of 15 or 16 risers may be put together in the shop and set up in the building; the stair-builder in that case must be careful in taking the dimensions, also see that the walls are built straight; if between stud partitions there is not so much risk; if the walls are crooked and long wide flights, the best way is to put them together in the building.

When proceeding to cut out the steps and risers, consider the thickness of lath and plaster, the base and depth of housings; as the walls in this case are stud partitions,† allow ⅜″ on each side for lath and plaster; also allow the strings to project one inch [1″] on each side beyond the plaster for the thickness of base; allow three-quarters of an inch [¾″] on each side for the housings.

Now take a strip a little longer than the width of well, set off from left to right the width of opening [3′. 0″], then measure to the left for the plastering and base, [⅜″ + ⅜″ + 2″ = 3¼″] equals 3¼″. Now 3′. 0″ minus 3¼″ equals 2′ 8¼″ to which add the two housings [¾″ + ¾″ + 2′. 8¼″ = 2′. 9¾″] equals 2′. 9¾″ for the total length of steps and risers; they should be cut half an inch longer to allow for squaring the ends.

---

*A very good method to house out the nosings and scotias, is to take a step, shoulder the nosing ¾″ from the end down to the face of rise, then stand the step in the housing that is already made in the string; then with a fine scribe awl mark around the nosing carefully, then house out and the nosing will be sure to come up close. The same method is applied when the steps, risers and scotias are all glued up.

†For brick walls ⅝″ is allowed for plaster, and for stud partitions ⅞″ is allowed for lath and plaster.

The width of steps equals the tread [9″] plus the projecting nosing* [1¼″] plus the tongue [⅜″] into the rise at the internal angle *D*, of step and rise; thus 9″+1¼″+⅜″=10⅝″ equals 10⅝″ for the total width of step. The width to get out the risers equals the height of rise [7⅝″] unless the risers be tongued into the steps, then allow the tongue [⅜″] more; the steps should be ploughed ¼″ deep to receive the scotia unless in very common work.

Now square and cut the treads and risers to the exact length 2′, 9¾″: take two trestles, set them out of wind and place the strings on edge with the nosings down, enter a step at each end, and at the center, wedge them slightly and tack a nail in each end of step, then square the flight with a rod; brace and nail the steps firm; enter the balance of steps and risers, glue, wedge, and nail them firm; the landing step leave out until set in place at the building. If it be preferred to build them up in the building, place the two strings in place, and if brick walls, mark and plug the walls every tenth course in the horizontal beds, then cut and enter the first rise, and also the two upper steps. See that the strings are square to each other then fix in place. Now cut and fix the steps and risers by wedges and glue; also nailing the steps and risers from above and also below for good stairs; also glue and nail blocks *OO* firmly in the angle; *JK* shows a scantling underneath to which rough brackets may be nailed in case the steps are long.

Fig. 4. *Shows the plan of a close stairs having 13 risers* landing on a quarter pace, with one rise off on each side, this rise off the quarter pace, should be avoided if possible in all cases as it may cause stumbling at the head of stairs. The construction is the same as explained for Fig. 1.

Fig. 5. *Shows the plan of a close stairs having 15 risers* landing on a quarter pace level with the floor above; also having a quarter pace at the starting one rise from the floor, the rise is allowed to project to receive the door.

Fig. 6. *Exhibits the plan of a box stairs having 13 risers* with one winder and two risers on each side of the triangular pace. This form of a stair case would be bad in a dwelling house where there are children, and should be avoided if possible. The plan is introduced here to show how the difficulty may be overcome in a hampered place; the treads are 8″.

Fig. 7. *Shows the plan of a double quarter pace, box stair* case, having 20 risers. The landing rise is kept away from the door; at the starting the first rise projects out to receive the door. The treads are 7¾″; in this case where the tread is narrow the nosing of the step may be increased a little over the general rule, but not over a half inch; some would prefer to divide each quarter pace into two steps and take one rise from the short branch landing, so as to give more room at the door, and also take one rise from the middle branch, and thereby increase the treads to 8¼. At the starting the first rise could project out beyond the door far enough to receive the finish, this would improve the stairs, although some will not allow winders of any kind in a house.

Fig. 8. *Shows the plan of a double quarter pace winding* box stairs containing 16 risers. Part of the first step to gain "run"

*As a rule the nosing is allowed to project past the rise equal to the thickness of steps.

is allowed to stand out in the room, the step is made long enough to receive the finish around the door. For want of space three winders are placed at each quarter pace divided off equally on the quarter circle. This kind of a stair case should not be used in a first-class dwelling house; in small houses, and where cramped for space, the stair-builder has often to resort to winders as the last remedy.

Fig. 9. *Shows plan of an open flight in a hall having a platform or "half pace."* There are 12 risers to the platform, and 6 off, 18 risers in all. This type of a stair case is classed with the "dog-leg" style. There is no cylinder used. The rail occupies the center of hall on the different flights both ascending to and returning from the platform, and a vertical plane through the center of balusters would be the center of hall.

To gain room at the starting the center of newel post is placed at the face of second rise, and the first rise and step is rounded off, and is termed a "*bull nosed step.*" The newel at the platform and risers is so constructed that the face of No. 12 rise, landing, and the face of No. 13 rise, starting off the platform, is opposite, and lines with the center of newel. Sometimes these stairs are lined up with narrow flooring, smoothed and beaded, and cut off hand-rail high and caped. Sometimes they are closed in with stud partitions and plastered, in that case they are termed close or box stairs. Then again they are often finished with return nosings and brackets on an outer string, having rail, balusters and newels. If the risers be mitered to the string and no brackets, the strings are then termed "*quaker strings.*"

Light. Windows should be so placed in all close stairs that sufficient light and air may be introduced, so those passing up and down may not stumble: also that the dust which gathers in the corners may be dusted out and kept clean; and for ventilation, that the sun and air may enter, sweeten and purify the atmosphere within. Dark corners in all cases should be avoided; "better not" build at all, than build a house with disease breeding places in it; if not convenient to have windows, then introduce a skylight in the roof if possible.

PLATE 20.

Plate 20. [Scale $\frac{3}{4}$=1 foot]. *Exhibits the plan of a quarter pace having three winders for a box stairs, and the manner of lining off the strings and winding steps; the rise is $7\frac{1}{4}''$ by $9''$ tread.*

Fig. 1. *Shows the plan of three winders in a quarter pace connecting the flyers.*

The opening in the second story is framed in the rough 3'. $1\frac{1}{2}''$, **X, X, X,** shows the line of studs. Make **X***J* equal 3'. $1\frac{1}{4}''$ for the width of opening in the second story; at *J* is shown the thickness of the wainscoting [$1''$], then from the studs to center of wainscoting equals 3'. $1''$.

Make 1 2 and 1 3 each equal 3'. $1''$; at right angles to **XX**, draw 3 *O*; then at 2 and at right angles to **XX**, draw 2 *O*, establishing the point *O*; at *O* set off the newel to equal $5''\times5''$, the center *O* will be on line with the center of wainscoting. **A, A, A, A,** shows the face of wall string, set out from studs $1\frac{1}{8}''$; for the lath and plastering [$\frac{7}{8}''$] and for the thickness of base [$1''$]. **HH** shows the string [$1\frac{1}{2}''$] on the right.

From the center *O* sweep the arc *BC* to any radius; then divide the arc into three equal divisions *BD, DE* and *EC;* from the center *O* draw the rise *OE* produced, cutting the wall string at *F*. Again from *O*, draw the rise *OD* produced, cutting the wall string at *G*. Draw the straight treads 4, 5, 6, &c., parallel with the rise *O* 3, the dotted lines show the projecting nosing. It will be noticed that if the face side of No. 1 winder be turned over it will answer for No. 3 winder, but the grain of wood will run the wrong way.

The stair-builder will find it convenient in cutting out the winders to make two patterns as shown at Figs. 2 and 3. They should be made substantial from strips and braced, that they may keep their shape make them a little large at the nosing; also allow for the tongue on the back edge; they should be longer than shown on plan so they may be made to answer for longer steps. For shorter steps an additional strip tacked on at the wide end will save an extra pattern.

For four winders in a quarter pace two other patterns made in the same way will be found to save time. String them up for future use.

Laying out the wall strings for winders.

Fig. 4. *Shows the wall string starting.*

The rise equals $7\frac{1}{2}''$, No. 1 winder measures $20\frac{1}{2}''$ at the wall string, then take the steel square with $20\frac{1}{2}''$ on the blade and $7\frac{1}{2}''$ on the tongue, and apply it to the edge *AB* of string; draw the face of rise *CD* from the tongue. Now set a bevel to the line *CD* and draw No. 1 rise and winder. Set up at *D* the height of rise [$7\frac{1}{2}''$] and draw No. 2 step, then transfer the distance from No. 2 rise to the corner [$14\frac{1}{2}''$] on plan, Fig. 1, and allow $\frac{3}{4}''$ more for the tongue shown in the corner; make the easing at *F* to suit; glue on a triangular piece at *H* to form the easing connecting the regular base; draw the curves to please the eye and suit the height of base and string in the corner.

Proceed in the same manner to lay off the wall string at Fig. 5. The bevel is shown, also the divisions are laid off to correspond with the divisions on the plan; the joint at *R* connecting the straight string is $4\frac{1}{2}''$ from the face of No. 4 rise; instead of a tongue in the corner there will be a groove, and the string cut off $1\frac{7}{8}''$ from the face edge of groove.

Make the height of easing in the corner to agree with that at Fig. 4. in this case $8''$. At *R* a portion of the straight string is drawn to give the direction of the straight wall string; now with a flexible strip, draw the curve tangent to the straight string to suit the eye; it will be noticed that the distance from the external angle of No. 3 rise to the curve is less than the regular distance [$4''$], while at No. 4 rise the distance is greater; this will often happen and must not be considered a serious fault; of course, it should be the aim to have the margin regular, but a graceful curve must be considered, for that will be the first to catch the eye.

The splice at *R* is made with a tongue and groove; this is very nicely done on the shaper and afterwards fit up and glued; when dried and smoothed off, tack or screw a piece of board 2' long on temporarily to keep the joint firm while hauling to the building; this can be made a neat and substantial joint; the newel post is ploughed to receive the wainscoting.

Fig. 6. *Shows the manner of boring and cutting in the housings.*

AB shows the gauge line run on from the face of string far enough down to allow $3\frac{1}{4}''$ to $4''$ from the external angle of step and rise to the edge of string; at *C* four or five holes are bored ⅜″ deep; and at *D* they are shown mortised out ready to apply the back saw as explained for Fig. 2, Plate 19.

Fig. 7. *Shows how to find the stretch of pitchboard for setting the compasses.*

Run a light gauge line *AB* on a flat surface, turn the hypothenuse of pitchboard down on the gauge line, and with a thin pointed knife blade held along the slope of rise and tread, mark lightly on the gauge line the points 1 and 2; then set the compasses carefully to the distance 1 2, for the stretch of pitchboard.

Fig. 8. *Shows the housing pattern.*

In a hand shop this pattern will be found very handy when laying off the housings for the tread, rise and wedge room.

Fig. 9. *Shows a templet for sawing out the wedges with the circular saw.*

Where the stair-builder is favored with steam power, very little material in a stair shop need be wasted. *A* shows the saw guide; *B* a piece of board about 2′, 0″ long, and 5 wide; the thickness is [1″] shown in elevation at *C*, having a handle *D*, and notched out at *E*, the size of wedge, the saw is shown at *F*.

In a stair shop very little stock need go to waste; all the cuttings may be collected and piled away until a slack time comes, then sawed up into wedges and triangular blocks to glue in the internal angle of step and rise; also into circular nosings, scotias and casing on wall, and front strings, and many other little things for the turning lathe. Mind economy is the secret of success in all branches of business.

PLATE 21.

Plate 21. *Exhibits the construction of patterns for a wall rail on winders for a box stairs; the plan of risers and treads corresponds to Fig. 1, Plate 20. The rail is 2½″ wide by 3½″ deep.**

Figs. 1 and 2. [Scale ¾″ = 1 foot]. *Shows the plan and elevation;* 1, 2, 3, indicate the position of risers for the three winding treads on plan; 4, 5, 6, show the risers for the straight treads. *A, A, A,* shows the line of plaster from which the center of rail is set out 3½″. The wall rail is 2½″ wide, thus allowing a space for the hand between the wall and rail of 2¼″. This is optional with the stair-builder, the space, however, should not be less than 1½″ between the wall and rail.

The rail is shown starting out of a rosette at *H* and continuing up and terminating in the architrave or finish around door at the landing. At *XXX* are shown iron "hold-fasts," or brackets. To support the rail they should screw into the studs or into pieces cut between the studs as shown at *B;* this should be attended to before the lathing is done; if brick walls, then blocks should be placed in the walls every 4′. 0″ for the hold-fasts.

Now lay off the center line of rail *DDD* on plan 3½″ from the line of plaster, make quarter turn in the corner to whatever radius desired, say 6″, then make *DE* and *DF* each equal 6″ and at right angles to *DF* and *ED*, draw *EO* and *FO*, establishing the parallelogram *EDFO;* then with *O* as a center and *OE* for a

---

*In specifying timber the horizontal measure is first mentioned, and the vertical measure last; as for a joist 2″×10″ means that the 10″ way is vertical and the 2″ is horizontal.

radius draw the curve for the center line of rail from *E* to *F*. Join *FE* for the chord. Now mark the treads on the center line of rail; from the joint at *D* to face of No. 1 rise is 12″; from No. 1 rise to No. 2 equals 18½″. From No. 2 rise to *E*, the spring of quarter turn, 7½″. Then from *F* to No. 3 rise 7½, and from No. 3 rise to No. 4 rise 18½, and from No. 4 rise to No. 5 rise 9″. For the inclination of the straight rail the common pitch is 7½″ rise by 9″ tread.

Fig. 2. *Shows the elevation and development of the treads, risers and tangents corresponding to the center line of rail on plan.*

First take the average pitch of 5 risers around the winders on the center line of rail, thus: From *D* to face of No. 1 rise on plan, equals 12″, to No. 2 rise 18½″, to No. 3 rise around the angle of tangents equals 27″, to No. 4 rise equals 18½″, and one straight tread 9″, makes a total (12″+18½″+27″+18½″+9″ =85″) equal to 85″, which being divided by the number of risers (5÷85″=17″) equals 17″ for the average tread.

Now let *XX* indicate the edge of drawing board, then with the steel square take 17″ on the blade and the height of rise (7½″) on the tongue, apply to the edge of board and draw the perpendiculars *EG*, *DN* and *FJ* from the tongue to agree with tangents *ED* and *DF*, on plan, Fig. 1. Elevate the treads and risers, keeping the face of No. 2 and 3 rise 7½″ from the spring lines as shown, corresponding to plan, Fig. 1. At the external angle of the treads and risers set off the half depth [1¾″] of rail as shown by the arcs, then draw lines *AB* and *CK* indefinite, to tangent the arcs for the center of rail.

At *Q* set up 4″ to underside of rail and 1¾″ more to *L* the center of rail. Draw *LA* parallel to the floor line, cutting *AB* at *A*. Prolong No. 2 rise to cut *AB* at *B*, also prolong No. 3 rise. Make 3 *M* equal 2 *B*, join *BM* produced, cutting *CK* at *C*, also cutting the perpendiculars *EG*, *DH* and *FJ* at 6, 7 and 8; then 6 7 and 7 8 show the increased length of tangents in elevation.

Now ease off the angles at *A*, *B* and *C* to please the eye, using a flexible strip, being careful to draw the curves tangent to the center lines at the joints. Next set off the half depth of rail [1¾″] on each side of center line for the ramp patterns. The pattern for the level quarter turn at *L* is shown at *H* on plan. At right angles to *EG* draw 6 *N*, cutting *DH* at *R*, then *N* 6 is the height the wreath-piece will rise from *E* to *F* on plan.

Make *NP* equal the chord *EF*, Fig. 1; from *R* and at right angles to 6 8, draw *RS*. Parallel with *DH* draw the half width of rail, cutting the tangent 6 7 at 10 for the increased width of face-mould on the radial lines.

Fig. 3. *Shows the face-mould.*

The tangents 6 7 and 7 8 in elevation are the same length, hence there will be but one bevel required. Select a piece of heavy paper, draw the right line 7 8 produced to *t;* make 7 8 *t* equal 7 8 *T* in elevation; then with 8 *P* in elevation as a radius, and 8 for a center, draw arc at 6, then with 8 7 as a radius and 7 for a center, draw arc intersecting at 6; also with the same radius and the points 6 and 8 as centers draw arcs intersecting at *O;* join 6 7, 6 *O* and *O* 8, and we have the parallelogram *O* 8 7 6.

Proof. If the diagonal *O* 7 equals the diagonal *OD* on plan, Fig. 1, the parallelogram is correct.

On the radial lines 6 *O* and 8 *O*, make 6 1, 6 2 and 8 1, 8 2, each equal 7 10 in elevation. On the diagonal *O* 7, make *O* 3 equal the radius *O* 3 on plan. On each side of 3 set off the half width of rail (1¾).

Now pivot the trammel in *O* and set the arms at right angles to the diagonal *O* 7, for in this case the diagonal is the direction of the minor-axis. Set from pencil to minor-pin the distance *O* 3 for the center line, leaving the major-pin loose. Then place the pencil in 8, drop the pins in the grooves, hold the trammel firm. Now fasten the major-pin and draw the center line 6, 3, 8. Next draw the convex curve. set from pencil to minor-pin the distance *O* 4. (the trammel remaining as before) place the pencil in 2 and drop the pins in the grooves, then fasten the major-pin and trace the curve 2, 4, 2, for the outside of mould. For the inside or concave side set from pencil to minor-pin the distance 5 *O*. Now place the pencil in 1 and drop the pins in the grooves, then fasten the major-pin and trace the concave side 1, 5, 1, of mould.

Make the joint at 6 perpendicular to tangent 7 6; from 1 and 2 draw the width of shank parallel to tangent 7 *t*; at *t* make joint at right angles to tangent *t* 7.

Bevel. Make *OS* on plan equal *RS* in elevation; join *SE*, then in the angle *OSE* is found the bevel for both joints; they will cross the tangents.

The application of bevels are shown at sections *a* and *b*; the dotted line shows the gauge line and the tangent line squared across the joint, gives the center through which to apply the bevel; the block pattern is applied square to the bevel, and gives the twist of rail at the joints; the shaded parts show the amount of over wood that has to come off. The sliding of the mould is shown at Plate 24.

If a round rail is required, as shown at Fig. 4, then draw the parallelogram *O* 8 7 6, and draw the center line of rail 8 3 6, with the trammel, make joints at *t* and 6 as at Fig. 3. Then set off the half width of rail [1¼″] on each side of the center line as shown. For a round rail the thickness of plank required, need be only a slight increase over the diameter of rail, just enough to dress, because the elliptic curve, passing through the center of wreath-piece, gives the correct "falling line," and as the center of a round rail is equi-distant from the circumference in all its parts. the wreath when in position, must be correct.

At sections *a* and *b*, the shaded part shows the amount of over wood that has to come off; if the bevel be applied through the center, as at Fig. 3, it will give the direction to bore for the bolt nuts.

Fig. 5. *Shows the wreath-piece landing.*
This face-mould is the most simple to draw in stair building. as the plank is not sprung; the lines can all be taken from the pitchboard, (except the trace of mould), including the bevel shown at 8.

First draw the parallelogram *OAbD* for the center of rail on plan; elevate rise No. 16 perpendicular to *cD*, and at any point. draw the pitchboard *efg* at right angles to No. 16 rise; prolong the hypothenuse *eg* indefinite. From points *c*, *A*, 3, *D*, and 4, on plan. draw lines parallel with No. 16 rise, cutting the pitch line *eH* at 5, 6, 7, 8 and *H*. Then again, draw lines indefinite from the same points perpendicular to the inclination *eH*.

Face-mould. Now parallel with the inclination draw *cab* in elevation. make *ao* and *bd* equal *AO* and *bD* on plan; join *od* and prolonged, establishing the parallelogram *oabd* on the cutting plane; the points 3 and *h* show the increased width of mould at joint; add on straight wood parallel with 3 *h* sufficient to let in and fasten to the architrave.

The line *od* is the semi-major axis, and the line *oa* is the semi-minor axis, the trammel centers in *O;* make *aj* and *ak* each equal the half width of rail; now trace the curve for the inside and outside of mould, as has been explained. From *j* and *k* draw lines parallel with the tangents *cb* for the shank, the joint at *c* is at right angles to the tangent *cb*, and is drawn to agree with joint *c*, on plan.

The section at *b* shows the bevel applied in the usual way; at joint *A* the square is shown applied from the face of plank because there is no spring in this case; the shaded part shows the required thickness and breadth of plank to contain the twist of wreath-piece. In this case the pitchboard gives the correct **Bevel.**

Fig. 6. *Shows a section of round rail ¼ full size.*

The dark shade shows the iron bolt, the light shading shows the hollow dowel through which the rail bolt is to pass freely; this hollow dowel answers a good purpose; ¾″ is a good size, they enter the rail about ½″ on each side of the joint, and are glued in on one side at the bench. Then bore through the dowel for the bolt. For round rails and center joints of moulded rails, they suit well.

Figs. 7 and 8. *Exhibits a handled scraper one-half full size.*

This is found a good tool for moulding the twist part of a hand rail; they may be made of all sizes and patterns, the drawing explains itself. Fig. 7 shows the length of scraper. Fig. 8 shows a cross section of the same; *HH* shows the handles, *B*, the steel bit; *C*, the cap held down by the set screws *SS* in cross section; *T* shows the throat; apple tree is a very good wood from which to make this tool; the cap at *C* may be made from some harder wood.

Figs. 9, 10 and 11. *Shows a dovetail pattern,* (Scale ¼ full size).

Every stairbuilder has his own way of laying off dovetails. This pattern is introduced here as a handy means to lay off the work in a hand shop where something of the kind is needed. Mr. Parry has a dovetailer he furnishes with his router that saves all the trouble of laying off the dovetails.

Fig. 9. *Shows the front of tool.*

Fig. 10, the side and **Fig. 11,** a cross section. *A* is the stem 2¼″×¾″ thick, and is including the guard *B* 18″ long. A slot ¾″×10″ is shown at *C* rebated on one side as shown at *j*, Fig. 11, the guard is 11″ long and ¾″×1½″ in cross section, having a projecting lip *D*, Fig. 10. *E, E, E, E,* shows the size of mortise on top of the step. *F, F, F,* shows the size of dovetails and are made fast to the pieces *EE*, as shown at *H*, Fig. 11. *L* is the binder. *MM* are set screws, having washers *NN* and nut in the binder to adjust the pattern for the different widths of steps. The binder keeps the dovetail pattern square on the stem.

This pattern is intended to apply on the steps before the ends of steps are cut off for the return nosings.* Some stair-builders prefer this method. It will be observed the pattern is reversable for either right or left hand stairs, and should be made of cherry or some hard wood.

---

*The ends of steps are cut off when the nosings and brackets are to be fit on in the building when putting up the rail.

Figs. 12 and 13. *Exhibits the face and end view of the "Cupper gauge,"** [Scale ¼ full size].

A is the stock, *B* is the stem adjusted by the set screw *D*, and holding a long tooth *C* made of steel, and held in place by a key *E*.

Fig. 13. *Shows an end view of the same.*

The stair-builder should have different sizes of this tool, some holding a pencil and others steel points. They are very handy in squaring the wreath part of rail. After working the concave side of wreath-piece to the plumb, the convex or outside may be easily gauged; also when moulding the wreath part of rail the gauge will be found handy in tracing the different members around the twist, especially in double rails.

PLATE 22.

Plate 22. *Exhibits the plan and elevation of a platform or half-pace stair case; and also how to construct the cylinder and strings for the same.*

Figs. 1 and 2. *Shows the plan and elevation.* [Scale, ¼″=1 foot].

†The height of story is 10′, 6″; the width of hall equals 6′, 2″; width of joist in the second story equals 10″; the door under the platform is 6′, 8″ high; the run from the face of No. 1 rise, including the platform and cylinder, is 14′, 2″; the steps are to be 1¼″ thick, and returned on the outer string. The rail is 3¾″ wide by 2½″ deep; balusters are 2″×2″; the newel post, 7″×7″; the cylinder 7″ diameter; the rail is on the right ascending, therefore is termed a *"right hand rail."* There are to be 18 risers, and the height is 10′, 6″, then 10′, 6″ reduced to inches (10′, 6″×12″=126″) equals 126″, which being divided by the number of risers, 18. (126″÷18=7″) equals 7″ for each rise, as shown on story rod *XX* in elevation, Fig. 2.

The height of door under the platform is 6′, 8″, and we should have at least 6″ over the door for the casing or finish; the platform joist is 10″ deep; the lath and plaster is ⅝″ and the floor on the platform is ⅝″ thick. Then the whole height from door (6′, 8″+6″+⅝″+⅝″+10″ =97¾″) equals 97¾″; now 14 risers at 7″ each equals 98″, making 8′, 2″ from floor to top of platform, thus allowing the space required under the platform for door and finish.

For the relative width of tread to the height of rise for dwellings if practicable, use Bloudel's constant of 24 inches, from which take twice the rise (24″—7″+7″=10″) equals 10″ for the width of each tread.

Now we have for the run of stairs including the platform an cylinder, 14′, 2″; there is always one full step less than there are risers in the run of a flight of stairs, and as we have a run of 14 risers to the platform, there will be 13 full treads and one landing.

---

*Termed this because Mr. Cupper was the first to introduce the tool in print for the stairbuilder

†When taking the height of story the stair-builder will do well to try his rod at different points, as sometimes the joist are out of level and might cause trouble; therefore, care in this particular should not be neglected; the best point to take the height is at the starting of the first rise. Also let the young man think twice before setting down one item in his dimension book, for a mistake of a few inches may cause the whole flight to be got out the second time.

Then 13 treads at 10″ each, equals 130″, or 10′, 10″ for the run, and 4″ more for the cylinder, equals 11′, 2″; then 14′, 2″ minus 11′, 2″ leaves 3′, 0″ for to frame the platform in the rough, as shown at Fig. 1: the width of platform should equal the half width of hall, more is better and less crowds the passage between the rail and wall.

The next will be the flight off the platform, there are 4 risers and three full treads, at 10″ each, equals 2′, 6″, and one landing, for which allow 6″ for the rough bearer to catch well on to the joist at the landing; also allow 3′, 0″, for the platform, and 4″ for the cylinder, (2′, 6″+6″+3′, 0″+4=6′, 4″), thus making the whole distance from the wall to the joist at the landing 6′, 4″ to allow for the flight off the platform.

The next is to determine the "headway;" that should be 7′, 0″ at least, more is better, but in cramped places the stair-builder has often to do with less. When the headway is cut short it destroys the good effect that the stairs would otherwise have if there was more headroom. A good allowance is 8′, 0″, whenever it is convenient to have it.

Now we will count down 14 risers from the landing at 7″ each, minus the joist (10″), plastering (1″), flooring (1″). ($14 \times 7″ = 98″ - 10″ + 1″ + 1″ = 86″ \div 12″ = 7′, 2″$) equals 7′, 2″ for the headroom. Now place the face of headway joist plumb over No. 15 rise, numbering down from above as shown in elevation; or the horizontal distance from the wall to the headway joist will equal 3′, 0″ for the platform, 4″ for cylinder, and 10 treads at 10″ each, and 1″ for fascia ($3′, 0″ + 4″ + 10 \times 10″ \div 12″ = 8′, 4″ + 1″ = 11′, 9″$) equals 11′, 9″, as shown on plan.

The next is to decide the width of landing in the second floor. The width of hall is 6′, 2″ in the rough, and we have to provide for a 7″ cylinder, and the center of cylinder will be the center of hall. The face string is one (1″) inch thick. The center of hall is 3′, 1″ from wall. ($3′, 1″ + 3\frac{1}{2}″ + 1″ = 3′, 5\frac{1}{2}″$). Hence the width of well equals 3′, 5½″, and the width of framing will equal 6′, 2″ minus 3′, 5½″, or 2′, 8½″ for the width of framing at the landing. The length will be 11′, 9″ minus 6′, 4″, the space for the flight off the platform; equals ($11′, 9″ - 6′, 4″ = 5′, 5″$), for the length of trimming 5′, 5″ by 2′, 8½″ in width as shown on plan, Fig. 1.

Fig. 3. (Scale 1½″ = 1 foot). *Shows how to place the risers in the cylinder so as to give the same inclination to the wreath of cylinder that the straight part of string has.*

Draw **AB** indefinite and parallel to the edge of drawing board **XX**, set the compasses to 3½″, and with **O** as a center, draw the semi-circle **ACB**, draw **OC** at right angles to **AB**, also from **A** and **B** draw the direction of the straight part of outer string perpendicular to **XX**; with **A** for a center and **AB** as a radius, draw arc at **Y**; again with the same radius and **B** as a center draw the intersection at **Y**, draw **KL** parallel to **XX** and to tangent the point **C**. From **Y** and through **A** and **B** draw lines to intersect **KL** at the points **K** and **L**; then **KL** is the stretchout of the semi-circle **ACB**. The treads are 10″, make **CM** and **CN** each

The stair-builder should make the above calculation in the building when taking the dimensions for the stairs. He will save time by calling the attention of the foreman carpenter to the startings and landings, marking where the joist must be trimmed to and floors laid for all straight stairs. This can easily be done in the building. For winders the best way is to make a plan to a scale, and all trimming laid off from the drawing. All measurements should be carefully noted in the book for dimensions.

equal to half a tread (5″+5″=10″), draw **YM** and **YN**, cutting the line of cylinder at 2 and 3. Draw the face of risers 2 **F** and 3**D** parallel with **AB**, and we have the position of risers in the cylinder.

The manner of placing risers in the cylinder is explained at Plate 15.

Fig. 4. *Shows the same plan as at Fig. 3 on the string line.*

NN shows the nosing. **C** the string. The risers are shouldered to receive the thickness (1″) of string, and a ¼″ is allowed to project and miter with the bracket, the nosings project over the rise equal to their thickness (1¼″), and are shown mitered at the ends to return over the brackets. The treads are 10″, hence the balusters will be spaced half a tread (5″) from center to center as shown at **A** and **X**. Observe the two face sides of baluster at **A** line with the face of rise, and also with the face of bracket line. The mortise for dovetail is shown in the center of baluster.

Fig. 5. *Shows how to lay off the staves for a 7″ cylinder.*

AC indicates a gauge line run on the draft board a convenient distance from the edge. Set the compasses to a radius of 3½″, and with **O** as a center draw the semi-circle **IBD**. With the same radius space off the semi-circle into three equal parts as 1 2 for one stave, draw **O** 2 prolonged for the joint of stave, and join 1 2 for the face of stave. The shaded part shows its thickness (1½″).

The angle **O** 1 2 gives the bevel for the staves, or as shown, the angle **A O** 2 gives the bevel in this case.

The shaded part at **D** shows the stave for the quarter cylinder and the bevel for the same. One drawing, that at Fig. 4 will do for Fig. 3 and Fig. 5. To make the drawing plain and not confuse the learner, it is thought best to separate them, that the lines may be more easily understood.

Fig. 7. *Shows how to lay out the front string and connect the same with the cylinder.*

The mode of finding the stretch of pitchboard and how to lay off the wall string has been explained for Fig. 1, Plate 19, and also Fig. 7, Plate 20. The wall string should be laid off first, and is done in the same manner as above.

Now take the outer string run a light gauge line **BC** from the lower edge, a distance equal to ⅜″ for the lath and plaster, and 4″ for the rough horse, and 1″ more for the rough horse or scantling to clear the back of rise and tread, (⅜″+4″+1″=5⅜″) equal to 5⅜″ from the lower edge.

It is supposed the lines on the wall string have been laid off and the internal angles of step and rise are squared over to the edge of string as shown at the points 3, 3, 3, Fig. 2, Plate 19.

Now lay the wall string down on the bench with the face side up, take the outer string and turn the face side down on the wall string with the lower edge to the upper edge of wall string; then transfer the divisions 3, 3, 3, &c., from the wall string to the front or outer string, and square the divisions over to the gauge line, **BC**, then apply the pitchboard along the gauge line as shown at **A**, Fig. 7, and mark around the external angle of step and rise with a suitable blade, keeping the hypothenuse of pitchboard close to the gauge line **BC**; in this way the front and wall strings will agree and no trouble will be experienced when stepping up the stairs; the reason for running the gauge line on from lower edge of front string is, often the board selected for the string will not hold the full width, and the triangular pieces that cut out may be glued on, and thus increase the string to the required width. Make the distance from No. 13 rise to joint of cylinder equal to the corresponding distance *AB*, (8⅛″) on plan Fig. 7. Make joint *DE* perpendicular to No. 13 tread, parallel with the joint *DE* add on ⅜″ for tongue. At *F* glue on a triangular piece to form the casing. The easment pattern *K* is shown applied; *GH* shows the joint of cylinder at the turnout. The first rise is shown reduced the thickness of a step. (1¼″) so that the height of the rise will be the same as the regular height when the step is in place.

Fig. 8. *Shows the short front string off the platform.*

This string is laid off from the wall string in the same manner as Fig. 7. Make the distance from No. 16 rise to the joint of cylinder *AD* to equal 9⅜″ as shown on plan, Fig. 4, and draw *AD* perpendicular to No. 15 tread. Parallel with the joint *AD* add on ⅜″ for the tongue. At *KE* is shown the end view of same. At *M* the string is notched ¼″, because the steps are that much thicker than the flooring, and this allows the string at that point to come close under the flooring. For the width of string at the casing allow 10″ for the joist, and for lath and plaster ⅜″ equals 10⅜. Now make *MG* equal 10⅜, and draw the line at *G* parallel with the floor line *FM*. Then use the easing pattern for the curve of easment. A saw kerf is shown at the end for joining the level fascia or string.

Fig. 9. [Scale, ¾″=1 foot]. *Exhibits the elevation of staves, to obtain their different lenghts.*

This drawing may be made on the back of cylinder board, and used for subsequent like cylinders; apply the hypothenuse of pitchboard to the edge of draft board, and along the tread draw the line *AB* indefinite. Make 1 2, 2 3. 3 4, each equal the back of stave 2 3, Fig. 10; perpendicular to *AB* draw 1 8. 2 7, 3 6, 4 5, indefinite. Make 1 8 equal *DE*. Fig. 7, plus the height of a rise [15″]; also make 4 5 equal *HD*, Fig. 8. [7″]. Draw 8 5 for the length of staves, they should be cut longer for trimming, as shown.

For ordinary work that is painted, this method of staving up a cylinder can be made a good job, but for hard wood finish with large cylinders they should be built differently; that is, the grain of wood. instead of being perpendicular to the treads, should run in the direction of the straight string for all first-class work; this requires more labor, and consequently the cost will be greater; the manner of doing this will be explained when describing a 12″ cylinder.

To prepare the staves for glueing, first see that they are out of wind on the face 1 2, Fig. 5; then dress off on one edge 2 3. to the bevel at *O*, then gauge for the width 2 1, and reduce the other edge to the required bevel. After the staves have been brought to their width, make a cylinder pattern *DBI* 1, of thin stuff, and mark the ends to the curve 1, 2, 3, then with the cylinder plane dress down to the curve.

Where the stair-builder is favored with steam, take a circular saw having a diameter not over the diameter of cylinder, to use as a wabble; then place a guide across the table, held down with two hand screws, now run the staves over the saw several times until reduced sufficiently near the curve, leaving a small margin for a guide to keep the staves parallel when glueing them up. Also if having a hand jointer, with an adjustable guide, the staves may be reduced to the required splay, thus saving much time.

Glueing. For good work the glue must be of the best grade, and carefully prepared; have the glue so that it will run smooth from the brush without any lumps or being stringy, and the hotter the better.

Rub the joint well after applying the glue, to lessen the thickness of glue in the joint; now set the "dogs," Fig. 8, Plate 23, along the joint, on the outside, tapping them lightly with the hammer, then set them away to dry; afterwards to make the joints stronger, screws or nails may be used.

If there is any sap wood on the joints, rub a little chalk over the sap part before applying the glue to prevent the sap wood from absorbing the glue too fast. For all light work the dog will be found convenient; with their use, the staves for large cylinders may all be glued up with one heating of the glue.

Dress out the cylinder to the pattern with the "cylinder plane," then see that the two joints are out of wind, using the winding strips, or over the hand jointer, if one is at hand.

Fig. 10. *Shows plan of cylinder and the strings joining.*

Fig. 11. *Shows the same in elevation.* The joints AB and CD are reduced to the thickness of strings [1″]; take the cylinder square (that is, a right angle triangle, similar to the pitch-board, Fig. 6, made from pasteboard), and square the top line BD, from the edge BA: make BF equal the heighth of a rise [7″], make FA equal DE, Fig 7 [8″]; then BA will equal [7″+8″=15″] 15″; make DC equal DH, Fig. 8 [7″]; now take a thin pliable strip, bend it into the cylinder to the points A and C, let the ends of strip extend out from the joint, tack one end, and hold the other under the thumb, then apply the pitch-board to the joint of cylinder, and regulate the ends of strip to the pitch by raising or lowering that part of strip in the cylinder; when satisfactory, trace the falling line of cylinder with a lead pencil, and trim off the surplus wood as shown at Fig. 11. The shaded part shows the cut and also the plough on the face of joint to receive the tongues on the strings; the dotted lines show the staves as glued up.

Now, after the cylinder is fit on the strings, and the lower edge moulded, glue and nail the cylinder to the lower string, square to the face, tack a brace on, to hold the cylinder firm; cover all exposed joints so as to protect them.

Dimensions for jointing the rail on the bench.

Next, take the lengths off the strings, for jointing the rail, and enter them in the order book, to be used when getting out the rail.

At Fig. 7 the first length is shown, taken from the joint GH, along the guage line to the cylinder joint at the point D [11′, 8″].

At Fig. 8 the length is shown taken from the joint of cylinder at H, along the guage line BC, to plumb with the face of No. 18 rise [2′, 11¾″].

The level lengths must be taken at the building and afterwards entered in the order book.

Figs. 12, 13, 14. *Shows plan of cylinder and elevation of strings.*

In this case the strings are 1½ thick, and halved out to suit the sides of cylinder; the cylinder is made fast by screws driven from the back of string, sufficiently slanting to draw the joint close after being glued. This method makes a good firm job, but requires more time.

☞ The other method described above can all be done on the shaping machine, where steam power is used.

Preparing the steps and risers. The steps and risers will be next in order; take a rod, say half the width of hall [3′, 1″] in length, set off from right to left 3½″ for the radius of cylinder; then measure to the right ⅓″ for bracket; then 1¼″ for the nosing [3′, 1″—3½″+¼″+1¼″=2′, 11″] equals 2′, 11″ for the length to cut the steps in the rough; for the risers they may be cut the thickness of nosing [1¼″] less, or 2′, 9¾″; no allowance has been made for squaring the risers; as the length of steps has been taken between the rough walls, and the face of wall string projects out 1⅞″ for base, lath and plastering, the steps are housed ¾″ into the wall strings, leaving then 1⅛″ for squaring the ends and for uneven walls.

Now, there are 18 risers. the rise No. 1 and No. 15 starting both flights, will be the thickness of step [1¼″] narrower than the rest; there will be two landing steps 8″ wide; the one at the platform will extend across the platform having the well hole cut out to 6½″ diameter to receive the thickness of bracket; the other will be the regular length.

Then again, Nos. 1, 2 and 15 steps will be 2″ longer than the regular length; that will leave 13 steps that will cut off to the regular length. And the two landings deducted off the whole number will leave 16 steps that will require to be the full width.

Now after the steps and risers are cut off to their proper lengths, size them to width; the width for the regular risers will be the true height of rise 7″ plus ⅜″ for tongue equals 7⅜″, see Fig. 3, Plate 23.

The width of steps will be equal to the tread [10″] plus ⅜″ for tongue, at the internal angle *B*, and plus the thickness of step 1¼″ for the projection of nosing, thus : 10″+⅜″+1¼″ = 11⅝″, equals 11⅝ for the full width of treads, see Fig. 3, Plate 23. After the steps and risers are grooved and tongued, cut the miter on the steps for the return nosings; for a handy means, use the miter jack, Fig. 7, Plate 23.

The risers should be grooved so as to allow the rise to be a little full in width, so that when keying up they may be forced up tight; nothing but dry stuff should be used in the manufacture of stair work, as unseasoned material will be sure to give trouble.

Next square the ends of the risers for a right hand rail, then shoulder back ¼″ for the thickness of bracket [¼″] plus 1″ for the thickness of string, [¼″+1″=1¼″] equals 1¼″, as shown at *A*, Fig. 4, then miter the ends of risers to receive the brackets.

For the "platform step" use the platform pattern for a 7″ cylinder, see Fig. 10, Plate 23. With this pattern mark off the miter and the circular part to be sawed out, also the notch for the string off the platform.

The stair builder will find the above pattern answers a good purpose; the "circular end steps" at the turnout and how to find their location is shown at Figs. 1 and 2, Plate 24.

Fig. 4. The dovetails may now be laid off on the ends of steps, and also on the top at the same time; the balusters are 2″ square, the center of baluster should be the center of dovetail; then take the dovetail pattern and make from the guide to center of first dovetail 1¼″ for the projection of nosing, and 1″ more to center of baluster, equals 2¼″, thence to the center of next, the distance of half a tread, 5″ in this case.

To facilitate the operation of cutting in the dovetail on the steps, string them alongside of the bench, all face out, mark and rip them in to the proper distance. Now stock them on the trestles and mortise them half through on the back, leaving the core remaining to keep the mortise clean so the glue will adhere when glueing in the balusters.

Where there is steam power the dovetails may be cut in nicely on the band saw by having a beveled block to cant the step to the splay of mortise.

Place the short baluster with the two faces on line with the face of rise, and also the face of bracket, or end of step, as shown at **A** and **X**. For the circular end steps have a single pattern, with the size of mortise on top of the step tacked on, so that the mortise can be marked on top of the step, and also on the end, at the same time.

Glueing up the step and rise. Have the glue not too thin, place the step on the bench face down, glue the rise in place, being careful to keep the miter on rise in line with the miter on step; glue and nail the triangular blocks in the internal angle of step and rise. See **B,** Fig. 3, Plate 28. Now glue and nail scotia **D** into place; use the pitch-board in the angle of step and rise to keep them square; sponge off all surplus glue from the face side of step and rise, and lay away to dry.

Sometimes, as in oak, the step may be bowed and difficult to glue up. They may be managed in this way: Have a stout bench top, and, with two hand screws, draw the rise and step down to the bench top, then block and nail the rise to place.

Nosing the steps. After the glue is dry the nosings and scotias may be worked, being careful to have them all alike. In using the "nosing plane" work down to the round, being particular of the last shaving. This is done that they may fit snug in the housings.

Panel under the first flight, Fig. 1. The triangular panel terminates in this case at the joint of cylinder, and extends up back of the string $\frac{1}{8}''$; find the starting point **A**, say plumb with the face of second rise, then count the number of full treads from **A** to joint of cylinder. There are 11 full treads at 10$''$ each, and the last tread extends into the cylinder 1$''$, leaving 9$''$ to be counted into the panel; the total $[11\times10''=9''=119''\div12''=9', 11'']$ equals 9$'$, 11$''$, from **A** to **C**, along the floor.

Now make a scale drawing $1\frac{1}{2}''$ to the foot; make **AC** equal 9$'$, 11$''$; draw a perpendicular from **C**, then place the point of pitch-board at **A**, with the tread along the line **AC**, and draw the hypothenuse cutting the perpendicular from **C** at **D**; divide the right angle triangle **ACD** into panels to suit the fancy.

Brackets. For ornamenting, the front strings are usually $\frac{3}{4}''$ thick, made to fancy; they are mitered to the rise for good work, and the nosing returns at the end; those for the cylinder may be cut having the grain of wood perpendicular to the tread, then steaming and bending them over a heated stove pipe to the required curvature; or they may be kerfed on the back and sprung into place.

Circular Nosings. Are worked from the solid including the scotia; the scotia is sometimes worked separate, and each nailed to place in its turn; they also may be turned in the lathe for small cylinders.

Return Nosings. Are cut a shade longer between the heels of miters than the length of brackets,* to allow for smooth-

---

*The brackets are usually cut $\frac{1}{2}''$ longer than the width of tread; when fillets are used the fillet for the rise is mostly 1$''$ wide, then the nosing is cut one inch longer than the width of the tread to return around the fillet. Sometimes the brackets are made continuous, and the nosings return on themselves on top of the brackets.

ing the joints; for good work the returns should be sized, then fit
and glued, and may be cleaned off at the bench.

Building up the stairs. The "well" is supposed to be
trimmed to the dimensions laid down already at Fig. 1. and the
platform framed to the required width [3′, 0″], and set to the
proper height (8′, 2″), from top to top of joist or floor.

Now elevate the two wall strings to their places temporarily,
to see if they are correct and that the platform is in the proper
place. if so, then select three long scantling for bearers, the
straightest one to come against the front string; lay them on the
trestles, place the front string on the scantling selected for the
outer string, keep the scantling ⅞″ back from the lower edge of
string for the lath and plaster; mark and cut the upper and lower
ends of scantling, and also the two others to the same length, and
cut; now nail the string to the scantling and elevate the same to
place, keeping the center of cylinder to the center of hall at the
platform, and the face of string at the lower end 3½″ from the
center of hall.

Now drop a plumb line from the face of trimming at *A* and *B*
Fig. 1,to see if the proper allowance (8″), for the cylinder, and
thickness of level fascia is correct. Also see that the top of cylinder is down from the top of platform ¼″ for the thickness of step,
that is greater than the thickness of floor; when all is correct,
fasten temporarily at the bottom and also at the platform, then see
if the string is plumb on the face and at the cylinder, if so, nail
well at the floor and at the platform. try the plumb again, if
found all right, then nail up the middle scantling to line with the
first; by tacking on a few strips to the two scantling they will
facilitate getting up and down.

Squaring the wall string from the face string. The
front string is now supposed to be set straight and plumb on its
face; select two or three steps and risers, cut them off long
enough to enter the wall string and project over the face string
¼″ to receive the brackets, place them in the wall string at
different points and wedge them slightly. then move the wall
string in or out as required to bring the steps square with
the face string to receive the brackets; when found square
and level, make a mark on the floor at No. 1 rise, also with
chalk mark for the plugs (if brick walls) at several of the
housings and along the upper edge; now remove the string and
plug the walls, then reset the string to place, keeping the face
of string 1⅞″ from the wall to allow for plastering and the thickness of base: nail through the housings so that few nails may be
seen as possible; before the wall string is nailed the landing or
platform step should be cut to length and entered in place.

Now cut and put in the steps, beginning at the top and stepping down from the platform; when the steps to the platform are
cut and in place, then proceed to set the strings for the short flight
off the platform. Elevate the face string from the cylinder, keeping the upper end at *M*, Fig. 8, even with the joist; then fasten the
string temporarily. See that the step at the landing will come
level; also see if there is the proper distance [7″] between the
strings at the point *B*, Fig. 1; if so, then glue the joint at cylinder and nail up firm at *B;* next cut in and nail the bearers to
the platform, landing joist and front string, keeping the bearer
up the ⅞″ from the lower edge, for lath and plastering, then
nail up the middle bearer and square the wall string. Cut and
put in the steps as before.

Now proceed to glue in the wedges. Have the glue for this job thicker than for ordinary work. Begin to wedge from above, wedge up the rise first, then the step that is glued to the same rise. Two persons should help at this work, one above with hammer and block, tapping the step. This helps the step and rise to come up close at the nosing and scotia.

After the steps are all wedged up, set and nail the scantling at the walls to receive the lath. Where the scantling comes against stud partitions, keep the bearer out from the partition to allow the lathing on the partition to pass behind the bearer. Then cut rough brackets, as shown at *E*, Fig. 2, having the grain of wood vertical or perpendicular to the treads. They should be equal to a tread in width (10''). Keep them $\frac{1}{2}''$ above the lower edge of bearer, as shown. This is done in case there is any shrinkage of timber the plastering will not be injured by the ends of brackets.

After this cover the steps with rough boards to protect the steps while plastering. Put up the level fascia and $\frac{1}{4}$ cylinder, allowing the same to project down $\frac{1}{2}''$ below the joist to receive the lath and plaster; then put in the triangular panel: also, cut in a block, 2', 6'' high from floor to center, to receive the wall rosette at the upper end of hand rail, and also at *K* and *F*, Fig. 2, for solid nailing when putting down the base, mouldings and easements.

Now take the lengths of rail along the level from the face of landing rise to joint of $\frac{1}{4}$ circle, as *CH* in elevation. Fig. 2, (5', $6\frac{1}{2}''$); then from $\frac{1}{4}$ circle to wall (3', 1'') on plan Fig. 1. These lengths enter in the order book when returned to the shop.

PLATE 23.

Plate 23. (Scale $\frac{3}{4}''=1$ foot). *Exhibits the steps and risers and manner of constructing the same; also, how the steps are supported underneath.*

Fig. 1. *Shows the elevation of three steps at the starting of Fig. 1, Plate 22.*

AA shows the steps tongued into the rise, and grooved on the underside to receive the tongue on the risers *C, C, C.* At *D, D, D* is shown the scotias; at *F* the bearer is shown cut off to suit the floor; *E* shows a rough bracket nailed to the bearer, and through the rise into the step, the bracket is shown cut off a little above the lower edge of bearer to prevent damage to the plaster in case of shrinkage. The grain of wood should be perpendicular to the tread.

Fig. 2. *Shows the upper end of flight landing on the platform; also; the short flight starting off the same and landing on the second floor.*

AAA shows the full step; *C, C, C* the risers; *BB* the blocks glued and nailed in the internal angle of step and rise, on the underside, to give strength and prevent squeaking; *DD*, the scotias. $\frac{1}{4}''$ by $\frac{7}{8}''$ for $1\frac{1}{8}''$ steps, and $\frac{5}{8}''$ by 1'' for $1\frac{1}{4}''$ steps: *FF* shows the bearers fit up to the joist *HH* at the platform and landing; the upper bearer is shown "bird-mouthed" on to a cleat at the lower end; *EE* shows the rough brackets nailed to the bearers. having blocks *JJ* glued and nailed in the angles of tread, rise and bracket; in this case the brackets must be made from dressed lumber.

At **K** and **L** the platform and landing steps are sized down on the joist to agree with the thickness of flooring.

Fig. 3. *Shows a step and rise to a larger scale. (1½″=1 foot).*

A shows step 1¼″ thick, and the nosing projecting 1¼″; the rise is 7″, and tread 10″.

Fig. 4. *Shows the scotia **D** fit into a groove in the step **A**, and the riser **C** to come in behind, to be glued, blocked and nailed.*

The former method, Figs. 2 and 3, will give more wear, as the groove for the latter method cuts into the projecting nosing, leaving less solid wood to be worn away, but is the method usually adopted.

Fig. 5. *Shows the step extended to the back of rise, and the rise tongued down into the step.*

This method is more convenient when stepping up winders, as the stepping up is started from below instead of above, as shown at Fig. 2. More satisfaction, and a better job, can be made by the former method.

If the groove in the step at the internal angle **A** be the least open it shows, and will catch and hold the water; then again, in nailing up through the step into the rise, on the underside, there is more danger of splitting the step along the groove: and also, wider stuff is required for the steps.

Fig. 6. Shows the manner of shouldering and mitering the rise **C** to suit the thickness of string **D**; the miter is shown at **A**. Where there is steam power the tennon machine does the shouldering and mitering both at the same time, neat and speedy.

Fig. 7. *Shows the miter templet for mitering the ends of steps for the return nosings.*

S shows the step: **B** the box, the sides so set as to take in the thickness of step easily; **A** is a stop to come up to the end of step; **MM** is the miter, and **B** shows a guage line run on the side of box as a guide for the saw. In a hand shop this templet will be found convenient; use a guard on the back saw for the required depth.

Fig. 8. Shows the "dog," made from steel ¾″ square, for bench use. They should be heavier at the center, and drawn out gradually at the points; they should taper slightly on the inside towards the point of tusks, so that when driven they will gradually bite the harder. If the taper is too great they will spring out in hard wood.

Fig. 9. [Scale ½″=1 foot]. *Shows the size of bearer required under a flight of 15 risers, straight run, so as not to deflect over .03 of an inch per lineal foot.*

The length of bearer **SB** is 15′, 0″, from the joist starting to the joist landing; the horizontal distance **KL** between the joist starting and landing is 11.′ 2″; **DD** shows two timbers 4″ by 5″ flitched with a ¾″ by 4½″ iron plate, bolted together; at **S** is shown an iron "stirrup," forming a "shoe" for the lower end of bearer; **CC** shows the trimmers, above and below; **EF** shows the face string; **HH** the lower edge of same, or line of plastering; **W** shows the weight. The formula to find the size of material required is explained at the end of letter press for Plate 28.

Fig. 10. *Shows a circular step pattern to mark off the platform step for a 7″ cylinder.*

The face of rise No. 14 and 15 is in the cylinder ⅛″, as shown; the radius is 3¼″; at **A** a hole is shown to hang the pattern up. In a shop doing a large business a set of these patterns for the different cylinders will be found very economical.

PLATE 24.

Plate 24. (Scale, 1½″=1 foot). *Exhibits the construction of face-moulds for the stair-case, Plate 22. The balusters are 2″ ×2″; rail 4″ wide × 2½″ deep. and newel 7″ × 7″; the pitch is 7″×10″.*

Fig 1 and 2. *Shows how to place the risers and find the radius of turnout at the newel post.*

Draw the base line **AB**, Fig. 2, elevate No. 1, 2 and 3 risers and treads; through the center of balusters **XX**, draw the inclination of the under side of rail. Parallel with **XX** draw the center of rail **DC** indefinite; from the top of No. 1 step set up 4½″ to the under side of rail for the difference that the newel is longer than a short baluster; for example say the short baluster is 2′, 2″ from the top of first step to the underside of rail at the center of the baluster, then the newel post will be 2′.2″ plus 4½″, or 2′, 6½″ high from top of step to the under side of rail.

Then make **EF** equal 4½″ and **FG** equal 1¼″ to the center of rail: from **G**, and parallel to **AB**, draw **GK** indefinite, cutting the inclination of the center line of rail **DC** prolonged, at **H**. From **H**, and perpendicular to **AB**, draw **HB**, to Fig. 1. Draw **BC** indefinite and parallel to **AB**, to indicate the center of rail on plan, Fig. 1; draw No. 1, 2 and 3 rise opposite those at Fig. 2: place the center of newel post on line with the face of No. 1 rise, and out any distance from the center of rail that may be desired. say in this case, as the hall is narrow, we place the side of newel to line with the back of balusters; then the center of newel at **O** will be out from the center of baluster 2½″; draw **OB**, draw the size of cap, cutting **OB** at **H**. Make **HD** equal half width of rail [2″] for the point of miter,* make **BC** equal **BD**, then **BD** and **BC** are the tangents on plan. From **C**, and perpendicular to tangent **BC**, draw **CE** indefinite; also from **D**, and at right angles to tangent **BD**, draw **DF** prolonged to intersect **CE**, (for want of room not shown). Make **CK** equal ¾″ for the face of string; make **KL** equal ¼″ for the face of bracket; also make **LM** equal 1¼″ for the projection of nosing. From the intersection (not shown), draw the curve of turnout through the point **K**, for the cylinder, shown by the solid line; also draw the bracket and nosing lines. Now draw the risers to intersect the bracket line, and the projection of the nosings to intersect the nosing line; then through the intersections draw the miters, thus locating the risers and treads and the radius for the turnout at newel post.

This drawing should be made on paper to prepare the steps and risers, also the cylinder; afterwards rolled up until the rail is wanted. then the drawing may be completed for the construction of the face-mould.

Figs. 1, 2, 3 and 4. *Show the construction of face mould for the turnout at the newel post.*

The position of newel post. location of risers in the cylinder, tangents, and location of the first rise [No. 3] outside the spring of cylinder are shown [5″] on plan Fig. 1. This, together with so much of the elevation. Fig. 2. as the base line, the elevation of treads and risers, and the inclination of the center line of rail,

---

*Some prefer to extend the curve of turnout to the point of miter as here described, instead of terminating the curve at the intersection of cap, and adding on straight wood for the miter as shown at Figs. 12 and 14, Plate 29. By carrying the curve to the point of miter, and moulding the wreath-piece to suit the cap, gives the best results.

has been explained. The drawing, it is supposed, has been made on paper and laid away until the rail is wanted. Now, to prevent a confusion of lines on plan Fig. 1, we will make another plan, Fig. 3. Draw the tangents *DB* and *BC* to correspond in length with tangents on plan Fig. 1, and also in the angle at *B; D* 2 and *D* 3 show the miter into the cap; *DF* and *CE* indicate the radial lines. [For want of room their intersection is not shown].

Now, parallel with *DB* and *BC* draw *DH* and *CH* for the parallelogram *HDBC* on plan; prolong the tangent *BC* towards *K* for the direction of straight rail; from *D*, and at right angles to *CB* prolonged, draw *DJ;* join *CD* for the chord on plan; draw the diagonal *BH;* cutting the short chord at 4, draw the curve *CD* for the center line of rail on plan. Draw the width of rail as shown.

Now, at Fig. 1, draw the radial line *EC* on plan perpendicular to *AB*, cutting the inclination of the center of rail at *N* in elevation; prolong *GH* to cut *CN* at *K*, then *KN* will equal the height that the wreath-piece has to raise, and *HN* will be the length of tangent in elevation.

Make *K* 2 equal the chord *DC*, Fig. 3; make *K* 6 equal the diagonal *BH*, on plan Fig. 3; join *N* 2: make *H* 4 equal *BJ*, Fig. 3; from 4 and perpendicular to *NH* prolonged draw 4 5. Make joint at *D* plumb over No. 3 rise and perpendicular to the inclination *DH*.

Fig. 4. *Shows the face-mould for the turnout.*

At any convenient place on the paper for face-mould, draw *BC*, with *C* as a center, and *N* 2, Fig. 2, for a radius; draw arc at *D;* then with *BD*, Fig. 3, as a radius, and *B* for a center, draw arc intersecting at *D*. Join *BD*, draw *DO* and *CO* parallel with *BC* and *BD* for the parallelogram *ODBC* on the cutting plane, or plane of plank.

Proof. The diagonal *HO* must equal the distance *N* 6, Fig. 2; if so, the angle of tangents at *B* is correct.

Prolong tangent *BC*, 6″ to *E;* make joints at *D* and *E* perpendicular to the tangents *BD* and *BE*.

Bevels. To find the bevels return to Fig. 2. Suppose the base line *AB*, Fig. 2, to be the edge of draught-board; at any convenient distance over draw a gauge-line 7 8; perpendicular to *AB* draw *PR* equal to *DJ*, Fig. 3; make *P* 9 equal 4 5; make *P* 10 equal the height *KN;* draw *R* 9 and *R* 10 prolonged to edge of board, then the angles at 9 and 10 give the bevels required. Parallel with 7 8 draw the half width of rail as 1 12, cutting the hypothenuse of bevels at 13 and 14.

Return to Fig. 4. Make *DM* and *D* 13 each equal 10 13, Fig. 2; also, make *EN* and *E* 14 each equal 9 14, Fig. 2. Make 6 *T*, Fig. 2, equal *B* 4, Fig. 3; from *T*, and parallel to *KN*, draw *TS*, Fig. 2; prolong the joint *DM*, and also the diagonal *BO*, to intersect each other (not shown on plan), and from the intersection draw *KJ* indefinite.

Make *BF* equal 6 *S*, Fig. 2, join *FD*. From 13, and parallel with *DF*, draw the proportional line 13 *H*, cutting *OB* produced at *H;* make *FL* equal *FH;* from *N* and 14 draw lines parallel to *BE* to intersect the radial line at *K* and *J*.

Now, with a pliable strip applied to the points *DFC*, draw the curve for the center of rail; also, through the points 13, *H*, *J*, trace the curve for the convex side of mould, and through the points *MLK* trace the curve for the concave side of mould.

At sections *P* and *R* the tangents are shown carried across the joint intersecting the gauge-line. The bevel found in the angle at 10, Fig. 2, is shown applied from the face of crook, through the intersection. In like manner, the bevel found in the angle at 9, Fig. 2, is applied at section R, and the block pattern shows the twist of wreathpiece. The shaded part shows the amount of wood required to saw out the crooks; and the arcs, shown laid off from the center line on face mould, gives the lines to follow when sawing out the crook square through the plank. Observe the bevels do not cross the tangents in their application in this case because the minor axis is not in the mould, or there is no point in the width of mould that is equal to the true width of rail [4"]. Hence the bevels both apply the same way; also, observe the steepest bevel is applied to the widest end of mould. For sliding this kind of a mould on the crook see Fig. 5, Plate 10. Sight holes are shown on the face-mould to aid in adjusting the mould over the tangent on the crook.

Fig. 5. *Shows plan of the center line of rail for a 7" cylinder, and 2"$\times$2" balusters.*

The radius for a 7" cylinder will equal $3\frac{1}{2}$", and the bracket equals $\frac{1}{4}$" in thickness; the face of baluster will be flush with the line of bracket, and hence the center of baluster will project $\frac{3}{4}$" beyond the line of cylinder, making the radius for the center line of rail [$3\frac{1}{2}$"$+\frac{3}{4}$"$=4\frac{1}{4}$"] equal $4\frac{1}{4}$".

Draw AB indefinite; then with O as a center, and OB [$4\frac{1}{4}$"] for a radius, draw the semi-circle BCA; enclose the semi-circle with the rectilineal parallelogram $ABDE$; draw the radius OC. and we have the two square parallelograms $OBDC$ and $OCEA$, on plan.

Prolong tangents DB and EA towards M and N for the direction of straight rail; make the face of No. 13 and 14 rise $9\frac{1}{8}$" from the spring of cylinder to correspond with Fig. 4, Plate 22, then the face of No. 14 and 15 rise will be in the cylinder $\frac{1}{8}$".

Fig. 6. *Shows the development of tangents.*

Let XX indicate the edge of drawing board; make BD, DC, CE and EA equal tangents BD, DC, CE and EA on plan, Fig. 5. Through B, D, C, E and A draw perpendiculars to XX indefinite; now elevate the risers and treads, keeping the face of No. 13 and 16 rise $9\frac{1}{8}$" from the spring lines at A and B; (No. 16 rise not shown), through the center of baluster JJ and SS, draw the inclination of the under side of rail parallel with the under side of rail, draw the center line of rail, cutting the perpendiculars B and D at G and H; and also cutting the perpendiculars A and E at U and T; join TH, cutting the perpendicular from C at K. Parallel with XX, draw GL, cutting DH at 2; parallel with XX draw KM, cutting DH prolonged at 3. Now, LK will be the height the wreath-piece is required to raise, and as LK is one-half the whole height around the semi-circle, only one face-mould will be required.

Prolong tangent KH to intersect BM at N; prolong tangent GH to intersect MK at P; from 3, and at right angles to GP, draw 3 4; from 2, and perpendicular to NK, draw 2 5; parallel with DH, draw the half width of rail, cutting GH at 6, and KH at 7. Make GO equal the chord DC on plan, Fig. 5. A squared section of rail is shown at Q.

Joint Bevels. Parallel with XX draw the dotted line 8 9; draw 9 10 perpendicular to XX and equal to the radius OC, Fig. 5. Make 9 11 equal 3 4, Fig. 6; also, make 9 12 equal 2 5, Fig. 6; draw 10 12 and 10 11 prolonged to edge of board. The bevels are shown in the angles at 11 and 12.

Fig. 7. *Shows the face-mould.*

Make GH equal GH, Fig. 6; with G as a center, and OM, Fig. 6, for a radius, draw arc at K; again, with H as a center, and HK, Fig. 6, for a radius, draw arc intersecting at K; draw HK; parallel with HG and HK draw KO and GO for the parallelogram $OGHK$ on the cutting plane, or plane of plank.

Proof. The diagonal *OH* must equal *ON*, Fig. 6; if so, the angle of tangents at *H* is correct.

Prolong tangent *HG*, 6″ to *F* for length of shank; make joints at *F* and *K* at right angles to the tangents; prolong *OG* and *OK* indefinite: make *G* 5 and *G* 6 each equal *H* 7, Fig. 6; also, make *K* 7 and *K* 8 each equal *H* 6, Fig. 6; make *GA* equal *H P*, Fig. 6; draw *OA* for the direction of minor axis; let *O* 2 equal *OC*, Fig. 1, for the semi-minor axis; make 2 3 and 2 4 each equal the half width of rail [2″]. Draw 6 10 and 5 9 parallel to *GF* for the shank of mould. Now pivot the trammel at *O* with the arms at right angles to the minor axis as shown. Then set from pencil on rod to minor pin the distance *O* 4, place the pencil at 7, drop the pins in the grooves, and fasten the major pin; then trace the concave side of mould through the points 6, 4, 7. Again, set from pencil to minor pin the distance *O* 3, then place the pencil in 8, drop the pins in the grooves, fasten the major pin, and trace the convex s'de of mould through the points 5, 3, 8.

At section *B* the bevel found in the angle at 11, Fig. 6, is shown applied through the center of plank; at section *C* the bevel found in the angle at 12, Fig. 6, is applied in the same manner.

The block pattern shows the square section of rail; the shaded part indicates the amount of over wood that has to be removed in the formation of the wreath-piece, also the thickness of plank required for the twist, [4″]. In many cases less will do; this is owing to the style of rail, as the corners may work off or remain full

If a trammel is not at hand, draw the two right angles at *O*, and use a rod as previously described, or find another point on the diagonal *OH*, and use a flexible strip. The point on the diagonal *OH* is found on the diagonal *ON* in elevation from *O* to the intersection at the perpendicular. For a correct face-mould the trammel gives the curves absolutely correct for all cylindric sections that are circular on plan.

Figs. 8 and 9. *Show how to apply the tangents to the crook and slide the mould.*

The face-mould at Fig. 8, is made from ½″ stuff, and has three holes bored through on the tangents for sight holes to aid in sliding the mould over the tangents on the crook. The heavy line *XXXX*, Fig. 8, shows the crook sawed out to a parallel width and square through the plank.

First see that the crook is out of wind on the face and near a uniform thickness; now place the face-mould in the center of crook, and transfer the tangents from the mould to the crook, as shown by the heavy dotted lines 2 3 and 3 4. Mark the joints *X* 2 *X* and *X* 4 *X*; then cut and dress off the joints square to the tangents, and also to the face of plank. Now carry the tangents across the joints square to the face; then mark the tangents on the opposite side of crook. Where there is a shank 5″ or 6″ long, as *XA*, a good plan is to joint the shank *XA* square to the face of crook, then run a gauge-line on for the tangent 2 3; then place the mould to this line and mark the tangent 3 4. Then the shank joint can be squared from the face and side of shank.

Now center the joints as shown at sections *P* and *R* with a gauge shown by the dotted lines on the face of joints, making both centers the same distance from the face of crook.

Next apply the bevels through the points *P* and *R*; then, from where the bevels cut the upper and lower faces of crook, as 5 6 and 7 8, draw another set of tangents *FH* and *HK* parallel to 2 3 and 3 4; repeat the operation on the opposite side of crook: these last lines are the lines on which the mould has to slide. Now slide the face mould so that the tangents *FH* and *HK* on the mould will exactly coincide with the tangents **FH** and **HK** on the crook. The sight holes will aid in locating the mould, as shown. Now mark around the mould for the lines to dress off the overwood; before lifting the mould transfer the minor axis 9 10 to the face of crook; then apply the mould to the opposite side in the same way. It will be observed that at **B** and **D** the mould extends beyond the crook, and the line for working off to the plumb will be lost, while on the opposite side the line will show. A good plan for the learner in this case will be to tack the mould in its place, and the arris of mould will be a guide to work off the surplus wood to the plumb.

Fig. 9. *Shows the crook turned up, and the concave side is shown worked off to the plumb lines.*

Two patterns are here shown to give a better idea how the mould is applied. One pattern is all that is required in practice. By dressing down the concave side, as shown, and using the Cupper gauge shown at Fig. 12, Plate 21, the convex side of wreath-piece may be gauged to the required width without the aid of face-mould. As the bevels are applied they show the wreath-piece intended for a right hand rail and landing on the platform; for the wreath-piece off the platform apply the bevels the reverse way of this; or it will be seen that if the wreath-piece be turned face down it will answer for the wreath-piece off the platform.

One thing the beginner must remember; that is, when working off the surplus wood to the plumb he must hold his tools near as he can to the plumb. The minor axis that is marked on both sides of the crook will be the direction to hold the tools, as 9 9.

After the crooks have been dressed to the plumb bevels on the concave side, then bolt them together at the center joint, keeping the center lines on the joints opposite each other. Then stand the twist on the floor and cast the eye down on the concave side and see if the curve is correct, having no kinks or abrupt places, when all is satisfactory. Then use the Cupper gauge and gauge from the concave side for the width of rail, then unbolt and dress off the convex side. Then bolt them together again and dress off at the center joint carefully that the two wreath-pieces may join each other without kinks. Just here a good way to prove the correctness of center joint is, first, see that the center lines made from the bevel are exactly opposite, or parallel to, each other when bolted together. Then place the wreath down on a true surface on the side, as shown at Fig. 9, and see if the shank of upper wreath-piece is parallel with the true surface; if so, the joint is correct. Again, just here, the wreath for a platform may be tested, to see if the shanks have the right direction for the pitch to and off the platform, by laying down the inclination of the pitch to the platform, and also off the platform on the drawing board, forming the acute angle, as **CGE**, Fig. 2, Plate 29. Then place the wreath on its side, same as above, with the shank to agree with one inclination; then sight the other shank to see if it agrees with the other inclination; if so, the wreath is correct.

To find the twist lines. Carry the minor axis on the plumb across the wreath-piece, as 9 9; bisect 9 9, Fig. 9; center 9 9 at 13 with the gauge used at section **P**, for the center of plank; set off half the thickness of rail on each side of 13; do the same on the convex side of wreath. Now we have three points, 11, 14, 12, through which to bend a pliable strip. Be careful when bending the strip to keep it square with the joint at the shank.

Use the try square often at the shank joint when working off the over wood, applying the stock to the joint and the blade to the straight part of shank at times.

After the surplus wood is removed from the top side of wreath-piece. then gauge for the thickness using the Cupper gauge. On small wreaths, the learner will discover at the center joint, the gauge will cut below the block pattern at 15, as shown by the dotted line, while at the opposite side the gauge will cut at the corner of block pattern. This arises partly from the direction of the joint on the concave side; in small cylinders the joint is more of a plumb joint than a perfect butt joint; on the convex side the joint will be found to be, or nearly so, a perfect butt joint; in large cylinders and narrow rails the center joist is nearly a perfect butt joint both on the inside and also on the outside of rail.

The learner must be careful to allow plenty of over wood at the center joint until he has the two pieces bolted together, then dress down to please the eye and touch, so as to avoid all abrupt places.

Fig. 10. *Shows how to place the casement pattern for marking the points to cut the straight rail.*

Draw a tread [10″] and rise [7″] and the level landing: through the center of short baluster *XX* draw the under side of rail, place the lower edge of pattern along the line *XX*, and slide up until it will measure a half rise [3½″] from the floor line to the point *A*.

Now draw the face of landing rise across the pattern, marking the center at *B* for the point from which to measure for the length off the platform. Then from *C* to joint *A* equals 13¼″, to allow for the easement on the level.

At *F* the length of a regular long baluster is shown 3½″ longer than a regular short baluster, and at *H* the baluster is shown 2½″ longer than a regular short one, and at *J* the baluster is shown 3¾ longer than a regular short one.

Fig. 11. *Exhibits a straight easement starting from a newel post.*

Elevate 2 or more risers and treads; through the center of baluster *XX*, draw the under side of rail, parallel with *XX* draw the center line of rail *AB*; from the top of first steps set up to the under side of rail the difference that the newel is longer than a short baluster, say 4½″, and the half thickness of rail [1¼″] more to the center of rail at *O*. From *O*, draw a line parallel to the first step to intersect the inclination of the center of rail at *A*; plumb with No. 1 rise. draw the center *O* of cap; from the center *O*, draw the verge of cap [3½″], cutting *OA* at *F*. Make *FC* equal the half width of rail [2″], then *C* is the point of miter: parallel with *CA*. draw the half width of rail to intersect the verge of cap at *D* and *E*.

Through *E* and *D*, and at right angles to *CA*, draw *ED* indefinite, cutting *CA* at *J*. Make *AL* equal *AJ*; from *L* draw the radial line *LH*, at right angles to *AL*, then *H* is the center to draw the curves for the easing pattern. Prolong the face of No. 2 rise to intersect the center line of rail at *K*, then *KB* shows 7½″ to joint, to be deducted when cutting the straight rail.

Fig. 12. *Shows a square section of rail.*

The dark shade indicates the rail-bolt at the center, a dowel on each side of the bolt keeps the rail from turning at the joints, and should be used in all good work, so that when the joints are dressed off they remain substantial. The hollow dowel suits best at the center joint, for then the wreath-piece can be turned around on the joints, the dowel keeping them from sliding off the center.

Cutting and jointing the rail at the bench.

The first length from spring of turnout to the spring line of cylinder at platform is 11′ 8″. See Fig. 2, Plate 22. Now we have 6″ of straight wood on shank of face-mould, Fig. 4, and 6″ on shank of face-mould, Fig. 7. Then 11′ 8″—6″+6″=10′ 8″ for the measure to cut the straight piece for the first length.

Again, the second length from spring of cylinder at the platform to the face of rise landing equals 2′ 11¾″, and we have to allow 6″ for shank at face-mould, Fig. 7, and 6½″ for straight wood on lower end of easement, Fig. 10; then 2′ 11¾″—6″+6½″=1′ 11¼″ for the length to cut the straight rail off the platform. The third length from face of landing rise to spring of quarter cylinder equals 5′ 6½″, from which deduct 13¼″ for the easement landing, Fig. 10, [5′ 6½″—1′ 1¼″=4′ 5¼″] equals 4′ 5¼″ for the length to cut No. 3. From the spring of quarter cylinder to wall equals 3′ 1″, Fig. 1, Plate 22. from which deduct 6″ for shank on quarter turn, see Fig. 5. [3′ 1″—6″=2′ 7″] equals 2′ 7″ for to cut the straight rail for No. 4 length.

Hanging Rail. This part of the work every stair-builder has a way of his own; a very good plan is to first have the mortise for the balusters cleaned out, the brackets fit and nailed on, and the nosings fitted and dressed off. Now number the nosings and lay them aside, then mark the center of baluster 1″ from the end of step, and 2″ more to the convex side of rail, [1″+2″=3″] equals 3″ from the end of step or the bracket line, to the convex or outside of rail.

Then mark a few steps 3″ from the ends, also around the cylinder on the platform and along the level, for points to plumb the rail. Next place the first length of straight rail on the nosings, keeping the convex side to the points marked on the steps; now try the plumb bob at the end of wreath-piece at the platform, and down the side of rail when correct, plumb through the center of cap for the center of newel post on the floor.

While the rail is in this position, measure from the floor to under side of cap, say that it equals 13″; then at the center of a short baluster measure from the top of step to the under side of rail, say that it measures 1½″; then 13″ minus 1½″ equals 11½″ that the newel post is longer than a short baluster at its center when in position.

For example, 2′.1½″, say the height of a short baluster when in position measures 2.1½ at its center, from the top of step to the under side of rail; now the newel from floor to under side of cap equals [2′ 1½″+11½″=3′ 1″] three feet one inch.

Now set and fix the newel to the center on floor and height just found* [3′ 1″]; then hang the rail firmly on stanchions; glue and drive up the nuts on the rail bolts, plug the holes made for the nuts, see that the rail is straight between the crooks, then plumb and bore for the balusters; now dovetail and glue in the balusters. Before glueing be careful to see that the rail is straight, without any bends. Often the straight rail is bowed, and can be straightened nicely when putting in the balusters. Next nail on the nosings. Trim down the wall string and spandril under the stairs, leaving the hand rail for the last job to dress down, so the finisher may apply a coat of "filler" immediately after the stair-builder has completed his work.

---

*The post may be cut to length in the shop and set in place, and the rail hung at once in the building, but the method described above is considered the most economical in the end.

PLATE 25.

Plate 25. [Scale, ¼″=1 foot]. *Exhibits the plan and elevation of a two-story stair case. In the first story the stair-case is divided into two flights; the first flight lands on a platform level with the floor in the back building, then branches off, and lands on the floor in the second story. And in the second story, leading to the attic, the stair-case is composed of one continuous flight.*

The height of the first story is 11′ 1″ from top to top of joist; the height of the first story back equals 9′ 4″; the width of joist in the second story is 10″; the width of hall in the rough is 8′ 2″. The height of second story, from top to top of joist, equals 10′ 0″: width of joist in third floor is 10″; steps are 1¼″ thick; nosings are to be returned over brackets; size of rail 4⅛″x2¾″, flat moulded.

Now we have 11′ 1″ for the height of the first story, which, reduced to inches, [11′ 1″×12″=133″] equals 133″. to be divided by 7″, equals 19, for the number of risers in the first story. Now the height for the first story back equals 9′ 4″, which, reduced to inches [9′ 4″×12″=112″] equals 112″; that being divided by 7″ [112″÷7″=16] equals 16, for the number of risers to the platform. That leaves three [3] risers for the short flight landing in the second story.

For the tread take Blondel's formula, but use for a constant 25″. for an easy step [25″−$\overline{7″+7″}$=11″] equals 11″ for the tread or cut on horse.

For the flight in the second story leading to attic we have 10′ 0″ for the height, which, reduced to inches, [10′ 0″×12″=120″] equals 120″; that being divided by 8 [120″÷8″=15] equals 15 risers to the attic; then for the relative width of tread to the height of rise, by the above formula and constant [25″−$\overline{8″+8″}$ =9″] we have 9″ for the width of tread by 8″ rise for the cut out of horse.

Fig. 1. *Shows the plan for the first story.*

The well hole is 12″ between the outer strings; the cylinder will then have a radius of 6″. The width of half pace from the face of cylinder to wall should equal the half width of hall [4′ 1″]. But this cannot always be, for in cramped places the room will not allow more than the length of a step, and should never be less

Now in a 12″ cylinder with the steps laid out on the center line of rail, there will be about 2″ from the face of the landing rise [No. 16] to the face of platform joist, see Fig. 1, Plate 26. Then if we allow 4′ 0″ from the wall to the face of the platform, and 2″ more to face of the landing rise, and 15 treads at 11″ each, we will have [15×11″=165″÷12″=13′ 9″+2″+4′ 0″= 17′ 11″] for the run of first flight, including the platform 17′ 11″ as shown on plan, Fig. 1.

And for the flight off the platform we have 4′ 0″ for the width of platform, and 2″ from the face of platform to face of the first rise off the platform, and two treads at 11″ each; also allow 6″ beyond the face of last rise to the face of trimming joist to allow the bearers a good bearing against the joist for nailing; this then will give us [2×11″+2″+6″+4′ 0″=6′ 6″] from the wall to the face of joist landing including the platform 6′ 6″, as shown on plan.

The next to decide is the distance out from the back wall the second flight will come, as that will determine the head room for the first flight. The cylinder landing in the third story we will keep plumb over the cylinder at the platform in the first flight; then we will have 4' 0'' for the width of landing, and 1'' more to face of rise, then 14 treads at 9'' each, and ⅜'' more from the face of No. 1 rise to the rough joist to admit the cylinder.

Therefore [14×9''=126''÷12=10' 6''+4' 0''+1''+⅜''=14' 7⅜''] we will have for the whole distance from the back wall to the trimmer at the starting of the flight in the second story 14' 7⅜''. as shown, Fig. 3.

Headway for the First Flight. The horizontal distance from wall to face of trimmer in the second story equals 14' 7⅜'', from which deduct 4' 0'' for platform, and 2'' from platform to face of No. 16 rise [14' 7⅜''—4' 0''+2''=10' 5⅜''] equals say 10' 6'', which being reduced to inches and divided by the width of a tread [11''] in the first flight [10' 6''×12''=126''÷11''=11 4''] gives eleven full treads and four inches more to count down from the platform to plumb under the face of the trimming joist in the second story, which brings us 4'' over on No. 4 step. This then leaves the height of four risers (28'') at the starting plus the width of joist [10''] in the second story, also the thickness of floor [1''], and plastering [1'']. to be deducted from the whole height [11' 1''].

Then [28''+10''+1''+1''+12=3' 4''] the height of the story 11' 1'' minus 3' 4'' equals 7' 9'' for the headway as shown Fig. 2, the joist will round off at *D*, and allow perhaps 2'' more which will be ample headway, for the first flight.

Width of Landing Pace. For the width of framing for the landing pace. take the half width of hall [4' 1''], and deduct [6''] for half the cylinder. and 1'' for thickness of front string, [4' 1''—6''+1''=3' 6''] and we have 3' 6'' for the width of landing pace in the rough. which if deducted from the whole width of hall [8' 2''—3' 6''—4' 8''] equals 4' 8'' for the width to trim the well in the rough.

Length of Landing Pace. Now we have 14' 7¾'' from the wall to face of trimmer in the second story, and 6' 6'' from the wall to the face of joist at the landing, then 14' 7¾'' minus 6' 6'' equals 8' 2'' nearly. for the length of landing pace as shown.

The next will be the head room for the flight in the second story; the height of rise is 8'', and the tread 9''; we will count down 13 risers at 8'' each. [13×8''÷12''=8' 8''] that will equal 8' 8''. Then the depth of joist in the third floor is 10''. and the plastering and flooring may be counted at 2'' more, [8' 8''—10''÷2''=7' 8''] which equals 7' 8'' from the top of No. 2 step to the ceiling. We will then place the fascia on headway trimmer plumb over the center of No. 2 step and have very good head-room for the second story flight going to the attic.

The distance from back wall to the face of trimmer at headway will be equal to 12 treads at 9'' each. one-half tread 4½'', and 4' 0'' from the wall to the face of trimmer at the landing, and 2'' more from the trimmer to face of No. 15 rise and the thickness of fascia at headway, [12×9''—4½''—4' 0''+2''=13' 6½''] equals for the whole distance 13' 6½''. from the wall to the face of trimmer. Then 13' 6½''—4' 0''=9' 6½'', for the length to frame the well: and, as the cylinder in the attic has the same radius as in the first story, the well will have the same width of opening, 4′ 8″; then the trimming of the well in the attic will be 4′ 8″ by 9′ 6½″ in the rough.

Fig. 1. At *P* is shown the manner of building the platform. The flooring will run in the same direction as the steps wherever this can be done; more satisfaction will be the result. *A, A, A,* are the bearers, 3″ by 4″ scautling. They are doubled at the outer string on the long flight. At *B, B, B,* the dotted lines show the rough brackets, the center bearer having two rows, one on each side. The center of newel post is placed in the center of hall. The arc and radius for the turnout is determined from the difference that the newel post is longer than a short baluster, and the location of newel see explained Plate 26. Fig. 4

Fig. 2. *Shows the elevation of first flight of 16 risers landing on the platform, thence, with 3 risers more, branching off and landing in the second story.*

SS shows the front string; *WW* the wall string; *J, J. J,* shows the joints of cylinder connecting the front string: *AB* shows the story rod divided off to the required number of risers [19]. At *C* is shown the pitch-board, made to suit the height of rise.

At *EF* the run of treads is spaced off on a rod. *H* shows the pitch-board made to suit the tread. The correct rise and tread should be entered in the order book, as the pitch-board is liable to shrink. At *Q* is shown the panel work underneath the first flight continued to the joint of cylinder, having an arch-way for a wash-stand or coat closet. At *K* is shown the rough bracketing underneath the steps.

Fig. 3. *Shows elevation of the flight leading to the attic, having a straight run of 15 risers.*

MN shows the story rod spaced off; *AC* shows the run spaced off into the required number of treads: at *O* and *R* is shown the pitch-board dressed off neatly to the rise and tread.

At Figs. 2 and 3 are shown the lengths on the front string to cut the rail and make the joints at the bench, so as to save any work in jointing the rail in the building. The lengths for the levels must be taken in the building after the stairs are up, and afterwards entered in the order book.

The first, or No. 1 length, from joint of turnout to joint of cylinder at the platform, is 14′ 0¼″; No. 2 length, from joint of cylinder to the face of landing rise, is 1′ 9½″; No. 3 length is shown taken from the face of landing rise to joint of cylinder starting off the second flight, and is 8′ 0⅞″; No. 4 length, 12′ 8½″, is taken from joint to joint of cylinder; No. 5 length, 8′ 4½″, is shown taken from the joint of cylinder landing to joint of quarter cylinder; No. 6 length is taken from the joint of quarter cylinder to the wall, and equals 4′ 1″. All lengths must be taken parallel with the lower edge of string.

The stair-builder should take time and figure out the different dimensions around the well, on the spot, so that the carpenter can trim and lay the floors. By so doing he will give better satisfaction and be more economical to himself. For this reason the young man should familiarize himself in figuring out these dimensions.

PLATE 26.

Plate 26. [Scale, ¾″=1 foot]. *Exhibits the construction of the cylinders and strings; also, how to find the radius and position of the risers in the turnout at newel for the stair-case. Plate 25.*

Fig. 1. *Shows plan of a platform cylinder 12″ in diameter, and how to place the risers and treads on the center line of rail equal to those in the straight run [7″×11″].*

This has been fully explained at Plates 15 and 16, and is shown here, together with Figs. 2 and 3, more to illustrate the joining of the cylinders to the straight strings.

Now, the balusters are 2″ square, and must stand flush with the face of bracket, which is ¼″ thick. Then the center of baluster will be back from the face of outer string ¾″, and the radius for the center line of rail will equal 6¾″. With 6¾″ for a radius and *O* as a center, draw the semi-circle *ABC*; through *O*, draw *CA* prolonged; at right angles to *AC*, draw *AK* and *CS* for the direction of straight string.

With *OB* as a radius and *B* for a center, draw the arc intersecting the center line of rail at 2; through 2 and *B* draw a line produced, cutting *CA* at *X* and *SC* prolonged at 3; then *C* 3 is the stretchout for half the semi-circle.

Now, from 3 space off half a tread (5½″) to face of No. 17 rise; from the face of No. 17 rise set off a regular tread (11″) to No. 18 rise; draw Nos. 15 and 16 risers opposite to Nos. 17 and 18; locate a short baluster on Nos. 15 and 18 steps, and space off the balusters around the cylinder. Then curve Nos. 16 and 17 risers to suit the balusters.

At *S* is shown the thickness of string (1¼″). *NN* shows the nosings. The faces of Nos. 15 and 18 risers are located 5⅛″ from the diameter line *AC*.

Fig. 2. *Shows the cylinder starting from the level to rake in the second story.*

The manner of finding the stretchout and placing the risers is the same as described for Fig. 1, only in this the treads are 9″. Make from 3 to face of No. 1 rise equal half a tread (4½″), and make from No. 1 to No. 2 rise equal a regular tread (9″), thus locating the face of No. 2 rise 2⅛″ from the spring or diameter of cylinder. Locate the short baluster on No. 2 step from that; space off the required number of balusters around the cylinder, and curve No. 1 rise to suit the balusters.

Fig. 3. *Shows the plan of cylinder landing on the level in the third story.*

The solid lines show the cylinder and the face of rises. The outside dotted line *ABC* shows the center line of rail ¾″ out from the cylinder line; *C* 3 shows the stretchout from *C* to *B* From the point 3 set off half a tread (4½″) to face of No. 15 rise, which is drawn on the opposite side. From face of No. 15 to No. 14 rise equals a regular tread (9″), making the face of No. 14 rise 2⅛″ from the spring of cylinder. Locate the short baluster on No. 14 tread; from that space off around the cylinder on the center line of rail the required number, then curve No. 15 rise to suit the baluster. A better way to place the risers in the cylinder for startings and level landings is shown in Figs. 1 and 5, Plate 16, where one set of face moulds is made to answer for both cylinders.

Fig. 4. *Shows how to determine the radius of the turnout from the height and position of the newel post.*

We will say the newel post is 6″ higher than a short balnster from the top of step to the under side of rail, at the center of baluster.

Elevate two or three risers as Nos. 1, 2, 3 and 4; through the center of short baluster **XX** draw the under side of rail; make **XC** half the depth of rail (1⅜″); draw **CD** parallel with **XX** for the center of rail; from the top of No. 1 step set up 6″ to the under side of rail, and 1⅜″ more for the center of rail at **E**, draw **ED** parallel with top of first step to intersect **CD** at **D**. At any convenient point, and parallel with **ED**, draw **AB** to indicate the center line of rail. Now set the center of newel **O** on line with the face of No. 1 rise, and 6¾″ out from the center line of rail; from **D** drop the perpendicular to intersect **AB** at **F**. Join **OF**; from the center **O** draw the verge of cap 7″ in diameter, and cutting **OF** at **H**. Make **H** 2 equal half the width of rail (2¼″) also set off on each side of **OF** half the width of rail to cut the cap at 3 and 4; join 3 4, intersecting **OF** at 5; then make **FJ** equal **F** 5. Then **FJ** and **F** 5 are the length of tangents on the plan.

From **J**, and perpendicular to **FJ**, draw **JR** indefinite; from 5, and at right angles to 5 **F**, draw 5 **R**, intersecting **JR** at **R**; then **R** 5 is the radius (2′ 2″) for the turnout at the center of rail, and ¾″ less, or 2′ 1¼″, is the radius for the curve of front string 6 7; draw 7 8 parallel with **AB**.

Now carry down the face of No. 1. 2. 3 and 4 risers from the elevation to plan. Nos. 1, 2, 3 and 4 show their position on plan. The face of No. 3 riser is shown on plan 4½″ out from the joint of the turnout; the radius and position of risers for the turnout are now shown as required for preparing the turnout, steps and risers for the same.

This drawing should be made on paper, then after the steps are prepared, the drawing can be rolled up until the rail is required.

Fig. 5. *Shows the semi-circle divided off into an odd number (5) of staves.*

Then the back surface of the center stave will lay solid against the face of platform. **AB** shows the edge of drawing board; **CD** is a gauge-line run on for the diameter of cylinder. From **O** draw the semi-circle to a radius of 6″; space off the semi-circle into the required number of staves, as **D** 2, 2 3; join 2 **D** prolonged to edge of board at **H** for a handy means to set the bevel from the edge of board as shown. **SS** shows the edge of face string and manner of connecting the cylinder by splicing and drawing the joint up with screws from the back.

Fig. 6. *Shows the quarter circle divided into two staves.*

The face of one stave is prolonged to cut the edge of drawing-board to set the bevel as shown.

Fig. 7. *Shows the upper and lower ends of wall string for the first flight, and is laid off as has been described at Fig. 2, Plate 19.*

AB is the gauge e, run on 10¾″ from the upper edge; one inch is allowed for e grounds, which is worked on the solid as shown at **C**; the compasses are set to the hypothenuse of pitchboard, and the required number of risers are spaced off on the gauge line as **OO**; **DD** shows the wedges; the wedge for riser being entered first and those for the step last.

At **EE** the string is gained half through to join with the base; **FF** shows the base moulding, it is rebated on the lower edge to drop down on the base ¼″ as shown at **C**.

Fig. 8. *Shows the upper and lower ends of the front or outer string.*

AB shows a gauge line run on lightly as a guide for the pitchboard as shown at *P*, Fig. 10; the points *O, O, O,* &c., along the lower edge are transferred from *O, O, O,* &c., on the wall string, Fig. 7, then squared over to intersect the gauge line *AB* at *XXX,* &c.; if the pitchboard is applied to these points carefully, the two strings cannot fail to be both of the same length.

Cylinder Joints. At Fig. 1 the face of No. 15 rise is shown $5\frac{5}{8}''$ from the joint of cylinder. Now as the end of rise is reduced to $\frac{1}{4}''$ thick for to miter with the brackets, the distance from the cut out of string to joint of cylinder will be $\frac{1}{4}''$ less, making $5\frac{5}{8}''$, as shown; the joint *CD* is $10\frac{3}{4}''$ long. Then the joint of turnout at Fig. 4 is shown from the face of No. 3 rise to joint $4\frac{1}{2}''$ in this case, the $\frac{1}{4}''$ will be added, making $4\frac{3}{4}''$ from the cut out of No. 3 rise to the spring *FE* of turnout.

No, 1 rise is shown reduced to $5\frac{3}{4}''$, allowing the thickness of a step $1\frac{1}{4}''$, that when the step is in place, the risers will all be uniform in height. The points from which to take the length, to cut the rail are shown from joint to joint of cylinders, [14' $0\frac{1}{4}''$].

Fig. 9. *Shows the outer string having three risers landing in the second story.*

The wall string is not shown, but the points *O, O,* on the lower edge of string are transferred from corresponding points on the wall string as above; the points are squared over to intersect the gauge line, from which to apply the pitchboard.

At Fig. 1 the face of No. 18 rise is shown $5\frac{5}{8}''$ from the joint of cylinder, then $\frac{1}{4}''$ more for the reduced thickness of rise will equal $6\frac{1}{8}''$ from the joint of cylinder *AB* to the cut out of the face string as shown. The joint is $11\frac{1}{4}''$ long. At *C* the string is notched $\frac{1}{4}''$ for the difference between the thickness of step ($1\frac{1}{4}''$) and the flooring ($1''$) in the second story.

For the full easement landing allow $10''$ for the width of joist, and $\frac{1}{8}''$ more for the lath and plaster equals $10\frac{1}{8}''$. Then draw *FG* parallel with *CD*, and ease off the angle *OFG* with the easement pattern. *HH* shows two balusters on the level. At No. 19 rise the landing step and rise are shown returned over the bracket. The lengths to joint the rail are shown, $1'\,9\frac{1}{2}''$ for the short string and $8'\,0\frac{1}{8}''$ for the level length, which is taken from the face of No. 19 rise to joint of cylinder starting second flight.

Fig. 10. *Shows the upper and lower end of the wall string in the second story.*

The lining off is the same as has been described for Fig. 7. The lower end is shown lined off to the pitch-board, and afterwards with the housing pattern. At the upper end the pitchboard *P* is shown applied along the gauge-line and ready to apply the housing pattern. The upper end is notched out to fit up against the joist at the landing. At *A* is shown a triangular piece glued on to form the easement. The string is shown rebated on the upper edge forming the grounds.

Fig. 11. *Shows the upper and lower ends of the outer string.*

It is lined out from the wall string in the same manner as Fig. 8. The joint *AB* is shown on plan Fig. 2 to be $2\frac{1}{8}''$ from the face of No. 2 rise. The rise is shouldered, allowing $\frac{1}{4}''$ to connect the bracket. Then from the joint to cut-out for No. 2 rise will equal $3\frac{1}{8}''$. The joint is $10\frac{3}{4}''$ long and parallel to the risers.

At the upper end the face of No. 14 rise is shown on plan Fig. 3 to be 2⅝″ from the joint of cylinder. In this case the ¼″ for rise must be taken off, leaving from the cut-out of No. 14 rise to the joint CD equal to 2⅜″, as shown. Make the joints perpendicular to the treads; the length of joint equals 13¾″. The length, 12′ 8½″, for jointing the straight rail is taken from joint to joint of cylinders, and parallel to the lower edge of string. The first level length in the attic (8′ 4⅛″) is taken from joint of cylinder landing to joint of quarter cylinder; and, again, from joint of quarter cylinder to wall (4′ 1″) for the last length.

PLATE 27.

Plate 27. [Scale ¾″=1 foot]. *Exhibits a method how to obtain the length of staves for the cylinders at Plate 26.*

Fig. 1. *Shows the development of staves for the cylinder, Fig. 1, Plate 26.*

Let *AB* indicate the edge of drawing board; draw Nos. 15, 16, 17 and 18 risers and treads 7″×11″. Make *CD* equal 6⅛″ perpendicular to *AC* draw *DF*; then with the breadth of a stave as *D* 2, Fig. 5, Plate 26, space off five staves and draw them parallel to *DF*; make *LO* [10⅝″] equal *DC*, Fig. 8, Plate 26· also make *DF* (11⅛″) equal *AB*, Fig. 9, Plate 26, join *OF* for the length of staves as shown. Observe the staves extend beyond the steps at the upper ends and also below the inclination *OF* at the lower end for over wood. *MN* and *CP* show the width of string (6″) at the internal angle of step and rise.

Fig. 2. *Shows the development of staves from the concave side of cylinder, Fig. 2, Plate 26, starting from the level to rake.*

Let *AB* indicate the edge of drawing board; from *AB* draw Nos. 1 and 2 treads and risers; also line off joist; No. 1 rise is reduced ¼″ for the difference in thickness of the steps and flooring boards. From the cut out of No. 2 rise at *C*, make *CD* equal 3⅛″ as shown at Fig. 11, Plate 26.

Draw *DF* perpendicular to No. 1 step; from *F* space off five staves equal to *D* 2, Fig. 5, Plate 26, draw the staves parallel to *DF*; from *C*, set off 6″ to lower edge of string *FG*, which is parallel to *AB*; the joist is 10″, and lath and plastering is ⅛″. Then drop down from the joist 10⅛″ to *K*; draw *KH* parallel to the joist line, cutting *GF* prolonged, at *H* for the length of staves as shown; the staves are shown to be cut longer to allow for trimming.

Fig. 3. *Shows the development and length of staves for Fig. 3, Plate 26, landing on the level in the third story.*

Let *AB* indicate the edge of drawing-board. Draw Nos. 14 and 15 treads and risers; draw *BC* for line of joist. As the steps are ¼″ thicker than the flooring, No. 15 rise is drawn a ¼″ higher. The cylinder is notched out, as shown, to receive the step. From the face of No. 14 rise set off 2⅝″ to *D*. Draw *DF* perpendicular to No. 14 tread; from *DF* space off five staves, each equal to *D* 2, Fig. 5, Plate 26. Make *DF* (13¼″) equal *DC*, Fig. 11, Plate 26. Make *CK* equal the width of joist (10″), plus the thickness of lath and plaster (⅛″), equals 10⅛″. Draw *KH* parallel to the joist line *BC*; also, draw *FH* parallel to *AB* for the length of staves as shown. Cut the staves long enough to allow for trimming.

Fig. 4. *Shows the staves for Fig. 1 jointed and glued up, forming the cylinder, ready to trim off and splice to the strings.*

At *A* and *B* the strings are shown gained in to receive the joints *C* and *D* of cylinder. The joint at *C* is 10⅝″ long, and the joint at *D* is 11⅛″ long. The twist line 6, 5, 4, 3, 2, 1, is obtained by bending a pliable strip in the cylinder from 1 to 6, governing its direction at the joints with the pitch-board by the use of a tack at points 1, 6, 4, 5 and 2; then by shifting the tacks at 5 and 2 the direction of strip at the joints is easily adjusted to the inclination of pitch-board.

The jointing and preparing of the staves for glueing is explained for Plate 22.

Fig. 5. Shows the cylinder, for the starting from the level to the rake, for the flight in the second story, and repeats Fig. 4 only in this case: A full easing is required to connect the level with the rake. The width of face string along the level is 10″ for the joist and ⅜″ for the lath and plaster; equals 10⅜″. Then the length of joint at *D* will be 10⅜″; the length of joint at *C* is shown 10¾″. At *A* and *B* are shown the splice joints on the ends of straight strings to receive the joints of cylinder shown at *D* and *C*, which are to be glued and screwed from the back of strings. The twist line is found as described at Fig. 4. Only the direction of strip at joint *D* is regulated by the square and at joint *C* the pitch-board gives the direction of the twist line to agree with the straight string. At the intermediate points 5, 4, 3, 2, the learner must use his judgment as to the direction so as to avoid any abruptness in the curve. Also the learner will discover from experience that if the direction of twist lines at the joints be a little steeper than the pitch-board it will improve the curve at the joints. The steps are 1¼″ thick and the floor in the second story is one inch thick. For this reason observe that No. 1 rise is 7¾″ high and the regular rise is 8″. This allows the level part of cylinder to come close up under the flooring.

Fig. 6. *Shows the cylinder for the rake to level landing in the third story.*

For laying out the treads and risers in the cylinder use a flexible square made from card board. The joint at *D* is 10¼″ long and the joint at *C* 13½″ long. Always lay off the treads and risers in the cylinder to agree with the plan first, then measure down from the tread line for the length of joints. The twist line is obtained in the same manner as the preceding. As the steps are a ¼″ thicker than the flooring No. 15 rise is first marked a ¼″ higher, then afterward notched out to admit the landing step; then the level fascia and that part of the cylinder not notched out will come close up under the flooring.

The lengths for jointing the straight rail to the wreath-pieces are shown taken from joint to joint of cylinders, and should be entered in the order book; those on the level are taken after the stairs have been stepped up. However, if the trimming of the well is all right, the level string connecting the easement at the landing of the first flight, also the level fascia in the third story at the quarter cylinder, may have all their joints made at the bench, glued and screwed up in sections ready to set in place in the building.

Fig. 7. *Shows plan of turnout to accompany Fig. 1, Plate 26.*

One plan will be all that is required, but to make it plainer to the learner, it is best to divide it into two or more plans; the solid lines show the face of string; **SS** shows the thickness (1½″) of string; **N** shows the nosings.

The position of risers to the radius and curve of turnout is shown at Fig. 4, Plate 26. **B** is the newel post, **O** the center from which the segment of cylinder is drawn. it is shown divided into two staves; the bevel for the staves is shown at **C**. The face of No. 3 rise is 4½″ out from the spring of cylinder; the baluster (2″×2″) at **A** is shown to line on two faces with the face of rise and bracket, then the center of rail will be ¾″ from the face of string.

Fig. 8. *Shows the elevation of Nos. 1, 2, 3 and 4 risers, and the lower end of front string.*

The newel post is shown having a tenon **A** through the floor, with two pair of folding keys made to press against a piece of timber, **B**, that is cut between the joist and mortised out to slip over the tenon **A**, so that when the keys are driven home the post will have a firm foundation. The cut out of front string is shown 4¾″ from the joint of turnout **CD**. No. 1 step shows the manner of constructing the step and riser. At No. 3 and 4 rise the brackets **HH**, and nosings **JJ**, are shown returned over the brackets on the front string. The best way to fasten the balusters in the steps is to dove-tail, glue and nail them, if the material is dry and No. 1 glue is used, the work will remain substantial; **F** and **G** shows the base of a short and long baluster in position. Observe they are cut a little short of the thickness of step, so they will not bind on the cut out of string, but will draw down close at the shoulders.

Fig. 9. *Shows the moulding on the lower edge of front string.* (Scale ½ full size.)

Fig. 10. *Shows the upper edge of wall string.*

S shows the string, G the grounds. P the plaster, **B** the base moulding, O the rebate of base, **H** the housing for step. The grounds to receive the plaster is shown worked on the solid; this string is usually 1½″ thick, and the steps are housed in ¾″ deep; on brick walls allow ⅝″ for plaster,* and on partions ⅞″ for lath and plaster.

Preparing the steps are the same as has been described in Plate 22 for a 7″ cylinder. This being a 12″ cylinder, there will be more circular end steps. Patterns may be made the same as shown for a 7″ cylinder, or they may be laid off from the drawing. If the drawing be made on thick paper the curves may be pricked through on to the stuff and afterward traced and dressed to the required shape. For the construction of the concave and convex risers, see Fig. 5 and 6, Plate 31.

---

*If adamantine or Keen's cement be used for the walls, then allow ½″ for brick and ¾″ for lath and plaster.

PLATE 28.

Plate 28. [Scale ¾=1′]. *Exhibits the manner of veneering the cylinder. The true pitch of stairs is laid off on the cylinder line instead of on the center line of rail, as at Fig. 1, Plate 26.*

Fig. 1. *Shows the semi-circle 12″ in diameter and the stretchout C 3, for the quarter circle is drawn in the same way as at Fig. 1, Plate 26.*

On the stretchout 3 *C* set off half a tread (5½″) to 4, or the face of No. 17 rise; from the face of No. 17 rise to the face of No. 18 will equal a tread or 11″, draw No. 15 and 16 rise opposite to No. 18 and 17 rise ; now locate the short baluster on No. 15 and 18 treads, then space off the intervening baluster equal and curve No. 16 and 17 rise to suit the baluster. The face of No. 15 and 18 rise is shown 7″ from the spring of cylinder.

Fig. 2. *Shows the thickness of veneer.*

The shaded part shows the staves. The string **AA** is 1½″ thick and is shown reduced at the circular part sufficiently to bend around the drum, the reduced part is extended beyond the spring line from 1″ to 2″, so as to relieve the spring at the junction of the straight with the circular part and thus avoid a possible fracture. To avoid making the recess on the back of string a better way is to make the veneer of an even thickness throughout, then after the veneer is lapped over the drum, lag out for the full thickness of string, thus avoid a tedious job in reducing the string to the required thickness.

How to Determine the Thickness of Veneer:

Barlow in his experiments on the curvature of different woods has formulated a rule for the safe elastic limit before fracture for three kinds of wood, oak, fir and larch.

Rule. Multiply the radius in feet or a decimal of a foot by the constant for the kind of wood used and the result will be the thickness in inches, or the decimal of an inch. Thus the formula reads;

For Oak=the radius in feet × 0.05=thickness in inches.
" Fir=the radius in feet × 0.035=thickness in inches.
" Larch=the radius in feet × 0.077=thickness in inches.

For Example, suppose the radius of curve to be 33″, which is equal to 2′ 9″, or the inches reduced to the decimal of a foot (9″÷12=.75) would equal 2.75′.

Now 2.75′×0.05 for oak equals .1375 of inch. This reduced to sixteenths (.1375×16=2.2000) equals 2.200. or say two-sixteenths strong.

For white pine the constant 0.0625 will be about right and would not injure the elasticity of the wood. Of course straight grained lumber should be selected for veneering in all cases. Suppose then we use the decimal 0.0625 for white pine and the radius of curvature is 6″, or the decimal of a foot equals .5. Then 0.0625×.5=0.03125 of an inch. Now the decimal 0.03125 reduced to thirty seconds (.03125×32=1.00000) equals one-thirty-second (1/32) of an inch for the thickness of pine veneer, and for every additional 6″ that the radius increases the thickness of veneer will increase one-thirty-second of an inch.

By steaming the veneer, this thickness may be increased by 2, but in steaming hard wood, the grain becomes discolored and is not to be recommended for fine work unless the wood be pine and then painted; or of walnut the discoloring does not show so much when varnished.

Fig. 3. *Shows the Veneer.*

The treads and risers should be lined off with lead pencil and not cut out until removed from the drum. After the treads and risers Nos. 14, 15, 16, 17, 18 and 19 are lined off, make from the cut out of No. 18 rise to spring of cylinder equal $7\frac{1}{4}''$; and from the cut out of No. 15 rise to spring of cylinder $6\frac{3}{4}''$; draw **AB** and **CD**, each perpendicular to the treads for the spring lines of cylinder; the points from which to take the lengths for jointing the rail at the bench are shown taken from the spring of cylinder and parallel with the lower edge of string.

The length of the platform is $1'.\ 10\frac{1}{2}''$, and the level length is $8'\ 0\frac{1}{2}''$ to the joint of cylinder; at **F** the string is notched $\frac{1}{4}''$ to fit up close to the floor at the back of landing step; at **H** the string is gained in for joining the level fascia; at **K** is shown a splice joint connecting the straight string.

Fig. 4. *Shows what is termed a drum*, made to the size of well hole in diameter, having straight sides; **AB** indicates the spring line.

Fig. 5. *Shows the string* with the veneered part bent over the form; fasten the straight part at one end firmly to the side of drum with two hand screws, keeping the spring line **AB** on the string, over the spring line **AB** on the drum, if the spring line on the string agrees with the spring line on the drum at the opposite side, then clamp the string down firmly, pressing the veneered part down close to the "form." As a precaution on small cylinders when bending the veneer over the drum, put a few staves across the veneer with a screw at each end temporarily every few inches apart, this may save a fracture of the veneer; **DD** shows staves cut out a little longer than required, when putting them on commence at one end and fit one down, put a screw at each end into the drum, thus drawing them closely to the veneer; then fit, glue and screw the next, finishing up at the other end. After the glue is dry, dress off the high places on the back of staves, then tack and glue on two courses of hard wood strips $\frac{1}{8}''$ thick and $2''$ wide, in two thicknesses. Let the lower course be $1''$ above the lower edge of string, and the other course far enough down from the upper edge not to interfere with the cut out of string.

After the glue is dry remove the string from the form, and dress off the over wood to the edge of veneer. If there are mouldings to be worked on the lower edge of string, the staves can be extended and rebated to form grounds for the mouldings.

The well-hole finished in this way makes first-class work, and in hard wood finish should always be done; for the character of finish in a house is often determined by the appearance and workmanship of the stairs, thus adding to or diminishing the value of the building.

Fig. 6. *Shows a method of curving the front string at the turnout, shown at Fig. 7, Plate 27.*

There the curve is shown built with two staves, but for hard wood that is varnished the grain in the straight part of front string should continue, if possible, to include the cylinder as shown.

The radius of the curve is $2'\ 1\frac{1}{4}''$, and the string **B** can be easily bent over the form **A** by cutting grooves as shown at 1, 2, 3, perpendicular to the treads with a cutting thrus; or having steam power, the grooves can be cut in a few minutes with the circular saw over the saw table, and all the same depth, as that is very important to avoid kinks and have the curve regular.

After the grooves are cut, bend the string over the form keeping the spring line on the string over the spring line on the form, and fasten down with hand screws; size the grooves with thin glue, let dry, then make keys of hard wood, and fit them into the grooves neatly, so that when glued and gently driven home, they will not spring the curve at one place more than at another, and when taken off the form the curve will be regular, having no kinks.

At *B*, it will be observed that one key is placed beyond the spring line to relieve the curve at that point. When the glue is dry, dress off the keys to the curve; then glue and tack on thin strips as above, extending them over on the straight part binding the whole; the treads and risers in the curved part must not be cut out until the bending is complete.

The space to allow from center to center of grooves or dadoes is $\frac{1}{32}''$ for every inch of radius, plus the width of groove, may be taken as a rule.

Example, suppose the radius of curve to be $12''$, which equals $1\frac{3}{8}$ plus the width of groove ($\frac{1}{4}''$), equals ($1\frac{9}{16}'' + \frac{1}{4} = 1\frac{0}{8}$) for each space $\frac{5}{8}''$, to space off the grooves for a cylinder $24''$ diameter.

In this case the radius equals $25\frac{1}{4}''$, which equals $\frac{3}{4}$, plus the width of groove $\frac{1}{4}''$, equals one inch ($1''$) for each space, nearly.

At *F* is shown the manner of splicing and screwing the joint from the back, the splice joint should be near the spring of cylinder at the platform. where it would not be so noticeable, for it is very difficult to make a joint of this kind in hard wood that will not show more or less.

Fig. 7. At *A* is shown a method of grooving the steps to receive the full thickness of rise, and the scotia *F,* is glued and nailed in the angle under the nosing *H*.

Another method is shown at *B*. The step is grooved to receive both the scotia and rise, and at the internal angle *K,* the step is made to extend to the back of rise, and the rise is side-tongued down into the step. At *C* the rise is allowed to extend down to the underside of step, and the step is side-tongued into the rise. The method shown at *K* allows the stepping up to begin at the bottom.

At *DD* blocks are shown glued in the internal angle to give strength and prevent squeaking.

For description of Figs. 8, 9 and 10, see at the end of letter press for Plate 29.

Steps. The cylinder, front and back strings have been lined off. The next will be to cut out the steps and risers. The steps are to be $1\frac{1}{4}''$ thick; that will take plank $1\frac{1}{4}''$ thick, and the risers are specified $\frac{7}{8}''$ thick.

Now take a rod and measure off from left to right the half width of hall ($4'\ 1''$), then to the left half the width of well-hole ($6''$); then to the right for the thickness of bracket, $\frac{1}{4}''$ and $1\frac{1}{4}''$ more for the projection of nosing. This will ($4'\ 1'' - 6'' = 3'\ 7''$) $+ 1\frac{1}{4}'' + \frac{1}{4}'' = 3'\ 8\frac{1}{2}''$) equals $3'\ 8\frac{1}{2}''$ for length of the regular steps.

Step No, 1, is $5''$ longer, No. 2 is $1\frac{1}{2}''$ longer, and No. 17 is $2\frac{1}{2}''$ longer than the regular length above. The platform step may be $8'\ 2''$ long to extend the full length of platform. In the flight to attic No. 1 step is $3\frac{1}{2}''$ longer than the regular length and the landing step may be long enough to include the diameter of cylinder and $2''$ more to bed on the joist, or $13''$ longer than a regular straight step.

The risers may be cut the thickness of step less or $3'\ 7\frac{1}{4}''$ long. These lengths are taken between the walls, the steps on that account will be long enough for fitting into the housings. However, when taking the dimensions preparatory to getting out the stairs, see that the walls are plumb, and note the "set offs" of brick work, if any, at the height of the different storys.

Width of Steps. The tread or cut out of front string is 11″, the projection of nosing is usually equal to the thickness of steps in this case 1¼″. The tongue at the back of step is ⅜″, then the width [11″+1¼″+⅜″=12⅝″] of steps equals 12⅝″ for the first story. And the steps in the second story will equal 9″ for the tread, plus 1¼ for the projection of nosing, and ⅜″ more for the tongue at the back of step, (9″+1¼″+⅜″=10⅝″) equals 10⅝″ for the width of steps in the second story.

Risers. The risers for the first story are to be dressed up neatly to 7″, and in the flight to the attic they are to be dressed 8″ wide. If the risers are to be tongued ¼″ into the step as shown at *B*, Fig. 7, then the width of rise will be increased ¼″, or 7¼ wide for the first flight and 8¼″ for the second flight. Should they be joined as at the external angle *F* and internal angle *K* tongued into the step above and below, then the width of rise would be minus the thickness of step, plus the depth of tongue above ¼″, and also the tongue below ¼″ equals (7″—1¼″ =5¾″+¼″+¼″=6¼″) for the net width of rise 6¼″, and the step would be increased in width to the back of rise as shown.

The Circular End Steps can be laid off on the ground plan. From the center with the dividers strike the curves and lay off the miters. Or lay off the plan on thick paper and prick through on to the stuff for steps and trace the curves on the steps. For a guide, cut sight holes through the paper at different points along the edge of steps so the drawing may be easily regulated on the step. The system of patterns shown and explained for Fig. 10, Plate 23, will be found the most convenient for a large stair shop.

The mitering of steps, risers and glueing the same has been explained in connection with Plate 22.

After the panel work under the first flight is prepared, steps nosed and together with the scotia cleaned off, the nosings let into the wall strings, cylinders glued on to the long front strings, and joints dressed off, the work is ready for the building.

If the work has to be handled a good deal in shipping, then cover the miters on the steps and risers; also protect the exposed joints of cylinders and strings. The cylinders that are glued to the string should be well braced before leaving the shop for the building. The height of the platform may be marked on the cylinder before leaving the shop. When the stairs are stepped up take the level length and enter them in the order book when returned to the shop. Also have blocks well fastened in the walls at the termination of rail so that the rail and rosette may be securely fastened to the wall. Also at the starting and landing of all flights, see that blocks are cut between the studs and the walls plugged that solid railing may be had for the easements.

Bracket well, underneath the stairs, always have the grain of wood perpendicular to the step. Keep the ends of brackets ½″ above the lower edge of carriage or bearer so that in case of shrinkage the ends of brackets would not break the plaster.

In the first flight to the platform two 3″×4″ scantling, *AA*, Fig. 1, Plate 25, are shown placed against the front string, and rough brackets on the opposite side from the string, the center bearer is bracketed on both sides to distribute the weight equally, and also deafen the walking line.

In the flight to the attic, there is no support from a panel, as in the first flight; therefore, double the center and also the outer bearer and bracket the same as shown for the first flight to the platform.

Scantling 3″×4″, doubled in this case, will give ample strength, but will deflect in time, and cause the plaster to crack.

A good and economical way to prevent the bearer deflecting whenever it can be done, is to put a ½″ rod through the outer bearer parallel to the risers, and anchored well into or through the wall;

give the rod all the inclination possible from the lower edge of bearer to the internal angle of step and rise on the under side. The rods may be used every four [4' 0"] feet. Also, brace well between the outer bearer and the wall horizontally.

Strength of bearers underneath the stairs to prevent the cracking of plaster.

At Fig. 9, Plate 23 is shown the outer bearer for the flight to the attic, Fig. 3, Plate 25.

For stiffness of joist to prevent the cracking of plaster, Tredgold allows a flexure of $\frac{1}{25}$ of an inch for every foot in length. Mr. R. G. Hatfield, in his valuable treatise on *Transverse Strains*, recommends $\frac{1}{33}$ of an inch, or the decimal .03" per foot in length for a full load. D. Copet Berg, in his article on safe building, in the *American Architect*, makes use of the same constant, stating the deflection should not exceed 0.03 of an inch per foot of span, or else the plastering will be apt to crack.

The stair-builder should know how to calculate the dimensions of his beams, to suit the weights likely to come upon the stairs. Mr. R. G. Hatfield, in his work on *Transverse Strains*, has given us the benefit of his experiments in the weight of crowds per superficial foot. He states the greatest load to be provided for is 70 lbs. per superficial foot for a crowd. We will now see what load likely to come on the bearers in the flight to the attic in this case.

For the dead load we have:

14 yellow pine steps $4\frac{6}{12}$ cubic ft. @ 33 lbs. per ft.=151 lbs.
15 white pine risers and front string, say 4 cubic ft.
For bearers and rough brackets, . . $\underline{13}$ " "
$ 17$

Equals 17 cubic ft. of white pine @ 28 lbs., cubic ft.=476 lbs.

Plastering.

The soffit measures 14' 6"×3' 6" =50¾" square ft.
50.75 square feet of plastering @ 9 lb. per foot =456.75
Walnut rail and balusters, say 3⅓ cubic ft. @ 33 lbs. =$\underline{110.00}$
 Total, 1193.75

This gives us 1,193¾ lbs for the dead load. Should iron be used as flitches for the bearers, or rods for trusses or hangers, their weight should be added.

For the live load we will use Mr. Hatfield's constant of 70 lbs per superficial foot. The horizontal distance between the trimmers is 10' 6", and width of stairway between the plastering and hand rail equals 3' 3", then 10' 6" by 3' 3" equals say 34 square feet at 70 lbs per foot [34×70=2,380] equals 2,380 lbs plus the dead load, [2,380 + 1,193¾=3,573¾] equals 3,574 lbs for the whole load likely to come upon the stairs uniformly distributed.

To distribute this load on the bearer underneath the stairs, two methods may be considered. First, by placing one bearer at the outer string sufficiently strong to take up one-half the whole load, allowing the wall to take up the other half. Second, or by using a center bearer which would divide the load into four equal parts, thus giving to the center bearer one-half the whole load, and the outer bearer and the wall each one-fourth the whole load. We will consider the former method in this case as the most economical.

Rule to find the size of bearers allowing .03 of an inch for every foot in length for deflection. Tredgold is quoted as good authority among engineers; he gives a formula for inclining beams, and is formulated there by Mr. F. E. Kidder, author of the *Architects' and Builders' Pocket Book.*

FORMULA No. 1.

$$\text{Safe load at the center} = \frac{\text{Breadth} \times \text{cube of the depth} \times e.}{\text{Length} \times \text{horizontal distance between supports}}$$

FORMULA No 2.

$$\text{Breadth} = \frac{\text{Load} \times \text{length} \times \text{horizontal distance between supports.}}{\text{Cube of the depth} \times e.}$$

e is a constant and equals for white pine, 82. '
e is a constant and equals for hemlock, 80.
e is a constant and equals for white oak, 95.
e is a constant and equals for wrought iron, 2,000.

The deflection from a weight uniformly distributed, is to the deflection caused by the same weight placed in the center as 5 is to 8; or in other words, ⅝ of the uniformly distributed load will deflect the same beam to the same extent if the load be placed at the center.*

Now we have a uniformly distributed load of 3,574 lbs. to be divided into 2 equal parts [3,574÷2 =1,787 lbs.] equals 1,787 lbs; allowing ⅝ of this for a center load, equals [(1,787×5)÷8=1,1169] or say 1,118 lbs. for the center load on the outer bearer.

Example. †What must be the breadth of a white pine bearer to carry a load at the center of 1.118 lbs.? The length of bearer on the rake being 14′.5, and the horizontal distance between supports being 10′.5, and the depth of bearer to equal 6″.
Breadth equals (1.118×14.5′×10.5′÷6.3″×82=9.6″, equals 9.6″ by 6″ deep, or say 10″×6″, making 60″ for the cross section of timber. Then by placing 2 bearers 5″×6″ side by side at the outer string, and by bolting and spiking them together, will give the area of cross section and be amply stiff enough to carry the load and not deflect a sufficient amount to injure the plastering. In this case, a center bearer will be required to nail up the brackets, and afford nailing for the lath; lighter material as two 3″×1″ scantling spiked together will be ample.

If brackets be nailed on both sides of the bearer, they will deafen the steps on the treading line. In this case the length of bearer is 14.5′ long, and at .03 of an inch per foot for deflection, would deflect [14.5′×.03=.435] the bearer equal to .435 of an inch; this decimal reduced to sixteenths would equal [.435×16=6.960], very near $\frac{7}{16}$ of an inch.

If the bearers be kerfed in from the upper side ⅔ their depth, and oak wedges driven in the kerfs, so as to give them a camber, this will add $\frac{1}{6}$ to their stiffness for flexure.‡ Very dry material should be used in this case to make the work substantial.

Stuff for bearers should be kept on hand perfectly seasoned, for it is impossible to make substantial work without good, dry material. Where two scantlings are thus spiked together, reduce the two inner edges to form a V shape so the plastering may have a chance to key.

In long and heavy flights iron flitches or angle irons should be bolted to the bearers, for to depend all together on wood for bearers would increase the width of front string too much, and give to the stair-case a clumsy appearance.

---

*See Nicholson's Dictionary, Vol 2, Page 530.

†Note.—The student will notice the length of bearer, 14′.6″, and also the horizontal distance, or run, 10′.6″, has been substituted for 15.0″, and 11′ 2″, shown at Fig. 9, Plate 23.

‡Nicholson dictionary, Vol. 2, Page 530.

A stirrup iron or cast iron shoe should be used at the lower end to support the bearer and its load.   Also the floor joist at the lower end of bearers should be well bridged, for where cracks show in the plastering nine cases out of ten they will appear there first.

In case the outer bearer be flitched with wrought iron at its center the scantling may be reduced in size.   The proportion for the thickness of iron to the wood being equal to one-twelfth.

Suppose we try two white pine bearers 4″ by 5″ flitched at the center, the thickness of flitch will equal one-twelfth the thickness of the two bearers (8″), which equals ⅔ of an inch, and for the depth we will allow 4½″, or half an inch less than the depth of scantling to allow for shrinkage of timber and for the plaster to key.

We will first find the safe load at the center for the wrought iron flitch by Formula No. 1.

$$\text{Safe load at the center}=\frac{5\times4^3.5\times2,000}{8\times14.5\times10.5}=748.1 \text{ pounds.}$$

which equals say 749 lbs as the safe load for the iron flitch. We will next find the safe load at the center for one of the white pine bearers 4″×5″, by Formula No. 1.

$$\text{Safe load at the center}=\frac{4\times5^3\times82}{14.5\times10.5}=269.3 \text{ pounds.}$$

which equals 269 lbs as the safe load for one bearer.

Then the two bearers (269+269=538 lbs), will equal 538 lbs, plus the safe load for the iron flitch (749 lbs), which (538+749= 1,287 lbs) equals 1,287 lbs and not deflect .03 of an inch per lineal foot.   This over-runs the whole load [1,287—1.118=169 lbs] at the center of outer bearer 169 lbs, which will make up for the iron flitch, the weight of same being 139 lbs.

The two bearers and flitch are to be bolted together, let the bolts pass through the center of the pine bearers, for the stress in the fibers of wood are less on that line, it being the neutral axis between the tensile and compressive stresses.   At the upper ends the bearers should be well spiked to the trimmer, but on account of the extra weight the outer bearer must be supported by a stirrup iron, or a cast iron shoe bolted to the trimmer at the lower end, as shown at Fig. 9, Plate 23.

The resistance of wrought iron to a tensile strain equals 60,000 lbs to the square inch, a factor of 6 is usually allowed for safety, hence 10,000 lbs per square inch is allowed as a safe working load for wrought iron.

In this case then a stirrup made from a light iron bar, say ¼″×1, will be more than enough to support the load at the lower end.   The area of cross section for one side [¼″×1″=0.25] equals 0.25 square inches, plus the area of the other side (0.25+ 0.25=0.50) equals for both sides 0.5 of a square inch.

Then 10,000 lbs by 0.5 equals 5,000 lbs as the safe load for the stirrup iron.   In using the light iron the ends that lap over the trimmer had better be upset, thus increasing their stiffness.   In addition to the stirrup iron the bearer can be well spiked to the trimmer, thus insuring good and substantial work.

PLATE 29.

Plate 29. [Scale, ¾″=1 foot]. *Exhibits a simple method how to construct the face-mould for the stair-case, Plate 25.*

Fig. 1. *Shows the plan of the center line of rail for the cylinder, Fig. 1, Plate 26.*

The rise is 7″×11″ tread, with 6″ for a radius, and O as a center, draw the semi-circle as shown by the dotted line for the face of cylinder; the balusters are 2″×2″, and the bracket is ¼″ thick; the face of baluster is flush with the face of bracket, that will locate the center of baluster back from the face of front string ¾″; the radius for the center line of rail will then equal 6¾″. Now with 6¾″ for a radius, and O as a center, draw the semi-circle ACE; through O draw the diameter AE. Draw the rectilineal parallelogram $ABDE$ to tangent the curve at the points A, C and E. Prolong tangents BA and DE indefinite towards 3 for direction of straight rail; draw OC parallel with AB for the two square parallelograms $ABCO$ and $EDCO$ on plan. The face of No. 15 and 18 rise is 5⅜″ from the spring of cylinder as shown.

Fig. 2. *Shows the length of tangents in elevation; the tangents as developed from plan, are folded.*

Let XX indicate the edge of drawing board; make AB equal AB on plan, Fig. 1; draw AC and BD perpendicular to XX; elevate Nos. 15, 16, 17 and 18 rise and tread, keeping the face of No. 15 and 18 rise 5⅜″ from the spring line AC as shown.

From the external angle of No. 15 and 18 rise, draw the true inclination of rail, cutting the perpendiculars from A and B at E and F, and also at C and P; prolong the inclination to intersect at G. Draw GH parallel to XX, cutting BD at K; draw EL indefinite and parallel to XX, cutting BD at M; then MK is the *height* for the lower wreath-piece, and HC is the *height* for the upper wreath piece. As the pitch to and from the platform is the same, the two heights will be equal; draw FJ and PQ parallel to XX; draw KJ prolonged; then EF and KJ show the increased length of tangents AB and BC on the cutting plane.

Make EL equal the chord AC on plan, Fig. 1; parallel with BD draw the half width of rail [2¼″], cutting FE and KJ at 4 and 3; from K, and at right angles to EG, draw K 5; also from E, and at right angles to KJ prolonged, draw E 6; make JN equal JH.

Bevels. The dotted line R 9 indicates a gauge line drawn parallel to XX; draw 9 T perpendicular to XX, and equal to the radius OC, Fig. 1; make 9 7 equal K 5; also make 9 8 equal E 6; draw T 7 and T 8 prolonged to edge of board; the bevels are found in the angles at 7 and 8.

Fig. 3. *Shows how to construct the face-mould.*

Draw BP indefinite; make BA equal EF in elevation, Fig. 2; with A as a center, and the distance LH, Fig. 2, for a radius, draw arc at C; again, with B as a center, and KJ, Fig. 2, for a radius; draw arc intersecting at C; join BC; parallel with BC and BA, draw AO and CO for the parallelogram $OABC$ on the cutting plane.

Proof. The diagonal OB must equal the distance LN, Fig. 2, if so, the angle of tangents at B must be correct. Make AJ

equal *FG*, Fig. 2; draw *JO* for the direction of minor axis; make *O* 2 equal *OC*, Fig. 1 for the length of semi-minor axis; make 2 3 and 2 4 each equal the half width of rail [2¼″]. Let *A* 5 and *A* 6 each equal *K* 3, Fig. 2; also make *C* 7 and *C* 8 each equal *F* 4, Fig. 2; prolong shank 6″ from *A* to *P*. Make joints at *P* and *C* at right angles to *BP* and *BC*; draw 6 9 and 5 10 parallel to *AP* for the shank. Now pivot the trammel in *O*, with the arms *XX* at right angles to *O* 2; then with the rod, set from pencil to minor pin the distance *O* 3; place the pencil in the point at 7, and drop the pins in the grooves, then fasten the major pin, and trace the curve 5, 3, 7, for the concave side of mould. Again, set from pencil to minor pin, to equal the distance *O* 4, then place the pencil in the point 8, and drop the pins in the grooves and fasten the major pin, then trace the curve for the convex side of mould through the points 8, 4, 6; the curve for the center line is drawn in the same way.

At sections *D* and *N* the tangent lines are shown carried across the joints intersecting the dotted gauge line. At *D* the bevel found in the angle at 7, Fig. 2, is applied through the intersection. At *N* the bevel found in the angle at 8, Fig. 2, is applied through the center of plank. It will be observed the bevel as applied at section *D* will pitch the joint at *C* up. while the bevel as applied at section *N*, will pitch the shank at *P*, down, thus showing the wreath-piece is intended to land on the platform for a right hand rail; for the wreath-piece off the platform turn the stock of bevel reverse to what is shown.

The shaded parts at section *D* and *N* show the thickness and width of plank required to saw out the crook and the amount of over wood to be removed in the formation of wreath-piece.

Fig. 4. *Shows the plan of the center line of rail for the cylinder starting from the level to rake, Fig. 2, Plate 26.*

The dotted line indicates the face of cylinder, the radius is 6″, the solid line shows the center of baluster or the center line of rail, the radius of which is 6¾″. Then with *O* as a center and *OA* (6¾) for a radius, draw the semi-circle *ACE*. Through *O* draw the diameter *AE*; draw the rectilineal parallelogram *EDBA* to tangent the curve at *EC* and *A*; draw *OC* at right angles to *AE* for the parallelograms *OCDE* and *OCBA* on plan; prolong tangents *DE* and *BA* to the right for the direction of straight rail. The face of No. 2 rise is shown located 3″ from the spring of cylinder, the rise is 8″ and tread 9″.

Fig. 5. *Shows the elevation and development of tangents from Plan, Fig. 4.*

In this case let it be observed the tangents are spread out or unfolded from the plan. In the former case, Fig. 2, they are shown folded, only two perpendiculars being drawn. This is done to give the learner a clear idea how to get the correct height * of each wreath-piece.

Let *XX* represent the edge of draft board, make *ED*, *DC*, *CB* and *BA* equal the tangents on plan, Fig. 4; perpendicular to *XX* draw *AF*, *BG*, *CH*, *DJ* and *EK* indefinite. Now elevate the risers and treads, keeping the face of No. 2 rise 3″ from the spring line *EK*, as shown. Through the center of baluster *OO*, draw the inclination of the underside of rail, parallel with the underside of rail draw the center of rail prolonged, cutting the

---

*The student must be careful to obtain the exact height in the elevation to have the wreath rail the proper height, as the drawing may be correct in every other particular, and a mistake in the height will spoil the wreath.

spring line at K and also DJ at P.   From A to F set up
the height of half a rise (4″) and the half depth of rail 1⅜″ additional, (4″+1⅜″=5⅜) equals 5⅜″ for the center line of level
rail.   Parallel with XX draw FR prolonged, cutting the perpendicular from B at G; draw GP prolonged, cutting the perpendicular from C at H and also the spring line EK at S.   From H
and parallel to XX, draw HT, cutting the perpendicular from D
at U, then HR is the height for the level wreath-piece and TK
is the height for the raking wreath-piece.   Prolong KP to intersect HT at N.   From K and parallel to XX draw kJ prolonged,
Make KW equal the chord EC, Fig. 4.   From U and at right
angles to NK draw U, 2.   From J and at right angles to HP prolonged, draw J 3.   Make RY equal the chord CA, Fig. 4.   Parallel to DJ draw the half width of rail, cutting the inclination of
tangents KP at 4, and also the tangent HP at 5.

Bevels.   Draw the dotted line 6 7 parallel to XX; perpendicular to XX, draw 6 9 equal to the radius OC, Fig. 4; make 6
8 equal U 2; make 6 7 equal J 3; draw 9 8 and 9 7 prolonged to
edge of board for the bevels required for the inclining wreath-
piece; also the angle GHR gives the bevel for the level wreath-
piece at the shank.

Fig. 6.   *Shows the face-mould for the level wreath-piece.*

Draw BP indefinite; make BA equal BA on plan; draw
BC at right angles to BP, and equal to GH, Fig. 5; draw
CO and AO parallel to BA and BC for the rectilineal parallelogram $ABCO$.

Proof.   If the diagonals AC and BO equal the distance Hy,
Fig. 5, the parallologram is correct, and OC is the semi-minor
axis, and OA is the semi-major axis of the elliptic curve for the
center of mould.   Make AP equal 6″ for length of shank; make
joint at P square to BP; make C 2 and C 3, each equal the half
width of rail [2¼″]; make A 4 and A 5, each equal P 5, Fig. 5;
draw 4 6 and 5 7 parallel to AP for width of shank.   Now
pivot the trammel at O, and set from pencil to minor pin the distance O 2, and from pencil to major pin set to the distance O 4,
and trace the curve from 2 to 4, for the concave side of mould.
Again, set from pencil to minor pin the distance O 3, and from
pencil to major pin to equal the distance O 5, then trace the curve
from 3 to 5, for the convex side of mould; proceed in like manner
to trace the center line if required.

In tracing the curves for this mould, the string will answer to
draw the elliptic curve, see Fig. 8, Plate 5.   As the difference between
the two axis is so little, the curves may be drawn from different centers on the major axis with the compasses near enough for practice.
The minor axis OC gives the joint at C, and is at right angles to tangent BC.

At section D the tangent is shown carried across the joint square
to the face of crook, and intersecting the dotted line; the bevel
found in the angle at H, Fig. 5, is shown applied from the face of
crook, through the center of plank to pitch the joint at C up.   At
section N the tangent is squared across the joint, intersecting the
dotted line; the block pattern is centered at the intersection, and
applied square to the face of plank, thus allowing the shank AP
to have a horizontal position; the shaded part shows the amount
of over wood to be removed at the shank.

Fig. 7.   *Shows the face-mould for the wreath-piece that is
inclining.*

Draw DP indefinite and at any convenient place on the
paper that will suit best for saving the material.   Make DE equal

KP, Fig. 5. With *E* for a center and the distance *WT*, Fig. 5, for a radius, draw arc at *C*. Again with *D* for a center and *HP*, Fig. 5, as a radius, draw arc intersecting at *C*, connect *DC*. Parallel to *DC* and *DE*, draw *EO* and *CO* for the parallelogram *OCDE* on the cutting plane.

Proof. The diagonal *OD* must equal the distance *SW*, Fig. 5. If so the angle of tangents at *D* must be correct.

Make *EJ* equal *PN*, Fig. 5, draw *OJ* for the direction of minor axis. Make *O* 2 equal the radius *OC*, Fig 4 (6¾″). Let 2 3 and 2 4 each equal the half width of rail (2¼). Make *E* 6 and *E* 5 each equal *P* 5, Fig. 5. Also make *C* 7 and *C* 8 each equal *P* 4, Fig. 5. Now pivot the trammel in *O* with the arms at right angles to *O* 2 and proceed to trace the curves for the concave and convex sides of mould as described for Fig. 3.

From *E* add 6″ for straight wood to *P* for shank. Make joints at *P* and *C* at right angles to the tangents *DE* and *DC*, draw 6 9 and 5 10 parallel to *EP* for the width of shank.

The sections at *N* and *D* show the application of bevels. The bevel at *N* is found in the angle at 7, Fig. 5. and the bevel at *D* is found in the angle at 8, Fig. 5; as applied, they show the correct position of wreath-piece.

Fig. 8. *Shows the plan of the center line of rail for the "rake to level twist" landing in the third story, shown at Fig. 3, Plate 26.*

The dotted line indicates the face of cylinder, the radius being 6″. The solid line shows the center of rail, and is struck with a radius of 6¾″ from the center *O*.

Through the center *O*, draw *AE* indefinite, enclose the semicircle *ACE* with the rectilineal parallelogram *ABDE*; draw *OC* at right angles to *AE*, and we have the two square parallelograms *OABC* and *OCDE* on plan; now *AB* and *BC* are the tangents for the inclining wreath-piece, and *ED*, *DC* are the tangents for the wreath-piece on the level; prolong *BA* and *DE* to the left for the direction of straight rail.

*The face of first rise outside the cylinder is No. 14, being 3″ from the spring line; the face of No. 15 rise will then extend into the cylinder 6″.

Fig. 9. *Shows the elevation of tangents; in this case they are folded similar to those at Fig. 2, the shaded part shows the twist of rail.*

Let *XX* indicate the edge of drawing board. Make *AB* equal *AB*, Fig. 8, [6¾″]; draw *AC* and *BD* perpendicular to *XX*, and of indefinite length; now elevate Nos. 13, 14 and 15 treads and risers, keeping the face of No. 14 rise 3″ from the spring line *AC* as shown. Through the center of baluster *OO*, draw the inclination of the under side of rail; parallel with the under side of rail draw the center of rail, cutting the perpendiculars *AC* and *BD* at *E* and *h;* the top of No. 15 rise gives the floor line; from the floor line set up 4″ to the under side of rail, and the half depth of rail [1¾″] more, making 5¾″ to the center of rail at *J;* draw *JK* parallel to *XX*. From *h* and *E*, draw *hL* and *EM* prolonged: bisect *LJ* at *n;* draw *nP* parallel to *XX*, draw *pL* prolonged; join *Kn;* then *Mp* is the *height* for the inclining wreath-piece, and *nJ* is the *height* for the wreath-piece on the level; prolong *Eh* to intersect *np* prolonged at *R*. From

---

*To correspond with that at Plate 26, this should read 2½″ instead of 3″. Also the same at Fig. 4.

E, and at right angles to *pL*, draw *E* 6; from *p*, and at right angles to *ER*, draw *p* 7; make *Ly* equal *Ln;* make *EQ* equal the chord *A C*, Fig. 8.

Parallel with *BD* draw the half width of rail, cutting *Eh* at 3 and *LP* at 4, and also *nK* at 5. The bevel shown at *O* indicates the point of pitch-board at the center of baluster, giving the inclination of the underside of rail.

Bevels. The dotted line 8 9 indicates a gauge line parallel with *XX*. Perpendicular to *XX* draw *ST* and equal to the radius *OC* (6¾″) Fig. 8. Make *S* 10, equal *P* 7. Fig. 9. Make *S* 12, equal *E* 6. Fig. 9. Make *S* 8, equal *nJ*, Fig. 9. Draw *T* 12, *T* 10, and *T* 8, prolonged to edge of board for the bevels as shown.

Fig. 10. *Shows the face-mould for the wreath-piece landing.*

Draw *BP* indefinite; make *BA* equal *Eh* in elevation Fig. 9. With *A* for a center and *Qn*, Fig 9. as a radius, draw arc at *C*. Again with *B* for a center and *LP*, Fig. 9, as a radius, draw arc intersecting at *C*, connect *BC*. Parallel with tangent *BC* and *BA* draw the radial lines *AO* and *CO*, forming the parallelogram *OABC* on the cutting plane.

Proof. The diagonal *BO* must equal the distance *QY*, Fig. 9. If so, the angle of tangents at *B* is correct.

Make *AJ* equal *hR*, Fig. 9, draw *OJ* for the direction of minor axis, make *O* 2 equal *OC*, Fig. 8, make 2 3 and 2 4 each equal the half width of rail (2¼″). Make *A* 5 and *A* 6 each equal *P* 4, Fig 9. Let *C* 7 and *C* 8 each equal *h* 3, Fig. 9.

Now pivot the trammel in the center at *O*, with the arms *XX*, at right angles to the semi-minor axis *O* 2. Then set from pencil to minor pin on the trammel rod the distance *O* 3. Now place the pencil in the point at 7 and drop both pins in the grooves, then fasten the major-pin and trace the curves through the points 7, 3, 5, for the concave side of mould. Again set from pencil to minor pin the distance *O* 4. place the pencil in the point at 8 and drop both pins in the grooves, then fasten the major-pin and trace the curve through the points 8, 4, 6, for the convex side of mould. Set off 6″ from *A* to *P* for length of shank. Make joints at *P* and *C* at right angles to the tangents *BP* and *BC*. Draw 5 9 and 6 10 parallel to *AP* for the width of mould at the shank.

The section at *D* shows the bevel taken from the angle at 10, Fig. 9, and applied through the center of plank; the section at *N* shows the bevel taken from the angle at 12. Fig. 9, and applied from the face of crook through the center of plank, so as to pitch the shank down, as required.

Fig. 11. *Shows the face-mould for the wreath-piece on the level.*

This face-mould may be drawn with the compasses from different points on the major axis line *OE;* the parallel sides *ED* and *OC*, of the parallelogram equal the radius *OC*, Fig. 8, and the parallel sides *OE* and *CD* equal *Kn*, Fig. 9.

The bevel at section *D* is shown in the angle at 8. Fig. 9, and is applied so as to pitch the joint at *C* down; at section *N* the square is applied, thus allowing the shank to conform to the line of floor. The block pattern is shown applied at right angles to the lines made from the bevel and try square, showing the twist of wreath-piece in the crook.

Fig. 12. *Shows the plan of turnout corresponding to Fig. 4, Plate 26, which is supposed to be made on heavy building* *paper, and after the steps are got out, the drawing is rolled up, and when the patterns are required for the rail, the face-mould is laid off on the paper.*

The tangents *HF* and *FJ* produced, and the position of risers all correspond to Fig. 4, Plate 26. Draw *HO* and *JO* parallel to *FJ* and *FH*, forming the parallelogram *OHFJ*; prolong tangent *JF* indefinite; from *H* draw *HC* at right angles to *JC*; the face of No. 3 rise is shown 4½″ from the spring of curve.

Fig. 13. *Shows the elevation of tangents.*

Let *XX* indicate the floor line. Make *FH* and *FJ* equal the tangents *FH* and *FJ* on plan, Fig. 12. Parallel with *FD*, draw *JG*, cutting the inclination of the center line of rail at *Q*, prolong *ED* to intersect *JG* at *L*, then *LQ* equals the *height* the wreath-piece will rise in the curve at the center of wreath-piece.

Make *LM* equal the chord *HJ*, Fig. 12; let *DN* equal *FC*, Fig. 12. From *N* and at right angles to *QD* prolonged draw *NK*; draw *HP* parallel to *FD*. Make *P* 2 equal *H* 2 on plan for the point of miter. Make *LT* equal *FO*, Fig. 12.

Bevels. Let *S* 5 indicate a gauge line parallel to *XX*. Perpendicular to *XX* draw *SR* and equal to *HC*, Fig. 12. Make *S* 5 equal the *height LQ*. Let *S* 6 equal *NK*, draw *R* 5 and *R* 6 prolonged to edge of board *XX*. Parallel to *S* 5, draw the half width of rail (2¼″), cutting the hypothenuse of bevels at 7 and 8.

Fig. 14. *Shows the face-mould.*

At any convenient place on the paper draw *FP* indefinite. Make *FJ* equal *DQ*, Fig. 13. With *J* as a center and *MQ*, Fig. 13, for a radius, draw arc at *H*. Again with *F* as a center and *FH*, Fig. 12, for a radius, draw arc intersecting at *H*; draw *FH* prolonged to equal *H* 2 on plan, Fig. 12. Draw *HO* and *JO* parallel to *FJ* and *FH* for the parallelogram *OHFJ* on the cutting plane, which will coincide when in position with the parallelogram *OHFJ* on plan, Fig. 12.

Proof. The diagonal *FO* must equal the distance *TQ*, Fig. 13. If so, the angle of tangents at *F* must be correct.

Make *JP* equal 6″ for length of shank, make joints at 2 and *P* at right angles to the tangents *F* 2 and *FP*. From *H* and at right angles to *FH*. draw a line indefinite. Prolong the diagonal *FO* to intersect the line from *H*; from the intersection (not shown) draw the radial line through *J* prolonged for the points of contact, or the connection of straight with the curved part of mould.

Make *P* 6 and *P* 13 each equal 6 7, Fig. 13. Make *H* 4 and *H* 3 each equal 5 8, Fig. 13; draw 13 7 and 6 8 parallel to *JP*; draw 3 11 and 4 12 parallel to *H* 2. Now the intersection (not shown) is the point to pivot the trammel, and from the intersection to the point 8 is the semi-major axis for the concave side of mould, and the minor axis would be at right angles, but on account of the extreme length of the axis as shown at *J*, Fig. 13, Plate 17, it would be attended with too much trouble. A better way to use the ordinates as previously explained, and thus find all the points in the curve that may be desired. Or points may be found on the diagonal *FO*[*]. through which the curves may be drawn by using the pliable

<hr>

*These points on the diagonal give another point in each curve and answers very well for small cylinders. But for the large cylinders and for face-moulds over winders more points in the curves are required for a correct trace of the face-mould. These three points may be found on the proof diagonal in elevation for any wreath-piece as shown by the dots on the line *YZ*, Fig. 2, Plate 32, for all wreath-pieces standing over a quarter circle on plan; and for all wreath-pieces less than a quarter circle the points are found on the proof diagonal as shown at Fig. 4, Plate 24.

strip. Thus return to the elevation Fig. 13, draw *TQ*, make *L* 3 equal *O* 5, Fig. 12, draw 3 4 parallel to *LQ*. Now return to Fig 14, make *O* 5 equal *Q* 4, Fig. 13, and draw the proportional line *H* 5, draw 4 10 parallel to *H* 5, make 5 9 equal 5 10. Now with a pliable strip, draw the curve 7, 9, 3, for the concave side of mould and through the points 8, 10, 4, draw the curve for the convex side of mould, and through the points *H* 5, *J*, draw the center line of mould. At section *N* the bevel found in the angle at 5, Fig, 13, is shown applied from the face of crook through the center of plank. At section *D* the bevel found in the angle at 6, Fig. 13, is shown applied through the center of plank, and the block pattern is applied square to the line made from the bevel, thus showing the twist of wreath-piece in the crook. Observe the bevels do not cross the tangents in their application. The shading shows the surplus wood to be removed, and also the thickness and width of plank required to saw out the crook.

Fig. 15. *Shows the easement pattern for the landing of the first flight. How to mark the point F on the pattern so as to cut and joint the rail at the bench.*
Draw a tread and rise and floor line anywhere on the draft-board; through the center of baluster *XX*, draw the under side of rail. Then take the easement pattern already made, and apply the lower edge to the inclination through *XX*, as shown; now slide the pattern until the lower edge at *AB* will equal the distance *XQ*, [4″] Fig. 5; then mark the pattern opposite the landing rise at center of rail, as shown at *F*, and we have 5″ to the joint at *C* on the inclination to allow when cutting the straight rail. And from *F* to *B*, parallel with the floor line, we have 20½″ to allow for the easement when cutting the straight rail for the level. At 1 is shown how much longer the long baluster is than the regular short baluster for the first flight; 4 5 shows how much longer the balusters for the level are to be over the regular short balusters; at 2 and 3 the difference over the regular short balusters is shown for these two odd balusters.

Figs. 8, 9 and 10, Plate 28. *Shows how to construct the face-mould over a quarter pace winding, so as to form two easings in the wreath-piece, thus avoiding the short ramp usually at the lower end of wreath-piece.*

Fig. 8. Shows the plan of quarter cylinder having three winders in the quarter pace; *AB* and *BC* are the tangents enclosing the center line of rail; *AD* and *CE* indicate the direction of straight rail; *OABC* shows the parallelogram on plan.

Fig. 9. *Shows the elevation of tangents.*
Let *XX* indicate the edge of drawing board. Make *AB* equal *AB*, Fig. 8. Draw *AC* and *BD* perpendicular to *XX* and of indefinite length. Now elevate the treads and risers, keeping the face of No. 9 rise 2″, and also the face of No. 13 rise 10″ from the spring line *AC*; through the center of baluster *OO* and *OO* draw the under side of rail; parallel with the under side of rail, draw the center of rail, intersecting *AC* at *E*, and at the upper end prolong the inclination indefinite, cutting *BD* at *H*; draw *HE* prolonged indefinite; perpendicular to *AF* draw *FD* to cut *EH* prolonged at *G*; make *EJ* perpendicular to *AC*; make *EK* equal the chord *AC*, Fig. 8; make *FL* equal twice *DH*; parallel with *BD*, draw the half width of rail, cutting *EH* and *FH* at 2 and 3; ease the angle at *E*; at right angles to *ME*, and at the spring of easing, draw the joint line 4 5, cutting the center of straight rail at 6, and also *HE* prolonged at 7; parallel

with *HE* prolonged, draw the half thickness of plank, cutting the joint line 4 7 at 5; from 5, and perpendicular to *HE* prolonged, draw 5 8, cutting *HE* prolonged at *N*. Now *NE* is the length required for the shank of face-mould at the lower end; the shank of mould at the upper end may be any length, as the wreath-piece contains a natural easing.

Bevels. From the center *D*, draw a line to tangent *HG*, and intersect *HD* at *P*; join *PF*; the angle at *P* gives the bevel for the lower end of wreath-piece; again, from the center *J* draw a line to tangent *FH* prolonged, and intersect *BD* at *Q*; join *QE* for the bevel required at the upper end of wreath-piece. The bevel shown in the angle at 5, applies from the joint after the sides of wreath-piece are worked off to the plumb.

Fig. 10. *Shows the face-mould.*

Make *NEH* equal *NEH*, Fig. 9; with *E* as a center, and the distance *FK*, Fig. 9, for a radius, draw arc at *F*; again, with *H* for a center, and *FH*, Fig. 9, for a radius, draw arc, cutting at *F*; draw *FH* prolonged; parallel with *EH* and *HF*, draw *FO* and *EO* for the parallelogram *OFHE* on the cutting plane.

Proof. The diagonal *HO* must equal the distance *LK*, Fig. 9, if so, the angle of tangents at *H* must be correct.

Make *EG* equal *HG*, Fig. 9; draw *GO* indefinite for the direction of minor axis; make *OC* equal *OC* on plan, Fig. 9; make *C* 2 and *C* 3 each equal the half width of rail [1¼″]; make *E* 4 and *E* 5 each equal *H* 3, Fig. 9; make *F* 6 and *F* 7 each equal *H* 2, Fig. 9; make joints at *N* and *S* perpendicular to the tangents *HE* and *HF*; from the points 6, 7, and 5, 4, draw lines for the straight wood parallel to the tangents *HS* and *HN* to intersect the joints at 8, 9, and 10, 11; now draw the curves of face-mould in the usual way.

The bevel found in the angle at *Q*, Fig. 9, is shown applied at section *B*; and the bevel found in the angle at *P*, Fig. 9, is shown applied at section *A*; the block pattern is shown applied in the usual way.

Now work off the sides of wreath-piece to the plumb, then through the center of rail section draw *ab* as shown at section *A*; from *a* and *b* draw lines on the sides of wreath-piece square to the joint, then mark on these lines from the joint the distance *N* 7, Fig. 9. Now apply the bevel shown in the angle at 5, Fig. 9, from the joint and through the points just found on the sides of wreath-piece which will give the cripple joint 5 4, Fig. 9; a section of this joint is shown at *D*, the points 7 and 6 correspond to the two centers 7 and 6, Fig. 9; after the cripple joint is cut, then carry the line *ab* across the joint, and also the plumb line made from the bevel; raise up the distance 7 6, Fig. 9, for the center of block pattern, and shape the casing square from the joint last made; the points 7 and 6 correspond to the two centers 7 and 6, Fig. 9. Observe a piece may be glued on the top of wreath-piece to accommodate the easing; the crook must be sawn out wider on the concave side to allow the block pattern to raise up the required height, 7 6, Fig. 9. This method of forming the unnatural or forced easing in the wreath-piece at the lower end is not preferred by the author; in a case of this kind, when the inclination of pitches is less steep then an easing may be worked on the shank of wreath-piece and carried into the twist part with good results. At Fig. 9, the parallelogram *FHWZ* is shown projected from the tangent *FH* in elevation.

Some prefer in this way to find the angle of tangents on the cutting plane, then transfer them to the material for pattern by using a bevel.

PLATE 30.

Plate 30. [Scale ¾″=1 foot]. *Exhibits how to construct the face-mould when the risers are placed at any point in the cylinder without reference to what effect they may have on the wreath part of rail as is sometimes the case, with ordered rails, and also in the capping of iron balustrades.*

Figs. 1 and 2. *Show how to find the length of tangents and treatment of the wreath over a cylinder 12″ in diameter starting from the level to a rake, when the face of No. 1 rise is 1″ outside the spring of cylinder, the balusters are 2″×2″, bracket ¼″ thick. Then the radius for the center line of rail will equal 6¾″. The rise is 8″ by 9″ tread. The size of rail is 4½″ by 2¾″. The rail is to be a "right-hand rail."*

Fig. 1. *Shows the plan.*
From the center *O* draw the semi-circle *ACE* to a radius of 6¾″ for the center line of rail. Enclose the semicircle with the rectilineal parallelogram *ABDE*, draw *OC*, forming the two square parallelograms *OABC* and *OCDE*. Prolong tangents *BA* and *DE* to the right for the direction of straight string. The dotted line shows the face of outer string. The face of No. 1 rise is one (1″) inch outside the spring of cylinder.

Fig. 2. *Shows the elevation of tangents, as developed from plan, they are folded.*
Let *XX* indicate the edge of drawing board, make *AB* equal *AB* on plan, Fig. 1, (6¾″), draw *AE* and *BD* perpendicular to *XX*, elevate No. 1 and 2 rise and tread, keeping the face of No. 1 rise 1″ from the spring line *AE*. At *B* set up 4″ to the underside of rail plus the half thickness of rail (1¾″+4″=5¾″) equals 5¾″ to the center of rail as *BC*; draw *CF* parallel to *XX*.

Through the center of baluster *OO* draw the underside of rail, parallel with *OO* draw the inclination for the center line of rail to intersect *AE* at *h*.

Let it be observed that if the center line of rail *Gh*, were prolonged to intersect the perpendicular *BD*, it would fall below the point *C*, and as the point *C* is a fixed point, we will have to assume an inclination for the wreath-piece different from the regular pitch and make what is termed a "cripple joint" at the shank end of mould.

Then draw *CJ* for the assumed pitch, cutting *AE* at *K*. The point *J* is not arbitrary, the stair-builder can use his judgment as to what inclination or length to make the shank *JK*. At *C* is shown a section of rail. *C* 2 shows the increased width of mould for half the rail at the center joint. In the angle at *K* is shown the bevel for the center joint. At the shank joint of mould the square will be applied because there is no spring in this case.

The joint at *J* is made at right angles to the true pitch, and the bevel shown at *J* gives the cut for the cripple joint as shown. The shaded part shows the curve of wreath-piece flowing into the straight rail. In the hands of a skillful stair-builder this treatment of the wreath-piece will give a beautiful twist as the curve is carried more into the shank.

The dotted lines drawn parallel with *CJ* show the thickness (5″) of plank required, less thickness would answer by taking off the corners as shown at section *N*, Fig. 5, for they will come off in moulding the wreath-piece.

The face-mould for this wreath-piece is shown at Fig. 5.

Figs. 3 and 4. Repeats Figs. 1 and 2, only the former is shown for a wreath-piece landing, or from the rake to a level. The face of No. 16 rise is one inch (1″) outside the spring of cylinder. The tangents *AB, BC, CD* and *DE* coincide with those at plan, Fig. 1.

Fig. 4. *Shows the elevation of tangents, they being folded.*

Let *XX* indicate the edge of draught board, make *AB* equal *AB*, Fig. 3. Draw *AE* and *BD* perpendicular to *XX*. Elevate No. 15 and 16 treads and risers, also floor line, keeping the face of No. 16 rise 1″ from the spring line *AE*. Draw the floor line *OS*. Through the center of baluster *OO* draw the inclination for the underside of rail, parallel with *OO* draw the center line of rail intersecting *AE* at *h*. At the floor line *S* set up 4″ to the underside of rail and 1⅜″ more or 5¾″ to the center *C*, then *C* is a fixed point. Draw *CT* parallel to *XX*, cutting *AE* at *W*.

Now let it be observed that if the true inclination *Gh* were prolonged to intersect *BD*, it would raise above the fixed point *C*, which would be too high, so we will make a cripple joint at the shank same as at Fig. 2. Now in drawing this, to save time draw the assumed pitch to agree with that at Fig. 2, and make one face-mould answer for both wreath-pieces.

Then make *CF* equal *FK*, Fig. 2, draw *FK* parallel to *XX*, draw *CK* prolonged to intersect *GH* at *J*, make the joint at *J* at right angles to *GJ*. The bevel in the angle at *J* gives the down cut for the cripple joint, the bevel in the angle at *C* is applied at the center joint. Parallel with *BD* draw the half width of rail, cutting *CK* at 2. At *C* is shown a square section of rail and the dotted lines cutting the angles of block pattern are drawn parallel to *JC* and give the thickness of plank (4½″) required to form the twist. Prolong *KF* to equal the chord *AC*, Fig. 3, as *KU*.

Fig. 5. *Shows the face-mould for both starting and landing.*

At any convenient place on the paper draw a line to equal *CKJ*, Fig. 4, as *BAJ*. At right angles to *JB* draw *AO* and *BC* each equal to *AB*, Fig. 3. Join *CO* for the rectilineal parallelogram *OABC* on the cutting plane.

Proof. The diagonal *OB* and chord *AC* must each equal the distance *UW*, Fig. 4. If so, the parallelogram is correct.

As all the angles are right angles, the face-mould will be a quarter of an ellipse with the joints on the axis lines. Make *C* 2 and *C* 3 each equal *C* 2, Fig. 4, make *A* 4 and *A* 5 each equal half width of rail (2¼), draw 4 6 and 5 7 parallel to *AJ*, make joint at *J* perpendicular to *AJ*. The dotted line at *J* indicates the overwood required for making the cripple joint.

Pivot the trammel at the point *O* and sweep the quarter ellipse in the usual way. The section *N* shows the bevel found in the angle at *C*, Fig. 4, applied from the face of crook. At section *D* the try square is shown applied. The shaded part shows the thickness of plank and the width at joints to saw out the crooks. The center point at section *D* should equal from the face of crook the distance 4 *J*, Fig. 4, and at section *N* the distance 3 *C*. Fig. 4, from the upper side of crook.

Make *J* 8 equal *Jh*, Fig. 4, then *J* 8 will be the amount to deduct for shank when cutting the straight rail.

In the two elevations, Figs. 2 and 4, the shaded parts show the two wreath pieces, the one starting, and the other for a landing; it will be observed if they were bolted together at the center joint *C*, they would answer for a platform twist. The quarter turn connecting the wreath-piece, is taken from plank the same thickness as for the straight rail, there being no spring bevel required at the shank of quarter turn.

Figs. 6 to 10. *Shows a different treatment of a landing and starting twist.*

Fig. 6. *Shows the plan, starting from the level to a rake similar to Fig. 1.*

Only in this case the face of rise is placed on line with the diameter or spring line of cylinder, the rise is 8″ $\times$ 9″ tread, the tangents *AB*, *BC*, *CD* and *DE,* coincide with Fig. 1.

Fig. 7. *Shows the elevation; the tangents are folded.*

Allow *BA* prolonged to indicate a base line; make *BA* equal tangent *AB* on plan, Fig. 6; draw *AG* and *BF* perpendicular to *BA.* Now elevate No. 1 and 2 rise and tread, keeping the face of No. 1 rise on the spring line; from the base or floor line *BA,* set up 4″ to the under side of rail plus the half thickness [1⅜″] of rail, [1⅜″+4″=5⅜″] equals 5⅜″ to *L.* Draw *LK* for the center of level rail, thus establishing the point *L;* through the center of balusters *OO,* draw the inclination for the under side of rail; parallel with *OO,* draw the center line of rail, intersecting *AG* at *J.* From *L,* and parallel to *OO,* draw *Lm.* (In this case, *Lm* happens to come on line with the upper side of rail.) The block pattern shows the section of rail at *L.* Make shank joint at pleasure, say at 2, and perpendicular to *OO.*

The dotted lines show the thickness of plank required to form the twist, the thickness of rail being gauged off from the lower side, and all the over wood is to be removed from the top side of crook at the shank; *L* 4 is the distance from the lower side of crook to center the block pattern at *L.* The bevel for the center joint is shown in the angle at *m;* as the plank in this case is canted but one way, only one bevel will be required; the try square will apply at the shank joint; the face-mould is shown at Fig. 10.

Fig. 8. *Shows the plan from the rake to a level, similar to Fig. 3.*

Only the face of No. 16 rise is on line with the spring of cylinder. The tangents *AB*, *BC*, *CD* and *DE,* and also the tread and rise agree with Fig. 6.

Fig. 9. *Shows the elevation of tangents from plan, Fig. 8. they are folded.*

Let *BA* prolonged, indicate a base line or line of floor; perpendicular to *BA,* draw *BF* and *AG;* elevate No. 15 and 16 rise and tread, keeping the face of No. 16 rise on the spring line *AG.*

Through the center of balusters *OO* draw the inclination for the under side of rail, parallel with *OO* draw the center of rail intersecting *AG* at *J;* also draw the upper side of rail *S* 3, to intersect the perpendicular from *B* at *F.* From the floor line set up 4″ to the underside of rail plus the half thickness (1⅜″) of rail (4″+1⅜″=5⅜″) equals 5⅜″ to *L.* Draw *LK* prolonged and parallel to *BA,* draw *LM* parallel to *SF;* draw *MN* at right angles to *AG;* parallel to *BF* draw the half width of rail (2¼″), cutting *SF* at *X.* The block pattern is shown centered at *L,* the dotted line shows the thickness of plank required for the wreath piece. [4¾″.] Make shank joint at pleasure, say 3 2.

Let *LU* equal the chord *AC* on plan, Fig. 8. In the angle at *L* is shown the bevel for the center joint.

Fig. 10. *Shows the face-mould.*

Make *BA* and *AJ* equal *F* 3 and 3 2 Fig. 9. From *A* and *B* and perpendicular to *jB* draw *BC* and *AO* each equal to *OC,* Fig. 8, for the rectilineal parallelogram *OABC* on the cutting plane or plane of plank.

Proof. The diagonal *BO* and chord *AC* must be equal and of the same length as *NU,* Fig. 9. Make joint at *J* at right angles to tangent *BJ.* Let *C* 2 and *C* 3 each equal *Fx,* Fig. 9. Also make *A* 4 and *A* 5 each equal the half width of rail (2¼″).

Draw 4 6 and 5 7 parallel to *AJ.* Now pivot the trammel in *O* and trace the curves for the face-mould as has been explained. The joint at *C* is on line with the major axis *OC* in this case because the plank is not sprung and the angles of the parallelogram on plan and face-mould are all right angles.

The section at *N* shows the tangent *BC* carried across the joint square to the face of plank and the dotted line run on from the face of crook equal to the distance *L* 4, Fig. 9. The bevel found in the angle at *L*, Fig. 9. is applied through the intersection. At section *D* the full thickness of rail is shown gauged from the face or upper side of crook and the surplus wood at the shank is removed from the under side of crook.

At elevation Fig. 7. the surplus wood at the shank is shown gauged from the under side of crook, and most of the surplus wood is removed from the top.

It will be observed that if the wreath-piece for Fig. 8 were bolted to that of Fig. 10, it would answer for a platform twist, the face of risers being on line with the spring of cylinder. *KJ* is the correct height of wreath-piece from center to center of rail.

Make *J* 9 on face-mould equal *J* 2 in elevation Fig. 9, for the amount to be deducted for shank when jointing the straight rail. The quarter turns connecting the wreath-pieces are level as described for Fig. 5.

Figs. 11, 12 and 13. *Shows a third method how to obtain the face-mould when the risers are misplaced.*

Fig. 11. *Shows the plan and agrees with Fig. 8; the face of No. 16 or landing, rise is on line with the spring of cylinder.*

With 6¾″ as a radius and *O* for a center draw the semicircle *ACE.* The dotted line indicates the face of cylinder. Draw the diameter *AOE,* draw the direction of straight rail from *A* and *E* at right angles to *AE.*

Fig. 12. *Shows the elevation of a step and rise and inclination of rail from which to determine the length of tangents on the plan. The rise is 8″ by 9″ tread.*

Let *XX* indicate the edge of draught board, elevate No. 15 and 16 tread and rise and the floor line at the landing. From *A* draw the spring line *AE* indefinite. Through the center of balusters *OO* draw the under side of rail, parallel with *OO* draw the center line of rail *RJ* and prolonged indefinite. From the floor line set up 4″ to the under side of rail and the half thickness of rail 1⅜″ more, or 5⅜″ to the center of rail at *B* through *B*, draw a line parallel to the floor line, cutting the inclination for the center of rail at *C* and prolonged indefinite. From *C* draw *CD* parallel to *AB.*

Now return to plan, Fig. 11, draw tangent *AD* indefinite. Make *AD* equal *AD,* Fig. 12. Make *DF* equal *AD* and to tangent the semicircle at *F.* Draw *FO* for the joint on plan, then the wreath-piece will cover so much of the plan that lays between *A* and the joint at *F.* From *F* to *E* will be level, the solid lines shows the pattern for the same, it being a little over a quarter of a circle. Parallel with tangents *DA* and *DF* draw *FH* and *AH,* From *F* and at right angles to *AD* prolonged draw *FG,* draw the diagonal *OD.*

Now return to the elevation Fig. 12, draw *JM* parallel to *XX* and prolonged to the left. Make *MN* equal the chord *AF,* Fig.

11. Make *CK* equal *DG*, Fig 11, make *CQ* equal *DH*, Fig. 11;
also make *CL* equal *DO* on plan, Fig. 11; draw *MQ* prolonged,
cutting the perpendicular from *L* at *U*. From *K* and at right
angles to *RC* draw *KP*.

Bevels. The dotted line 2 4 is drawn parallel to and at any
distance from the edge of board *XX*; draw 2 5 perpendicular to *XX*
and equal to *GF*, Fig. 11.   Make 2 3 equal *KP*, also make 2 4
equal the height *MC*, draw 5 3 and 5 4 to edge of board and the
angles at 3 and 4 give the bevels required.   Parallel with 2 4
draw the half width of rail, cutting the hypothenuse of bevels at
7 and 8.

Fig. 13.   *Shows the face-mould.*

Make *DA* equal *JC*, Fig. 12; with *A* for a center, and the
distance *NC*, Fig. 12, as a radius, draw arc at *F;* again, with *D*
as a center, and *DF*, Fig. 11, for a radius, draw arc intersecting
at *F;* join *DF;* parallel with *DA* and *DF*, draw *FH* and *AH*
for the parallelogram *HADF* on the cutting plane, that will
agree when in position, with the parallelogram *HADF* on plan,
Fig. 11.

Proof.   The diagonal *DH* must equal the distance *MQ*, Fig.
12.   Prolong *DA* 6″ to *J* for length of shank; make joint at *J* at
right angles to *JD;* make joint at *F* perpendicular to *DF;* prolong joint at *F* indefinite; draw the diagonal *DH* to intersect the
joint line from *F* at *O;* draw *OA* prolonged for the trapezium
OADF on the cutting plane, that will coincide with the trapezium *OADF* on plan, Fig. 11; proof: the diagonal *DO* must equal
the distance *MU*, Fig. 12, if so, the quodrilateral is correct.

Draw *OC* perpendicular to *OF;* make *OC* equal the radius
OA, Fig. 11; then *O* is the center to pivot the trammel, and *OF*
is the semi-major axis, and *OA* the semi-minor axis.   Make *F* 2
and *F* 3 each equal 4 8, Fig. 12; make *J* 6 and *J* 7 each equal 3
7, Fig. 12; draw 6 4 and 6 5 parallel with *AJ;* make *C* 8 and *C* 9
each equal the half width of rail [2¼″].

Now pivot the trammel at *O*, with the arms at right angles to
the minor axis *OC*, then set from pencil to minor pin the distance
O 8, and from pencil to major pin the distance *O* 2; now trace the
curve from 2 to 4 for the concave side of mould; proceed in like
manner to trace the convex and center line of mould.   At section
B the bevel shown in the angle at 3, Fig. 12, is applied from the
face of crook; at section *N* the bevel shown in the angle at 4, is
applied from the face of crook.   Observe the bevels do not cross
the tangents in their application, because the minor axis is not
within the parallelogram, as shown.

Fig. 14.   *Shows how to place the risers in the cylinder
so as to have the rail the proper height at the landing, and
make the wreath-piece without any spring or joint bevel at the
shank; thus canting the plank only one way.*

This gives the most simple method to construct the face-
mould; the rise is 8″, and tread 9″, the elevation is first drawn,
then the plan.

Let *XX* indicate the edge of drawing board; draw *BF* at
right angles to *XX;* any where on the line *BF*, place the rise of
pitchboard, and draw the inclination *CJ* indefinite for the center
of rail.   Parallel with *CJ* draw the under side of rail; at *C*, draw
a section of rail, from the under side of rail section, measure down
half a rise [4″] to the floor line *V;* draw the floor line parallel to
XX, cutting the under side of rail at *O*, then *O* is the center of
short baluster, and the balusters are 2″×2″, then the face of No.

16 rise will be 1″ to the left of *O*, and No. 15 rise will be 9″ to the left of that again. Now determine the radius for the cylinder say 6″, then the radius for the center line of rail will equal 6¾″. Make *BA* equal 6¾″; perpendicular to *XX*, draw *AE*, cutting *JC* at *H*; draw *HM* prolonged, and parallel to *XX*; draw *CK* parallel to *XX*, and of indefinite length for the direction of level rail.

Fig. 15. *Shows the plan.*

Draw the two right angles *AOC* and *COE* indefinite; make *OC* equal *AB*, Fig. 14; with *OC* [6¾″] as a radius, draw the semi-circle *ACE*; draw the tangents *AB*, *BC*, *CD* and *DE*. Prolong tangent *BA* and *DE* to the left for the direction of straight rail; place the face of No. 15 and 16 rise to agree with risers in elevation, relative to the spring of cylinder; the face of No. 15 rise is located 7½″ from the diameter, then the face of No. 16 rise will be in the cylinder 1½″.

Return to Fig. 14, make *HG* equal the chord *AC*, Fig. 15; parallel with *BF*, draw the half width of rail [2¼″], cutting *HC* at 3; the dotted line shows the thickness of plank [4″] required for the wreath-piece.

Fig. 16. *Shows the face-mould*, and is drawn in the same manner as at Fig. 5 and 10. Observe at sections *N* and *D* the block pattern is applied at the center of plank in this case; the bevel for section *N* is found in the angle at *C*, Fig. 14; there being no spring in this case, the try square is applied at the shank joint section *D*.

Figs. 17 and 18. Shows the same principal as at Fig. 14 and 15 applied to a platform twist, the manner to find the location of risers in the cylinder, and the construction of face-mould repeats, and in this case is the same as shown at Fig. 16, the lettering being the same.

Let it be noticed the face of No. 15 rise is 7½″ from the spring of cylinder and the face of No. 18 rise is 6½″ from the spring line, the difference being equal to half the thickness of baluster. This method allows in this case two more balusters (4) to be placed in the cylinder on the platform. Also observe at section *N*, Fig. 16, that if the wreath-piece were turned upside down it would suit for the wreath-piece starting off the platform.

This method of placing the risers in the cylinder makes the construction of face-mould and formation of the wreath an easy matter. One fault is in a "level to rake," and "rake to a level" twist, the joining of the wreath-piece with the level quarter turn at the center joint in small cylinders does not please the eye so well as when both the raking and level wreath pieces are sprung at the shanks, then the "helix" or twist line, in passing from *C* to *E*, Fig. 15, gradually lowers into the straight part of rail resulting in a graceful curve pleasing to the eye. Of course by using a spring bevel more work is required, and in cheap work the easiest method is mostly resorted to. The objective feature referred to above may be remedied by cutting the level crook from stuff half an inch thicker than the rail, and raising the twist strip so as to carry the curve gradually from the rake to the level, and taking the surplus wood off at the top at the center joint, and off from the underside at shank for the landing twist, and for the level part of twist starting the block pattern is applied so as to take the surplus wood from the underside at the center joint, and from the upper side at the shank as shown at Figs. 22 and 23. This would increase the length of balusters ½″ at each turn, but may be counteracted by raising or lowering the block pattern at the shank of the raking wreath piece, as shown at section *D*, Fig. 10. As the center joint is plumb this treatment of the above wreath-pieces makes the center joint a splice joint and thereby detracts from its appearance to some extent.

Fig. 19. *Shows the plan of a 12″ cylinder for a platform stairs having two different pitches; the rise to the platform is 8″×9″ tread, and off the platform the rise is 6″×12″ tread; this often happens in a stairs going to the attic, where the flight off the platform has to be constructed to give head room at the landing under the rafters.*

*The method here shown is to construct the face-mould so that one pattern and one set of bevels will answer for both wreath-pieces.**

AB, BC, CD and *DE* are the tangents for the center of rail on plan; the face of No. 8 rise is 3″, and the face of No. 11 rise is 7½″ from the joint or spring of cylinder; No. 9 and 10 rise is in the cylinder.

Fig. 20. *Shows the elevation of tangents, they being folded.*

Let *XX* represent the edge of drawing board; make *AB* equal *AB*, Fig. 19; perpendicular to *XX*, draw *AE* and *BD*; elevate Nos. 8, 9, 10 and 11 rise and treads, keeping the face of No. 8 rise 3″, and No. 11 rise 7½″ from the spring line *AE*, as shown.

Through the center of balusters *OO, OO*, draw the inclination of the under side of rail for both inclinations; parallel with *OO, OO*, draw the center of rail, intersecting at *F*; bisect the two pitches at *G*, and draw *GF* indefinite, cutting *AE* and *BD* at *C* and *H*; perpendicular to *GF*, and through *H* and *C*, draw *JHP* and *LCM*, cutting the center of rail *FN* at *P* and *Q*. Perpendicular to *LM*, draw *QR;* join *CR* and produced. At right angles to *JP*, draw *PT* equal to the chord *AC*, Fig. 19; from *C*, and at right angles to *FN*, draw *C 2*; again, from *P*, and perpendicular to *CR* produced, draw *P 3*; parallel with *ML*, draw the half width of rail, cutting *CR* and *QP* at 4 and 5 for the increased width of mould on the radial lines.

Bevels. The dotted line *UV* indicates a gauge line run on parallel to edge of board *XX;* draw *UW* perpendicular to *XX*, and equal to *HC*, Fig. 20; make *U 6* equal *C 2*, and *U 7* equal *P 3;* draw *W 6* and *W 7* prolonged to edge of board. Then in the angle *U6W*, is found the bevel for the shank joint, and the angle *U7W* gives the bevel for the center joint.

Fig. 21. *Shows the face mould.*

At any convenient place on the pattern paper draw *BJ* indefinite, make *BA* and *AJ* each equal *QP* and *PN*, Fig. 20. Then with *A* as a center and *TH*, Fig. 20, for a radius, draw arc at *C*. Again with *B* as a center and *RC*, Fig. 20, as a radius, draw arc intersecting at *C*, join *BC*. Parallel with the tangents *AB* and *BC* draw *CO* and *AO* prolonged at *A* and *C* for the parallelogram *OACB* on the cutting plane. Make *AD* equal *QF*, Fig. 20. Join *DO* and prolonged for the direction of the minor axis, then at right angles to *DO* and through *O* draw the direction of the major axis *EF*.

Make *O 2* equal *HC*, Fig. 20, let 2 3 and 2 4 each equal the half width of rail. Make *C 5* and *C 6* each equal *Q 5*, Fig. 20.

*This method of solving this problem in hand-railing, first appeared in "Carpentry and Building," for July, 1884, Vol. 6, Page 146. This journal is published in New York, by DAVID WILLIAMS, and should be studied and preserved by every carpenter in the country; by having the numbers bound, they serve as a ready reference and encyclopædia on all that appertains to the trade; especially to the young man it is a valuable, practical instructor.

Let *A* 7 and *A* 8 each equal *C* 4, Fig. 20, draw 8 10 and 7 9 parallel with *AJ*. Make joint at *j* at right angles to the tangent *JB* and the joint at *C* make perpendicular to the tangent *BC*.

Now pivot the trammel at *O* and trace the curves for the inside, outside and center line of the face-mould as explained at former plates.

The application of the bevels is shown at sections *P* and *N*. For the points on the pattern, to cut the straight rail, make *JM* equal *N* 8, Fig. 20, for the length to the platform, and for the length of the platform make *JL* equal *Y* 9, Fig. 20. Now measure from these two points *M* and *L* instead of the point *A*, as in other cases.

It will be observed that in drawing the face-mould in this way so as to make one pattern and one set of bevels answer for the two different inclinations, the twist when blocked out will not be plumb at the center joint. This will not be noticed much for a small flat rail, but for a high double rail the sides will show. This can be remedied some by working the wreath a little full at the center joint and dressing off agreeable to the eye, after the two wreath pieces are bolted together.

Figs. 22 and 23. *Show two quarter turns to connect a starting and landing twist. The tangents agree with those on plan.*

The explanation for Fig. 4, Plate 16, will apply in this case and needs no other explanation further than to say better results will follow by springing the plank for both wreath-pieces, similar to Fig. 4, plate 16, but will take more time.

PLATE 31.

Plate 31. [Scale ¼″=1 foot]. *Exhibits plan and elevation of a one-story platform staircase.*

The height of story from top to top of joist equals 12′ 3″, width of joist in the second story is 10″, width of hall 10′ 3″ in the rough; run of first flight including the platform 18′ 0″; the door under the platform is 7′ 6″ high; steps are 1¼″ thick, rail 3½″ by 5,″ double moulded; balusters 2″ by 2″; newel post 10″ by 10″, and a left hand rail.

Fig. 1. *Shows the plan.* Having sixteen risers to the platform in the first flight and five risers in the return flight to the landing in the second story, making twenty-one risers in the height of story. The cylinder is 24″ in diameter and the steps are spaced off on the cylinder line equal to the regular tread. The center of newel is placed in the center of hall. The three first treads at the wall string are increased gradually in width 10½″, 11½″ and 13½″, while at the front string they are equal to the regular tread in width, allowing a gradual "swell" on the nosing line.

Fig. 2. *Shows the elevation.*

The height of story 12′ 3″ is divided off on the story rod *AB*, into 21 risers, thus 12′ 3″ reduced to inches (10′ 3″×12″=147″) equals 147″, which divided into 21 divisions (147″÷21=7″), equals 7″ for the height of each rise. If we use the constant of 24″ (24″—7″+7″=10″) as before we will have 10″ for the width of the regular tread. Now there are 16 risers to the platform at 7″ each (16″×7″=112″÷12″=9′ 4″), equals 9′ 4″ for the height of platform. The height of door under the platform

Is specified to be 7' 6", then 9' 4" minus 7' 6" equals 1' 10" for the space from top of door to top of platform. The depth of joist is 10 and thickness of floor is 1" and plaster 1" (10"+1"+1"=12") equals twelve inches, leaving 10". That amount is ample for the finish over the door.

The run, including the platform, is required to be 18' 0", there being 12 treads in the first flight at 10" each [12×10=120] plus three odd treads that are 10½", 11½" and 13½" wide (120×10½"+11½"+13½"=155½") equals 155½ inches, which reduced to feet (155½"÷12=12' 11½") equals 12' 11½" for the horizontal run of the treads to the platform. Then the width of platform to the face of No. 16 rise will equal 18' 0" minus 12' 11½" (18' 0"—12' 11½"=5' 0½") or 5' 0½" as shown on plan.

Again, the thickness of rise equals 1" and allow 1½" for uneven walls, the platform may be framed 4' 10" (5' 0½"—1"+1½"=2½")=4' 10") for the neat width.

The flight off the platform has 5 risers and 4 full treads at 10" each, then there should be 6" from the last rise to the face of joist at the landing, so that the bearers may have good nailing against the joist. The width of platform from the face of No. 16 rise to wall equals 5' 0½", the distance then from the wall to face of joist at the landing **A**, (4×10"+5' 0½"=8' 10½") equals 8' 10½", as shown on plan.

Headway. For the headway count down from the landing, say 16 risers at 7" each minus the width of joist 10" in the second story, thickness of floor 1" and 1" for the plastering (16×7"=112)—10"+1"+1"—100"÷12"=8' 4") equals 8' 4" plumb over and including No. 6 rise. In this case No. 6 rise should be deducted from 8' 4", leaving 7' 9" for the head-room. So we will locate the face of trimmer plumb over the center of No. 5 step. This will give ample head-room.

Then from the back of platform to the face of trimmer marked **C** at the headway will equal 5' 0½" from the back of platform to the face of No. 16 rise plus 10 treads at 10" each 5' 0½" + (10×10"=100")÷12=8' 4"+5"+5' 0½"=13' 9½") equals 13' 9½".) And the length of quarter pace landing marked **AB** on plan will equal 13' 9½" minus 8' 10½" (13' 9½"—8' 10½"=4' 11"), or 4' 11" for the length of trimming at the landing, and the width of quarter pace will equal the width of hall (10' 3") minus the half width of hall (5' 1½") plus the radius of silver 12" and the thickness of fascia (1½") or outer string (10' 3"—[5' 1½"+12"+1½"=63] 4' 0") equals 4' 0" for the width of landing from the rough wall to the face of header marked **C**, on plan, Fig. 1. This completes the trimming for the well of staircase.

The joist at the landing should be well bridged and spiked to prevent sagging; if the walls are brick, the platform should be framed and built in when the walls are going up, by leaving a space over each joist, the platform may be leveled up when putting up the stairs. At the terminus of the rail, a block should be built in the wall 2' 8" from the floor to its center, for to fasten the rosette and rail; if stud partitions, see that the block is set far enough back for the plastering to key.

At **h, h,** are shown the rough brackets underneath the stairs cut and nailed to 3"×4" bearers, having the grain perpendicular to the treads. At **H** is shown the panel work under the first flight, having an arched opening into a coat closet or wash-stand; the size and variety of panels may be arranged to suit the taste of architect or stair-builder.

Fig. 3. [Scale ¾″=1 foot]. *Shows the plan of cylinder* 24″ *in diameter.*

The risers Nos. 15, 16, 17 and 18 are spaced off on the stretch-out **AD**, and are drawn into the cylinder at **L** and **N** to suit the position of balusters in the same manner as explained at Plate 15, which should be well studied.

From **D,** on the stretchout, to **F,** equals half a tread (5″), and is the face of No. 16 rise; and from **F** to **K,** and **K** to **G,** each equal to a full tread (10″), and are the face of No. 14 and 15 risers, thus establishing the face of No. 14 rise 6″ from the spring line **AC.** as shown.

Draw No. 17, 18 and 19 rise opposite to No. 16, 15 and 14 rise, and locate the short balusters on No. 14 and 19 treads; then space off the intervening balusters equally, and curve the face of risers No. 16 and 17 to suit the balusters as shown.

The outer solid line **ABC** shows the face of cylinder; the outer dotted line, indicates the center line of rail ¾″ from the cylinder line; the inner dotted line shows the thickness of bracket (¼″), and the inner solid line 1, 2, 3, 4, shows the projection of nosing, (1¼″).

Fig. 4. *Shows the semi-circle* **ABC,** divided off into an odd number of staves (11); the chord or the segment for No. 1 stave is extended to the edge **DE,** of drawing board; for a convenient means to adjust the bevel **F,** a greater or less number of staves may be used, as the stair-builder may desire; this width of staves answers very well for the treads, and is intended to be made from stuff 1½″ thick. At Fig. 1, Plate 33, is shown how to obtain the length of staves.

Figs. 5 and 6. [Scale 1½″=1′]. *Shows the convex and concave risers.*

The end of risers are slit, forming a veneer **CC,** about ⅟₁₆″ thick, steamed, bent, glued and clamped to the cores **A** and **B,** for the proper curve; "cauls" are clamped down over the veneer to press them close and even to the core.

Fig. 7. *Shows plan of the turnout at the newel, divided into three staves, and spliced to the outer string; then screwed from the back.*

The face of No. 4 rise is 5″ from the spring of cylinder, the radius is 2′ 1¼″, and should be drawn on heavy paper, as shown at Fig. 9, Plate 32. The bevel for jointing the staves is shown at **A.**

The cut-out for No. 14 rise is 5¾″ from the joint of cylinder; at No. 19 rise the cut-out of outer string is 6¼″ from the joint of cylinder; the width of string at the internal angle of thread and rise is 6″. The jointing of the staves, glueing and splicing to the strings has been described under a 7″ cylinder. Also preparing the steps and stepping up is the same as has been explained for a 7″ and 12″ cylinder, at Plates 22 and 25.

Measuring for jointing the rail at the bench. The first length [11′ 6″], for jointing the rail, is shown taken from spring of turnout to the spring of cylinder; the second length [2′ 8″] is taken from the spring of cylinder to the face of last rise landing; the third length [4′ 9¼″] is taken from the face of last rise landing to the spring of quarter cylinder; and the fourth and last length [5′ 1½″] is taken from the spring of quarter cylinder to wall. All these lengths, and also the dimensions of pitch-board [7″×10″], should be entered in the order book.

PLATE 32.

Plate 32. [Scale ¾″=1′]. *Exhibits the construction of face-moulds for a stair-case, Plate 31.*

Fig. 1. *Shows the plan of the center line of rail, and the tangents for the same.*

Draw the diameter line *AE*, and the radius *OC*, indefinite, and at right angles to each other; then with 12¾″ for a radius, and *O* as a center, draw the semi-circle *ACE*, for the center of rail; the dotted line shows the face of cylinder or outer string line.

Enclose the semi-circle with the rectilineal parallelogram to tangent the semi-circle at the points *A*, *C* and *E*, and we have the two square parallelograms *OABC* and *OCDE*, on plan. Prolong tangents *BA* and *DE*, to the right for the direction of straight rail. The position of risers in the semi-circle are the same as at Fig. 3. Plate 31; the face of No. 14 and 19 rise is 6″ from the spring of cylinder. The balusters No. 1, 2, 3, &c., are spaced off on the center line of rail and drawn normal to the curve at their centers.

Fig. 2. *Shows the elevation of tangents; they are unfolded.*

Let *XX* indicate the edge of drawing board. Make *AB*, *BC*, *CD* and *DE*, each equal *AB*, *BC*, *CD* and *DE* on plan, Fig. 1. Perpendicular to *XX*, draw *AF*, *BG*, *CH*, *DJ* and *EK* indefinite. Now elevate Nos. 13, 14, 15, 16, 17, 18, 19 and 20 risers and treads, keeping the face of No. 14 and 19 rise 6″ from the spring lines *AF* and *EK*.

Through the center of baluster *SOO*, on the right, and *OO*, on the left, draw the inclination for the under side of rail; parallel with *OO*, draw the center of rail, cutting *EK* and *JD* at *L* and *M*, on the left. And on the right, cutting *AF* and *BG*, at *N* and *P*; connect *PM*, cutting *CH* at *Q*. At right angles to *CH*, draw *QR* and *LS*, cutting *DJ* at *T* and *U*; then *RL* is the height of the wreath-piece for the quarter circle, from *C* to *E*, on plan, Fig. 1; and the height for the quarter circle from *A* to *C* is the same as shown at *NV*. Prolong *LM* to intersect *RQ* at *W*; also prolong *QM* to intersect *EK* at *Y*.

Make *LZ* equal to the chord *AC*, Fig. 1; at *M* set off the half width of rail on each side of *DJ*; parallel with *DJ* draw the half width of rail, cutting the tangent *MQ* at 2, and the tangent *LM* at 3. From *T*, and at right angles to *LW*, draw *T* 4; from *U*, and perpendicular to *YQ*, draw *U* 5.

Bevels. Let 6 6 indicate the edge of drawing board, and the dotted line indicate a gauge line parallel with the edge of board. Make 7 8 perpendicular to 6 6, and equal to the radius [12¾″] *OC*, Fig. 1. Make 7 9 equal to *T* 4, and 7 10 equal *U* 5; draw 8 9 and 8 10 prolonged to 6 6; the angle at 9 gives the joint bevel for the shank, and the angle at 10 gives the bevel for center joint.

Fig. 3. *Shows the face-mould.*

At any convenient place on the pattern paper draw *JD* indefinite; make *DE* equal *LM*, Fig. 2; let *EJ* equal 6″ more or less, for length of shank. With *E* for a center, and the distance *RZ*, Fig. 2, as a radius, draw arc at *C*; again, with *D* for a center, and the tangent *MQ*, Fig. 2, as a radius, draw arc intersecting at *C;* connect *DC* parallel with tangents *DE* and *DC;* draw *CO* and *EO*, establishing the center *O* for the trammel, and the parallelogram *OEDC* on the cutting plane that will agree when in position with the parallelogram *OABC* on plan Fig. 1.

Proof. If the diagonal *OD* equals the distance *ZY*, Fig. 2, the angle at *D* must be correct.

Prolong *OE* and *OC*. Make *EF* equal *MW*, Fig. 2; draw *OF* produced, through *O*, and at right angles to *OF*, draw *AB*, for the direction of the major axis; make *O 2* equal *OC*, Fig. 1, (12¾″), Let 2 3 and 2 4 each equal the half width of rail (1¾″); make *C* 5 and *C* 6, each equal *M* 3, Fig. 2. Also *E* 7 and *E* 8, each equal *M* 2, Fig. 2. Parallel with *EJ*, draw 7 9, and 8 10; make joints at *J* and *C* perpendicular to the tangents *DJ* and *DC*. Now pivot the trammel at *O*, with the arms centered on the axis line *AB;* then set from pencil to minor pin the distance *O 2*, (12¾″), place the pencil at *C*, and slide the major pin until both pins drop into the grooves; then fasten the major pin, and trace the elliptic curve through the points *C2E*, for the center line of rail; proceed in the same manner to trace the concave and convex curves of face-mould.

At section *M* and *N*, the bevels are shown applied through the center of plank; the shaded part shows the amount of over wood to be removed, and also the thickness of plank required for the wreath-piece.

FIG 4. Repeats Fig. 3, the lettering being the same, and indicates the face-mould, Fig. 3, turned over, and the tangents lined off on the opposite side; the figure is introduced here to show the learner how the bevels are applied, so as to mate them for a platform twist. Observe at *N*, Fig. 3, the bevel is applied so as to pitch the shank *EJ*, down; and at section *N*, Fig. 4, the bevel is shown applied from the face of plank, and the reverse way, so as to pitch the shank *EJ*, up; and at the shank, section *M* shows the bevel applied so as to pitch the joint at *C*, down; and at Fig. 3, section *M* shows the bevel applied so as to pitch the joint at *C*, up, thus mating the two crooks. Fig. 3 forms the wreath-piece landing on the platform; and Fig. 4, the wreath-piece off the platform. The learner, by trying the two crooks together, will see if the bevels are applied correctly.

Fig. 5. Shows the elevation of the two wreath-pieces; the tangents being folded.

Fig. 2 shows the tangents unfolded; It will be obvious to the learner, after a little study, that for a platform twist, all the lines necessary to obtain the face-mould may be found in this way, without the trouble of unfolding all the tangents, See Fig. 2 Plate 29; also, Figs. 9 and 11, Plate 33; unless it be required to find the lengths of odd balusters; then the development of tangents together with the treads and risers becomes necessary.

How to obtain the length of odd balusters. Return to Fig. 1; prolong tangents *AB* and *ED* to the left; make *BF* and *DG*, each equal *WT*, Fig. 2. Connect *FC* and *GC*, for the directors; from the center of balusters 2, 3, 4, draw lines parallel to *CF*, intersecting the tangents *AB* and *BC*, at 9, 10 and 11. Also from the center of balusters 6, 7 and 8, draw lines parallel to the director *GC*, intersecting the tangents at the points 12, 13 and 14, as shown.

Now we have the position of balusters on the tangents on plan, relative to their position on the tangents, on the cutting plane.

Return to elevation, Fig. 2, and transfer the location of each baluster from the tangents on plan, Fig. 1, to corresponding position in elevation, Fig. 2, as shown at 9, 10, 11, 12, &c. Set off the under side of rail parallel to the line of tangents; draw the center of baluster perpendicular to the treads, to intersect the under side of rail, as 9 2, 10 3, 11 4, 12 5, &c.

Now as the under side of rail is drawn through the center of the regular short balusters at *OO*, and the length of a regular short baluster is 2′ 1″ from the top of step to the under side of rail measured at its center; then the baluster marked No. 9, will be ½″ longer than a regular short one; and the baluster marked No. 10, will equal 4½″ longer; and No. 11 baluster will equal 1½″ longer; No. 12 will be 3½″ longer; No. 13 will equal ½″ shorter; No. 14 will equal 1¾″ longer; and No. 15 baluster will be ¼″ shorter than a regular short baluster, 2′ 0¾″, from the top of No. 18 step to the under side of rail at the center of baluster, and a regular long baluster will be half a rise or 3½″ longer than a regular short one.   The length of short baluster is taken for the standard because the under side of rail is drawn through the center of balusters *OO* and *OO;* and the length of balusters at those points is naught, as shown in elevation.*

Figs. 6, 7 and 8.   *Show the plan, elevation and face-mould for the turnout.*

Fig. 6.   *Shows the plan.*

Let *D* indicate the center of newel, set off 12″ to the face of outer string, and ¾″ more to the center of rail at *L.*   Draw *LA* indefinite.   If the post be a pedestal newel, set the same to show the two sides to the best advantage; draw *DB* at right angles to the side of newel; make the end of wreath-piece at *C* to enter the newel ½″.   Make *BA* equal *BC,* locating the point *A* in this case 5″ from the face of No. 4 rise.

From *A* and *C,* draw lines perpendicular to *AB* and *BC,* converging at *O;* then with *O* for a center, and *OA* as a radius, draw the center line of rail from *A* to *C;* then *AB* and *BC* will be tangent to the curve at the points *A* and *C.*   The dotted line at *A* shows the face of outer string, and makes the radius ¾″ less for the curve of cylinder or 2′ 1¼″.   Locate the short baluster on No. 4 step, and space off the intermediate balusters towards the newel.

Now curve the risers to suit the spacing of balusters and position of newel; parallel with the tangents *BA* and *BC,* draw *AP* and *CP* for the parallelogram *PCBA* on plan; from *C,* and perpendicular to *AB* prolonged, draw *CL.*

Fig. 7.   *Shows the elevation of tangents, they are folded; also the treads and risers.*

Let *XX* indicate the edge of drawing board.   Make *AB* equal *AB* on plan Fig. 6, perpendicular to *XX,* draw *AR* and *BD* indefinite; now elevate Nos. 1, 2, 3 and 4 risers and treads, being careful to keep the face of No. 4 rise 5″ from the spring *AR.*

From the top of No. 1 step set up 6″ to the underside of rail and 2½″ additional, plus the height of a rise (15½″) to the center of rail at F, making 15½″ from the floor line to the center of rail. Then the height of newel from the floor line to the center of rail will equal 15½″ plus the length of a short baluster (2′ 1″), or (1′ 3½″+2′ 1″=3′ 4½″) equal to 3′ 4½″.

---

*The standard lengths for balusters, as furnished to the market, are cut 2′ 4″ to 2′ 6″ for short ones, and 2′ 8″ to 2′ 10″ for long balusters, in proportion of one short baluster to three long ones; the standard length for solid newels is 4′ 0″, or cut in scantling lengths of 8′, 10′, 12′ and 16′. and in squares of 5s, 6s, 7s, 8s and 10s; for angle newels, the lengths run from 5′ 6″ to 6′ 6″ long.   Plank for stair-builders' use is sawed 2⅛″, 2⅜″, 3⅛″, 3⅝″, 4⅛″, 4⅝″, 5⅛″ and 6⅛″ in thickness, from forest timber, straight in the grain, and free from shakes, knots and sap wood.

Draw *FE* parallel to *XX*, cutting *BD* at *W;* through the center of balusters *OO* draw the under side of rail; parallel to *OO* draw the inclination for the center of rail, cutting the spring and angle lines at *R* and *K*, and also cutting *FE* at *J;* draw *KE*.* Make *EQ* equal the diagonal *BP*, Fig. 6; make *EM* equal the chord *AC* on plan Fig. 6; let *RN* equal twice *KW;* make *WP* equal *BL*, Fig. 6, from *P*, and at right angles to *GJ* prolonged draw *PH;* make *EL* equal the diagonal *BO*, Fig. 6; draw *NQ* prolonged to intersect the perpendicular from *L* at *Z*.

As the radius on plan in this case is 2′ 2″ for the center line of rail, it will require a large trammel, and also more room to draw the curves of mould; therefore we will find points in the elliptic curve, from the chord line, through which to trace the curves of face-mould.

Return to plan Fig. 6.   From the center *O* draw the half width of rail equally on each side of the center line (1¾″).   Make *BJ* equal *WJ*, Fig. 7; connect *J C* for the directing ordinate; draw the chord *AC;* bisect *AC* at *R;* bisect *RC* and *RA* at *T* and *S*. From the points *A, S, R, T* and *C* draw ordinates parallel to *JC*, cutting the inside, center and outside of rail on plan at the points 2, 3 and 4; from *A*, and at right angles to *CJ* prolonged, draw *AK;* draw *CM* indefinite and at right angles to *JC*, cutting the curve of rail on plan at 5 and 6.

Bevels.   Return to elevation Fig. 7; let *YY* indicate a base line; draw 2 2 parallel to *YY;* draw 3 14 perpendicular to *XX*, and equal to *AK*, Fig. 6.   Make 3 5 equal to *CL*, Fig. 6; make 3 6 equal *HP;* also make 3 7 equal the height *ER*.   Draw 14 7 and 5 6 prolonged.   The angle at 7 gives the bevel for the joint connecting the newel, and the angle at 6 gives the bevel for the shank joint.   Parallel to 2 2, draw the half width of rail (1¾″), cutting the hypothenuse 5 6 at 10; also make 2 9 and 2 15 each equal *C*5 and *C*6, Fig. 6.   From 9 and 15, and parallel to 2 2, draw 9 12 and 15 16.

Fig. 8.   *Shows the face-mould.*

Draw *GJ* indefinite; make *RK* equal *RK*, Fig. 7; with *R* for a center and the distance *RM*, Fig. 7, as a radius, draw arc at *C;* again, with *K* for a center, and *KE*, Fig. 7, as a radius, draw arc intersecting at *C;* draw *KC* prolonged.   Parallel to *KR* and *KC* draw *CO* and *RO* for the parallelogram *OCKR* on the cutting plane.

Proof.   The diagonal *OK* must equal the distance *QN*, Fig. 7; if so, the angle of tangents at *K* is correct.

Make *KJ* equal *KJ*, Fig. 7; join *JC* for the director; draw the chord *RC;* bisect *RC* at *A;* bisect *AR* and *AC* at *S* and *T;* from the points *T, A, S* and *R* draw ordinates indefinite and parallel to the director *JC*.   Now transfer the points 2, 3, 4 on ordinates on plan Fig. 6 to corresponding ordinates on face-mould, as *A*. 2, 3, 4; make shank *RG* equal 6″; make joint at *G* at right angles to tangent *GK;* make joint at *C* perpendicular to the director *JC;* make *C*5 and *C*6 each equal 7 12 and 7 16, Fig. 7, respectively; make *G* 7 and *G* 8 each equal 6 10, Fig. 7.   Prolong the diagonal *KO* to equal the distance *NZ*, Fig. 7, at *D;* draw *DR* at 9 and 10 for the points of contact.   Now trace the curve for the concave side of mould through the points 2, 2, 2, &c., and through the points 4, 4, 4, &c., for the convex side, using a flexible strip.

---

*The intention here is to show how the face-mould may be drawn for a turnout, when both tangents are inclining.

The section at *N,* shows the bevel found in the angle at 6, Fig. 7; the block pattern determines the thickness of plank required; the section at *B,* shows the rail larger than the regular size, because the joint 5 6, on plan, Fig. 6, is drawn oblique to the curve of rail on plan, thus increasing the section of rail on the joint; if the joint was made on the line *OC,* then the joint would be normal to the curve; but we have thought best in this case, to make the joint at right angles to the director *JG.* instead of the tangent *BC;* for this reason the joint will be plumb, or perpendicular to a horizontal surface when the wreath-piece is elevated into position; then if the wreath-piece be required to miter into a cap, the casing in the wreath-piece can be forced at right angles to the joint.

The bevel applied at section *B,* is found in the angle at 7, Fig. 7. Observe the bevels in this case do not cross the tangents. If the rail be required to miter into a cap, as shown at Fig. 9, then return to Fig. 7, make *EU* equal the amount required for miter [1¾″], as shown at Fig. 9; through *U,* and parallel to *AR,* draw *US;* prolong *KE* to *V;* return to Fig. 8, and prolong *KC* on face-mould, Fig. 8, to equal *EV,* Fig. 7, as *C* 13; draw the joint parallel to 5 6, draw 5 11 and 6 12 parallel to *C* 13 for the amount of wood required to make the miter.

Observe at Fig. 7, the tangent *KV,* drops below the horizontal line at *U;* this will cause the block pattern at section *B,* to be raised up the distance *UV,* above the centering of the plank at that joint.

This method of inclining the lower tangent at the newel, allows the wreath-piece to fall lower so as to accommodate a shorter newel post, but must not incline too much, as the wreath-piece should ease off into the cap, graceful as possible.

Six [6″] inches is allowed on shanks for straight wood, and must be deducted from the lengths shown in elevation, Fig. 2, Plate 31, when jointing the straight rail.

Fig. 9. *Shows the plan of the turnout and the three swelled steps.*

The treads on the circle are spaced off equal to the regular treads, and graduated on the wall string, as shown. The nosings may be curved by using a pliable strip thinned down at one end; the nosings at the wall strings should be at right angles to the strings.

This drawing should be made full size on suitable paper, then the outline of steps can be transferred to the plank by pricking through the paper with an awl; also, the stair-builder can draw the face-mould on the same.

PLATE 33.

Plate 33. [Scale ¾″=1 foot]. *Exhibits the treatment of the cylinder, Fig. 3, Plate 31, when the outer or front string is of hard wood, and the cylinder is veneered.*

Fig. 1. Shows the length of staves for the cylinder, Fig. 4, Plate 31; laid off in the same way as has been explained for a 7″ and 12″ cylinder.

Fig. 2. Shows the cylinder 24″ diameter, the veneer is to be bent over a drum, and the staves 1, 2, 3, glued on the back with the joints perpendicular to the treads. At *A* and *B,* is shown the splice connecting the straight part, and is intended to be glued and screwed from the back, as shown.

Fig. 3. Shows the veneer. **AB** is the stretchout of semicircle, draw **AD** and **BE** perpendicular to **AB**; from the center **C**, set off No. 16 rise 4¾", and No. 17 rise 5¼"; then elevate Nos. 15, 14, 18 and 19 risers and treads, making No. 19 rise 6¼" from the spring line **AD**, and No. 14 rise 5¾" from the spring line **LE**.

The joints to connect the straight strings are made at No. 14 and 19 rise; the veneer is made the same thickness throughout, and the staves 1, 2, 3, &c., are shown extended beyond the veneer to allow for trimming off, and to have room for a screw to bring the stave and veneer down close on the drum. At **G** and **F**. the stave is shown wider, and should be glued to the veneer before bending over the drum; keep the joint of stave to the springing lines **AD** and **LE**; after the two staves **G** and **F,** have been glued to the veneer, and the glueing is thoroughly dry, dampen the veneer with hot water; then clamp one end to the drum, being careful to keep the spring line on the veneer over the spring line on the drum. Then bend the veneer over the drum gently, and at the same time screwing down a stave at intervals temporarily, to bring the veneer down close to the drum; if the other spring line agrees with the spring on the drum, then clamp firmly to the drum, and leave stand until the veneer is dry, then glue and rub the staves to place, using a screw at each end to bring all down firm.

This makes clean, nice work; the tread and rise is cut out, after being lifted from the drum. When laying off the lines on the veneer use a lead pencil; if a knife be used there will be danger of causing the veneer to kink.

Fig. 4. *Shows another method of doing the same thing by bending the veneer* **AA** *over a drum* **B;** *then kerfing and steaming the back part* **CC,** *and bending it over the veneer.*

In this case the back part **CC** must be of an even thickness throughout, say 1½", and the kerfs should be extended beyond the springing lines as shown, and to within ⅛" of the back, if possible; the kerfs must be cut perpendicular to the treads, and made from straight-grained stuff; the kerfed part should be well softened by steaming, then bent over the drum and let stand until dry, being careful to have the springing lines on the kerfed part parallel with the spring lines on the drum. After it has set, lift from the drum, tack on two braces, then soften the veneer and bend over the drum, being careful to keep the plumb lines on the veneer to the spring lines on the drum; leave the veneer in this way until dry; then glue and clamp the kerfed part down firmly to the veneer. *The distance apart to make the kerfs so as to close is shown next.*

Fig. 5. [Scale ¼" equals 1'.]

Take a strip, the thickness being equal to the thickness of plank intended to be kerfed, say 1½"; run a gauge line on to whatever is allowed to remain solid, say ⅛", shown by the dotted line **AB**; then make a kerf **OC** with the saw that is to be used for the kerfing. Now draw the arc of a circle **DE** to whatever radius required, in this case 12½"; then through the center **O** draw a straight line **DO**, and place the strip to the line, keeping the kerf to the center at **O**; now fasten with two nails at 2 and 3; then move the other end **F** until the kerf will close, and mark the edge of strip cutting the arc at **H**, then **DH** will be the distance apart to space off the kerf. The saw should have guides clamped to the sides, so the kerfs will be all the same depth, for good work.

Fig. 6. *Shows another method for constructing the cylinder.*

The piece intended to bend over the drum *BB* to form the cylinder should be straight in the grain, and be made of an even thickness throughout. The dadoes are cut perpendicular to the treads, and all to the same depth. This is very speedily and neatly done on the saw table with a dado head. The piece to be dadoed can be arranged across the table to the proper inclination in a frame, and in a few minutes the work is done. One or two grooves should be cut beyond the spring lines *CC*, as shown. This is done to prevent too sudden departure from the straight to the circular part, and thus avoid perhaps fracture. The string should be laid out with a pencil so as not to abraid the surface, as that may cause fracture or kinks. The laying out should be done before bending, but not cut out until the work is lifted from the drum.

After the dadoing is done the work require to be well softened by by steam or hot water; a steam box is very handy and economical for work of this kind. By turning on the live steam the work is soon softened, and the moisture is speedily evaporated from the work. After the work is sufficiently softened clamp one end to the drum, keeping the spring lines opposite, and gently bend over the drum, adding a stay every few inches to avoid kinks, and clamp the other end firmly to the drum, being sure the spring line on the work comes opposite or parallel to the spring line on the drum.

Now size the dadoes with thin glue, and leave the work in this shape to dry out. Then fit hard wood keys into the grooves, glue and drive them in lightly, not too hard, as the work may raise off the drum and cause kinks. After the glue is hard dress off the keys to the curve; then glue and nail on the back of cylinder two lines of hard wood strips ¼″ thick and 2″ wide; one line ⅜″ from the lower edge, and the other near the internal angle of the tread and rise. The strips laminated in two thicknesses would be best, as shown at 2 and 3.

The distance apart to make the dadoes and the thickness of veneer, or solid part, is explained for Plate 28, Fig. 6.

This treatment of circular strings for any circle over 10″ radius makes good and substantial work. All circular wall strings should be constructed in this way.   *e*

Fig. 8. Shows the lower end of cylinder increased in thickness to form grounds for plastering and offer solid nailing for a heavy plaster moulding *D; B* shows the lagging glued on to the back of cylinder, and the moulding *D*, is shown one-half full size; *F* shows the veneer; *A*, the stave, and *C*, the plastering. This heavy moulding will have to be constructed same as the wreath-piece of a hand rail, and fit to the cylinder in the shop and put up after the plastering is done.

At Fig. 7, the tangents *AB* and *BC* are shown for the plaster moulding *D*, the radius for the center of which is 1½″ more than the radius of cylinder, or 13½″.

Fig. 9. *Shows the elevation of tangents; they are folded.*

Let *XX* indicate the edge of drawing board. Make *AB* equal *OA*, Fig. 7, [13½″]; perpendicular to *XX*, draw *AC* and *BD* indefinite; anywhere on *XX*, place the pitchboard, and draw the inclination indefinite, cutting *AC* at *E*, and *BD* at *F*; return to Fig. 8, draw *CJ* perpendicular to the treads, and to intersect the inclination *GF* at *J*; from *J*, and perpendicular to *EL* prolonged, draw *JK*; then *KL* is the height that the wreath-piece will raise for the quarter circle from *A* to *C*, Fig. 7. Now make *EC* equal the height *KL*, Fig. 8; perpendicular to *AC*, draw *CD* prolonged, intersecting *EF* prolonged at *G*; from *D*, and perpendicular to *GE*, draw *DH*; parallel with *CD*, draw *FJ*; draw *DJ* indefinite; From *E*, and at right angles to *DJ*, draw *EK*; make *B* 2 equal half width of the plaster moulding [2½″]; parallel with *BD*, draw the half width of moulding, cutting the tangents *FE* and *DJ*, at 3 and 4; Parallel with *XX*, draw *EL* indefinite; make *EL* equal the chord *AC*, Fig. 7; make *JM* equal *JC*.

Bevels. From the edge of board **XX**, run the gauge line **ab**; perpendicular to **XX**, draw **bf** equal to the radius **OA**, Fig. 7, (13½″). Make **bh** equal **DH**, and **bg** equal **EK**; draw **fh** and **fg** prolonged, to **XX** for convenience when setting the bevels.

Fig. 10. *Shows the face-mould.*

At any convenient place on the pattern paper, lay down the steel square, and draw the right angle **JHC** indefinite. Make **HF** and **HE**, each equal **HF** and **HE**, Fig. 9; with **F** for a center, and **DJ**, Fig. 9, as a radius, draw arc intersecting **HC** at **C**; Connect **FC**; parallel with **FC** and **FE**, draw **EO** and **CO**, establishing the center **O**, and the parallelogram **OEFC**, on the cutting plane.

Proof. The diagonal **OF** must equal the distance **LM**, Fig. 9, if so, the angle of tangents at **F** is correct.

Make **EN** equal **FG**, Fig. 9; draw **NO** prolonged; through **O**, and at right angles to **ON**, draw **PQ** for the position of trammel; make joints at **J** and **C**, at right angles to the tangents **JF** and **FC**. Make **O** 2 equal the radius **OA**, Fig. 7 [13½″]. Let 2 3 and 2 4, each equal the half width of moulding (2⅛″); make **C** 5 and **C** 6, each equal **F** 3, Fig. 9, and **E** 7 and **E** 8, each equal **D** 4, Fig. 9; parallel with **JF**, draw 8 10 and 7 9 for the shank.

Now pivot the trammel at **O**, and trace the elliptic curves of face-mould as has been described for the preceding Plates. At **R** and **S**, the bevels are shown applied to cross the tangents; the block pattern shows the twist of rail and the thickness of plank required; the shaded parts show the surplus wood to be removed.

Figs. 11 and 12. *Show another method how to construct the wreath part of moulding by making both tangents equal, and using a cripple joint at the shank.*

Fig. 11. *Shows the elevation of tangents; they are folded.*

Let **XX** indicate a base line; make **AB** equal **OC**, Fig. 7; draw **AC** and **BD** perpendicular to **XX**; draw the inclination of the center line of rail as **EZ**; make **EC** equal the height **LK**, Fig. 3; draw **CD** and **EL** parallel to **XX**; **EL** cuts **BD** at **N**; bisect **ND** at **F**; connect **CF**; draw **FE** prolonged; make **EL** equal the chord **AC**, Fig. 7. From the center **D**, draw arc to tangent **FC** as **DH**; join **HC** for the bevel for both joints; parallel to **BD**, draw the half width of rail to intersect **FE** at 3. On **EZ**, set off 6″ to **S** for shank; make joint at **S** perpendicular to **EZ**; prolong **FE** to allow over wood for cripple joint, say to **J**; through **J**, draw 4 5 perpendicular to **FJ** for a temporary joint on shank.

Fig. 12. *Shows the face-mould.*

Make **EC** equal **CL**, Fig. 11; with **C** and **E** for centers, and **EF**, Fig. 11, as a radius, draw arcs intersecting at **F** and **O**; draw **FE**, **FC**, **EO** and **CO** for the parallelogram **OEFC** on the plane of plank. *Proof.* The diagonal **OF** must equal the diagonal **OB** on plan Fig. 7; if so, the angle of tangents at **F** must be correct; prolong **FE** to **J**, equal to **EJ**, Fig. 11. Prolong the radial lines **OC** and **OE** indefinite; make joints at **C** and **J** perpendicular to the tangents **FC** and **FJ**; make **C** 5 and **C** 6, also **E** 7 and **E** 8 each equal **F** 3, Fig. 11. As both tangents in elevation are the same length in this case, the diagonal **OF** becomes the direction of minor axis. Make **O** 2 equal **OA**, Fig. 7, for the semi-minor axis, Let 2 3 and 2 4 each equal the half width of rail (2″). Now pivot the trammel at *O*, with the arms at right angles to *O* 2; then set from pencil to minor pin on the rod to equal *O* 4, and place the pencil in the point at 6, then slide the major pin until both pins drop into the grooves, then fasten the major pin and trace the curve for the convex side of mould through the points 6, 4, 3; proceed in like manner to trace the curves for the concave and center lines of face-mould ; draw 7 9 and 8 10 parallel to *EJ*.

Sections *R* and *S* show the bevels applied. Observe the block pattern is first applied the same distance down from the face of crook at both joints; then work off the sides of shank to the joint bevel; afterwards apply the cripple bevel shown in the angle at 4, and cut the cripple joint. See first that all lines on the temporary joint are squared over from the joint on to the upper and lower and also the vertical sides of shank, so that when the temporary joint is cut away the lines required on the cripple joint may be easily carried over the joint again.

Now slide the block pattern down on the cripple joint the distance *JS*, Fig. 11; then lay off the direction of straight moulding at right angles to the cripple joint, and ease the angle to please the eye, and fit the lower end of string.

PLATE 34.

Plate 34. *Exhibits a two-story stair-case with a half pace winding* in the first flight, and a double quarter pace winding flight in the second story. Figs. 1 to 4 are drawn to a ¼″ scale [scale ¼″=1 foot]; and Figs. 5 and 6 are drawn to a ¾″ scale [scale ¾″=1 foot].*

The height of first story from top to top of joist is 11′ 4″; the hall is 6′ 0″ wide in the rough; the joist is 9″ deep in the second story; the back door under stairs is 6′ 6″ high; and there is 10′ 8″ at the starting, and at the landing 5′ 8″ to the door jamb.

The height of second story from top to top of joist is 10′ 0″; depth of joist in the third floor equals 9″; the soffit of stairs will clear the window in the second story as they land with a quarter pace winding, and the window is set plumb over the opening below on the one side; the horizontal space between the walls for the stairs equals 11′ 4″.

The newel is 7″×7″, to be set in the center of hall; size of rail 4″×2½″; balusters 2″×2″; height of base exclusive of the moulding is 8″ for the first story, and 7″ in the second story.

Fig. 1. *Shows the plan of the first flight.*

The height of story is 11′ 0″, which reduced to inches equals 136″, divided by 17 risers [136″÷17=8″] equals 8″ for each rise, if we allow 25″ for a constant, the relative proportion of

---

*The plan of the above stair-case is not intended as a model for the young man to copy from in practice, for winders in small and contracted halls are objectionable, and should be avoided at all times if possible. The grand circular or elliptical stair-case can be made an object of beauty, that cannot be excelled in stair-casing, in that case having more room, the winders can be increased in width at the outer string, and thus give to the rail easy flowing curves, and a gentle ascent to the grade of steps; but as the stair-builder has to adapt the stair-case to the space allotted, hence he will have to exercise his judgment as to what will suit the space, and give the best results; the above plan is given as an extreme, and is intended to show how such stairs may be treated, the principle being the same for all.

tread to rise will equal 9″ [25″—(8″+8″=16″)=9″], then the pitch of stairs for the first flight will equal 8″✕9″, if there be room to allow a tread equal to 9″.

The well hole is in the center of hall, and the cylinder is 8″ diameter, the winders should be laid off on heavy paper. First lay off the line of rough walls; parallel with the walls, draw the wall strings, allowing ⅜″ for plaster on brick walls, and ⅛″ on stud partitions, then ⅞″ for the thickness of base, making 1¼″ for the stud partition wall, and 1⅜″ for the brick walls, that must be allowed from the rough walls to face of the wall strings; the thickness of wall strings is usually 1⅜″, this thickness allows sufficient to work the grounds on the solid for the plastering.

Draw the cylinder in the center 3′ 0″ from the walls; draw the outer string; set off in this case from the string line 14″ for the regular tread line around the cylinder. Right here the workman may have to make several trials in spacing off the winders on the walking line, either shifting the walking line further out, or bringing it nearer to the well hole, so as to locate the first rise to admit an casing and the finish around door at the starting; the walking line should not be over 18″ from the string line, and may be located at any point between, the nearer to the string line the better, as then the winders at the narrow ends will be increased in width.

Now with the dividers set to 9″ begin at the center (No. 12 rise) of semi-circle, and space off towards the starting 11 threads on the walking line, which leaves about 18″ from No. 1 rise to the face of door-jamb, to allow for the "trim" and easement on the wall string. Also, step off towards the landing five (5) full treads, and we have 9″ from the face of No. 17 rise to the door-jamb; this is too scant if it could be avoided, but less has to do in many cases.

In all cases for a half-pace winding stairs at the center (No. 12 rise) there should be a rise, or the center of a tread. In locating the risers at the outer string first space off the balusters around the cylinder, beginning at the center of cylinder (No. 12 rise in this case), and spacing them equal to half a tread or less; in this case they are less, so the balusters will appear evenly spaced. Nos. 8, 9, 14 and 15 threads may be graduated to help the casing on the lower edge of string, while the balusters, instead of being over the rise, may sit over on the treads to show them evenly spaced, as shown at step No. 17, Fig. 16, Plate 15. In stairs cramped for room this has to be done. When the points for the risers are spaced off on the cylinder and front string to connect the "flyers" or straight treads, then draw the face of risers to suit the balusters and through the points just found on the walking line to intersect the wall string. It will be observed the rise Nos. 11 and 13 do not radiate to the center of cylinder, and Nos. 9, 10, 14 and 15 cut the front string very oblique. This should be avoided whenever possible to do so by allowing the risers to radiate from the center of cylinder and allowing but one graduating step outside the cylinder. This case has been introduced to give the learner an idea how to manage a flight when the steps have to be crowded. In small buildings, for want of space, the stairs are often too much crowded.

Observe, that the temporary step patterns for Nos. 8, 9, 10 and 11 winders will answer for Nos. 15, 14, 13 and 12 winders by reversing the patterns. For the trimming of the well in the second story, allow 6″ from the back of No. 17 rise to the joist, or 5′ 0″ from the wall, as shown. The width to trim the well in the second story at the starting of the second flight will equal the half width of hall (3′ 0″) plus the radius of cylinder (4″), and the thickness of fascia (1″) [3′ 0″+4″+1′]=3′ 5″] equals 3′ 5″ as shown on plan.

The trimmer at the starting of second flight should be at the back of cylinder, and at right angles to the wall, if that will allow enough head room. In this case there will be ample head room, the face of trimmer being over the middle of first tread, thus allowing the ceiling to carry around level to back of cylinder starting in the second flight, and at right angles to the level fascia. The soffit of the second flight will then curve down at right angles to the face string, instead of following the twisting line of treads and risers. The face of trimmer is shown 8′ 7½″ from the face of joist at the landing, or 8′ 7½″ from the wall; the landing will then be trimmed out to 2′ 7″ by 3′ 7½″ in the rough.

The dotted lines show the manner of putting in the bearers; dry 3″ by 4″ scantling should be selected for this purpose, neatly cut, fit and well nailed, and rough brackets, with the grain perpendicular to the treads. The brackets are nailed to the bearers, and through the back of rise into the tread.

Fig. 2. *Shows the elevation of threads and risers.*

AB shows the story rod; the height of story 11′ 4″ is divided into 17 risers; the first length (6′ 8″) to measure for the straight rail is shown taken from the spring of turnout to the spring of cylinder. No. 2 length (2′ 1″ is taken from the spring of cylinder to plumb with the face of last rise, No. 17, and the length of level (3′ 9″) is taken from the face of No. 17 rise to the spring of cylinder starting of the second flight.

Fig. 3. *Shows plan of the flight landing in the third story.*

The height equals 10′ 0″, being reduced to inches equals 120″, and divided by 15, the number of risers for a trial, equals 8″ for each rise, and the relative width of thread will equal 9″.

The well will be trimmed to the width of that in the second story 3′ 5″ wide, and the space between the walls is 11′ 4″; allowing the space for the second flight to equal 11′ 4″ by 3′ 5″ in the rough. Allow 3′ 0″ at each of the quarter pace winders to the center of cylinder, plus 4½″ for graduating the treads at the spring of cylinders (3′ 0″+3′ 0″+4½″+4½″=6′ 9″), which equals 6′ 9″ to be deducted from the whole space, 11′ 4″ (11′ 4″ —6′ 9″=4′ 7″) equals 4′ 7″, to be divided by the width of a tread, (9″) gives us six straight treads; that will place a rise in the center of well. In this case, No. 8 rise comes in the center.

We will make the walking line 14″ from the face of front string on trial.

Now, with the dividers set to the width of a tread (9″), begin at No. 8 rise and step off the treads either way on the walking line; the face of Nos. 1 and 15 rise comes on line with the face of level front string. This will answer very well; from No. 5 and No. 11 riser, space off the balusters in the cylinder to equal the spacing of the balusters on the straight steps (4½″) or a little less in small cylinders. The spaces in this case are less. Nos. 1 and 15 rise should be curved to suit the circular nosing without too much peak at the point of miter, and also help the casing at the joining of the cylinder with the level string. It will be observed that Nos. 4 and 11 winders are the same, only reversed. The front of the former is back of the latter, and one set of patterns will answer for the winders of both quarter paces in this case, thus saving time and material when cutting them from the plank, and also adds to the general appearance of the stairs.

After the measures are taken for stairs of this kind, the first thing the stair-builder should do is to make a plan to a scale of say ¾″ to equal one foot. By so doing fewer mistakes will occur, and much time be saved.

For the head-room. Count down from the landing 12 risers at 8″ each equals 96″ ($\frac{96}{12}″=8′\ 0″$) equals 8′ 0″, minus the joist, flooring and plastering, say 11″, will equal 7′ 1″ from the top of No. 3 step to the line of ceiling; this will answer.

Fig. 4. *Shows the elevations of treads, risers and strings.*

The story rod **AB** is divided into 15 risers. **SSS,** &c., show the springing of the cylinders. The measure for cutting the straight rail is shown taken from spring to spring of cylinder. No. 4 length is shown 7′ 0¾″, and No. 5 length (6′ 7″) is taken from the spring of cylinder landing to spring of quarter cylinder, and from quarter cylinder to wall 3′ 0″, measured on plan. The raking lengths are taken at the bench, and the level lengths after the stairs are stepped up, and all entered in the order book.

Fig. 5. *Exhibits plan of No. 1 cylinder.* [Scale ¾″=1′] Showing the angle that the steps and risers make with the outer string and cylinder. The nosing line is drawn parallel with the risers, and intersects with the nosing line, which is drawn parallel with the face string; the face of risers is drawn to intersect the bracket line, determining two points through which to draw the miters of nosings. It will be observed at No. 10 step the point of miter is very acute. To avoid so long and pointed miter it will be better to round it off, and connect the nosing and scotia of step with the return nosing, making a joint at right angles to the face string, as shown at **A.** The nosings of Nos. 11 and 12 steps are rounded off to connect the return nosings.

Fig. 6. [Scale ¾″=1 foot]. Shows the cylinder connecting the straight string; the shaded part shows the staves, the angle that the risers make with the face string, and the cylinder, for the cut-out of front string, is shown.

The joint of cylinder is ½″ from the cut-out of No. 10 rise; Nos. 9, 8 and 7 treads are 4″, 4½″ and 9″ respectively: Nos. 11, 12 and 13 rise come in the cylinder, and the staves can be divided off, glued up and trimmed to suit the direction of risers; the joint of cylinder is 1½″ from the cut-out of No. 14 rise, and Nos. 14, 15 and 16 treads are 4″, 4½″ and 9″ respectively.

Fig. 7. [¾″ Scale]. Shows the well hole, starting second flight; through the intersection of the steps and risers, with the return nosings and brackets, draw the miter lines for the ends of steps; No. 1 and 2 step have the nosings rounded to avoid too long a miter, and allow the baluster to enter the mortise easily. The joint of cylinder is ¾″ from the face of No. 4 rise.

Fig. 8. [¾″ Scale]. Shows the width of staves, they are made to suit the spacing of the risers; the spring line of cylinder is 1½″ from the cut-out of No. 4 rise; and the cut-out of outer string for No. 4 and 5 treads are 3½″ and 9″ respectively.

Fig. 9. [¾″ Scale]. Shows the angle of steps and risers intersecting the bracket line and return nosing; from those two points draw the miters for the ends of winding steps, for the return nosings and brackets. The landing and starting rise, Fig. 7, is made concave and convex to help the width of cylinder connecting the level fascia or string, and also the spacing of the balusters; the face of No. 12 rise is shown 1¼″ from the joint of cylinder.

Fig. 10. [¾″ Scale]. Shows the staves lined off to suit the spacing of risers, the cut-out of face string is shown for Nos. 10 and 11 tread to be 9″ and 8½″, and the joint of cylinder is shown ¾″ from the cut-out of No. 12 riser. The plan of winders should be drawn full size on manilla paper, and rolled up until needed; the intersection of risers with the wall strings, give the width of winders, as shown on plan, Fig. 1' No. 8 tread is 15″ from face to face of rise, and No. 9 is 21″; No. 10 is 8½″ from face of rise to wall string in the angle; and from the angle to face of No. 11 rise is 17½″; No. 11 and 12 treads are 16½″ each, and No. 13 tread is 17½″ from face of rise to face of wall string in the angle; then 8½″ from the face of string in the angle to face of No. 14 rise; No. 14 tread is 21″, and No. 15 tread is 15″ from face to face of rise; No. 16 tread is the regular width 9″.

When laying out the wall string, a very good way is to note down these widths on a piece of paper, and thus avoid referring to the drawing. The face strings are shown to be 1″ thick, and are halved on to the cylinders at their joinings, and should be glued and screwed from the back for good work.

PLATE 35.

Plate 35. [Scale ¾″=1 foot.] *Shows the front and wall strings, and the development of staves in the cylinder for the first flight of winders, Plate 34.*

Fig. 1. *Shows the front string,* at the starting and landing, and broken at the middle, connecting which is shown the development of staves, as taken from the chords shown at Fig. 6, Plate 34, and is intended to show how the length of staves may be obtained. The stave for No. 10 tread is 3″ wide on the chord; Nos. 11 and 12 is 3½″, and No. 13 is shown 3″. See Fig 6, Plate 34.

The face string is spaced off with the dividers for the regular treads, as has been explained at former plates. No. 8 tread is 4½″; No. 9 is 4″, and the spring of cylinder *AB* is½″ from the cut out of No. 10 rise; No. 16 is a regular tread; No. 15 tread is 4½″, and No. 14, 3¾″, and the joint or spring of cylinder is 1½″ from the cut-out of No. 14 rise. The steps are 1¼″ thick. It will be noticed at the landing *F* the string is notched ¼″ to come level with the joist; make the width of level string at that point 9″ for joist, and ¾″ for plastering (9″+¾″=9¾″) equals 9¾″. The width of inclining string is 6″ from the internal angle of step and rise to the lower edge of plaster. Opposite No. 15 and 16 rise the string is increased in width, and at No. 8 rise the width is diminished some to allow the easings a graceful curve.

The easings connecting the staves are imperfect, and is done to get the length of staves in the rough. After the staves are glued up, the cylinder formed and connected to the strings, then the perfect easings are made agreeable to the eye and taste. A triangular piece, *H*, is glued on the lower end to relieve the acute angle formed by the inclination of the string with the floor line with an easing. The casing is short to allow the base board along the panel work to join flush and square with the string. *JK* shows the joint or spring of turnout 6″ from the cut-out of No. 3 rise.

The dotted line *M* shows the thickness of step (1¼″) cut off the lower end of string, making No. 1 rise 6¾″ high, so that when the step is in place the rise will be equal in height to the rest.

The first length for jointing the rail is is 6′ 8″; the second is 2′ 1″; and the third is 3′ 9″ on the level.

Fig. 2.   *Shows the wall string for the first 10 risers.*

EF shows a joint; to make this string in one piece would require the plank to be 22″ wide. So wide a plank is not always at hand and it is better to make the string in two pieces. Let the piece containing the winders, take in so many regular treads as the width of plank will admit. In this case we have two and a half regular treads in addition to the winders, so we will make the joint *EF* at the center of No. 5 tread.

To find the bevel *C*, take the average of the treads by the rise; thus add together the width of each tread at the wall string, and divide by the number of risers to be included in the string piece, [8½″+21″+15″+9″+9″+4½″=65″] [65″÷5=15″], equals 15″ as the average tread. Now with the steel square take 15″ on the blade, and the rise 8″ on the tongue, and apply from the edge *FH*, of plank. The tongue will give the bevel or plumb cut shown at *C* for each rise. Now space off the risers from the plan, Fig. 1, Plate 34, using the bevel to give the direction. Then set the dividers to the height of a rise [8″], and mark each rise, and draw the treads at right angles to the rise, using the steel square.

The regular treads at the lower end of string, are stepped off on the gauge line, as has been described. The joint *EF*, may either be lapped or grooved and tongued in the joint, and a strip nailed on the face of string to hold the joint firm. It may be removed when the string is in place.

At the upper end 1⅝″ is added on to receive the wall string, Fig. 3, and a groove at *AB*, is shown to admit the tongue *AB*, Fig. 3.

Fig. 3.   *Shows the wall string No. 2.*

The two center treads, No. 11 and 12, are alike 16½″×8″ rise and the bevel *E*, may be set to that pitch for the direction of each rise. The width of treads on the string 17½″, 16½″, 16½″, 17½″, are taken from the plan, Fig. 1, Plate 34. At the upper end, 1⅝″ is added on to receive string No. 4. The shaded part *CD*, shows a groove ½″ deep to receive the tongue *DC*, Fig. 4. The dotted line at the lower end shows the face of No. 1 string, and ⅛″ is added on to allow for tongue.

Fig. 4.   *Shows No. 3 wall string.*

The bevel for the direction of risers may be found by taking the average of the treads, the same as for No. 1 string. The width of treads on plan equals 8½″, 21″, 15″, 9″, plus 11″, for easment at the landing; equals 64½″, which being divided by 4 risers, gives 16⅛″ for the average. Then apply the steel square to the edge of plank, with 16⅛″ on the blade and 8″ on the tongue, the tongue will give the bevel *A* for the direction of risers. Now line off the treads at right angles to the risers; No. 14 rise is 8½″ from the face of No. 2 string, shown by the dotted line; *DC* shows the limit of the tongue.

The treads and risers are now lined off on the wall strings; the next will be to ease off the angles and connect them in the corners with curves that will be graceful and pleasing to the eye. From the external angle of tread and rise set off 4″, as shown by the arcs, as *JZ*, Fig. 2. Now it will be obvious, that at the lower end of No. 3 wall string, the casing to connect No. 2 string must raise up sufficiently high to clear No. 14 rise with the 4″ face above the treads at the angle; 7″ is allowed at the landing for height of base, and on trial we will set up 11″ at the lower end and trace the curve AXD for the upper edge of string, using a pliable strip. At D care must be taken to have the curve to tangent a line at right angles to the plumb cut DC.

From the top of tread, at the upper end of No. 1 wall string, set up on trial 6½″, and trace the curve for the upper edge of wall string to tangent the straight part at G, also keeping the strip near to the arcs, as consistent with a curve agreeable to the eye.

Now at the lower end of No. 2 string set up 6½″ to agree with the casing at the upper end of No. 1 wall string; also set up 11″ at the upper end of No. 2 wall string to agree with the lower end of No. 3 wall string, and ease off the angles at F and G. As the treads in No. 2 wall string are near alike, the upper edge may be straight. It will be noticed that opposite Nos. 15 and 16 rise, No. 3 string, the curve does not tangent the arcs, passing above the former and under the latter. This cannot be avoided always. The stair-builder must make his curves agreeable to the eye and free from abruptness as ne possibly can make them, for in that consists the pride of his profession.

The upper and lower edge of wall string may next be trimmed off, and the steps and risers housed in. The nosings and scotias for the straight steps are marked on the string from the step and rise after being glued up, as has been explained for Plate 22. When marking the nosings and scotias on the strings for housings, for the winders, cut a piece of straight nosing to the oblique angle that the winder makes with the string for a pattern, and trace the contour of nosing and scotia for the housing, as previously explained.

PLATE 36.

Plate 36. [Scale ¾″=1 foot]. *Exhibits the front and wall strings for the flight Fig. 3, Plate 34. Also the development of staves in the cylinder to obtain their lengths in the rough.*

Fig. 1. *Shows the lower end of face string connecting the cylinder.*

AB shows the joint of cylinder 1½″ from the cut-out of No. 4 rise. No. 4 tread is 3½″ wide on the face string, and No. 5 tread equals 9″. The dotted line AC, shows a gauge line run on 6″ from the lower edge as a guide for the internal angles of the regular treads and risers. The width of each stave is taken from the chord, Fig. 8, Plate 34. DE shows the joint of cylinder connecting the level string, which is 9½″ wide to cover the rough joist and receive the plaster.

It will be noticed that No. 1 rise is 7¾″ high, instead of 8″, the regular height of rise. This occurs from the step being 1¼″ thick, and the floor 1″. By reducing the first rise ¼″, the first stave will then come close up under the flooring. This does not reduce the whole height any, for it will be seen at the landing, Fig. 2, a ¼″ is added on, so that the level fascia will come chuck up under the floor, and at the same time the casing will drop ⅛″ below the joist to receive the plastering.

The casing on the string and at the lower end in the cylinder is temporary, and intended to show the length to cut the staves in the rough. After they are glued up and the cylinder spliced to the strings, the easements can be better studied, and the defects remedied to please the eye.

Fig. 2. *Shows the development of staves for the cylinder landing in the third story; the widths are taken from the chords Fig. 10, Plate 34.*

AB shows the joint of cylinder connecting the inclining string, and ¾″ from the cut-out of No. 12 rise. *DC* shows the joint connecting the level string. A triangular piece at *E,* will be required to glue on the lower edge of level string to help the easing at the joining of the cylinder. The stave at No. 12 tread is 2¾″ wide; No. 13 and 14 are 2½″ wide, and No. 15 is 3″ wide. The dotted lines show the length of staves in the rough.

Fig. 3. *Shows the wall string No. 1 at the starting.*

No. 1 tread is 15″ wide, and No. 2 is 23″ wide on the wall string, as taken from plan, Fig. 3, Plate 34. The part dotted line *CD* shows the face of No. 2 wall string connecting; in the angle a ½″ is added to enter the wall string No. 2.

Fig. 4. *Shows wall string No. 2*

As there are winders at both ends, it had better be made in two parts. The bevels at *X* and *O,* for the direction of risers, may be found in the same manner, as explained for Fig. 2, Plate 35. Nos. 3 and 13 rise come in the corners in this case. *AB* and *CD* show grooves into which the tongue on No. 1 and No. 3 wall strings are fitted; *EF* shows the splice joint.

Another and convenient way to line off the strings for veneers is to make an elevation of each string to a scale drawing, as shown at Nos. 1, 2, 3, wall string, then draw a line *GH,* so as to divide the breadth of string at *HG* and *EL* about equal at its widest part; then set the bevel *X,* or *O,* to agree with the risers and the line *GH,* or *EL.* The width of treads is taken from plan, Fig. 3, Plate 34, on a slip of paper for convenience. The bevel at *B,* Fig. 5, may be found in the same way. Care must be taken to line off all the treads at right angles to the risers. By drawing the elevation of treads and risers, also the curves on the upper edge of string, to a scale, the young man will gain experience in the use of the drawing instruments.

At the lower end of No. 1 wall string 7″ is allowed for the height of base; also the same is allowed at the landing, exclusive of the moulding.

A rule for the width of base, including the moulding, relative to the height of story, is one inch for every foot in height of story from floor to ceiling. A suitable easing is found in this case at the lower end of No. 3 string, by allowing 3½″ for height of string above No. 13 step at the angle. At the upper end of No. 2 string, from the top of No. 12 tread to the upper edge of wall string will equal (8″+3½″=11½″) 11½″. This also allows an easing agreeable to the eye.

And at the lower end of No. 2 wall string a suitable easing is formed, leaving the string 6½″ above No. 3 tread. Then the height at the upper end of No. 1 string, above No. 2 tread, will equal 8″ for rise, plus 6½″ to connect the lower end of No. 2 string, equals 14½″, which allows a favorable easing at the upper end of No. 1 string, as shown. After the curves on the wall strings are made, mark all the easings on a board intended for the mouldings, and thus save time in working them out when needed.

PLATE 37.

Plate 37. [Scale ¾″=1 foot]. *Exhibits how to find the length of tangents and radius for the turnout at the newel post; also the face-mould for the same. The face-moulds for the half pace winding in the first flight, and the two quarter pace windings, starting and landing, in the upper flight, for the stair-case, Plate 34.*

Figs. 1 and 2. *Show how to locate the radius of turnout relative to the height of newel post and inclination of rail.*

The newel post is $7″\times7″$. Through the center at **O**, draw the face of No. 1 rise perpendicular to one side of newel; extend the side of post by a line to **A**, as **CA**, for the center of rail shown by the dotted line. Parallel with No. 1 rise, draw No. 2 and 3 rise. Now draw a base line **XX**, Fig. 2, and elevate No. 1, 2 and 3 rise. Through the center of baluster **O, O**, draw the under side of rail, and parallel with **OO**, draw the center of rail **AB** indefinite.

From the top of No. 1 step set up $6″$ to the under side of rail, and $1\frac{1}{4}″$ additional to the center of rail. $(6″+1\frac{1}{4}″=7\frac{1}{4}″)$, equals $7\frac{1}{4}″$ from the top of No. 1 step to the center of rail at **F**: from **F**, and parallel to **XX**, draw a line to intersect the inclination of rail at **B**; from **B**, let fall the perpendicular, intersecting the center line of rail, Fig. 1, at **C**; draw **CO**, intersecting the cap at **D**.

Make **CE** equal **CD** for the length of tangents on plan. Perpendicular to the tangents, and from the points **E** and **D**, draw the radial lines, converging at **F**: with **FE** as a radius, draw the curve for the center line of rail from **E** to **D**. Now draw the string, bracket and nosing lines, and miters connecting the return nosings, thus completing the plan of turnout for getting out the steps. The face of No. 3 rise is shown $6″$ from the spring of turnout; the face of string is the solid line on plan.

Fig. 3. *Shows the plan of tangents for the face-mould.*
EC and **C** 5 correspond to Fig. 1; draw **EF** and 5 **F** parallel to **CE** and **C** 5; prolong **EC** indefinite; draw 5 **H** perpendicular to **EC** prolonged. Draw the diagonal **CF**, cutting the chord line of rail at 3; draw the chord **E** 5; 5 3 shows the amount ($2″$) of straight wood required to point of the miter from the verge of cap.

Fig. 4. *Shows the elevation of tangents and how to find the bevels.*

Let **XX** indicate the edge of drawing board. Make **AB**, **BC**, each equal **EC** and **C** 5, on plan, Fig. 3. Perpendicular to **XX**, draw **AD**, **BE** and **CF** indefinite. Now elevate Nos. 1, 2 and 3 risers, making the face of No. 3 rise $6″$ from the spring line **AD**; through the center of balusters **O, O**, draw the under side of rail.

Parallel to the under side of rail, draw the inclination for the center of rail indefinite, cutting **AD** and **BE**, at **D** and **J**; through **J**, and parallel with **XX**, draw **KJL**, intersecting **AD**, at **K**, and **CF**, at **N**; then **KD** is the height of the wreath-piece. **JD** is the increased length of tangent **EC**, on plan; **JN** is a level tangent, and remains the same length as **C** 5, on plan. Make

Kh equal *CF*, Fig. 3. Now make *K* 4 equal the chord *E* 5, Fig. 3. Also make *J* 5 equal *CH*, on plan, Fig. 3. From 5, and perpendicular to *DJ* produced, draw 5 6.

Bevels. Parallel with *XX*, draw the gauge line *PQ;* perpendicular to *XX*, draw *QR* equal to *H* 5, Fig. 3. Make *QS* equal 5 6; also make *QP* equal the height *KD;* draw *RS* and *RP* produced to *XX*. for convenience when adjusting the bevel.

Parallel with *XX*, draw the half width of rail (2″), cutting *PR* and *SR*, at 8 and 7. Now the bevel in the angle at *P* is for the joint at miter, and the bevel in the angle at *S* is for the shank joint, and *X* 8 is the increased width of half the face-mould at the miter, and *X* 7 shows the increased width of half the mould at the shank. Make *DG* equal 6″ for shank connecting the straight rail.

Fig. 5. *Shows the race-mould.*

With the steel square, draw the right angle *G* 6 5 indefinite. Make 6 *J* and 6 *D*, equal 6 *J* and 6 *D*, Fig. 4. With *J* for a center, and *C* 5, Fig. 3. as a radius, draw arc cutting 6 5 at 5. Draw *J* 5 prolonged 2″ to point of miter. Parallel with *DJ* and *J* 5, draw 5 *O* and *DO*, for the parallelogram *ODJ5*, that will agree, when in position, with the parallelogram *FEC5*, on plan, Fig. 3.

Proof. The chord *D* 5, must equal the distance *D* 4, Fig. 4, and the diagonal *OJ*, must equal the distance *Dh*, Fig. 4, if so, the angle of tangents at *J*, must be correct.

Prolong *JD* 6″ to *G*, for shank. Make joint at *G* perpendicular to *GJ*; from 5, and at right angles to *J* 5, draw a line indefinite to the left, also prolong the diagonal *JO*, to intersect the line from 5: and from the intersection (not shown), draw a line through *D*, for the point of contact. Make 5 2 and 5 3 each equal 8 *X*, Fig. 4. Make *G* 4 and *G* 10 equal 7 *X*. Fig. 4. Draw 4 8 and 10 9 parallel to *GD;* add on 2″ to point of miter parallel to 2 3. Now trace the concave side of mould from 9 to 3, and for the convex side from 8 to 2, using a flexible strip, being careful to tangent the straight lines at the points 2, 3 and 8, 9.

If it be desirable to find another point in each curve as 1 and 7, on the diagonal, then proceed as directed * for Fig. 4, Plate 24.

Fig. 6. *Shows the plan of an 8″ cylinder, agreeable to Fig. 2, Plate 34.*

The balusters are 2″ by 2″, making the radius for the center line of rail equal 4¾″.

Draw *AF* and *OC* indefinite and at right angles; then with *O* as a center and 4¾″ for a radius, draw the semi-circle *ACF;* from *A* and *F* draw the direction of straight string to the right.

Now show the graduating winders outside the spring of cylinder. The face of Nos. 10 and 14 rise is 1½″ from the spring of cylinder; Nos. 9 and 15 rise is 3½″ more, and Nos. 8 and 16

*Mr. Secor in his work on Hand-railing has fully described this method for finding the points on the diagonal from the plan. Also Mr. James H. Monckton, in his 1878 edition on stair-building, has described the points correctly on the diagonal from the plan. Others have shown a center point on the diagonal, but not correct in all cases.

At sections *L* and *N* the dotted line indicates the center of plank; the tangent line is carried across the section square to the face of crook, and intersects the dotted line; then through the intersection the bevel is shown applied from the face of crook. The block pattern is applied at right angles to the line made from bevel; the shaded part indicates the thickness of plank required. Observe the bevels do not cross the tangents in their application.

rise are each 4½″ still further out from the spring line **AF** of cylinder to the commencement of the regular treads (9″).

Next draw the tangents **AB**, **BC**, **CD** and **DF**, forming the two square parallelograms **OCBA** and **OCDF** on plan Fig. 6.

Fig. 7. *Shows the elevation of tangents and the treads and risers, which are unfolded from plan Fig. 6.*

In a case of this kind, it will be more economical to find the average pitch of the tangents; then the drawing may be made on a board not over 24″ wide and 9′ 0″ long. Thus, add together the width of treads on the center line of rail, and around on the tangents, including Nos. 7 and 10 treads. First, from the face of No. 7 rise to joint of cylinder (9″+5″+4″+½″=18½″), equals 18½″ plus 4¾″ for the tangent **AB**; the opposite side will equal the same, 23¼″. Then the two tangents **BC** and **CD** will equal 9½″ more. The sum total (23¼″+23¼″+9½″=56″) will equal 56″, which being divided by 10 risers, equals 5⅗″ nearly for the average tread. The rise is 8″; therefore the average pitch will be 8″ by 5⅗″. Now let **XX** indicate the edge of drawing board; then apply the steel square to the edge of board, with 8″ on the tongue and 5½″ on the blade; the tongue will give the pitch **FL** for all the vertical lines.

Now set a bevel from the edge of board to the line **FL**, as shown, and draw the perpendiculars **DK**, **CJ**, **BH** and **AG**, parallel to **F L** and equal to **AB**, **BC**, **CD** and **DF**, (4¾″) Fig. 6.

Next elevate the treads and risers, measured from the center line of rail on plan Fig. 6, keeping No. 10 rise ½″ from the spring of cylinder **AG**, and No. 14 rise ½″ from the spring **FL**; No. 9 tread measures 4″, and No. 8 tread is 5″; No. 7 tread equals 9″ wide: the measurement on the opposite side is the same on the center line of rail.

Through the center of balusters **O, O** draw the inclination for the underside of rail; parallel with **O, O** and **O, O** draw the center of rail to intersect **AG** at **M**, and **FL** at **N**.

The next is to give the inclination of tangents over the winders. This requires the best judgment of the stair-builder. By referring to Fig. 1, Plate 34, observe the direction of Nos· 9, 10 and 11 risers, they fall back from the rail, while at Nos, 13, 14 and 15 rise, they come out towards the rail. Or, in other words, when going up the stairs at No. 10 step, the person will be beyond the rail, and consequently the rail will feel high, and when coming down the stairs at No. 14 rise, the person will be forward of the rail, and the rail if set at the regular height would be too low. To obviate this, the rail must be "lifted" over the winders at Nos. 13, 14 and 15 treads, and kept down to about the regular height or less on Nos. 8, 9 and 10 winders.

If by lifting the rail, it should come a little high, that will be a good fault, but if the stair-builder should miss it, and the rail be low, then the owner would find fault, as then there would be danger when going down the stairs.

The worst difficulty the stair-builder will have, and where his best judgment will be required in lifting the rail, will be over Nos. 13, 14 and 15 treads. At Nos. 8, 9, 10 and 11 treads, there will be no danger, as the direction of risers fall back of the rail, and the rail will naturally appear high even when kept a little below the height of a regular short baluster.

If the risers in the cylinder were to radiate from the center **O**, then the difficulty of regulating the height of tangents in the cylinder would be obviated, as the person would then be normal to the curve in the direction of any of the treads, but it is only where there is ample room that the winders can be so placed.

At Fig. 1, Plate 34, the diameter line is extended to the walking line, and happens to cut the walking line at Nos. 9 and 15 rise. Now let it be observed that the diameter line being extended cuts across Nos. 10 and 14 rise, thus indicating that the point on the walking line at No. 9 rise, is one rise lower than at the joint of cylinder. At the opposite side the joint of cylinder will be two risers lower than at the point of intersection with the walking line, consequently we will have to lift the tangent at the angle *D*, on plan, say nearly two risers.

Then set up from No. 13 tread to *L* 14″, and from any point, say *Q*, on the line *PN*, draw the inclination for the upper tangent, cutting the perpendiculars *FL* and *DK*, at *L* and *I*, and intersecting *CJ* at *S*. From *I*, draw the inclination of tangents to touch the arc at *T*, and cut the perpendiculars *JC*, *HB* and *GA*, at *U*, *H* and *W*, and prolonged to intersect *ME* at *y*. Perpendicular to *FL* draw *LJ* and *UF*, cutting *DK* at 2 and 3. At right angles to *AG*, draw *WC*, cutting *BH* at 4; then *CU* will be the height of the lower wreath-piece, and *FL* will be the height of the upper wreath-piece.

Prolong *HI* to intersect *LJ* at *V;* from 3, and at right angles to *VU*, draw 3 5; from 2, and at right angles to *LS*, draw 2 19; from 4, and at right angles to *HW*, draw 4 6. Make *C* 22 and *U* 18 each equal the chord *AC*, on plan, Fig. 6. Parallel with *DK*, draw the half width of rail (2″), intersecting *IL* and *UI*, at 20 and 21. At *W*, allow 4″, and at *L*, allow 2″ for shank. Ease the angles at *y* and *Q*, to please the eye. Opposite the face of Nos. 8 and 16 rise, draw the face of rise to intersect the center of rail at *OO* and *OO*, for points to measure from when jointing the straight rail. These points should be marked on the patterns, also the distance *M*, *OO* (13¼″), and *N*, *OO* (12½″), to be convenient when jointing the straight rail.

Bevels. *aa* indicate the edge of drawing board, and the dotted line indicates a gauge line parallel with *aa;* perpendicular to *aa*, draw *bf* equal to *OC*, on plan, Fig. 6. Make *bh* equal 2 19; also make *bm* equal 5 3; let *bn* equal 4 6; draw *fm*, *fn* and *fh* prolonged to the edge of board.

Now in the angle at *h* is found the bevel for the shank joint 24, and in the angle at *m* is found the bevel for the joint at *U* on the upper wreath-piece. As the tangents *UH* and *HW* are of the same length, only one bevel will be required at the lower wreath-piece. The angle at *n* gives the bevel for both joints of the lower wreath-piece.

Fig. 8. *Shows the face mould for the lower wreath-piece.*

Draw *BAF* to equal *HWT*. Fig. 7; with *A* for a center and *U* 22, Fig. 7, as a radius, draw arc at *C*; then with *B* for a center and *BA* as a radius, draw arc intersecting at *C*, join *BC* parallel with *AB* and *CB*; draw *CO* and *AO* prolonged.

Proof. *OB* must equal the diagonal *OD*, Fig. 6; if so, the angle of tangents at *B* must be correct.

Make *A* 2, *A* 3 and *C* 4, *C* 5 each equal *I* 21, Fig. 7; make *OD* equal the radius (4¾″) of the center line of rail; let *D* 6 and *D* 7 each equal the half width of rail (2″).

Make joints at *C* and *F* perpendicular to tangents *BF* and *BC*; parallel with *BF* draw 2 8 and 3 9 for the shank; now pivot the trammel at *O* at right angles to *BO*, and set from pencil to minor pin the distance *OD* for the center or *falling line* of rail; then place the pencil in *C*, and drop the pins in the grooves, and fasten the major pin; then trace the curve *CDA;* repeat the operation for the concave and convex side of mould. The bevels are shown applied through the center of plank at sections *L* and *N;* the bevel at *L* is applied so as to elevate the joint at *C,* and at *N* the bevel is applied so as to pitch the joint at *F* down.

Fig. 9. *Shows the face-mould for the upper wreath-piece.*

The tangents being of unequal length, there will be two bevels required, as the shortest tangent connects with the easing at the upper end, the steepest bevel will apply to that joint.* Draw *CB* equal to tangent *IU,* Fig. 7. With *C* as a center and *J* 18, Fig. 7, for a radius, draw arc at *A;* with *B* as a center and tangent *IL* for a radius, draw arc intersecting at *A;* join *BA* prolonged to *H,* equal to *I* 24, Fig. 7. Parallel with *CB* and *BA* draw *AO* and *CO,* for the parallelogram *OABC,* on the cutting plane.

Proof. The diagonal *BO* must equal *S* 18, Fig. 7; make *CD* equal *IV,* Fig. 7; draw *DO* produced; let *OF* equal the radius *OC,* Fig. 6; make *F* 6 and *F* 7 each equal the half width of rail (3″); make *A* 2 and *A* 3 each equal *I* 21, Fig. 7. Make *C* 4 and *C* 5 each equal *I* 20, Fig. 7; make joints at *C* and *H* at right angles to the tangents *CB* and *BH;* draw 2 8 parallel with *BH* for the shank on the concave side. On the convex side the joint intersects the curve.

Now pivot the trammel at *O,* with the arms resting perpendicular to the semi-minor axis *OF,* and trace the inside and outside curves of face-mould in the same manner as has been explained. The letters *P* and *Q* show the sections of the joints *H* and *C;* the bevels are applied through the center of plank. The bevel at *Q,* let it be observed, is applied so as to throw the shank end up, while at the shank end the bevel is applied so as to throw the center joint at *C* down.

Fig. 10. *Shows the plan of the center line of rail for the cylinder, starting in the second story. See Fig. 7, Plate 34.*

Make *AE* equal the diameter (9½″) for the center line of rail, with *O* as a center; draw the semi-circle *ACE;* enclose the semi-circle with the tangents *AB, BC, CD* and *DE;* prolong *DE* and *BA* indefinite to the left. The face and directions of risers are made to agree with Fig. 7, Plate 34. On the center line of rail the face of No. 4 rise is shown ¾″ from the spring of cylinder; No. 4 tread measures 4″, and No. 5 tread measures 9″ on the center line of rail; the regular pitch is 8″ rise by 9″ tread.

Fig. 11. *Shows the development of tangents and the elevation of treads and risers, measured from the center line of rail on the line of tangents on plan, Fig. 10.*

First find the average pitch on the center line from *E,* around the tangents to No. 6 rise from plan. Fig. 10. From the face of No. 6 rise to *B* equals 18½″; from *B* to *D* equals 9½″, and from *D* to *E* equals 4¾″, total (18½″+9½″+4¾″=33″) equals 33″, which being divided by 6 risers, equals 5½″ for the average tread. Then with the square, take 5½″ on the blade and the rise (8″) on the tongue, and apply to the edge of board *XX;* the tongue will give the line *AJ* required for the average pitch from the edge of drawing board. Parallel with *AJ,* draw *BK, CH, DG* and *E,* equal to *AB, BC, CD* and *DE,* on plan, Fig. 10. (4¾″ each). Now draw the floor line *LL,* at right angles to *CH.*

---

* It is well to note this, as some use a parallel face-mould.

Make the position of No. 1 rise from *D,* equal that on plan, Fig. 10, (2″); then elevate the risers and treads from the tangents on plan, making the risers parallel and the treads at right angles to the perpendicular lines, keeping No. 4 rise ¾″ from the spring line *AJ;* No. 4 and No. 5 treads equal 4″ and 9″ each. Now through the center of baluster *mm,* draw the inclination for the under side of rail. Parallel with *mm,* draw the center of rail *MN;* it will be observed that the regular pitch intersects the spring of cylinder at *N.* On the plan, Fig. 3, Plate 34, extend the diameter line to cut the walking line at *A;* let it be observed that the joint of cylinder comes in No. 3 tread at *C,* and the diameter line cuts across No. 4 rise; and will rest at about the center of No. 4 tread, thus indicating the point *A.* will be one rise and a half above the point *C,* on the inclination of rail. Then that is about the height above No. 3 tread, that the inclination of the upper tangent should cross the perpendicular *AJ,* in the elevation say at *P;* now allow from *N* to *Q* sufficient to make an easing on the straight rail to connect the shank of wreath-piece.

Then from *Q.* through *P.* draw tangent cutting *BK* at *O,* and prolonged to intersect *CH* at *R.* From the floor line at *L* set up half a rise to the under side of rail taken from the first flight (4″ in this case), and 1¼″ more to the center of rail, making 5¼″ from the floor line *LL* to the center of rail at *S.* Parallel to *LL* draw *SC,* cutting *DG* at *T:* connect *TO,* cutting *CH* at *U.* From *U* and *P,* and at right angles to *CH,* draw *UA* and *PH,* cutting *BK* at *V* and 9. Then *CU* will be the height for the lower wreath-piece, and *AP* will be the height for the upper wreath-piece.

Prolong *UO* to intersect *PH* at *Y;* make *U* 7 and *C* 8 each equal to the chord *AC,* on plan Fig. 10. From 9, and perpendicular to *PR* produced, draw 9 10; from *V* and at right angles to *UY,* draw *V* 12; at *O* draw the half width of rail (2″) parallel with *BK,* cutting *PR* at 13 and *OU* at 14.

Bevels. Parallel with *LL* draw the dotted line *W* 18; perpendicular to *LL* draw *WZ,* equal to the radius *OC,* Fig. 10; make *W* 16 equal *V* 12, and *W* 17 equal to 9 10; make W 18 equal the height *CU;* draw *Z* 18, *Z* 17 and *Z* 16 prolonged to *LL,* for the bevels required.

Fig. 12. *Shows the face-mould at the starting.*

Draw the rectilineal parallelogram *OEDC,* making *EO* and *DC,* also *OC* and *ED* each equal *UT* and *TC,* Fig. 11.

Proof. The chord *EC* and the diagonal *OD* must each equal *U* 8, Fig. 11. If so, the parallelogram is correct.

Make *E* 2 and *E* 3 each equal *O* 14, Fig. 11. Let *C* 4 and *C* 5 each equal the half width of rail (2″). Pivot the trammel in *O,* with the arms centered on the semi-major axis *OE,* and trace the concave and convex sides of face-mould, as has been described; add on 2″ or more straight wood at *E* parallel to *OE,* to help the easing at the joint connecting the straight rail. The minor axis *OC* forms the joint at *C.* The section at *N* shows the bevel found in the angle at 18, Fig. 11, applied so as to pitch the joint at *C* up, and at section *M* the square is shown applied from the face of crook, allowing the tangent *ED* to be horizontal.

Fig. 13. *Shows the face-mould for the upper wreath-piece, connecting the casement. Fig. 11.*

Make *CB* equal tangent *OU,* Fig. 11. With *C* as a center and 7 *H,* Fig. 11, for a radius, draw arc at *A;* with *B* as a center, and tangent *OP*, Fig. 11, for a radius, draw arc intersecting at *A*; join *BA* and produced; draw *AO* and *CO* parallel with *BC* and *BA* prolonged, for the parallelogram *OABC* on the cutting plane.

Proof. The diagonal *BO* must equal the distance *R* 7, Fig. 11. If so, the angle of tangents at *B* is correct.

Make *AE* equal *P* 19, Fig. 11; make joints at *E* and *C* at right angles to tangents *BE* and *BC*; make *A* 2 and *A* 3 each equal *O* 14, Fig. 11; also make *C* 4 and *C* 5 each equal *O* 13, Fig. 11. Let *CF* equal *OY*, Fig. 11; join *OF*, and prolonged, for the direction of minor axis; make *OJ* equal to radius *OC*, on plan Fig. 10. Make *J* 6 and *J* 7 each equal the half width of rail (2″); draw the shank 2 8 parallel with *BA*.

Pivot the trammel at *O* with the arms at right angles to the semi-minor axis *OJ*, and set from pencil to minor pin the distance *OJ*, for the center line of rail; then place the pencil in *A*, and slide the major pin until they both drop into the grooves, then fasten the major pin and trace the center or *falling line*: proceed in the same manner to trace the concave and convex sides of face-mould.

At *D* and *P*, the sections show the bevels applied through the center of plank; the bevel found in the angle at 17, is applied at *D*, and the bevel found in the angle at 16, Fig. 11, is applied at *P*, always from the face or upper side of crook, which must be true, or out of wind.

Fig. 14. *Shows plan of the center line of rail for the quarter pace winding landing in the third story.*

The diameter of cylinder is 8″, and the radius for the center line of rail is 4¾″.

Make *AE* equal 9½″; with a radius of 4¾″, and *O* for a center, draw the semi-circle *ACE*, for the center of rail. Draw the rectilineal parallelogram *ABDE*, tangent to the curve at the points *A*, *C* and *E*; prolong *BA* and *DE* for the direction of straight rail.

In practice for a working drawing, the direction of winders and flyers showing how oblique they cut the string line, are supposed to be laid out on paper full size from the scale drawing. Fig. 3, Plate 34. The plan shows No. 11 tread measures 4″ on the center line, and No. 12 rise ¾″ from joint or spring of cylinder.

Fig. 15. *Shows the development of tangents and the elevation of treads and risers measured from the tangents and straight part on plan, Fig. 14.*

For convenience, first find the average tread from the face of No. 10 rise, around the tangents to face of No. 15 rise; thus from No. 10 rise to spring of cylinder (9″+4″+¾″ = 13¾″) equals 13¾″, plus *AB*, (4¾″), plus from *B* to face of No. 15 rise (8½″), equals (13¾″+4¾″+8½″ = 27″) for the total 27″, which being divided by 5 risers (27″÷5 = 5⅜″) equals 5⅜″, nearly for the average tread.

Let *XX* indicate the edge of board; then with 5¾″ on the blade, and 8″ on the tongue, draw the direction of the perpendicular *EF* from the tongue. Parallel with *EF*, draw *DG*, *CH*, *BJ* and *AK* indefinite.

Now elevate Nos. 10, 11, 12, 13, 14 and 15 risers and treads, keeping No. 12 rise ¾″ from the spring line *AK*, as shown. Draw the floor line at the landing; from the floor line set up 4″

to under side of rail, and 1¼″ more, or 5¼″ to the center of rail at *L*. At right angles to *EF*, draw *LN*, cutting *EF* at *F*, and *DG* at *N*.

Through the center of balusters *O, O*, draw the under side of rail; parallel with *OO;* draw the center of rail *PM*, intersecting *AK* at *M;* draw arc equal to the half thickness of rail at the center of baluster No. 12 tread, then from the point *N*, draw a line tangent to the arc, intersecting the inclination *MP* at *Q*, and cutting the perpendiculars *CR*, *BJ* and *AK*, at *R*, *y* and *S*.

From *S*, and at right angles to *AK*, draw *SC*, cutting *JB* at *T;* from *R*. and perpendicular to *CH*, draw *RU*, cutting *GD* at *V;* then *UF* is the height for the upper wreath-piece, and *RC* is the height for the lower wreath-piece; and *NR*, *Ry* and *yS* show the increased length of tangents in elevation; make joint at *W* at right angles to *QS;* ease off the angle at *Q* to please the eye, and to tangent the joint at *W;* make *U* 2 and *C* 3, each equal the chord *CE*, on plan, Fig. 14.   Parallel with *DG*, draw the half width of rail. cutting the tangent *NR* at 4: from *T*, and at right angles to *RS*, draw *T* 5.

Bevels.   As the tangent *FN* is level, there will be but one bevel for the landing wreath-piece, and as both tangents *Ry* and *yS*, for the lower wreath-piece, have the same inclination, there will be but one bevel required for both joints.   Let *aa* indicate the edge of board, and the dotted line be a gauge line parallel to *aa;* draw 6 7 perpendicular to *aa*, and equal to *OC*, on plan. Fig. 14; make 6 8 equal *T* 5, and 6 9 equal the height *UF;* draw 7 8 and 7 9 produced, to edge of board *aa* for the bevels in the angles at 8 and 9.

Fig. 16.   *Shows the face-mould for the quadrant ACO, Fig, 14.*

Make *WAB* equal *WSY*, Fig. 15.   With *A* as a center, and *R*, 3. Fig. 15, for a radius, draw arc at *C*, again with *B* as a center and *AB* as a radius, draw arc intersecting at *C;* with the same radius and *C*, also *A*, as centers, draw arcs intersecting at *O;* draw *OA* and *OC* indefinite, and we have the parallelogram *OABC* on the cutting plane, that will agree with the parallelogram *OABC*, on Plan Fig. 14. when in position.

Proof.   The diagonal *OB* must equal the diagonal *OB*, on plan Fig. 14.   Draw *BO* indefinite for the direction of minor axis.   Make *OD* equal *OC*, on plan Fig. 14; make *A* 2, *A* 3, *C* 4 and *C* 5 each equal *N* 4, Fig. 15.   Let D 6 and *D* 7 each equal the half width of rail (2″).   Make joints at *C* and *W* at right angles to the tangents *BA* and *BC*.   Parallel with *BW* draw 2 8 for the shank.   Now pivot the trammel at *O*, with the arms at right angles to the semi-minor axis *OD*.   Set from pencil to minor pin the distance *OD;* then rest the pencil in *C*, drop the pins in the grooves.   Now fasten the major pin, and trace the center curve of face-mould.   Proceed in the same manner to trace the concave and convex sides of mould.

The sections *G* and *H* show the application of the joint bevel, which is taken from the angle at 8, Fig. 15.

Fig. 17.   *Shows the face-mould for the quadrant OEC, Fig. 14.*

Draw the rectilineal parallelogram *OCDE*, making *OC* and *DE*, also *OE* and *CD*, to equal *FN* and *NR*, Fig. 15, respectively.

Proof.   The diagonals *OD* and *EC* must equal *F* 2, Fig. 15.   Make *C* 2 and *C* 3 each equal the half width of rail (2″); let

E 4 and *E* 5 each equal *N* 4, Fig. 15. Now pivot the trammel at *O*, with the arms resting on the semi-major axis *OE*. Then set from pencil to minor pin, equal to *OC*, and from pencil to major pin to equal *OE*. Now trace the center line on face-mould from *E* to *C*; proceed in like manner to trace the concave side of face-mould through the points 4, 2, and convex side through the points 5, 3. Parallel with 4 5 add 2″ of straight wood *EF*, to help the easing in wreath-piece, to connect the straight rail *LF*, Fig. 15. The bevel at section *M* is taken from the angle at 9, Fig. 15, and applied from the face and through the center of plank, so as to pitch the joint at *C* down. At section *N* the block pattern is applied parallel to the face of crook, and at the center of plank.

Fig. 18. *Shows the easement required at the landing of the first flight.*

Through the center of balusters *O, O* draw the underside of rail parallel with *O, O*; draw the center of rail *AB* indefinite. From the floor line set up 4″ to underside of rail, and 1¼″ more to *C* for center of rail (4″+1¼″=5¼″), equals 5¼″. Parallel with floor line draw *CB*, intersecting *AB* at *B*. Now ease off the angle *ABC*, to please the eye; plumb over the face of No. 17 rise; make a point *D*, showing the face of landing rise No. 17 on the easement pattern. Now mark on the pattern the distance (14½″) from *D* to join *C*, for the amount to allow for easement when jointing the straight rail.

Jointing the rail. No. 1 length. *The length from th[c] spring of turnout to spring of cylinder equals 6′ 8″, Fig. 2, Plate 34; the length of shank on face-mould, Fig. 5, equals 6″, and the distance, *M, OO*, Fig. 7, equals 12½″, and from *OO* to joint at *E* equals 1′ 3″, or 2′ 3½″ from *M* to joint at *E*, as the allowance for ramp. Then the dimension to cut No. 1 length (6′ 8″—(2′ 3½″+6″=2′ 9½″)=3′ 10½″.

No. 2 length. From joint of cylinder to face of No. 17 rise landing equals 2′ 1″, Fig. 2, Plate 34. The easement connecting the wreath-piece at the upper end measures from *N* to *OO* 12½″; then 2′ 1″ minus 12½″ (2′ 1″—1′ 0½″=1′ 0½″), equals 1′ 0½″, as the distance between the two points *OO*, Fig. 7, and the point *D*, Fig. 18. This will allow 6¼″ from *D* to joint at *A*, Fig. 18, and 6¼″ from *OO* to joint near *P*, Fig. 7. as shown.

No. 3 length. The length from face of No. 17 rise to spring of cylinder starting second flight equals 3′ 9″. Now the horizontal distance from *D* to *C*, Fig. 18, equals 14½″ for the level length on easement landing of the first flight, and we have 2″ of straight wood, *EB*, added on to the lower end of wreath-piece, Fig. 12 (14½″+2″=1′ 4½″), which equals 1′ 4½″ to be deducted from the whole length (3′ 9″—1′ 4½″=2′ 4½″), equals 2′ 4½″, the length to cut No. 3.

No. 4 Length. The length from spring of cylinder starting to spring of cylinder landing in the second flight equals 7′ 0¾″, see Fig. 4, Plate 34. The length of easement, Fig. 11, measures from spring of cylinder at *N* to *Q*, 6″, and from *Q* to joint at *M*, 9½″; (6″+9½″=15½″) equals 15½″ to allow for the easement; and for the ramp, Fig. 15, allow 6″ from *M* to the point plumb over the face of No. 11 rise, and 14½″ more to the lower joint of ramp at *P*, which being added (14½″+6″=1′ 8½″), equals 1′ 8½″ plus the length of easing above (15½″) [1.8½+1′ 3½″=3′

8″], equals 3′ 0″ to be deducted from 7′ 0¾″ (7′ 0¾″—3′ 0″ =4′ 0¾″), equals 4′ 0¾″, the length to cut No. 4.

No. 5 length. Is the second level, and is marked 6′ 7″ from spring of cylinder landing in the third story to the spring of quarter cylinder. Now we have allowed 2″ of straight wood *FE,* on face-mould, Fig. 17; then deduct 2″ from the whole length, 6′ 7″, equals 6′ 5″ to cut No. 5 length. In case there be straight wood on the quarter turn, deduct the amount of straight wood in addition to the 2″ allowed on the wreath-piece.

The short piece to wall equals 3′ 0″ in length. After the joints are made, bolted and dressed off, the rail is ready to hang.

HANGING THE RAIL. In large stair shops it is customary for one set of men to step up, and another to hang rails and complete the job, while neither get them out. So a few words in addition to what has been said for a platform stair-case, will not be out of place here.

When proceeding to hang the rail over winders, as in this case, a very good plan is to elevate the rail on stanchions notched out to receive the rail. Let the rail be raised or lowered to suit the height of the regular balusters, and plumb carefully on the convex side to points made at intervals on the steps and around the cylinder. The distance in to mark the points from the face of bracket line equals half the thickness of balusters (1″) plus the half width of rail (2″), equals 3″ for the convex side of rail. Now when the rail is plumb to the points around the cylinder and the straight part, and also the height to suit the baluster is correct, then plumb through the center of cap for the center of newel on the floor, and take the height from floor to under side of cap for the height of newel. The newel may now be cut, set, and the rail placed in position, using stanchions for supports, set near the joints and out of the way for glueing and driving up the nuts.

Next if the straight rail have any bends, they may now be straightened by bracing; plumb and bore for the balusters, dress off the under side of rail and put the balusters in place, using a thick glue for this purpose.

After the balusters have been set and glued at intervals, remove the stanchions and complete glueing in the balusters. Some prefer to hang the rail at once on a few balusters; the stanchions make the rail more solid, and may save a broken twist, and is better for straightening the crooked part of straight rail, which often has to be done.

If the stairs are got out and stepped up carefully, the newel and balusters may be cut at the bench. It will be noticed at Fig. 4, that the under side of rail is drawn through the center of baluster, and its length is naught at that point, while the under side of rail is raised up 6″ above the first step to allow for casing at the newel; then whatever height from top of step to under side of rail, we make the short baluster, the newel will be 6″ longer from the top of first step to the under side of rail, or from the floor to under side of rail will be the height of a rise [8″] more, or 14″, in this case; for instance, the height of a short baluster from the top of the step to under side of rail at the center is 2′ 1½″. and the newel is 6″ higher than a short baluster, plus the height of first rise 8″, will equal for the whole height of newel from the floor to under side of cap 3′ 3½″, (2′ 1½″ + 6″ + 8″ = 3′ 3½″).

For pin top balusters allow 1½″ to enter the rail; the height of square is half a rise for the short ones, and the length of turning being all the same, will make the squares for the base of long baluster equal the height of a rise; sometimes the balusters are square at the top and also at the base; the squares at the base and top for both balusters being the same height, then the turning for the shafts will be the difference of half a rise; sometimes the squares at the base are one height and the shafts, also one length in turning, and the squares at the top of different lengths.

To find the length of odd balusters under the wreath part of rail, study Figs. 1 and 2, Plate 32; to prevent a confusion of lines, this is omitted here, however, for common work, if the balusters have their shafts all turned the same length, the difference will be in the square at the base, and will not be objectionable unless the proportion is too much out of the way.

BORING THE RAIL. This is best done on the stairs after the rail is hung, the plumbing and boring for the balusters is a short job for a flight of stairs; for boring around the winders, use a ratchet or angle brace.

PLATE 38.

Plate 38, Figs. 1 and 2. [Scale ¼″=1′.] *Exhibits plan elevation of a double quarter-pace winding stair-case, having a quarter pace and four risers to the landing in the second story; the quarter pace at the starting has a circular wall string, and the circular corner is ornamented with a nitch.*

The height of story is 12′ 6″ from top to top of joist; the joist are 10″ wide in the second story, and they are to be stripped across for lath and plastering with 1″ by 2″ strips, making 11″ for the depth of joist. The width of hall is 8′ 2″; the height of door under the stairs is 7′ 6″; the length of well to receive the stairs 13′ 9″; the rail is 4″ by 2½″. Balusters are to be 2″ by 2″.

Fig. 1. Shows the plan, having 20 risers and starting with a quarter pace winding around a cylinder of 8″ radius, and landing with a quarter pace winding on a cylinder of 6″ radius to a level quarter pace at No. 16 rise; thence with four flyers to the landing in the second story.

The height of story from top to top of joist equals 12′ 6″, which reduced to inches equals 150″, being divided by 20 risers (150″÷20 =7½″), equals 7½″, as the height of each rise, and if we use a constant of 25″ in this case, the relative width of tread to rise will be 10″, or 7½″ by 10″ for the pitch. See rule for width of step in proportion to height of rise, page 87.

The cylinders are laid off so as to have the well hole in the center of well; then Nos. 2 and 16 rise will be about the same length as at the flyers or straight steps, 3′ 7″.

The walking line is drawn 15″ from the face and parallel with the outer string. No. 9 tread is placed at the center of well in this case, and the balance of treads is spaced off on the walking line either way equal to a regular tread (10″). Nos. 1 and 2 treads are slightly curved and increased in width on the walking line. The length of Nos. 2 and 16 treads should never be less than those at Nos. 9 or 20, but if anything, they should be longer 3″ or 4″. If shorter the stair-case will have a contracted appearance. An inch or two at these points makes a great difference either way. Draw Nos. 7 to 11 and also No. 17 rise at right angles to the outer string; then locate the short balusters on Nos. 11 and 17 treads, and space off for the intermediate balusters on the center line of rail. The face of risers may now be drawn to suit the balusters, and through the points on the walking line to intersect the wall string.

It will be observed at Fig. 4, that the baluster on No. 12 step is located near the center of tread; this is done to allow the balusters to appear near the same from centers; the tread is graduated to aid the easing on the lower edge of string.. The face of wall string projects 1⅜″ from the line of studs, allowing ⅜″ for lath and plastering, and 1″ for the thickness of base; No. 11 winding tread is 12″ wide at the face of wall string No. 12 and 13 treads are 19½″ and 26¾″ each. No. 14 is 6″ to the face of string in the corner, and 24½″ from the corner to face of No. 15 rise. No. 15 winding tread is 24½″ wide; No. 7 rise is 8″ from the spring of circular wall string, and No. 2 rise is 6″ from the spring at the starting. Nos. 1, 2, 3, 4 and 5 treads are each 18¾″ wide, and No. 6 is 16½″ wide at the wall string. This quarter pace winding for a working drawing should be drawn full size on heavy paper. **AA** shows the bearers 3″×4″

scantling, to which rough brackets are nailed for supports; they are placed in position so as to transmit the weight from the outer string to the walls. **BB** shows the bridging on the quarter pace opposite the bearers, the same should be done at the landing.

Fig. 2. *Shows the elevation.*
The height **AB**, [12′ 6″] being divided into 20 risers at 7½″ each, the joist is shown 10″ wide and 1″ stripping for lathing, making 11″ as the depth to allow for joist.

The height from floor to top of platform is 10′ 0″, and the joist, plastering and flooring of platform, equals 12″, and the carriage, lath and plastering, plumb under and including No. 15 rise, will equal 16″ more, (12″+ 16″=2′ 4″) equals 2′ 4″. Now the door under the platform is 7′ 0″ plus 2′ 4″ [7′ 0″+ 2′ 4″=9′ 4″] equals 9′ 4″, this deducted from the height of platform [10′ 0″—9′ 4″=0′ 8″] equals 8″ for the finish over the door plumb under No. 15 rise.

Often a full finish over the doors and windows under the platforms cannot be had. In this the stair-builder has to arrange as best he can, but whenever practicable, let the finish be complete, as that improves the work.

Headway. Count down from the landing 14 risers at 7½″ each (14×7½″= 105″/12 =8′ 9″), equals 8′ 9″ from the top of floor to and including No. 7 rise. The width of joist, stripping, flooring, lath and plastering equals 13″. Then 8′ 9″ minus 1′ 1″ equals 7′ 8″ as the height from No. 6 tread, plumb over No. 7 rise to the line of plastering. We will locate the face of trimmer plumb over the center of No. 6 tread, at the walking line. This will allow ample head room. This locates the trimmer in the second floor 9′ 3″ from the wall for the length of well.

For the quarter pace at the landing in the second story, the face of joist is located 6″ from the face of No. 20 rise, and 7′ 2″ from the wall; the half width of hall is 4′ 1″, and the radius of cylinder equals 6″, and the thickness of level fascia is 1″. Then the width to trim the landing [4′ 1″—(6″+1″) =3′ 6″], will equal 3′ 6″ by 2′ 1″, as shown on plan Fig. 1. **SS** shows the spring of cylinder.

The lengths to measure for jointing the rail are shown taken from spring to spring of cylinder (6′ 9″) for No. 1 length; No. 2 length is taken from spring of cylinder to face of No. 20 rise (3′ 1½″); No. 3 length is taken from the face of landing rise to the spring of quarter cylinder (2′ 0″), and No. 4 length is taken from spring of quarter cylinder to wall on plan (4′ 1″); all inclining lengths must be taken parallel to the true pitch, and all level lengths parallel to the floors.

Fig 3. *Shows the plan of cylinder at the newel drawn to a ¾″ scale.*
The balusters are shown spaced off on the center line of rail, and the risers are drawn in to suit; the radius **OA** equals 8″ for the line of cylinder. The face of No. 6 rise is 2¾″ from the spring of cylinder. The cut-out of No. 6 tread is 5¼″; No. 2 step should be increased in width, so as to give the proper space between Nos. 2 and 3 balusters and at the newel post.

Fig. 4. *Shows the balusters spaced off around the 12″ cylinder, and face of risers drawn to suit the spacing of balusters.*
The nosing line of steps intersects with the return nosings and gives the miters for the return nosings. The miter on No. 14 step is very acute, and may be relieved by rounding off at the

point, as shown in Fig. 5, Plate 34. The face of No. 13 rise is
3½″ from the spring of cylinder. The width of Nos. 11 and 12
tread on the face string is 8¼″ and 5″ each.

Fig. 5. *Shows how to obtain the curve of grounds around
the head of a nitch.*

The solid line **AB** shows the line of plaster, and the dotted
line **CD** shows the line of studs, the radius being 4′ 2″; **HJ** shows
the diameter of nitch. With **H** and **J** for centers, draw focus at
Q from **Q**; through **H** and **J** draw the radial lines indefinite;
parallel with **HJ** draw a line tangent to the semi-circle at **K**, intersecting the radial lines at **L** and **M**; then **LM** is the stretchout
of the semi-circle **HKJ**; now divide the diameter **HJ** into any
number of spaces, as 1, 2, 3, 4, &c.; then draw 1 **X**, 2 **X**, 3 **X**,
&c., perpendicular to **HJ**, and intersecting the semi-circle **HKJ**
at 5, 5, &c. From **Q** and through 5, 5, &c., draw lines to intersect
the stretchout **LM** at 6, 6, &c. From **L** 6, 6, and **M** draw lines
perpendicular to **LM** indefinite. Draw **PR** indefinite and parallel to **LM**, cutting the perpendicular at 7, 7, 7, &c., to indicate the edge of nitch.

Now transfer 4 **X**, 3 **X**, &c., to corresponding points 7 4, 7 3,
&c., as shown, and through the points **P**, 1, 2, 3, 4, &c., trace the
curve for the head of nitch. Then kerf between **P** and **R**, and
bend to the required circle.

PLATE 39.

Plate 39. [Scale ¾″ =1 foot]. *Shows the front and wall
string for the stair-case, Figs. 1 and 2, Plate 38.*

Fig. 1. *Shows part of the outer string and the panel
work underneath, connecting the cylinder at the starting.*

AB is the spring of cylinder, **CD**, **EF** and **GH** show the
length of staves in the rough, and are taken from the cylinder,
Fig. 3, Plate 38, in the same manner as explained for Figs. 5 and 6,
Plate 34. The cut-out for No. 6 rise is 3″ from the spring of
cylinder, and the cut-out for No 6 tread is 5¼″. The width of
outer string below the internal angle of tread and rise is 7″. The
lower edge of string is cased off in this case down to the floor,
and the panel work is made to suit.

The first length [6′ 9″] for rail is taken parallel with the
internal angle of the regular treads from joint to joint of cylinders. No. 1 rise is shown reduced to 6¼″, to allow for the step.

Fig. 2. Shows the upper end of outer string, Fig. 1, connecting the 12″ cylinder at **AB**, and also the lower end of face
string, Fig. 3, connecting the cylinder at **CD**. The regular
straight treads 7, 8, 9 and 10, are spaced off with the dividers, and
the pitchboard is applied to the gauge line **NP**.

. No. 11 tread is 8¼″, and No. 12 is 5″ on the face string.
The joint of cylinder is 3¼″ from the cut-out of No. 13 rise;
LM, **KJ**, **HG** and **EF** show the length of staves in the rough;
the angles **R** and **S** are eased off to please the eye; the length 6′
9″ for the straight part of rail is shown taken from the spring of
cylinder **AB**. The two cylinders may be tongued and glued to
this string at the bench, and set up in the building.

Fig. 3. *Shows the upper end of front string landing in the second story.*

The string is notched ¼″, the difference between the thickness of step and flooring. The joist is 10″ deep, and are furred down one inch with 1″×2″ strips, nailed at right angles to the direction of joist to prevent cracks in the plastering. The lath and plastering is ⅞″. Then the width of level fascia (10″ +1″÷⅞″=11⅞″) will equal 11⅞″, as shown; the face of joist is set back 6″ from the face of No. 20 rise to allow the bearers **B**, room to catch well up on the joist; the angle at **A**, is eased off with the easement pattern. The dotted line **CD**, shows a saw kerf, the end of string being halved out to receive the level fascia, thus forming a butt joint; some prefer to make a splice joint at this point.

Fig. 4. *Shows the wall string for the circular part, the risers and treads are lined off, but no housing is done until taken from the form.*

Make a convex pattern to suit the curve for the face of circular wall string. Fig. 1, Plate 38; make No. 1 tread 18¾″ wide as shown on plan; No. 2 tread is 6″ to the spring line **AB**; then transfer the balance of No. 2 winder (12″) with the convex pattern; next develop the stretchout of No. 3, 4, 5 and part of No. 6 tread to the spring line **CD**, in the same way. No. 7 rise is 8″ from the spring line as shown. In this case as the treads at the lower end are alike, a pitchboard 7½″×18¾″ may be used. With the above pattern, the stretchout of each step may be developed on the wall string correct enough for practice.

No. 7 tread is regular and equals 10″. The joint **EF** is made in the center of No. 8 tread. The height for base at the lower end is 8″; the angles at **J** and **H** are eased off to please the eye. The plank for this string should be dressed up to an even thickness throughout. The riser lines on the face of string should be very light; they should be pencil lines at first; then after the string is taken from the drum they may be traced with the knife. This is done to avoid weakening the surface of string before bending.

The string may now be grooved on the back for keys. Space them off to the rule given in letter press for Fig. 6, Plate 28, making them parallel to the spring lines **AB** and **CD**, or perpendicular to the treads.

Fig. 5. *Shows the upper end of Fig. 4.*

The joint **FE** is made in the center of No. 8 tread. The treads and risers are laid off in the same manner as described for Plates 35 and 36. The dimension of each winder may be taken from the plan Fig. 1, Plate 38, on a slip of paper for convenience when lining off the string. In the corner 1⅞″ is added on to receive the short string, Fig. 6; **AB** shows a groove in the corner.

Fig. 6. *Shows the wall string connecting Fig. 5, and landing on the quarter pace.*

At the lower end **AB** shows a tongue to enter the groove in the corner, shown at Fig. 5. By raising up 6½″ in the angle a suitable easing is found on the lower end of Fig. 6, and also on the upper end of Fig. 5. This will increase the width of string at the external angles of Nos. 13 and 14 rise, but this cannot be avoided at all times. The straight part of wall string is lined off from the pitch-board.

PLATE 40.

Plate 40. [Scale ¾″ 1 foot.] *Shows how to construct the face-moulds for the stair-case. Fig. 1, Plate 38; the plan of cylinder starting being greater than a quarter circle and less than a semi-circle.*

Fig. 1. *Shows the plan of tangents, enclosing the center line of rail for the wreath-piece, starting from the newel; the angle of tangents on plan is acute, and the wreath to be worked out in one piece.*

The center line of rail *ABC* is struck from the center *O*, with a radius *AO*, equal to 8¾″. The dotted line indicates the face of cylinder; *X* is the center of newel, and *D* is the point of miter; *C* is the termination of the curve at the cap.

From *C* draw *CO;* perpendicular to *CO* draw *CE* indefinite; perpendicular to *AO* draw the tangent to intersect *CE* at *E;* prolong the tangent *EA* to *S* for direction of straight rail. From *O*, and parallel to *CE*, draw *OK;* the face of No. 6 rise is 2¼″ from the spring of cylinder on the center line of rail, and No. 6 tread measures 5¾″ as shown. No. 7 tread is a regular tread 10″ wide.

Fig. 2. *Shows the elevation of risers, treads and the length of tangents.*

Let *XX* indicate the edge of drawing board; make *AJ* and *JB* equal *AK* and *KE*, Fig. 1; perpendicular to *XX*, draw *AC*, *JM* and *BD* indefinite; on the line *AC*, set up the height of five risers, then elevate Nos. 6, 7 and 8 risers, keeping the face of No. 6 rise 2¼″ from the spring line *AC;* No. 6 tread is 5¾″, and No. 7 tread is 10″. Through the center of balusters *O, O*, draw the under side of rail; parallel with *OO*, draw the center of rail, intersecting *AC* at *C;* from the top of No. 1 step set up 4½″ to the under side of rail, and 1¼″ more to the center of rail, making 5¾″ from top of No. 1 tread to center of rail at *L;* make *DF* equal *CD* on plan, Fig. 1, (1¼″).

From *L*, and parallel to *XX*, draw *LG*. Now let it be observed at Fig. 1, Plate 38, that the diameter is prolonged to intersect the walking line at *H*, on No. 6 tread, that the radial line enters No. 5 tread and across No. 6 rise, and in on No. 6 tread, indicating that the tangents should be lifted above No. 5 tread on the spring line *AC*, over one rise, we will say to *K*, 8½″ in this case, as that will allow at the same time a suitable easing to connect the wreath-piece with the straight rail.

Draw *LK* prolonged to intersect the center of rail at *N*, and cutting the perpendicular from *J* at *M;* from *M*, and parallel to *XX*, draw *MP*. Make *GR* equal the diagonal *DE*, Fig. 1; make *GQ* equal the chord *AC*, Fig. 1; make *KS* equal 2¼″ for shank; make joint at *S* at right angles to *NK*. Draw the point *H* on the center of rail opposite the face of No. 7 rise for a point on the pattern to measure from, when jointing the rail; the distance *HC* is 10″, which should be marked on the pattern: from *P*, draw *PT*, at right angles to *LK*.

Bevels. Let *ZZ* indicate the edge of a board; parallel with *ZZ*, draw 9 10; perpendicular to *ZZ*, draw 9 11, equal to the radius *OA*, Fig. 1, (8¾″). Make 9 12 equal *PT*, and 9 13 equal *GP;* draw 11 12 and 11 13 prolonged to edge of board; the angle at 13 gives the bevel at the miter cap, and the angle at 12 gives the bevel for the shank.

Parallel with 9 10, draw the half width of rail (2″), cutting the hypothenuse of bevels at 14 and 15.

Fig. 3. *Shows the construction of face-mould.*

Make *SKML* equal *SKML,* Fig. 2; with *K* as a center, and *KQ* in elevation, Fig. 2, for a radius, draw arc at *C;* then with *L* as a center, and the director *EC,* Fig. 1, for a radius, draw arc intersecting at *C;* join *LC* prolonged to equal *CD* (1¼″) on plan, Fig. 1.

Perpendicular to *LC,* draw *CO* indefinite; parallel with *LC,* draw *MO;* draw *OK* prolonged, and we have the trapezium *OKLC,* on the cutting plane, that when in position, will agree with the trapezium *OAEC,* on plan, Fig. 1.

Proof. The diagonal *OL²* must equal the distance *RP,* Fig. 2. If so, the angle of tangents at *L* must be correct.

Make joint at *S* at right angles to *SL;* make *OA* equal the radius *OA,* Fig. 1, (8¾″); make *A* 4 and *A* 5 each equal the half width of rail (2″); make *C* 2 and *C* 3 each equal 13 15, Fig. 2; also make *S* 7 and *S* 8 each equal 12 14, Fig. 2; draw 8 6 and 7 9 parallel to *SL,* to intersect the radial line *OK* produced. Now *OC* is the semi-major axis, and *OA* the semi-minor axis.

Pivot the trammel at *O* with the arms resting on the major axis line; for the concave side of mould, set from the pencil to minor pin the distance *OA,* then place the pencil in the point at 3, and drop the pins into the grooves, then fasten the major pin at *O,* and trace the curve for the convex side of mould; proceed in like manner to trace the center and concave curves; from *D* draw the straight wood required for miter parallel to *OC.*

Sections *P* and *R* show the application of bevels. Observe they cross the tangents in their application.

Fig. 4. Shows how to obtain the face-mould for the same plan by the use of ordinates, drawn from the chord line as a base, which is more convenient than using a trammel in long face-moulds. The correctness of curve depends on the number of ordinates; the greater number of ordinates the more correct will be the face-mould. The lettering is the same as Fig. 1; *AE* and *EC* are tangents to the center line of rail at the points *A* and *C.* Draw the chord *AC;* bisect the same at *M;* bisect *AM* and *MC* at *N* and *P;* bisect again at *Q* and *R;* from these bisections draw ordinates parallel with the director *CE,* cutting the concave and convex sides of rail at 1, 1, 1, and 2, 2, 2, &c.

Fig. 5. *Shows the face-mould similar to Fig. 3.*

Draw *SKVL* equal to *SKML,* Fig. 2. With *KQ,* Fig. 2, as a radius and *K* for a center, draw arc at *C;* with *GL,* Fig. 2, as a radius and *L* for a center, draw arc intersecting at *C;* draw *LC* produced. Draw the chord *KC;* bisect *KC* at *M;* bisect *MK* and *MC* at *N* and *P;* bisect again at *R* and *Q;* draw ordinates from the points *K. M, N, P, R, Q,* parallel to the director *CL.* Now transfer the points on ordinates on Plan Fig. 4 to corresponding ordinates on face-mould, using the chords as base lines.

` Make joint at *S* perpendicular to *SL;* make *CD* equal *CD* on plan; make joint at *D* perpendicular to *DL;* make *C* 3 and *C* 4 each equal 15 13, Fig. 2; make *S* 8 and *S* 7 each equal 14 12, Fig. 2. Draw the direction of straight wood at 7, 8 and 3, 4, parallel with the tangents **KL** and **LC**. Then trace the concave and convex sides of face-mould through the points 3, 1, 1, 1, 8, and 4, 2, 2, 2, 7, using a flexible strip.

If the points of contact are required, draw **CO** indefinite and perpendicular to **DL**; parallel with **CL** draw **VO**; from the intersection at **O** draw **OK** prolonged. Then the radial lines **OC** and **OK** give the points of contact connecting the straights with the curved part. The sections at **A** and **B** show the bevels applied, same as at Fig. 3.

Proof. The diagonal **OL** must equal the distance **PR**, Fig. 2; if so, the triangle **KLC** is correct.

If it be required to find the length of odd balusters at the newel, then return to plan Fig. 1. Parallel with the director **CE**, draw lines from the intersection of each rise with the center of rail to intersect the tangent **AE** at **F, G, H** and **J**. Now from the points **F, G, H** and **J** on plan draw lines perpendicular to **XX** in elevation, Fig. 2, showing the treads and risers 1, 2, 3, 4 and 5, in elevation.

Then if lines be drawn from the center of each baluster in the same manner to intersect the under side of rail as shown for No. 3 baluster on No. 4 step, which intersects the tangent at **L**, and again intersects No. 4 step at **Y**, and the underside of rail at **U**; then No. 3 baluster is equal to **UY**, longer than a regular short baluster. The other balusters may be elevated in the same way.

Fig. 6. *Shows plan of the center line of rail for the 12″ cylinder, Fig. 4, Plate 38.*

The radius **OA** for the center line of rail equals $6\frac{3}{4}''$; **AB, BC, CD** and **DE** show the tangents enclosing the semi-circle **ACE**; draw the direction of the straight string **AF** and **EG**. Now show the direction of the risers cutting the tangents. The face of No. 13 rise is $3\frac{1}{2}''$ from the spring of cylinder measured on the face of outer string, if measured on the center line of rail, it equals $3''$. When proceeding to draw the elevation of treads and risers, take the width of treads from the center line of rail on the straight part, and in the cylinder follow the line of tangents.

Fig. 7. *Shows the elevation of tangents; they being unfolded.*

Let **ZZ** indicate the edge of drawing board; find the average pitch from the face of No. 10 rise to the face of No. 18 rise. Thus $(10''+8\frac{1}{2}''+5\frac{1}{2}''+3''+6\frac{3}{4}''+6\frac{3}{4}''+6\frac{3}{4}''+6\frac{3}{4}''+10''-64'')$ equals $64''$, measured around the tangents. Now this includes 8 risers and 8 treads. Divide $64''$ by 8, the number of risers, equals $8''$, for the average tread, the regular rise is $7\frac{1}{2}''$, then with $8''$ on the blade of square, and $7\frac{1}{2}''$ on the tongue, the tongue will give the average pitch.

Now set a bevel to that pitch, and draw the perpendiculars **AF, BG, CH, DJ** and **EK**, each to equal **AB, BC, CD** and **DE**, on plan, Fig. 6.

Next elevate the treads and risers, keeping the face of No. 13 rise $3''$ from the spring line **AF**, and No. 17 rise comes on the spring line **EK**; Nos. 12 and 11 treads equal $5\frac{1}{2}''$ and $8\frac{1}{2}''$ each; and No. 10 and 17 treads equal $10''$ each.

Through the center of balusters **O, O,** and **O, O,** draw the inclination for the underside of rail. Parallel with **OO** and **OO** draw the center of rail intersecting **AF** at **L** on the right, and on the left extend to intersect **BG** at **M**, cutting **CH, DJ** and

EK at *HJ* and *K* respectively. *M* is a fixed point; from *M* draw *MP* to tangent arc at No. 12 rise, and intersecting the center of rail at *P*, and cutting *AF* at *Q*. From *Q* and at right angles to *AF*, draw *QR*, cutting *BG* at *S*. Through *H*, and perpendicular to *AF*, draw *FHE*, cutting *BG* and *DJ* at *G* and *N*; then *RH* will be the height for the lower wreath-piece, and *EK* will be the height for the upper wreath-piece. Prolong tangent *QM* to intersect *HF* at *T*; also prolong tangent *HM* to intersect *FQ* at *V*; from *S* and perpendicular to *MV* draw *SW*; from *G* and at right angles to *TQ* draw *GY*; from *N* and perpendicular to *JH* draw *NU*; make *Q* 2 and *E* 3 each equal to the chord *AC*, on plan Fig. 6; parallel with *BG* draw the half width of rail (2″), cutting *HM* and *MQ* at 4 and 5; at *K*, 6″ is allowed for straight wood, and at *Q* 4″ is allowed.

Ease off the angle at *P* to form the ramp agreeable to the eye.

Bevels. Let *XX* indicate the edge of board; draw the dotted line 6 20 parallel to *XX*; draw 6 7 perpendicular to *XX*, and equal to the radius *OC*, Fig. 6 (6¾″). Make 6 8 equal *GY*, and 6 9 equal *UN*, and 6 20 equal *SW*; draw 7 8 and 7 9 and 7 20 to the edge of board for convenience when setting the bevel.

If it be required to find the length of odd balusters in the cylinder, then return to plan, Fig. 6; make *BK* equal *GT*, Fig. 7; connect *KC* for the director, or level line on plan. Now from the center of each baluster draw lines parallel to *CK*, to intersect the tangents *AB* and *BC* for the lower quadrant *OABC*; for the upper quadrant *OCDE*, the diagonal *OD*, becomes the director in this case, because both tangents in elevation are the same length. Then from the center of each baluster in the upper quadrant, draw lines parallel to *OD*, to intersect the tangents *CD* and *DE*. Now transfer the points on tangents on plan to their position on the treads, relative to the tangents as shown in elevation, Fig. 7. Observe the baluster on No. 14 tread is one [1″] inch longer than a regular short baluster; also the long baluster on No. 12 tread is 3½″ longer than a regular short one.

Fig. 8. *Shows the face-mould for the lower wreath-piece.*

Make *AB* equal *QM*, Fig. 7; with *A* as a center, and 2 *F*, Fig. 7, for a radius, draw arc at *C*; again with *B* as a center, and tangent *HM*, for a radius, draw arc intersecting at *C*; join *BC*; parallel with *BC* and *BA*, draw *AO* and *CO*, for the parallelogram *OCBA*, on the cutting plane.

Proof. The diagonal *OB* must equal *V* 2, Fig. 7; make *AD* equal *TM*, Fig. 7. Draw *OD* for the director; make *OF* equal *OC*, on plan, Fig. 6; make *F* 2 and *F* 3 each equal the half width of rail; make *A* 4 and *A* 5 each equal *M* 4, Fig. 7, and *C* 6, *C* 7 each equal *M* 5, Fig. 7. Pivot the trammel at *O* with the arms at right angles to *OF*, and set from the pencil to minor pin the distance *OF* for the center of rail; then place the pencil in *C*, and drop the pins into the grooves, and trace the center line on the face-mould For the concave side, set from pencil to minor pin the distance *O* 2, then place the pencil in the point at 6, and drop the pins into the grooves, then fasten the major pin and trace the curve 6, 2, 4; repeat the operation for the convex side.

Make joint at *H* 4″ from *A*, and at right angles to *BA*, draw 4 8 and 5 9 parallel to *BH*; make joint at *C* perpendicular to *BC*.

The sections **Q** and **S** show the application of bevels. The bevel shown at 20, Fig. 7, applies at **Q**, and the bevel shown at 8, Fig. 7, applies at the section marked **S**. Note the bevels cross the tangents.

Fig. 9. Shows the face-mould for the upper wreath-piece, the tangents being both the one length, hence, the diagonal on the cutting plane will be the director, or direction of the minor axis, and only one bevel will be required for both joints.

Make **ED** equal tangent **KJ**, Fig. 7; let **EL** equal 6″ for shank, as shown at **K**, Fig. 7; with **E** as a center, and 3 **K**, Fig. 7, for a radius, draw arc at **C**; then with **DE** as a radius, and **D** for a center, draw arc intersecting at **C**; join **DC**; parallel to **DE** and **DC**, draw the radial lines **CO** and **EO** for the parallelogram **OEDC**, on the cutting plane.

Proof. The diagonal **OD** must equal the diagonal **OD**, on plan, Fig. 6.

Make **OA** equal the radius **OC**, Fig. 6; let **A** 2 and **A** 3 each equal the half width of rail (2″); make **C** 4, **C** 5 and **E** 6, **E** 7, each equal **M** 4, Fig. 7; make joints at **L** and **C** perpendicular to the tangents **DL** and **DC**; draw 6 8 and 7 9 parallel with **EL**.

Pivot the trammel at **O**, with the arms at right angles to the director **OD**; set from pencil to minor pin the distance **OA**, then place the pencil at **C**, and enter the minor pin in the groove; at the same time slide the major pin until both pins enter the grooves, then fasten the major pin and sweep the curve through the points **CAE**; the curve must tangent **DE** and **DC** at the points **C** and **E** always, if not, the work must be gone over again and corrected. If the elliptic curve should cross the tangents at the points **C** and **E**, or should it fall short, the learner will be sure the mould is not correct.

The sections **B** and **J** show the bevels applied through the center of mould. The bevel shown at 9, Fig. 7, is applied at both joints. The distance **LE** shows the amount of straight wood (6″ to allow when cutting the straight rail.

Fig. 10. Shows the easement pattern landing in the second story. The under side of inclining rail is made to pass through the center of balusters **O, O**, on No. 19 and 20 tread, and the under side of level rail is lifted above the floor half a rise (3¾″); the face of No. 20 rise is shown on pattern at 2. The amount of straight wood is 3″ as shown for the inclining part, and for the level from the face of No. 20 rise to the joint on easement, equals 1′ 3″ to allow when cutting and jointing the rail. For convenience, these measurements should be marked on the pattern.

Jointing the rail. The easement pattern over Nos. 6 and 7 treads, Fig. 2, shows 10″ from the spring of cylinder to the fixed point **H**, marked on the pattern. And the ramp pattern over Nos. 11 and 12 treads, Fig. 7, shows 1′ 9″ from the spring of cylinder to the fixed point **I**, also mark on the pattern. These points should be transferred to the crook, so as to be seen on the under side of rail, when bolted together for proving the exact lengths before leaving the shop.

The length from spring to spring of cylinder equals 6′ 9″ for *No. 1 length*, (see Fig. 2. Plate 38); now deduct the two measurements above (10″+1′ 9″=2′ 7″) from the whole length (6′ 9″— 2′ 7″=4′ 2″) equals 4′ 2″ between the two fixed points **H**, Fig. 2, and **I**, Fig. 7.

For No. 2 length. The shank at Fig. 9, is 6'' long, and the easement pattern at Fig. 10, shows 3'' from the joint to the fixed point 2, and the whole length from spring of cylinder to face of landing rise, equals 3' 1½''; from which deduct the above (3' 1½''—(6''+3'')=2' 4½'') equals 2' 4½'', the length to cut No. 2.

For No. 3 length. We have 1' 3'' to the joint on easement pattern to be deducted from the whole length 2' 0'' from face of No. 20 rise to spring of quarter cylinder, which (2' 0''—1' 3''= 0' 9'') equals 9'' for the short length, the shank of quarter turn may be increased, and one joint made to answer; from quarter turn to wall is 4' 1''.

PLATE 41.

Plate 41. [Scale ¾''=1 foot]. *Exhibits two different face-moulds for a quarter pace winding, starting from a newel, and having five winders; the regular tread is 10''×7'' rise.*

Fig. 1. *Shows a quarter circle starting from a 6''×6'' newel, with five winders.*

The radius *OA* for the face of outer string equals 12'', the distance *AB* is 15'' from the face of string for the walking line. The regular tread 10'', is spaced off on the walking line; No. 1 tread is swelled and increased to 11¼'' on the regular tread line; the balusters should be spaced off equal, and the risers drawn from the balusters through the spacing on the walking line; in this case it will be observed that No. 3, 4 and 5 risers radiate to the center *O*, and No. 2 rise nearly so; now if the radius *OA* be prolonged to cut the walking line at *B*, it will be seen in this case that the line *BO* remains on No. 6 step from the intersection at the spring of cylinder to the intersection of the walking line, hence a person walking up or down the stairs, the hand will be normal to the curve of rail. Wherever the stair-builder can arrange his winders in this way, more satisfaction will be the result.

The center of newel is 5'', and the point of mitre is 4'' from the spring line *OC*, Fig. 2. On the face of wall string, No. 1 tread is 15''; No. 2, 18¼''; No. 3 is 27'' to corner; No. 4, 27''; No. 5, 19'', and No. 6 is the regular tread 10'' wide; these measurements may be marked from the drawing made to the full size, on to the scale drawing, or a slip of paper for convenience, when lining off the wall string.

At No. 3 winder, a temporary pattern made of thin lath is shown tacked and braced; this pattern, by turning over, will answer for No. 4 winder; patterns may be made for the other winders and all strung up until needed, and the drawing, if made on paper, may be rolled up for future use. The lining out of the wall and front strings is the same as previously described.

Fig. 2. *Shows the plan of tangents AB and BC, inclosing the center line of rail ADC.*

The radius *OA*, of the quarter circle *ADC*, equals 12¾''; the center of newel is located 6'' from the quarter circle, and the point of miter is 4'' from the spring line *OC*; the face of No. 7 rise is 8¼'' from the spring line *OA*; the dotted line *EF* indicates the face of cylinder, the radius of which is 12''.

Fig. 3. *Shows the development of tangents from plan Fig. 2, the elevation of treads and risers, and also the tangents for face-mould.*

Let **XX** indicate the edge of drawing board; make **AB** and **BC** equal **AB** and **BC**, Fig. 2, perpendicular to **XX**; draw **AD**, **BE** and **CF**, indefinite. At **A**, set up the height of 6 risers, and elevate the treads and risers from their intersection with the tangents on plan, Fig. 2; make the face of No. 7 rise 8¼″ from the spring line **AD**. Through the center of balusters **O**, **O**, draw the underside of rail parallel with **OO**, draw the center of rail, cutting **AD** at **G**; mark the point **H**, on the center of rail, plumb over No. 7 rise, for a fixed point when cutting the straight rail.

Now 4″ to the right, and parallel with **CF**, draw the point of miter **JK**; from the top of first step set up 5″ to the underside of rail, and 1¼ more, or 6¼″ to the center of rail at **Z**. We are now ready to elevate the tangents; if a radial line be drawn to the center of No. 2 step, Fig. 1, on the walking line, as **OC**, it will be seen. The line is all on No. 2 step, and indicates that the direction of steps is very near normal to the curve of cylinder or rail, and the position at **C** will therefore admit of keeping the rail down to the regular height of a short baluster. Then we will in this case give the lower tangent the inclination of No. 2 tread and rise, as shown at **SS**; draw the underside of rail parallel with **SS**; draw the tangent indefinite for the center of rail, cutting **CF** at **L** and **BE** at **N**, and at the same time intersecting a level line from **Z**, say at **n**, so as to allow a small easing into the cap.

From **N**, draw the upper tangent to intersect **GH**, at any point beyond **G**, sufficient to form an easing connecting the wreath with the straight rail, we will say at **M**, and cutting **AD** at **P**, prolong **PN** to intersect **CF** at **Q**; parallel with **XX** draw **LR**, cutting **BE** at **T**; parallel with **XX** draw **GU**, cutting **LN**, produced at **V**. From **U**, and perpendicular to **VL**, draw **UW**; from **T**, and perpendicular to **PQ**, draw **TY**; parallel with **BE**, draw the half width of rail, cutting **LN** and **NP** at 9 and 10. Make **R** 12 equal the chord **AC** on plan, Fig. 2; make **P** 19 equal twice **NU**, prolong the tangent **NL** to intersect **JK** at 13.

Bevels. The dotted line 14 15, indicates a gauge line parallel with **XX**; at right angles to **XX**, draw 15 16, equal to the radius **OC**, Fig. 2; make 15 17 equal **UW**, and 15 14 equal **TY**, join 14 and 16, and 17 16; the angles at 14 and 17; give the bevels required; make **P** 18 equal 2″ for shank on face-mould.

Fig. 4. *Shows the face-mould.*

At any convenient place on the pattern paper draw **BC** 13, equal to **NL** 13, Fig. 3; with **C** as a center and **P** 12, Fig. 3, for a radius, draw arc at **A**; again, with **B** as a center, and the tangent **PN**, Fig. 3, for a radius, draw arc intersecting at **A**; draw **BA** prolonged, parallel with **AB** and **BC**, draw **CO**, and **AO** produced, for the parallelogram **OABC**, on the cutting plane, or plane of plank.

Proof. The diagonal **OB** must equal the distance 13 19, Fig. 3; if so, the angle of tangents at **B** must be correct. Make **CD** equal **NV**, Fig. 3, draw **DO**, produced, for the direction of the minor axis; make **OF** equal the radius **OC**, Fig. 2; make **F** 2 and **F** 3 each equal the half width of rail [2″]; make **A** 4 and **A** 5 each equal **N** 9, Fig. 3; make **C** 6 and **C** 7 each equal **N** 10, Fig. 3; draw 6 8 and 7 9 parallel with **B** 13; make joint at 13, perpendicular to tangent **B** 13, and the joint at **H**, make at right angles to tangent **AB**; draw 4 10 parallel to **HB**. Now pivot the trammel at *O*, and set from pencil to minor pin the distance *OF*, for the center of rail on the face-mould; then place the pencil in the point at *A*, and drop the pins in the grooves; then fasten the major pin and trace the curve for the center of rail on the face-mould shown by the dotted line *AFC*: now draw the concave and convex sides of mould in the same way.

The bevel shown in the angle at 17, Fig. 3. is applied at section *L*, and the bevel shown in the angle at 14, Fig. 3, is shown applied at section *N*.

For the joint at *L*, connecting the newel cap, make the joint and apply the bevel in the usual way.   After the bevels have been applied, and the wreath piece dressed off to the plumb on the concave and convex sides, then draw the line 2 2 through the center of crook as shown at section *L*, and apply the bevel shown in the angle at 13, Fig. 3, from the joint and through the points 2, 2 giving the plumb cut *JK*, Fig. 3, from which lay off the center of rail *Zn*, Fig. 3, the distance to 13 *Z* above the point 13. A short piece may be glued on the upper side of crook to increase the thickness of plank for the easing, if required. as shown at *OO*.

The section at *L* shows the block pattern lifted up from 13 to *Z*, at the center.   Now shape the easing at right angles to the joint *JK*, as shown.

To obtain the length of odd balasters, make *CH* on plan, Fig. 2, equal *VU* in elevation, Fig. 3; join *OH* for the director on plan.   From the center of Nos. 3, 4 and 5 baluster, draw lines to intersect *CB* and *BA* at 9, *B*, and 10; now transfer the point marked 10 on No. 5 tread, also the point 9 on No. 3 tread, and the intersection at *B* on No. 4 tread on plan, Fig. 2 to corresponding treads in elevation, Fig. 3, as shown.

The baluster on No. 4 tread happens to come on the angle line *BE;* now elevate the balusters parallel to the perpendicular, to intersect the underside of rail as shown.

As the short baluster at *O* is naught, then the baluster on No. 3 step will be equal to ½″ longer, and on No. 4 step 1¼″, and on No. 5 step 1¾″ longer than a regular short baluster.

Fig. 8.   *Shows how the easing at the upper end of wreath-piece may be worked on the shank of same, and thus avoid the short easing* **HM,** *Fig. 3.*

PA shows the tangent *NG*, Fig. 3, prolonged; also *GB* for the inclination *GH*, Fig. 3.   Through 5, draw the joint 3 4 perpendicular to the straight rail *BG;* set off on each side of *PA*, the half thickness of plank required for the wreath-piece, shown at section *N*, Fig. 4; make a temporary joint at *A*, at right angles to *AP*, as 2 3; to this joint apply the bevel in the usual way, shown at N, Fig. 4, and work off the wreath-piece to the plumb on the concave and convex sides; then apply the bevel shown at 2, from the temporary joint, for the cripple joint 3 4.   Now drop the block pattern on the joint just made the distance *A* 5, below the center of plank for the center of rail as shown; then ease off into the wreath part, from a tangent at right angles to the joint 4 3, thus saving the short straight easing.

Fig. 5.   *Shows another treatment of the plan, Fig. 2; the radius* [12¾″] *for center of rail, the position of treads and risers being the same.*

AB, BC, are the tangents; the face of No. 7 rise is 8¼″ from the spring of cylinder.

Fig. 6. *Shows the elevation of treads and risers, also the tangents.*

The upper tangent is allowed to have the same inclination in this case as the straight rail; hence the wreath-piece will contain its own natural easing all in the wreath part of rail, at the upper end. In this case a joint is made at the spring line at the lower end, and a small easing is added to connect the newel cap, as shown.

Let XX indicate the edge of drawing board, make AB and BC each equal AB, BC, on plan, Fig. 5. Perpendicular to XX draw AD, BE and CF indefinite. Now elevate the treads and risers from the tangents on plan, Fig. 5, making No. 7 rise $8\frac{1}{4}''$ from the spring line AD. Through the center of balusters O, O, draw the underside of rail. Parallel with OO, draw the center of rail, cutting AD at P, and BE at N, and prolonged to intersect CF at Q; from the top of No, 1 step set up $5''$ to the underside of rail, and $1\frac{1}{4}''$ more, or $6\frac{1}{4}''$ to the center of rail at Z; draw Zn parallel to XX.

From the center of baluster on No. 2 tread, draw the arc for center of inclining rail. From N, draw a line to tangent the arc and intersect the horizontal line from Z at n, and also cutting CF at L; make joint at L perpendicular to LN, and draw easing to suit. From P draw PU parallel with XX, cutting LN produced at V. From L draw LR parallel with XX, cutting BE at T; from T and at right angles to PQ, draw Ty; from U, and at right angles to LV, draw WU; parallel with BE, draw the half width of rail ($2''$) cutting the tangent PN at 10, and the tangent NL at 9; make R 12 equal the chord AC, on plan, Fig. 5; at P allow $6''$ for straight wood on the shank of face-mould; make R 19 equal LQ.

Bevels. Let 14 15 indicate a gauge line parallel with XX; perpendicular to XX, draw 15 16 equal to the radius OC, Fig. 5. Make 15 18 equal Ty, Fig. 6, and 15 17 equal WU, Fig. 6; draw 16 18 and 16 17 prolonged to edge of board.

Fig. 7. *Shows the face-mould lined off from the chord line, by the use of ordinates transferred from the plan direct.*

Make BC equal NL, Fig. 6; with C as a center, and P 12, Fig. 6, for a radius, draw arc at A; again with B as a center, and PN for a radius, draw arc intersecting at A; join BA and prolonged to H, allowing $6''$ for shank. Parallel with AB and BC, draw CO and AO, for the parallelogram $OABC$, on the cutting plane.

Proof. The diagonal OB must equal the distance 12 19 Fig. 6, if so, the angle of tangents at B must be correct.

Make joints at H and C perpendicular to the tangents AB and BC; make CD equal NV Fig. 6; join OD and produced for the points in face-mould, through which to trace the concave and convex curve using a pliable strip.

Draw the inside and outside curve of rail on plan, Fig. 5; make CH equal UV Fig. 6, connect OH for the director; bisect the chord AC at D; bisect AD and DC at E and F; now parallel with OH, and from the points A, E, D, F and C, draw ordinates to cut the concave and convex curves of rail on plan, as E, 2, 3, 4, &c.

Now return to Fig. 7, bisect the chord AC at D; bisect DA and DC at E and F; parallel to the director OD, draw ordinates indefinite from the points A, E, D, F and C, then transfer the points on the ordinates on plan, Fig. 5, to corresponding ordinates on face-mould, using the chords for base lines; make *OJ* equal the radius *OC* on plan, Fig. 5; make *J* 4 and *J* 5 each equal the half width of rail (2″); make *C* 2 and *C* 3 each equal *N* 10, Fig. 6, also make *A* 6 and *A* 7 each equal *N* 9, Fig. 6; parallel with *HB*, draw 6 8 and 7 9 for the width of face-mould at the shank. The curves may now be drawn through the points just found, using a pliable strip.

At sections *P* and *R* the bevels are shown applied to cross the tangents.

Balusters. If required to find the length of odd baluster in the quarter circle on the center line of rail, then from the center of each baluster on plan, Fig. 5, draw lines parallel with the directing ordinate *OH*, to intersect the tangents as at *XXX*, Fig. 5.

Now transfer their intersection with the treads on tangents on plan, to corresponding treads in elevation. It will be noticed that the balusters on No. 4 winder does cross No. 4 rise and on to No. 3 winder on plan, and is set over on line with No. 4 tread in elevation, Fig. 6, as the proper place for its length. Now parallel with the risers, draw the balusters to intersect the underside of rail at *ff*, &c., for their respective lengths, as explained for Fig. 3.

It will be observed that after the director *OH* on plan, is located, the position of risers under the tangents in elevation, relative to the cutting plane may be established; for each ordinate on face-mould is horizontal and parallel to corresponding ordinates on plan, and all parallel to the directing ordinates.

It will be observed at Fig. 6, the tangent *PN*, is in line with the center of straight rail, thus avoiding the easing shown at Fig. 3. This has caused the rail to raise at *N*, and as a result, the balusters are longer, and the rail will feel high when standing on No. 4 step; while at Fig. 3, the rail will have an agreeable height; but it is a good fault that the rail on winders be high better than to feel low.

On quarter and half pace winding stairs the rail should never be constructed so that the wreath-piece would line with the nosings, unless the risers all radiate to the center, and at the same time, be for a large cylinder, or in a circular stair-case, then the wreath may be constructed so that when placed on the stairs, the underside of rail will touch every nosing. When as in this case the tangent *PN*, Fig. 6, is the continuation of the straight rail; there should not be more than one graduating step outside the cylinder, or the space of a regular tread, may start from the spring of cylinder at the upper end of winders, while at the lower end, they should be graduated; one fault to this method is, without the use of graduated steps at the upper end, the easing on the lower edge of front string will be difficult to make satisfactory, as the string has to be increased more than usual at the angle in the formation of the easing connecting the regular treads with the winders.

PLATE 42.

Plate 42. *Exhibits plan* (Fig. 1) *of a half pace divided into two quarter paces by placing two risers across the half pace.*

This is done in many cases to gain room and avoid winders. The well hole is 10″ diameter, and the pitch is 8″ wide by 9″ tread. No. 14 tread is placed in the center of half pace, and the balusters are to be spaced off on the center line of rail equally, and then the risers are curved to suit the balusters and the miters at the return nosings.

Also at Fig. 2 is shown a quarter pace winding; the radius of quarter cylinder is 12″. In this case we have placed No. 16 tread in the center, and spaced the others either way on the walking line. Nos. 13 and 20 are the first square risers outside the winding treads. Locate a short baluster on Nos. 13 and 20 tread;

then space the intervening balusters equally, and draw the risers through the points on the walking line to suit the balusters. The scale for Figs, 1 and 2 is ¼″ equal 1 foot.

Fig. 3.   [Scale ¾″=1′.]   *Shows plan of the 10″ cylinder, Fig. 1.*

The dotted line indicates the string, and solid line the center line of rail.   *AB. BC, CD* and *DE* show the tangents enclosing the center line of rail.   The balusters are spaced off around the cylinder, and the concave and convex risers are curved into the cylinder to suit the balusters.   The face of Nos. 12 and 17 rise are 2¼″ from the spring of cylinder, the radius of cylinder being 5″, and balusters 2″×2″.   Then the radius for the center line of rail will equal 5¾″, or the diameter for the center line of rail will equal 11½″.

Fig. 4.   *Shows the elevation of tangents, treads and risers, unfolded from the tangents on plan Fig. 3.*

Let *XX* indicate the edge of drawing board; the points *A, B, C, D* and *E* show perpendiculars drawn from *XX*, and indicating the spring *A* and angle *B*, center *C* and angle *D* and spring *E*, on plan Fig. 3.   Now elevate the risers and treads from the tangents on plan Fig. 3, being careful to keep the face of No. 12 and 17 rise 2¼″ from the spring lines *A* and *E*, as shown on plan Fig. 3.   Through the center of balusters *O, O* and *O, O* draw the underside of rail; parallel with *OO*, on the right, draw the center of rail, cutting the spring line at *E*, and to intersect the angle and center lines at *D* and *F*, and also intersecting the spring line on the left at *G*.   Now *D* becomes a fixed point.   At the external angle of No, 12 rise draw arc equal to the half thickness of rail (1¼″), and from *D* draw a line to tangent the arc and intersect the center of rail at *H*, and cutting the center, angle and spring lines at *C. B* and *A*; from *A,* and square to the spring line *C*, draw *AJ.* cutting the angle line *B* at *K;* then *JC* will be the height for the lower wreath-piece; from *C*, and square to the spring line *E.* draw *CL*, cutting the angle line *D* at *M;* then *LE* is the height for the upper wreath-piece.

Square to *LE*, draw *EN*, cutting the angle line *D* at *P;* prolong the tangent *CD* to intersect *NE* at *Q;* from *P*, and perpendicular to *CQ*, draw *PR;* from *M*, draw *MS* square to *EF*: make *CT* and *JU* equal the chord *AC*, Fig. 3; draw *KV* at right angles to *AB;* parallel with the angle line *D*, draw the half width of rail, cutting the tangent *DE* at 2, and the tangent *CD* at 3; ease the angle on the left at *H* to please the eye; make joint on easement so as to allow 3″ of straight wood on the shank of face-mould.

Bevels.   Let 4 5 indicate a gauge line parallel with *XX;* square to *XX*, draw 4 6, and equal to the radius *OC*, Fig. 3; make 4 7 equal *PR*, make 4 8 equal *KV*, also make 4 5 to equal *MS;* draw 6 5, 6 8 and 6 7 to the edge of board.

As the two tangents *AB* and *BC* for the lower wreath-piece are both the same length, and inclination, one bevel only will be required for both joints, the angle at 8 gives that bevel.

The tangents *CD* and *DE* for the upper wreath-piece are of different inclinations and will require two bevels; the angle at 5 gives the bevel for shank, and the bevel in the angle at 7 gives the bevel for center joint.

Fig. 5. *Exhibits the face-mould for the lower wreath-piece.*

Make *AB* equal the tangent *AB*, Fig. 4: with *A* as a center and *CU*, Fig. 4 for a radius, draw arc at *C*: again with *B* as a center, and *BA* for a radius, draw arc intersecting at *C*, join *BC*. Parallel with *BA* and *BC*, draw *CO* and *AO* for the parallelogram on the cutting plane, that will coincide with the parallelogram *OABC* on plan, Fig. 3, when in position.

Proof. The diagonal *BO* must equal *BO* on plan, Fig. 3. Draw the diagonal *BO* for the direction of minor axis: prolong the radial lines *OA* and *OC*; make *A* 2, *A* 3, also *C* 4, each equal *D* 3, Fig. 4; make *OD* equal the radius *OC*, Fig. 3; make *D* 6, *D* 7, each equal the half width of rail [2″]; make from *A* to *F* equal 3″ for shank; make joint at *F* square to the tangent. Now draw the right angle at *O*, and trace the concave and convex sides of mould by using the rod as described at Fig. 9, Plate 13.

The sections at *H* and *J* show the bevels applied to cross the tangents, and through the center of plank. The shaded part shows the width at the joints to saw out the crooks. At the crossing of minor axis, ⅜″ wider than the mould on the concave side, is all the over-wood that will be required in this case; that amount will allow the twist of rail; at this point the bevels blend, and the section is at right angles to the face of crook.

Fig. 6. *Exhibits the face-mould for the upper wreath-piece.*

Make *CD* equal tangent *CD*, Fig. 4, with *C*, as a center, and *NT*, Fig. 4, for a radius; draw arc at *E*; again, with *D* as a center and *DE*, Fig. 4, for a radius, draw arc intersecting at *E*, draw *DE*, prolonged 6″ to *H*; parallel with *DE* and *DC*, draw *CO* and *EO*, for the parallelogram on the cutting plane.

Proof. The diagonal *DO* must equal *TF* in elevation, Fig. 4; make *CA* equal *DQ*, Fig. 4. Draw *OA* indefinite for the direction of minor axis. Make *OB* equal the radius *OC*, Fig. 3. Prolong the radial lines *OC* and *OE*; make *E* 2 and *E* 3 each equal *D* 3, Fig. 4; make *B* 5 and *B* 4 each equal the half width of rail (2″); make *C* 6 and *C* 7 each equal *D* 2, Fig. 4.

Make joints at *C* and *H* square to the tangents *CD* and *DE*. Draw 3 9 and 2 8 parallel with *DH*. Draw the right angle to the minor axis at *O*, and trace the concave, convex and center curves of face-mould, using a rod to make points in the curve, then use a pliable strip in tracing the curves.

The section at *P* shows the bevel at the angle 7, Fig. 4, applied through the center of plank; the section at *R* shows the bevel found in the angle at 5, Fig. 4, applied through the center of plank, for the shank end of wreath-piece.

Fig. 7. *Exhibits the plan for the quarter pace winding.* [*Scale ¾″—1 foot*].

The dotted line indicates the face of outer string, and the solid line the centre line of rail. The radius for the center line of rail equals 12¾″; the tangents *AB* and *BC* inclose the quarter circle and are at right angles to each other; the face of No 14 and 19 rise is 2¼ from the spring of cylinder; Nos. 13 and 19 treads are 6¼″ on the center line of rail; Nos. 12 and 20 treads are the regular width, 9″.

Fig. 8. *Exhibits the development of tangents AB and BC, from the plan, Fig. 7, and also the treads and risers.*

Let *XX* indicate the edge of drawing board; at right angles to *XX* draw the spring and angle lines *A*, *B*, *C*; elevate the treads and risers from the tangents on plan, keeping the face of

Nos. 14 and 19 rise, 2¼″, from the spring lines; Nos. 13 and 19 treads are 6¼″ wide, and Nos. 12 and 20 are 9″ wide. Note, at Fig. 2, the radial lines intersect the regular tread line by crossing No. 19 rise, and also crossing No. 14 rise, thus indicating that the rail should be kept up at No. 19 rise, while at No. 14 the rail should be kept down.*

Through the centre of balusters *O, O* and *O, O* draw the underside of rail parallel with the underside of rail; draw the center of rail, intersecting the spring line at *D* on the left and at *E* on the right; now we will allow the direction of upper tangent to cross the spring line at *C,* level with No. 19 tread, making a small easing to connect the wreath-piece. Take a point say at *G,* and draw *GC* prolonged, cutting the angle line at *B,* and intersecting the spring line at *F.* At the center of baluster on No. 14 tread draw arc equal to the half thickness of rail; from *B* draw line to tangent the arc, cutting the spring line at *A,* and intersecting the center of rail at *H,* square to the spring line; from *A* draw *AJ,* cutting the angle line at *K;* then *JC* will be the height the wreath-piece will raise from center to center.

From *C,* and square to *CJ,* draw *CL,* cutting the angle line at *M;* prolong the tangent *AB,* to intersect *CM* at *N;* from *M,* and square to *BN,* draw *MP;* from *K,* and square to *BF,* draw *KQ;* make *AR* equal the chord *AC,* Fig. 7. Parallel with the angle line at *B* draw the half width of rail (2″), cutting the tangents at 2 and 3. Allow 2″ at *A* and *C* for straight wood on the shank of face-mould. Make the joints square with the tangents *AB* and *BC;* ease off the angles at *H* and *G* to please the eye.

A plumb line over Nos. 13 and 20 rise at the center of rail, will serve as points to calculate the length of straight rail. To the points *D* and *E* there are 11½″; mark this on the pattern, as shown.

Bevels. The dotted line 4 5 indicates a gauge line parallel with *XX;* make 4 *S* on the perpendicular line equal the radius *OC,* Fig. 7; make 4 6 equal *MP;* let 4 5 equal *KQ;* draw *S* 6 and *S* 5 prolonged to edge of board.

Fig. 9. *Shows the face-mould.*

Make *AB* equal the tangent *AB,* Fig. 8; with *A* as a center, and *RL,* Fig. 8, for a radius, draw arc at *C;* again with *B* as a center, and *BC,* Fig. 8, for a radius, draw arc intersecting at *C;* connect *BC;* parallel with tangents *BA* and *BC,* draw *AO* and *CO,* for the parallelogram *ABCO,* on the cutting plane.

Proof. The diagonal *BO* must equal *RF,* Fig. 8; make *AD* equal *BN,* Fig. 8. Draw *DO* for the director, at right angles to the director at *O* draw the seat for the trammel; make *OF* equal *OC* on plan; make *F* 2 and *F* 3 each equal half width of rail (2″). Let *A* 4, *A* 5 each equal *B* 3, Fig. 8, and *C* 6, *C* 7 each equal *B* 2, Fig. 8; make *AH* and *CJ* each 2″ for straight wood connecting the ramp and easing; make joints at *H* and *J,* at right angles to the tangents *BA* and *BC;* draw 4 8 and 6 9 parallel with the tangents.

---

* The inclination to give the tangents over winders in elevation in many cases will require the best judgment of the stair-builder. This he will learn from practice — where to raise or lower the tangents, so that the rail will have an agreeable height, neither too high nor dangerously low.

Now if a trammel is not at hand, and this being a long face-mould, less room will be required by making use of the ordinates; or the stair-builder can make use of the rod and find points in the curve, then use a flexible strip in tracing the concave and convex sides of mould; when the trammel is used to trace the contour of face-mould, the center line should also be traced on the mould, for it serves as a guide to the correctness of mould, as the curve must tangent the tangents at the points A and C; if the trammel should fail in this, then either the trammel or pins on the rod are misplaced.

The section at N shows the bevel at 6, Fig. 8, applied through the center of plank; the section at L shows the bevel found in the angle at 5, Fig. 8, and is applied from the face of plank, through its center.

If it be required to find the length of odd balusters, then prolong tangent AB on plan, Fig. 7, making BD equal MN, Fig. 8, join DC for the director on plan; from the center of each baluster, draw lines parallel with the director to intersect the tangents on plan.

Now transfer these points on the tangents to the corresponding treads in elevation, and erect perpendiculars to intersect the underside of rail as shown. The regular short baluster at No. 13 tread is naught, and on No. 14 tread a ¼″ longer; No. 15 is ⅞″ longer; on No. 16 tread the baluster is 2½″ longer; No. 17 is 4½″ longer; No. 18, 4¾″ longer, and on No. 19 tread 3″ longer than a regular short baluster. Supposing the regular short baluster to be 2′ 2″ from top of step to underside of rail, then the baluster on No. 19 tread would be 2′ 2″ plus 3″ equals 2′ 5″ for its length from top of step to underside of rail at the center of baluster.

PLATE 43.

Plate 43. *Exhibits how to obtain the face-moulds in three pieces* around a semi-circle containing seven winders; the rail is shown for a right hand.*

Fig. 1. [Scale ¼″ = 1 foot.] *Shows plan of a half pace winder.*

There are two graduating treads outside of the cylinder on each side. The diameter of cylinder is 20″; the regular tread line is 15″ from the face of cylinder; the tread is 10″ by 7″ rise. No. 12 rise is placed on the center of half pace, and the regular tread (10″) is spaced off from that, right and left on the walking line. The balusters are then spaced off equally, and the risers drawn through the points on the walking line to the wall string and the outer string to suit the spacing of balusters; the balusters are 2″ by 2″, and rail 3″ by 4″, double moulded.

Fig. 2. [Scale ¾″ = 1 foot.] *Exhibits the plan for the center line of rail; the radius* OA *for the semi-circle* ABC *equals* 10¾″. *The dotted line shows the face of outer string.*

The face of Nos. 8 and 16 rise are 3½″ from the spring of cylinder on the outer string, the width of No. 7 and 16 treads, is 5″, and No. 6 and 17, are regular treads 10″ wide on the horse; the balusters are 2″ × 2″.

----

*Mr. Simon DeGraff claims the first to advance the system of making three pieces in the wreath around a semi-circle.

Divide the semi-circle ABC into three equal parts * as AD, DE and EC; draw the joints at D and E, radiating to the center O, draw the tangents AF, FD, DG, GE, EH and HC, each perpendicular to the radial lines OA, OD, OE and OC; they must equal each other in this case to be correct.

Parallel with tangents AF and FD, draw DJ and AJ for the parallelogram $AFDJ$, on plan; the semi-circle being divided into three parts at E and D, then the tangent AF will equal half the diagonal OF, and the diagonal JF will equal the length of tangent AF; prolong the tangent AF. From D, and at right angles to AF prolonged, draw DK.

Fig. 3. *Shows the development of tangents from the plan, Fig. 2; the treads and risers are elevated from the tangents on plan.*

Let XX indicate the edge of drawing board; now find the average pitch from tangents on plan, as explained at Plate 37; then draw the perpendiculars AB, CD, EF, GH, JK, SM and NP, to the average pitch, from the edge of board XX, all parallel to each other and the same distance apart, and equal to AF, FD, DG, GE, EH and HC, on plan, Fig. 2.

Now elevate the treads and risers from the tangents on plan, being careful to keep Nos. 5 and 16 rise $3\frac{1}{2}''$ from the spring lines AB and NP. Nos. 7 and 16 treads are each $5''$, and Nos. 6 and 17 treads are $10''$ each; the risers and treads are shown by the dotted lines, as taken from the tangents on plan Fig. 2. Through the center of balusters O, O and O, O draw the underside of rail parallel with the underside of rail; draw the center line of straight rail, cutting the spring line AB at Q for the lower end, and at the upper end prolong the center line to intersect the perpendicular JK at R, and cutting LM at S, and NP at N. At the center of baluster on No. 8 tread draw arc equal to the half depth of rail ($2''$); from S draw a line to tangent the arc and intersect the center of rail at T, and also cutting the perpendiculars at A, C, E, G and J. Make joints at E and J, as they are points of contact† with the center line of rail, as shown at D and E, on plan Fig 2.

At right angles to AB, draw AF, cutting the perpendicular CD at D, then FE will be the height for the lower wreath-piece; perpendicular to EF draw EK, cutting GH at H, then KJ will be the height for the middle wreath-piece; at right angles to JK draw JP, cutting the perpendicular from L at M, then PN is the height for the upper wreath-piece. Parallel with JP draw NL, cutting JS prolonged at u; make LV, MW and DY each equal FK on plan, Fig. 2; from V, and perpendicular to tangent JS produced, draw $V3$, and from W, and at right angles to NR draw $W4$; from y, and at right angles to AC, draw $y2$; make FZ and $P9$ each equal the chord AD on plan, Fig. 2.

----

*The radius of any circle will divide that circle into 6 equal parts, or the semi-circle into 3 equal parts, because the radius is the chord of 60 degrees of the circle. When dividing a circle into segments, it will be found the better way to make the chord of each segment equal the radius of the circle, then the length of each tangent AF, FD, on plan, will equal the diagonal FJ of their parallelograms, and will also equal one-half the diagonal OF, of the trapezium $OAFD$, both on plan and face-mould, as shown at Figs. 4 and 5, and also at Figs. 5, 6 and 7, Plate 44.

†At these points of contact the direction of the tangents cannot be changed. The points C, G and S are the angles, and answer to the angles F, G, H, on plan Fig. 2. At these points the direction of tangents may be changed. The student in stair-building will do well to remember this.

Bevels. Let 5 5 indicate the edge of a board, and the dotted line indicates a gauge line; perpendicular to 5 5 draw 20 21 equal to KD on plan, Fig. 2; make 20 22 equal V 3, and 20 23 equal y 2, and 20 24 equal W 4; draw 21 22, 21 23 and 21 24 prolonged to the edge of board 5 5 for the bevels required; parallel with 5 5 draw the half width of rail, cutting the hypothenuse of triangles at a, b and d.

Fig. 4. *Shows the face-mould for the lower wreath-piece connecting the ramp.*

Make AB equal AC in elevation, Fig. 3; with A as a center, and EZ, Fig. 3 for a radius, draw arc at C; again with B as a center, and BA for a radius, draw arc intersecting at C, join BC; parallel with BA and BC draw CD and AD for the parallelogram $ABCD$ on the cutting plane.

Proof. The diagonal BD must equal the diagonal FJ on plan, Fig. 2, if so, the parallelogram is correct.

Make BO equal FO, on plan, Fig. 2, and OF equal the radius AO on plan, Fig. 2. Make AH equal 3″ for the shank connecting the ramp; make joints at H and C perpendicular to tangents AB and BC. Draw the radial lines AO and CO for the points of tangency; make F 2 and F 3 each equal the half width of rail (1⅜″); make H 4, H 5, also C 6, C 7, each equal 5 b, Fig. 3; parallel with HB draw 4 8 and 5 9. Now pivot the trammel at O, and trace the concave and convex sides of face-mould. If preferred, bisect the chord AC, and draw the ordinates as has been explained. By making a joint at A, shown by the dotted line, this face-mould will answer for the middle wreath-piece, because the length of tangents and heights is equal in both cases.

The sections at L and N show the application of the bevel. Only one bevel is required for both joints, and is shown at the angle 23, Fig. 3. The same bevel applies for the middle wreath-piece. Observe the bevels cross the tangents.

Fig. 5. *Shows the face-mould for the upper wreath-piece.*

In this case, the tangents being unequal, two bevels will be required, and also observe from the elevation, Fig. 3, they will not cross the tangents, as the long tangent JS produced cuts the horizontal line LN between the perpendicular LM and the point V. The learner will find this explained at Fig. 9, Plate 14.

Make AB equal to JS, Fig. 3. With A as a center and 9 N, Fig. 3, for a radius, draw arc at C; then with B as a center, and tangent SN, Fig. 3 for a radius, draw arc intersecting at C; draw BC produced to F, equal to 6″ for the length of straight wood on shank. Parallel with AB and BC draw CO and AO for the parallelogram on the cutting plane.

Proof. The diagonal BO must equal the distance MR, Fig. 3. Prolong tangent AB, to D, equal to Su, Fig. 3; join DC for the director; the curve of face mould may now be drawn by ordinates or with the trammel, if with the trammel, prolong the diagonal BO equal to itself, to H; through H, and parallel to the director DC, draw HJ equal to the radius OA, Fig. 2, 10¾″, then JH is the semi-minor axis; draw the radial line HC prolonged, which gives the point of tangency on mould; make joints at A and F perpendicular to tangents BA and BF; make F 2 and F 3 each equal 5 d, Fig. 3; draw 2 4 and 3 5 parallel with the tangent BC; make A 6, A 7 each equal 5 a, Fig. 3; make J 8 and J 9 each equal the half width of rail (1⅜″). Now pivot the trammel at H, with the arms perpendicular to JH, and set from pencil to minor pin the distance *HJ* for the center line on face-mould, then place the pencil in *C* and the minor pin in the groove, at the same time sliding the major pin on the stem until both pins drop into the grooves, then fasten the major pin and trace the center line; proceed in like manner to trace the concave and convex sides of mould.

Ramp. Mark the face of No. 7 rise on the ramp at *T*; then *TQ* shows the amount (10″) to allow when jointing the rail; at the upper end the shank of face-mould shows 6″ to be deducted.

The sections at *M* and *N* show the application of the bevels. The bevel shown at 22, Fig. 3, is applied at *M*, and the bevel shown at 24, Fig. 3, is applied at *N*. Observe they do not cross the tangents. The shaded part shows the required width to saw out the crook from the plank, also the thickness of plank required to contain the twist of wreath-piece.

If ordinates be preferred for tracing the curve of face-mould instead of a trammel, then prolong tangent *EH*, on plan Fig. 2, to *L*, equal to *LU*, Fig. 3. Join *LC* for the director on plan; *DC* is the director on mould Fig. 5. Now bisect the chords, draw ordinates and transfer points from plan to face-mould, as described in former plates.

Fig. 6. [Scale ¼″=1 foot,]. *Exhibits the plan of a quarter pace winding at the landing.*

The cylinder being struck from two different radii, 12″ and 6″, as shown for the cylinder line; the tread line on the winders is 13″ from the face of cylinder; the balusters are 2″ by 2″, and the rail is 3″ by 4″, double moulded; the rise is 8″, and the regular tread 10″.

Fig. 7. *Shows the plan of the center line of rail ACE, struck from the centers M and N, their radius being 12¾″ and 5¾″, respectively.* [Scale ¾″=1 foot.]

Draw the tangents *AB*, *BC*, *CD* and *DE* at right angles to the radial lines. The tangents for the upper wreath-piece form an acute angle at *D*, and the two lower tangents form an obtuse angle on plan at *B*: parallel with *AB* and *BC* draw *CO* and *AO*; draw the chord *CE*, and the diagonal *BO* produced to *M*.

Bisect *CE* at *F*; draw the diagonal *FD*. The face of No. 14 rise is 1½″ from the spring line of cylinder; No. 13 tread is 8½″; No. 12, the regular tread, 10″. From *C* draw *CH* perpendicular to *AB* prolonged; again from *C* draw *CJ* perpendicular to tangent *DE*.

Fig. 8. *Shows the tangents unfolded from plan, and the elevation of the treads and risers from the tangents on plan; also the increased length of the tangents in elevation, for the face-mould.*

Let *XX* indicate the edge of drawing-board, then with the bevel set to the average pitch, draw *AB*, *CD*, *EF*, *GH* and *JK*, to correspond to tangents *AB*, *BC*, *CD* and *DE*, on plan, Fig. 7. Now elevate the treads and risers, keeping the face of No. 14 rise 1½″ from the spring line *AB*, as shown on plan. No. 13 tread is 8½″ wide, and No. 12 tread is the regular width 10″. Through the center of balusters *O*, *O*, draw the underside of rail. Parallel with the underside of rail, draw the center of rail, to cut the spring line *AB* at *L*. Mark the face of No. 13 rise on the center line of rail at *M*, then *ML* equals 12¾″ to allow when jointing the straight rail to the ramp. At the landing set up half a rise (4″) to the underside of rail, plus the half thickness of rail (2''), equals 6'' to the center of rail from the floor line. Then draw *PN* parallel to the floor line. Now *P* is a fixed point. At the external angle of No. 14 rise, draw arc equal to the half thickness of rail, and from the fixed point *P*, draw the inclination of tangents, to tangent the arc and intersect the center of inclining rail. This happens to be at *Q*. The inclination of tangents cuts the perpendiculars at *A*, *C*, *E* and *P*, and the level tangent at *P* and *N*. From *A*, and perpendicular to *AB*, draw *AF*, cutting the angle line *C* at *D*. Then *FE* is the height for the lower wreath-piece. From *E*, and perpendicular to *EF*, draw *EH*, then *HP* is the height for the upper wreath-piece. Make *HR* equal the chord *EC*, on plan, Fig. 7. Let *HS* equal the diagonal *DF*, on plan, Fig. 7. Make *DU* equal *BH*, on plan, and *PV* equal *DJ*, on plan, Fig. 7. From *V*, and perpendicular to tangent *EP* prolonged, draw *VW*, and from *U*, and perpendicular to tangent *AC*, draw *Uy*. Bisect *PH* at *Z*. Make *FT* equal the chord *AC*, on plan, Fig. 7.

Bevels. Let 3 3 indicate the edge of board, and 4 4 a gauge line, make 4 5 equal *HC* on plan, Fig. 7, and 4 6 equal *JC* on plan, Fig. 7. Make 4 7 equal *Uy*, Fig. 8, and 4 8 equal *VW*, Fig. 8, and 4 9 equal the height *HP*, Fig. 8; draw 6 4, 6 8 and 5 7 prolonged to 3 3. Then the angle at 7 gives the bevel for both joints on the lower wreath-piece, as both tangents have the same inclination. The angle at 8 gives the bevel for the lower joint on the upper wreath-piece, and the angle at 4 gives the bevel for the upper joint.

Parallel with 4 4 draw the half width of rail, cutting the hypothenuse of triangles at *a*, *b* and *d*.

Fig. 9. *Shows the face-mould for the lower wreath-piece.*

Make tangent *AB* equal *AC*, Fig. 8; with *A* as a center, and *TE*, Fig. 8 for a radius, draw arc at *C*; again with *B* as a center, and *BA* for a radius, draw arc intersecting at *C*, join *BC*; parallel with *AB* and *BC*, draw *CO* and *AO* for the parallelogram *ABCO* on cutting plane.

Proof. The diagonal *BO* must equal the diagonal *BO* on plan, Fig. 7. Prolong *BO* to equal *BM* on plan, Fig. 7; through *A* and *C* draw the radial lines *MC* and *MA* to give the points of tangency; prolong *BA* 3'' to *D* for straight shank, as shown at ramp in elevation, Fig. 8; make joints at *D* and *C* square to the tangents; make *D* 2 and *D* 3, also *C* 4 and *C* 5 each equal 7 *a*, Fig. 8; make *MF* equal the radius *MC*, Fig. 7. Let *F* 6 and *F* 7 each equal the half width of rail [1½'']: parallel with *DB* draw 2 8 and 3 9. Now pivot the trammel at *M*, with the arms at right angles to *MF*, then set from pencil to minor pin the distance *MF*, place the pencil in the point *A* and drop the pins into the grooves, and trace the center line of rail through the points *AFC*; repeat the operation for the concave and convex side of face-mould. At sections *P* and *N*, one bevel is shown applied to both joints taken from the angle at 7, Fig. 8.

Fig. 10. *Shows the face-mould for the landing wreath-piece.*

Make tangent *AB* equal *EP*, Fig. 8. With *A* as a center, and *RP*, Fig. 8, for a radius, draw arc at *C*; again with *B* as a center, and *PN* for a radius, draw arc intersecting at *C*; draw *BC* prolonged to *D*, 2'' for straight wood connecting the level rail. Draw the chord line *CA* perpendicular to tangent *CB*;

draw *CE* indefinite. Bisect the chord *AC* at *F;* draw the diagonal *BF* prolonged, intersecting *CE* at *H;* draw *HJ* parallel with *BC*, and equal to *EN*, (6¾''), Fig. 7.

Proof. The diagonal *BF* must equal the distance *SZ*, Fig. 8.

Make *J* 2 and *J* 3 each equal the half width of rail (1½''). Make joints at *D* and *A* square to the tangents *AB* and *BC;* make *C* 4 and *C* 5 equal 9 *d*, Fig. 8, and *A* 6, *A* 7, each equal to 8 *b*, Fig. 8. Now pivot the trammel in *H* with the arms resting in the major axis *CH;* then for the center line of rail, set from pencil to minor pin the distance *HJ*, and from the pencil to major pin the distance *HC*, now trace the curve through the points *C*, *J* and *A* for the center line of rail on mould, repeat the operation for the concave and convex curves of mould; 2'' of straight wood is added on at *D* to help the easing at the joint connecting the straight rail.

At sections *L* and *M* the bevels are shown applied to cross the tangents; the bevels shown in the angles 8 and 9, Fig. 8 are applied at sections *M* and *L*, respectively.

If a trammel be not at hand, then bisect the chords and use ordinates as previously described, *BC* will be the director on face-mould, and *DE* will be the director on plan, Fig. 7.

For the face-mould, Fig. 9, the diagonal will be the director, both on the mould and on plan, because both tangents have the same inclination.

At *N*, Fig. 3, observe the tangent *NS* is drawn with the same inclination as the straight rail, thus lifting the falling line of rail at the upper end of winders; if kept down at this point, and a short easing made to connect the wreath rail, the wreath would be improved and be still high enough; it is thought well to show the tangents in elevation in this way, so as to develop a face-mould having the minor axis outside the mould and near the joint, and thus exhibit an extreme in hand-railing, in a practical way; for in practice the stair-builder has various shapes of moulds to make, and how to construct and prove their correctness is the aim here sought.

PLATE 44.

Plate 44. *Exhibits the construction of face-moulds for a flight of geometrical stairs circular on plan and starting from a newel.*

Fig. 1. [Scale ¼''=1 foot.] *Shows the plan.*

The regular tread equals 10½'' by 6¾'' rise; they are spaced off on the regular tread line 18 inches from the outer string, the corners remaining square to give more room, and by using a wall rail will suit the ascent and descent of old people better than if the wall string were concentric with the outer string. For effect, in grand circular stairways the wall string should be circular to correspond with the front string, and the wall space ornamented with niches for statuary. The rail is 4'' wide by 5'' deep, to be double moulded.

Fig. 2. [Scale ¾''=1 foot.] *Shows plan of tangents.*

The radius for the cylinder equals 15'', and the balusters are 2'' by 2'', and by allowing ¼'' for the projection of bracket, the radius for the center line of rail will equal 15¾''. At the newel the cylinder is contracted, which increases the length of first step and make the stairs more inviting to ascend. The direction of risers and threads are given on plan; the width of rail (4″) is laid off on plan, so that ordinates may be used in drawing the face-moulds. The plan of rail is divided into five wreath-pieces; the chord of the segments for Nos. 2, 3, 4 and 5 wreath-pieces equals the radius OB; the joints shown at A, B, C and D all radiate to the center O; the joint at E shows 2″ of straight wood added to connect the straight rail on the level.

Draw the tangent FH perpendicular to radius Fg, and tangents AH, AJ, BJ, BK, CK, CL, DL, DM and EM, all perpendicular to the joints A, B, C, D and E; parallel with the tangents HF and HA, draw FN and AN; parallel with tangents AJ and BJ, draw BP and AP, forming the parallelogram $AJBP$ on plan. The parallelograms for Nos. 3, 4 and 5 are the same, because the chords BC, CD, DE, are of one length.

From F No. 1 and perpendicular to tangent AH, draw FG; from A No. 2, and at right angles to BJ prolonged, draw AS; from C No. 4, and perpendicular to tangent DL prolonged, draw CT; from D No. 5, and perpendicular to tangent EM prolonged, draw DU.

The treads, risers, joints of rail and tangents on plan being located, we are ready to draw the increased length of tangents in elevation.

Fig. 3. *Exhibits the elevation of tangents, treads and risers, as developed from tangents on plan Fig. 2, for the increased length of tangents for the face-moulds.*

To economize room, first find the average pitch on the line of tangents; then elevate the treads and risers from the tangents on plan. The stretchout of tangents from F to M equals, we will say, 94½″ which being divided by 14 (the number of risers) equals say 6¾″ for the average tread; then set a bevel to the average pitch, 6¾″ by 6¾″ rise, and draw the perpendiculars F, H, A, J, B, K, C, L, D, M and E. Now elevate Nos. 1 to 15 treads and risers from the tangents on plan Fig. 2; then determine which tangents will be level. Tangent FH connects the newel cap, and should be level, or nearly so, to make the curve connecting the cap graceful as possible, we will give the tangent HF No. 1 a slight inclination, and by forcing the curve at the miter joint, a more graceful curve will be obtained than if the tangent HF in elevation was to remain level. Again, tangent ME, at the landing, should be level, for a full easing at that point is required.

From the top of No. 1 step set up to F, the height to underside of rail, 5″, plus the half depth of rail [2½″], equals 7½″; at the landing set up to E, 4″ to the underside of rail, plus the half depth of rail [2½″] equals 6½″ to the center of rail at E; draw EM at right angles to the spring line E; now M and H are fixed points; from the external angle of Nos. 4 and 12 rise, draw arcs equal to the half depth of rail [2½″], and draw the inclination of tangents, cutting the perpendicular at H, A, J, B, K, C, and L; now L and M are fixed points, draw ML prolonged to cut the perpendicular C at N; draw FH prolonged, cutting the perpendicular A at D; from F draw the horizontal line FO, cutting the perpendicular H at P, and also cutting the tangent AH prolonged at y; draw AQ at right angles to AO, cutting the perpendicular J at R; draw BS at right angles to BQ, cutting the perpendicular K at T; draw CU square to CS, cutting the perpendicular L at V; from D, and at right angles to DU, draw DW, cutting the perpendiculars M and L at X and Z, and also cutting the tangent CL prolonged at I.

Now *OA* is the *height* for No. 1 wreath-piece; *BQ* and *CS*
are the *heights* for Nos. 2 and 3 wreath-piece, they being both the
same. *DU* is the *height* for No. 4 wreath-piece, and *XM* the
height for No. 5 wreath-piece. Make *Oa* equal the chord *FA* on
plan; prolong *QA* to the right and make *Ab* equal the diagonal
NH on plan; make *Qd* equal the chord *BA* No. 2 on plan; make *Ui*
and *WH* equal the chords *DC* and *DE* Nos. 4 and 5 on plan,
Fig. 2; make *Pm* equal *GH* No. 1 on plan, Fig. 2; let *Rn* equal *JS*
No. 2 on plan; make *Vt* and *Zc* equal *LT* No. 4 on plan; let *Mg*
equal *UM* No. 5 on plan, Fig. 2. From the points *m, n, t, c*
and *g*, draw *me, nh, tl, CP* and *gS* square to the tangents *AH*,
JA, DL, CL and *DM* produced.

Bevels.* Return to plan, Fig. 2, make *HV* No. 1 equal
Py, Fig. 3, draw *VF* indefinite for the director; from *A*, and
perpendicular to *FV*, draw *AW*; make *Wa* equal *OA*, Fig. 3;
join *Aa*, and in the angle at *a* the bevel is found for the joint *F*,
at the miter cap; for the joint at *A* on No. 1 wreath-piece, make
GX equal *me*, Fig. 3; join *XF*, and in the angle *X* is found the
bevel as shown.

For Nos. 2 and 3 wreath-piece, make *Sy* equal *nh*, Fig. 3;
join *yA* for the bevel required for the two wreath-pieces on each
joint; for No. 4 wreath-piece, make *Tb* equal *CP*, Fig. 3, and
Td equal *tl*, Fig. 3; join *bc* and *dc*, and in the angle *b* is found
the bevel for the joint at *C*, and the bevel shown at *d* applies at
joint marked *D*; for No. 5 wreath-piece, make *Um* equal *gS*,
Fig. 3; make *Un* equal the height *XM*, Fig. 3; connect *mD* and
nD and the angle at *m* gives the bevel for the joint at *D*, and the
angle at *n* gives the bevel for the upper joint at *E*.

Now draw the half width of rail [2″] parallel with the tangents to cut the hypothenuse of triangles forming the bevels; for
No. 1 wreath-piece the dotted line cuts at 2 and 3, and for Nos. 2
and 3 wreath-piece the dotted line cuts at 4; for No. 4 wreath-
piece the dotted line cuts at 5 and 6, and at No. 5 wreath-piece
the dotted line cuts at 7 and 8.

Face-moulds. *Fig. 4 shows the face-mould for No. 1
wreath-piece, starting from the newel post.*

Make *AH* equal *AH*, Fig. 3; with *A* as a center, and *Aa*,
Fig. 3, for a radius, draw arc at *F*; with *H* as a center, and *HF*,
Fig. 3, for a radius, draw arc intersecting at *F*; draw *HF* prolonged, parallel with *HA* and *HF*, draw *FN* and *AN*, for the
parallelogram *NAHF*, on the cutting plane.

Proof. The diagonal *HN* must equal the distance *Db*, Fig.
3; if so, the parallelogram is correct.

Make *Hy* equal *Hy*, Fig. 3. Connect *yF* for the director on
face-mould. Draw *F* 2 indefinite, and at right angles to *Fy*.
Make joint at *A* at right angles to *AH*. Make *F* 2 and *F* 3, each
equal *a* 2, Fig. 3. Make *A* 4 and *A* 5, each equal *X* 3, Fig. 3.
Draw the chord *AF*. Bisect the chord *AF* at *B*; bisect *BA* and
BF at *D* and *C*; from the points *A, D, B* and *C*, draw ordinates
parallel with the director *Fy*; now on plan, at No. 1, bisect *AF*
at *B*; bisect *BA* and *BF* at *D* and *C*.

From the points *A, D, B, C* and *F*, draw ordinates parallel
with the director *FV*, to cut the concave, convex and center line

---

of rail on plan; then transfer the points on the ordinates from the plan Fig. 3 to corresponding ordinates on face-mould Fig. 4, and trace the curves through the points, using a flexible strip. At F add on 1½″ for miter on the line of tangent HF, but make the splice joint at right angles to the director Fy, instead of the tangent HF, as is done for a butt joint; by drawing the joint at right angles to the director Fy, the joint will be plumb when the wreath-piece is elevated into position, and at the same time will be square to the face of plank, because the joint is parallel to the major axis.

Observe in this case the joint made from the director cuts the rail oblique at F, on plan Fig. 3, and not normal to the curve, as it would if drawn at right angles to the tangent HF, Fig. 2; hence the block pattern must be increased in width equal to the oblique cut at this joint.

The sections M and N show the bevels applied through the center of plank; they cross the tangents in their application. The block pattern is applied square to the lines made from the bevels; the shaded parts show the thickness of plank and the amount of overwood to be taken off.

Fig. 5. *Shows the face-mould for Nos. 2 and 3 wreath-piece.*

Make BJ equal the tangent BJ, Fig. 3; with B for a center and Bd, Fig. 3, as a radius, draw arc at A; then with J for a center and JB as a radius, draw arc intersecting at A, join AJ; parallel with JB and JA draw AP and BP. Then $PBJA$ will be the parallelogram on the cutting plane.

Proof. The diagonal JP must equal the diagonal JP on plan Fig. 2. Make joints at A and B perpendicular to the tangents BJ and AJ; as both tangents are of equal length, the diagonal JP becomes the director on the face-mould, and also on plan Fig. 2. Draw the chord AB on mould and also on plan; bisect them at CF and D. Draw the ordinates parallel with the directors PJ at Fig. 5, and also on plan Fig. 2; then transfer the distances from the plan Fig. 2, to the face-mould, Fig. 5, using chords for base lines; make $A\,2$, $A\,3$, and $B\,4$, $B\,5$, each equal $y\,4$, Fig. 2. Now trace the curve through the points for the concave and convex sides of mould.

If a trammel or rod is desired in preference to the ordinates, then extend the diagonal JP indefinite; make PO equal to the diagonal JP in this case. From the points 2, 3, 4, 5, draw lines indefinite, and at right angles to the joints; from O, draw the radial lines OB and OA, indefinite, which gives the points of contact, as 6, 7, 8, 9 on the radial lines; at right angles to OJ draw HK, to indicate the trammel and use the rod, making points, through which draw the elliptic curves, using a pliable strip.

The sections at M and N show the bevel at y, No. 2, Fig. 2, applied through the center of plank; observe they cross the tangents.

Fig. 6. *Exhibits the face-mould for No. 4 wreath-piece on plan.*

Make CLI equal CLI, at No. 4, in elevation, Fig. 3. With C as a center, and Df, Fig. 3, for a radius, draw arc at D; with L as a center, and tangent LD, Fig. 3, for a radius, draw arc intersecting at D. Connect LD; parallel with DL and CL, draw CQ and DQ for the parallelogram $QDLC$, on the cutting plane, or plane of plank.

Proof. The diagonal LQ must equal the distance VN, Fig. 3. Make joints at D and C square to the tangents DL and CL, join *DI* for the director; make *D* 8 and *D* 9 each equal *D* 5 No. 4 on plan, Fig. 2; make *C* 4, *C* 5 each equal *b* 6 No. 4 on plan; now draw the chord line *DC*, Fig. 6, also on plan, Fig. 2; make *LI*, Fig. 2 equal *Zi*, Fig. 3, draw *ID* for the director on plan. Bisect the chords as previously explained, and draw the ordinates parallel with the directing ordinate *DI* to cut the inside, center and outside of rail on plan, Fig. 2; now transfer the points on the ordinates on plan at No. 4, Fig. 2, to corresponding ordinates, Fig. 6, using the chords as base lines, then trace the elliptic curves through the points shown. If a trammel or rod be preferred, then prolong the diagonal *LQ* indefinite, make *Qo* equal *LQ;* from *O*, draw the radial lines *OC* and *OD* indefinite; at right angles to the joints, draw 3 2 and 9 3, also 4 6 and 5 7 for the points of contact; draw *OA* parallel to *DI* and equal to the radius *OB* on plan, for the semi-minor axis; draw the direction of major axis through *O* and at right angles to *OA;* make *AF* and *AB* each equal the half width of rail [2″]; now with a rod, find points in the elliptic curve, through which trace the curves using a pliable strip.

The sections *T* and *S* show the bevels applied through the center of plank, so as to cross the tangents; the shaded parts indicate the thickness of plank and also the width at the joints to saw out the crooks from the plank; at the minor axis, ½″ or less is all that will be required over the true width of rail, to allow for the twist of rail.

Fig. 7. *Exhibits the face-mould for No. 5 wreath-piece on plan.*

Make tangent *DM* equal *DM*, Fig. 3. With *D* as a center, and *Eh*, Fig. 3 for a radius, draw arc at *E*; with *M* as a center, and *EM*, Fig. 3 for a radius, draw arc intersecting at *E*, draw tangent *ME*, which becomes the director, make joints at *M* and *E* perpendicular to the tangents; at *E*, 2″ of straight wood is added on to help the easing connecting the straight rail on the level; parallel with tangents *MD* and *ME*, draw *ER* and *DR* for the parallelogram *RDME* on the cutting plane.

Proof. The diagonal *MR* must equal the distance *EX*, No. 5, Fig. 3; make *D* 2 and *D* 3, each equal *m* 8. at No. 5, Fig. 2. Make *E* 4 and *E* 5, each equal *n* 7, at No. 5 Fig. 2. Draw chord *DE;* bisect the same at *A*, also bisect *AD* and *AE* at *C* and *B;* now parallel with the director, draw ordinates indefinite. Bisect the chord *DE*, on plan, Fig. 2, in like manner, and draw ordinates parallel with the director *ME*, to cut the concave, center and convex sides of rail; now transfer the points on the ordinates at No. 5, Fig. 2, to corresponding ordinates on face-mould, Fig. 7, using the chord lines *DE* as a base; now trace the curves through the points, using a pliable strip.

The sections *W* and *y*, show the bevels applied through the center of plank; the shaded parts show the thickness of plank, and also the width at the joints to saw out the crooks from the plank; observe the bevels do not cross the tangents in this case.

If a trammel be preferred to the ordinates, then prolong the diagonal *MR*, and also the joint line 5 *E* 4, to intersect at *O*, then *OE* will be the semi-major axis; the semi-minor axis will be at right angles and equal to the radius *EO*, Fig. 2, (15¾″). Draw the radial line *OD* prolonged; at right angles to the joint, draw 2 7 and 3 6 for the points of tangency.

Proof. *RO* must equal *MR* in this case. The ordinates, however, will be found more convenient, as less space will be required in the construction of the moulds.

Balusters. If the length of odd balusters be required under the tangent in elevation, Fig. 3; the *directors* on plan. Fig. 2, for each wreath piece will give their location on the tangents, and may be transferred to their position in elevation as previously described.

SELF-SUPPORTING STAIRS.

Self-supporting stairs circular on plan may be constructed in several ways. The main object is to have them secure at the landing and at the starting with a substantial system of carriage underneath the steps. The string for the concave side should be made from 1½" plank, and dadoed on the back; then bent over a drum and keyed with hard wood keys set in glue. The string for the convex side should be dadoed and keyed in the same manner, and after being set in place a thin veneer may be bent over the same to cover the keys and joints. The steps and risers may be constructed in the usual way, all laid off from the working plan, which is drawn full size on the floor or large drawing board. When the stairs are to be set up in the building they should be lined off on the door, and the strings and risers set plumb over their lines on the floor. The string for the concave side should be set first and fastened to the joist above and floor below, and supported temporarily between by setting up several scantling and screwing them to the face of string. These scantling should be well braced, holding the string rigid and plumb over the lines on the floor.

Now the string for the convex side may be set up true to the lines on the floor, and supported temporarily in the same manner, as the concave string. Place the supports at the face of string, and brace them well to hold the string firm and true to the lines on floor. The steps and risers, being tongued blocked and all well glued, may now be set in place. Then take strips ½" thick and 3" or 4" wide, glue and nail them with the 3" way in a vertical position to the back of the concave string, extending them down into the joist at the starting, and also up into the joist at the landing. Keep the strips up to line with the under edge of risers; then the soffit will be regular. At intervals cut in brackets underneath each step, having the grain perpendicular to the tread. These brackets are nailed to the laminated soffit, and triangular blocks may be glued and nailed to the step, and also the bracket. After the soffit is covered in this way then strip for plastering, or a better way is to panel the soffit with Lincrusta Walton. Iron bolts should be placed across the stairs parallel with and at the back of every other rise; at the starting a spandrel should fill the triangular space to four feet high, which will give additional strength. At the landing two by half-inch flat iron [2"×½"] should be let into the joist and soffit of stairs where the soffit of stairs ease off to to the level. These irons should be well bolted to the same.

PLATE 45.

Plate 45. *Exhibits the construction of the face-mould for a stair-case elliptical on plan, and starting from a scroll.*

Fig. 1. [Scale ¼"=1 foot] Shows the plan.

The direction of risers in an elliptical stairs should be normal to the curve, or near to that as possible, so the rail may be constructed more readily to an even height for the hand, and at the same time obtain easy flowing and graceful curves; and if the front string be open, having return nosings and brackets, long miters on the return nosings will be avoided; or should the outer string be close, the nosings and string lines will show more even, and a more satisfactory job will be the result, and the angles of strings and risers will be less liable to collect the dust. Observe No. 16 tread is increased in width to receive two balusters, and thus allowing the rail to ease off gracefully at the landing. The construction of such stairs requires the skill of a practical stair-builder.

In the construction of the wall string, dado the back of string parallel with risers. Bend over a drum and insert dry, hard wood keys, well glued. A joint may be made at the center, and the drum made high enough to take in No. 10 rise. Then both the upper and lower pieces may be bent over the same drum by turning the notched

edges toward each other, and thus save room and material. The
outer string may be made in the same way; if for a close string,
while on the drum lag out to the required thickness to admit the
veneer on the convex side. Then house in the treads and risers;
cross-tongue and bolt the joints of string if made in two pieces;
light, thin mouldings may be easily bent and nailed to place; or if
large and heavy mouldings for panels; they should be worked from
the solid plank for first-class work. If large mouldings are used as
string mouldings, then work each member out separately and nail
them to place. A little ingenuity displayed in this line will avoid the
kerfing of mouldings, which should never be done, particularly when
the finish is in hard wood. In splicing winders or steps plough and
use slip tongues cut across the grain obliquely, and of very dry
material; beads may be steamed and bent to place; if large, they
will require to be nailed every few inches. The steaming of light
wood discolors the grain, and should be avoided for hard wood
finish, unless of walnut, which being a dark wood, the steaming is
not objectionable.

For intermediate rails between the string and hand rail, which
is intended to support balusters or panels of spindle work; these
intermediate rails may be laminated in several thicknesses of
strips by clamping and gluing three or four pieces at a time; over
the drum the strips should be thin enough to bend easily, the
clamps may be constructed on the drum, and wedges used every
few inches; paper should be laid over the drum before gluing, to
prevent the work adhering to the drum; string mouldings may
be built up in the same manner, and worked after being removed
from the drum. If heavy paneling be required, the drum will
answer for a form over which the paneling may be constructed.

Fig. 2.   [Scale ¾″=1 foot.]   *Shows the plan.*

The dotted line **CDEFG** shows the center line of rail,
which is a true ellipsis; the parallel lines show the width of rail.
Joints are shown at **A, B, C, D, E, F** and **G**, they are drawn
normal to the center line *; at right angles to the joints, draw
the tangents **AH** and **BH, BJ** and **CJ, CK** and **DK, DL** and
EL, EM and **FM, FN** and **GN,** at **G;** two or more inches of
straight wood is added on to connect the straight rail; parallel
with the tangents, draw lines from joints to form the parallelogram on plan.

OAHB shows the parallelogram for No. 1 wreath-piece on
plan; **PBJC** the parallelogram for No. 2 wreath-piece; **QCKD**
for No. 3 wreath-piece; **RDLE** for No. 4; **SEMF** for No. 5, and
TFNG shows the parallelogram for No. 6 wreath-piece.

From **C** and perpendicular to **DK** prolonged, draw **CU;** from
D and at right angles to tangent **CK** prolonged, draw **DV** for
No. 3; at No. 4 draw **EW** perpendicular to tangent **DL** prolonged; at No. 6 draw **FX** at right angles to tangent **GN** prolonged. The joints and tangents being now lined off on plan,
next proceed to unfold the tangents from plan, and elevate the
treads and risers to determine the increased length of tangents in
elevation.

Fig. 3.   *Exhibits the elevation of tangents.*

First find the average pitch on the line of tangents, as directed
at the preceding plate, to which set a bevel, and draw the perpendiculars **A, H, B, J, C, K,** &c., from the edge of drawing
board. The horizontal distance apart corresponds to those on
plan; next elevate the treads and risers from the tangents on plan
Fig. 2. They will all be square and parallel to the perpendiculars.
The perpendicular **A** indicates a joint, and **H** an angle; **B** a
joint, and **J** an angle; **C** a joint and **K** an angle; **D** a joint, and
L an angle; **E** a joint, and **M** an angle; **F** a joint, and **N** an angle;
and **G** a joint at the landing.

---

*See Plate 5, Fig. 8, how to draw a line normal to an elliptical
curve.

To give the scroll a graceful curve, set up 1″ from the top of No. 1 step to the under side of rail, plus 1¼″ to **A** for the center of rail (2½″); at right angles to the perpendicular **A**, draw **AH**; then **H** is a fixed point. From the floor line at the landing set up 4″ to the under side of rail, plus 1½″ to the center of rail at **G** (4″+1½″=5½″)=5½″; draw **GN** square to the perpendicular; then **N** is another fixed point. From the external angle of Nos. 7 and 12 tread draw arc to 1¼″ radius; then draw the inclination for the center of rail to tangent the arcs, and cutting the perpendiculars at **M, E, L, D** and **K**. Then **M** and **K** also become fixed points; connect **NM**, cutting the perpendicular at **F**. From **K** draw **KJ**, cutting the perpendicular at **C**. Join **JH**, cutting the perpendicular at **B**; from the point **H** the tangents should be drawn so as to give a gradual rise to the rail.

As stated elsewhere, the location of tangents is discretionary with the stair-builder: the higher they are raised above the treads, the rail will be correspondingly raised; if the rail be a little high the fault will not condemn the work, but on the other hand, if too low, then serious objections may be urged. The young man will learn with a little practice. The direction of tangents should be drawn so as to give the rail as easy flowing curves as the plan will admit of.

From **H**, and square to perpendicular **B** draw **HO**: then **OB** will be the *height* for No. 1 wreath-piece. From **B**, and square to perpendicular **C**, draw **BP**, cutting perpendicular **J** at **Q**; then **PC** is the *height* for No. 2 wreath-piece. From **C**, and at right angles to perpendicular **D**, draw **CR**, cutting perpendicular **K** at **S**; then **DR** is the *height* for No. 3 wreath-piece. From **D**, and square to perpendicular **E**, draw **DT**, cutting perpendicular **L** at **U**; then **TE** is the *height* for No. 4 wreath-piece. From **E**, and square to perpendicular **F**, draw **E, NN**; then **NN, F** is the *height* for No. 5 wreath-piece. From **F**, and square to perpendicular **G**, draw **FW**, cutting perpendicular **N** at **X**; then **WG** will be the *height* for No. 6 wreath-piece.

It will be observed that the tangents **EM** and **MF** for No. 5 wreath-piece are the same length, and also height as for No. 3 wreath-piece, and need not be described further, as the face-mould and bevels for No. 3 will apply to No. 5 wreath-piece; for by turning No. 3 wreath-piece upside down it will answer for No. 5.

Prolong the tangent **CJ** to intersect **BQ** at **a**; extend tangent **BJ** to intersect **PC** at **b**; prolong tangent **DK** to intersect **CS** at **d**; prolong tangent **CK** to intersect **DR** at **e**. Make **of** equal the chord **AB**, Fig. 2; let **Pg** and **Ck** No. 2 equal the chord **BC**, Fig. 2; make **Rh** equal the chord **CD**, Fig. 2; make **TJ** equal the chord **DE**, Fig. 2; let **Wm** equal the chord **FG**, Fig. 2, and **Wl** equal the diagonal **NT**, Fig. 2; make **Dn** equal the diagonal **MS** or **KQ**, Fig. 2.

Make **SP** equal **KU**, on plan, Fig. 2. Let **kr** equal **KV**, Fig. 2. Make **uq** equal **LW** on plan, Fig. 2. Let **Ns** equal **Ny**, on plan, Fig. 2. From **Q**, No. 2 and square to **CJ**, draw **Qt**; from **XX**, and square to tangent **BJ** prolonged, draw **XX Z**; from **p**, and square to tangent **DK** prolonged, draw **pv**; from **r**, and square to tangent **CK** prolonged, draw **r, OO**; from **q**, and square to tangent **DL**, draw **qw**; from **S**, and square to tangent **FN** prolonged, draw **Sy**.

Parallel with **JQ**, draw the half width of rail (2″), cutting the tangents **BJ** and **CJ** prolonged, at 18 and 20.

Bevels. Now return to plan, Fig. 2, and draw the bevels and the increased width of face-moulds at the joints. Make **Ja**

No. 2 equal Qt, Fig. 3.   Join aB; make Jb No. 2 equal XXZ, Fig. 3.   Join bC, which gives the bevels for No. 2 wreath-piece. No. 1 wreath-piece has one tangent raking, and one level, hence there will be but one bevel required, and that is found in the angle at B, Fig. 3.   No. 3 has both tangents inclining, and of different inclinations, hence two bevels will be required.

Make Nd No. 3, equal pv, Fig. 3.   Join dC; make Ve No. 3, equal r, OO, Fig. 3.   Join eD, and we have the bevels in the angles at d and e for No. 3 wreath-piece.   No. 4 wreath-piece has both tangents inclining the same, therefore only one bevel will be required for both joints.

Make Wf No. 4, equal qW, Fig. 3.   Join fE, the angle at f gives the bevel for No. 4 wreath-piece at both joints.

No. 5 wreath-piece is the same as No. 3.   No. 6 wreath-piece has one tangent inclining and the other horizontal, and as they form an obtuse angle, two bevels will be required.

Make xg No. 6 equal the height WG, Fig. 3; join gf; make yh equal ys, Fig. 3; join hG for the bevels in the angles at g and h for No. 6 wreath-piece.

For the increased width of moulds at the joints.

Draw parallel with the tangents the half width of rail to intersect hypothenuse of bevels: as for No. 3 wreath-piece at j and l; for No. 4 wreath-piece at m; for No. 6 wreath-piece the line cuts at n and p.

Fig. 4.   *Shows the face-mould for No. 1 wreath-piece; one tangent is inclining and the other horizontal in elevation, and as the tangents on plan form a right angle, only one bevel is required, and also the face-mould may be drawn with the trammel.*

Make BH equal BH, Fig. 3; make HA square to HB, and equal to the radius OB on plan Fig. 2; draw AO and BO parallel with HB and HA for the rectilineal parallelogram $OAHB$ on the cutting plane.

Proof.   The chord AB and diagonal HO must equal Bf in elevation, Fig. 3.   Make A 2 and A 3 each equal J 18, Fig. 3; make B 4 and B 5 each equal the half width of rail ($2''$); now pivot the trammel at O, with the arms on the major axis AO, and trace the concave, convex and falling lines of face-mould.

The section at M shows the bevel found in the angle at B, Fig. 3 applied through the center of plank; the section at N shows the try square is applied, and the block pattern shows the thickness and width to saw out the crook.

Fig. 5.   *Exhibits the face-mould for No. 2 wreath-piece; as the plan is the segment of a true curve, this face-mould may also be drawn with a trammel.*

Make CJa equal CJa, Fig. 3.   With C as a center, and Cg, Fig. 3 for a radius, draw arc at B; again, with J as a center, and JB, Fig. 3 for a radius, draw arc intersecting at B, connect BJ; parallel with JB and JC, draw CP and BP for the parallelogram $PBJC$ on cutting plane.

Proof.   The diagonal JP must equal the distance bK, Fig. 3.

Connect Ba for a director; parallel with Ba draw the direction of minor axis PF indefinite; make PF equal the radius PC, Fig. 2; make F 6 and F 7 each equal the half width of rail [$2''$]. Let C 2 and C 3 each equal J 18, Fig. 3, and B 4, B 5 each equal J 20, Fig. 3; pivot the trammel at P, with the arms at right angles to the minor axis PF; then for the center line on face-mould, set from pencil to minor pin the distance PF, now place the pencil in the point at *B*, and the minor pin in the major groove, at the same time slide the major pin to drop into the minor groove, fasten the major pin and trace the center line on mould.

Proceed in the same manner to trace the concave and convex sides of mould.

Make joints at *B* and *C* at right angles to the tangents *BJ* and *CJ*. The section at *A* shows the bevel taken from the angle at *b*, Fig. 2, and the section at *D* shows the bevel taken from the angle at *a*, Fig. 2. They are applied through the center of plank, and the shaded parts show the over wood to be removed.

Fig. 6. *Shows the face-mould for No. 3 wreath-piece, which is termed a "wreath-piece with an intermediate easing," or accommodation wreath; not because both tangents are inclining, but that one tangent has a greater inclination than the other.*

Make *DKd* equal *DKd*, Fig. 3; with *D* as a center and *Dh*, Fig. 3, for a radius, draw arc at *C*; again, with *K* as a center and *KC*, Fig. 3, as a radius, draw arc intersecting at *C*; connect *KC*; parallel with *CK* and *DK* draw *DQ* and *CQ* for the parallelogram *QCKD* on the cutting plane.

Proof. The diagonal *KQ* must equal the distance *en*, Fig. 3. Join *Cd* for the director; draw the chord *CD*; bisect *CD* at 2; bisect 2 *C* and 2 *D* at 3 and 4; parallel with the director *Cd* draw ordinates indefinite from the points 3, 2, 4, and *D*; now on plan Fig. 2 bisect the chord *CD*, in like manner at the points 3, 2, 4 and *D*; make *K XX* equal *Sd*, Fig. 3. Join *C XX* for the director on plan; parallel with the director *C XX* draw ordinates from the points 3, 2, 4 and *D* to cut the concave, center and convex sides of rail on plan at 5, 6 and 7. Now transfer the points 2, 5, 6 and 7 from the ordinates on plan Fig. 2 to corresponding ordinates on face-mould, Fig. 6; make joints at *C* and *D*, square to the tangents *CK* and *DK*; let *C* 8 and *C* 9 each equal *dJ*, Fig. 2. Let *D* 10 and *D* 11 equal *1e*, Fig. 2. Through the points trace the concave, center and convex sides of face-mould.

The section *A* shows the bevel found at *e*, Fig. 2, and at section *B*, the bevel found in the angle at *d*, Fig. 2. The bevels are applied from the upper or face side of crook, and through the center of plank; observe they cross the tangents.

Fig. 7. *Exhibits the face-mould for No. 4 wreath piece; the tangents both have the same inclination, hence only one bevel will be required for both joints, and the wreath-piece is termed a wreath-piece without an easing.*

Make *DL* equal *DL*, in elevation, Fig. 3. With *D* as a center, and the distance *EJ*, for a radius, draw arc at *E*; again, with *L* as a center, and *LD* for a radius, draw arc intersecting at *E*; join *LE*; parallel with *LE* and *LD*, draw *DR* and *ER*, for the parallelogram *RDLE*, on the cutting plane.

Proof. The diagonal *LR* must equal the diagonal *LR*, on plan, Fig. 2. In all cases when the two tangents have the same inclination and length, the diagonal becomes the *director*.

Make the joints at *E* and *D* at right angles to the tangents *LE* and *LD*. Draw the chord *DE*; also the diagonal *RL* bisects the chord at 5. Bisect 5 *E* and 5 *D* at 6 and 7. Parallel with the director *LR*, draw ordinates indefinite from the points *D*, 7, 5, 6 and *E*; draw the diagonal *RL*, on plan, Fig. 2, bisects the chord *DE* at 5. Bisect 5 *E* and 5 *D* at 6 and 7. Parallel with the director *LR*, draw ordinates to cut the concave, center and convex sides of rail, then transfer the points on the ordinates, Fig. 2, to corresponding ordinates on the face-mould, Fig. 7, as 5, 8, 9, 10.

For the increased width of mould at the joints, make E 2 and E 3 also D 4 and D 5, each equal *fm*, Fig. 2. The concave, center and convex curves of face-mould may now be drawn through the points indicated, using a flexible strip. The bevels for both joints as shown at sections H and J, are found in the angle at f, Fig. 2, the bevel is applied so as to cross the tangents; the shaded parts show the width at the joints to saw out the crooks. At the narrow part of mould ⅜″ of overwood may be allowed on the concave side, and less on the convex side. At that part of the mould the bevels blend, and the side of rail is at right angles to the face of plank.

Fig. 8. *Exhibits the face-mould for No. 6 wreath-piece;* *one tangent GN, is horizontal, and the other NF, is inclining; the wreath-piece is termed "a wreath-piece with a full easing."*

Make FN equal FN, in elevation, Fig. 3. With F as a center, and the distance Gm, Fig. 3, for a radius, draw arc at G; again, with N as a center, and GN, Fig. 3, for a radius, draw arc intersecting at G: join NG; let it be observed NG becomes the director for the ordinates. Parallel with NG and NF, draw FT and GT, and we have the parallelogram $TGNF$, on the cutting plane.

Proof. The diagonal NT must equal the distance Gl in elevation, Fig. 3; if so, the angle of tangents is correct.

Draw the chord GF; bisect GF at 18; bisect F 18 and G 18 at 20 and 19. From the points 19, 18, 20 and F, draw ordinates indefinite, and parallel to the director GN. In like manner on plan, Fig. 2, bisect the chord in 18, 19, 20 and draw the ordinates parallel with the director GN to cut the concave, center and convex curves of rail on plan, as shown at 18, 21, 22 and 23. Now transfer points from plan to corresponding lines on face-mould, Fig. 7. For the increased width of mould at the joints, make F 2 and F 3 each equal *hp* on plan, Fig. 2; also make G 4 and G 5 each equal *gn* on plan, Fig. 2, then trace through the points for the concave, center and convex curves of mould, using a pliable strip. Add on two or more inches at the joint G, to help the easing in the wreath-piece to connect the straight rail.

The bevel shown at section L is taken from the angle at g, Fig. 8, and the bevel shown at section P is taken from the angle at h, Fig. 2. Observe they do not cross the tangents, as there is no point in the mould that is equal to the true width of rail |4″|. The bevels are applied from the upper side of crook, the shaded parts show the width at the joints to saw out the crook.

Balusters. If it be required to find the length and location of balusters under the wreath rail, then make J 24 No. 2 on plan, equal Qa at No. 2 in elevation, connect 24 B for the director of No. 2 wreath-piece on plan, Fig. 2. Also make E 25, No. 5 wreath-piece on plan equal Sd in elevation, Fig. 3. Connect S 25 for the director of No. 5 wreath-piece on plan. The small circles indicate the location of balusters on plan.

At Nos. 1, 2, 3, 4, 5 and 6 wreath-piece on plan draw from the center of each baluster parallel with their directors, lines to intersect the tangents; the black dots show their intersection on the tangents.

Now transfer the position of balusters on the tangents to their respective treads in elevation, being careful to space them

---

between the perpendiculars, as they are shown on the tangents on plan. The small circles at each tread show their location in elevation. From the center of each baluster draw perpendiculars to intersect the under side of rail as shown. The height of scroll from the top of No. 1 step to the under side of rail we will say is 2′ 3″, and the elevation Fig. 3 shows No. 1 baluster to be 1″ from top of No. 1 step to the under side of rail. Then this one inch (1″) has to be deducted from the odd balusters, as shown in elevation; thus, the second baluster measures 2¼″ from the top of step to under side of rail; then (2¼″—1″+2′ 3″=2′ 4¼″); No. 2 baluster equals 2′ 4¼″ from top of step to under side of rail. The third baluster on No. 1 step equals 5¼″; then 5¼″ plus 2′ 3″ and minus 1″ equals 2′ 7¼″ for No. 3 baluster, from the top of No. 1 step to under side of rail when in position.

The balusters on No. 4, 7, 8, 13, treads, and the first baluster on the landing No. 17, are the same length as the first baluster; those on No. 3, 6, 9, 12 and 14 treads are ½″ longer than the first; the balusters on No. 10 and 11 treads are ¾″ longer; on No. 5 tread a ¼″ longer; on No. 2 tread 2½″ longer; on No. 15 tread 1″ longer; on No. 16 tread 4″ longer, and the second baluster at the landing No. 17 equals 1¾″ longer than the first baluster; the balusters on the level will be 3″ longer than the first. The balusters under a wreath having an easing, may vary a trifle, but this system will be correct enough for all practical purposes.

If desired, the exact location of each baluster may be found on the face-mould and transferred to the wreath-piece in the rough. When the mould is shifted on the tangents to its exact position on the crook, then the center of each baluster may be pricked through, and also the direction of each ordinate, then bored for the balusters to a template made to the pitch.

To do this, extend the center of balusters to intersect the tangents as shown in elevation, Fig. 3, for No. 4 wreath-piece; now transfer from the tangents in elevation to face-mould, Fig. 7, as shown by the dots; then parallel with the director, draw lines to intersect the center or falling line of mould, thus establishing their location.

To find the pitch to cut the template for the wreath-piece, Fig, 6, make *E, PP*, No. 5 in elevation, Fig. 3, equal the shortest distance from *D* to the director *C, XX* No. 3 on plan, Fig. 2; draw *RR, PP*, Fig. 3 for the angles at *RR* or *PP*, which gives the cut for the template *PP, E, RR*, to guide the bit when boring. For No. 7 mould the template is made to the pitch *TEJ* No. 4 in elevation, Fig. 3. For Fig. 8 mould the template is made to the pitch *XgF* No. 6 on plan, Fig. 3, and held at right angles to the ordinates, as *ab*, Fig. 7, or *C a*, Fig. 6.

As the face-mould is drawn the upper or back of rail is shown. The opposite side will be the underside or *breast* of rail. The boring of a rail for balusters is easily done, and the best results will be obtained by doing the boring on the stairs after the rail is hung and in its proper place. If the balusters be square at the top, then each baluster is plumbed to place and filled in between.

The lower end of scroll, containing the eye, may be worked from a thick piece of plank by marking out the plank to the pattern No. 1 on plan Fig. 2, and sawing out the same neat and square from the face of plank, and making the joint to the bevel shown by the dotted lines at No. 1 in elevation, Fig. 3; thus avoiding the face-mould No. 1, Fig. 4, and also the joint at *A*, on plan Fig. 2. In this case the twist line must be carried around so as to give a graceful curve. The reciprocal scroll shown at Fig. 5, Plate 6, may be applied here with pleasing effect.

PLATE 46.

Plate 46. *Exhibits 14 profiles of hand-rails one-half full size.*

Figs. 3 and 4 show the "pew back" pattern; Fig. 8 suits well for an altar or office rail; Fig. 9 for capping; Fig. 11 for capping on iron; Fig. 12 suits well for a wall rail. For square top balusters, the underside or "breast" of rail should be rebated out, as at *A* and *B*, Figs. 3 and 6; then filled in between. Fig. 5 shows the straight rail made in two pieces. These rails are classed as "double rails," with the exception of Nos. 9 and 11.

STRAIGHT RAIL. If the material is dry, the straight rail may be made from plank as the cheapest way; if very large double rails, then use inch stuff glued to a pine core, as shown at Fig. 3, or in several thicknesses, as shown at Figs. 2 and 7.

When ripping out the straight rail select plank that have squared edges and thoroughly dry. Then they will not spring much, if any. If the plank be springey, then rip up the center and joint off straight. If the rail be bowed up or down, it will be easy to straighten on the stairs when putting in the balusters, but if crooked sideways, it is more difficult to straighten, but it can be done by bracing the rail a little over straight the other way, and allowing the braces to remain over night after the balusters have all been well glued to place; then when the braces are removed the rail will come about straight. To do this requires one to have some experience in hanging rails. By thoroughly wetting the concave side of the crooked part, then forcing it out of straight the other way and leaving until dry, the rail will be about straight. Short kinks in the straight rail will sometimes occur in this way: the material being cross-grained, or a knot curl on the side of rail, will cause short kinks, particularly if the stuff be not thoroughly dry. When rails are worked out for some time before they are required these defects should be avoided much as possible, for a rail may be worked out nice and straight, then placed on the rack until wanted, and upon examination will be found crooked. This is a difficulty the stair-builder labors under, and hence the necessity that the material for straight rail should be made from the best lumber, straight in grain and thoroughly dry.

Black walnut requires one year for every inch in thickness to dry, and then it must be well "stuck" on strips up from the ground, where the air can circulate freely around the pile. Owing to being a dark wood it does not dry out so soon as any of the light-colored woods, and if near the ground will never dry. It is the best native wood we have to-day for hand-rails, balusters and newels; the sap part is objectionable, and should not be used in first-class work, but in second-class work may be stained * to imitate the heart wood. The sap in ash wood is like the heart wood, and therefore may be used. The sap part of oak should be avoided, as it is mostly damaged by the worm, and in cherry the sap should be cut away, as it is very inferior to the heart wood.

THE WREATH PART. For double rails the wreath-piece should be made in one piece from well seasoned lumber, as it is very tedious work to make the wreath part of double rails in two or more pieces when fitting them together. It may be difficult to find plank thick enough for large double rails. In that case the thickness may be increased by gluing the required amount to the underside of crook. This, however, should never be done, if possible, as the glued joints work out to a feather edge, and, if exposed to dampness, may ruin the wreath; plank thick enough for the wreath rail should in all cases be used for first-class work.

PLATE 47.

Plate 47. *Shows the construction of an open newel staircase having a quadrangular well-hole and close front string, finished with string mouldings and rosettes.*

---

* *To color the sap of black walnut.* Take one-half gallon of water, one-half pound of dry burnt umber, one-quarter pound of rose pink, one-quarter pound of Vandyke brown; mix thoroughly, apply with a sponge, allow to dry and rub off; when oiled will be uniform with

Fig. 1. [Scale ¼″=1 foot]. *Shows the plan having 18 risers. The main newel is 8″✕8″, and the minor newels are 6″✕6″.*

This style of a stair-case belongs to the dog-leg type, having newels in the angles, and the rails to butt the newels, either straight or with the old style "ramp and knee" or "goose neck"; sometimes the minor newels are allowed to extend up and finish with turned finals, at other times the rail is mitered around the newel, forming a cap with turned top, and the lower end of newel extends down below the ceiling, far enough to receive the lower edge of string and finish with a drop.

Fig. 2. [Scale ⅜″=1 foot]. *Shows the plan of the minor newel at Nos. 8 and 9 rise.*

The face of risers is located at the center of newels; **A** and **B** show the front string housed into the posts half an inch; the dotted lines show the steps housed into the posts and string ¾″.

Fig. 3. *Shows the elevation of four sides **A, B, C, D,** of post, Fig. 2, and also the strings connecting the same.*

⁺ The treads, risers and strings are housed into the newels, and the string mouldings are allowed to butt against the posts. The post is mortised to receive the rail, which should be tenoned and bolted at the joint.

If hard wood finish, the strings may be veneered on a pine core. **H** shows the core, and **K** the veneer ½″ thick, which is glued and well clamped to the pine core. **J** shows the shoe grooved out on the underside to straddle the string, and on the upperside to receive the balusters. **L** shows the filler cut in between the balusters. **N** shows the plaster, and **P** a moulded strip to cover the joint of plaster. **R** shows the carriage. **S**, the joist at the platform and landing.

The posts and strings may be chamfered, paneled and moulded in a variety of ways to suit the style and taste of the architect and stair-builder. The post at Nos. 12 and 13 rise is lined off similar to Figs. 2 and 3.

Fig. 4. *Shows the plan of post at the landing No. 18 rise· The face of rise being at the center of post.*

Fig. 5. *Shows the elevation of post and the raking and level strings connecting the same.*

C, D, E, F, shows the sides of post lined off to correspond with plan, Fig. 4. The rail **T** extends to the post straight. **U** shows the floor. **V,** the rough flooring. **X** shows the stripping underneath the joist for lathing. **N** indicates the plastering.

The rail is set 2′ 8″ from the floor to the top on the level, and on the rake 2′ 4″ from the top of step to the upper side of rail, plumb over the face of rise.

Fig. 6. *Shows a method of making and gluing up box or built posts.*

C and **E** are the two narrow, and **D** and **F** are the two wide pieces; **J** and **J** show the pine core. The sides **C, D, E** and **F** should be made from two inch stuff, and of perfectly dry material. A jointer, to joint and take the sides out of wind, and a pony planer to size them to an even thickness, are the best tools for preparing the material for box or pedestal posts. The pine core **JJ** is made to the proper width and glued to the wide sides **D** and **F**, first, then let dry, afterwards glue the internal angles and the edges of the narrow pieces, put a clamp at each end and one at the center, so as to draw up the narrow pieces close to the pine core; then put all the clamps on the wide pieces **D** and **F** that will be thought necessary to make the joints close.

Carpentry and Joinery.

Carpentry. Is properly divided into three branches, *constructive, descriptive* and *mechanical.*

Constructive Carpentry. Is divided into "carpentry and joinery," the distinguishing feature being less tools required for the carpenter proper, who takes charge and erects the naked carcase of the building. Then afterwards the joiner prepares the doors, sash, shutters, stairs and other finish for and completes the structure. In our country the difference, however, is very artificial, as most carpenters have all the tools required in the art of joinery, with the exception of the stairs. In large cities that branch of joinery is made a separate business.

Constructive Carpentry shows the practice of shaping and jointing the different pieces of wood in the erection and completion of a building, according to the design and intention of the architect.

Descriptive Carpentry. Shows the lines or methods for forming various kinds of work on plan, elevation and detail, according to and by the rules of geometry.

Mechanical Carpentry. Shows how to arrange the different timbers of a building relative to their strength, and the strain to which they may be subjected. This branch of carpentry is becoming more studied by the young carpenter who aspires to the upper rung in the ladder of that noble and honored occupation. The best and most practical books for the young American to study in this branch of carpentry is the "American House Carpenter," and also "Transverse Strains," by Mr. R. G. Hatfield. In this branch of carpentry we will give a few rules to calculate the strength of timber, and recommend the student to the different works herein referred to for a more extensive elucidation of the subject.

PLATE 48.

Plate 48. *Exhibits the construction of the "Hip," "Valley" and "Jack" Rafters for a roof having the angles on plan, all right angles.*

Fig. 1. [Scale ¼"=1 foot]. *Shows two right angles of a building to be hiped.*

‡ *KG*, *GA* and *AL* indicate the outside line of walls; *ZZ*, the inside of walls. Bisect *GA* at *N*; make *GK* and *AL*, each equal *AN*; draw *KL* parallel to *GA*; at right angles to *GA*, draw a line from *N* to intersect *KL* at *H*; draw *GH* and *AH* for the seat of the center line of hip. Now space off for the seat of jack rafters, *B, B,* &c.

Fig. 2. *Shows the elevation of "common rafters."*

GA is the width of building (12′ 0″), and agrees with **GA**, Fig. 1. **XX** shows the walls. **yy**, the ceiling joist resting on the "wall plates" **VV**; **bb** indicates the "raising plate" flush with the walls on the outside.

Bisect **GA** at **h**; draw **hD** perpendicular to **AG**; make the height from top of raising plate at **J** to **D**, to equal one-third the span **GA** (4′ 0″), which is termed a "third pitch." Draw **DG** and **DA** to the top edge of raising plate **bb**, for the length of common rafter from the "toe" to the center of "ridge plate" at **F**; allow the half thickness of ridge plate less, when cutting the rafter.

Now return to Fig. 1. Draw **HE** at right angles to **HG**, and equal to **hD**, Fig. 2. Draw **EG** from the top edge of raising plate **b** to the center of ridge plate at **F**, for the length of hip. When cutting the hip to the proper length, deduct the half thickness of ridge plate, which is equal to **Ed** on the inclination of hip as shown, carried up from the intersection of the seat of hip with the seat of ridge plate at **H**.

To find the length of jack rafters.   Make **HJ**, Fig. 1 equal **DA**, Fig. 2, the length of common rafter from the toe to the center of ridge plate.   From **J**, draw a line parallel to **LA**, intersecting **GA** prolonged; at **S**, draw **SH** for the center line of hip, set off the half thickness of hip parallel to **SH**.

Proof. **SH** must equal the length of hip **GE**; **CH** is the same length; now extend the jacks from **L** to **J** shown by the dotted lines. Then **J** 3, 2 3, &c., are the lengths of the jack rafters, and **SH** or **CH** is the length of the hip. Now, if the development **HJS** were elevated into position, it would coincide with **HLA** on plan.

Bevels. The bevel in the angle at **D** gives the down cut for both the common and jack rafters; the bevel at **G** gives the cut for the "foot" of both common and jack rafters. The bevel in the angle at **M** gives the down cut at the upper end of hip rafter, and the bevel shown in the angle at **J** gives the cut for the foot of hip rafter. The angle at **D** gives the bevel for the upper end of hip against the ridge plate, if applied on the plane of backing from the side which is done after the hip is backed; the angle at **T** gives the side cut of jack rafter against the hip.

To "back" the hip so as to range with the jack rafters; anywhere on the seat of hip **GH**, say at **O**, draw a line at right angles to **GH**, intersecting **GK** and **GN** at **P** and **Q**; from the center **O**, draw an arc to tangent the inclination **GE** of hip, and intersect the seat of hip **GH** at **R**, join **RP** and **RQ**, and the angle at **R** gives the bevel to back the hip; a section of hip is shown at **R**. * A more practical method is shown at next plate.

At **C** in elevation, Fig. 2, is shown the position of "Purlin" having the plane of its vertical sides perpendicular to plan. To find the cuts for a purlin against the hip, in a case of this kind there is no difficulty; if the plane of the sides of hip be plumb, and the purlin be parallel with the walls, then the down cut on purlin will be a right angle to the upper edge, and the side cut against the hip will be equal to the angle that the seat of purlin makes with the seat of hip on plan. In this case the bevel shown in the angle at **U**, Fig. 1, gives the side cut.

---

*This method of finding the backing for the hip rafter is ascribed to William Pope by Godfrey Richards, in his translation of the First Book of Andrew Palladio, 1676.—*Stuart's Dictionary of Arch.*

At **B** is shown another position for the purlin, the sides being oblique to plan, or perpendicular to the inclination of the common rafter. The method to find the cuts for a purlin in this position is shown at Figs. 3, 4 and 5. [Scale ½″= 1 foot.]

Fig. 3. *Shows a section of purlin 5″ by 9″.*

Apply the bevel shown at **D**, Fig. 2, from the upper side of purlin, and draw the plumb line **AC** across the section; at right angles to **AC** draw **E** 2 and **D** 3.

Fig. 4. *Shows how to find the down cut against the hip.*

Let **AB** indicate the "arris" of purlin shown at **E**, Fig. 3; parallel with **AB** draw the depth of purlin at **C** (9″); set a gauge to equal **D** 3, Fig. 3. The dotted line **DE** indicates the gauge line drawn parallel to **AB**; now set a bevel to the angle that the purlin makes with the hip on plan, which in this case, the hip being square, the bevel will be an angle of 45 degrees, and is shown in the angle at **U**, Fig. 1.

Then apply the bevel found in the angle at **U**, Fig. 1, from the arris **AB** as **FG**, intersecting **DE** at 2; from 2, and at right angles to **AB**, draw 2 3; join **F** 3 for the bevel in the angle at **AF** 3, required for the down cut.

Fig. 5. *Shows how to find the side cut of purlin against the hip rafter.*

Let **AB** indicate the arris **E**, Fig. 3. Make **BC** equal the breadth **AE**, Fig. 3 [5″]. Let **BE** equal **E** 2, Fig. 3. Draw the gauge line **DE** parallel to **AB**; from the arris **AB**, apply the bevel found in the angle at **U**, Fig. 1, cutting the gauge line **DE** at 3. At right angles to **AB**, draw 3 4. Join **H** 4 for the bevel required in the angle **AH4**.

This method of finding the bevels for the cut of purlin butting the hip, is practical, as they may be lined off on the timber, when the material is on the "trestles." *

Fig. 6. *Exhibits the rear and part of a main building on plan.*

AE, FC and **BD** indicate the line of walls. The internal angle at **F** must have a valley to form a junction with the rear wing; also the plane of that part of roof between the hip and valley will intersect with the plane of roof on the opposite side forming a short hip. The width **AB**, of main building is 32′ 0″, and the wing **CD**, 20′ 0″.

How to find the length and cuts of hip and valley rafters, also the length and cut of jack rafters between the hip and valley rafter.

Bisect **EG** at **H**, draw a line from **H** indefinite and parallel to **AE**; make **HL** equal **HE**, connect **EL** for the seat of long hip on center line; join **LG** for the seat of short hip on the center line; draw **CD** at right angles to **DB**; bisect **CD** at **M**; draw **MN** indefinite, intersecting **EG** at **P**, also intersecting **LG** at **Q**; join **QF** for the seat of valley rafter on its center line. Prolong the short hip **LQ** to intersect the common rafter at **R**, or the hip may be continued to **G**, and the common rafters cut to butt the hip from **R** to **G**. Now set off on each side of the center line of hips and valley the half thickness of hip and valley rafters;

---

*This system of bevels for the cut of purlins against the hip was first published by Mr. PETER NICHOLSON, in 1793. The system is shown more at large on Plate 50, where the student is referred for a more comprehensive study of the principle.

draw the jack rafters 2 3, 2 3, &c., to suit the space as shown. This completes the plan for the two hips *EL* and *LQ*, also the valley *QF* and jack rafters 2 3, &c., as required for the plan.

Fig. 7. *Shows the elevation of common and hip rafters for the main building.*

Draw *AB* parallel to *EG*, intersecting *HJ* at *K*; make *KJ* equal half the span *AB*, or 16' 0", for the pitch of roof, which is termed a "half pitch"; join *JA* and *JB* for the length of common rafter. Prolong *KA* equal to the seat *EL* of hip on plan, Fig. 6, as *KS*; join *JS* for the length of hip.

Fig. 8. *Shows the elevation and length of the common rafter for the rear building, and also the length of valley rafter connecting the main building.*

Make *MT* at right angles to *CD* and equal to *CM*, for a half pitch. Join *TC* and *TD* for the length of common rafter. Prolong *MC* to *U* equal to *FQ*, on plan, for the seat of valley rafter. Join *TU* for the length of valley rafter.

Now return to plan, Fig. 6. Make *PV* equal *TC*, Fig. 8, also make *HW* equal *AJ*, Fig. 7. Join *EW* and *VF*, also connect *VW* for the center lines of hips and valley rafters. Then when the trapezoid *EWVF* is elevated into position, it will agree with the trapezoid *ELQF*, on plan.

Proof. The center line *EW* of hip, must agree with the length of hip *JS*, in elevation, Fig. 7; also the center line *FV*, of valley rafter, must agree with the length *TU*, in elevation, Fig. 8.

Now after the hip is backed, set off on each side of the center line of hips and valley, the half thickness of timber measured on the plane of backing. Then extend the jacks to intersect the hips and valley rafters as 2 4 and 5 4, &c., for their different lengths. If at the point *R*, a line be drawn parallel to *PN*, cutting *WV* prolonged at *X*, then *WX* will be the length of short hip at the center, to butt the common rafter at *R*, when in position. Draw the joint at *X* at right angles to *RX*.

The bevel in the angle at *Y* gives the side cut against the common rafter, if the bevel be carefully applied from the outer edge *VW* after the hip has been backed. The down cut is shown at *T*, Fig. 8, and is applied to all hips and valley rafters. The bevel shown at 6, Fig. 8, applies to the foot of all hips and valleys. The bevel in the angle at *Z* gives the side cut for the jacks against the hips and valley rafters. The down cut for all jack and common rafters are alike, and the bevel is shown at *O*, Fig. 7. The bevel for the foot of all common and jack rafters that rest on the raising plate is shown at *X*, Fig. 7.

The bevel at *Z* will give the cut of hip against the ridge plate at *W*, but must be applied from the inner side 4 4 after the hip is backed. The valley rafter will need no backing, the edge being left square in this case. If exposed and the sheathing to form a finish, then the top edge of rafter must be worked into a V shape, the bevel being the same as for the backing of the hip.

As the valley rafter forms a right angle with the hip at *Q* on the plan, then the cut against the hip rafter *WV* will be a square cut, if applied before any backing is done to the valley rafter; 7, 7, shows the raising plate; the "foot" of rafter is notched out, forming a "heel" to butt the raising plate and neutralize the thrust of rafter.

Fig. 9. *Shows a graphical method to determine the stiffest beam that can be cut from round timber.*

Let **AB** indicate the diameter of a round log; bisect **AB** at **C**; with **A** and **B** as centers, draw arcs from **C** to intersect the circumference of log at **E** and **D**; join **AE**, **EB**, **BD** and **AD**, forming the rectilineal parallelogram **AEBD** for the size of beam.

PLATE 49.

Plate 49. *Shows an easy method how to find the length of hip and jack rafters, and cuts for the same, when the angles of building are obtuse or acute.*

Fig. 1. [Scale ¼″=1 foot]. *Shows the plan.*

AB, BC and **CD** show the outside line of walls; **ZZ** shows the inside line of walls; **yy**, &c., indicate the line of raising plate, which has to be well nailed to the joist to resist the thrust of rafters; **XX** show the "lookout joist" for cornice.

Bisect **AD** at **G**, draw **GH** parallel to **AB** for the center of ridge plate; bisect the angle **ABC**, also the angle **BCD**, at **E** and **F**; draw **BE**, also **CF** prolonged, to intersect **GH** at **K**; then **KB** and **KC** are the seat lines for the center of hips. On each side of **GH**, set off the half thickness of ridge plate, also set off the half thickness of hips on each side of the seat lines **BK** and **CK**. Now space off 2, **U**, **V**, **W**, &c., for the seat of common and jack rafters, and draw **U** 3, **Q** 4, **R** 5, **M** 6, &c., at right angles to the line of walls, to intersect the seat of hips at 3, 3, 4, 4, 5, 5 and 6, 6; in this case the rafters occupy position directly over the joist.

Fig. 2. *Exhibits the length of common and jack rafters, in elevation, the length of each jack is given on the common rafter.*

Draw **Xy** for the span [12′ 0″]; bisect **Xy** at **W**, draw the height **WV** at right angles to **Xy** and equal to **XW** 6′ 0″, plus the thickness of raising plate [1″] equals 6′ 1″. Draw the inclination of rafter from the center of ridge plate at **V**, to the edge of raising plate at **X** and **Y** for the length of common rafters, less the half thickness of ridge plate.

Now from the intersection of the seat of jack rafters, with the seat of hip at 3, 3, &c., on plan Fig. 1, draw lines parallel to **AB**, Fig. 1, to intersect the common rafter in elevation, Fig. 2, at the points **J**, **H**, **G**, **F**, **E**, **D**, **C**, **B**, **A**, then **XJ** is the shortest, and **XA** is next to the longest jack rafter. On the opposite side of hip, the jacks correspond in length.

On the short hip, **CK** for the obtuse angle, the length of jacks are found in the same manner. In elevation, Fig. 2, **yK** shows the length of jack rafter corresponding to **M** 6, Fig. 1.

Make **WK** equal **BK**, Fig. 1. Draw **VK** to the upper arris of raising plate, as shown for the inclination and length of the long hip, to the center of ridge plate. Make **WS** equal **KC**, Fig. 1. Draw **VS** to the edge of raising plate, as shown for the length of short hip to the center of ridge plate. When cutting the rafters, the half thickness of ridge plate must be deducted.

Bevels. The bevel in the angle at **M** gives the cut for the foot of the long hip **VK**; and the bevel shown at **O** gives the down cut for the long hip; the bevel at **N** gives the cut for the foot of short hip, and the bevel shown at *V* gives the down cut for the short hip. For all the common and also the jack rafters, the bevel at *P* gives the foot cut, and the bevel at *Q*, gives the down cut.

Fig. 3. [Scale ¾″=1 foot.] *Shows a practical method to get the side cut of jack rafters against the long hip BK, Fig. 1.*

A indicates the rafter having the foot cut to suit the raising plate; *B* indicates the "sole" of rafter turned up, and the bevel found in the angle at 9, Fig. 1, is drawn across the "foot cut," as 2 3; then at right angles to the foot cut draw line from the points 2, 3, to intersect the upper side of rafter marked *C*, at 4 and 5; connect 4 5 for the bevel, shown; that will give the side cut for the jack rafters *XJ, XA*, &c., Fig. 2. The rafters butting the hip *BK*, on the opposite side, are the same length and have like cuts, but made to match those on the opposite side.

Fig. 4. *Shows the side cut for the jack rafters butting the short hip CK.*

A shows the inclination and foot cut of jack rafter; *B* shows the sole of rafter turned up, and the bevel found in the angle at 8, on plan Fig. 1, is drawn across the sole at 2 3, from 2 and 3, and at right angles to the sole draw 2 4 and 3 5, intersecting the top of rafter from its opposite sides, as shown at *C*; connect 5 4 for the bevel to cut the jack rafters shown at *LY* and *KY*, Fig. 2; the jacks on the opposite side of hip are the same length and cuts; the bevel for the down cut is shown in the angle at *Q*, Fig. 2, for all the jacks and common rafters.

Fig. 5. *Shows how to get the side cut of long hip against the ridge plate HG, Fig. 1.*

A indicates the lower end of hip rafter; *B* shows the foot cut turned up, the bevel shown at 10, Fig. 1*, is applied across the sole as 2 3. Draw 3 4 and 2 5 square to the sole, and to intersect the upper side of rafter marked *C*; join 4 5 for the bevel to cut the upper end of long hip against the ridge plate, as required; this bevel must be applied before the backing is done.

The point of hip rafter at 6, is shown cut off to the angle that the hip makes with the angle of building at *B*, Fig. 1; this gives a point at 7 on *A* to set a gauge to back the hip shown by the gauge line 7 8; this is a practical way to find the backing of hips. No bevel is required for backing the hip when done in this way, although one is shown at section *H*. †

Fig. 6. *A* shows the lower end of short hip *CK*, Fig. 1; *B* shows the sole turned up; *C* shows the upper side of hip; the bevel 2 3 across the foot cut is found in the angle at 12, Fig. 1. The bevel in the angle at 5 gives the cut against the ridge plate *GK*, Fig. 1, but must be applied before the backing is done; the bevel in the angle *V* gives the down cut; the lettering and manner of finding the gauge line for backing the hip is the same as shown at Fig. 5.

A practical method to line off the jack rafters is to place the number of rafters required for one side of hip on the trestles,

---

*The bevels shown at 10 and 12 should be taken from the angles that the hips make at their intersection with the ridge plate at *K*, as *BKG* and *CKG*, because the direction of ridge plate may not always be parallel to the walls, as in this case.

†This method of backing a hip was first shown by MR. WILLIAM PAIN, 1774, in his *Practical Builder*.

side by side, and square the one end to line; set off on one side
from the squared end, the length of the shortest jack, measured
to the long point. On the other side, measure off the longest jack
to the extreme point, then use a straight edge to connect the two
points, which will give the intermediate lengths at the long points
for each rafter.

PLATE 50.

Plate 50. *Exhibits how to find the bevels for splayed work
on any angle, such as splayed jambs, boxes, mill hoppers, purlins, inclining posts or braces, struts and girts, in spire framing, or any cut in which the material is canted or raking, as the
cuts and length of hip, valley and jack rafters, all are obtained
by this principle, and should be well studied by every young man
in the trade.*

Fig. 1. [Scale $\frac{3}{4}''$=1 foot]. *Shows how to obtain the cuts
for an inclining strut A, against a post B, and also the foot-cut
on the sill S; the strut being canted, as shown on plan, Fig. 2.*

Draw the inclination **KL**, for the center of strut. Draw the
section **CDEF**; draw the upper arris **GH**, parallel to the center
line **LK**; with **E** as a center. and **EF** for a radius, draw the arc
FJ; draw a line parallel to **HG**, to tangent the arc at **J**, as shown
by the dotted line. From **H** and **G**, draw lines at right angles to
GH, intersecting the dotted line at 2 and 3; join 2 **K** and 3 **L** for
the bevel required.

Fig. 3. *Shows the same principle applied to the upper end of
an inclining post; the bevel is found in the same manner as at the
foot of the inclining strut, Fig. 1, the lettering being the same.*

If the post be on a corner and the strut on an angle, and the
arris **GH**, Fig. 1, is required to be backed, then to find the angle
of backing. turn up the foot cut as shown at **A**. Fig. 2. and draw
the angle of plan as 4 3 5; continue the side 4 3 to intersect the
side 5 6 at 7; then set a gauge from the arris **HG**. Fig. 1. to cut
the point 7 for the line of backing. If the angle of plan be
acute or obtuse. then make the angle 4 3 5, Fig. 2. agreeable to
the plan. In the above case the angle is shown on the foot cut
as a right angle.

Fig. 4. *Shows how to find the side cuts for splayed jamb
casing, or soffits, the angles being either square. acute or obtuse
on plan.*

A and **B** are square angles, **C** an acute, and **D** shows an obtuse angle. **ABCD**, **EFGH** show the plan; **B H** and **AE**
show the square miter on plan; **CG** shows the miter on plan for
the acute angle. and **DF** the miter on plan for the obtuse angle;
JK shows the inclination or splay required, and equals the width
of splayed work.

From the points **E, F, G, H**. draw perpendiculars to **EF**,
FG, **GH**, and **HE**; set off the width of splay **JK**, parallel to
AD, **DC**, **CB** and **BA**, to intersect the perpendiculars at 2, 3,
4, 5, 6, 7 and 8; connect 8 **B**, 7 **B**, 6 **C**, 5 **C**, 4 **D**, 3 **D** and 2 **A**
for the bevels required to cut the ends of splayed work, as
shown for their respective miters. If the ends are to be mitered,
or a butt joint be required, then proceed as directed at Figs. 5,
6, 7 or 8.

Fig. 5. *Shows how to proceed in obtaining the three different bevels that may be required for a right, obtuse or acute
angle for a splayed box or hopper.*

JK indicates the splay given to the side of box, and agrees
with the splay *JK*, Fig. 4, the upper edge *KA* being square to
JK, and equal to the thickness of stuff. Draw the horizontal
line *AB*, draw the perpendicular line *KL* indefinite, and cutting *AB* at *C*. With *K* for a center and *KA* as a radius,
draw arc *AX* indefinite; again, with *K* for a center and *KB* for
a radius, draw the arc *BY* indefinite.

Now the two right angle triangles *ACK* and *BCK* form
the base for all the bevels that may be required. If the splay
was equal to an angle of 45 degrees from a horizontal plane, then
only two bevels would be required; for then the perpendicular
CK would divide the right angle triangle *AKB* equally, and
the bevel for the side cut would also apply for the butt cut, because the two inclinations *AK* and *KB* would be alike, as
shown at *EDCF* for Fig. 1.

Fig. 6. *Shows the bevels for an obtuse angle.*

Let *KF* and *FG* indicate the side of box, and *FD* the miter
on plan corresponding to *FD*, Fig. 4; prolong *DF* to the left;
now from the points *A* and *B*, Fig 5, draw lines parallel to
KL indefinite, cutting the miter *FD*, on plan Fig. 6, at 2 and 3.
Again, draw lines to tangent the arcs at *X* and *Y*, Fig. 5, and
parallel to *KL*, as shown by the outside dotted lines; from 2 and
parallel to the side of box *GF*, draw 2 4; draw 2 5, 3 6 and
4 7, all at right angles to *KL;* connect *F* 5, *F* 6 and *F* 7 for the
bevels.

The bevel shown in the angle at *F* is for a butt cut; the bevel
in the angle at 6 is for the miter at the ends; and the bevel shown
in the angle at 5 is for the side cut, and is the same as shown in
the angle at 3, Fig. 4.

Fig. 7. *Shows the bevels when angle on plan is acute.*

Let *FG* and *GH* indicate the sides of box, and *GC* the miter
on plan which corresponds to *GC* on plan, Fig. 4. Prolong the
dotted lines from *A*, *B* and *X*, *y*, Fig. 5, parallel to *LK*; the
lines from *A* and *B* cut the miter on plan at 2 and 3. From 2,
and parallel to the side of box *GH*, draw 2 4; draw 2 5, 3 6 and
4 7 all perpendicular to the center line *KL;* join *G* 5, *G* 6 and
G 7 for the bevels. The bevel in the angle at 5 is the side cut,
and is the same as shown in the angle at 6, Fig. 4. The bevel in
the angle at *G* gives the butt cut, and the bevel in the angle at 6
gives the miter cut if required.

Fig. 8. *Shows the bevels when the angle on plan is a right
angle.*

Let *GH* and *HE* indicate the sides of box, and *HB* the
miter on plan corresponding to *HB* on plan, Fig. 4. Observe the
dotted lines that are drawn from the points *A* and *B*, Fig. 5;
parallel to the center line *KL*, intersect the miter *BH* on plan at
2 and 3; from the points 2 and 3, draw lines at right angles to the
center line *KL* to intersect the outside dotted lines at 5, 7 and 6;
draw *H* 5, *H* 6 and *H* 7 for the bevels. The bevel in the angle
at 5 gives the side cut, and is the same as shown in the angle at
7, Fig. 4. The bevel in the angle at *H* gives the butt cut, and
the bevel in the angle at 6 gives the miter cut if required.

" The student, by a diligent study of these eight figures, may
find the cuts for any splay.

Figs. 9 and 10. *Show how to find the veneer for a circular door-head having splayed jambs; the splay being carried around the head agreeable to the jambs.*

Fig. 9. *Shows the plan.*

AB and *CD* show the splay of jambs. Prolong *AB* and *CD* to converge at *O;* with *O* for a center, and *OD* and *OC* as radius, draw the arcs *DE* and *DF* indefinite.

Fig. 10. *Shows the elevation of arch.*

BD is the lesser diameter, and corresponds to *BD*, on plan, Fig. 9. From the center *O*, draw the semi-circle *BCD*; with the dividers, divide the semi-circle into 11 equal parts, as 1, 2, 3, &c.

Now return to plan, Fig. 1, and with the dividers, step off on the arc *DE*, the same number of equal spaces, as 1, 2, 3, &c., to *H;* draw the radial line *OH* to *J* for the length of veneer *DEHJFC* required.

This veneer is made from thin stuff and bent over a semi-conical drum made to the lines *AOC*, then tapered staves glued on the back, and cleaned off afterwards, thin strips may be glued on the back to stiffen. The radial lines from *O*, will give the taper for the staves, as shown at *EF*; for painted work, the splayed head may be glued up with staves.

For the joint bevel of staves, draw the two staves *ab, dc,* Fig. 10. Draw the radial line *ob;* return to Fig. 9, make *Kb* equal *Ob,* Fig. 10; draw *ba* parallel to *OC;* from *K*, and at right angles to *ba*, draw *Kc;* return to plan, from *O*, and perpendicular to *Ob*, draw a line indefinite; prolong the back of stave *bc,* to intersect the perpendicular from *O* at *Z;* make *Of* equal *Kc*, Fig. 9. Join *fZ*, and the angle at *f*, gives the joint bevel for the staves.

Figs. 11 and 12. *Shows the above principle applied to the construction of a splayed "Pue Back" circular on plan.*

Fig. 11. *Shows the plan of circular pue.* [Scale ⅛″= 1 foot].

O is the center, and *OA* shows the radius for the intersection of the back with the seat.

At Fig. 12, *DE* shows the splay of back. Prolong the inclination of the splay *ED* to intersect the perpendiculars from *O*, and from the intersection (not shown), sweep the curves *DF* and *EH* indefinite. Now divide the line *ACE*. Fig. 11, into any number of equal parts, as 1, 2, 3, &c. Then carry the dividers to the line *DF*, Fig. 12, and space off the same number of parts from *D* towards *F;* from the point of intersection (not shown), through *F*, draw *FH;* then *DEFH* shows the veneer that will bend to the curve *ACB*, Fig. 11, and at the same time gives the required splay to the pue back.*

Figs. 13 and 14. [Scale ⅛″=1 foot.] *Shows how to find the curve of a veneer for a circular window or door-head in a circular wall.*

Fig. 13. *Shows the plan; the shaded part shows the circular wall.*

AB, CD indicates the width of opening in the clear, and *AC* or *BD* shows the width of jambs; draw the chords *AB* and *CD;* perpendicular to *CD* draw *CE* and *DF;* parallel to *CD*

---

*For a long radius, use wire or find three points in the curve, then apply the problem, Fig. 11, Plate 2. Or from a ¾″ scale drawing, increase to full size by ordinates.

draw *EF*. Bisect *EF* at *O*; from *O* draw the semi-circle *EGF*; space off the semi-circle into any number of equal spaces, as 1, 2, 3, &c.; from 1, 2, 3, &c., draw lines parallel to *CE*, intersecting the chords at 4, 5, 6, &c., and 7, 8, 9, &c.; also cutting the curve of wall at 2, 2, 2, &c., on the convex side, and 3, 3, 3, &c., on the concave side.

Fig. 14. *Shows the veneer.*

Draw the base line *XX* from *A*; set off the spaces 7, 8, 9, &c., to equal 1, 2, 3, &c., in the semi-circle *E. G. F.* Draw 7 4, 8 5 and 9 6 parallel to the spring lines *AC* and *BD*.

Make 7 3, 8 3, 9 3, and 4 2, 5 2, 6 2, &c., equal corresponding spaces on ordinates Fig. 13; then trace the curve through the points *C*, 2, 2, 2, &c., for the convex side, and through the points *A*, 3, 3, 3, &c., for the concave side of veneer, being careful to tangent the straight part at the spring lines *AC* and *BD*. The veneer may be bent over a drum and staves glued on the back. The staves should be made from very dry material, and so for all work in which glue is used.

PLATE 51.

Plate 51. *Exhibits how to find the angle and jack ribs for an arched ceiling in a recess back of a pulpit; and also how to find the angle brackets for a stucco cornice.*

Fig. 1. [Scale ¼″=1 foot]. *Shows the plan of arched ceiling.*

The shaded part shows the jambs of proscenium arch; *AB* and *BC* indicate the seats of angle rib or "groin"; *EB* and *FB* show the seat of side ribs, the curve of which is determined from the main rib *EB*; divide *AG* into 6 equal parts; also divide *AE* into 6 equal parts; 8 *J* and *J* 3 show the seats of jack ribs.

Fig. 2. *Shows the elevation.*

Draw the base line *XX* indefinite. Make *BE* and *BF* equal *BE* and *BF*, Fig. 1; make *BA* equal the seat of angle rib *BA* on plan, Fig. 1. From *B* and *A*, erect perpendiculars indefinite; *BM* is the height. From *M*, draw a line parallel to *XX*, to intersect the perpendicular from *A*, at *R*; with *SS* for centers, draw the segments *EPM* and *FQM* for the main arch back of the proscenium arch. Divide *EB* into 6 equal parts, as 2, 2, 2, &c.; also divide *RM* into 6 equal parts, as 3, 3, 3, &c. From 2, 2, 2, &c., erect perpendiculars to *XX*, to intersect the arch *EPM* at 4, 4, 4, &c. From 4, 4, 4, &c., draw horizontal lines to intersect perpendicular lines from the points 3, 3, 3, &c., at *C, C, C*, &c. Through *A, C, C, C* and *M*, draw the curve for the angle rib or groin; if another point is required between *A* and *C*, then bisect the space *E* 2 and *R* 3, and draw the perpendicular and horizontal lines as before, and as shown. Then *ACC–M* is the angle rib for the seat line *AR* on plan, Fig. 1, and will agree with the main rib *EPM* when in position.

For the side rib *BG* on plan, Fig. 1, to agree with the angle rib. Make *BG* equal *BG* on plan, Fig. 1; draw *GT* parallel to *BM*; divide *MT* into 6 * equal parts, as 5, 5, 5, &c.; from 5, 5, 5,

---

*The number of points may be more or less. The greater the number of points the more correct the curve, will be.

let fall perpendiculars to intersect horizontal lines from 4, 4, 4, &c., at *D, D, D,* &c. Through *M, D, D, D* and *G,* draw the curve for the side rib that will agree with the angle rib *ACC–M;* if another point, *H,* is required between *G* and *D,* then bisect 5 *T,* and draw lines as before.

Extend the horizontal lines to intersect the main arch *FQM* at 6, 7, 8, &c: from the points 6, 7, 8, 9, draw perpendiculars as shown by the dotted lines 6 *L,* or 9 *N.* Then *FQ* 9 is the jack rib, to agree with *J* 8, on plan Fig. 1, less the half thickness of angle rib; 9 *N* is the vertical cut, and the butt cut against the angle rib may be found in a practical way, as shown for the cut at 6 *L.*

From the intersection of the two sides of jack rib with the angle rib Fig. 1, draw *a* and *b,* at right angles to 8 *J;* then make 6 *a,* Fig. 2, equal *ab,* Fig. 1; draw *ab* parallel to 6 *L;* now set off the thickness of jack rib as *KJ,* parallel to the upper side of rib, and draw *Ld* and *be* to the opposite sides of rib; then connect *de* for the bevel. Mind the exact length of jack rib is the the half thickness of groin rib less than the cut here shown, measured square from this cut.

The distance *cd.* on plan Fig. 1, is to be taken from the jack *J* 8, and shown at *DV,* Fig. 2; *GDV* shows the length of jack rib less the half thickness of angle rib, which agrees with *J* 8 on plan Fig. 1. These ribs may be made in two thicknesses of 1¼″ plank, and allowed to lap at the joints.

For the bevels at the upper end of angle ribs, return to plan Fig. 1. From *t* and *s,* and at right angles to the seat *BA,* draw *tg* and *sf;* also from *n* and *r,* and perpendicular to the seat *BA,* draw *nJ* and *rh;* make *Mh* and *Mf.* Fig. 2, equal *fg,* and *jh.* Fig. 1; draw *hJ* and *fg* parallel to *MB;* let *ZZ* equal the inclination and thickness* of groin at the upper end; draw *go, ju* and *MS* at right angles to the inclination of groin, as shown. Join *OS* and *NS* for the bevels required.

Fig. 3. *Shows a common bracket for a plaster cornice.*
AB is the projection along the ceiling, and *AC* is the distance down the wall. From the projections and curvature of bracket, as 1, 1, 1, &c., draw perpendicular lines to, and intersect *AB,* as 2, 2, 2, &c.

Fig. 4. Shows the seat *DE,* of angle bracket for a right angle *ADF;* how to find the curve for the angle bracket to agree with the common bracket, Fig. 3. From the points 2, 2, 2, Fig. 3, draw lines parallel to *AD,* intersecting *DE* at 3, 3, 3.

Fig. 5. Shows the angle bracket. Draw the right angle *CDE;* make *D,* 3, 3, 3–*E,* Fig. 5, equal *D,* 3, 3, 3–*E,* Fig. 4. Make *DC,* 3 1, 3 1—*E* 1, equal *AC,* 2 1, 2 1, 2 1–*B* 1, Fig. 3, then trace the contour of bracket through the points 1, 1, 1, 1, as shown.

Fig. 6. Shows the seat *KH* for an obtuse angle *AKD,* the projection *CD,* being the same as at Fig. 3. How to find the trace of angle bracket. With *KH* for a radius, and any point on *AD,* Fig. 3, for a center, as *K,* draw arc at *H;* join *KH,* cutting the perpendiculars from *AB,* Fig. 3, at 4, 4, 4.

Fig. 7. *Shows the angle bracket.*
Draw the right angle *CKH;* make *K,* 4, 4, 4–*H* equal *K,* 4, 4, 4–*H,* Fig. 7. From 4, 4, 4–*H,* draw perpendiculars to *KH*

---

* Remember the thickness of the angle rib must equal that on plan.

Indefinite.   Now make *KC.* 4 1, 4 1-*H* 1, equal *AC*, 2 1. 2 1—*B*
1. Fig. 3, and trace the profile of bracket through the points *C.* 1,
1, 1, &c.

Fig. 8. *Shows the seat, KL, of an angle bracket for an
acute angle, ALB.*

The projection *CA* agrees with *AB*, Fig. 3; how to find the
trace of angle bracket. With *KL* as a radius, and *K*, Fig. 3, for
a center, draw arc, cutting *BE* at *L;* join *KL*, cutting the perpendiculars at 5, 5, 5, &c.

Fig. 9. *Shows the angle bracket.*

Draw the right angle *CKL* indefinite; make *K* 5 5-*L* equal
K. 5, 5, 5 *L*, Fig. 3. From 5, 5, 5-*L*, draw perpendiculars to
KL indefinite. Make *KC*, 5 1, 5 1, 5 1-*L* 1 equal *AC*, 2 1, 2 1-
B 1. Fig. 3; then trace the outline of bracket through the points
C, 1. 1, 1, &c.

These angle brackets may be cut out square to the face of plank,
and the lath allowed to joint at the center of bracket for internal
angles; for external angles, the two outside corners have to be taken
off to the center of bracket, that the lath may miter and nail solid,

Mechanical Carpentry.

Transverse strength of rectangular wooden beams.

The transverse strength of rectangular wooden beams is in proportion to the breadth, by the square of the depth, and inversely as the length. Rule—multiply the breadth by the square of the depth in inches, and that product by the constant for the kind of material required; then divide by the length between the supports, in feet, for the breaking weight in pounds.

Formulated thus: $$B = \frac{b \; d^2 \; C}{L}$$

B equals the breaking weight in pounds; b equals the breadth, and d equals the depth, both in inches; L equals the length in feet between the supports; C equals a constant found by experiment tests on a unit of material, by taking a bar one inch square and $12''$ long between supports, and loading the bar at the center until it breaks. The weight that breaks the bar is termed the "constant" for that kind of material.

The unit of material, when of hemlock, breaks with 450 lbs.; white pine 500 lbs.; spruce 550 lbs.; white oak 650 lbs.; Georgia yellow pine 850 lbs.; locust 1,200 lbs.; cast iron 2,500 lbs.; wrought iron 2,600 lbs.; and steel breaks with a load of 6,000 lbs.—*Hatfield.*

Fig. 7. Plate 49 indicates a white pine joist $2''$ by $10''$ deep. The length between the supports AB equals $16'$, required the breaking weight, with the load at the center.

Formula: $$B = \frac{bd^2C}{L} = \frac{2'' \times 10'' \times 10'' \times 500}{16'} = 6,250 \text{ lbs.}$$

equals 6250 lbs. The young man should study this first formula well, for the breaking weight of material subject to a cross strain.

It is a well-known fact that if the weight be uniformly distributed, as at Fig. 8, the load may be doubled on the beam, or equal to 12,500 lbs., and the formula would read

$$B = \frac{2db^2C}{L} = \frac{2 \times 2'' \times 10'' \times 10'' \times 500}{16'} = 12,500 \text{ lbs.}$$

It is also proven from experiment that if the same beam be firmly fixed at one end and weighted at the free end, as shown at Fig. 9, the breaking weight would equal one-fourth the first example, or $\dfrac{6250}{4} = 1562.5$ lbs., and the formula would read

$$B = \frac{bd^2C}{4\,L} = \frac{2'' \times 10'' \times 10'' \times 500}{4 \times 16'} = 1,562.5 \text{ lbs.}$$

And for a uniformly distributed load, as shown at Fig, 10 would be doubled, or equal to 3125 lbs.

It is also a fixed rule that if the beam be firmly fixed at both ends and weighted at the center, as shown at Fig. 11, then the breaking weight would be one and a half times the first example, or 9375 lbs., and the formula would read :

$$B = \frac{1\frac{1}{2}\ bd^2 C}{L} = \frac{1\frac{1}{2} \times 2'' \times 10'' \times 10'' \times 500}{16'} = 9,375 \text{ lbs.,}$$

and the uniformly distributed load, as shown at Fig. 12, would be doubled, or equal to 18,750 lbs.

If the beam be firmly fixed at one end and supported at the other, as shown at Fig. 13, then the breaking weight would equal $1\frac{1}{4}$ times the first example, or 7812 lbs., and the formula would read :

$$B = \frac{1\frac{1}{4}\ bd^2 C}{L} = \frac{1\frac{1}{4} \times 2'' \times 10'' \times 10'' \times 500 \text{ lbs.}}{16'} = 7,813 \text{ lbs.}$$

and the uniformly distributed load, as shown at Fig. 14, would be double, or equal to 15,624 lbs.

The foregoing rules as set forth, are for the breaking strength of timber, and are established from the average of several tests made on each kind of wood; the bars selected for the tests are supposed to be perfect, or nearly so, hence a factor of safety is required to avoid accident.

Mr. G. Hatfield puts the factor of safety for the above formula at 3 and 4; The New York building laws also provide a factor of 3 for safety. Valuable data has recently been added to the transverse strength of timber by Professor Lanza and his students at the Massachusetts Institute of Technology. They experimented on full sized timbers, and made the discovery, that the usual factor 3 for safety is too low for the general run of timber as supplied from the mills and yards. The knots proved to be the weakest part of the timber. A factor of 6 will nearly harmonize Mr. Hatfield's formula with Prof. Lanza's experiments.

Then if the breaking weight in the first example be divided by 6, the result will be the *safe* or working load for the timber.

The formula would then read :

$$S = \frac{bd^2 C}{6L} = \frac{2'' \times 10'' \times 10'' \times 500}{6 \times 16'} = 1,041 \text{ lbs.;}$$

equals 1,041 lbs. for the safe load concentrated at the center W, Fig. 7. And the uniformly distributed load would be doubled, or equal to 2082 lbs.; the formula would read : $S = \dfrac{2b\ d^2 C}{6\ L}$

S equals safe load.

The safe load for the same beam firmly fixed at one end and loaded at the free end, as shown at Fig. 9, the formula would read:

$$S = \frac{b\ d^2\ C}{4,\ 6\ L} = \frac{2'' \times 10'' \times 10'' \times 500}{4 \times 6 \times 16'} = 260 \text{ lbs.;}$$

and the uniformly distributed load, Fig. 10, would equal twice that, or 520 lbs. for a safe load.

And the safe load for the beam Fig. 11, firmly fixed at both ends and load at the center, would be formulated thus :

$$S = \frac{1\frac{1}{2}\ b\ d^2 C}{6\ L} = \frac{1\frac{1}{2} \times 2'' \times 10'' \times 10'' \times 500}{6'' \times 16'} = 1,563\ 5 \text{ lbs.;}$$

and for the uniformly distributed load, Fig. 12, the safe load would be twice 1562 lbs, or 3125 lbs.; and the formula would be;

$$S = \frac{1\frac{1}{2}\ 2\ b\ d^2\ C}{6\ L}$$

The safe load for the beam, Fig. 13, firmly fixed at one end and supported at the other, is formulated thus:

$$S = \frac{1\frac{1}{4}\ bd^2 C}{6\ L} = \frac{1\frac{1}{4}\times 2''\times 10''\times 10''\times 500}{6\times 16'} = 1,302\ \text{lbs.}$$

equals 1,302 lbs. And the uniformly distributed load, Fig. 14, would be twice 1,302, or equal to 2,604 lbs. for the safe load. Formulated thus:

$$S = \frac{2,\ 1\frac{1}{4}\ b\ d^2\ C}{6\ L} = \frac{2\times 1\frac{1}{4}\times 2''\times 10''\times 10''\times 500}{6\times 16'\ 0''} = 2,604\ \text{lbs.}$$

The best form for rectangular beams is when the proportion of the breadth is to the depth, (or nearly so), as 5 is to 7; as for example 3″×4″ scantling, 4″×6″, 6″×8″, 8″×10″, 9″×12″, 10″×14″ timbers.

How to find the reaction at the walls, when a load is concentrated at any point other than at the center of the beam. Of course, if a beam be loaded at the center, as at W, Fig. 7, one-half the load is transmitted to each of the supports A and B, and the reaction at each of the supports is equal to one-half the load at W; but if the weight be changed towards either end, then the reaction at the walls will be in the inverse proportion to its distance from each end.

Fig. 7, Plate 49. Shows a beam 16′ 0″ between supports. Load, say 100 lbs. at C, 4′ 0″ from the support at A; required the reaction at the supports A and B. *

Rule. Multiply the weight at C (100 lbs.) by the distance to the near support (4′ 0″), and divide the product by the length AB (16′ 0″), for the reaction at B; then subtract the reaction at B from the total load, for the reaction at A. Thus $\frac{100\times 4'\ 0''}{16'\ 0''} =$ 25 lbs. that are transmitted to the support B; then 100 lbs. minus 25 lbs. (100—25=75 lbs.) equals 75 lbs. carried to the near support A.

Again, suppose the beam, Fig. 15, to be loaded at three different points C, D and E. AB equals 16′ 0″; AC equals 4′ 0″; AD equals 7′ 0″; AE equals 10′ 0″, from the near support A. The weights C, D and E, equal 150, 200 and 900 lbs. respectively, or 1,250 lbs. for the total load, exclusive of the beam. Proceed as before, and find the reaction at the remote support B for each weight, separately; then add the results together and subtract that sum from the total load, for the reaction at the near support A.

$$\text{Thus } AC = \frac{4'\ 0''\times 150}{16'\ 0''} = 37.5\ \text{lbs. for the reaction at } B.$$

$$AD = \frac{7'\ 0''\times 200}{16'\ 0''} = 87.5\ \text{lbs. for the reaction at } B.$$

$$AE = \frac{10'\ 0''\times 900}{16'\ 0''} = 562.5\ \text{lbs. for the reaction at } B.$$

---

* A cipher is here added to denote inches. If inches should occur in any of these calculations, then reduce the inches to the decimal of a foot, to facilitate calculation. For instance, should the measurement be 4′ 9″, then the item would read, four feet and seventy-five hundredths [4.75′].

Then 37.5+87.5+562.5 equals 687.5 lbs. of the weight carried to the support B; hence the amount carried to the support A equals the weights C, D, E, 150+200+900=1250 lbs., minus the total reaction at the support B. Thus, 1250—687.5=562.5 for the total reaction at support A.

In the above calculation the weight of beam has not been considered. One-half the weight of beam should be added to each total reaction.

This problem is useful to the mechanic when framing around the well of stair-ways and skylights where one trimmer may have to support several concentrated weights.

Strains. RULE—The strain or bending moment at any point in a beam is equal to the reaction at the support multiplied by its distance from the point selected. The weight at the center of beam. Fig. 11, equals say 200 lbs. Then, of course, the reaction at the supports A and B equals 100 lbs. plus the half weight of beam or trimmer; then let be required to find the strain at the point D, the reaction at A equals 100 lbs.

Thus, AD equals $8'\,0''$; then $8''\times100$=800 lbs. for the strain at the point D, for a single load.

Find the strain at the point C, $3'\,0''$ from the support A; AC equals $3'\,0''$; then 3.0×100 lbs.=300 lbs. as the strain at the point C from the single load at D.

Find the strain at the point E; BE equal $5'\,0''$; then $5'\,0''\times100$ lbs.=500 lbs. as the strain at point E from the single load.

Let it be observed at Fig. 11 the weight is at the center of beam, and the strain is found at any other point from the reaction at the supports. At Fig. 15 three weights intercept each other in their passage to the supports. The weight at C is $4'\,0''$ from the support A; the weight at D is $7'\,0''$ from A, and the weight E is $10'\,0''$ from the support A, and the reaction at the support A equals 562.5 lbs.

To ascertain the strains at the points C, D and E, Fig. 15, commence at support A. Strain at C equals reaction at $A\times AC$=562.5$\times4'\,0''$=2250 lbs.

Strain at D equals reaction at $A\times AD - W$ at $C\times CD$=562.5$\times7'\,0''$—150$\times3$=3487.5 lbs.

Strain at E equals reaction at $A\times AE - W$ at $C\times CE - W$ at $D\times DE$=562.5$\times10'$—150$\times6'\,0''$—200$\times3'\,0''$=4125 lbs. W equals weight.*

The strain at E, being the greatest, and the depth of joist being known, required the breath of a white pine beam at that point to carry the load safely, the beam being uniform throughout to suit the width of joist.

The strain from the concentrated load at E equals 4125 lbs; depth of joist equals say $12''$; length between supports equals $16'\,0''$. a, is a factor for safety and equals 6. Formulated thus:

$$b = \frac{4125\ La}{Cd^2} = \frac{4125\times16'\,0''\times6}{500\times12\times12} = 5.5,$$

equals $5\frac{1}{2}''$ for the unknown breadth by $12''$ for the depth.

When floors sustain heavy loads the header that supports the tail joist instead of mortise and tenon they should be set in stirup irons at the joining with the trimmers, and also joint bolts should be used and located at the neutral axis, or center of the timber. The strength thus gained is from two to three times from the stirup irons alone.† Also, the tail joist should be supported by

---

*Wilson.

† Lanza's experiments, American Architect and Building News.

stirrup irons for heavy work.   The joint bolts may be omitted in the tail joist.

Posts and Struts. Are subject to compressive strains. The rule mostly followed is Mr. Tredgolds, modified by Mr. Shalor Smith, C. E., of Baltimore.   The formula reads for square or rectangular timber posts thus :

$$S = \frac{C \times A}{6 \left[1 + \left(\frac{L^2}{b^2} \times .004 \right) \right]}$$

S equals safe load; C equals a constant for the crushing force per square inch, for the kind of material used, as shown at table 7: L equals length of post in inches; 6 equals the factor for safety; .004 equals Mr. Smith's constant for any kind of material; and A equals the area of cross section of timber; b equals the least dimension of the post in inches.

Example.   Required the safe load for a dry white oak post 8″ by 10″ by 9′, or 108″ long.

$$\text{Safe load} = \frac{9108 \times 80}{6 \left[1 + \left(\frac{108 \times 108}{8 \times 8} \times .004 \right) \right]} = 70{:}237 \text{ lbs.}$$

equals 70,237 pounds as safe load.   Observe that if the post supports a beam of white pine, the upper end of post must have a bolster or pillow of some hard wood, or else the post would sink into the pine girder, as shown at column 5, table 7, where the shearing force across the grain per square inch for white pine is 800 pounds, and the area of cross section of post equals 80 square inches.   Then 80×800=64,000 pounds, allowed to crush the girder $\frac{1}{10}$ of an inch; hence the post should be capped with an oak bolster* projecting a foot on each side.   The effect of the post on the oak bolster from the load of 70,237 pounds would be immaterial, as seen from column six, table 7, where 1060 pounds is allowed per square inch for a sensible impression.   Hence, 1060×80=84,800 pounds as the amount to load the oak bolster to leave a sensible impression.

Posts should be carefully set, being plumb and well bedded, if allowed to incline; then in addition to the load they carry, a strain is set up in the fibers that is not provided for in the dimensions; hence accidents may occur.   Metal or wrought iron columns set over each other, their flanges should all be trued up, being centered in a lathe.   It is not safe to bed the flanges in sheet lead, the lead is liable to work an injury, especially under a heavy and concentrated weight.

For wood posts supporting heavy loads, the posts should have metal caps and shoes in the form of sockets, to receive the ends of posts; the caps may be recessed to receive the end of the next post, and also project beyond the post as a support for the girder, or a metal cap may be fit down over the end of post, having two sides continued up, forming a shoe to receive the ends of girder, and the metal sides forming supports for the shoe to receive the next post above.

For warehouses and factories, the above construction will give the best satisfaction.   The end of wooden posts should never be set directly on a wooden girder, as the wood will shrink, often more on one side than the other, thus cause the post to deflect from

---

* Cast iron preferred.

a perpendicular, and result in cracks in the walls, floors out of level, and final ruin of the building.

If the posts or girders be made from green or part dry lumber, they should be allowed to stand until dry before painting, as the paint will close up the pores, and thus prevent the moisture from reaching the surface; dry rot will then commence at the center of timber, weaken, and perhaps cause accident. By boring a hole in the center of the posts to admit air, will prevent dry rot; the caps and shoes should be cast with a hollow space, so as to admit a free circulation of air through the post.

If posts be made from green timber, the strength of same will be reduced one-half; therefore the constant for crushing, in No. 2 Column, Table 7, should not be taken at more than one-half.

Fig. 15, Plate 50. *Exhibits how to find the strain from a load on a brace or strut; the same rule applies to a pair of rafters; and from the strain, how to calculate the dimensions of timber required to support the load with safety.*

Let *AC* and *AB* pass through the center or neutral axis of the strut and tie, and *BC* equal the perpendicular height, connect the two at the center of timber, forming the triangle of forces *ABC*.

Now the length of strut from center to center of timbers is 10′ 0″. set out 6′ 0″ from the perpendicular height, which is 8′ 0″, and loaded with 40 tons at its apex; there are two struts meeting at the same point; therefore each strut has to support 20 tons each; required the strain in each strut.

Rule. *As the perpendicular height (8′ 0″) is to the weight (20 tons), so is the length of strut (10′ 0″) to the strain in the strut.*

Example: 8′ 0″:20::10:25 equals 25 tons, for the strain in the strut *AC.*

Required the strain in the tie *AB*.

Rule. *As the perpendicular height (8′ 0″) is to the load (20 tons), so is the horizontal tie (6′ 0″) to the strain in the tie.*

Example; 8′ 0″:25::6′ 0″:15 equals 15 tons, for the strain n the horizontal tie *AB.*

Then 25 tons the strain in the strut *AC* being reduced to pounds (2240×25=56,000 lbs.), equals 56,000 pounds, and 15 tons the strain in the tie *AB* reduced to pounds (2240×15=33,600 lbs.) equals 33,600 pounds.

Required the dimensions of a spruce strut to safely support the compressive strain of 56,000 pounds.

Now from column two, Table 7, we find the crushing force per square inch for spruce pine equals 6862, and if we allow a factor of 6 for safety, or 1000 pounds per square inch, then $\frac{56000}{1000}$=56 square inches in section, or a timber 7″ by 8″ will give ample strength, provided the stiffness is sufficient in proportion to the length, for when the length of a column or strut exceeds 15 times its least diameter there is danger from bending.

Now to ascertain if the above 7×8 timber is stiff enough for flexure, proceed by the formula of Shalor Smith's for the strength of columns or posts, as previously shown. Thus;

$$\text{Safe load} = \frac{6862 \times 56}{6[1 + (\frac{120 \times 120}{7 \times 7} \times .004)]} = 21,778 \text{ lbs.}$$

equals 21,778 pounds, this being too light; try an 8″×10″ yellow pine timber, by the above formula, which will sustain a safe pressure of 63,663 pounds; this allows ample for stiffness of strut *AC*, 10′ long.

Next required the dimension of the tie **AB** to safely resist the tensile strain of 33,600.

From table 7, column 3, we find the tensile strain for a yellow pine to be 11,400 pounds to a square inch, and if we use a factor of 6 for safety, ($\frac{11400}{6}=1900$), or 1,900 pounds per square inch, then the area of tie (33,600÷1,900=17′), will equal 17 square inches, or a timber of yellow pine $2\frac{1}{8}''×8''$ will be ample to neutralize the strain on the tie **AB**.

ALGEBRAIC SIGNS AND SYMBOLS.

+   Plus—Sign of addition.

—   Minus—Sign of subtraction.

×   Times—Sign of multiplication.

÷   Divided by—Sign of division.

:   Is to—Sign of ratio.

::   So is—Sign of equality of ratio 4:8::16:32.

=   Equals—Sign of equality.

▢   Signifies square inches.

▧   Signifies cubic inches.

$\sqrt{}$ Radical sign of square root.

$\sqrt[3]{}$ Radical sign of cube root.

l   Represents length.

b   Represents breadth.

d   Represents depth.

h   Represents height.

$\dfrac{l+b}{d}$ Indicates the length is to be added to the breadth and divided by the depth.

$\dfrac{lb}{d}$ Indicates the length to be multiplied by the breadth and divided by the depth.

$\dfrac{l-b}{d}$ Indicates the breadth to be subtracted from the length and divided by the depth.

$l^2 b^3$ Indicates the square of the length is to be multiplied by the cube of the breadth.

$\dfrac{\sqrt{l}}{\sqrt[3]{b}}$ Indicates the square root of the length is divided by the cube root of the breadth.

$6\sqrt{\left(\dfrac{bd^2}{h}\right)+1}=Z.$ Indicates the breadth is multiplied by the square of the depth and divided by the height plus unity, and the square root of this sum, multiplied by 6, and the product equals **Z**.

[ ]   Bracket—Indicates that all the figures within are to be taken together as one.

——   Bar—Indicates that the figures over which it is placed are to be taken together.

TABLE 1.

LONG MEASURE.

```
    12'' =     1  '
    36'' =     3  ' =     1  yd.
    72'' =     6  ' =     2  '' =    1 fath.
   198'' =  16.5' =    5.5 '' =   2.75 '' =    1pch. or pole
 7,920'' =   660 ' =   220  '' = 110    '' =  40 '' = 1fur.
63,360'' = 5,280 ' = 1,760 '' = 880    '' = 320 '' = 8 '' = 1mi.
```

1 French meter=39.37 inches.
1   "   centimeter=about ⅜ of an inch.

TABLE 2.

MEASURE OF SURFACE.   (SUPERFICIAL.)

```
144   square inches =  1 square foot.
  9   square feet   =  1 square yard.
30¼   square yards  =  1 square rod   =       272¼ square feet.
 40   square rods   =  1 square rood  =      10,890  square feet.
  4   square roods  =  1 square acre  =      43,560  square feet.
640   square acres  =  1 square mile  =  27,878,400  square feet.
  1   square mile   =  1 square section, land measure.
  1   square = 100 sq. ft. architect's and builder's measure.
```

TABLE 3.

CUBIC MEASURE.

```
1728   cubic inches =  1 cubic foot.
  27   cubic feet   =  1 cubic yard.
 128   cubic feet   =  1 cord.
24.75  cubic feet   =  1 perch of stone.
   1   cubic foot   = 2200 cylindrical inches.
   1   cubic foot   = 3300 spherical inches.
   1   cubic foot   = 6000 conical inches.
```

TABLE 4.

AVERDUPOIS WEIGHT.—U. S. STANDARD.

```
16 drachms              = 1 ounce.
16 ounces               = 1 pound.
28 pounds               = 1 cwt.—112 pounds.
 4 quarters or 112 lbs. = 1 hundred weight.
20 hundred weight       = 1 ton=2240 pounds.
14 pounds               = 1 stone.
100 pounds              = 1 quintal.
American Commercial ton = 2000 pounds.
```

TABLE 5.

DRY MEASURE.

2 pints=1 quart=67.2 cubic inches.
4 quarts=1 gallon=268.8025 cubic inches.
2 gallons=1 peck=537.605 cubic inches.
4 pecks=1 bushel=2150.42 cubic inches.   [Winchester.]

TABLE 6.

LIQUID MEASURE.

4 gills=1 pint=28.875 cubic inches.
2 pints=1 quart=57.75 cubic inches.
4 quarts=1 gallon=231 cubic inches.

TABLE 7.

RESISTANCE TO COMPRESSION, SHEARING, TENSILE AND TRANSVERSE STRAIN.

MATERIAL.	Crushing force per square inch with the grain. [Rodman.] $=C$ lbs. average.	Tensile strength per square inch. [Rodman.] lbs. average.	Shearing strength per square inch with the grain. [Hatfield.] lbs. average.	Shearing strength to crush the fibers 1-20 of an inch across the grain. Per square inch. [Hatfield.] lbs. average.	Sensible impression on the side of timber from shearing across the timber. Per square inch. [Hatfield.] lbs. average.	Transverse strain constant for ultimate breaking load per square inch. $B=\dfrac{Wl}{bd^2}$ [Hatfield.] lbs. average.
Georgia Pine	8,947	11,400	840	2,250	900	850
White Pine	5,017	11,433	480	800	320	500
Spruce	6,862	13,666	540	650	260	550
Hemlock	6,817	16,533	550	800	320	450
White Oak	9,108	19,466	1,250	2,650	1,060	650
Locust	9,113	27,517	1,160	2,800	1,120	1,200
Birch	7,969	15,333	......	5,600	......	650
Hickory	9,887	25,900	......	4,000	1,640	625
White Wood	5,742	14,923	......	......	......	600
Wrought Iron	70,000	60,000	......	......	......	......
Cast Iron	145,000	20,000	......	......	......	2,800
Steel	110,000	160,000	......	......	......	2,500

TABLE 8.

CRUSHING STRENGTH OF BUILDING MATERIAL.

MATERIAL.	Crushing per sq. inch In pounds		Weight per cu. foot in pounds.	
Fox Island Granite,	14,875	Gilmore	164	Maine.
Quincy "	17,750	"	166	Massachusetts.
Hurricane Island "	14,425	"	166	
Bay of Fundy	11,812	"	162	
Joliet, Ill. Limestone	12,775	"	158	Illinois.
Com. Italian Marble	11.250	"	168	
Berea Sandstone,	8,300	"	133	Ohio.
Brown "	9,850	"	140	Little Falls, N. Y.
Amherst "	6,650	"	136	Ohio.
Cleveland "	6,800	"	140	"
Massillon "	8,750	"	131	"
Medina "	17,250	"	150	New York
Brick (Common), ...	375 to 3,000	Thurston	112	
Brick-work, ordin'y,	300 to 500		112	
Brick-work, good in cement, ...	450 to 1000		112	
Press Brick, ...	12,000	Kidder		
Mortar, common, ...	120 to 240	Haswell	98	
" year after setting, ...	440 to 580	Rondelet		
Good Cement, pure...	7,500		81	
Concrete, ...	600		125	

TABLE 9.

Average weight per cubic foot for materials used in the construction and loading of buildings.

Woods.

	POUNDS.		POUNDS.
Apple tree	49	Larch	33
Ash	52	Lignum vitæ	83
Beech	43	Locust	46
Birch (American)	40	Mahogany (Honduras)	40
Butternut (white walnut)	23	Mahogany (San Domingo)	50
Cedar—red	40	Maple	49
Cedar—Canadian	56	Oak, white	50
Cherry	44	Oak, live	59
Chestnut	41	Poplar, or white wood	24
Cypress	27	Pine, Georgia	48
Dogwood	47	Pine, white	28
Ebony	79	Rosewood	45
Elm	36	Red wood	23
Fir (Norway spruce)	33	Spruce	30
Blue gum	52	Walnut, black	33
Hemlock	26	Sycamore	37
Hickory	58		

Metals.

	POUNDS.		POUNDS.
Brass cast	525	Silver (standard)	644
Copper cast	555	Steel	490
Cast iron	450	Tin cast	459
Gold (standard)	1108	Wrought iron	485
Lead	712	Zinc cast	450

Stones.

	POUNDS.		POUNDS.
Alabaster	173	Granite	170
Asphalt	156	Glass, flint	192
Asphaltum	87	Gypsum	143
Bricks, pressed	150	Lime, quick	53
Bricks common hard	125	Lime, stone	169
Bricks, soft	100	Lime, stone, broken loose	96
Brick work, press	140	Marble	170
Brick work, ordinary	112	Masonry, granite or limestone	165
Cement, Portland	81	Masonry of ruble	140
Cement, Rosendale	56	Masonry of sandstone, dressed	144
Coal, anthracite, solid	93	Mortar, hardened	103
Coal, anthracite, broken loose	54	Porphyry	180
Coal, bituminous, solid	84	Quartz	165
Coal, broken loose	49	Rotten stone	124
Earth loose	76	Sand, coarse	112
Earth rammed	95	Sand, moist	130
Earth, with gravel	126	Slate, American	175
Glass, common window	157	Tiles	115
Glass, plate	172		

Miscellaneous.

	POUNDS.		POUNDS.
Ashes, wood	58	Snow, just fallen	5 to 12
Bark, Peruvian	49	Snow, moistened by rain	15 to 50
Butter	59	Sulphur	125
Coke	27	Saltpeter	131
Camphor	62	Tar	62
Charcoal	26	Water, rain at 60° F	62½
Cotton, baled	20	Water, sea	64
Fat	58	Wax, bees	60
Gunpowder	57	Whale bone	81
Gneiss, common	168	Mercury at 32° F	849
Hay, baled	17	Mud, wet fluid	120
Ice	58	Mud, dry compact	110
Ivory	114	Talc	156
Plaster of paris	73	Soap	56
Petroleum	55	Sugar	100
Platinum	1342	Honey	90
Red lead	559	Milk	64
Rosin	69	Fire brick	137
Salt, coarse	45	Clay	125
Salt, wet	140		

TABLE 10.

WEIGHT PER LINEAL FOOT OF SQUARE AND ROUND IRON.

[Fry.]

Thickness or Diameter.	Square Bar in Pounds.	Round in Pounds.	Thickness or Diameter.	Square Bar in Pounds	Round in Pounds.
1/16	0.0132	0.0104	7/8	2.5790	2.0250
1/8	0.0526	0.0414	1	3.3680	2.6450
3/16	0.1184	0.0930	1 1/4	5.2630	4.1330
1/4	0.2105	0.1653	1 1/2	7.578	5.052
5/16	0.3290	0.2583	1 3/4	10.310	8.101
3/8	0.4736	0.3720	2	13.470	10.580
7/16	0.6446	0.5063	2 1/4	17.050	13.390
1/2	0.8420	0.6613	2 1/2	21.050	16.530
5/8	1.3166	1.0330	2 3/4	25 470	20.010
3/4	1.8950	1.4880	3	30.310	23.810

To find the weight of a square bar ¼″ thick, and 1½″ wide and 1′ long from the above table, take the decimal .2105. opposite ¼, and multiply by 6. or take one-sixth of the sum opposite 1½ (7.578) for the weight of a foot lineal; thus, 7.578÷6=1.263 pounds.

TABLE 11.

To Find the Weight of Castings from their Patterns.

Multiply weight of white pine pattern by 16 for cast iron.
    "   "   "   "   "   " 18 " brass.
    "   "   "   "   "   " 19 " copper.
    "   "   "   "   "   " 25 " lead.

TABLE 12.

The Weight of Various Metals Per Superficial Foot.

[Fry.]

Thickness in fractions of an inch. lbs.	Cast Iron. lbs.	Wrought Iron. lbs.	Steel. lbs.	Brass. lbs.	Copper. lbs.	Lead. lbs.	Zinc. lbs.
$\frac{1}{16}$	2.344	2.526	2.552	2.734	2.891	3.708	2.344
$\frac{1}{8}$	4.687	5.052	5.104	5.469	5.781	7.417	4.687
$\frac{3}{16}$	7.031	7.578	7.656	8.203	8.672	11.125	7.031
$\frac{1}{4}$	9.375	10.104	10.208	10.938	11.563	14.833	9.375
$\frac{5}{16}$	11.719	12.630	12.760	13.672	14.453	18.543	11.719
$\frac{3}{8}$	14.062	15.156	15.312	16.406	17.344	22.250	14.062
$\frac{7}{16}$	16.406	17.682	17.865	19.141	20.234	25.958	16.406
$\frac{1}{2}$	18.750	20.208	20.417	21.875	23.125	29.667	18.750
$\frac{3}{4}$	28.125	30.312	30.625	32.813	34.688	44.500	28.125
1	37.500	40.417	40.833	43.750	46.250	59.333	37.500

TABLE 13.

Weight per Superficial Foot on Roofs from Various Causes.—[Thurston.]

                                                       LBS.

Weight of ⅛ slating on 1 inch sheathing............................ 6.75
    " of ³⁄₁₆ slating on 1 inch sheathing...................... 9.00
    " of ¼ slating on 1 inch sheathing......................... 11.25
    " if slate-felt be used, add............................... .25
    " or laid in mortar, add.................................... 3.00
    " of snow on roof.. 20.00
    " from wind pressure—[Trautwine]........................... 40.00

FOR ROOFS NOT OVER SEVENTY-FIVE FOOT SPAN.

Weight, if covered with corrugated iron, unboarded.......... 28.00
    " if plastered below the rafters........................... 38.00
    " if corrugated iron on sheathing boards................... 31.00
    " if plastered below the rafters........................... 41.00
    " if slated on laths....................................... 33.00
    " if slated on 1¼ inch boards.............................. 35.00
    " if plastered below the rafters........................... 46.00
    " if shingled on lath...................................... 30.00
    " if plastered below the tie beam.......................... 40.00
    " if roof be from 75 to 100 foot span add to each.......... 4.00

Excavators' Memoranda.

Excavating is computed by the cubic yard of 27 cubic feet; and paving by the superficial yard of 9 square feet.

To ascertain the number of cubic yards, multiply the length by the breadth, and that sum by the depth, all in feet; then divide by 27. If to find the number of bushels, divide by 2,150.42; or to find the number of gallons. divide by 231.

If the plot to be excavated is uneven, and apt to lead to disputes after being excavated; then survey the portion to be dug out, with a Comstock level, by taking levels at regular intervals over the surface, and from the average calculate the amount of earth to be removed, before commencing the work.

To take the levels, locate the instrument at the highest point, say four feet above the earth surface. Now the level of foundation below the earth surface at the high point is 10′; then take levels at intervals over the plot to be excavated from the level of instrument to the earth surface, and deduct the perpendicular heights from the 10′. Now suppose levels at regular intervals for 25 points have been taken, and the remainders summed up and divided by 25 will give the average depth of excavation or earth to be removed.

TABLE 14.

Clean dry Sand and *Gravel* in excavation, will retain a vertical face of one foot for a short time without caving in.................................. = 0 to 1 foot.
Moist Sand and ordinary *Surface Mould*........... = 1 to 3 feet.
Loamy Soil, well drained,................................ = 5 to 10 "
Clay,.. = 9 to 12 "
Compact Gravel Soil, for a short time................ = 10 to 15 "
                  Hurst.

A cubic yard of earth, when dug up, will occupy from $1\frac{1}{4}$ to $1\frac{1}{2}$ cubic yards.

Paving Brick should measure $9''\times4\frac{1}{2}''\times1\frac{3}{4}''$, and weigh from 4 to $4\frac{1}{2}$ pounds each. One yard of paving requires 32 paving brick, laid flat, and 83 on edge.

14	cubic feet	of	Chalk	weighs	1	Ton,
18	"	"	Clay	"	1	"
21	"	"	Earth	"	1	"
19	"	"	Gravel	"	1	"
22	"	"	Sand	"	1	"

TABLE 15.

NUMBER OF CUBIC FEET TO BE REMOVED, AND THE NUMBER OF
BRICK REQUIRED FOR WELLS FROM 3' 0" TO 12' 0" IN
DIAMETER.

Diameter of well in the clear.	No. of brick in thickness.	No. of cubic feet per ft. in height.	No. of bricks per foot in height.	Diameter of well in the clear.	No. of brick in thickness.	No. of cubic feet per ft. in height.	No. of bricks per foot in height.
3' 0"	½	11.0446	66	7' 6"	1	63.6174	347
3' 6"	½	14.1862	77	8' 0"	1	70.8823	368
4' 0"	½	17.7205	88	8' 6"	1	78.54	390
4' 6"	½	21.6475	99	9' 0"	1	86.5903	413
5' 0"	½	25.9672	110	10' 0"	1	103.8691	457
5' 6"	½	30.6796	121	10' 6"	1	113.0976	479
6' 0"	½	35.7847	132	11' 0"	1	122.7187	500
6' 6"	1	50.2656	302	11' 6"	1	132.7326	523
7' 0"	1	56.7451	324	12' 0"	1	143.1391	546

Stonemasons' Memoranda.

Cellar walls should be constructed of stone, carried up above the ground. Brick should not be used for outside cellar walls, as the dampness will rise by capillary attraction injuring the joist and render the rooms unhealthy; this may be obviated by providing a damp course of slate and pitch under the first floor of joist.

Footings. The New York City Building Laws require them 12" wider than the thickness of wall next above them, and 12" projection around all foundations for piers, columns, posts or pillars, and 18" in thickness, and all laid in cement mortar.

Stone foundations shall be at least 8" thicker than the wall next above, to a depth of 16 feet below the curb level, and shall be increased 4" in thickness for every additional five feet the wall is deeper. All foundation walls, either of brick or stone, are required to be built in cement mortar, for all high buildings. For ordinary dwelling houses of two or three stories, the basement walls are usually of common rubic 18" thick, built in common mortar, and having a footing course of heavy stone projecting 6" on each side whenever practicable.

For high and massive buildings in the city of Chicago, owing to the yielding nature of the soil, the entire excavation is sometimes covered over with rail road iron, bedded in concrete; then the foundation walls are started off the concrete.

Where the soil is compressible, piling is resorted to as a base for foundation walls; wooden piles should not be used in dry soils, but in water they have proved to be durable; they are usually 20 to 25 feet long, owing to the depth required for a solid base.

Load on piles. When a wooden pile refuses to sink over ¼ inch under a blow from a ram, weighing 2,500 lbs., falling 30 feet, it is considered home. Brevet Major John Sanders, U. S. Engineer, gives a formula for a safe load, thus :

$$\frac{R \times \overline{h \div d}}{8} = \text{Safe load.}$$

R equals the weight of ram in pounds.

h equals the height of fall in inches.

d equals the distance the pile sinks from the last blow in inches.

Example. Required the safe load of a pile, the ram weighing 1,200 pounds, dropping 6 feet and driving the pile 3 inches.

$$\frac{1,200 \times 72 \div 3}{8} = 3,600 \text{ pounds as the safe load;}$$

if the pile refused to sink over ¼″ under the above conditions, then the safe load would be 43,200 pounds.

For the crushing strength of stones and mortars, the student is referred to Tables 7 and 8.

Ruble masonry is valued by the perch, containing 24¾ cubic feet. To lay a perch of ruble masonry, it requires about 3 bushels of sand and 1 bushel of lime; for good ruble work, the stone on the corners and jambs should be lapped, and through stones every five superfical feet in all straight walls, and no stones built in on edge, but on their natural bed. The proportion for mortar is 3 bushels of sand to 1 of lime. Concrete is made by mixing gravel, broken stone, brick or slag, with 1 part of cement, 6 parts of clean sand and other solid components, and 1½ parts of water; and thoroughly mixed and carefully rammed in place; and is measured by the actual contents.

Measuring Stonework. Girt around the building, adding twice the thickness of walls at the internal angles, including all openings that are not over 4 feet wide, in walls under two feet thick; also including all openings five feet wide, when the walls rae two feet to 2′ 6″ in thickness. When the openings are over 5 feet wide, add one thickness of wall to the width of each jamb only.

Footings measured same as main wall. All arches to be girt and one-half. All safety arches to be considered extra. All abutments that project out from the wall six inches and under to have 12 inches added on each end. All abutments above 6 inches, and not over 18 inches, to be girt measure only.

All piers that are built by themselves, and are 3 feet square and under, to be girt and one-half by one foot thick; and all piers that are three feet square and upward, to be measured solid, with 9 feet added for each foot in height for corners. Circular walls to be girt and one-half.

Recesses and slots to be measured solid. No reductions made for cut stone trimmings and lintels. Quarry measure in all cases to be solid.

Cut Stone Setting. Measure vault covers, flagging and ashler by the superficial foot. Coping and belt courses by the lineal foot; all other cut stone by the cubic foot.—*Hand Book of the Pittsburgh Builders' Exchange.*

For the number of brick per superficial foot in a wall, add seven brick for every half brick the wall is thick.

Bricklayers' Memoranda.

TABLE 16.

NUMBER OF HALF BRICKS IN THE THICKNESS OF WALL PER
SUPERFICIAL FOOT OF WALL SURFACE.

No of half brick... ...	1	2	3	4	5	6	7	8
No. of brick per super-ficial feet...............	7	14	21	28	35	42	49	56

Example : Required the number of brick in a wall 40 feet long, 25 feet high and 4 half brick in thickness. Under 4 in the above table is 28 brick to the superficial foot.

Then $40 \times 25 \times 28 = 28,000$; equals 28,000 brick.

The size and quality of brick vary in different localities. The standard size in Western Pennsylvania is $8\frac{1}{2} \times 4\frac{1}{4} \times 2\frac{1}{4}$ thick, and weight 5 to 6 pounds each, and for a good quality they should not absorb over one-twentieth their weight of water when dry.

A bricklayer's hod measures $9'' \times 9'' \times 16''$ long, and holds 16 brick; the V angle should be 60 degrees. Ladder rungs should not be over $9''$ from centers; 1000 brick closely stacked occupy about 56 cubic feet; 1000 old brick cleaned and loosely stacked occupy about 72 cubic feet; 1000 brick require about $3\frac{1}{2}$ bushels of lime and 9 bushels sharp sand.

A load of mortar measures 1 cubic yard, or 27 cubic feet; a double load measures twice the above quantity.

Strength of Brick Work. Mr. Trautwine, Civil Engineer, states ordinary brick work cracks with 20 to 30 tons pressure per square foot, or 311 to 466 pounds per square inch, and for good brick work in cement, 770 to 1088 pounds per square inch.

The New York City building laws require that brick cellar walls shall be four inches thicker than the walls next above, and the increase below the curb level is the same as for stone foundations, which see : For buildings not over 55 feet high, external walls, $12''$ thick; exceeding 55 feet and not over 80 feet, $16''$ to top of first story, thence if not over 40 feet to be $12''$ thick; more than 80 feet then $4''$ to be added for every 15 feet the building is higher than 80 feet. If brick be used for foundation walls, they must be laid in cement for all large buildings.

Mr. F. E. Kidder, March 30th, 1882, at the U. S. Arsenal in Watertown, Mass., made some experimental tests on brick piers, for the purpose of comparing different kinds of cements with common mortar and sand. The common mortar was taken from a building in course of erection near by. Seven different tests are shown in Table 17. The Portland cement used in the building of these piers is known as Brooks, Shoobridge & Co.'s cement.

TABLE 17.

COMMON BRICK LAID IN	Ultimate strength of pier. lbs.	Pressure per sq. in. under which the pier commenced to crack. lbs.	Ultimate strength per square inch.	Size of pier 8"×12".	Length of course. in.	Weight in pounds.	Age; 4 months, 26 days. m.	d.	Time of test in minutes. n.	First crack.
No. 1. Lime mortar, 2 days old	150,000	833	1,562	96	20¾	144	4.	26	45	80,000
No. 2. Lime mortar, 3 parts; Portland cement, 1 part	200,000	1,875	3,020	96	22¼	161	4.	26	55	180,000
No. 3. Lime mortar, 3 parts: Newark and Rosendale cement, 1 part	245,000	1,354	2,552	96	22⅛	159	4.	26	20	130,000
No. 4. Lime mortar, 3 parts; Roman cement, 1 part	195,000	1,041	2,030	96	22⅝	158	4.	26	25	100,000
No. 5. Portland cement, 1 part; sand 2 parts	240,000	1,302	2,500	96	23	166	4.	26	30	125,000
No. 6. Newark and Rosendale cement, 1 part; sand, 2 parts	205,000	708	2,135	96	23⅛	167	4.	26	20	68,000
No. 7. Roman cement, 1 part; sand, 2 parts	185,000	1.770	1,927	96	23¼	164	4.	26	20	170,000

TABLE 18.

TABLE SHOWING THE THICKNESS OF WALLS FOR DWELLINGS AND STORES, AS SET FORTH IN THE BUILDING LAWS OF THE CITY OF CHICAGO.

	Basement.	1st story.	2d story.	3d story.	4th story.
Basement and two stories	12"	8"	8"		
Basement and three stories	16"	12"	12"	8"	
Division walls, basement and two stories	12"	8"	8"		
More than three stories	16"	16"	12"	12"	12"
Division walls, basement and three stories	12"	12"	8"	8"	
Division walls, basement and four stories	16"	12"	12"	12"	12"
When first story, or basement and first story, are for shop or stores, then:					
Two stories and basement	12"	12"	8"		
Three stories and basement	16"	16"	12"	8"	
Four stories and basement	20"	16"	12"	12"	12"
Three-story building, division wall	12"	12"	12"	8"	
Four-story building, division wall	16"	16"	12"	12"	12"

Plasterers' Memoranda.

TABLE 19.

MATERIAL REQUIRED FOR 100 YARDS OF PLASTERING, THREE
COATS COMMON.

Lime,................................ ....12 bushels.
Sand,...36 "
Hair,.. 2 "
3 d Nails (fine) for joist spaced 2' 0'' from centers, 6½ pounds.
3 d   "   "   "   "   1' 4'' "   "   8½   "
3 d   "   "   "   "   1' 0'' "   "   10½   "
Number of lath required,...1,600.

Laths are cut 4' 0'' by 1½'' by ⅜'' standard.

One bushel of hair equals 8 pounds standard.

One yard of plastering, three coat work, requires nearly one-
half peck of unslacked lime, and nearly a peck and a half of sand,
and 16 lath.

One load of mortar or sand meaures one cubic yard, and will
fill 21 hods.

A plasterer's hod measures 15'' by 15'' by 23'' long, the **V**
is 60 degrees, and contains a bushel of mortar.

Plain plastering is valued by the yard, of 9 square feet; when
the material is furnished by the plasterer, deduct the half of all
openings over 9 square feet, and add all openings that are 9 square
feet and under; deduct all openings measuring 100 square feet
and over.

When materials are not furnished by the plasterer, no deduc-
tions for openings are made.

All cupboards, closets, pantries, and all circular work, are
measured double full height to the ceiling; Soffits of staircases are
measured one and a half times. All arrises, quirks and chamfered corners are measured by the lineal foot. Stucco cornice is
measured by the square foot. Girt around all members, and add
one foot lineal for every miter for the length, by the girt; any cornice or moulding less than 12'' girt, shall be measured as 12'' girt.
Ellipsis are measured three times. For enrichments, charge by
the piece.

Carpenters' Memoranda.*

TABLE 20.

BOARD MEASURE.

LENGTH IN FEET.

Width, Inches.	1	2	3	4	5	6	7	8	9	10	12	14	16	18	20	22	24	26	28	30	32	34	36
¼	0 0¼	0 0½	0 0¾	0 1	0 1¼	0 1½	0 1¾	0 2	0 2¼	0 2½	0 3	0 3½	0 4	0 4½	0 5	0 5½	0 6	0 6½	0 7	0 7½	0 8	0 8½	0 9
½	0 0½	0 1	0 1½	0 2	0 2½	0 3	0 3½	0 4	0 4½	0 5	0 6	0 7	0 8	0 9	0 10	0 11	1 0	1 1	1 2	1 3	1 4	1 5	1 6
¾	0 0¾	0 1½	0 2¼	0 3	0 3¾	0 4½	0 5¼	0 6	0 6¾	0 7½	0 9	0 10½	1 0	1 1½	1 3	1 4½	1 6	1 7½	1 9	1 10½	2 0	2 1½	2 3
1	0 1	0 2	0 3	0 4	0 5	0 6	0 7	0 8	0 9	0 10	1 0	1 2	1 4	1 6	1 8	1 10	2 0	2 2	2 4	2 6	2 8	2 10	3 0
2	0 2	0 4	0 6	0 8	0 10	1 0	1 2	1 4	1 6	1 8	2 0	2 4	2 8	3 0	3 4	3 8	4 0	4 4	4 8	5 0	5 4	5 8	6 0
3	0 3	0 6	0 9	1 0	1 3	1 6	1 9	2 0	2 3	2 6	3 0	3 6	4 0	4 6	5 0	5 6	6 0	6 6	7 0	7 6	8 0	8 6	9 0
4	0 4	0 8	1 0	1 4	1 8	2 0	2 4	2 8	3 0	3 4	4 0	4 8	5 4	6 0	6 8	7 4	8 0	8 8	9 4	10 0	10 8	11 4	12 0
5	0 5	0 10	1 3	1 8	2 1	2 6	2 11	3 4	3 9	4 2	5 0	5 10	6 8	7 6	8 4	9 2	10 0	10 10	11 8	12 6	13 4	14 2	15 0
6	0 6	1 0	1 6	2 0	2 6	3 0	3 6	4 0	4 6	5 0	6 0	7 0	8 0	9 0	10 0	11 0	12 0	13 0	14 0	15 0	16 0	17 0	18 0
7	0 7	1 2	1 9	2 4	2 11	3 6	4 1	4 8	5 3	5 10	7 0	8 2	9 4	10 6	11 8	12 10	14 0	15 2	16 4	17 6	18 8	19 10	21 0
8	0 8	1 4	2 0	2 8	3 4	4 0	4 8	5 4	6 0	6 8	8 0	9 4	10 8	12 0	13 4	14 8	16 0	17 4	18 8	20 0	21 4	22 8	24 0
9	0 9	1 6	2 3	3 0	3 9	4 6	5 3	6 0	6 9	7 6	9 0	10 6	12 0	13 6	15 0	16 6	18 0	19 6	21 0	22 6	24 0	25 6	27 0
10	0 10	1 8	2 6	3 4	4 2	5 0	5 10	6 8	7 6	8 4	10 0	11 8	13 4	15 0	16 8	18 4	20 0	21 8	23 4	25 0	26 8	28 4	30 0
11	0 11	1 10	2 9	3 8	4 7	5 6	6 5	7 4	8 3	9 2	11 0	12 10	14 8	16 6	18 4	20 2	22 0	23 10	25 8	27 6	29 4	31 2	33 0
12	1 0	2 0	3 0	4 0	5 0	6 0	7 0	8 0	9 0	10 0	12 0	14 0	16 0	18 0	20 0	22 0	24 0	26 0	28 0	30 0	32 0	34 0	36 0
13	1 1	2 2	3 3	4 4	5 5	6 6	7 7	8 8	9 9	10 10	13 0	15 2	17 4	19 6	21 8	23 10	26 0	28 2	30 4	32 6	34 8	36 10	39 0
14	1 2	2 4	3 6	4 8	5 10	7 0	8 2	9 4	10 6	11 8	14 0	16 4	18 8	21 0	23 4	25 8	28 0	30 4	32 8	35 0	37 4	39 8	42 0
15	1 3	2 6	3 9	5 0	6 3	7 6	8 9	10 0	11 3	12 6	15 0	17 6	20 0	22 6	25 0	27 6	30 0	32 6	35 0	37 6	40 0	42 6	45 0
16	1 4	2 8	4 0	5 4	6 8	8 0	9 4	10 8	12 0	13 4	16 0	18 8	21 4	24 0	26 8	29 4	32 0	34 8	37 4	40 0	42 8	45 4	48 0
17	1 5	2 10	4 3	5 8	7 1	8 6	9 11	11 4	12 9	14 2	17 0	19 10	22 8	25 6	28 4	31 2	34 0	36 10	39 8	42 6	45 4	48 2	51 0
18	1 6	3 0	4 6	6 0	7 6	9 0	10 6	12 0	13 6	15 0	18 0	21 0	24 0	27 0	30 0	33 0	36 0	39 0	42 0	45 0	48 0	51 0	54 0
19	1 7	3 2	4 9	6 4	7 11	9 6	11 1	12 8	14 3	15 10	19 0	22 2	25 4	28 6	31 8	34 10	38 0	41 2	44 4	47 6	50 8	53 10	57 0
20	1 8	3 4	5 0	6 8	8 4	10 0	11 8	13 4	15 0	16 8	20 0	23 4	26 8	30 0	33 4	36 8	40 0	43 4	46 8	50 0	53 4	56 8	60 0
21	1 9	3 6	5 3	7 0	8 9	10 6	12 3	14 0	15 9	17 6	21 0	24 6	28 0	31 6	35 0	38 6	42 0	45 6	49 0	52 6	56 0	59 6	63 0
22	1 10	3 8	5 6	7 4	9 2	11 0	12 10	14 8	16 6	18 4	22 0	25 8	29 4	33 0	36 8	40 4	44 0	47 8	51 4	55 0	58 8	62 4	66 0
23	1 11	3 10	5 9	7 8	9 7	11 6	13 5	15 4	17 3	19 2	23 0	26 10	30 8	34 6	38 4	42 2	46 0	49 10	53 8	57 6	61 4	65 2	69 0

	2'	4'	6'	8'	10'	12'	14'	16'	18'	20'	24'	28'	32'	36'	40'	44'	48'	52'	56'	60'	64'	68'	72'
24	2' 0"	4' 0"	6' 0"	8' 0"	10' 0"	12' 0"	14' 0"	16' 0"	18' 0"	20' 0"	24' 0"	28' 0"	32' 0"	36' 0"	40' 0"	44' 0"	48' 0"	52' 0"	56' 0"	60' 0"	64' 0"	68' 0"	72' 0"
25	2 1	4 2	6 3	8 4	10 5	12 6	14 7	16 8	18 9	20 10	25 0	29 2	33 4	37 6	41 8	45 10	50 0	54 2	58 4	62 6	66 8	70 10	75 0
26	2 2	4 4	6 6	8 8	10 10	13 0	15 2	17 4	19 6	21 8	26 0	30 4	34 8	39 0	43 4	47 8	52 0	56 4	60 8	65 0	69 4	73 8	78 0
27	2 3	4 6	6 9	9 0	11 3	13 6	15 9	18 0	20 3	22 6	27 0	31 6	36 0	40 6	45 0	49 6	54 0	58 6	63 0	67 6	72 0	76 6	81 0
28	2 4	4 8	7 0	9 4	11 8	14 0	16 4	18 8	21 0	23 4	28 0	32 8	37 4	42 0	46 8	51 4	56 0	60 8	65 4	70 0	74 8	79 4	84 0
29	2 5	4 10	7 3	9 8	12 1	14 6	16 11	19 4	21 9	24 2	29 0	33 10	38 8	43 6	48 4	53 2	58 0	62 10	67 8	72 6	77 4	82 2	87 0
30	2 6	5 0	7 6	10 0	12 6	15 0	17 6	20 0	22 6	25 0	30 0	35 0	40 0	45 0	50 0	55 0	60 0	65 0	70 0	75 0	80 0	85 0	90 0
31	2 7	5 2	7 9	10 4	12 11	15 6	18 1	20 8	23 3	25 10	31 0	36 2	41 4	46 6	51 8	56 10	62 0	67 2	72 4	77 6	82 8	87 10	93 0
32	2 8	5 4	8 0	10 8	13 4	16 0	18 8	21 4	24 0	26 8	32 0	37 4	42 8	48 0	53 4	58 8	64 0	69 4	74 8	80 0	85 4	90 8	96 0
33	2 9	5 6	8 3	11 0	13 9	16 6	19 3	22 0	24 9	27 6	33 0	38 6	44 0	49 6	55 0	60 6	66 0	71 6	77 0	82 6	88 0	93 6	99 0
34	2 10	5 8	8 6	11 4	14 2	17 0	19 10	22 8	25 6	28 4	34 0	39 8	45 4	51 0	56 8	62 4	68 0	73 8	79 4	85 0	90 8	96 4	102 0
35	2 11	5 10	8 9	11 8	14 7	17 6	20 5	23 4	26 3	29 2	35 0	40 10	46 8	52 6	58 4	64 2	70 0	75 10	81 8	87 6	93 4	99 2	105 0
36	3 0	6 0	9 0	12 0	15 0	18 0	21 0	24 0	27 0	30 0	36 0	42 0	48 0	54 0	60 0	66 0	72 0	78 0	84 0	90 0	96 0	102 0	108 0

*Masters Builders Memoranda includes all the building trades; he is the first and last man on the works, and should be well informed on all that enters into the construction of a building.

To ascertain from the above table the number of feet in a board 10" wide and 22' long, then in column under 22' and opposite 10" in first column is found 18' 4", answer.

If the above be 2" thick, or equal to 20" wide, then opposite 20" is found 36' 8", answer.

If the above be 8" thick, then 8 times 18' 4" equals 146' 8", answer.

$$18'\ 4''$$
$$8$$
$$146'\ 8''$$

If the above timber be 40' long, then in column under 36' and opposite 10" is found 30' 0"

and in column under 4' and opposite 10" is found 3' 4"

$$30'\ 0''$$
$$3'\ 4''$$
$$33'\ 4''$$

Then 30' 0" plus 3' 4" equals 33' 4", which being multiplied by 8 equals 266' 8", answer.

$$8$$
$$266'\ 8''$$

If a board be 11¾" wide and 9' long, then in column under 9' and opposite 11" is found

And in the same column and opposite ¾" is found

Then 8' 3" plus 6¾" equals 8' 9¾", answer.

$$8'\ 3''$$
$$0'\ 6¾''$$
$$8'\ 9¾''$$

If the same board be 1½" thick, then 8' 9¾"

Plus one-half of 8' 9¾"

equals 13' 2⅝", answer.

$$8'\ 9¾''$$
$$4'\ 4⅞''$$
$$13'\ 2⅝''$$

TABLE 21.

NUMBER OF SHINGLES AND NAILS PER 100 SQUARE FEET.

Laid to the weather.	Number per 100 square feet.	Number of 5 d nails. lbs.
4″	1,000	5
4½″	890	4½
5″	800	4
5½″	727	3¾
6″	667	3⅜

TABLE 22.

The standard width of shingles is 4″.

1000 feet of sheathing on rafters spaced 2′ 0″ from centers requires 29 lbs. 10d nails.

1000 feet of sheathing on rafters spaced 1′ 6″ from centers requires 40 lbs. 10d nails.

1000 feet of sheathing on rafters spaced 1′ 4″ from centers requires 45 lbs. 10d nails.

1000 feet of sheathing on rafters spaced 1′ 0″ from centers requires 60 lbs. 10d nails.

1000 feet flooring joist spaced 1′ 4″ from centers requires 40 lbs. 8d nails.

1000 feet 6″ weather boarding studding spaced 1′ 4″ from centers requires 35½ lbs. 8d nails.

1000 feet lath on studding spaced 1′ 4″ from centers requires 5¼ lbs. 3d fine.

For flooring and weather boarding allow one-fifth for waste and matching.

TABLE 23.

Approximate Number of Cut and Wire Nails to the Pound.

	Length in inches	Cut nails	Wire finishing	Wire fence nails	Wire slating	Wire roofing	Wire common
2d	1	......	1,558	......	411	411	1,200
3d fine.	1⅛	700	....	......	.....	.....	......
3d	1¼	480	980	......	329	251	720
4d	1½	300	760	......	209	165	432
5d	1¾	200	500	142	142	142	300
6d	2	160	350	124	.....	103	252
7d	2¼	128	275	92	.....	....	186
8d	2½	92	190	82	.....	....	132
9d	2¾	72	173	62	.....	.....	105
10d	3	60	137	50	.....	.....	87
12d	3¼	44	98	38	.....	.....	66
16d	3½	32	81	30	.....	.....	51
20d	4	24	71	23	.....	.....	35
30d	4½	18	....	....	.....	....	27
40d	5	14	....	....	.....	.....	21
50d	5½	12	....	....	.....	.....	15
60d	6	10	....	....	.....	.....	12
6d fence nails.	2	80	....	....	.....	....	......
8d "	2½	50	....	....	.....	.....	......
10d "	3	39	....	....	.....	.....	......
12d "	3¼	24	....	....	.....	.....	......

Speeding Pulleys. *The diameter in inches and number of revolutions of the driver being given, required the number of revolutions of the driven.*

Rule. Multiply the diameter of the driver in inches by its number of revolutions, and divide by the diameter of the driven in inches, for its number of revolutions.

The diameter in inches and number of revolutions of the driven being given, required the diameter of the driver for a given number of revolutions.

Rule. Multiply the diameter of the driven in inches by its number of revolutions, and divide by the given number of revolutions, for the diameter of the driven required in inches.

The diameter in inches and number of revolutions of the driven being given, required the diameter of the driven in inches.

Rule. Multiply the diameter of the driven in inches by its number of revolutions, and divide by the number of revolutions of driver for its diameter in inches.

Pulleys. Are of two kinds, "straight face" for shifting belt, and "crown face" for non-shifting.

Belting. To give durability to fast running belts, grease them well with castor oil.

When endless belts can be used splice them about 4″, glue and clamp, let stand over night, then peg with wooden pegs set in glue. This is better by far than leather lacing.

The best lacing for belts in fast speed is annealed brass wire of No. 55 gauge for narrow belts.

Weight of Grindstone. Rule. Square the diameter in inches and multiply by the thickness in inches, and that sum again by the decimal 0.06363. for the number of pounds.

To find the pressure per square inch of water in a tank 10′ square and 10′ deep.

A cubic foot of water at a temperature of 60 degrees F. weighs 62½ pounds, or 8.3 pounds to the gallon; at 212 degrees weight is 59.80, or 8.3 pounds per gallon. The pressure per square inch of a column of water one foot high equals 0.434 pounds; hence a column of water 12 inches square and 10 feet high at a temperature of 60 degrees will exert a pressure on the bottom of tank equal $(10 \times 62\frac{1}{2} = 625 \text{ lbs.})$ to 625 pounds, or equal $(625 \div 144 = 4.34)$ to 4.34 pounds per square inch nearly; then $120'' \times 120'' \times 4.34 = 62,496$, equals 62.496 pounds as the pressure on the bottom of the tank. The pressure on the sides of tank diminishes as the height decreases; at the top the pressure is nothing, while at the bottom the pressure per square inch is equal to the height (10′) in feet multiplied by 4.34; hence the average pressure on one side of the tank will equal one-half 4.34 (2.17) multiplied by its area in inches; thus, $120 \times 120 \times 2.17 = 31248$; equals 31,248 pounds on one side of the tank.

Glue. The cohesion of solid glue, Mr. Bevan found to be 4,000 pounds per square inch; his experiments on pieces of wood glued together, required a force per square inch, of 350 to 715 pounds to separate them.

Good glue is very hard and tough, and of a brown color; is transparent if held to the light, the fracture is ragged and oblique to the edge, is almost tasteless, and no bad smell, swells when soaked in cold water, requires to be boiled before it will thoroughly dissolve, requires about ten times its weight of water; it also forms a stiff jelly when cold, which is a fair test for good glue.

Poor glue is dark and cloudy, breaks easy, having a straight or conchoidal fracture and glass edge, is easily dissolved in cold water; if exposed to dampness, will emit a bad smell in a short time.

To prepare the glue. Place the amount of glue to be used. in a bag of some strong material, then pound with a mallet; place the glue in the pot, cover with clean cold water, let stand over night; then place the pot in the kettle filled with water, let boil, and stir well, remove the scum, and when the glue will run from the brush, smooth and free, having no lumps, is ready for use. Apply hot, the hotter the glue is the better will be the joint. In cold weather, warm the joints to be glued, but not too hot to burn the glue; after applying the glue, rub the joint well, to lessen the film of glue in the joint, and thus form a grain and suction in the joint: the work may now be clamped and let stand until dry, which for heavy work will require from two to three days, for light work less time will suffice; if the glue is a little thick, only apply it to one side of the joint. A spoonful of whitening to a pot of glue is said to improve the strength of same; a little alcohol will keep the glue sweet; fresh glue is always the best. When re-melted its strength decreases, and if burnt it is worthless. Clean boiling water should be used to thin down if too thick; the pot should be thoroughly cleansed when making fresh glue, as the old will taint and ruin the new. When not in use, place the pot in a cool place apart from the kettle; if a cover be placed over the pot, the moisture will keep the glue from crisping on the sides.

Turners' Cement.   To one pound of melted rosin, add a quarter pound of pitch; while boiling, add brick dust until considered thick enough, roll into sticks same as grafting wax.   When turning rosettes or other light work, by heating the above cement the work may be attached to the face-plate, and removed with a light tap from the hammer; in winter add a little tallow.

Glossary of Technical Terms
—AND—
GENERAL INDEX.

Aaron's Rod.—An enrichment consisting of a straight rod from which almond leaves are represented sprouting on each side; the term has been applied incorrectly to a rod around which a serpent is coiled.—[Audsley.

Abacus. — The upper number in the capital of a column, on which the architrave in classic and the springers in Gothic architecture immediately rest; in the Tuscan, Doric and Ionic orders it is rectangular; in the Corinthian and Composite orders the abacus is curved outward at the angles termed the *horns*; the curve is ornamented at the center with a rosette, termed the *rose* of the abacus.

Abutment. — A construction of stone, brick or other material which receives the thrust of an arch, vault or strut.

Acroteria. — A small pedestal placed on the apex or angles of a pediment for the support of a statue or other ornament.

Acute Angle.—Page 21.

Alburnum.—Sap-wood.

Alcove.—A recess in a room for a bed, sometimes curtained off and hid from view during the day.

Altar-Rail.—The railing of stone, marble, metal or wood in front of the communion table, and in front of which communicants kneel while receiving the sacrament; the height from the top of kneeling step is about 2' 2".

Algebraic Symbols.—230.

Angle-Bracket—A bracket placed in an interior or exterior angle, and not at right angles with the wall; to find the length and curve. 222, 223.

Angle-tie. —The timber that gives support to the *dragon-beam* in a roof; the diagonal piece cut in the angles of a square frame to reduce the same to an octagon.

Angle-Bead.—Or sometimes termed *staff bead*, is used as a saddle on the external angles of plastered walls to protect them from injury; if a column, it is termed an *angle column*; if a corbel, it is termed an *angle corbel*.

Angular-Capital. — In the Ionic capital where the three volutes are made to the angle of 135 degrees from all four sides.

Annulet.—A small fillet circular on plan, and square in section.

Antique—In architectural nomenclature, a term applied to works executed by the ancient Greeks and Romans.

Apron-piece.—The cap and fascia completing the inside finish for the window sill, and on which the architrave, or moulding finish around the window sometimes rest; is also termed the *window stool*. The horizontal piece of timber in a stair-case for supporting the rough horses at platforms, and quarter paces; is also termed the apron piece.—[Nicholson

Arc of a Circle.—In geometry, any part of the circumference of a circle that is less than a semicircle. 24. Applied to transfer angle. 26.

Architect.—Chief of the works; a person competent to design and superintend the execution of any building. The knowledge he ought to possess is wide and va-varied, comprehending all the trades and materials in the construction of buildings; he should be kind and gentle with those who are called upon to carry out his designs, and in so doing he should be positive and determined to check any effort to slight or deceive in the work.

Arch.—A concave structure raised or built over a center, and serving as the support of some superstructure. When several arches are built in a row it is termed an *arcade*. The line from which the arch springs is termed the *springing line*; the first arch stone is termed the *springer*; the *impost moulding* is the cap from which the arch springs. The arch stones are termed *voussiors*; the concave side of arch is termed the *intrados*, the opposite or convex side is termed the *extrados*; the solid extremities on or against which the arch rest are termed the *abutments*; the horizontal distance on the concave side from spring to spring of the arch is termed the span. The perpendicular height from springing to the concave side at its highest point is termed the *rise of arch*; the crown of the arch is its highest point on the intrados; the center stone at the crown is called the *keystone*; the *haunches* of an arch are the parts between the crown and the springing. The surface of the concave side is termed the *soffit*; and when a collection of mouldings is carried around the arch concentric with the intrados this ornamentation is termed the *archivolt*; and the mixed right angle triangle formed by the curve of extrados intersecting horizontal and perpendicular lines draw tangent to the extradoes, is termed the *spandrel*. The spandrel is sometimes pierced with a round opening termed an *o-r-cyc*. Various names are given to arches, owing to their profile. When a semi-circle it is termed a *circular arch;* when a semi-ellipse is termed an *elliptical arch;* when less than a semi-circle it is termed a *segmental arch;* when more than a semi-circle it is termed a *horse-shoe or sarasenic arch;* when an arch is drawn from two centers on the springing line it is termed a *pointed arch,* or *Gothic arch;* when springing from imposts at different heights it is termed a *rampant arch;* when a portion of straight exists between the impost moulding and the springing of the arch it is termed a *stilted arch.*

Architrave.—The band or finish carried around a window or door, composed of one or more members; also one of the three divisions in the entablature of the classic orders, resting immediately on the abacus.

Archivolt.—An ornamental band of mouldings concentric with the concave side and worked on the arch stones, and terminating at the impost moulding. Sometimes the keystone divides the archivolt at the crown of arch.

Area.—In geometry the superficial contents of any figure. In architecture, an open space allowed below the surface of ground for basement steps, or a court.

Arris.—The external angle formed by the meeting of any two planes.

Ashlerings.—Short studding cut under the rafters in the garret to cut off the acute angle made by the rafters.

Astragal.—A small projecting semi-circular moulding; it is also termed a *bead,* or *cocked bead,* and often cut into a *bead-and-reel* enrichment, or to represent a string of beads or berries.

Atlantes.—Figures of males used instead of columns to support an entablature; if females, they are termed *caryatides.*

Attic Order.—It is employed to decorate the facade of a story of small height, terminating the upper part of building.

Attic Story.—A term applied to upper story of a house where the ceiling is square with the sides to distinguish it from the garret.

Axis.—The spindle or center of any rotative motion.

Back.—The upper side of a hand-rail. (The under side is termed the *breast.*) The term is also applied to the hip and common rafter, as the back of a hip, and the *back of a rafter.*

Backing a Hip.—213; a practical method. 217.

Backing Up a Wall.—The term is applied to backing up a wall with brick or other material when the face is veneered with more expensive material. This should be carefully done with close joints, as the mortar will shrink, and apt to buckle the wall.

Badigeon.—A mixture of sawdust and strong glue used to fill up the defects in woodwork after being dressed off. The application should be very light, as it is liable to shrink. A mixture of freestone and plaster used by the mason to fill defects in dressed stonework.

Balcony.—A platform in front of a window or other opening, supported on brackets, and made safe by a balustrade, and sheltered sometimes by a large projecting *hood* or *canopy.*

Baluster.—The vertical supports to a hand-rail; a small column with turned shaft; standard lengths of, 152; to find the odd lengths under the tangents, 208, 151, 203; spacing around the cylinder, 69, 70, 71, 149; to find their position for boring on the crook, 209; to find the pitch of templet for boring, 209; boring for balusters, best results, 209.

Balustrade.—A number of balusters placed in a row supporting a cap or rail. In the colonial style it has a beautiful effect when used as a cresting surmounting the cornice or a truncated roof.

Banker.—A bench on which the stonecutter works the stone.

Base.—The finish at the floor skirting the sides of a room to protect the walls. The members are for the better class of work, composed of *plinth, subplinth,* base moulding, and *shoe* or *quarter* round, the base being tongued down into the shoe, and also into the base moulding.

Batten.—A piece of wood from one to six inches wide; the horizontal pieces on a *ledge* or *batten door,* to which the boards are secured; also used for stripping stone or brick walls for lath and plaster.

Batter.—The slope or inclination given to a wall or buttress, as in retaining walls, piers and abutments.

Barge-board.—The board that covers the rafters at the gable end of a roof; in the Elizabethan style of architecture it was placed at the verge of the raking cornice and enriched with scroll work and carvings. It is also termed a *verge-board.*

Bead.—A moulding semi-circular in section. When the bead is flush with the surface it is termed a *quirk-bead;* when raised it is termed a *cock-bead;* when worked from two sides it is termed a *returned bead* or *double-quirked bead.* A series of beads worked parallel to each other is termed *reeding.*

Beam.—Either of timber or iron, used to counteract a weight by compression or extension. When used to resist the thrust of a rafter it is termed a *tie-beam,* the strain being one of tension; when used as a *collar beam* (see collar beam), or as a *straining beam,* it is in a state of compression: or if used to support the ends of joist, or as a lintel, the strain is a transverse or cross strain. (See strain.) To find the safe load for an inclining beam, 130; to find the safe load for a horizontal beam, 225; to find the strongest beam that can be cut from a log, 216; the best form for rectangular timbers, 227.

Bed.—The horizontal surface of a brick or stone when built in a wall; when stone are built in a wall with their laminations horizontal they are said to be *quarry headed*.

Bed-Moulding. — The moulding under the plancier of a cornice carried around the brackets or over and in front of the dentil course; also in the angle formed by the shelf and frieze of a mantel.

Belt Course.—The course of stone in a wall immediately above the ground. It projects usually one inch and is also termed the *plinth*.

Bearer.—A term given to the support under a flight of stairs. Also termed the *carriage* or *rough horses*. (See *Horsing up*.) To find the dimension of timber so the soffit will not deflect more than .03 of an inch per foot of its length, 129, 130, 131; to calculate the load likely to come upon the bearers, 129; for self-supporting stairs, 203.

Belvedere.—A small portion of a building carried above the roof to view the surroundings; also termed a *turret, lantern* or *cupola*.

Bevel. — A tool similar to a *try square*, only the blade is adjustable to any angle with the stock. Application to the crook for the twist of a hand rail, 39, 43, 61, 63; crossing the tangents explained, 67, 43, 68, 66; to prove the correctness of bevel and application, 61, 170; for hip, valley and jack rafters, framing, or any splayed work, 218.

Beveled.—Two planers meeting at any angle less or greater than a right angle. It is termed *splayed* in many cases.

Bird's-mouth.—An interior angle cut on the end of a timber, to fit and rest on the external angle of another timber.

Black Walnut.—210; to color the sap part, 210.

Blockings.—Small pieces of wood glued in the unexposed internal angles of step and rise of stairs to strengthen the joint.

Block-stone. — Heavy stones, as they come from the quarry.

Bolt.—To find the size of bolt to resist the strain likely to come upon the bolt; divide the strain by 2,200 and take the square root of the product for the diameter of bolt. (*Farey*).

Bond-Course.—In brick work every sixth course is laid as a header across the wall to bind the whole. In stone work, bond stones for common ruble work is usually specified, every 2½ or 3 feet super-

ficial, so as to make the whole aggregate act together, and be mutually dependent on each other.

Bond-Timber.—Timbers built in the walls to tie them longitudinal, and also to nail the wainscoting and other finish thereto. Hoop iron, notched or serrated on the edge and coated with pitch, and built in the wall, is preferred, being more durable in case of fire.

Bond-Stones.—Sometimes termed *through stones*, are such as extend through the thickness of wall; in good ruble work they should be built in every 2½ or 3 feet superficial of wall surface, and in very thick walls every course should be *heart bounded*.

Boss.—An enrichment at the intersection of groins, or cross vaulted ceilings.

Bossage.—Stones that are left projecting from a wall to be ornamented in the future.

Boudoir.—French, a term used to designate a room especially appropriated to the mistress of the house, as her sitting room. (*Gwilt*).

Boxing.—Window frames are such when boxed out at the sides to receive sash weights; for inside shutters in first-class houses the jambs are boxed, either splayed or square to the window frame, to receive the inside shutters; the shutters are then termed *box shutters*.

Brace or Strut. — An inclined piece of timber forming a triangle to give strength to a building or any part of the same. It is also termed a strut. To find the strain from a given load, 229; from a given strain to find the dimension of timber, 229.

Bracket.—How to diminish the size, 27, 105.

Breadth.—The greatest width of a body at right angles to its length.

Bressummer.—The meaning is restricted to a beam or lintel across the opening of a shop front, to support the superincumbent load.

Brick-Layers.—Memoranda, 239.

Brick-Work. — When brick are laid in a wall at right angles to the face of wall, it is termed a *header*. When laid parallel to the face of wall it is termed a *stretcher*. When every alternate brick is laid as stretcher and header, and to break joints with the next course above and also under, it is termed *Flemish bond*.

Bridging.—Strips 1½"×3", cut and fixed from the lower edge of one joist to the upper edge of the next, crossing each other, is termed *herring-bone, truss* or *cross-bridging*. The joist is usually bridged in this way every five feet of their length; the strength gained by bridging in this way is three times over those that are not bridged. (See Hatfield's Transverse Stairs).

Builder.—One who contracts for the erection and completion of a building in all its parts.

Building—An edifice constructed for use or convenience, as a house, a church, a shop, &c.

Buttress.—A pier or heavy projection carried up to support a wall; a cheif feature in Gothic architecture. When carried from one buttress to another by arching, as in large mediæval churches, where the outer buttress is made to give support to the buttress of the *clear story* by arching over the roof of the *triforium* or *gallery*, it is termed a *flying buttress*.

Butt-Joint.—A joint at right angles to the direction of the straight part of anything, or that is normal to any curve at its intersection with the curve; a term applied to the center joint of the wreath rail, which is at right angles to the tangents of two wreath pieces of a hand-rail.

Cabling.—A staff or reed ornament placed in the flutes at the base of a column, the height of same being about one-third the height of the shaft.

Cage.—An outer work of timber surrounding another. Thus the cage of a stair is the wooden enclosure that confines it. [*Nicholson.*]

Camber.—A slight arching given to the upper edge of joist about ½″ in 16 feet of span.

Campanile.—In Italy a detached tower, erected for the purpose of containing bells.

Canted.—A position taken oblique to the horizon.

Canopy.—See balcony.

Canting-Strip.—In frame buildings the strip immediately above the base-board, and on which the weather boarding and corner strips rest; it is canted so as to carry the water from the building. It is also termed a *water table.*

Cantilever.—The joist that are made to extend out from a building to support a balcony or cornice; sometimes termed *lookouts.*

Capital—The crowning division of a column. In classic architecture the different orders have their respective capitals; but in the Egyptian, Indian, Byzantine and Gothic architectures there is an endless variety.

Carpenters.—Memoranda, 244.

Carpentry and Joinery.—212-224; descriptive, 212; mechanical, 224.

Carpet-Strip.—The strip under a door when closed, allowing the door to clear the carpet when open; also termed *threshold,* or *saddle strips.*

Casement.—A glazed sash, made to open and shut on hinges.

Carving.—When carving stands out from its ground it is termed in *alto relievo;* when projecting one-half it is termed in *mezzo relievo;* and when slightly raised it is termed *basso relievo,* which is the opposite when carved in *intaglio,* or sunk.

Carcase.—A building roofed in; ready for the joiner, plasterer and other artizans to ornament and complete the work.

Caul.—A devise used hot in veneering to press the veneer close to the form, and at the same time keep the glue moist in circular work. The caul is made to the curvature. At other times bags of sawdust are used, being easily adjusted by clamping to the required curve.

Cavetto. — A hollow moulding whose profile is a quadrant of a circle and is termed a *cove moulding.* It is the *scape* from the shaft at the base, and also from the shaft to the capital of a column. It is also termed the *apopoge.* [*Weale.*]

Centering.—Temporary supports over which arches and vaults are constructed; they are chiefly built of wood.

Chancel-Rail.—The rail and balusters around the chancel or altar in churches, and the bar in the courts of justice.

Chamfer. — An arris reduced equally on both sides forming two obtuse angles. If the chamfer is stopped short at the end, it is then termed a *stop chamfer.*

Chimney.—An appendage to the house in which the fire place is located and serves to convey away the smoke and ventilate the rooms.

Chord.—24.

Cheveron.—A moulding having a zig-zag or serrated edge; peculiar to the Norman style; it is also termed a *zig-zag* and *dancette* moulding.

Circular Winding Stair-Case—A stair-case that is circular on plan having all the steps winding. If the steps are supported by a wall at one end and open at the other, it is termed a *geometrical stair-case.* 198.

Circle.—To find the area, 23, 24; circumference, 23.

Cincture. — A fillet or narrow band connecting one moulding with another, as the *cavetto* at the top of a column is connected with the *astragal,* or at the base with the torus.

Clamp.—A narrow piece of wood joined to the end of a wide piece to prevent its warping; a device with screws used when gluing two pieces, to force out the surplus glue from the joint.

Cleat.—A narrow strip of wood nailed on in joinery; as a piece of wood nailed on a door, a shutter, &c. [*Webster.*]

Close-Outer-String. — Is meant that the steps and risers are housed into the outer string, same as the wall string. When such is the case the face of outer string is either paneled or otherwise ornamented with string mouldings, instead of brackets and return nosings, as in open strings. 210, 211.

Closer.—A brick either less than a half or a whole brick, used to close up a course of brick work; when less than a whole brick and greater than a half brick, it is called a *king closer;* when less than a half brick, it is termed a *queen closer.*

Cockle-Stairs.—A term used to denote a winding or spiral stairs. (*Chambers*).

Coffer.—A deep sunk panel in a ceiling, dome or vault. It is also termed *Caisson.*

Collar-Beam. — A beam used above the lower end of rafters to cut off the angle of rafters at the ridge, and also to stiffen the roof. If there be a tie-bearer, then the collar-bearer is in a state of compression; if no tie-bearer, then the strain is one of tension.

Column.—A long round body of wood, stone or iron; the part on which it rests is termed the *base.* The head is termed the *capital,* and the intermediate part is termed the *shaft.* The capital is surmounted by the *abacus* immediately on which the *architrave* rests. There are five orders of column the Tuscan, Doric, Ionic, Corinthian and the Composite. The column was a chief decorative feature in the porticoes of the ancient Greeks and Romans. They are termed *engaged or attached columns* when projecting three-quarters or less from a wall, and *insulated columns* when they stand clear of the walls.

Common Rafter.—The rafter to which the sheathing is nailed; it is supported by the *purlin,* which in turn are supported by the *principal rafters,* in a trussed roof.

Common Rafter.—215.

Concentric. — Circles, 24, and ellipses, 33.

Concrete.—Proportions of cement and stone, 238.

Concave.—24, and *Convex,* 24.

Cone.—Rule to find the area, 29.

Conic Sections.—29, 30.

Conge.—A cove, same as the apopoge and the *Cavetto.*

Console.—An ornamental bracket placed on the pilaster of a frontispiece to support the cornice; also to ornament the keystone of an arch; termed, also, *Ancone* and *Trusses.*

Conservatory.—A building for the propagation and preservation of rare plants and flowers. A superior greenhouse, it should be in a very dry situation, and the walls should be at least three bricks thick. [*Stuart.*

Coping.—A course of stone or wood on top of a wall for a protection. When the coping is one thickness it is termed *parallel coping;* when thicker in the middle and the top slanting two ways it is termed *saddle-back coping;* when thinner on one edge than

the other, it is termed *feather-edge coping.*

Corbel.—A term denoting a projecting stone or piece of timber which supports a weight or strain. A row of corbels connected with small arches or otherwise is termed a *corbel table.*

Cornice.—The upper division of the entablature directly over the frieze; when the frieze is omitted the cornice is termed an *architrave cornice.*

Corona.—The outer fascia of a cornice to which the crown moulding is nailed; the corona is allowed to drop below the plancier, and thus form a *drip.*

Corridor.—A passage or gallery, from which an entrance may be had to various apartments; sometimes running around a quadrangle.

Coved-Ceiling.—The walls of an apartment made to join the ceiling with a curve instead of a right angle.

Crockets.—Ornaments of foliage, or animals used to decorate the angles of spires, pinnacles or gables.

Crown Moulding.—The upper moulding of a cornice, the *cyma recta* being mostly used for that purpose, as it forms a good water drip.

Crossetts.—The projection or ears on arch stones to allow one arch stone to hang on the adjacent stone; the *breaks* in architraves around openingr, as doors, windows, &c.

Curtail-Step.—The first step in a stairway when the end is finished, in the form of a scroll; also termed the *scroll step;* how to draw, 35; manner of constructing, 35.

Copper Gauge.—Construction of, 99.

Cupola. — A dome or spherical vault crowning an edifice.

Cutting Plane.—A plane cutting a solid into two parts in any direction. In hand railing, the plane on which is developed the face-mould for the wreath-piece, 38, 43, 48, 51, 54, 47.

Cylinder.—In geometry, a solid figure whose base is a circle and whose curved superfices is everywhere at an equal distance from the axis or line supposed to pass through the middle. The term throughout this book is applied to the wreath or circular part of the outer string. To find the location of rises in a platform cylinder, so the wreath-piece will raise the proper height without springing the plank, 144; to determine the position of risers in a platform cylinder, so the inclination of rail will have the common pitch on the center line of rail, 70; to establish the position of rise in a quarter cylinder, so the wreath-piece will raise the proper height on the level and not spring the plank, 144; to locate the position of rise in a quarter cylinder, so the wreath-piece may be constructed in one piece when there are flyers above and below the cylinder, 71, 72; to find the position of risers in a quarter cylinder having flyers above and below, so that two wreath-pieces may form the twist, and that they may be constructed from the least thickness of plank, 72; to find the position of risers in cylinders, so the wreath part of outer string may have the same inclination as the straight part, 70, 69, 100; to determine the location of risers in a cylinder at turnout, 84, 119, 123, 120; number of staves in a platform cylinder, 149; veneering a cylinder over a drum, 154, 155; thickness of veneer, rule for, 125; dadoing and bending over a drum, 127; distance apart to make the grooves, 127; glueing up staves, 102, 103; that is, veneered, 127; how to place the risers in a semi-circular cylinder starting and landing, so that one set of face-moulds will answer for both wreaths, 73, 75; how to place the risers when less or more than a quarter circle, 80; how to place the risers in platform cylinders, 69; how to place the risers in a platform cylinder on the center line of rail, 70; joints of cylinder, 121; to find the length of staves, 122, 123, 124, 165.

Cyma-recta.—An Ogee moulding with the concave portion above. When the convex part is above, it is termed a *cyma-reversa* moulding or *talon.*

Dado.—The middle division of the pedestal of a column, termed the *die.* The term is also applied to the wainscoting around a room, vestibule or hall. (See pedestal.) A plane also termed *cutting-thrush;* used to cut grooves in a board across the grain, termed *dadoing* or *gaining.* 156.

Damp-Course.—A course of slate or asphalt laid in cement on outside walls about 18″ above the earth surface to prevent the dampness rising in the wall.

Dead Shore.—An upright piece of timber built in a wall to support a superincumbent weight until the brick which is to carry the load has set or become hard.

Dentils.—Small cubes resembling teeth arranged in a course to ornament a cornice or plain surface. Their width is one-half the length, and the space between each dentil is one-half their width, and the projection is equal to their face width.

Details. — Drawings made to a large scale or full size, furnished by the architect to the builder, and termed *working drawings.*

Diagonal.—22.

Diameter.—24.

Dimension.—The length, breadth or thickness of a body.

Directing Ordinate. — A line that governs the direction of an ordinate. 43, 44.

Discharging Arch. — An arch built in a wall over a lintel, or above another arch to discharge the weight to the piers. Also termed a *relieving arch.*

Dog-Legged Stairs. — Such as are solid between the upper flights; or those which have no well hole; the center of rail and balusters of the different flights being in one plane.—[*Nicholson.* 86-93.

Dome.—A circular, elliptical or polygonal covering of a part or whole of a building. The dome of the Pantheon at Rome is spherical in form, and 142½ feet in diameter.

Door.—The entrance into a house or an apartment.

Door-Frame—The wooden jambs and head enclosing a door; also including the sill if made of wood.

Dormer —A window in the roof of a house having the frame in a vertical position. When the window lies in the plane of the roof it is termed a skylight.

Dormitory. — A large sleeping apartment containing many beds.

Dove-Tail.—A tenon in the shape of a dove's tail which is made to fit into a mortise shaped like a trapezoid, forming a joint much used by cabinet makers in making drawers, boxes, &c. 104, 105; pattern, 98.

Dowel.—A pin used in a joint to give strength and prevent the joint from shifting, termed *doweling* the joint. 98.

Dragon Beam.—A short beam forming a seat for the foot of a hip rafter, and is held in place by the *angle tie.*

Draught-Board.—And draughting instruments, 3.

Drawing-Knife.—37.

Drawings.—In carpentry the description of a building made on paper to a scale, describing the different parts thereof, both interior and exterior, by *plans, elevations, cross-sections* and *details.* They are considered the property of the architect when the building is completed.

Drawing-Room.—The room to which the company retire after a meal.

Draw-Bore and Pin.—In framing, the hole through the tenon is bored closer to the shoulder by ⅛″ than the hole in the header is from the cheek; this allows the oak pin to draw the shoulders up close. When the tenon extends through and the pin driven on the outside of trimmer it is termed *through bore and pin.*

Dressings—In a brick front, stone is often used for lintels, sills, arches, quoins, cornices, terminals, string courses and other facings, which is termed *stone dressings.* The front may be of stone and *brick* or *terra-cotta* used for dressings; if wood be used it would be termed *wooden dressings.*

Dwarf Walls.—Low walls of less height than the story of a building; sometimes the joist of a ground floor rest upon dwarf walls; and the enclosures of courts are frequently formed by them, with a railing of iron on their top.—[*Nicholson.*]

Die or **Dye.**—The plain shaft of a pedestal.

Eave.—The lower edge of a roof which overhangs the wall to carry the drip beyond its outer surface. The eave course in shingling should be in three thicknesses tapered.

Easing.—To draw, 164, 163, 165; pattern to make for cutting straight rail, 114, 138; starting from a newel, 114.

Echinus.—An ovolo, a member in the capital of a column under the abacus, which is carved into the *egg-and-dart moulding*; also termed *egg-and-tongue* or *egg-and-anchor* moulding.

Ellipsis.—To draw with a trammel, 31; with a string, 32; straight edge, 34; described on the cutting plane, 34; rule to find the area, 31; and also the circumference, 31.

Elliptic. — Winding stairs and manner of constructing the same, 203, 204.

Embattled Building. — Resembling a castle having *merlons* and *embrasures* on the top of walls, forming a parapet above the roof, as in castelated architecture in mediæval times.

Embossed Work. — In Gothic architecture a kind of sculptured work; the figure is raised and chiseled into foliage heads and animals, serving as a *stop* at the intersection of ribs in groined ceilings, and also weather mouldings around doors and windows. Any raised figure relieving a plain surface may be termed embossed work.

Embrasure. — Also termed *Crenelles*; the space between the merlons, for the battery in ancient military architecture.

Eendecagon. — A polygon of eleven sides.

Entablature.—The whole of the parts of an order, above the abacus; in the Greek, Roman and Italian architecture it is divided into three divisions, the *architrave*, *frieze* and *cornice*.

Entasis.—In the Greek classic orders, a slight swell in the shaft of a column or baluster.

Equilateral.—triangle, 23.

Escape.—The cove at the bottom and top of the shaft of a column, where the shaft escapes from the base, and also the capital; also termed the *apophyge.*

External Angle.—22

Excavators.—Memoranda, 236.

Eye.—Eye of a scroll is the circle from which the spiral line commences; the center of a volute, 35, 36

Facade. — The main front of a building.

Face-Mould.—The profile of a cylindric section as it is developed on the cutting plane; the pattern is used to line off the crook for the wreath-piece of a hand-rail; to draw for a turnout slightly inclining at the newel, 152, 153; for a turnout level at the newel, 109, 110; for level to a rake, 73, 77, 135; for rake to a level, 73, 80, 135; for platform twist, 111; without springing the plank, 144; when the risers are misplaced, 140, 143; when the pitch off the platform is different to the pitch to the platform, to draw one mould to answer for both wreath-pieces, 146; for a quarter turn starting and landing, 140, 144; for over winders in a cylinder greater than a quarter circle, starting from a newel, 180, 181; to connect the straight rail above and below the quarter pace, 80, 82; for winders in a semi-circle having two wreath-pieces, 167, 168, 183, 184; for winders in a semi-circle having three wreath-pieces, 193; for winders in a quarter circle to connect the straight rail above and below the quarter circle and work the ramp in the wreath piece, 138; for a quarter circle having winders starting from a newel, 185; to draw over winders to contain the casing connecting the straight rail at the upper or lower end, 187, 138; for a circular well hole on plan, 198; elliptical, 203, 209, 64, 69; wreath-piece with a full casing for a quarter circle on plan, 130, 37; for a wreath-piece with an intermediate casing for a quarter circle on plan, 41; for a wreath-piece with no casing over a quarter circle on plan, 46; for a wreath-piece with a full casing over a less than a quarter circle on plan, 49; for a wreath-piece with an intermediate casing over a less than a quarter circle on plan, 53; for a wreath-piece with no casing over a less than a quarter circle on plan, 56; for a wreath-piece with an intermediate casing over a greater than a quarter circle on plan, 62; for a wreath-piece with an intermediate casing over an elliptic curve on plan, 65; for casing patterns and wreath-piece for a wall rail on the wide end of winders in box stairs, 95; for 6″ to 20″ platform cylinders, 134, 135; for a wreath over winders in a cylinder struck from different radii, 196; to draw so that one set of moulds and bevels will answer for a wreath starting, and also landing, the plan being a semi-circle, 75; to draw so that one set of moulds and bevels will answer for a wreath-piece starting or landing over a plan less or greater than a quarter circle, 76, 80; to draw for the wreath part of a plaster moulding underneath the wreathed part of outer string, 157; application to the plank, for sawing out the crooks, 51, 57;

Foliage.—An ornamental distribution of leaves on various parts of a building, as on panels, rosettes, bosses, corbels, capitals, &c.

Foliated.—Gothic cusped tracery formed of tre-foils, quarter-foils and cinque foils.

Footings.—The first stones in the foundation of a wall. They are large, heavy and project six inches or more beyond the next course above to distribute the load over a greater surface of ground, and thus give greater security to the superstructure. There may be two or more offsets to the footings, according to the weight of the superstructure and the compressibility of the soil; provided for in the New York and Chicago building laws. 257.

Fox-Tail Wedge. — In fox-tail wedging the mortise is increased at the bottom in the direction of the grain; then the tenon is checked and a glued wedge inserted and allowed to project; then afterwards driven home. This method of joining is used by the chair makers, and is suitable in spindle work.

Foundation.—The ground as prepared, either mother earth, piling, concrete, timbering, planking, or by any other means on which to lay the foundation stones.

Framer.—In carpentry, one that is expert in the construction of frame buildings and heavy timbered structures, such as trussed roofs, wooden bridges, factories, rolling mills, &c., is known as a *good framer*.

Freestone.—Any stone that works freely.

Frieze.—A broad surface under a projecting cap or cornice. In the classic orders, the middle division of the entablature usually ornamented with sculpture. The wide space under the shelf of a mantle between the fire front and the shelf on which the bed moulding rests. The upper panel in a six panel door is termed a *frieze panel*, and the rail under is termed the *frieze rail*.

Furniture.—In architecture, the visible brass or other metallic furnishment of hardware for a house, as locks, bolts, hinges, knobs, latches, &c.

Furring-out.—Trimming out the joist around hearths to the proper length for the hearth-stones, or for the lathers where the joist or scantling have not been properly spaced, or in corners, for solid nailing, or where inside shutters are to shut into a box, the walls have to be *furred out*; also stone walls, to avoid dampness, are furred out for the lath and plaster.

Gable.—The triangular space at the end of a house from the level of the eaves to the ridge. It is termed a *pediment* when it does not rise the height of the main roof. When the triangular space is cut off by the continuation of the corona of the level cornice, the triangular panel is termed the *tympanium*.

Gablet.—A small gable used in skew blocks, crow-stepped gables, intakes, on buttresses, pinnacles, &c., for ornament.

Gain—In joinery, housing, the excavation made in a door or window head to admit the stiles their full thickness, and also wedge room for keying up; termed also *dadoing*.

Gagued Arch.—When the stones or bricks of an arch radiate to a common center it is termed a *gagued arch;* and the bricks are termed *gagued bricks*, being cut and rubbed until a perfect joint and taper is attained.

Gallery.—The projecting stories around the walls of a theater are termed *galleries*. A room for the purpose of exhibiting pictures is termed a *picture gallery*; also churches to increase the seating capacity project platforms from walls on three sides termed *galleries*. That part in which the singers perform is termed the *singers' gallery*.

Garret.—The room under the roof of a house, being lathed and plastered to the cellar beams, rafters and ashlerings.

Gas-Fitter.—(See plumber.)

Geometrical Stair-Case. — A stair-case having one end of the steps supported by the wall only at one end, the other end being free between the stories, with the rail continuous. If the steps are winding it is termed a *geometrical winding stairs*.

Geometry.—The science of extension, quantity or magnitude, 22.

Gin.—A portable hoisting machine, having three legs, one being moveable, used for lifting heavy weights from wells, or building low walls.

Girder.—A main beam to span openings and transmit heavy loads from support to support. When the loads are very heavy they are trussed, and are then termed trussed girders. Rule to determine the transverse strength of, 224.

Glazier. — An artizan that performs the work of fixing the glass in windows.

Glue.—Made from the hide and hoof of animals; the older the animal the better will be the glue, 102, 103, 246.

Griffin. — A nondescript animal, used in the sculptured decorations of the ancients.

Grindstone.—Rule to calculate the weight of, 241. To true-up a grindstone use a piece of gas-pipe.

Groin.—A line traced through the intersection of two arches, termed the line of curved hip or groin. To find the length of and cuts, 221, 222.

Groove.—A sunken rectangular channel.

Ground Floor.—The floor level with or first above the curbstone, or roadway; the same may be termed the ground plan of the house.

Grounds--Are narrow strips about 2½″ wide and ¾″ thick nailed up straight, true and plumb around all doors, windows and walls, as a guide for the plasterer, and also for nailing up the finish.

Grout.—Is composed of quick-lime and fine sand thinned down to the consistency of cream and poured into the joints of masonry. In brick work it is applied every sixth course under each heading course, and every course in stone work to fill up the cavities.

Guilloche.—A string ornament in the form of a series of circles interlacing each other; a style of *fret*, or *basket work*.

Gurgoil.--A water spout projecting from a roof gutter to carry the water from the walls; it is sometimes carved into a grotesque head or animal, the water issuing from an open mouth.

Guttae.—Ornaments of conic form on the cornice of the Doric order; they are supposed to represent drops of water.--[*Stuart*.

Gypsum.—Sulphate of lime 21 per cent. water; when subjected to a moderate heat the water is withdrawn, and plaster of paris is the result.

Hall.—That part of a house in which the stairs are situated is termed the *stair hall*.

Half Pace.—The level platform between two parallel flights of stairs. See quarter pace.

Half Round.—A moulding that is semicircular in form, similar to a bead or torus.

Hammer Beam.—A short horizontal beam in the *hammer beam truss*, common in Gothic roofs.

Hand Rail of a Staircase.—A piece of wood smoothed and neatly moulded, set on balusters for a grip to assist one in ascending and descending a flight of stairs, and also to protect one from falling down the well hole; straight part of, 210; to straighten the crooked part of, 115, 210; cutting and jointing the, 115, 149, 174, 184; hanging and preparing for the balusters, 115, 175; taking the lengths for jointing, 107, 108; profiles of handrails, 210; scraper, 98; boring the rail, 175, 200; to stain the sap wood, 210; building up straight rail, 210.

Haunches of an Arch.—That portion of an arch between the keystone and the springing stone.

Header.—In carpentry, the double joist into which the tail joist are framed. In masonry, the stone that extends through the thickness of wall; they are also termed *bond* or *through stones*. In brick work, where the brick is laid lengthways across the thickness of wall, it is termed a *heading*. or *bond course*.

Head-Way.—The space allowed between a flight of stairs and the joist of the next floor above. How to calculate for trimming, 100, 117 148, 177.

Heel of a Rafter.—That part of the rafter that buts the *raising* or *pole plate* to receive the thrust of rafter.

Helical Line of a Hand Rail.—The spiral line twisting around the cylindric section, forming the twist of hand-rail for squaring up the wreath-piece, ready for moulding, 41.

Helix.—A small volute or twist under the abacus of the Corinthian capital; in every perfect capital there are sixteen helices, two at each angle and two meeting under the middle of each face of the abacus.

Heptagon.—22.

Hexagon.—22

Hip Knob.—A pinnacle placed at the apex of a hip roof; wrongly applied to the barge terminal at the summit of a gable.

Hip Rafter.—The angle rafter in the inclined ridge formed by the jack-rafters of a hip roof. To find the length when the angle on plan is a right angle, 214, 212, 213; to set a gauge for backing the, 217; to find the cut against the ridge plate after the backing is done, 215; to find the length of hip when the angle on plan is either acute or obtuse, 216; to find the cut against the ridge plate before the backing is done, 217; to find the backing for a hip, 217, 213; to find the bevels for hip framing of rafters, 213.

Hight or Height.—Either is correct.—[*Webster*.] The perpendicular hight of anything above its base or foundation.

History of Stair-Building.—9, 20.

Hoarding.—The timber enclosure about a building during erection or repairing.

Hod.—For plasterers, 241; for bricklayers, 239.

Hold-Fast.--A hook to drive into the wall to which a wall-rail is secured, 95.

Hollow Newel Stair-Case.—An open stair-case in contradistinction to a solid newel, into which the steps are secured and supported.

Horizontal Line.--21.

Hood.--A projecting cornice or roof over an outside opening to turn the rain or snow; usually held in place by a bracket on each side of the aperture.

Hood-Moulding.--A projecting moulding over an outside door or window as a projection to the finish from the weather; also termed *drip-moulding*, *label* or *weather moulding*.

Housing.—An excavation in a stair string into which is fit the steps and risers, 91, 94; pattern, 95.

Hyperbola.--30.

Horseing-Up Stairs.—A term used by stair-builders for supporting a flight of stairs; iron rods used for support, 128; to construct a truss bearer, 129; how to cut rough brackets, 128; the use of

Library. — The department or building provided with cases for the reception of books.

Lime. — By exposing limestone to a red heat the carbonic acid is expelled; the result is *quick-lime*; then if water be applied, it is termed a *hydrate of lime*, or *slacked lime*, 21.

Lining Out. — The lining or marking out of patterns and stuff required by the carpenter or joiner to be cut into smaller pieces.

Linings. — Door jambs and back linings, panel backs and elbows for inside shutters, the woodwork around doors, windows, or the covering of wall as wainscoating, soffits, &c., for the interior finish of a building; for the exterior, it is termed casing.

Lintel. — The horizontal timber or stone over an opening for a window or door to carry the superincumbent weight to the supports.

Loam. — A mixture of fine sand and clay; a little is sometimes used by the plasterer to make the mortar work easy.

Lobby. — An enclosed space from which entrance is made into one or more apartments.

Loggia — An open space recessed in a wall from which to obtain a view of the surroundings.

Luffer, or Louver-Boards. — Boards set inclining in an aperture and spaced so as to admit air and exclude rain; used in bell towers, stables, factories, to carry off the smoke and allow a free circulation of air.

Lozenge. — A quadrilateral, 22.

Loft. — A room in the roof of a building; a gallery or small chamber raised within a larger apartment, or in a church, as a music loft, a singing loft, a rood loft, &c. — *Parker.*

Mahogany. — A wood sometimes used for doors, sash and hand rails of stairs; the best quality comes from the mountains of Jamaica, that which comes from Honduras being soft and often spongy; it should be air dried and not forced. The genuine San Domingo mahogany is easily identified by the pores being filled with a white substance resembling flour. The Mexican mahogany is better than the Honduras.

Mean. — In mathematics, the average of the sum of all the quantities.

Measure. — That by which extent or dimension is ascertained; table of board, 242, 243.

Mechanical Carpentry. — 212, 224.

Midiæval Architecture. — The architecture of England, France, Germany and Italy during the middle ages, including the Norman and early Gothic styles, from A. D. 400 to 1500.

Medallion. — An oval, circular or sometimes square tablet, on which are embossed figures, busts and the like.

Member. — Different parts of a moulding, or the separate parts of a cornice, entablature or column, as the base, fillet, torus, conge, or capital.

Meter. — The French unit of length, 231.

Mezzanine Story. — Two stories within the height of one story, mostly divided at the platform of a stairway; it is also termed the *entresol story.*

Mixtilinear. — Angle, 21.

Modillion. — A cornice ornament similar to a bracket, having a greater projection than height.

Monkey. — Used as a weight in driving piles; from its weight and force to ascertain the stability of a driven pile, 238.

Mortar. — A mixture of lime and sand used to cement stone and brick in a wall and plaster in a building; is composed of two-thirds clean river sand and one-third well burnt lime. *Hydraulic mortar* is made from cement, and used in the construction of piers or walls under water, as it soon hardens by the action of the water.

Mortise. — A rectangular hollow made in a timber with auger and chisel, into which is fit a *tenon* made on the end of another piece of timber. The sides of the mortise are termed the *checks.*

Mouldings. — The ornamental forms applied to the projecting and receding members of an order. The contour of the Grecian mouldings have a curve of a conic section: the Roman form of the moulding was arcs of the true circle. In the five orders there are but eight regular mouldings, the *Ovolo*, the *Talon*, the *Cyma*, the *Cavetto*, the *Torus*, the *Astragal*, the *Scotia* and the *Fillet*. The projection of a moulding is about equal to its height as a rule.

Mullion-Frame. — A window frame divided into two or more openings by vertical posts. (See window.)

Muntin. — The short pieces in a door that are cut between the rails are termed muntins.

Net Measure — Is such when no allowance is made for waste of material.

Neutral Axis. — That plane in a beam in which the tensile and compressive forces terminate, and therefore nothing. 227, 230, 131.

Newel Post. — In close winding stairs the shaft around which the steps and risers wind at their narrow ends. In open stairs the post at the starting is termed the *newel post;* if posts be placed at the angles instead of cylinders, they are termed *angle newels;* box or built, 211; solid, 152; standard lengths, 152.

Niche. — A recess in a wall for the reception of a statue, vase or other ornament; they were a decorative feature and much used in the middle ages. 178.

are horizontal and made of wood. Lime slacked, sifted and mixed to a thickness of cream, then allowed to evaporate, forming a paste, is termed *fine stuff* or *putty*; it is used for the last coat, or *skim-coat*, after the floated coat is dry or nearly so. When fine stuff is mixed with plaster paris and a little white sand to form a hard surface at the corners, jambs, walls or running mouldings, it is termed *gauged stuff*. A half peck of white sand is allowed to a bushel of fine stuff for skimming; and for gauged work allow two quarts additional of plaster paris.

Point.—21.

Position. In geometry the situation of one thing in regard to another. [*Stuart.*

Post. A timber set upright as a support, termed a *corner post* in a house, *king* or *queen post* in a roof, *newel post* in stair-case; a *gate* or *fence post*; also a support to floors in warehouses and other structures. To calculate the strength of, 228; regard to its position for safety, 228; increased strain when inclining, 228, 229.

Principal Rafter. See truss roof.

Problem. In geometry a proposition in which some construction is required.

Produced. Extended in length.

Profile. In architecture, the contour of a moulding or mouldings, or the outline of a cross-section of a building, or any piece of work.

Prolonged. Continued in length.

Proscenium Arch. An arch over the stage, back of which the curtain drops.

Pulley. Speeding pulleys, 245.

Purlin. A horizontal piece of timber in a truss roof resting on the principal rafters and supporting the common rafters and their load To find the cuts against the hip rafter, 211, 213.

Quadrangle. Any figure with four angles and four sides, 22.

Quadrant. The quarter of a circle 21.

Quadrilateral. 22.

Quarter-pace. A landing in a stair case, where a person going either up or down, makes one right angle turn; if two right angle turns on the same pace, it is termed a half-pace.

Quarter Sawed. Lumber that is sawed from the log on the medullary rays is termed quarter sawed lumber.

Queen-Post Roof A roof in which a straining beam and two posts or bolts are used instead of one as in the king-post roof.

Quirk-Moulding. A moulding showing a deep narrow channel at its greatest projection to obscure the joint.

Radial Lines. Lines projecting in different directions from a common center; also termed *converging lines*.

Radius. 24.

Rafter. The inclining timber in a roof on which the sheathing is nailed: to find the length of common 213, 215, 216; to find the cuts, 213, 217.

Rake. An inclination or slope, as the pitch of a stair-case or roof, or anything that inclines to the horizon.

Ramp. A concave bend rising up. (See knee) to locate the points on pattern for jointing the rail, 196.

Raising-Plate. The board secured to the ends of the ceiling joist to receive the heel of rafters.

Rail. In joinery framing, the horizontal pieces in doors, sash, shutters or wainscoting.

Rebate. A rectilineal channel worked on the edge of a piece of stuff.

Rectangle. A figure whose angles are all right angles; 22.

Rectilinear. A figure whose boundaries are right lines.

Relieving Arch. An arch built over a stone or wood lintel, or over a flat arch, to carry the load to the pier.

Retaining Wall. A heavy strong wall constructed with a batter to prevent a bank of earth from sliding down.

Rhomboid. A quadrilateral; 22.

Rhombus. 22.

Reveal. A rectilineal rebate or recess at the sides of an opening for a door or window between the frame and the face of wall.

Rib. A curved timber, forming an arch, to which the lath are nailed; 221.

Ridge. The comb or highest part of a roof, where a pair of rafters butt the *ridge plate*.

Right Angle. An angle containing 90 degrees; 22, 21.

Right Line. A line absolutely straight; 21.

Rise. One of the divisions into which the height of a story is divided for a stair-case; 90.

Riser. The vertical board between two steps.

Sand. Proportion to lime in mortar, 241.

Sash. The frame holding the glass in a window

Scaffold. An assemblage of scantling, planks or boards erected to support workmen in the construction of a building.

Scalene Triangle. 23.

Scarfing. The splicing of two pieces of timber together to increase their length.

Scotia. A cove moulding, the contour of which is a quarter circle or a quarter ellipsis.

Scribing. The fitting up of any piece of work to an uneven surface with the dividers.

Scroll. A name given to spiral ornaments, as the termination sometimes given to a hand-rail at its starting, and also the volutes of the Ionic and Corinthian capitals. When a hand-rail starts with a wreathed scroll the first step is termed the *scroll* or *curtail* *step.* When a hand-rail starts from a newel with a straight easement worked into a scroll on top of the newel, it is termed a *vertical scroll.* How to draw, 35; reciprocal scroll to draw, 35; how the eye may be formed to the best advantage, 209.

Seasoned Timber. — Such as rendered sufficiently dry to be used for the rough framing timber.

Section of a Building.—A vertical plane or planes through any portion of a structure representing the walls, doors, windows, flues and finish on that particular plane.

Segment—24.

Semi-Circle. 24.

Self-Supporting Stairs. ... 203; mode of construction, 203.

Shaft....The body of a column between the base and the capital.

Shakey Lumber...That in which the growths or annual rings are disunited by the action of winds and frost.

Shank of a Wreath-Piece.... The straight part.

Shearing....Strength of timber per square inch, Table 7.

Shingles....Number to the square, 244.

Shoe....The inclined piece at the foot of a conductor to turn the water from the building; if long and cast of metal it is termed a *boot;* also an iron socket at the foot of a rafter or strut to receive the thrust.

Shutters....An appliance to shut out the light from a window.

Single or Double Worked Door....Means that the door is either moulded on one or both sides.

Skew-Back. ... In curved or straight arches, the abutment that slopes to receive the end of an arch.

Soffit....The ceiling or underside of a stair-case or archway, cornice or entablature.

Spandril....The triangular paneling under a flight of stairs is termed a *spandril.*

Splay... The term is applied to whatever has one side oblique to the other, as the walls or linings around doors or windows are sometimes splayed to admit light. Bevels for splayed work, 218; to find the veneer for a splayed circular door-head, and also of a pew-back, 220; to find the veneer for a circular door-head in a circular wall, the jambs being parallel, 220, 221.

Spring Bevel....The bevel applied to the shank of a wreath-piece. The bevel applied to the center joint is termed the *pitch-bevel,* and both are sometimes termed the *joint-bevels.*

Square. To construct, 26.

Stairs... A series of steps leading from one level to another. The horizontal distance from the face of first rise to the face of the rise landing is termed the *run.*

Stair-Case....The structure in a building by which communication is made with the different stories, and includes all the flights in a well for that stairway. When of one flight, landing on the next floor, is termed a *level landing stair-case;* when divided into two flights, running parallel to each other, is termed a *half pace-stair-case;* if winders fill the half pace, it is then termed a *half pace winding stair-case;* if winders fill a quarter pace, it is termed a *quarter pace winding stair-case;* if winding in two quarter paces, it is termed a *double quarterpace winding stair-case;* if all the steps are winding and circular on plan, it is termed a *circular geometrical stair case;* if the plan be an ellipsis, it is termed an *elliptical stair-case;* when stairs are supported only at the starting and landing, the sides being free, they are termed *self-supporting stairs.* To construct box, 90, 91, 92; to line off the string for box, 90; putting up box stairs, 90; preparing open stairs, 100, 101, 107, 108; setting up open stairs, 105, 107, 92; to line off winding stairs 158, 159, 160, 176; building self-supporting stairs, 203; building elliptical stairs, 203; directions for lining off strings, 163, 164, 165, 178, 179; rule to proportion the step to rise (Blondel's), 87, 99; to construct for a six-foot hall, 99; to construct for a two-story and seven-foot hall, 116; flight outside steps, 87; to construct step-ladder, 89; to construct box stairs, 90.

Staves of a Cylinder. To obtain their lengths, 102, 165; manner of preparing them by machinery, 102; number to a semi-circle, 101.

Stay...Same as brace.

Step... A step of a stair-case includes from the face of rise to the verge of nosing, 90; preparing the steps, mitering, dovetailing and gluing, 128, 104, 105; graduating the flyers and winders, 73; pattern for circular end steps, 104, 108; gluing up step and rise, 105; if crooked, 105; nosing the step, 105; mitering step for nosing, 108; grooving and tongueing, 108; thickness to length of step, 89; oak for outside steps, 89; making step ladder, 89; making cellar steps, 88; cutting out steps, 127.

Stile...In joinery the vertical pieces that bound a piece of framing and are made ridged to the horizontal pieces by tenon, mortise and glue.

Stirrup Iron...To calculate the strength of, 131; their value in framing, 227.

Stereotomy. The science or art of cutting solids into certain figures or sections, 43.

Stonemasons. Memoranda, 237, 238; measuring stonework, 238.

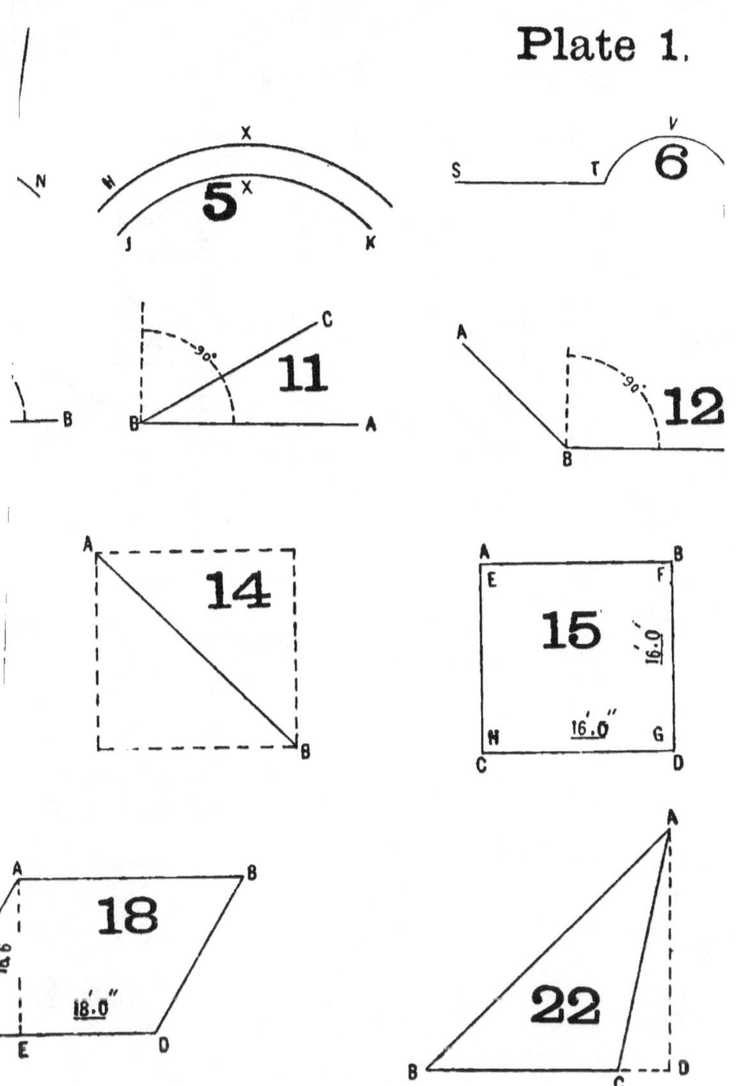
N
X
H
J
5
X
K
S
T
V
6
C
90°
11
B
A
B
A
90°
12
B
A
14
B
A
B
E
F
15
16.0'
C
H
16.0'"
G
D
A
B
18
16.6
18.0'"
E
D
A
22
B
C
D

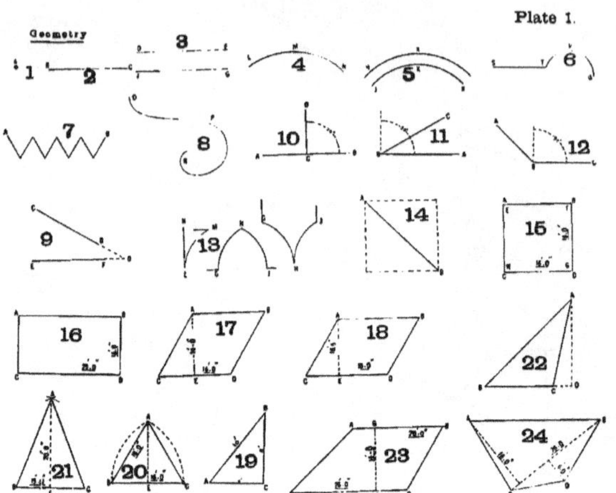
Geometry

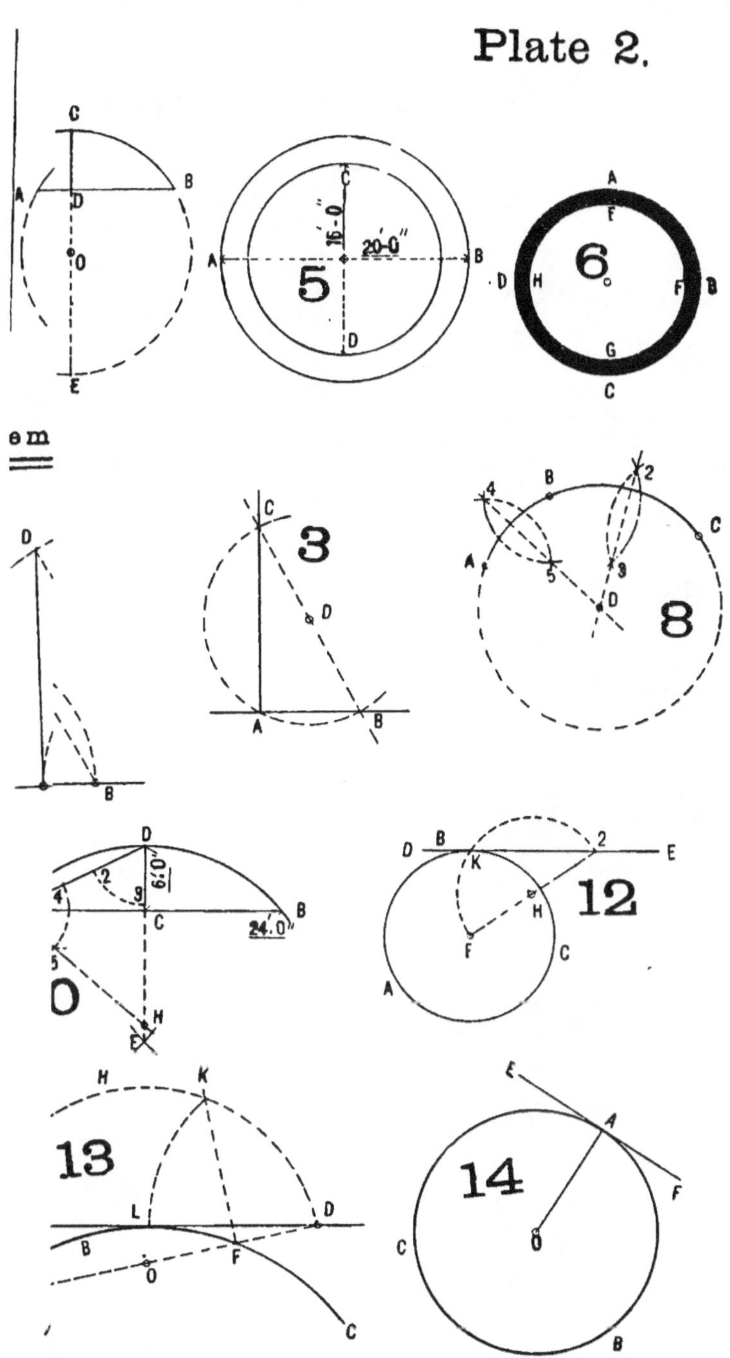

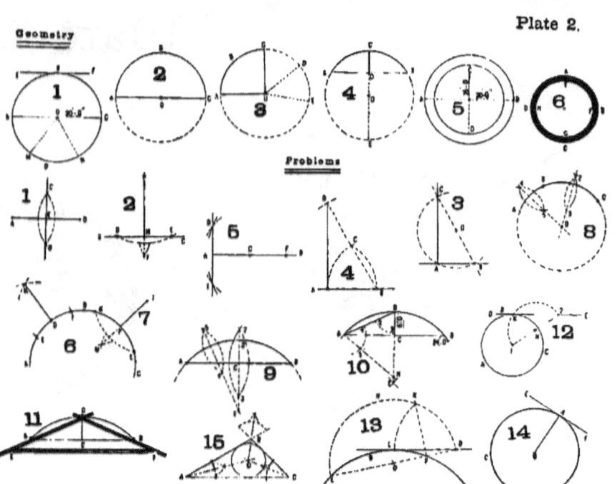
Geometry
Problems

Plate 3.

4

F
H
E
C
D
A
B

5
F
E
G
C
D
A
B

8
1
H
B
2
O
3
5
4
D

9
1 2 3 4 5 6
C
A
11 10 9 8 7
B

11
H
K
123456

12
B 1 2 3 4 5 E
C
A
13
C
E
A
B

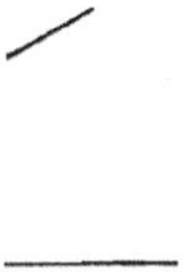

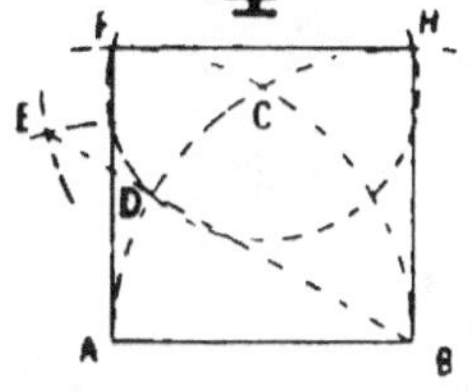

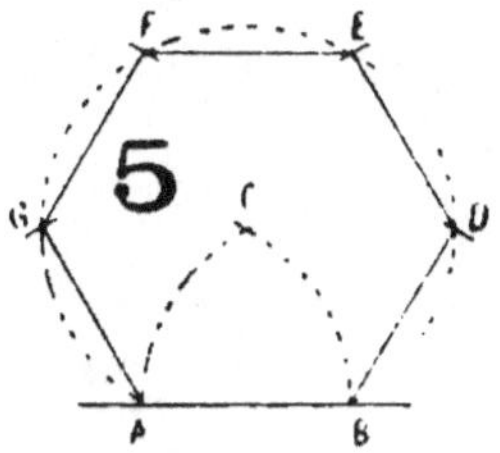

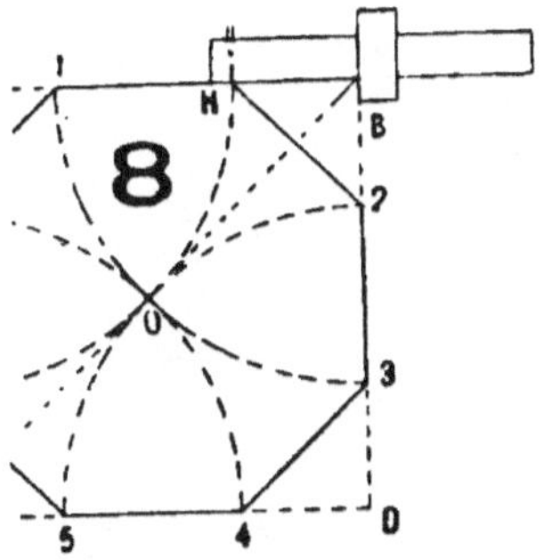

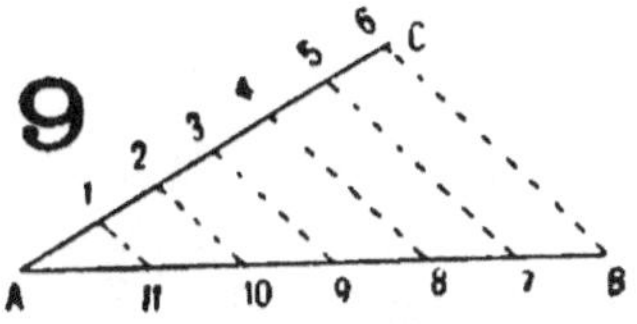

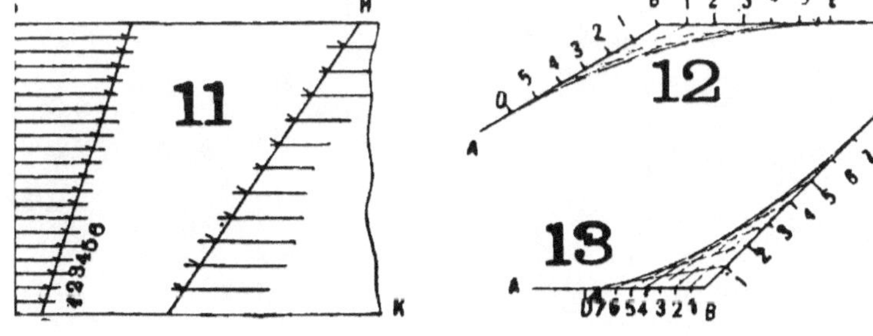

Problems

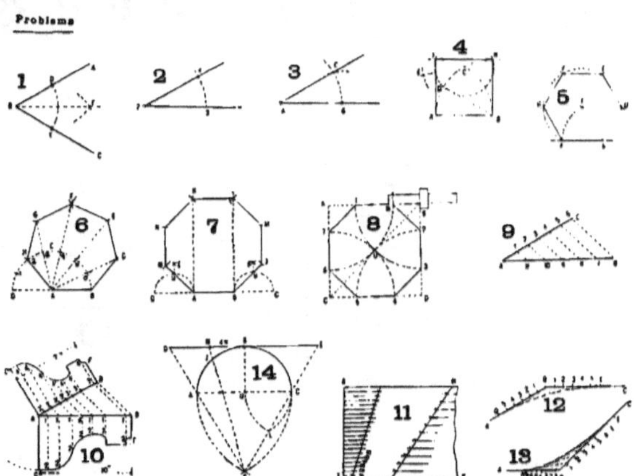

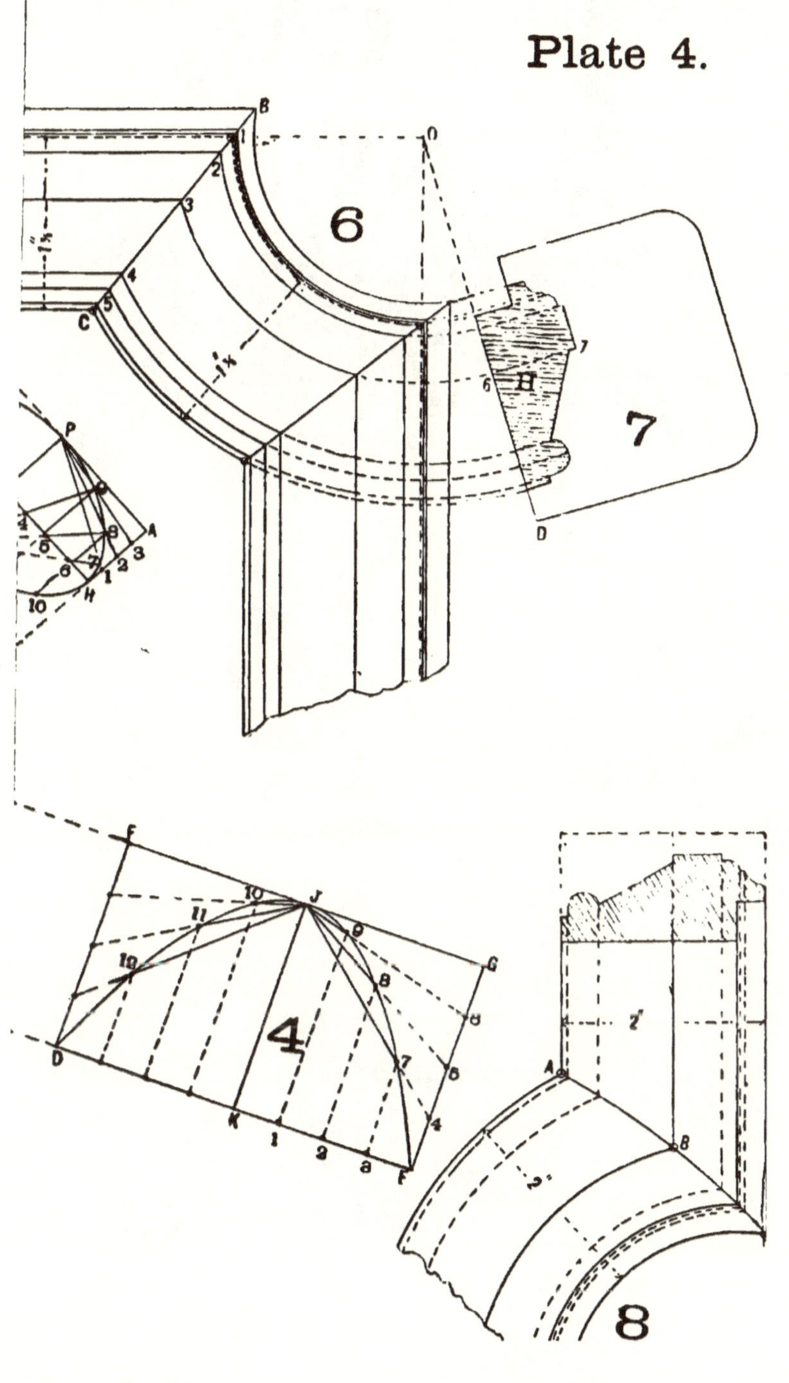

Plate 4.
6
7
4
8

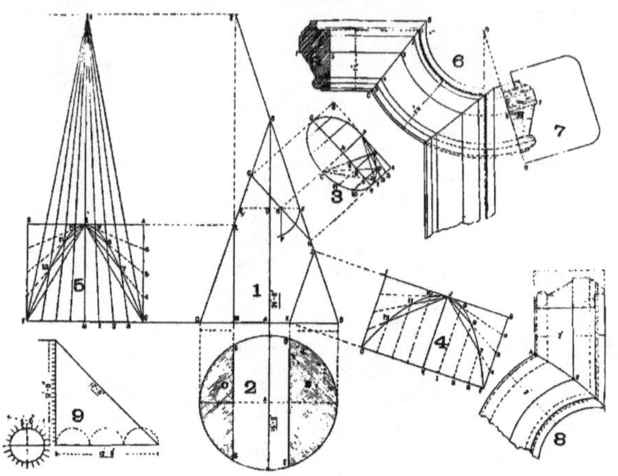

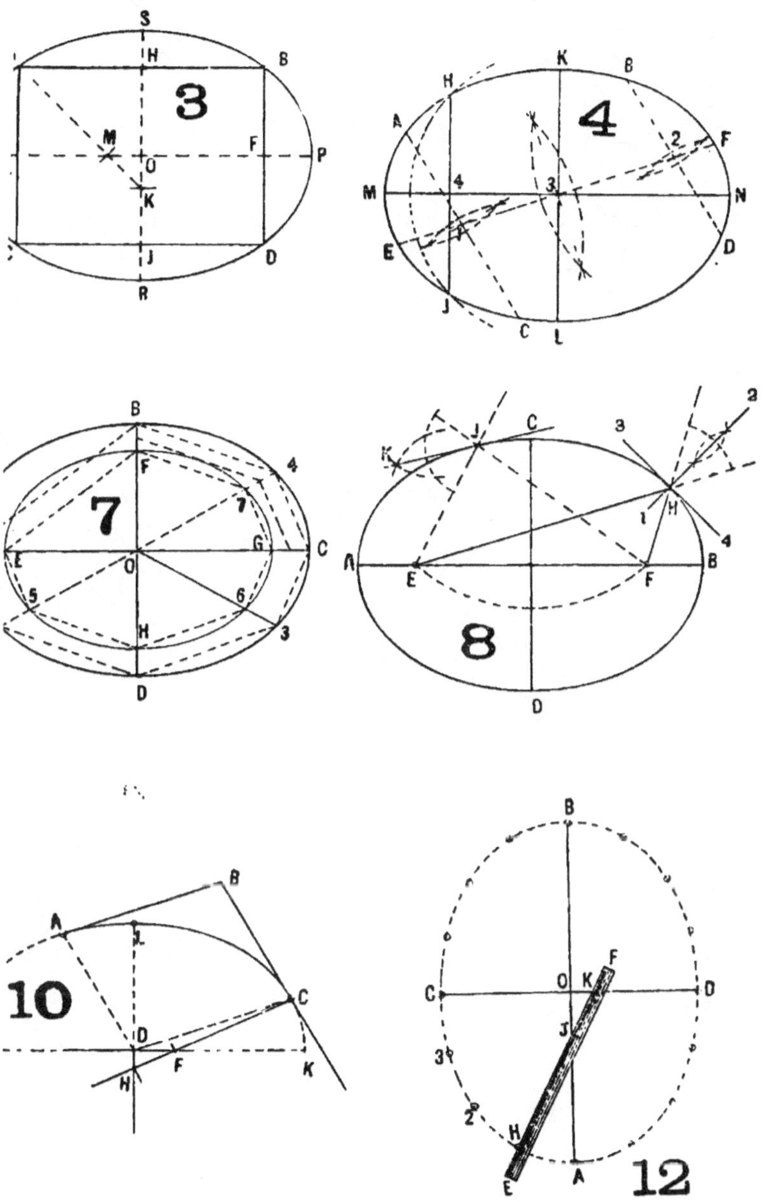
3
4
7
8
10
12

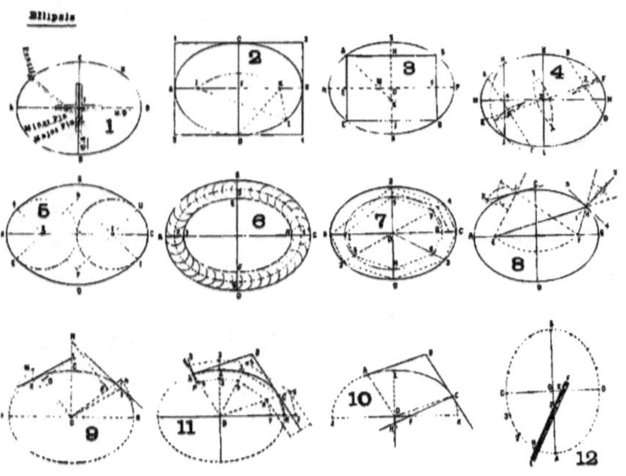

Ellipse

Plate 6.

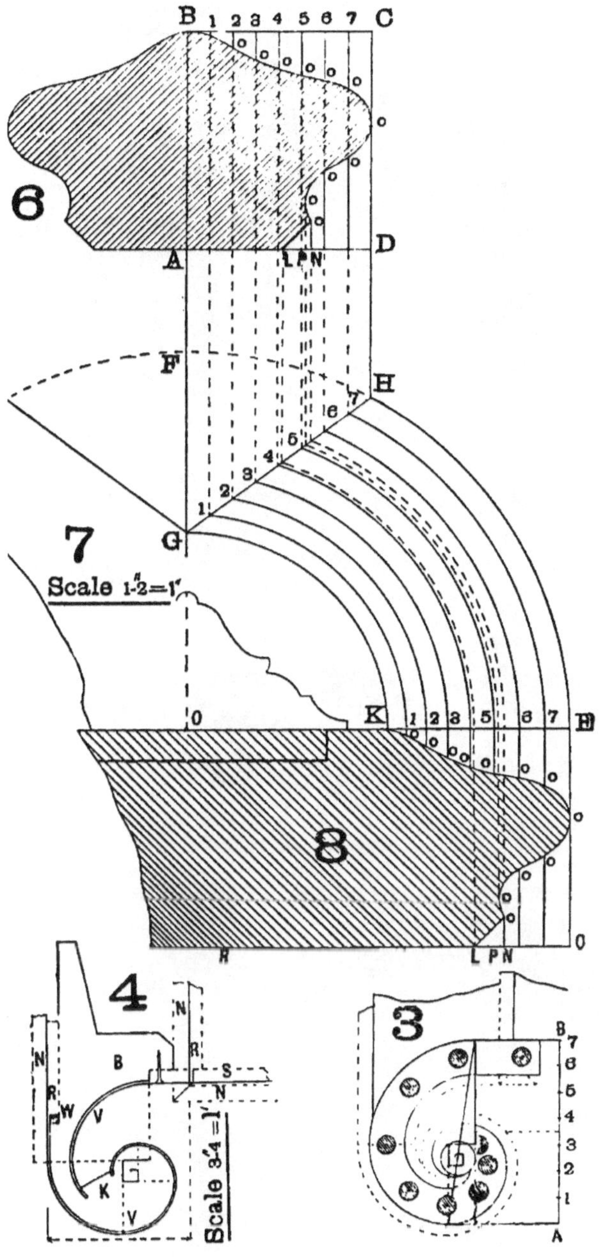

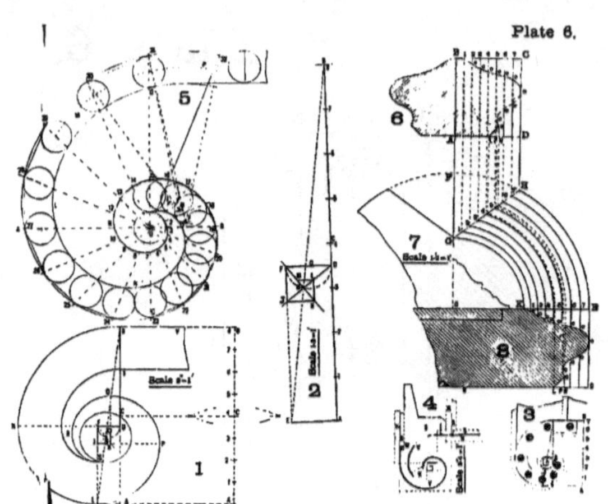

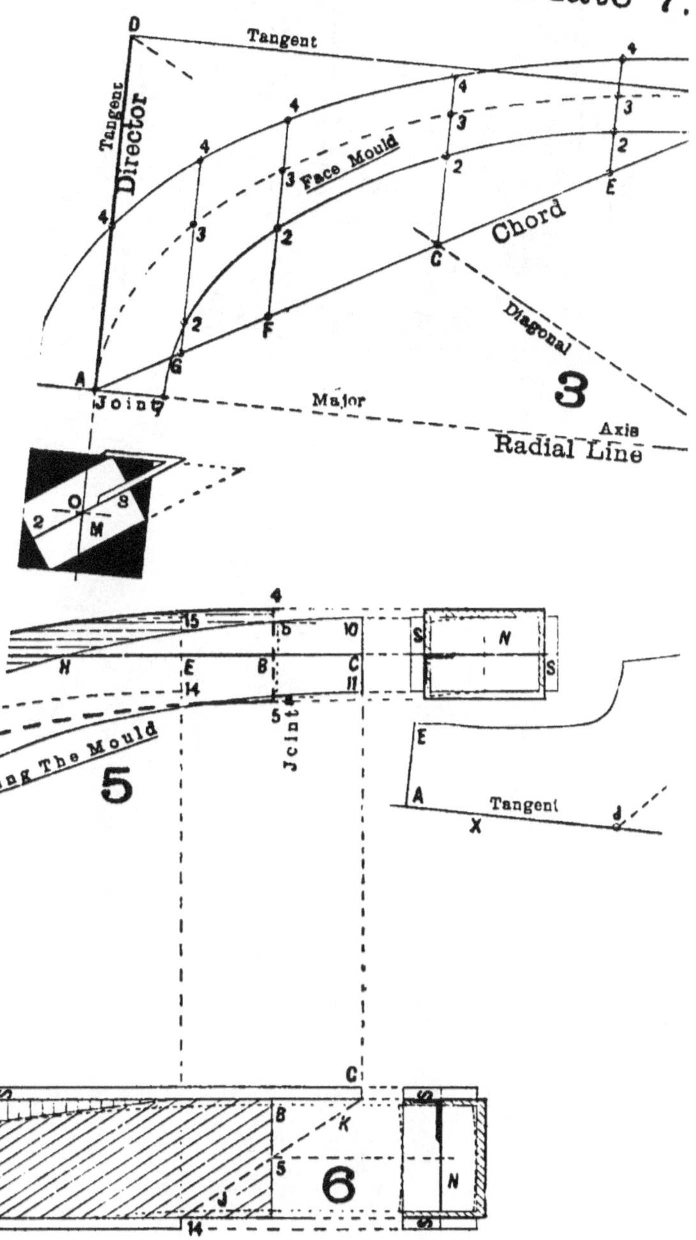
Tangent
Tangent
Director
Face Mould
4
4
4
4
3
3
3
2
2
2
E
C
Chord
Diagonal
3
2
F
G
A
Joint
Major
Axis
Radial Line
2
O
S
M
3
4
15
16
10
S
N
S
H
E
B
C
S
14
11
Joint
5
ing The Mould
5
E
A
Tangent
d
X
C
S
B
K
S
5
6
N
J
N
14

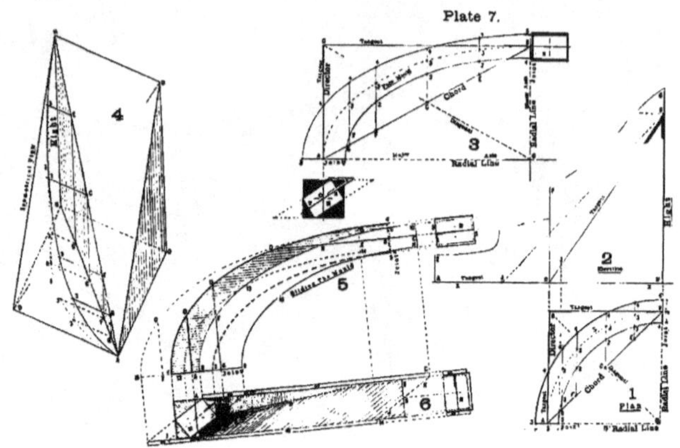

Plate 8.

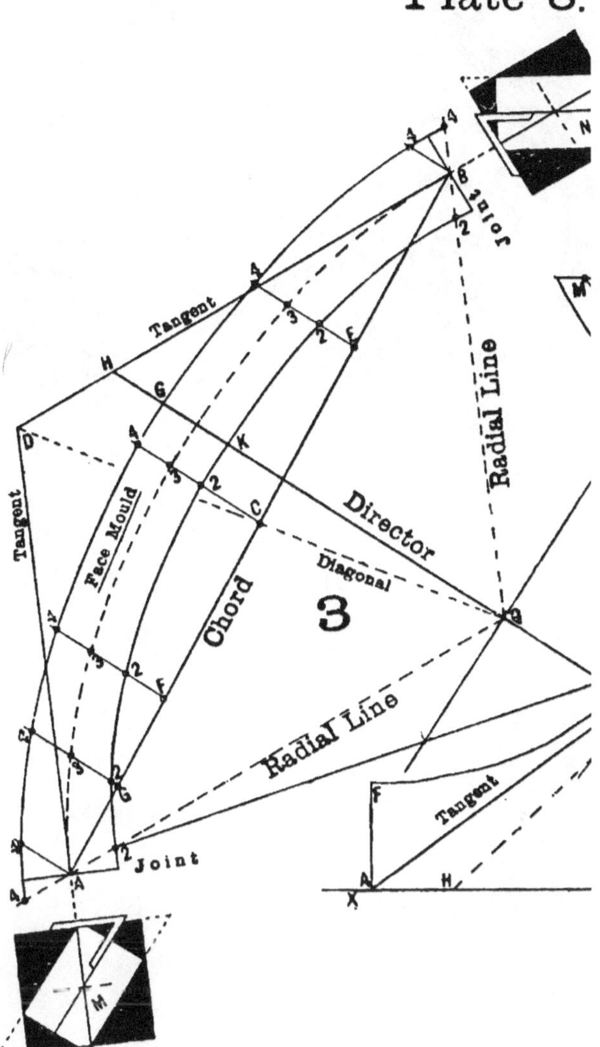

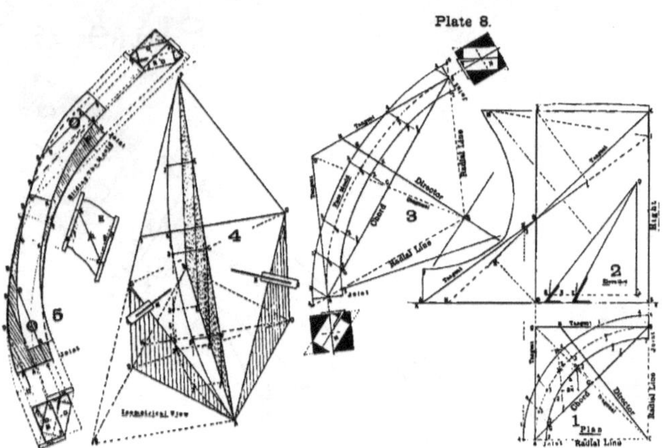

Plate 8.
Isometrical View
Radial Line
Joint
Soffit Point
Director
Chord
Radial Line
Tangent
Joint
Tangent
Height
Stretch
Plan
Radial Line
Joint
Chord
Director
Tangent

Plate 9

Tangent
Face Mould
Chord
Diagonal
Director
Radial Line
Radial Line
Joint
A Joint
Tangent
Elevation

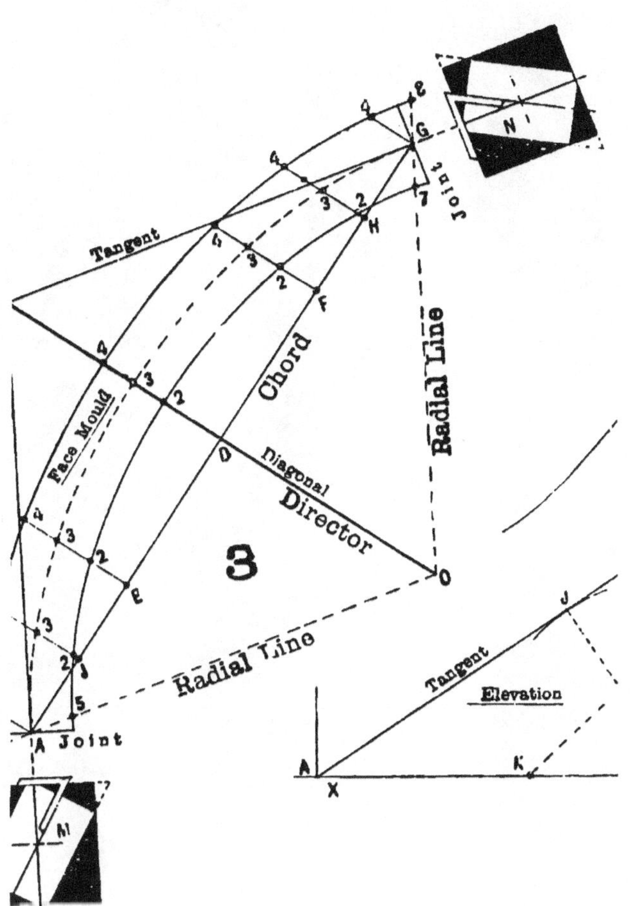

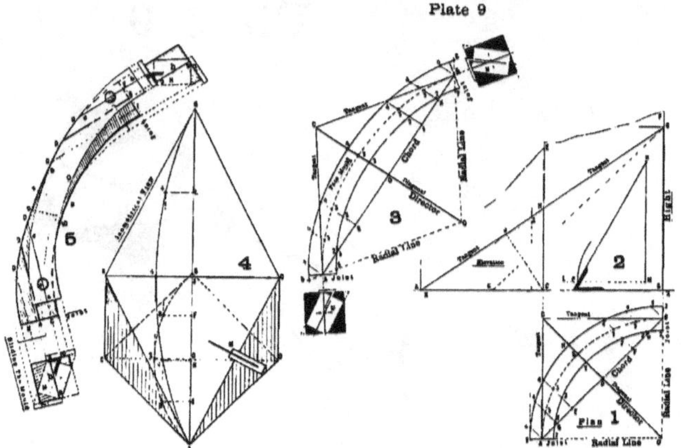

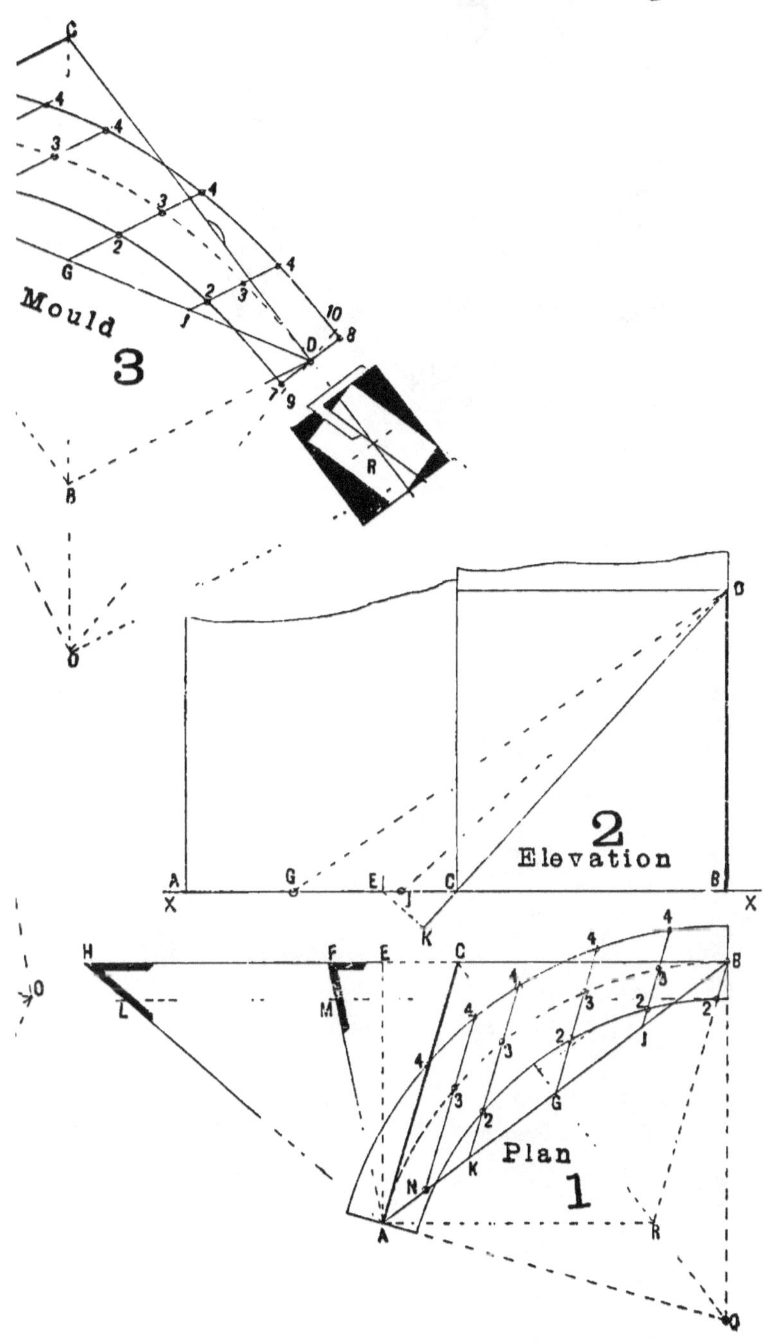
Mould
3
C
G
B
O
R
Elevation
2
A
G
E
C
B
X
X
J
K
O
Plan
1
H
F
E
C
B
L
M
G
N
K
A
R
O

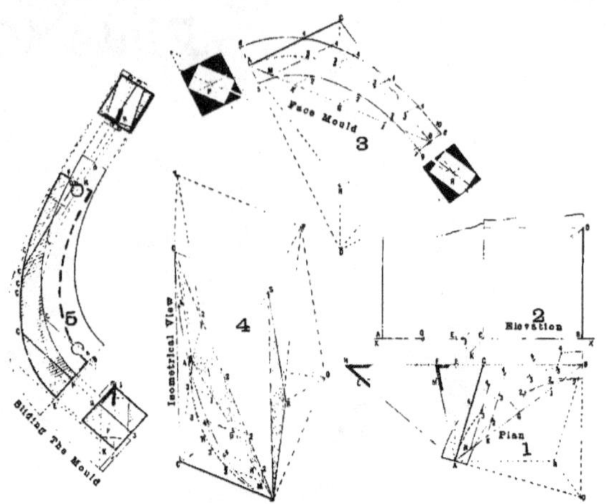

Face Mould
3
Isometrical View
4
Elevation
2
Plan
1
Sliding The Mould
5

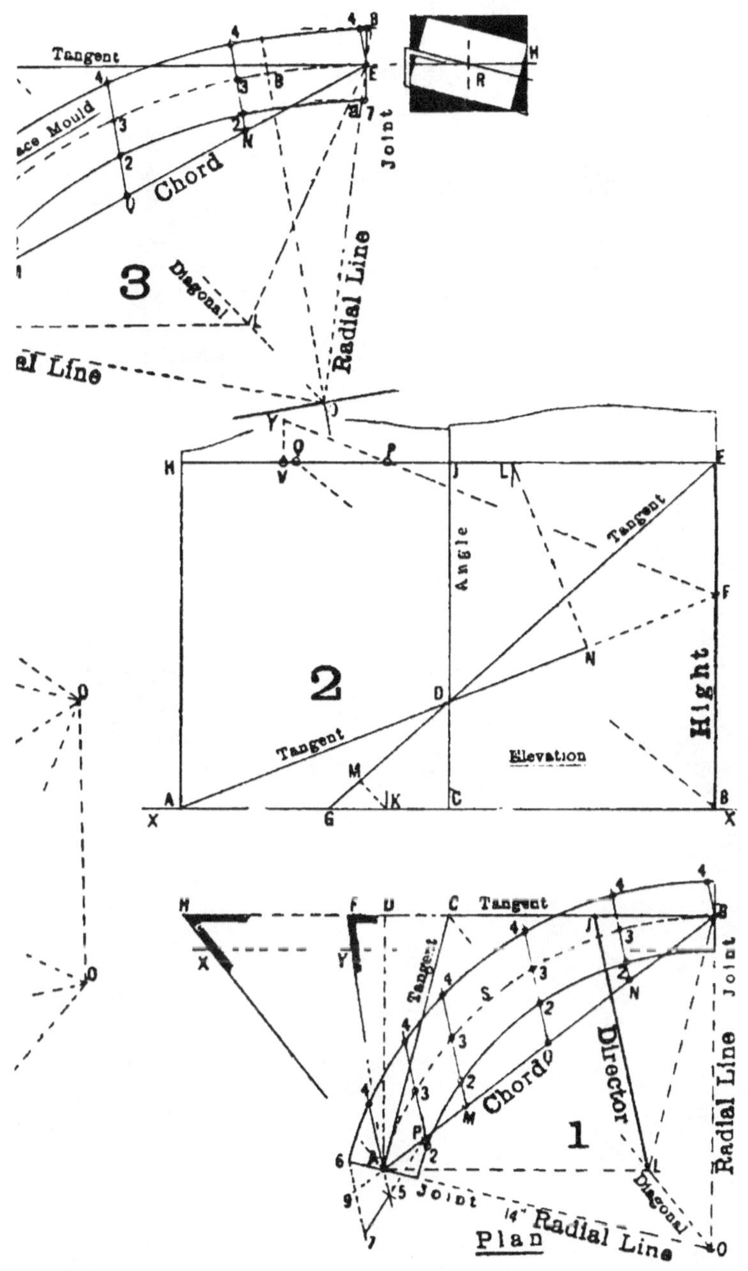

Tangent
ace Mould
Chord
3
Diagonal
al Line
Radial Line
Joint
R
H
O
V
Y
O
L
H
J
L
E
Angle
Tangent
F
Hight
2
D
N
Tangent
Elevation
M
O
A
X
G
JK
C
B
X
H
F
U
C
Tangent
4
X
Y
Tangent
S
N
Chord
Director
Radial Line
Joint
P
M
6
A
2
Diagonal
9
5
Joint
L
Radial Line
7
4
Plan
O
1

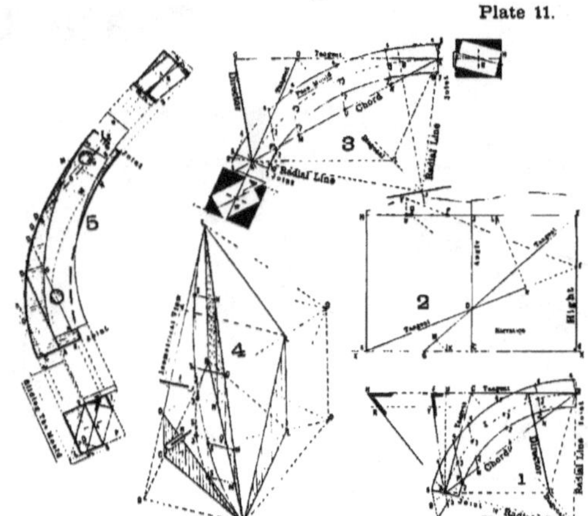

Plate 12. 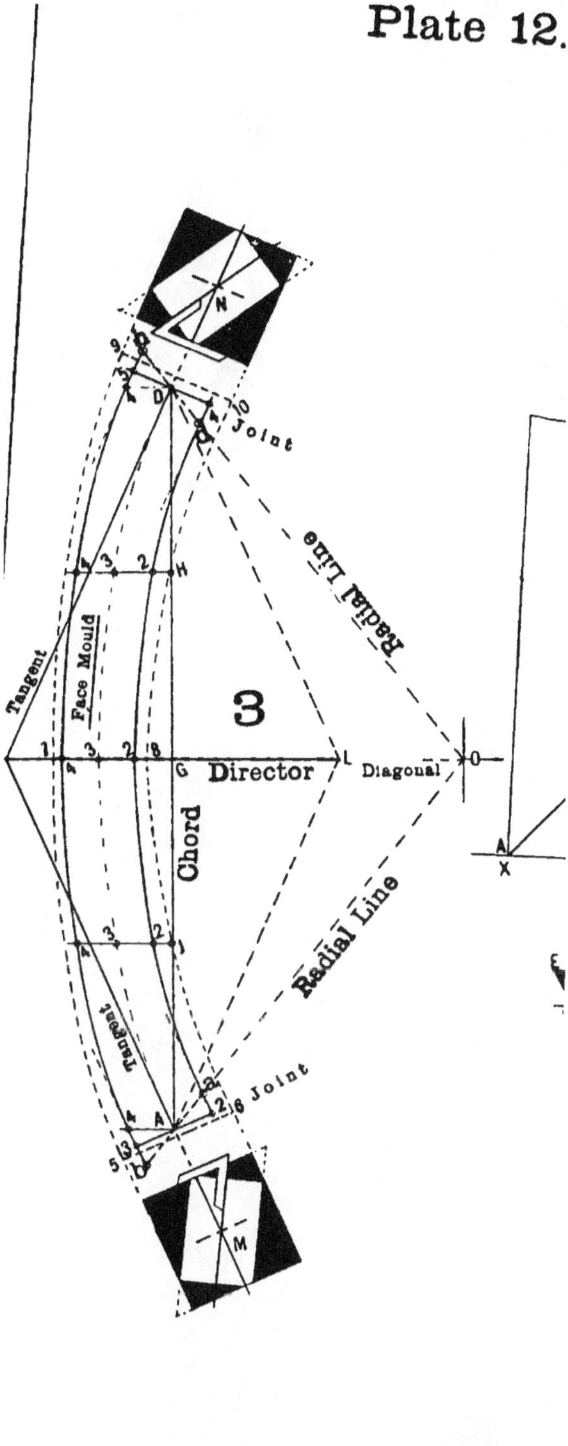
Joint
Radial Line
Tangent
Face Mould
Chord
Director
Diagonal
Radial Line
Tangent
Joint
N
M
3

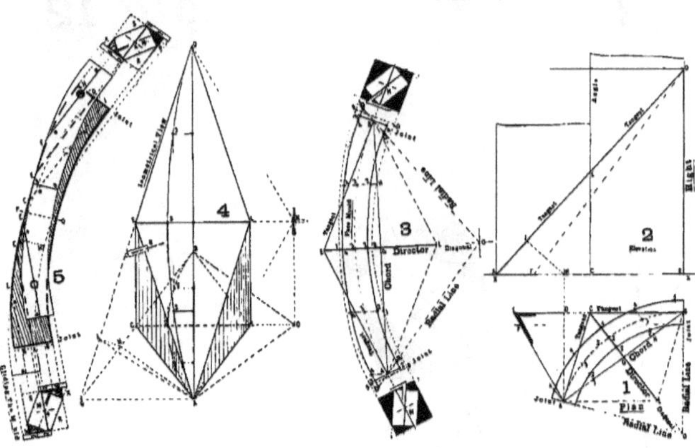

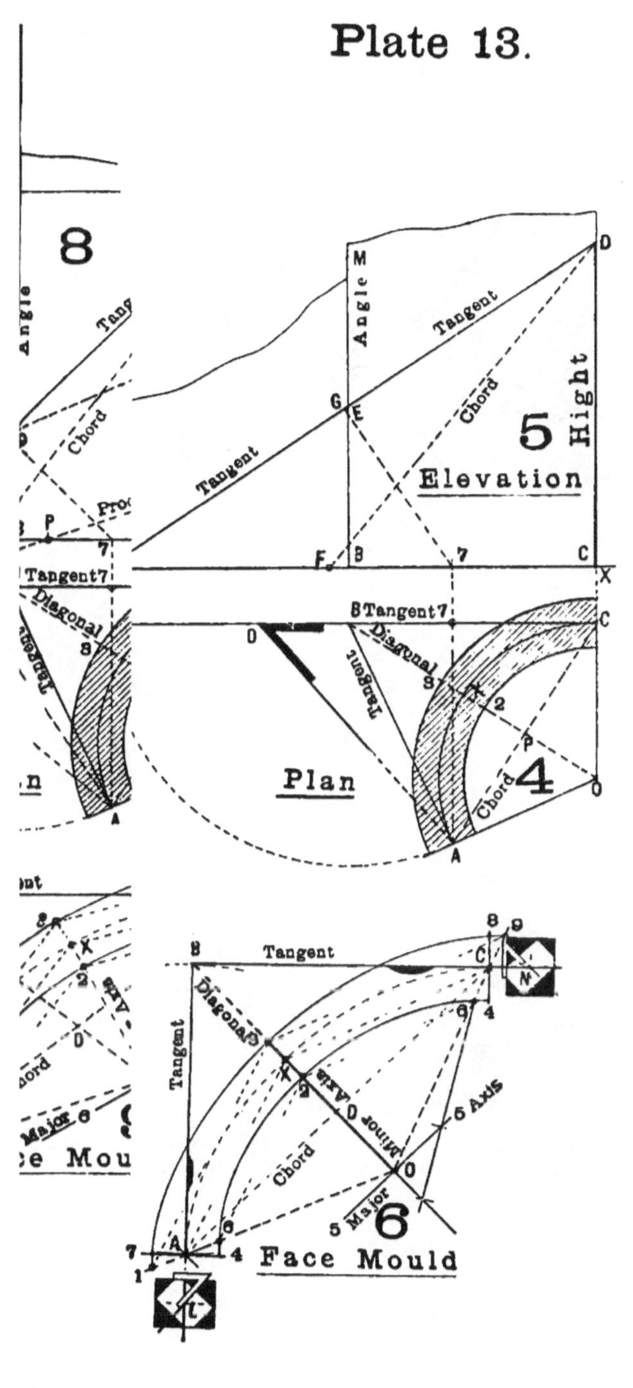
8
Angle
Tangent
Chord
Proc
P
7
Tangent7
Diagonal
8
Tangent
A
n
M
Angle
Tangent
Tangent
Chord
Hight
G
E
5
Elevation
F
B
7
C
X
8 Tangent 7
0
Tangent
Diagonal
8
Diagonal
C
2
P
Plan
Chord
4
O
A
nt
8
X
2
Axis
0
Chord
Major
e
ce Mou
8
Tangent
8 9
B
Tangent
C
N
Diagonal
Axis
5 Axis
Minor Axis
Chord
6
4
Major
0
5 Major
6
7
A
4
Face Mould
1

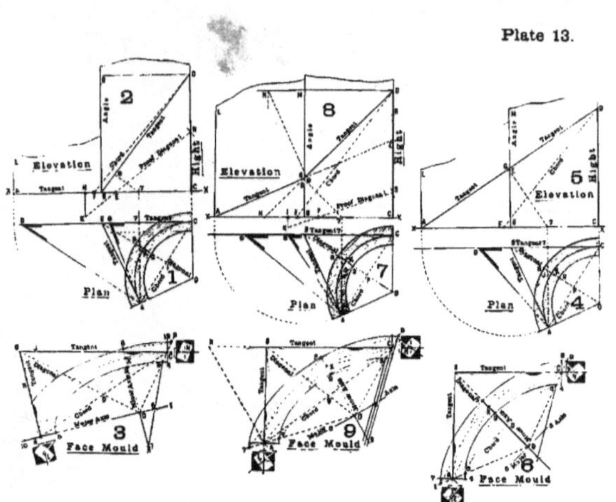

Plate 14.

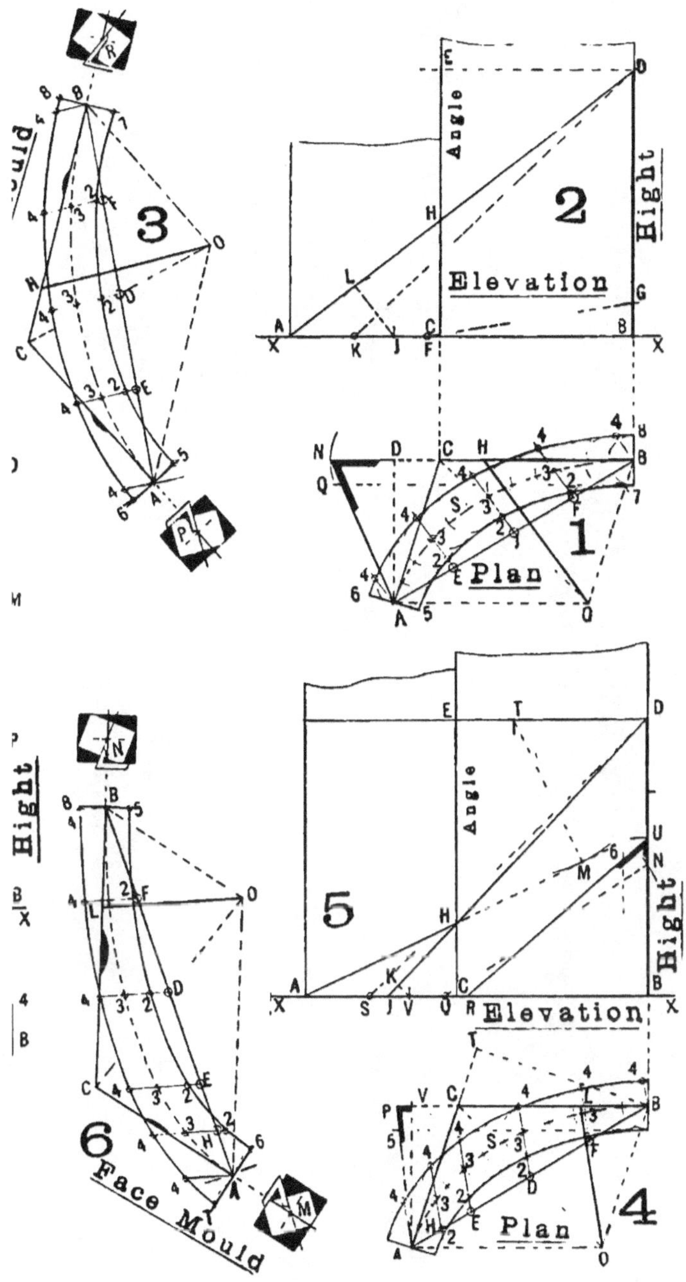

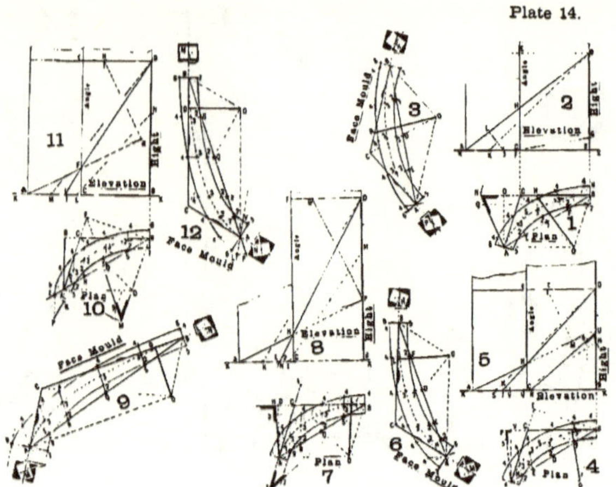

Plate 15.

Scale 3"4 = 1'
15
11"
16
D
B
6"
12
C
13
10"
14
5'
C
10
Plan
6"
8"K
6"
0
8"K
15
M
F
N
L
5"K
16
H
14
Q
O
R
P
17
K
B
9
Plan
10"
11"
10"
13
20"
21K
18
A
7
Plan
M
F
N
L
5"
16
H
O
10"
B
2K
2K
C
P
17
14"
I
A
15K"
D
8
Plan
13
M
F
N
L
5"K
14
H
10"
O
12"
12
K
B
1"
O
1"
P
15
A
16"
D
17K"
3
F
J
12
H
4K"K
13
K
B
O
C
11
7K"
9"
14
A
Plan
D
8"
4
F
J
14
H
5"
15
K
B
O
C
10"
13
8"
16
A
Plan
D
9"
5
F
J
17
H
5"K
18
K
B
O
N
L
16
10"
7"
C
10"
A
19
D
Plan
10"

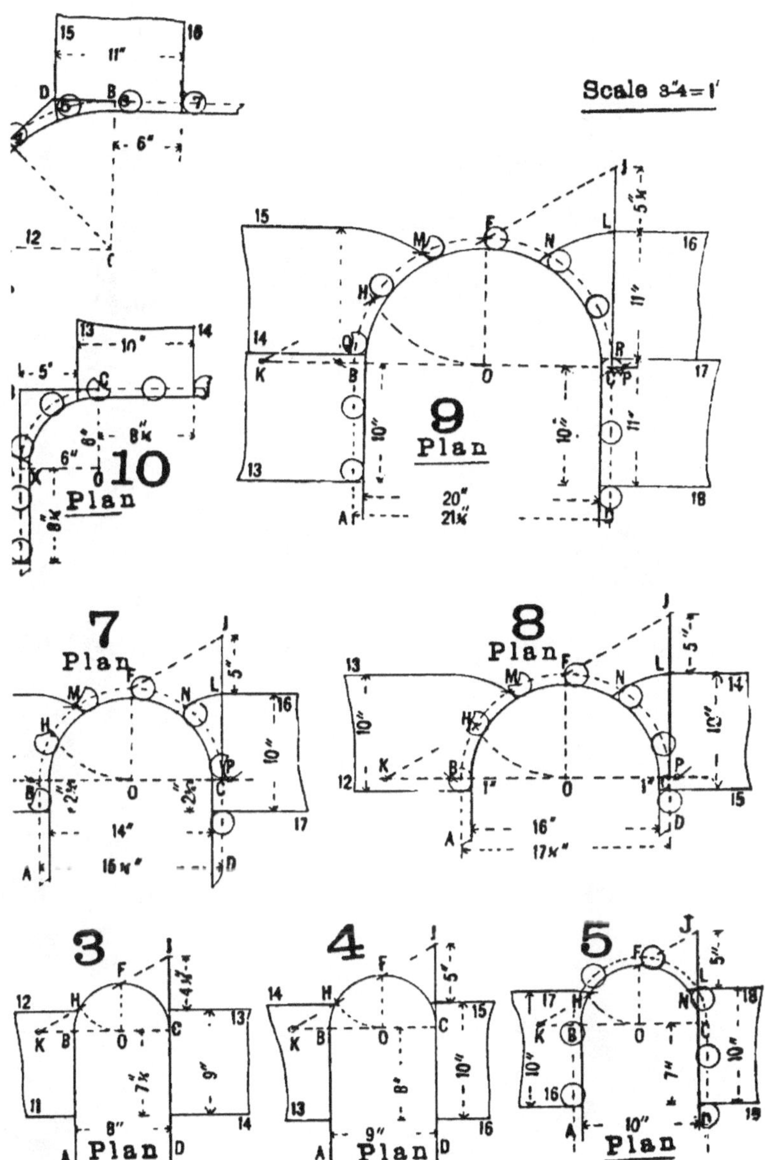

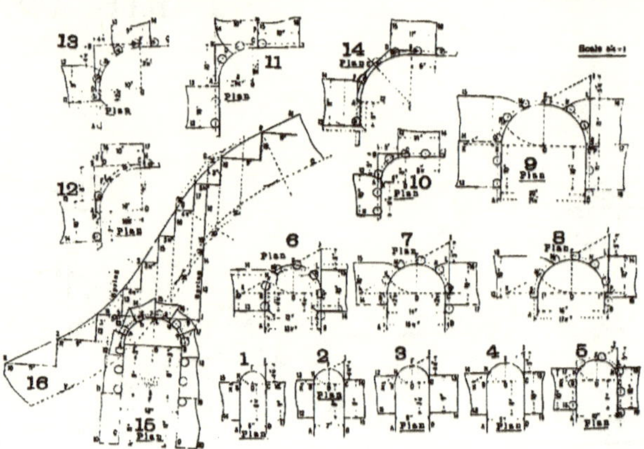

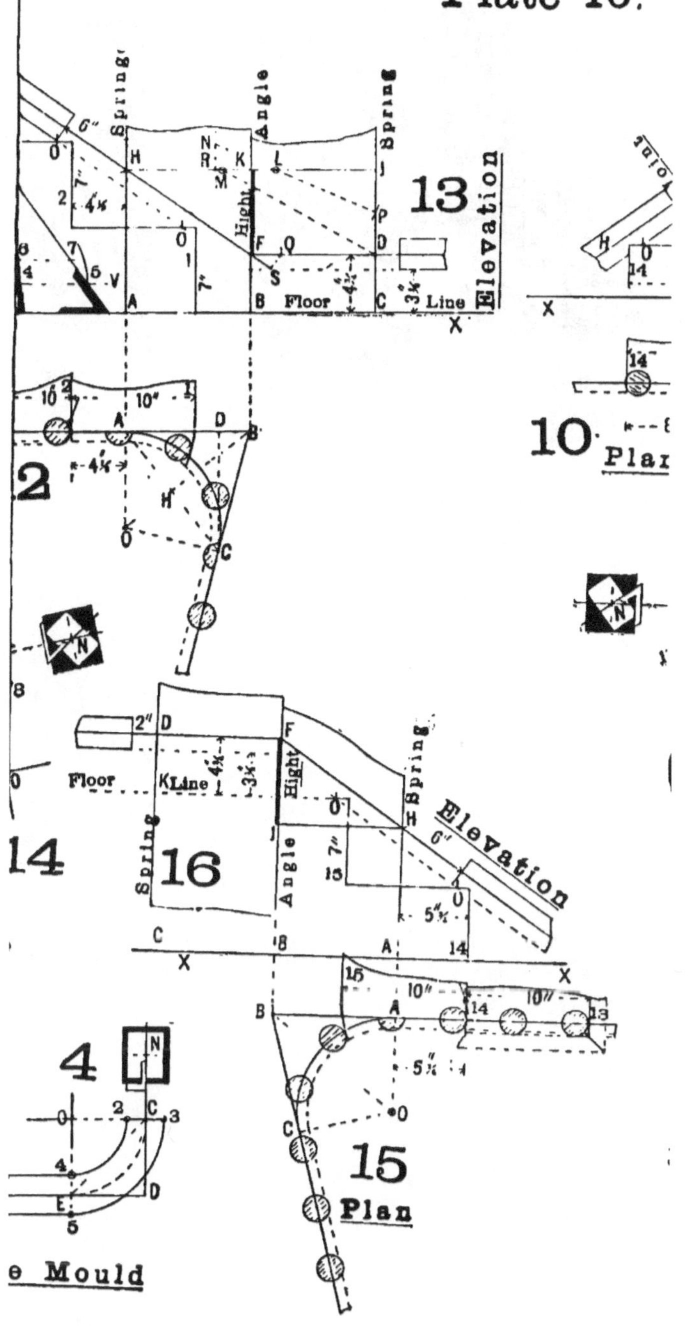
Spring
Angle
Spring
Elevation
13
Height
Floor Line
X
N
R
M
K
L
J
P
O
Q
F
S
A
B
C
D
4½
3¼
6"
7"
4½
7
5
V
2
10"
10"
2
A
D
B
H
O
C
N
4½
10
Point
H
O
14
X
14
10
Plan
E
N
2"
D
F
Spring
Floor
K Line
Spring
Angle
Height
14
16
Elevation
H
Spring
6"
O
7"
O
5½
5¾
13
4½
3¼
C
B
A
14
X
X
15
10"
10"
B
A
14
13
5½
5¾
O
C
15
Plan
4
N
O
2
C
3
4
D
E
5
e Mould

Plate 16.

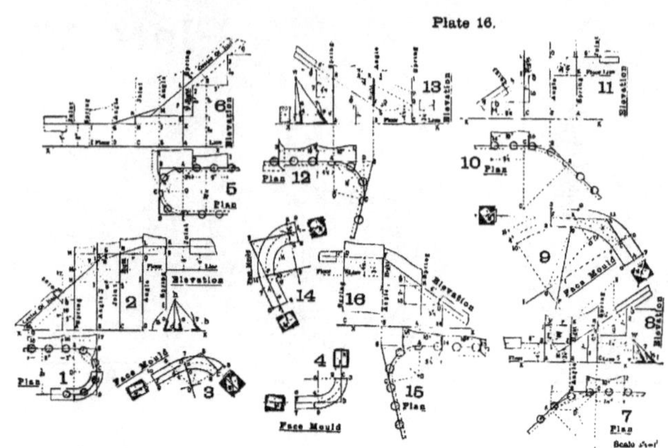

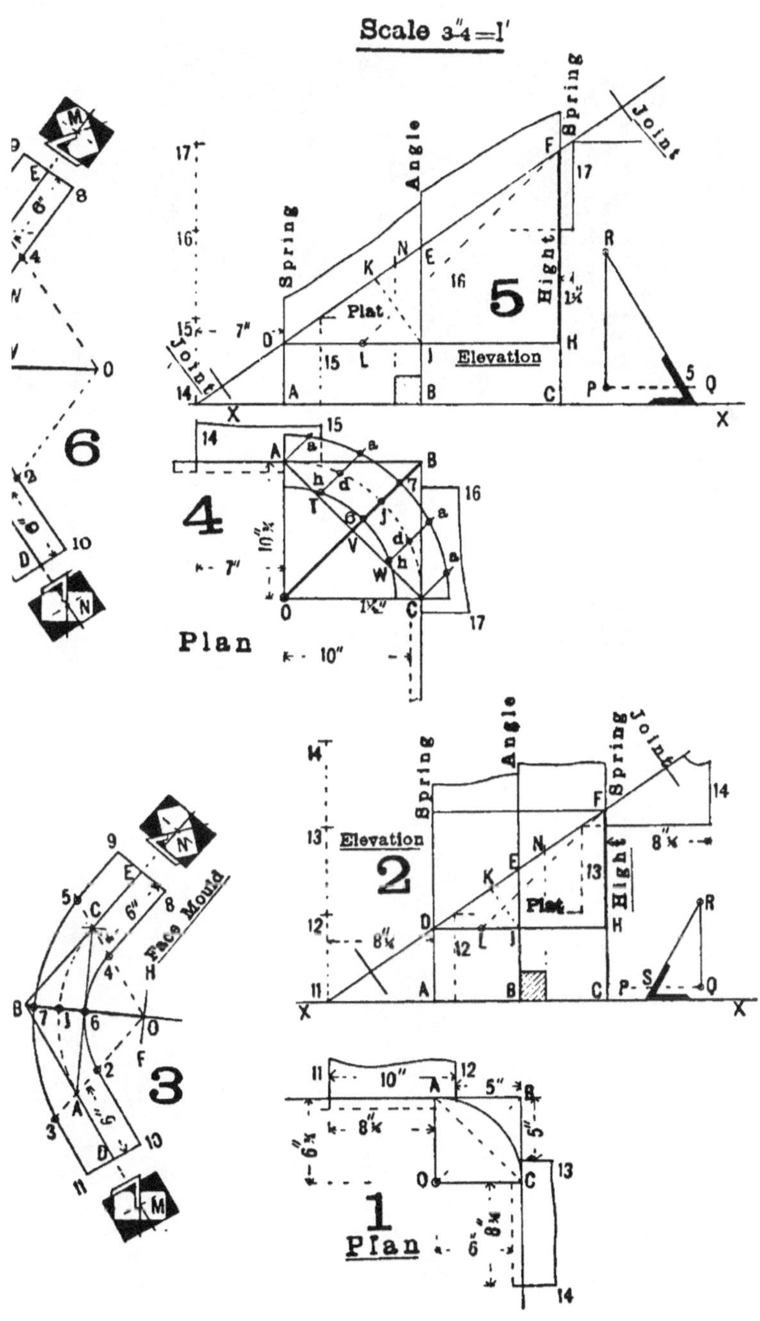
Scale 3″4=1′
Spring
Spring
Angle
Joint
Joint
Spring
Plat
Hight
Elevation
5
R
P
Q
X
X
A
B
C
K
N
E
L
J
H
F
17
17
16
15
14
15
16
17
7″
1¾
16
Plan
4
Joint
A
B
C
a
a
a
h
h
d
d
T
V
W
O
J
14
15
16
17
7″
10¾″
1¾″
10″
Face Mould
3
9
E
C
H
B
O
F
A
D
5
8
6″
7
1
6
2
4
3
10
11
M
N
Spring
Angle
Spring
Joint
Elevation
2
High
Plat
Hight
X
X
A
B
C
D
K
E
N
L
J
H
F
R
P
S
Q
14
13
12
11
13
12
14
13
8″¾
8¾
Plan
1
11
12
A
B
C
O
13
14
10″
5″
5″
5″
8¾
8¾
6″¾
6″
N
M
6
E
E
8
6″
4
N
V
O
2
D
10
6″

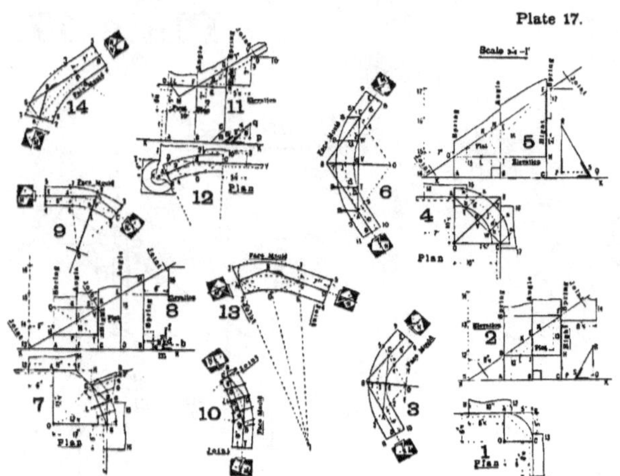

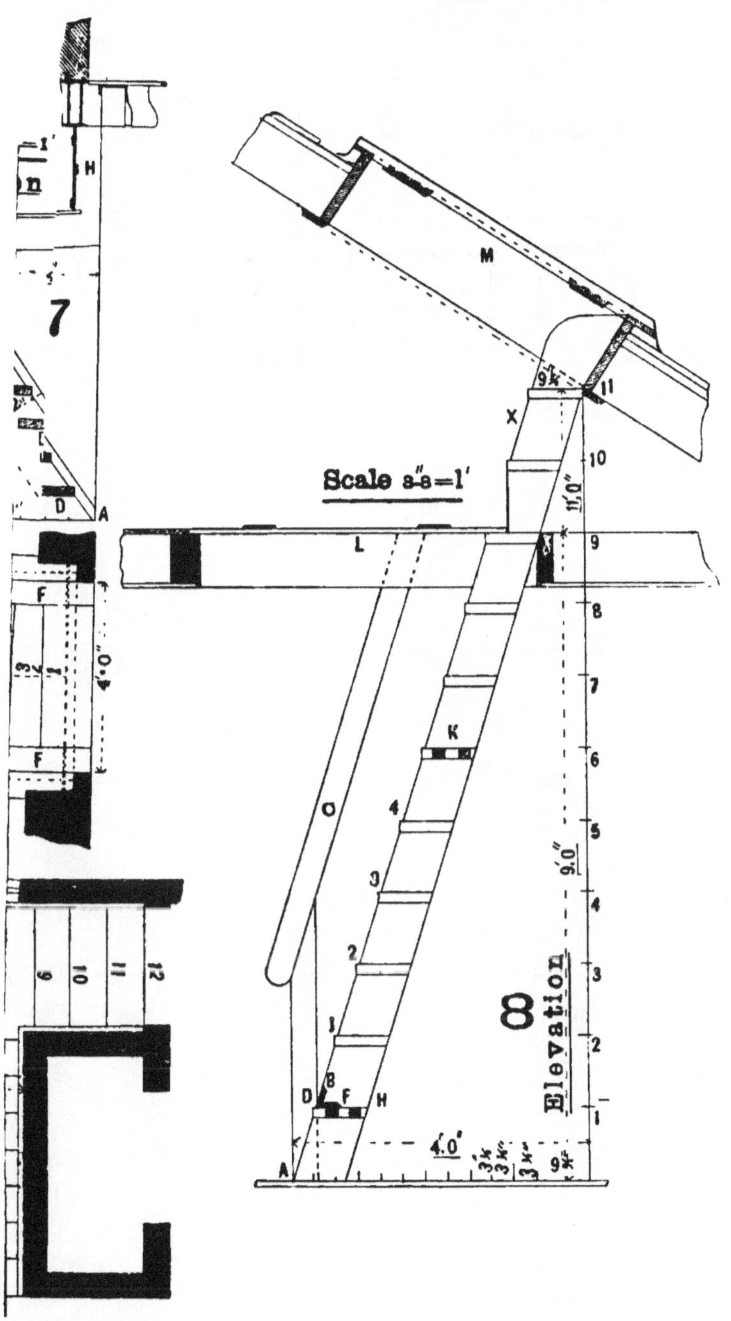
Scale 3"=1'
Elevation
7
8
M
X
L
K
O
4
3
2
1
D B F H
A
H
D
A
F
F
9 10 11 12
11,0"
9,0"
4,0"
4'0"
9 8 7 6 5 4 3 2 1
11
10
9
8
7
6
5
4
3
2
1

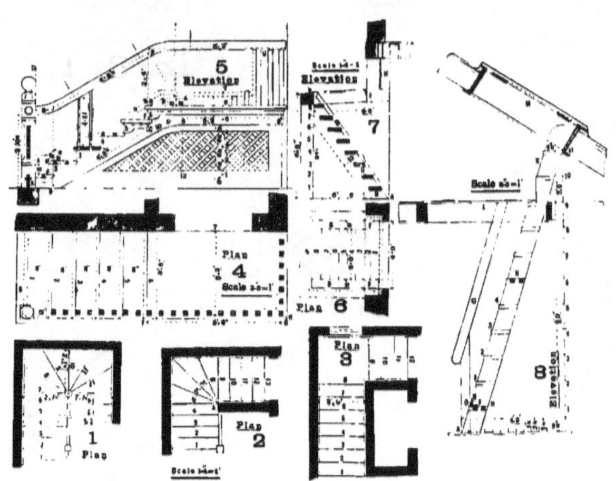

5
Elevation
Elevation
7
Plan
4
Scale ¾=1'
Plan 6
Scale ½=1'
Plan
3
1
Plan
Plan
2
Scale ¾=1'
Scale ¾=1'
Elevation
8

Plate 19.

Scale 1·4″=1′

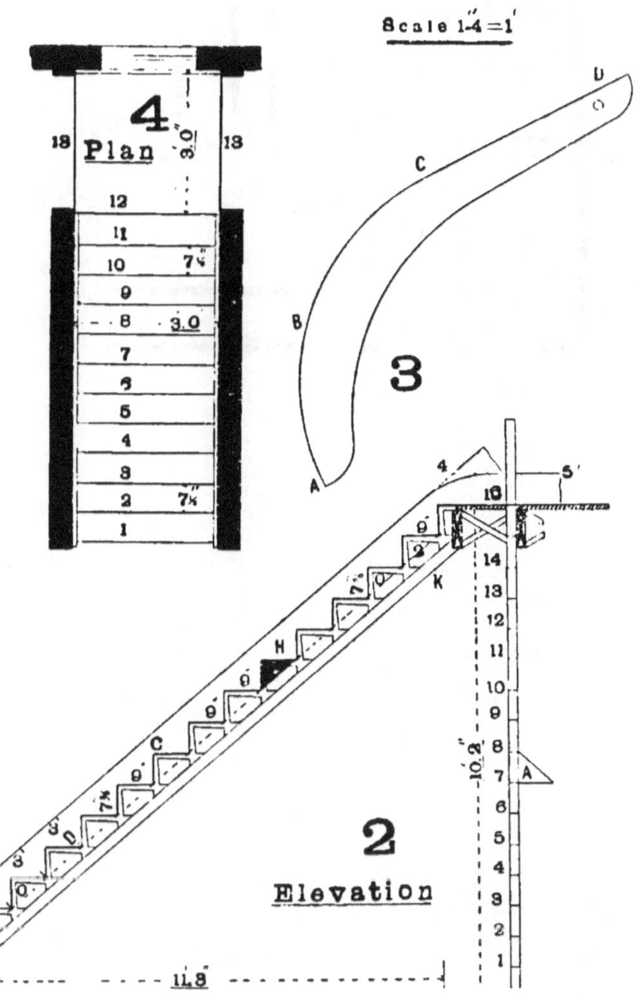

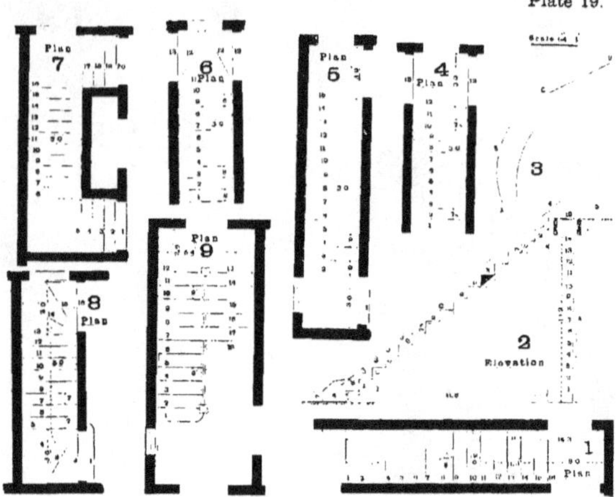

Plate 20.

Scale 3′4=1′

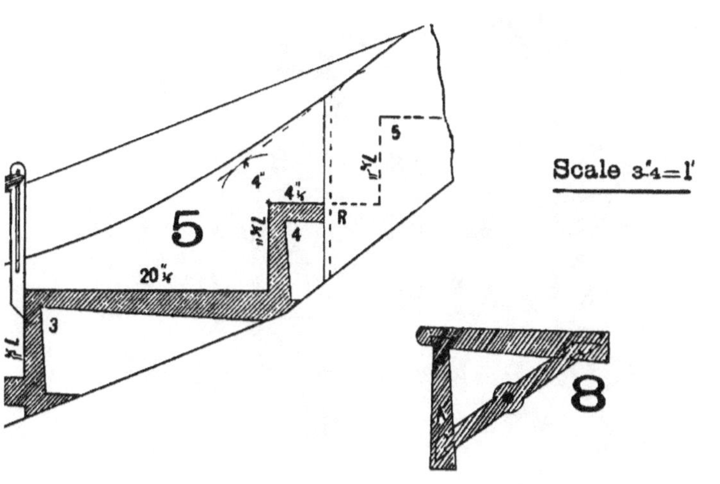

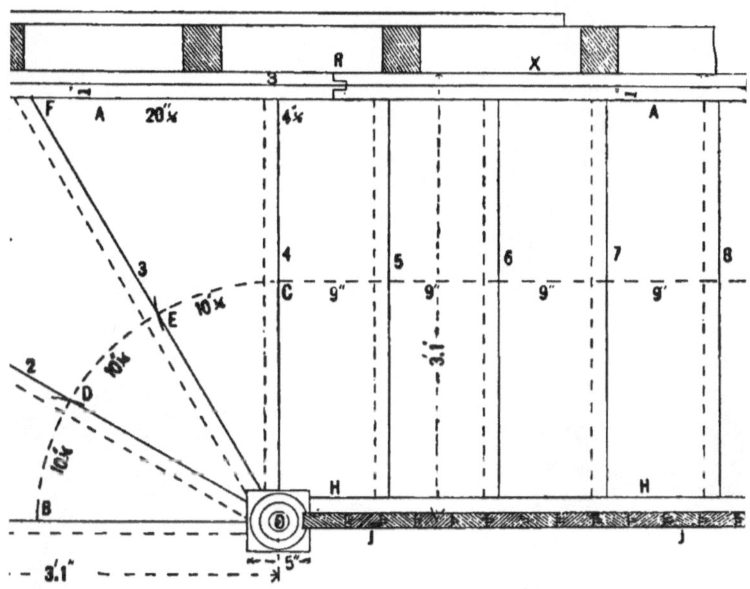

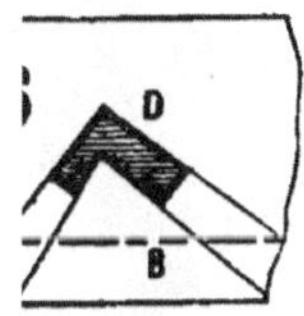

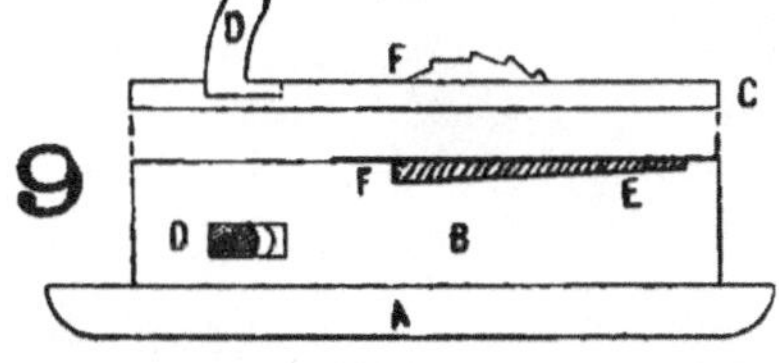

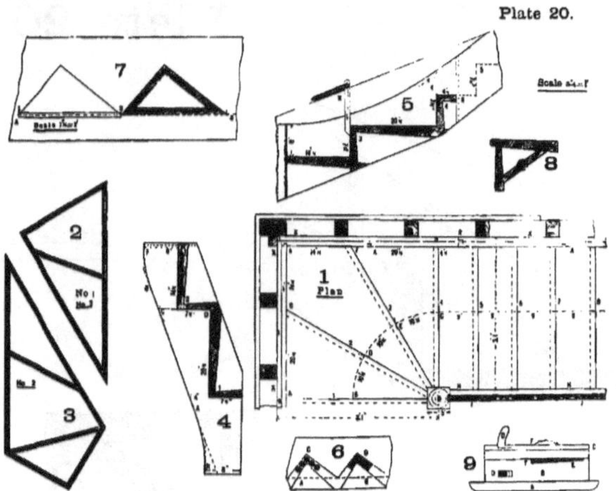

Plate 20.
7
Scale
5
8
2
No 1
No 2
3
1
Plan
4
6
9

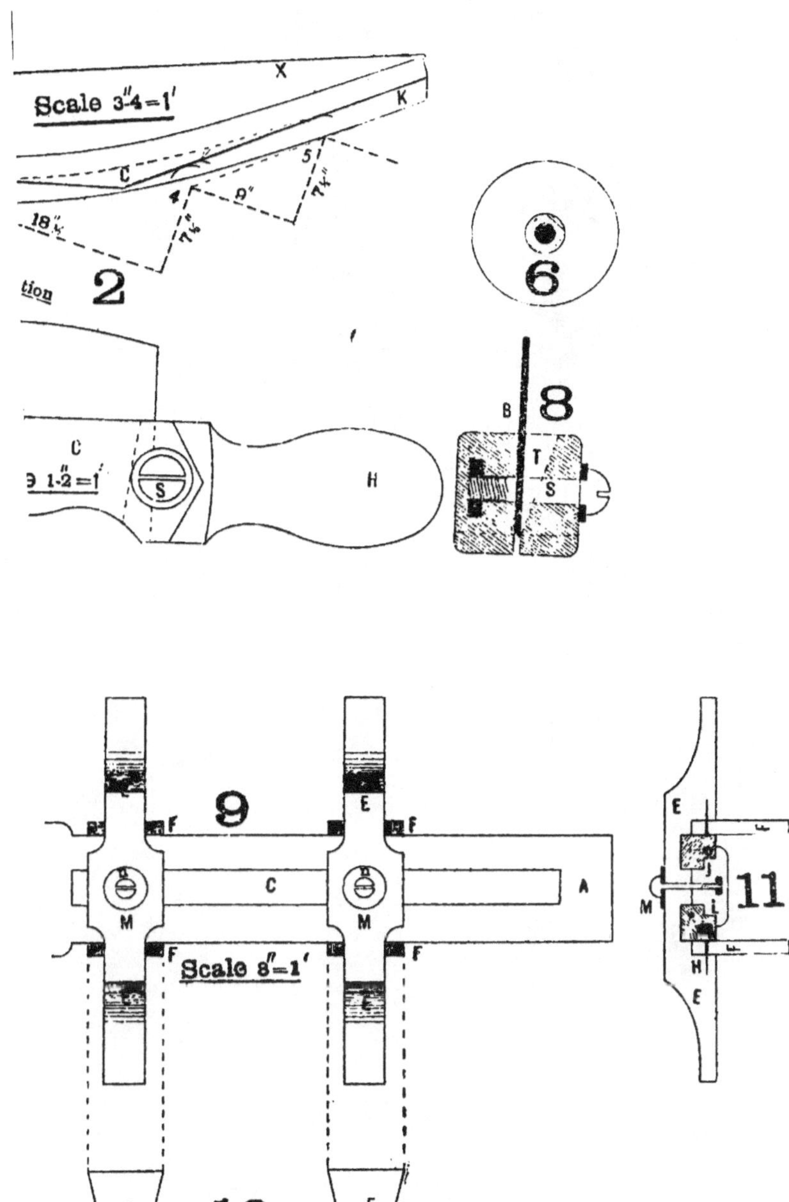
Scale 3"4=1'
X
K
C
5
4"
9"
7"
7½"
18"
tion
2
6
B
8
T
S
C
9 1-2=1'
S
H
9
E
F
F
C
A
M
M
F
Scale 8"=1'
F
E
F
J
11
M
L
H
E
10
F
L
F
L
M
M
A

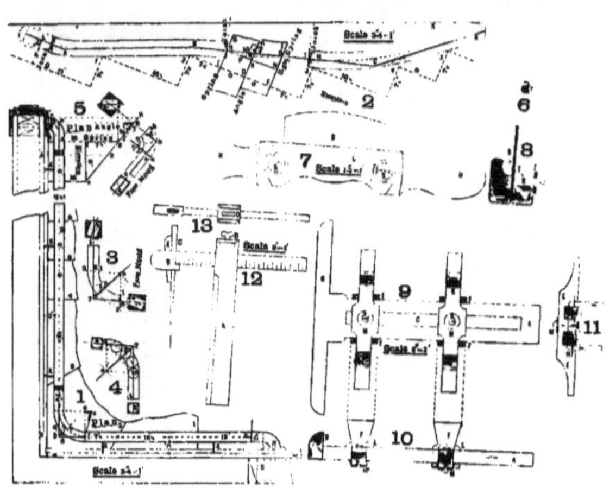

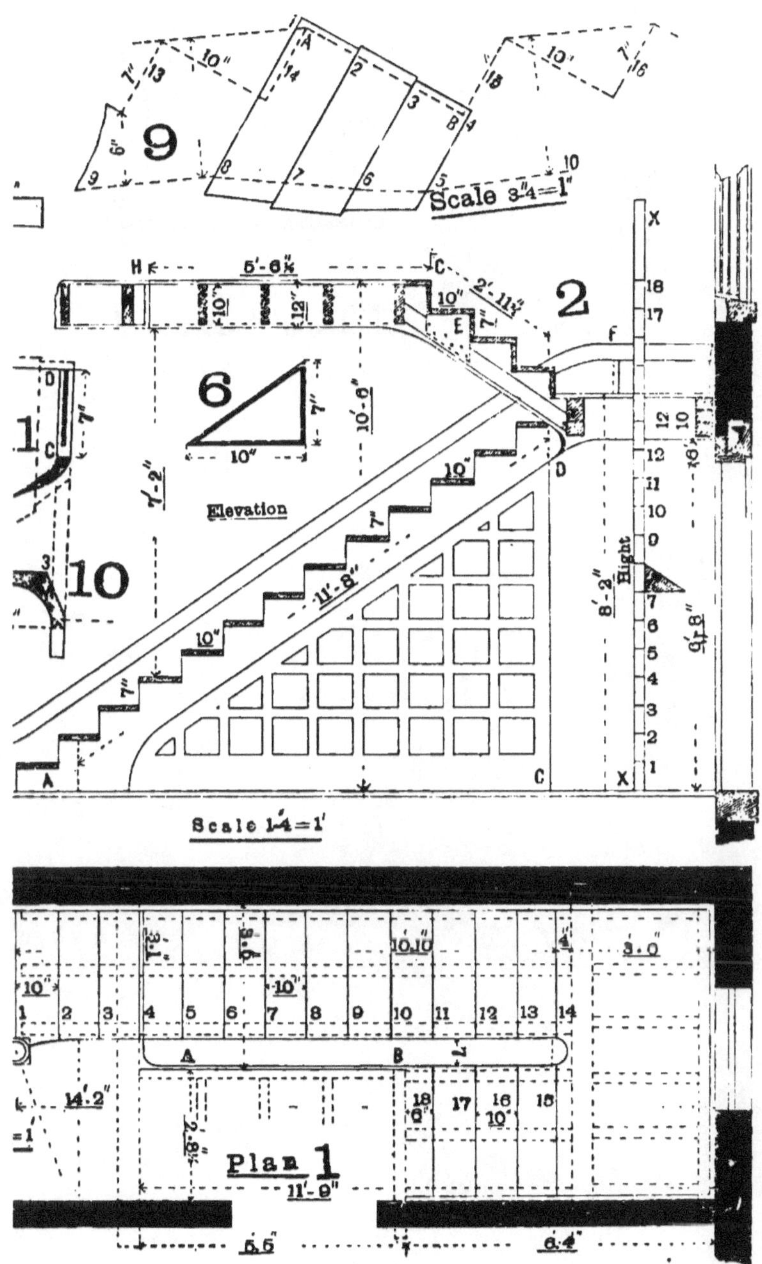
Scale 3"4=1'
9
H
5'-6"
C
10"
2'-11¼"
2
E
7"
X
18
17
f
6
7"
10"
1
7"
10'-6"
7'-2"
Elevation
D
12 10
12
11
10
9
8'-2"
Hight
8
7
6
5
4
3
2
1
9'-8"
11'-8"
10"
7"
10"
7"
10
A
C
X
Scale 1"4=1'
Plan 1
3'1"
5'8"
10.10
4
3.0
10"
10"
1 2 3 4 5 6 7 8 9 10 11 12 13 14
A B
14'-2"
2'-8½"
18 17 16 15
6" 10"
11'-0"
6.5
6.4

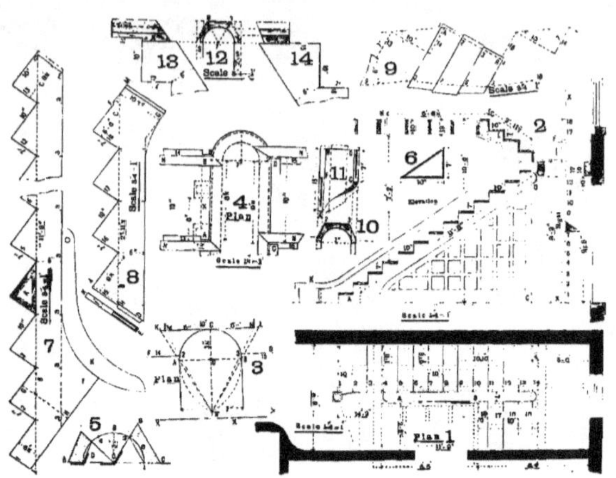

13
12
Scale
14
9
Scale
2
6
11
4
Plan
10
Elevation
Scale
8
7
Scale
3
Plan
5
Plan 1
Scale

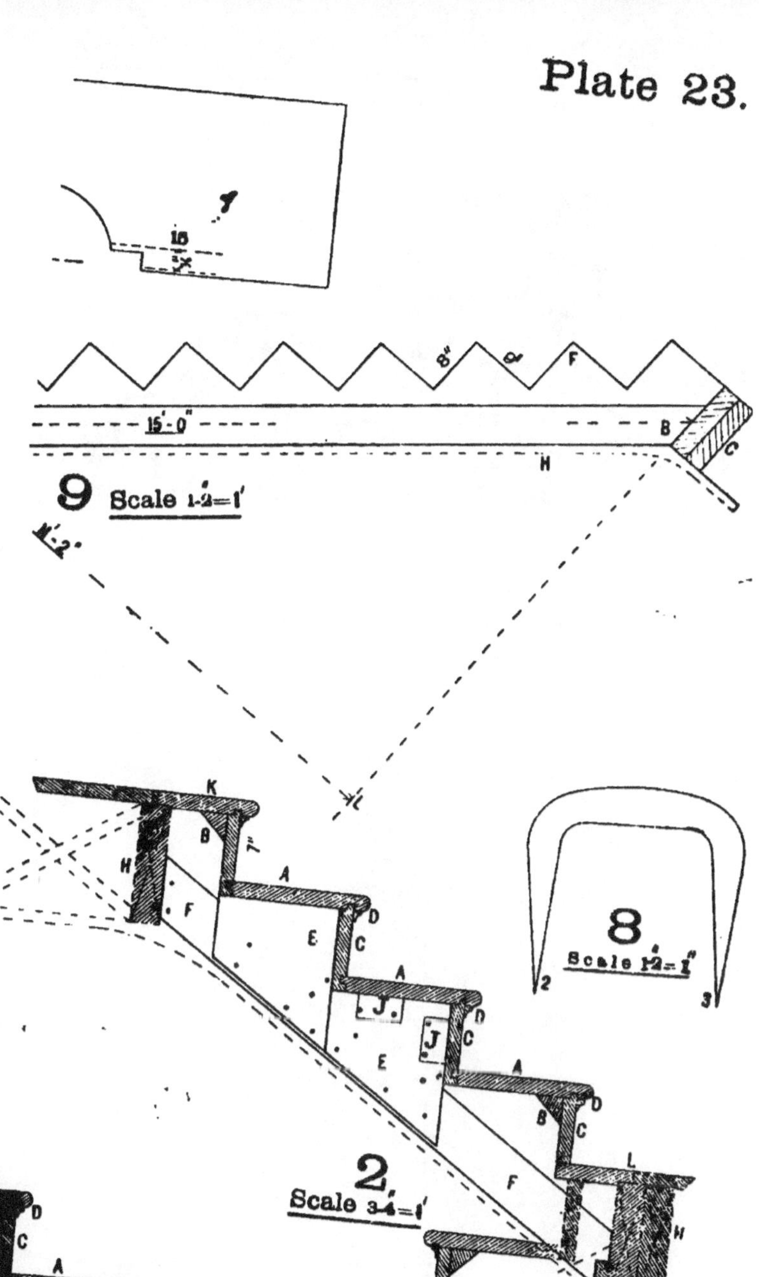
15'-0"
8"
F
B
C
H
9 Scale 1½=1'
K
B
H
F
A
D
E
C
A
J
D
J
C
E
A
B
D
C
L
F
H
2 Scale 3½=1'
8 Scale 1½=1"
B D
C
A
F
B
C
D

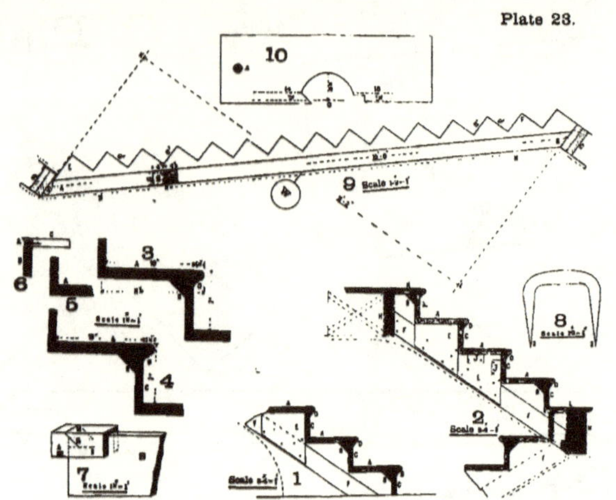

Plate 24.
4
H
J
13
B
C
F
D
O
L
M
4
6
P
7
3
J
B
4
H
D
3
2
F
3
D
X
1'.8"
3
M
3
N
5
G
6
R
14
J
2
6"
F
1'.8"
Pitch Board
Spring
9½"
X
13
J
X
13
14
M
B
X
X"
9¼
5
Plan
O
9¼
6"
N
A
X"
X
16
10"
16
2
10
6
9
B
3
X

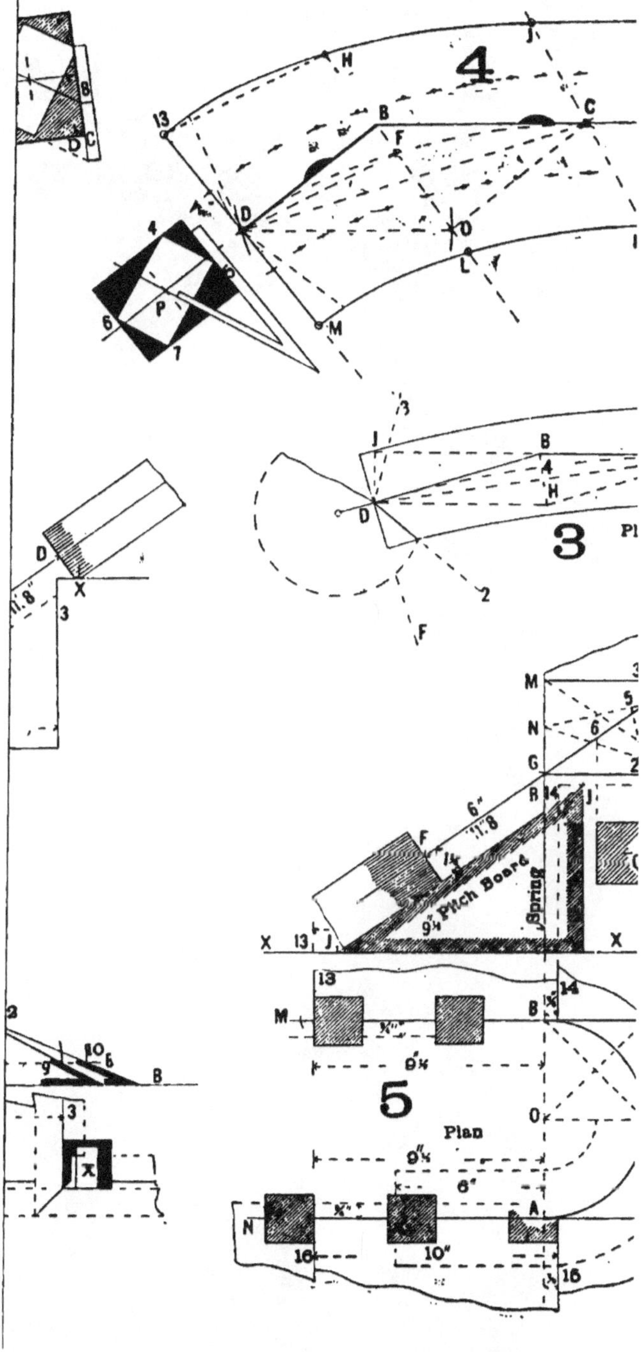

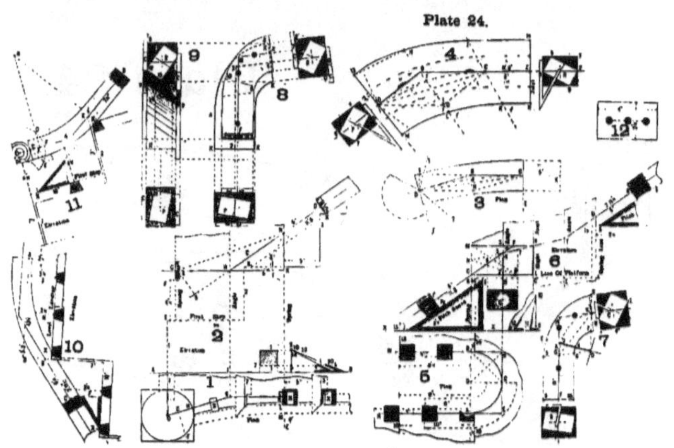

Plate 24.

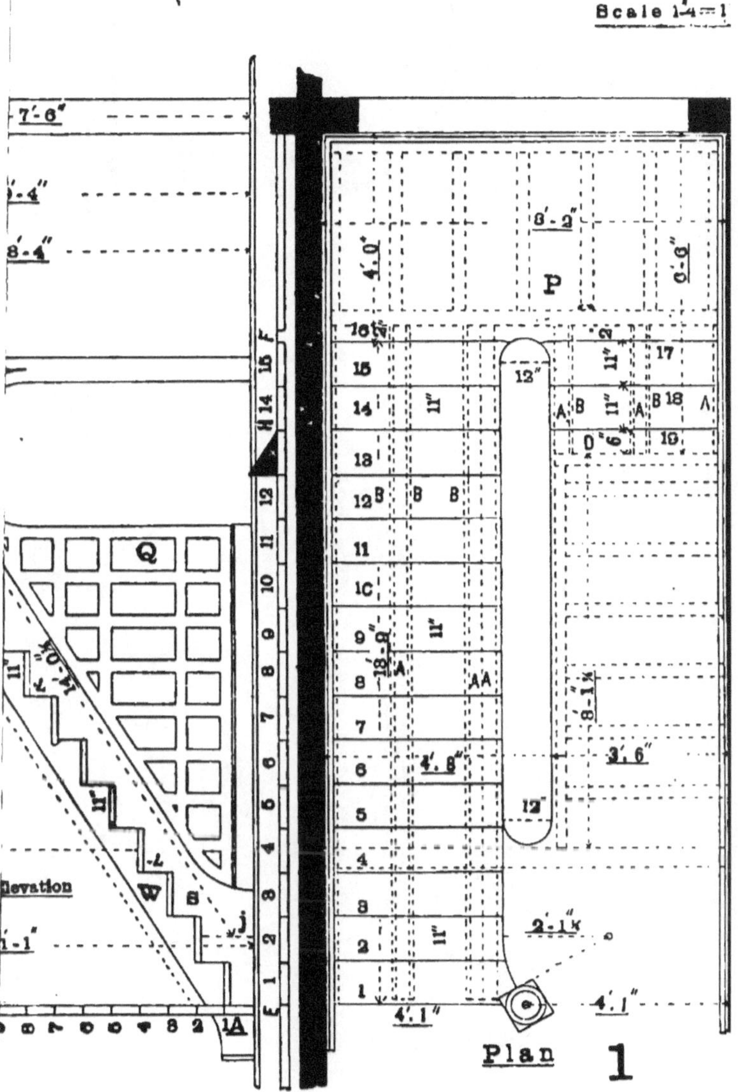
Scale 1¼"=1
7'-6"
'-4"
8'-4"
8'-2"
4'-0"
P
0'-6"
16
15
14
13
12
11
10
9
8
7
6
5
4
3
2
1
12"
12"
11"
17
18
19
A B A B
D
AA
A
Q
Elevation
4'-8"
3'-6"
8'-1¼"
2'-1¼"
4'-1"
4'-1"
Plan 1

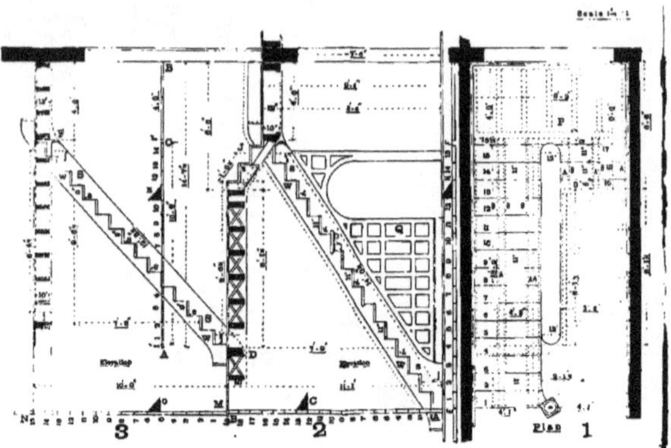

Scale 1/4 : 1
Plan
1
2
3

Plan

-B-

Plan

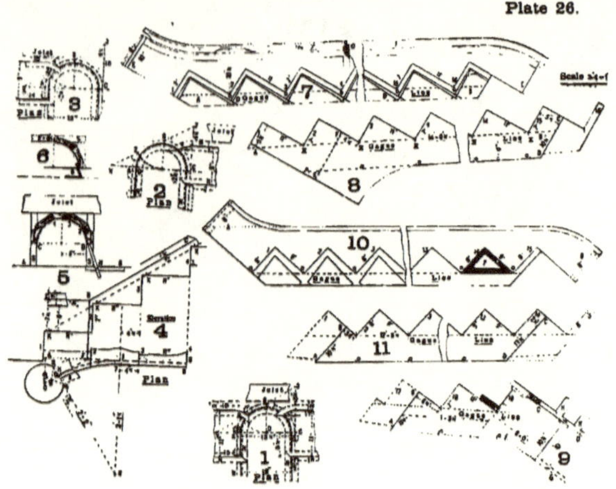

Plate 27.

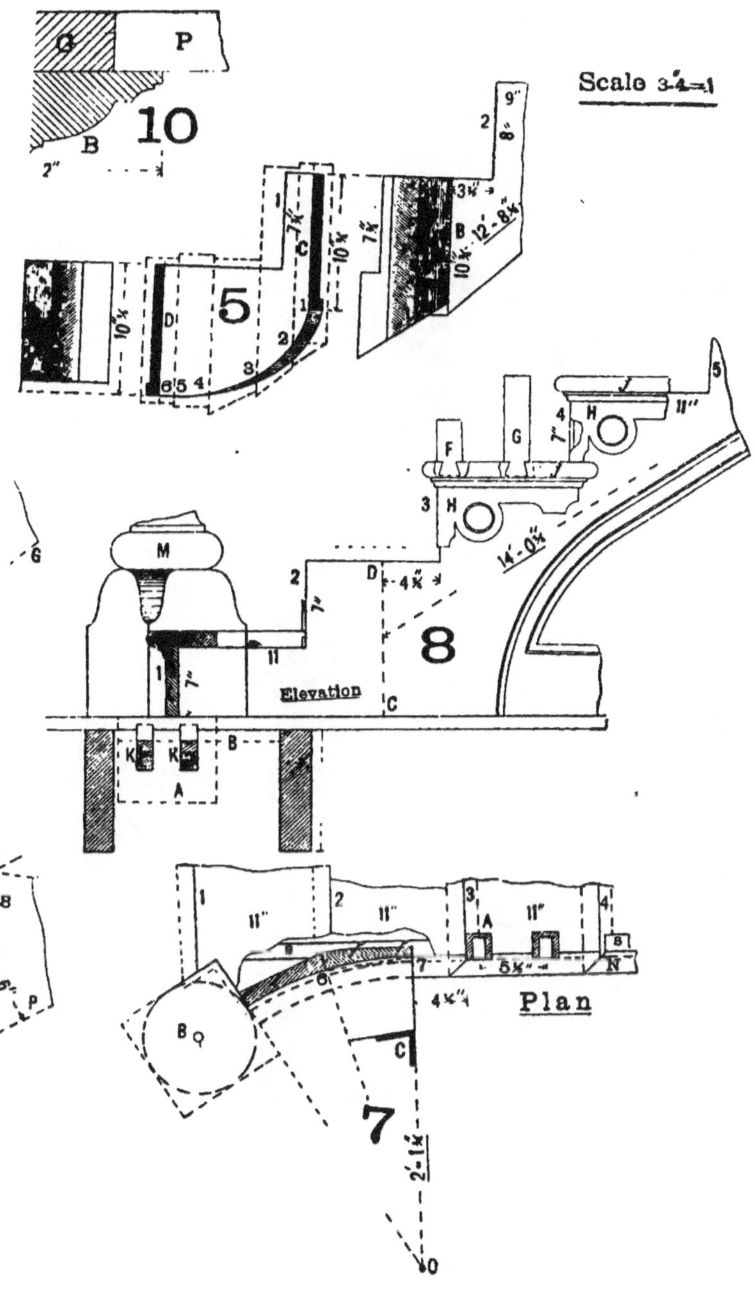

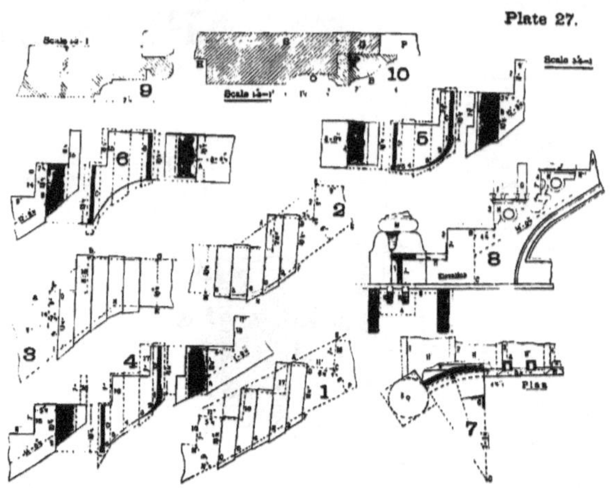

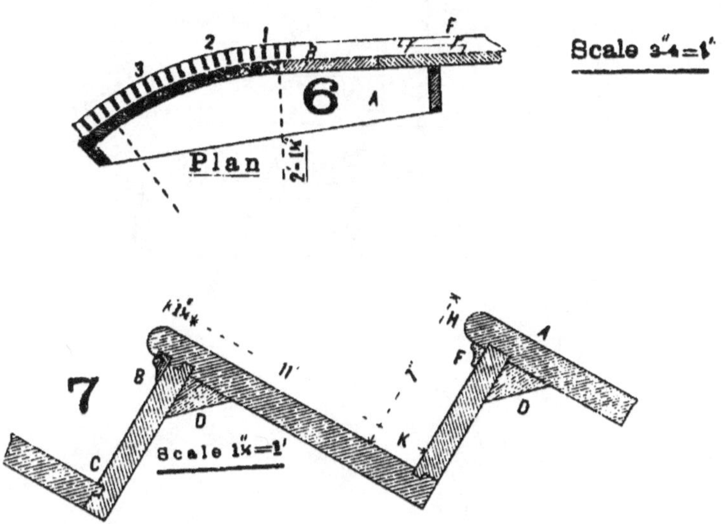
3
2
1
B
F
6
A
Plan
2'·1¼"
Scale 3"¼=1"
7
B
D
C
K 1¼"
H
H
F
A
D
K
Scale 1¼"=1'

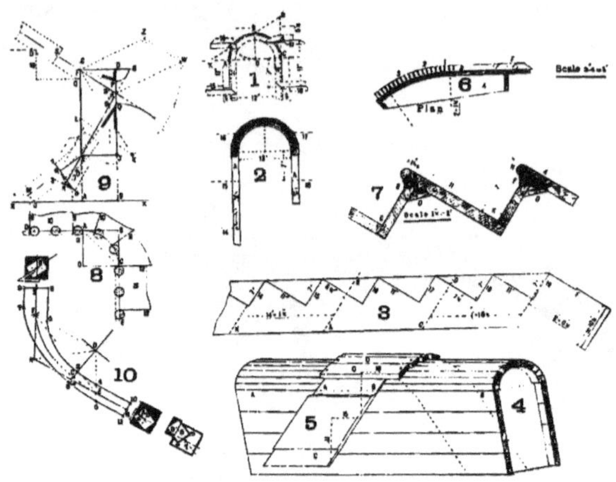

Plate 29.

Scale 3·4 = 1'

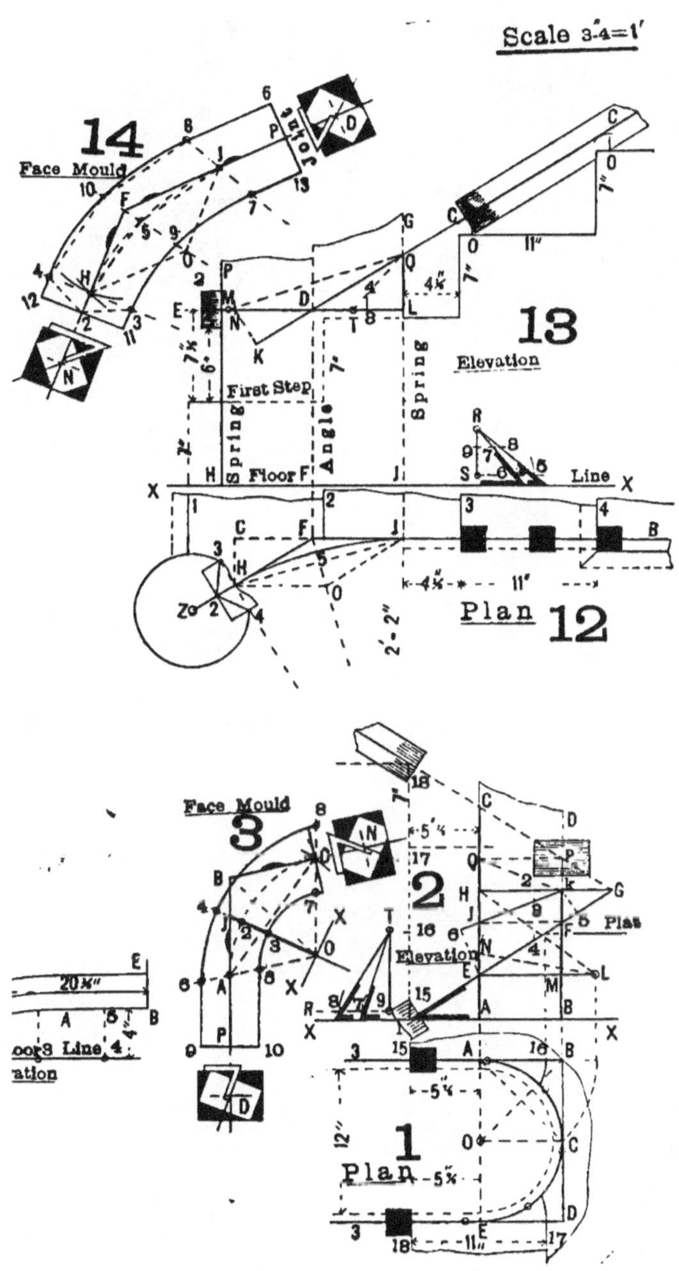

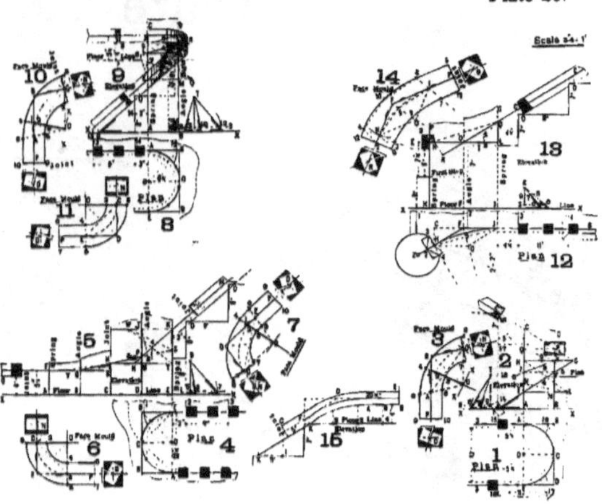
Scale ⅜=1'

Plate 30.

Scale 3-4=1'
17 Elevation
18 Plan
16 Face Mould
Floor Elevation
14
15 Plan
Spring
Angle
3 Elevation
4
Plan
2 Elevation
1 Plan
Spring
Angle
Floor
S Line

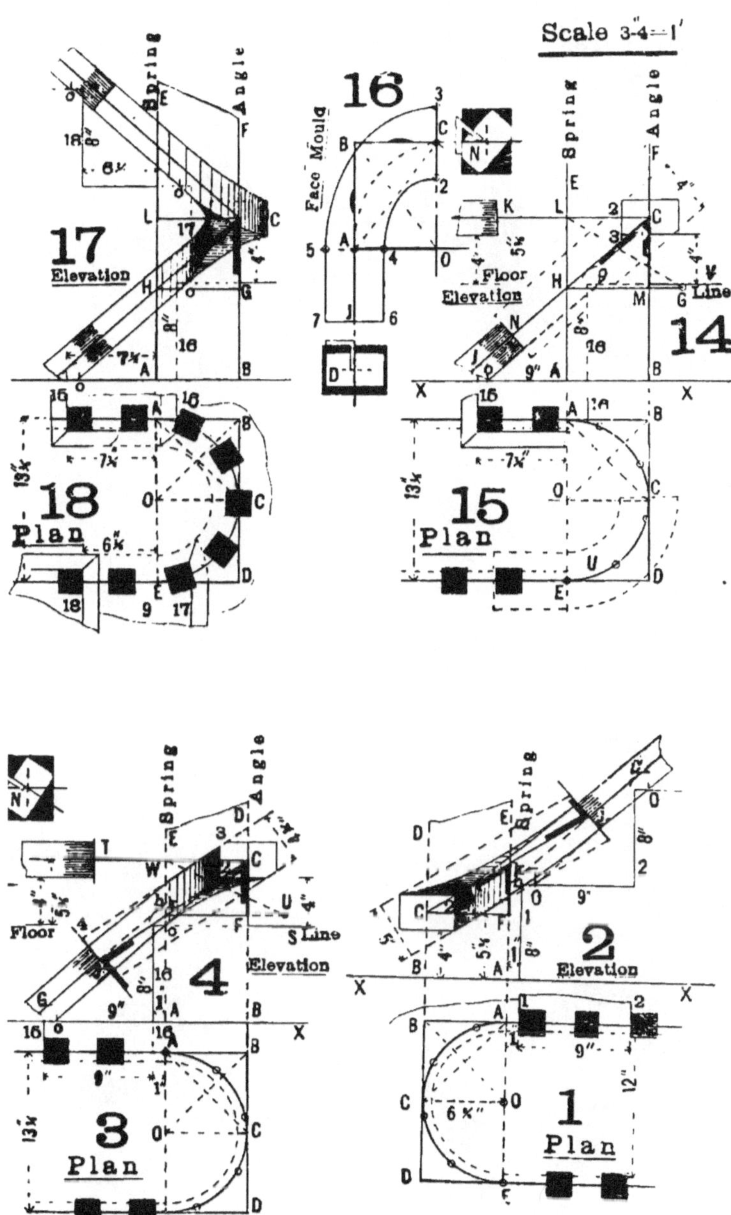

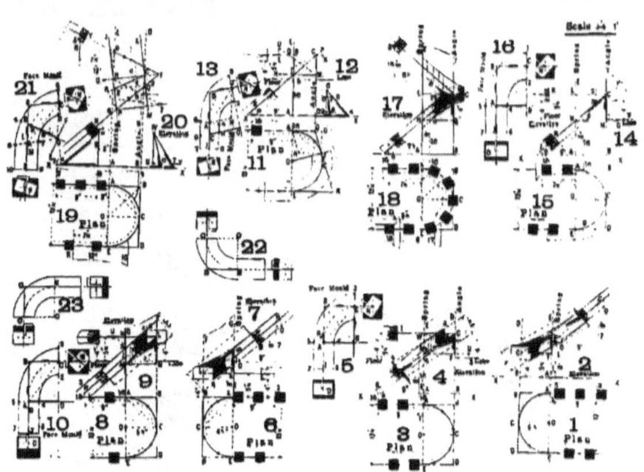

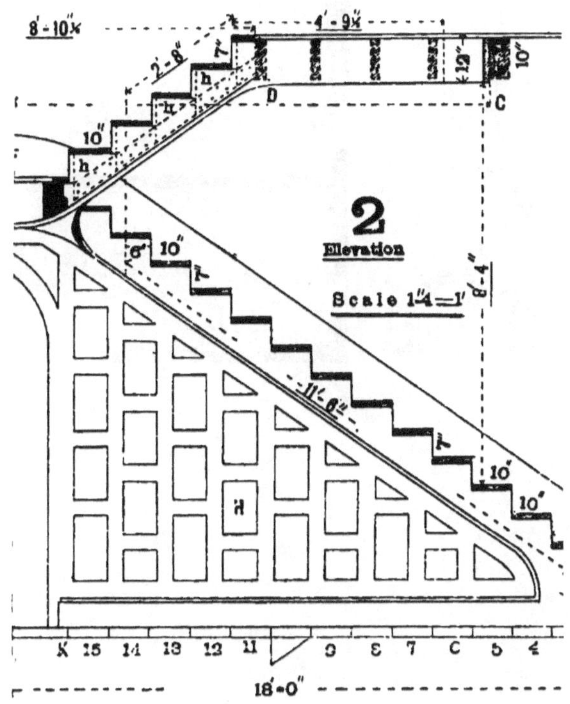
8'-10¼"
4'-9¼"
2'-8"
7"
h
h
h
D
C
12"
10"
10"
h
2
Elevation
Scale 1"/4=1'
8'-4"
6"
10"
7"
11'-8"
7"
10"
10"
h
16 15 14 13 12 11 10 9 8 7 6 5 4
18'-0"

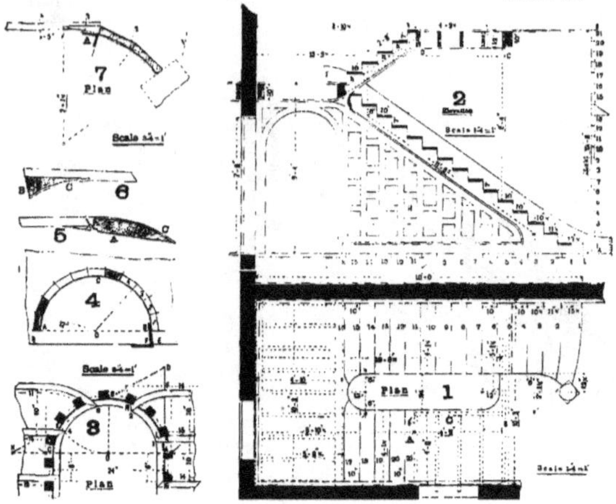

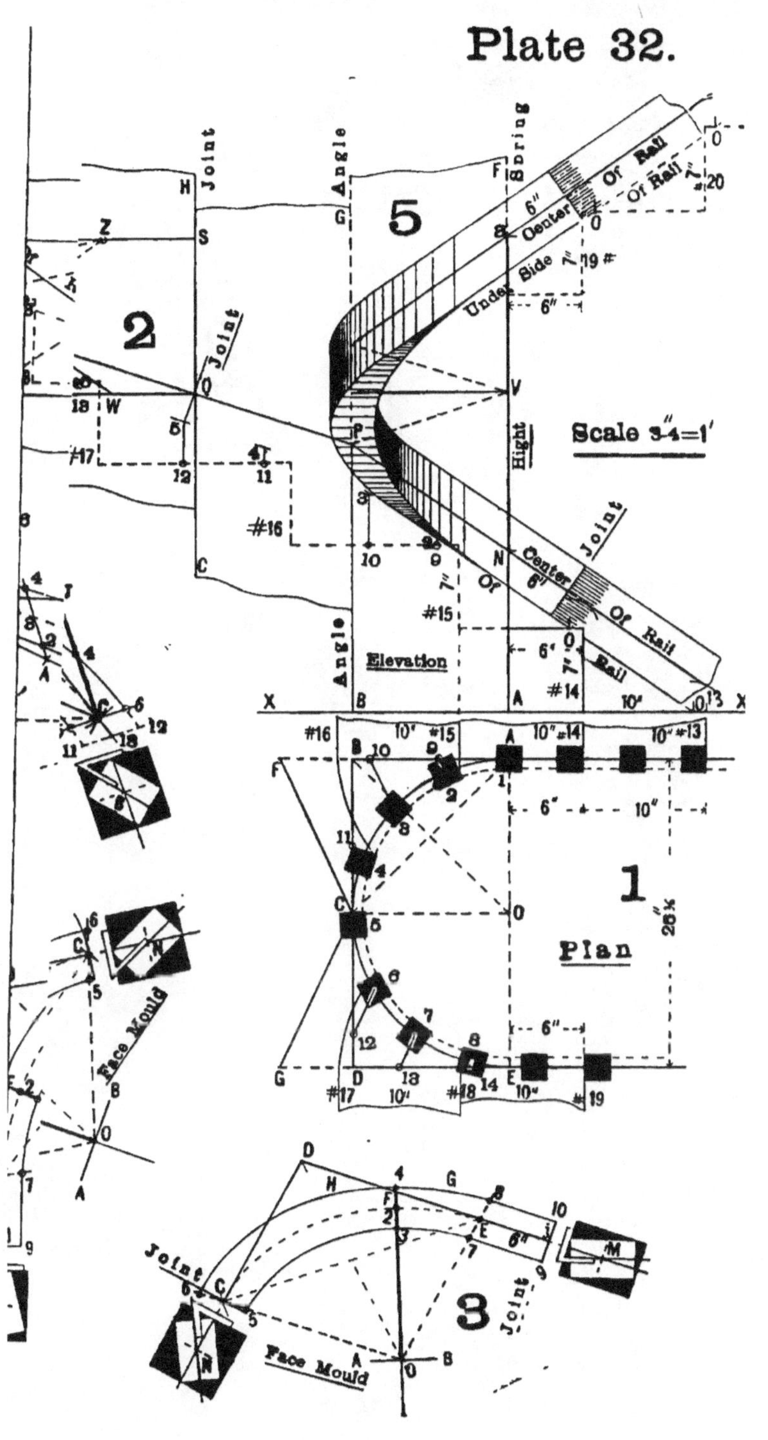

Plate 32.
5
2
Scale 3"4=1'
Joint
Angle
Spring
Center Of Rail
Of Rail
Under Side
Joint
Center Of Rail
Of Rail
Angle
Elevation
Hight
Face Mould
1
Plan
Joint
Joint
3
Face Mould

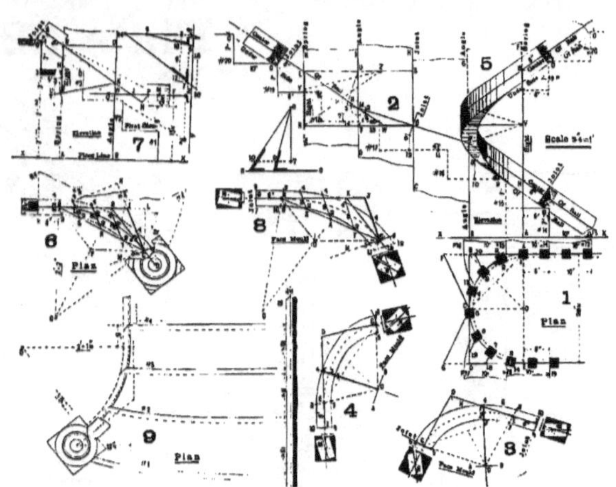

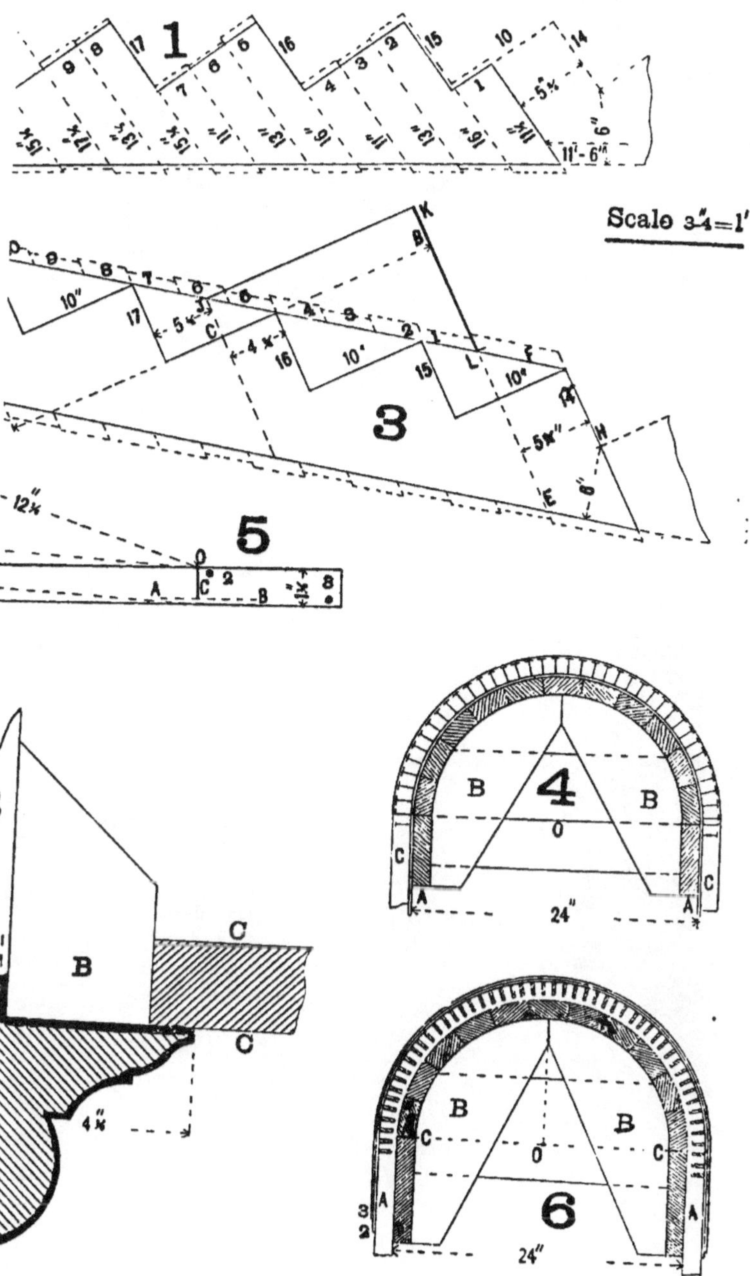
Scale 3"4=1'

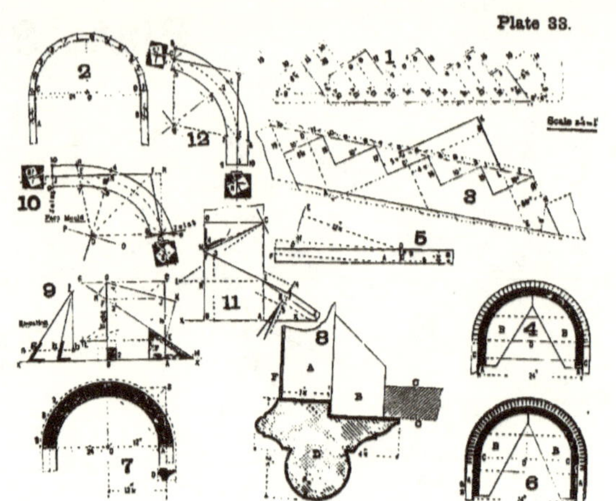

2
12
1
Scale ½=1'
3
10
5
9
11
8
4
7
6

Plate 34.

6'-0"
3'-9"
9"
B
17
2'-1"
9"
S
16
3'-7¼"
15
8'-7¼"
14
13
2
12
Elevation
11
6'-6"
10
Scale 1¼"=1'
9
Hight
8
11'-4"
7
9"
6
8"
5
4
6"
6"
3
8"
2
9"
1
A

10'-6"
18'-4"
18 ¼"
21"
10"
9"
9"
9"
17½"
16"
8'-6"
2'-8"
9"
8
7
6
5
4
3
2
1
10
6'-0"
16"
11
14"
12
8"
13
6"
18"
14
15
16
17
2'-8"
17½"
3'-7¼"
17½"
9"
21"
15"
9"
Plan
1
Scale 1¼"=1'
5'-0"

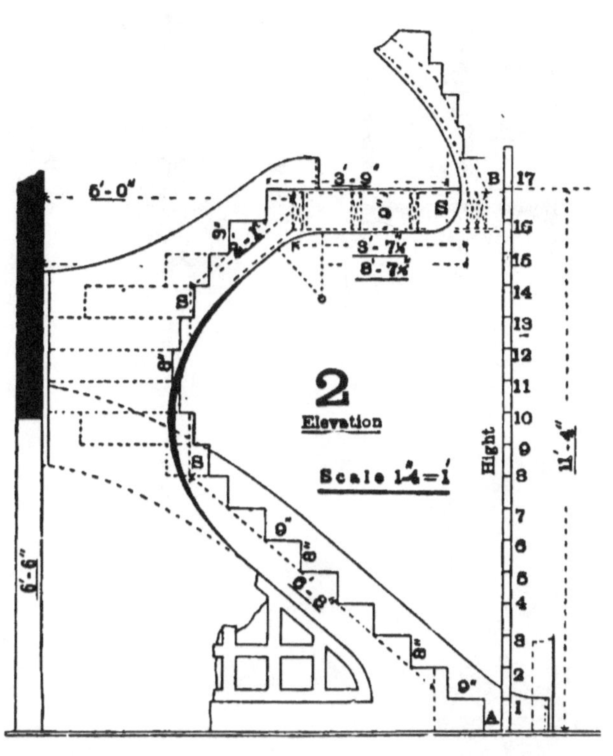

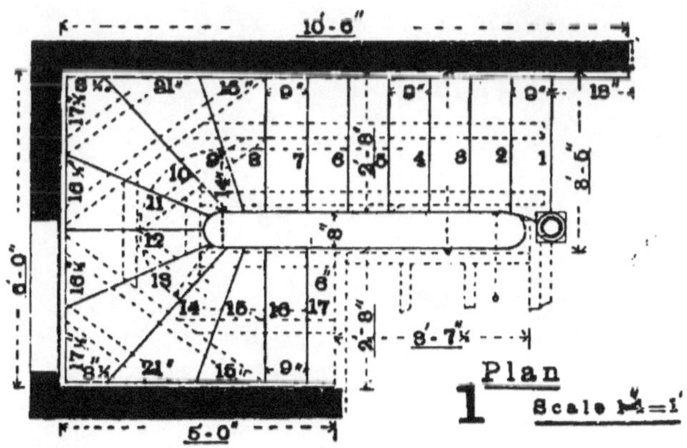

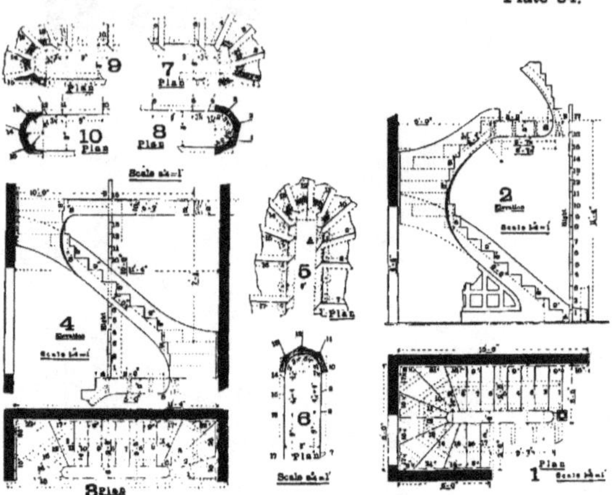

Plate 35.

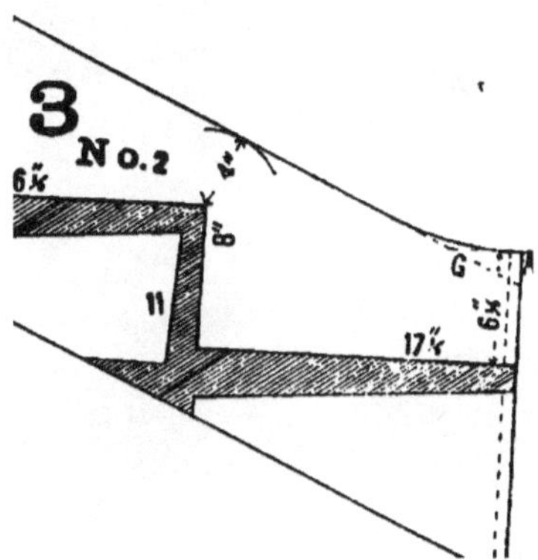

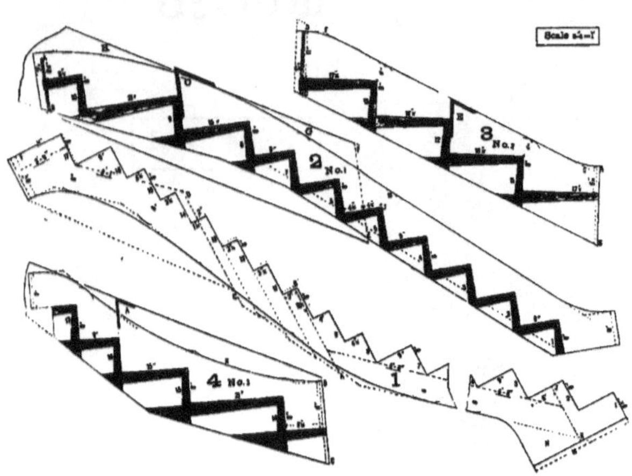
Scale ¼=1'
1
2 No.1
3 No.1
4 No.1

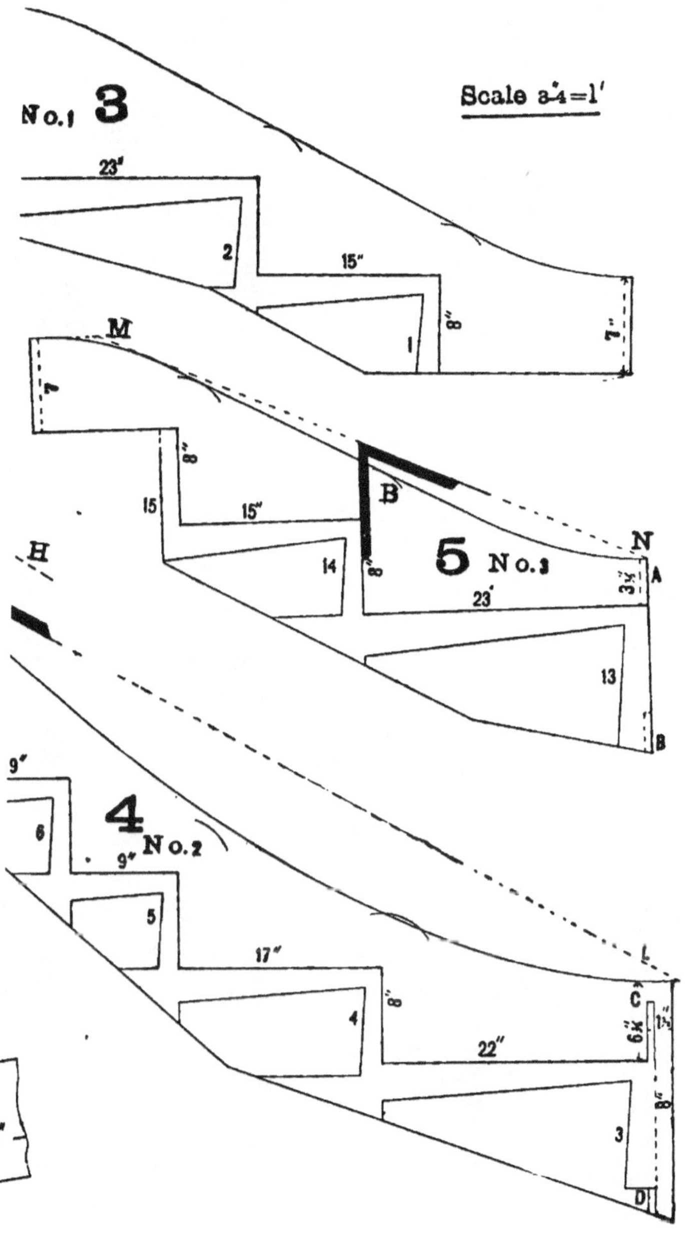

Plate 36.
No.1 3
Scale 3"=1'
23"
2
15"
8"
1
7"
M
7
8"
15
15"
B
14
8"
5 No.3
23'
N
A
3½"
13
B
H
9"
6
4 No.2
9"
5
17"
4
8"
22"
C
6½"
1½"
8"
3
D

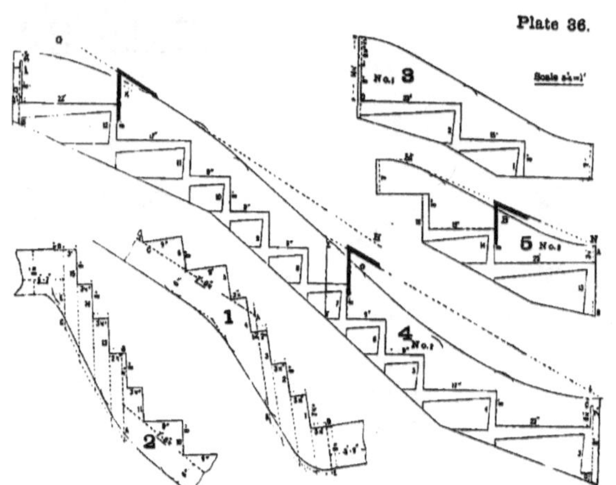

Plate 36.
Scale 3/4=1'
No. 3
No. 5
No. 4
1
2

Plate 37.

Plate 37.
4 Elevation
3 Plan
11 Elevation
13
18 Elevation
12
6
10 Plan
Joint
First Step
Spring
Angle
High
Face Mould
Scale 3"=1'

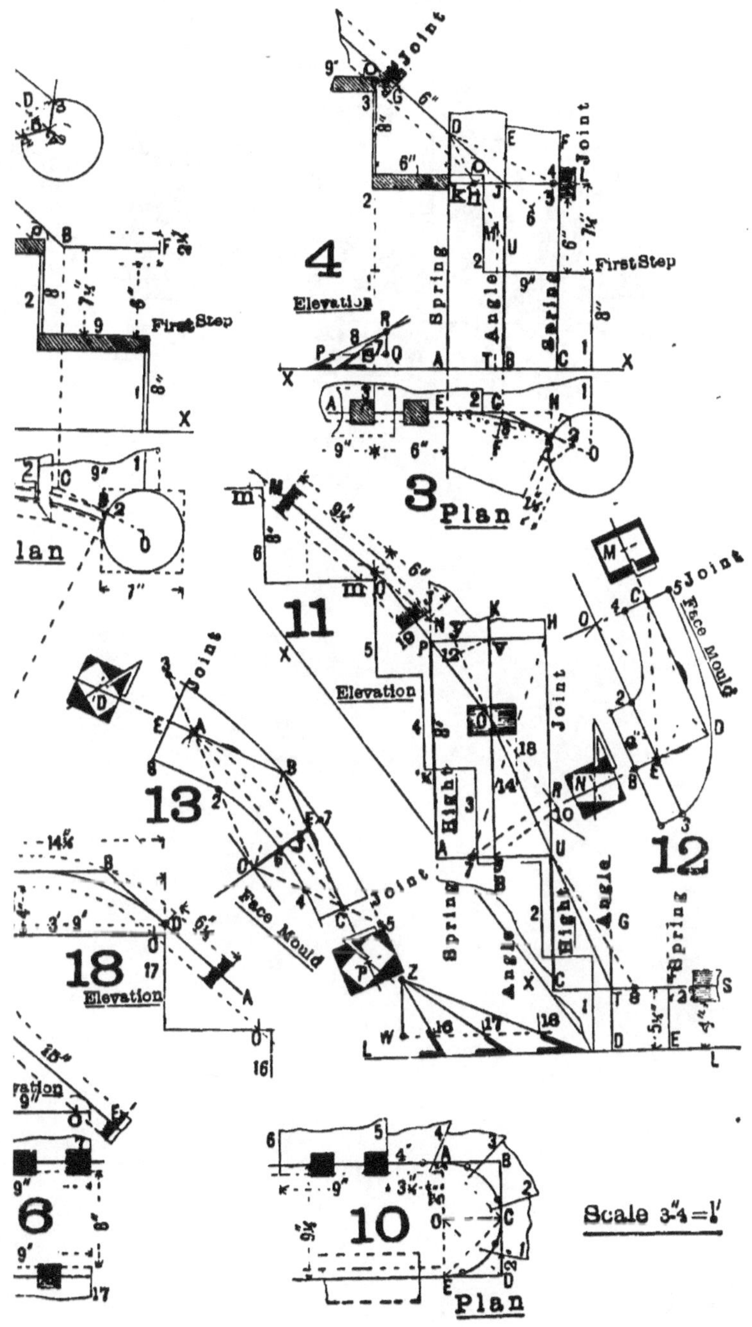

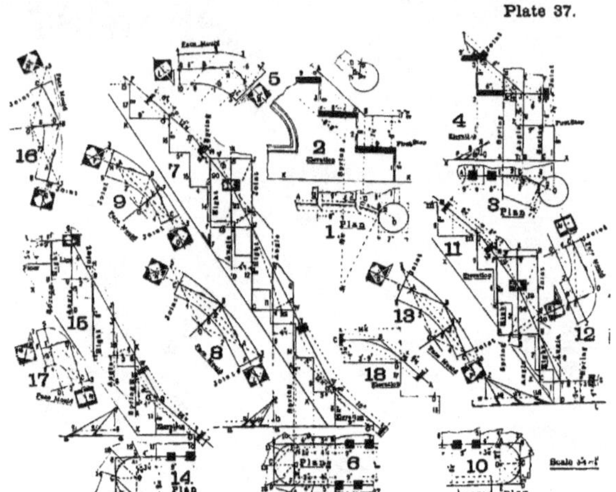

Plate 38.

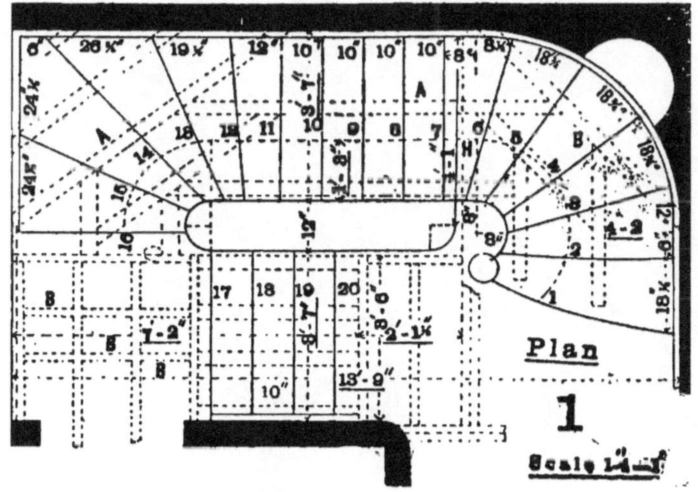

2
Elevation
Scale 1¼"=1'

Plan
1
Scale 1¼"=1'

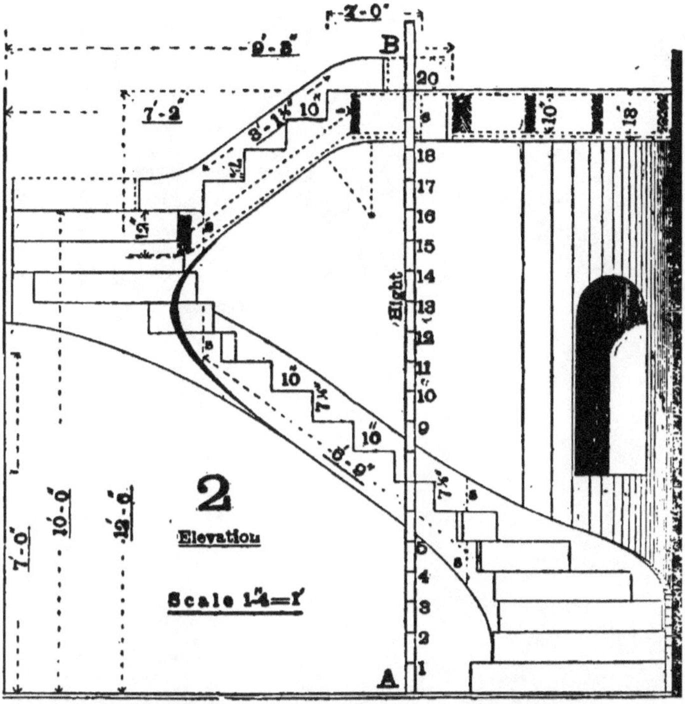

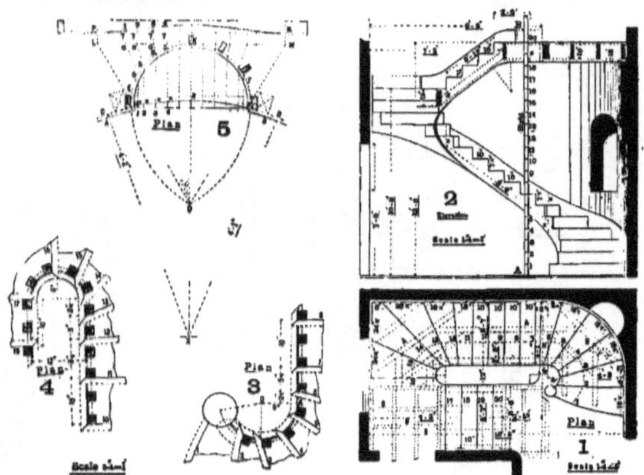

Plate 39.

6
24"¼
7½"
5
9½"
B
A
9
7½"
N
7°
6'-0"
10
0"
9"
10"
9
7½"
P
7"
2
5
7½"
18"¾
4
18"¾
18"¾
3
7½"
18"¾
B
10"
10"
9
7½"
Joint
F

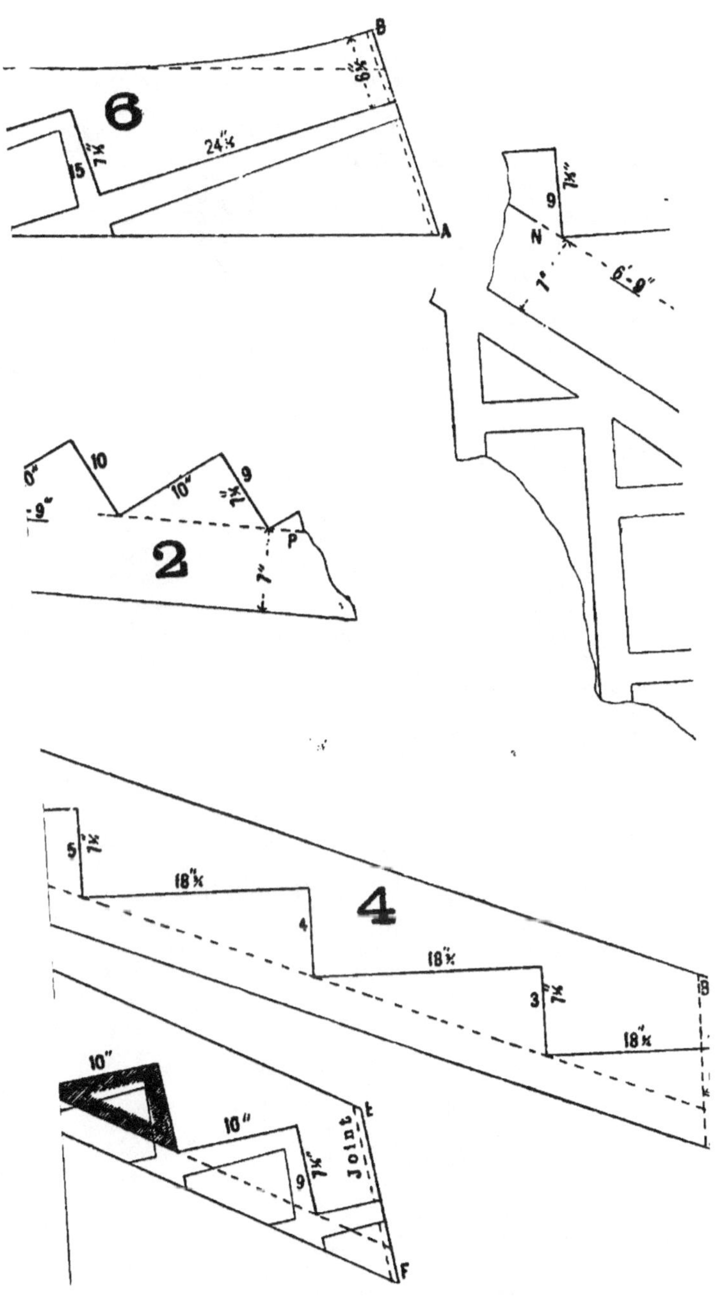

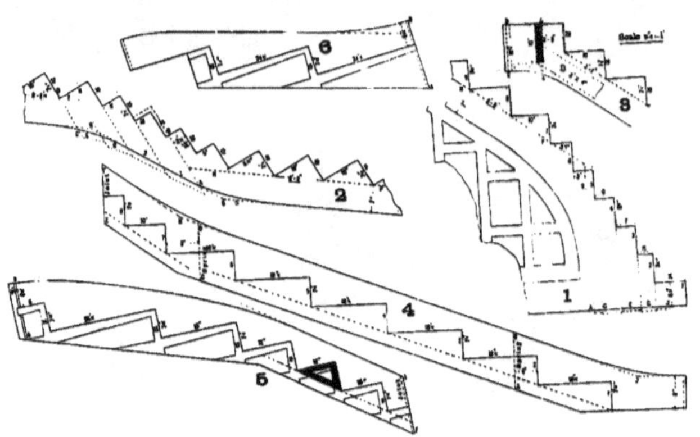

Plate 40.

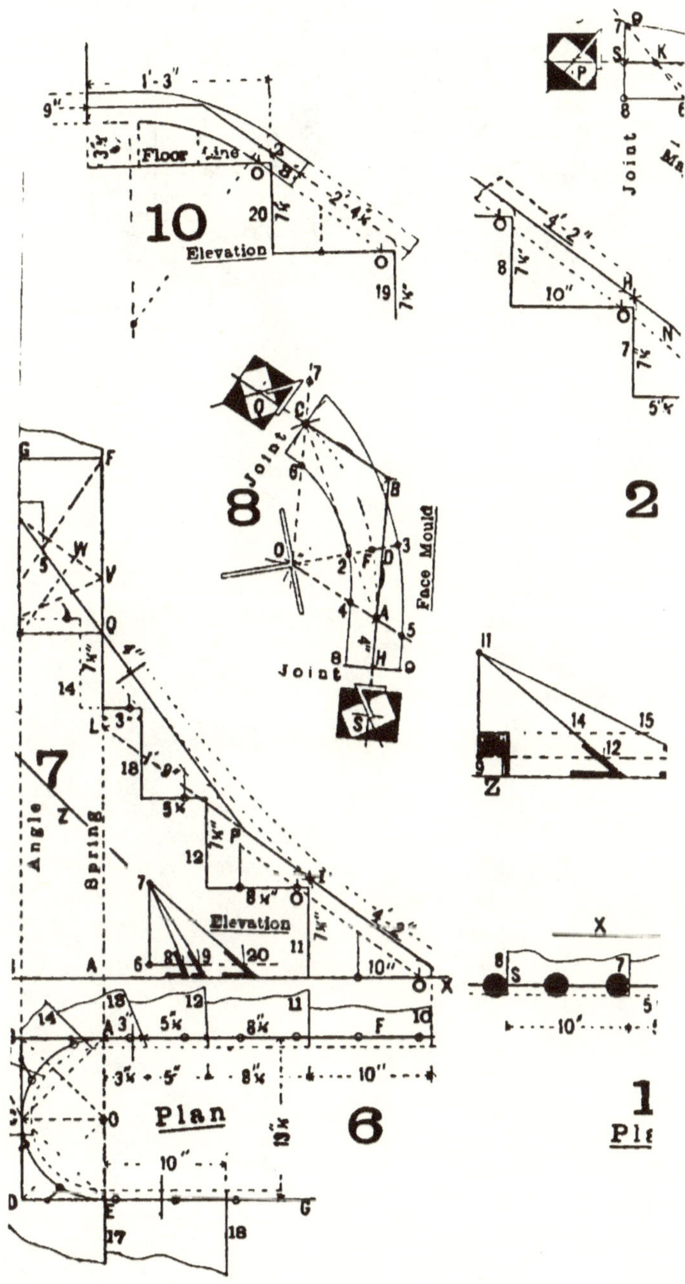

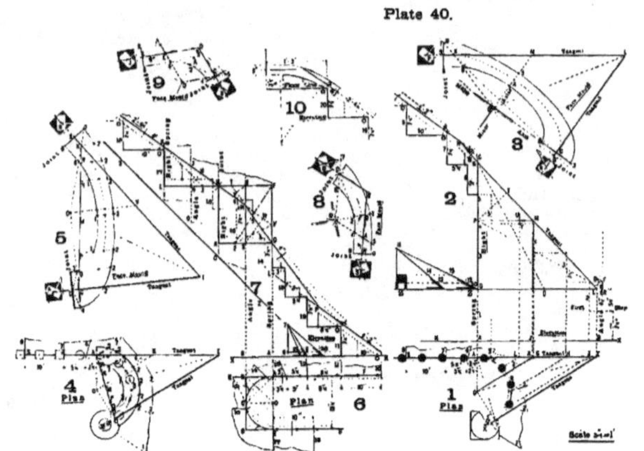

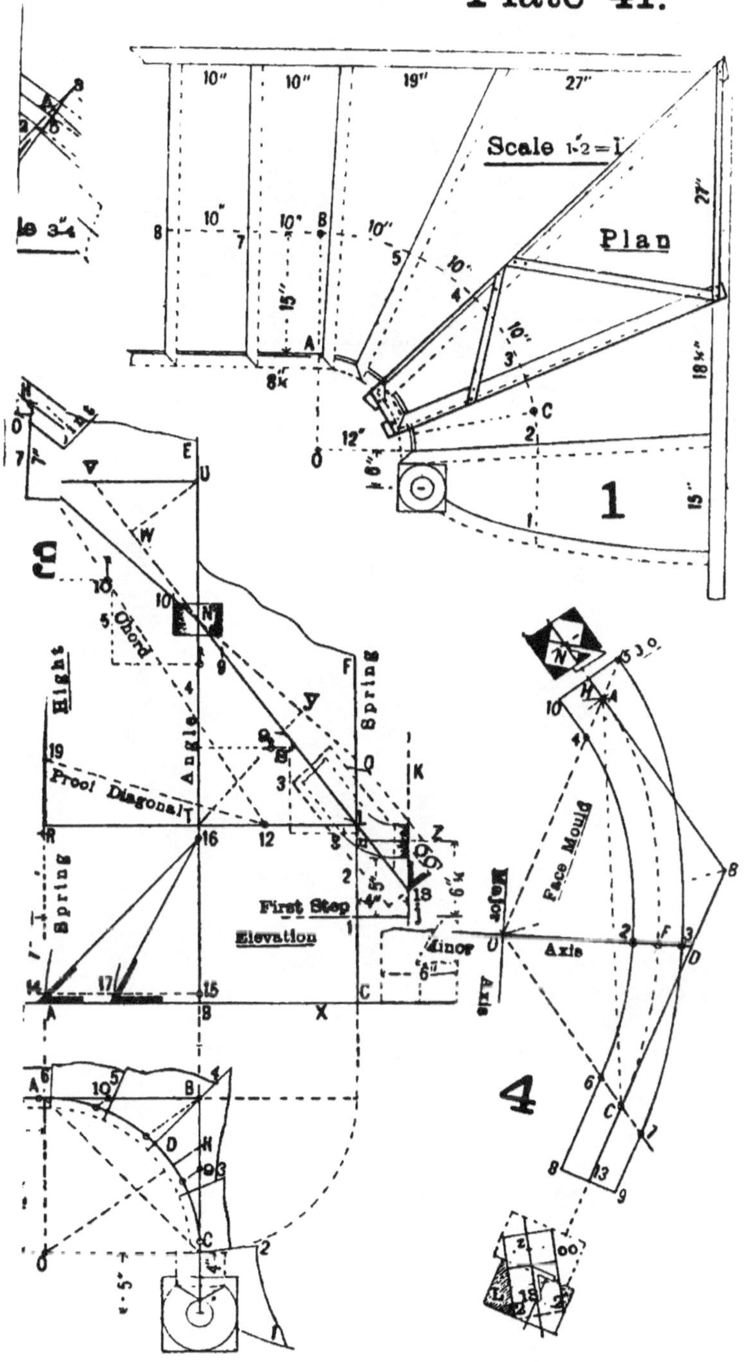

Plate 41.
Scale 1·2=1
Plan
10"   10"   19"   27"
27"
18½"
15"
1
15"
8½"
12"
Hight
Proof Diagonal
Chord
Angle
Spring
First Step
Elevation
Spring
Minor
Axis
Major Axis
Face Mould
2
3
4

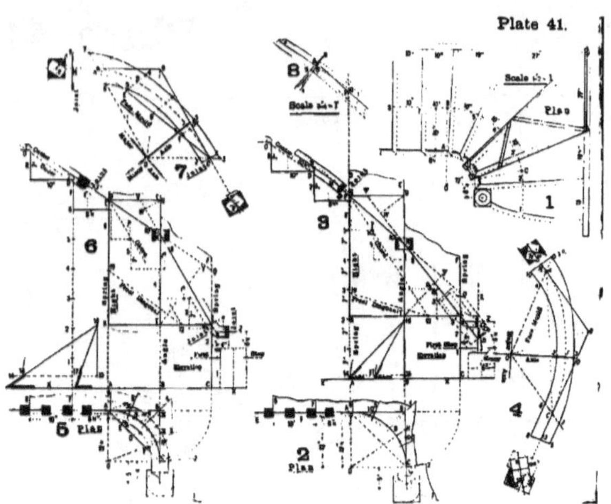

Plate 41.

Plate 42.

Scale 1-4=1'
9"
14 15
18
9" 12
11
10
16 17 18 19
9"
10"
3-2"
8-2"
Plan 1
Face Mould
Joint
Spring
Hight
Angle
5
Joint
Joint
Spring
Angle
Hight
Elevation
4
Face Mould
Joints
Joint
6
Plan 3
X
X
Scale 3-4=1'

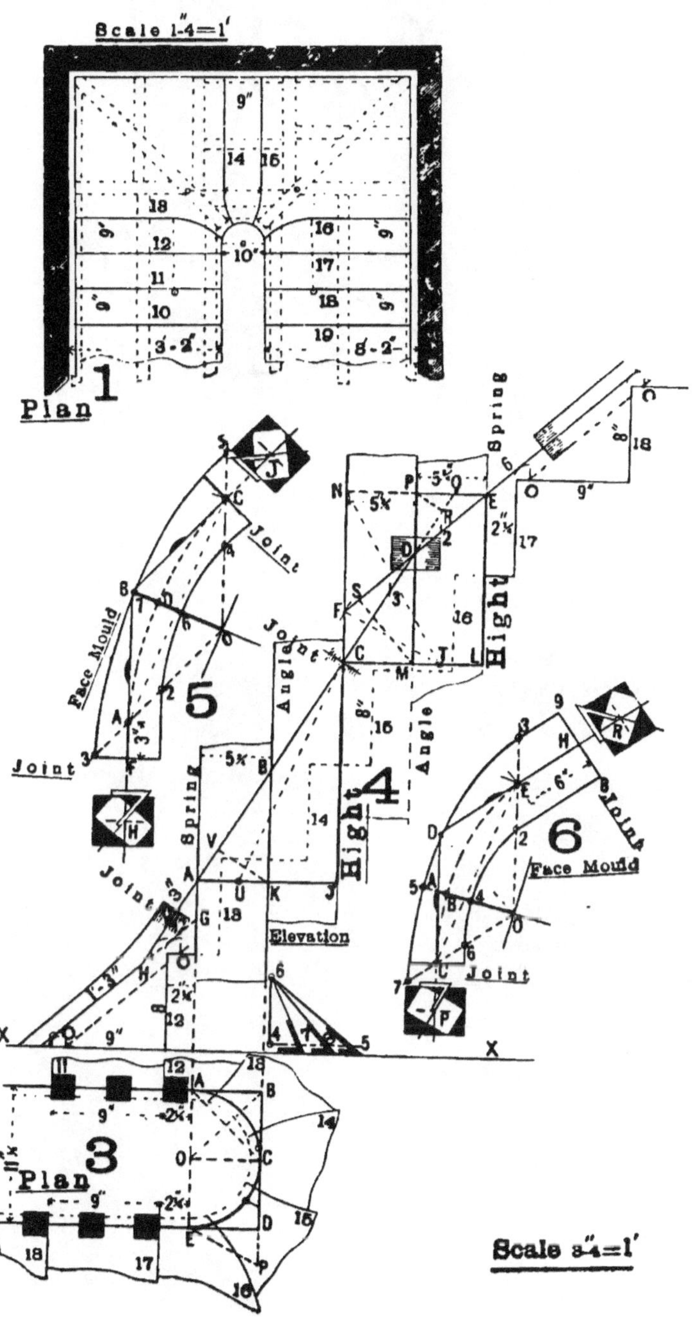

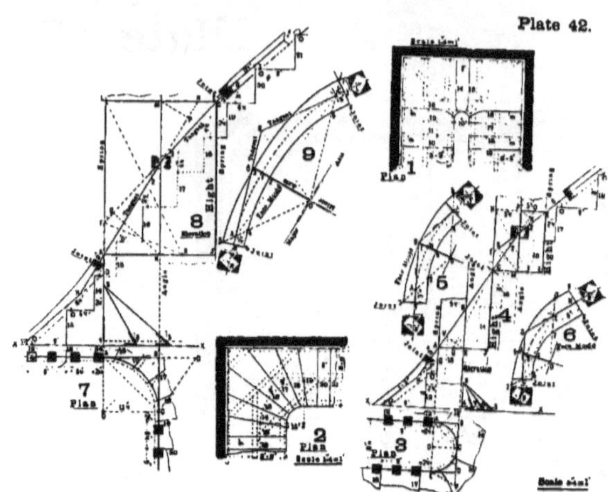

Plate 43.

Plan
6
Scale 1 4=1'
4
Joint
Face Mould
Joint
Floor Line
Spring Joint
Hight Angle
Hight Angle
Joint
10
Face Mould
8
Elevation
Spring Angle
7
Plan
9
Face Mould
Scale 3 4=1'

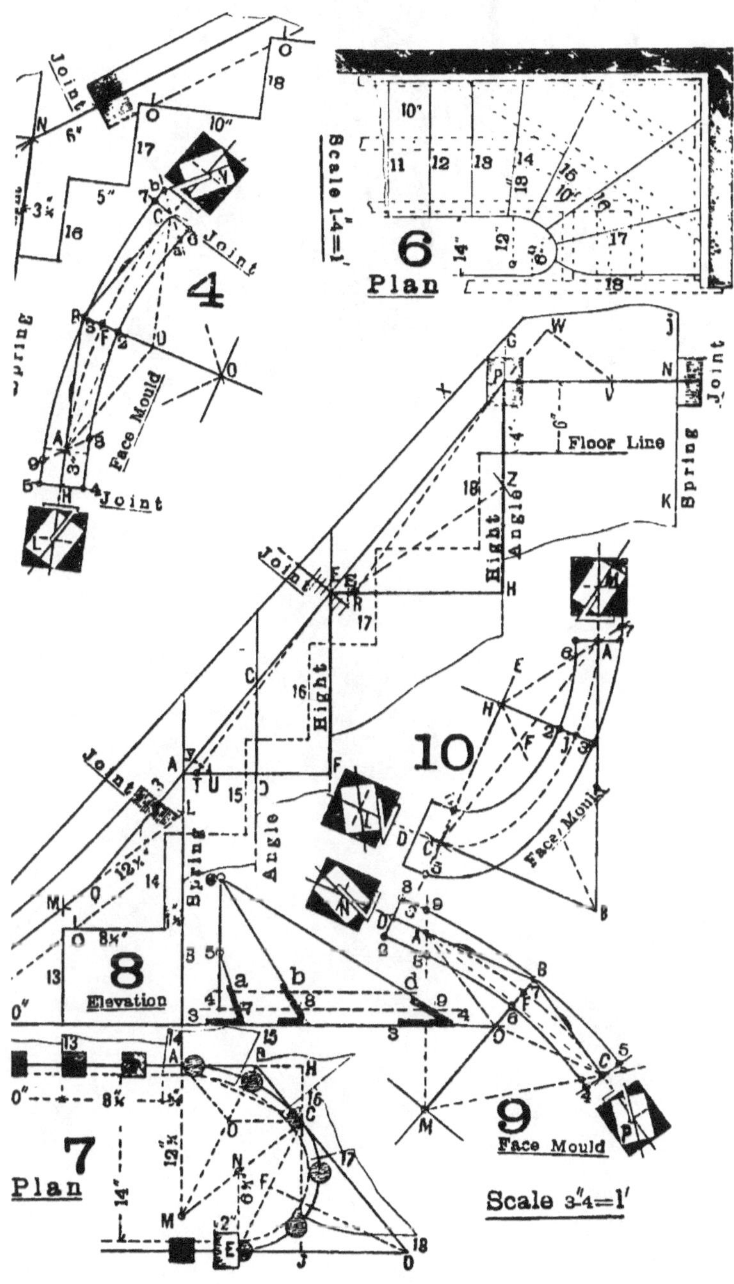

Plate 43.

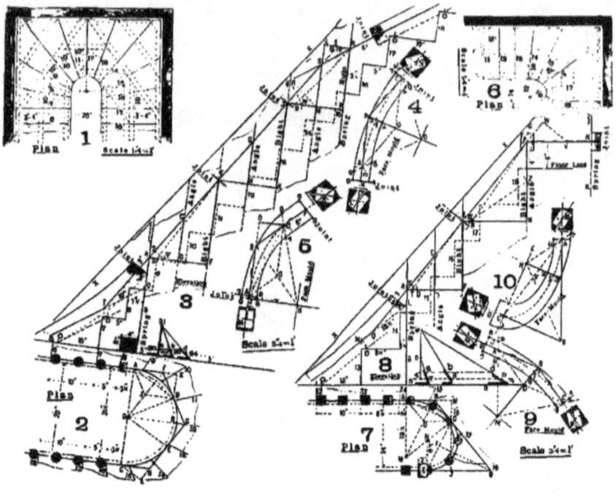
1
Plan
2
Plan
3
Elevation
4
5
6
Plan
7
Plan
8
9
Face Mould
10
Joint
Spring
Angle
Right
Floor Line

Plate 44.

Scale 3"4=1'

8
1
6
J
S
y
7
5
B
C
4
Joint
F
D
No-2
Joint
4
2
P
A
No-1
D
N
G
3
O
B
2
a n
B
K
G
C
H
V
R
W
2
L
F
E
1
Joint
K
b
No-1
Angle
3
Spring
Elevation
Joint
H
a
y a
F
2
5"
First Step
1
G
4
5
N
A
4
D
No-1
Face Mould
B
e
C
H
y
2
M
F
3

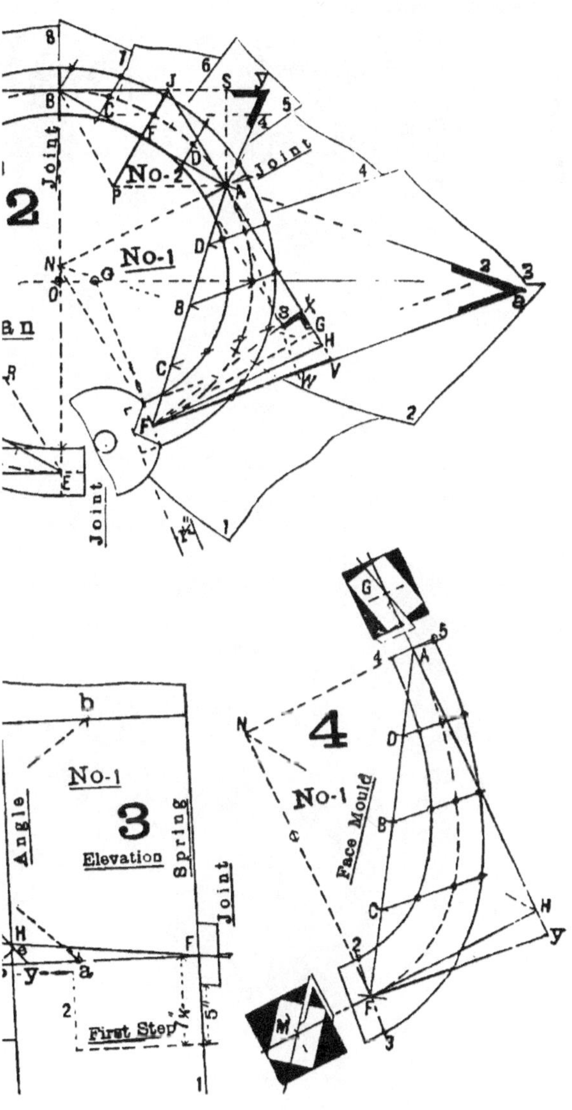

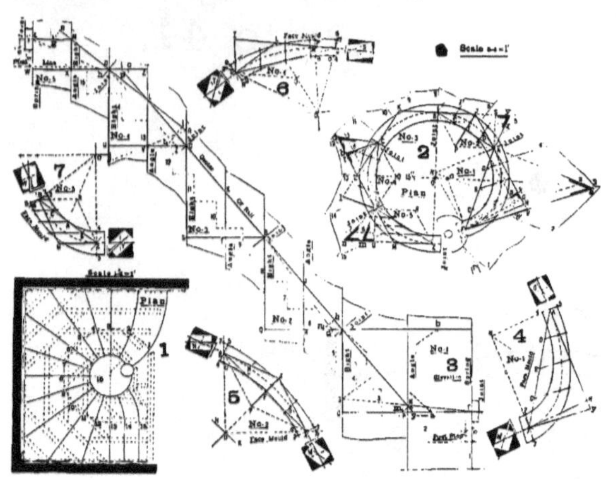

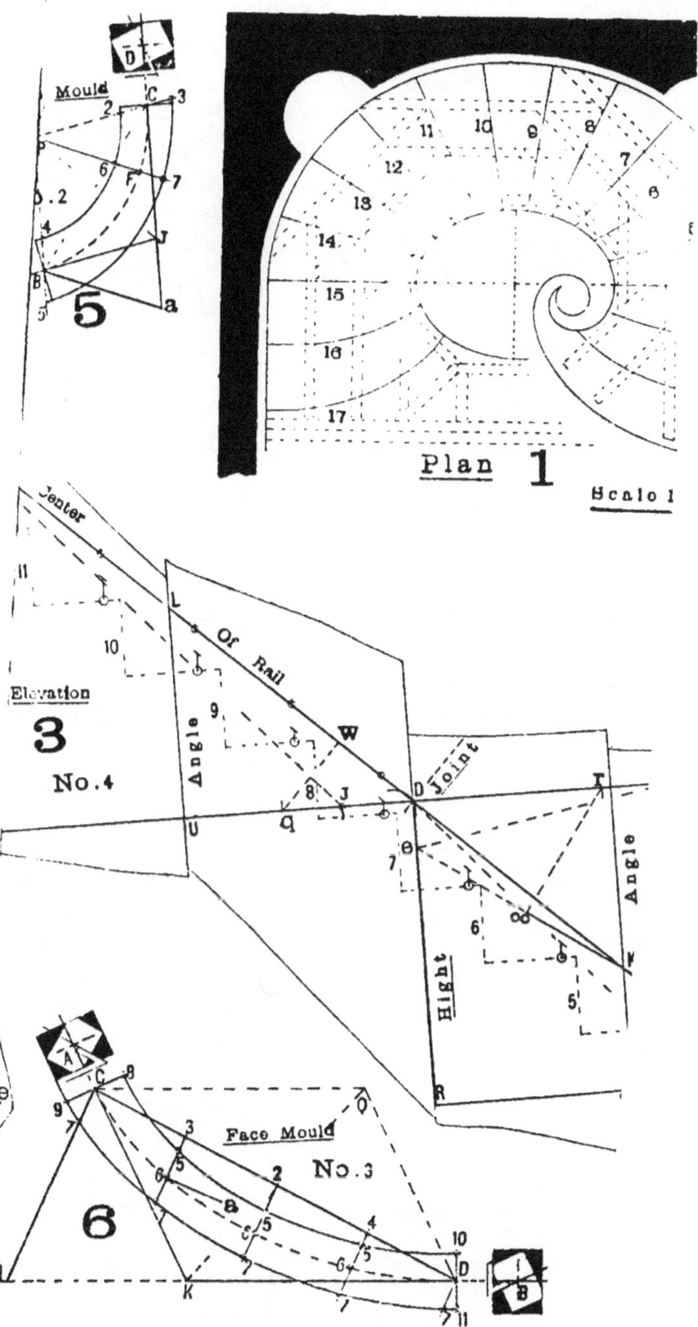

Plate 45.
Mould
5
D
C
2
3
6
7
2
4
B
a
Plan 1
Scale 1
11 10 9 8
12 7
13 6
14
15
16
17
Center
Of Rail
Elevation
3
No.4
Angle
Joint
Hight
Angle
9
W
J
q
U
D
T
Face Mould
No.3
6
A
C
9
7
3
2
5
6
5
4
10
D
B
d
K
11

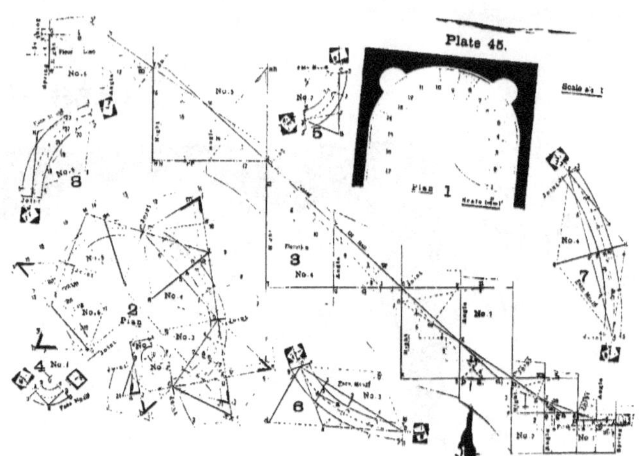

Plate 45.
Scale 2:1
Plan 1

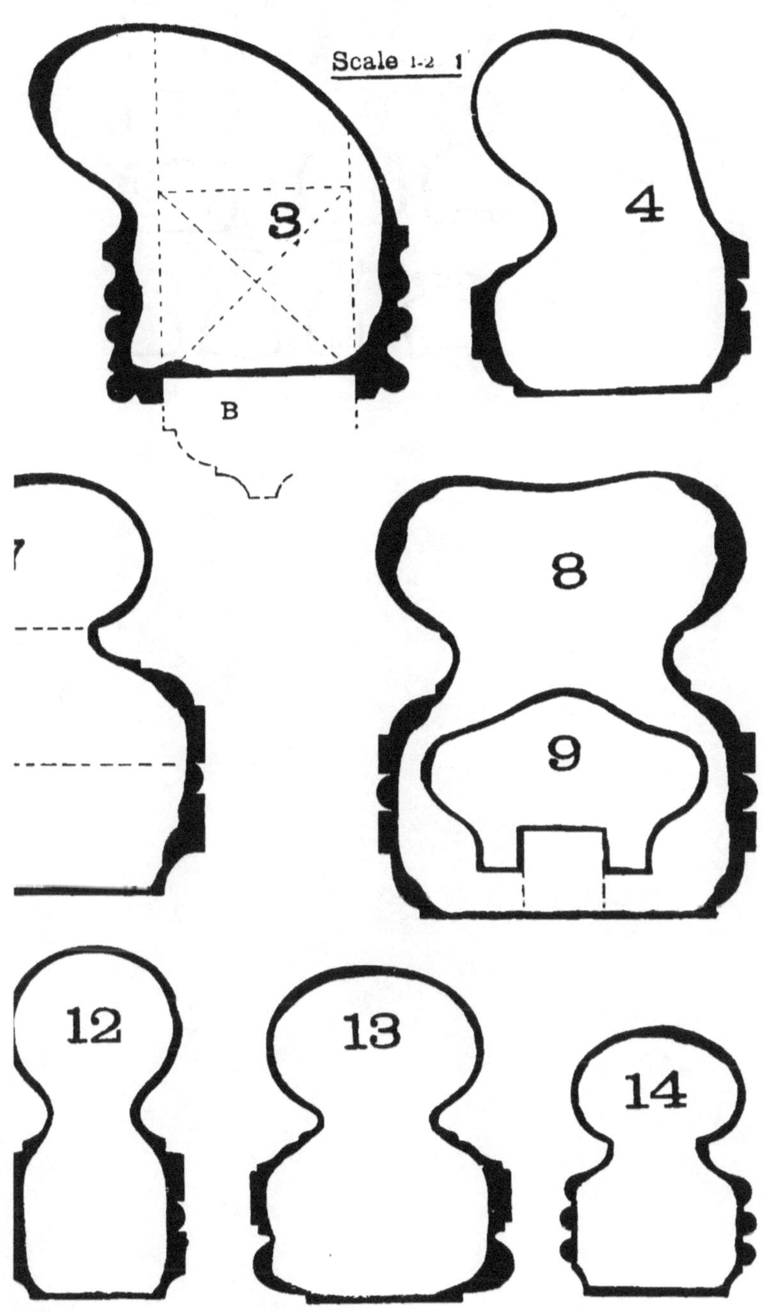
Scale 1·2 1
3
B
4
7
8
9
12
13
14

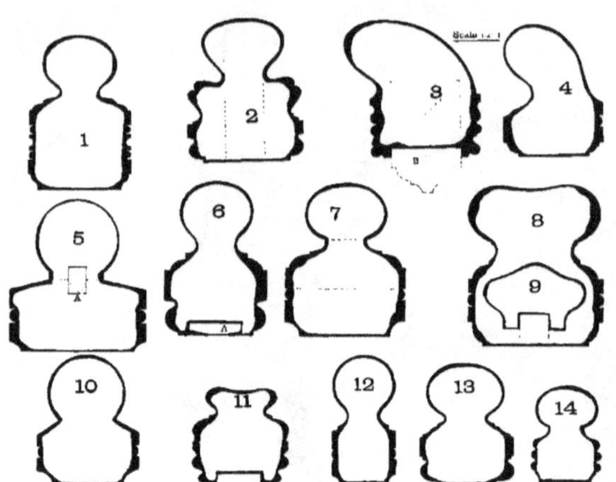

Scale 1:1

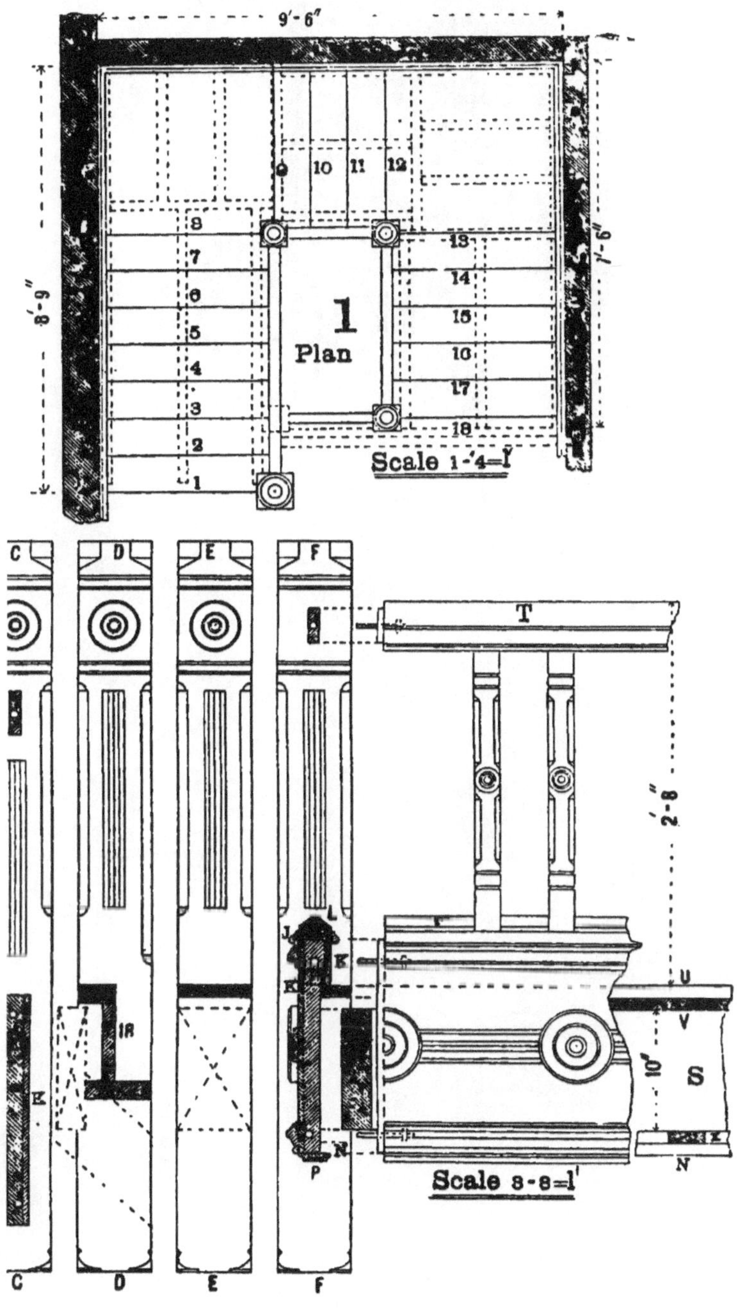
9'- 6"
1'- 6"
8'- 9"
10 11 12
8
7
6
5
4
3
2
1
13
14
15
16
17
18
1
Plan
Scale 1-4=1'
C D E F
T
2'-8"
L
J
K
K
N
P
U
V
10"
S
N
1R
C D E F
Scale 3-8=1'

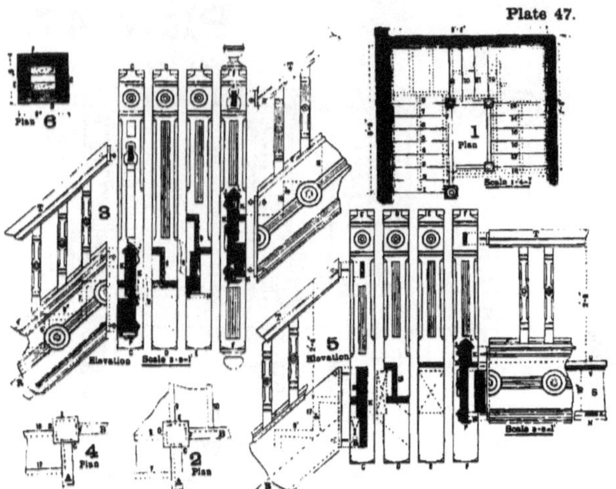

Plate 47.
Plan
6
Plan
Elevation
Scale
3
4
Plan
2
Plan
5
Elevation
1
Plan
Scale
Scale

Plate 48.

5
C
D
E
A
B
A
B
D
E
C
G
Scale 1"2=1'
3
A
E
D
C
B
D
F
Hight
B
C
2
Elevation
J
G
b
y
h
y
b
A
X
V
V
X
F
12-0
K
H
L
Z
B
Z
P
3
B
T
3
B
1
Plan
H
D
J
O
R
b
B
B
B
Z
B
U
G
O
N
A
S
C
Scale 1"4=1'

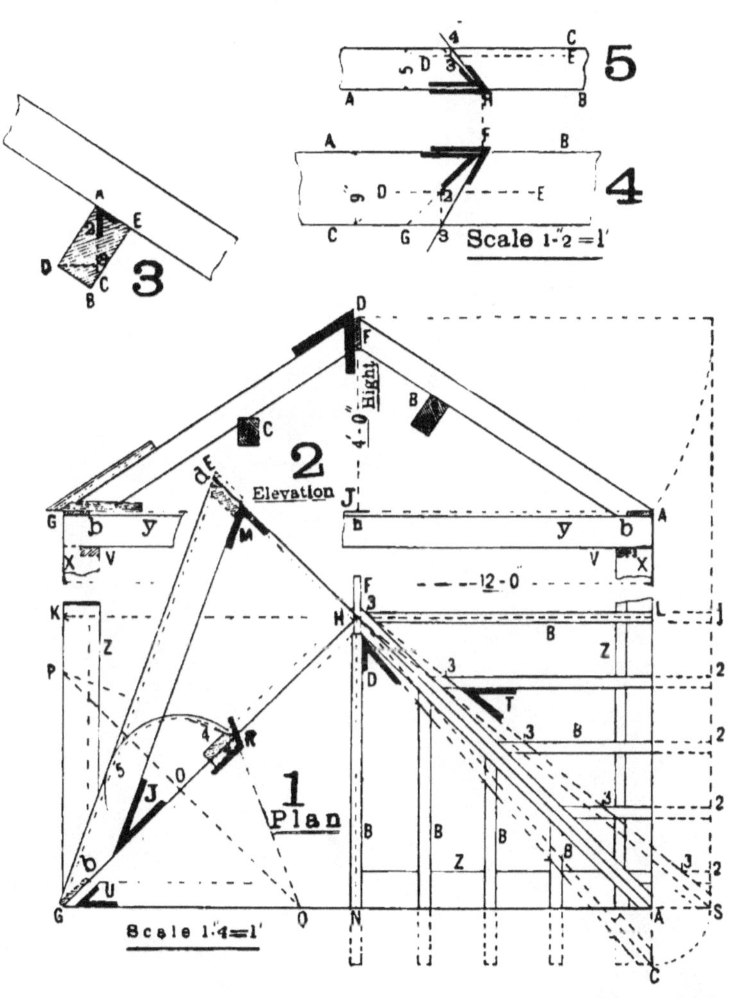

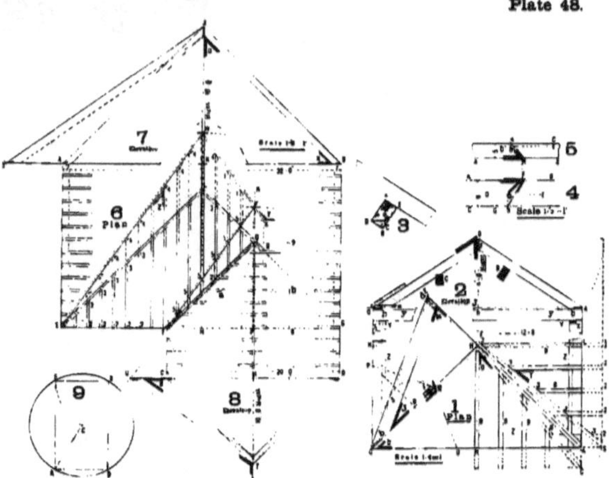

TABLE OF LENGTHS AND CUTS FOR COMMON AND HIP RAFTERS FOR A HIP SQUARE ON PLAN; ALSO, CUT OF JACK RAFTERS AGAINST HIP.

THE LENGTH OF RAFTERS, FOR A FOOT RUN, IS GIVEN IN FEET AND DECIMALS OF A FOOT.

Pitch *	1/12	1/10	1/9	1/8	1/7	1/6	1/5	1/4	1/3	1/2	2/3	3/4	Gothic †
Cut of common rafter,	12" × 2"	12" × 2.4"	12" × 2.666"	12" × 3"	12" × 3.428"	12" × 4"	12" × 4.8"	12" × 6"	12" × 8"	12" × 12"	12" × 16"	12" × 18"	12" × 20.784"
Cut of hip rafter,	17" × 2"	17" × 2.4"	17" × 2.666"	17" × 3"	17" × 3.428"	17" × 4"	17" × 4.8"	17" × 6"	17" × 8"	17" × 12"	17" × 16"	17" × 18"	17" × 20.784"
Cut of jack rafter against the hip.	12" × 12 3/16"	12" × 12 1/4"	12" × 12 5/16"	12" × 12 3/8"	12" × 12 1/2"	12" × 12 5/8"	12" × 12 7/8"	12" × 13 7/16"	12" × 14 1/2"	12" × 16 3/4"	12" × 20"	12" × 21 5/8"	12" × 24"
Length of common rafter, for 12" run, in feet.	1.013'	1.019'	1.024'	1.030'	1.040'	1.054'	1.077'	1.118'	1.201'	1.414'	1.666'	1.803'	1.999'
Length of hip rafter for 12" run of common rafter, in feet.	1.436'	1.440'	1.434'	1.439'	1.442'	1.453'	1.472'	1.502'	1.563'	1.734'	1.943'	2.043'	2.236'
Length of common rafter for 1" run, in decimals of a foot.	0.0845'	0.0849'	0.0854'	0.0859'	0.0866'	0.0878'	0.0898'	0.0931'	0.1001'	0.1178'	0.138'	0.150'	0.166'
Length of hip rafter for 1" run of common rafter, in decimals of a foot.	0.1187'	0.1192'	0.1195'	0.1197'	0.1204'	0.1217'	0.1227'	0.1252'	0.130'	0.144'	0.1621'	0.1718'	0.186'

EXAMPLE.—*Required the cuts and Length of a rafter ¾ pitch having a run of 14' 7''; also the cuts and length of hip for the same.*

FOR THE COMMON RAFTER.	FOR THE LENGTH OF HIP RAFTER.

FOR THE COMMON RAFTER.

In column under ¾ pitch, and on line for common rafter, take for one foot in length the constant ... 1.803'

And multiply the same by the length of rafter in feet, (14') ... 14

Cut off the decimals, and add the odd inches which equals for one inch in the same column 0.1502; that multiply by 7", thus [0.1502" × 7 = 1.0514] ...

run is 26 feet.
And the decimal .2906, which multiply by 12", ...

Equals three [3"] inches and the decimal .4872", that
Multiply by 16 ...

Equals ⁷⁄₁₆ and the decimal .7952", this
Multiply by 2, to reduce the same to thirty-seconds, ...

Equals for the length of rafter 26' 3 ⁷⁄₁₆", ⁷⁄₁₆", or 26' 3 ¹⁵⁄₃₂" ...

FOR THE LENGTH OF HIP RAFTER.

Take the constant 2.0616" in same column ... 2.0616

And multiply by the length of Common rafter, in feet, (14') ... 14

And add the odd inches; for this take the constant 0.1718 for hip rafters from same column, and multiply by the number of odd inches, thus [0.1718 × 7 = 1.2057] equals 1.2057 for the odd inches ...

Gives 30' and the decimal .9841' ...
This multiply by 12" ...

Equals one [1"] inch and the decimal .0672"
Which multiply by 16, ...

Equals ¹⁄₁₆ nearly, therefore we have for the length of rafter 30' 1 ¹⁄₁₆" ...

For the cut of common rafter.—In the same column, take 12" on the blade and 18" on the tongue. The blade gives the foot cut and tongue the plumb cut.

For the cut of hip rafter—In same column, take 17" on the blade and 18" on the tongue. The blade gives the foot cut and the tongue the plumb cut.

For the cut of jacks.—Take 12" on the tongue and 21 ⅝" on the blade. The blade gives the cut.

When cutting hip or jack rafters, take the lengths and apply the bevel on top and at the center of timber, dividing the miter equally each way.

For the cut of hip rafter against the ridge plate.—Take its length; the blade gives the blade and the side, which is equal to the run DE on the tongue; the blade gives the cut. Remember the run only applies when the hip is square on the plan, as at Fig. 1. When rectangular on plan, as of Fig. 2. Take the length CB on the blade and the side DR (as for a jack rafter) on the tongue. The blade gives the cut, provided the ridge plate is running in the direction of AD; if in the direction of JB, then take the length CB on the blade and DQ on the tongue, the blade gives the cut. These cuts are made before the backing is done.

---

* Any pitch defined as ¼, ½, &c., it means that the rise of rafter equals ¼ or ½ (or what it may be) the width of the building. As for a comb roof, having a span of 24 feet and a ¾ pitch, the rise would equal 18 feet, which would be a rise for a shed roof, or lean-to, equal to 36 feet.

† The rafter is equal in length to the span, forming an equilateral triangle for a gothic pitch.

‡ For struts and braces, having the same rise and run, 17" is allowed for each foot run for the length of brace. This is a little full; the correct measure being 16.9705", the difference being a scant ¹⁄₃₂ of an inch.

APPLICATION OF THE STEEL SQUARE IN ROOF FRAMING.

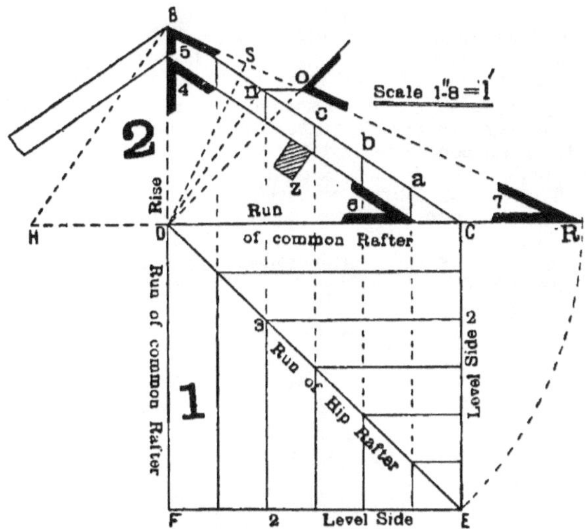

Fig. 1. *Shows plan of a square hip.* **Fig. 2.** *Shows the elevation.*

DCEF shows plan of hip and jack rafters; *DE* is the seat of the hip, having an angle of 45 degrees with the walls; *DC* is the run of a common rafter, and *DB* the rise; *BC* is the length of a common rafter. Make *DR* equal *DE,* join *BR* for the length of hip rafter; from *D* and at right angles to *BR* draw *DS;* perpendicular to *BC* draw *BH;* *Z* shows the purlin.

For the cuts and length of common rafter BC.—Take the run *DC* on the blade and the rise *DB* on the tongue all to a scale. The blade gives the foot cut and the tongue the plumb cut, as shown at 6 and 4; the hypothenuse *BC* gives the length.

For the cuts and length of hip rafter BR.—Take the run *DE* on the blade and the rise *DB* on the tongue to a scale. The blade gives the foot cut and the tongue the plumb cut, as shown at 7 and 5; the hypothenuse *BR* gives the length.

For the cut of jack rafter 2 3 against the hip.—Take *BC* on the blade and the level side *CE* on the tongue. The blade gives the cut, also the cut of hip against the ridge plate if applied on the plane of backing, and from the side of hip in which the jacks are parallel with the ridge, [if on the opposite side of hip, then the tongue gives the cut]. It also gives the miter for the gable mouldings and planceer in a raking cornice. The tongue gives the miter cut of purlin against the hip, also sheathing, gutter stop and level planceer when canted to the pitch of rafters; the foot and plumb cuts are the same as for the common rafter shown at 6 and 4. The length of jack rafters may be established by squaring up from plan to common rafter as shown at *abc,* and as described at Figs. 1 and 2, Plate 49.

For the cut on edge of sheathing.—Take **BH** on the blade and **DH** on the tongue. The tongue gives the cut, also the side cut of purlin against the hip, gutter stop, and level planceer, when canted to the pitch of rafters.

For the backing of hip rafter.—Take **DE** on the blade and **DS** on the tongue. The tongue gives the bevel; the angle for saddle on hip may be laid off from this bevel if required.

To find the cut on the lower end of a hip or valley rafter to line with the common rafter, when they are cut square instead of plumb, for the corona in a raking cornice.—From **D**, Fig. 2, and perpendicular to **CB** draw **Dn**, draw **no** parallel to **DC**, join **DO**. The angle at **O** gives the bevel. Take 12″ on the blade, and adjust the tongue to **DO** from the line **BO**, the tongue gives the cut.

The above cuts for jack rafters, purlins and hip backing, are for hips when square on plan. When rectangular on plan, follow Figs. 3, 4 and 5.

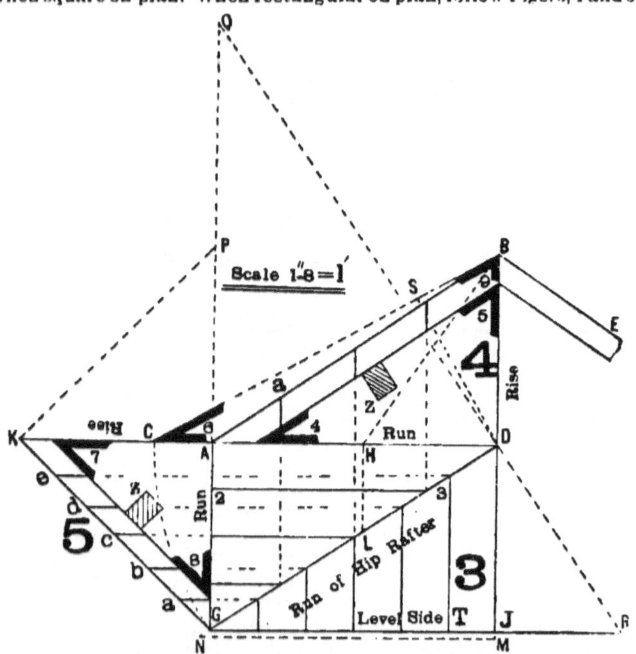

Fig. 3. *Shows plan of a hip accommodating two pitches, the seat **GD** of hip being the diagonal of a rectilineal parallelogram **ADJG** on plan. Figs. 4 and 5 show the elevation of common rafters.*

AD is the run and **DB** the rise for the rafter **AB**; **AG** is the run and **AK** the rise for the rafter **GK**; [**BE** has the same inclination as **AB**]. Perpendicular to **BE** draw **BH**; at right angles to **AD** draw **HL**. Make **DC** equal **DG**, join **BC** for length and inclination of hip rafter. From **D** and at right angles to **BC** draw **DS**; from **D** and square to **DG** draw a line to intersect **GA** prolonged at **Q**, also intersect **GJ** produced at **R**; at right angles to **KG** draw **KP**. Make **DM** equal **AP**; from **M** draw a line parallel with **GJ** to intersect **DG** prolonged at **N**.

For the cuts and length of common rafter **AB** *for the side* **AGD.**—Take the run **AD** on the blade and the rise **DB** on the tongue to a scale. The blade gives the foot cut and the tongue the plumb cut. as shown at 4 and 5 ; the hypothenuse **AB** gives the length.

For the cuts and length of hip rafter **CB.**—Take the run **GD** on the blade and the rise **DB** on the tongue to a scale. The blade gives the foot cut and the tongue the plumb cut, as shown at 6 and 9 ; the hypothenuse **CB** gives the length.

For the cut of jack rafters against the hip.—Take **AB** on the blade and the level side **AG** on the tongue. The blade gives the cut, also the cut of hip against the ridge plate, if applied on the plane of backing and from the side in which the jacks are parallel to the ridge plate—[if applied from the opposite side then the tongue gives the cut]. The blade also gives the miter cut for the gable mouldings and planceer in a raking cornice ; the tongue gives the miter cut for the purlin against the hip. sheathing. gutter stop and level planceer that is canted to the pitch of rafters. The foot and plumb cuts are shown at 4 and 5 for the jacks. and their lengths are found in the same manner as described for Figs. 1 and 2.

To find the side cut for purlin.—Take **BH** on the blade and and **HL** on the tongue. The tongue gives the cut, also the cut for sheathing on its edge, also the gutter stop, and level planceer when canted to the pitch of rafters.

To find the bevel for backing the hip.—Take **DQ** on the blade and **DS** on the tongue. The tongue gives the bevel for one side of hip.

For cuts and length of common rafter **GK,** *on the opposite side* **GDJ.**—Take the run **GA** on the blade and the rise **AK** on the tongue to a scale. The blade gives the foot cut, the tongue the plumb cut. as shown at 8 and 7 ; the hypothenuse **GK** gives the length ; **CB** shows the length and cuts of hip.

For the cut of jack rafter **T**3 *against the hip.*—Take **GK** on the blade and **GJ** on the tongue. The blade gives the cut, also cut of hip rafter against the ridge plate, provided it is applied on the plane of backing and from the side in which the jacks run parallel to the ridge plate—[if applied from the opposite side then the tongue gives the cut]. The blade also gives the miter cut for the gable mouldings and planceer in a raking cornice ; the tongue gives the miter cut for the purlin against the hip. sheathing. gutter stop. and level planceer to suit the pitch of rafters ; 4 and 5 show the foot and plum cuts : their several lengths are described at Figs. 1 2, and 5.

For the side cut of purlin.—Take **KP** on the blade and **MN** on the tongue. The tongue gives the cut, also the cut for edge of sheathing. gutter stop, and level planceer to suit the pitch of rafters.

Bevel for the backing of hip rafter.—Take **DR** on the blade and **DS** on the tongue. The tongue gives the bevel for the one side, and together with the bevel for the opposite side will give the angle for the saddle on hip if required.

The points *a, b, c, d, e,* Fig. 5. show the lengths of jack rafters for the side **GDJ;** the half thickness of hip must be deducted. Remember in deducting the half thickness of hip. or ridge plate when required. it must be measured square to the plane of the cut and not square to the plumb cut. The lengths **Ga, Gb,** &c , as here drawn, are to the center of hip. and the hips to the center of ridge plate.

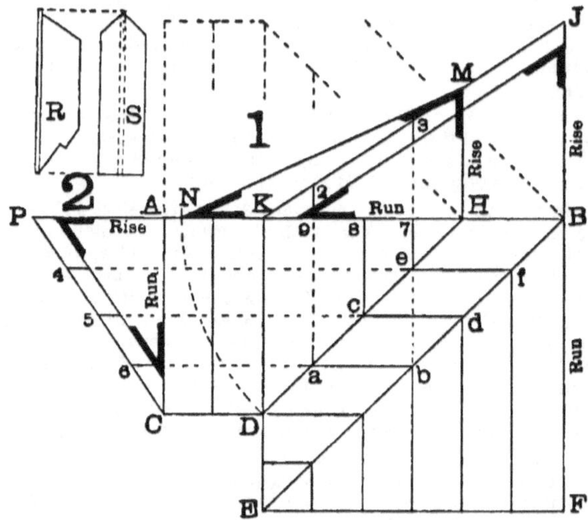

Fig. 1.—*(Scale, one-eighth inch equals one foot).* *Shows one side of a roof having a ¾ pitch and a square hip and valley. How to find the length of valley and cripples between the valley and hip.*

A, B, C, D, E, F, shows the plan of roof; **EB** shows hip, **DH** shows seat of valley; **ab, cd, ef** shows the seat of cripples; **CA** is a gable and **AH** the ridge.

Draw **BJ** for the rise; make **BK** equal **EF**; join **JK** for the length of common rafter. From **H**, and perpendicular to **AB**, draw a line to intersect the common rafter at **M**, then **MH** is the rise of valley rafter. Make **HN** equal **HD**; join **MN** for the length and cuts of valley rafter.

For the length of cripple **ab.**—From the points **a** and **b** erect perpendiculars to intersect the common rafter **JK** at 2 and 3; the valley and hip being both parallel, then the distance 2 3 is the length for all the cripples between the hip and valley rafters.

For the length of cripples between the ridge and valley rafter.—Make **AP** equal the rise **HM**; join **PC** for the length and cuts of the gable rafter. From the points **a, c, e**, erect perpendiculars to **CA**, cutting **PC** at 4, 5 and 6; then **P4, P5** and **P6** show the length of cripples e7, c8 and a9 on plan.

Fig. 2. *(Scale three-eighths inch equals one foot).* *Shows the template for marking the heel and side cuts of jack rafters.*

A shows the side and **B** the top.

The cuts for the cripples at the valley rafters are the same as for a hip rafter, only the plumb cut is the reverse way, the long point being on the under side.

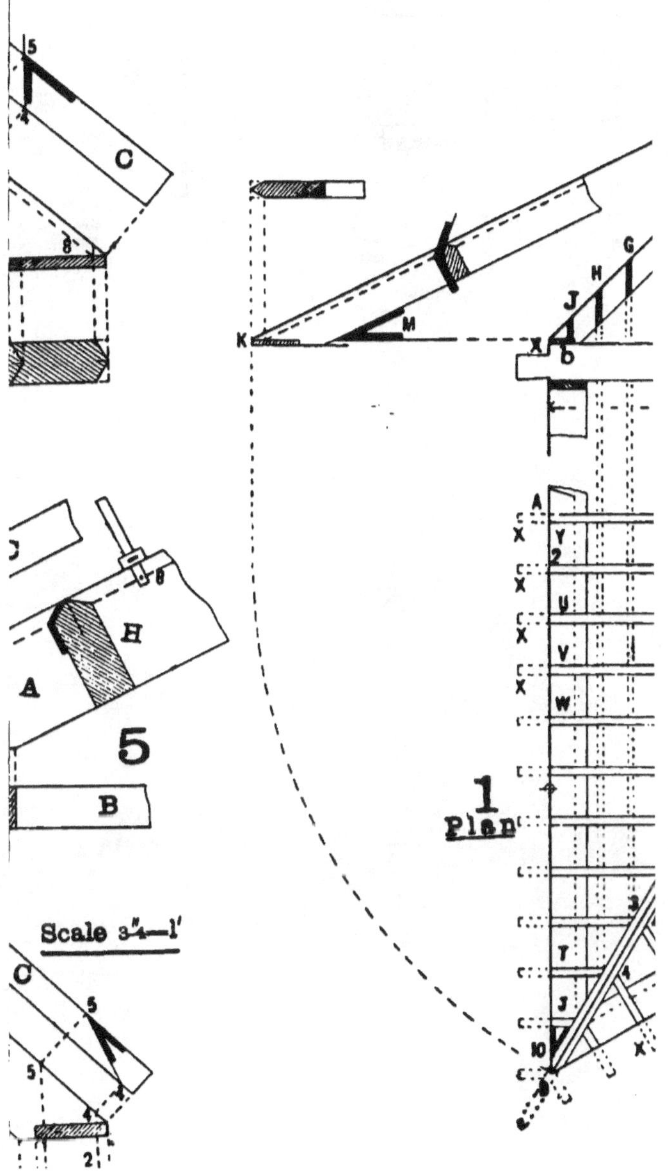
C
5
4
8
G
H
J
M
K
X
D
5
A
H
B
5
Scale 3"4=1'
C
5
5
Y
2
A
X
Y
2
X
U
X
V
X
W
1
Plan
T
J
3
4
T
J
10
X

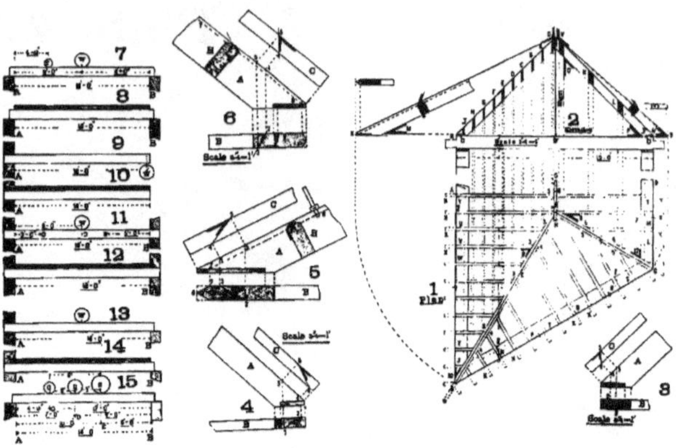

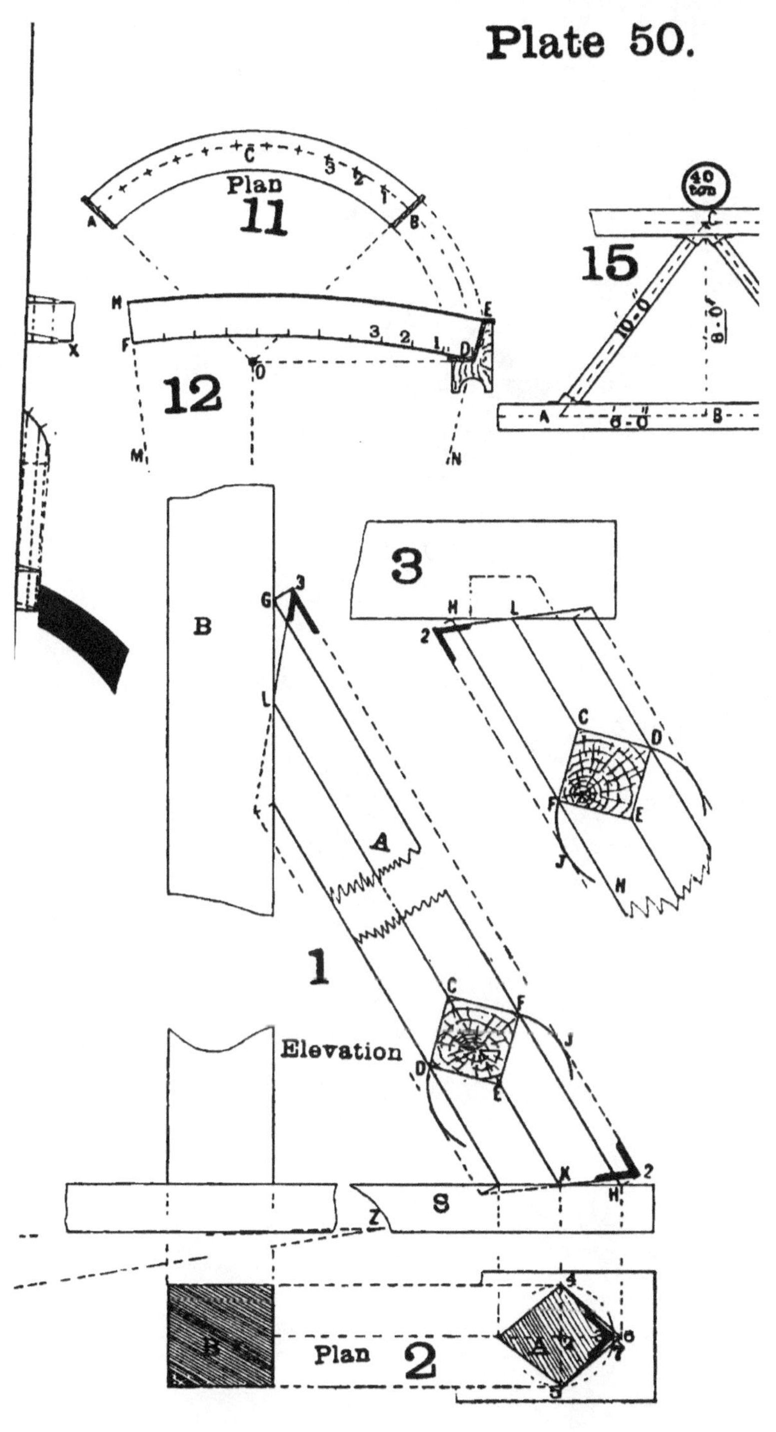

Plate 50.
Plan
11
12
15
40 TON
Elevation
1
Plan
2
3
B
A
S
Z
Plan

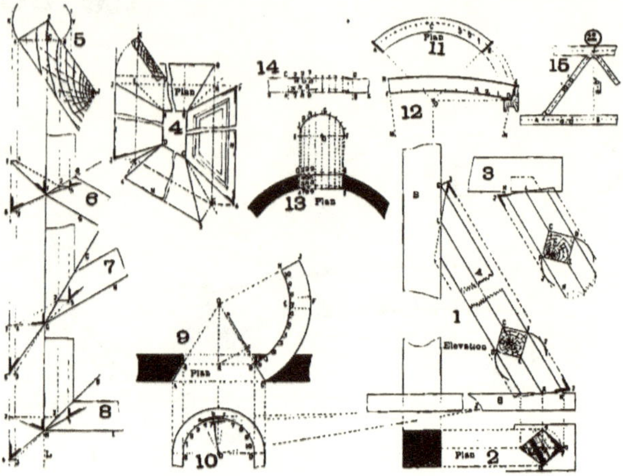
5
4
Plan
14
11
Plan
15
12
13
Plan
3
6
7
1
Elevation
9
Plan
8
10
Plan
2

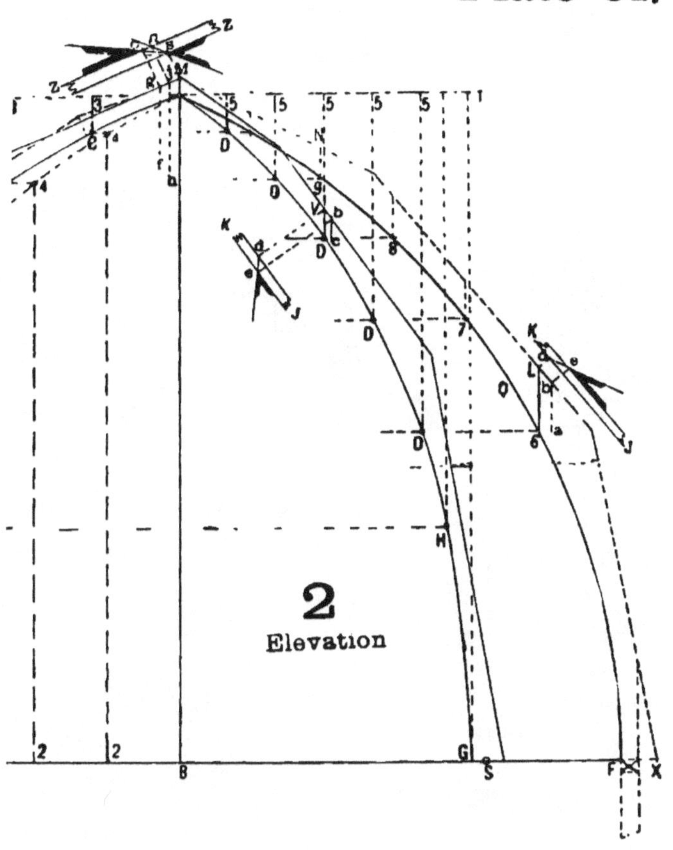
2
Elevation

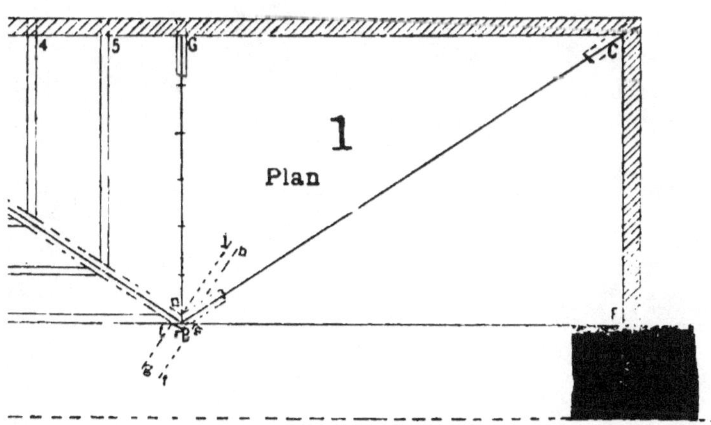
1
Plan

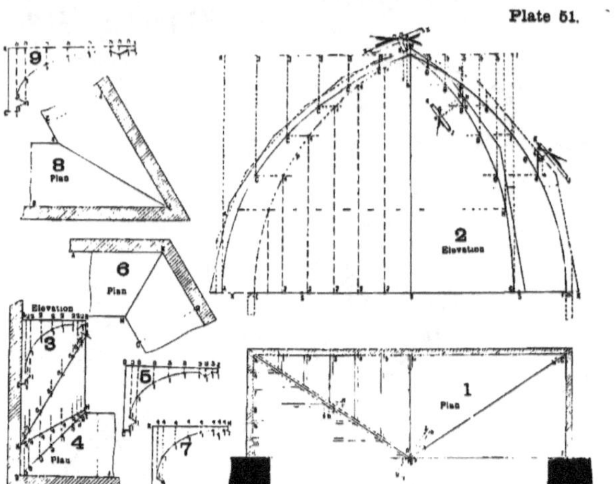

APPENDIX No. 2.

PLATE 52.

Plate 52. [Scale ⅛ =1] Square Hip and Octagon Roof Framing.

Fig. 8. *Shows a practical and simple method how to develope the length and cuts of the common hip and jack rafters on the pitching plane, for a square hip and for any pitch.*

Let *ABCD* be the plan for two square hips, and *AF*, *FB* be the seat of hips; draw the seat of jack rafters to intersect the seat line of hip, as *EF*, et. dr, &c. Make *EJ* equal *FB* join *FJ* for the length and cuts of the hip rafter. It will be observed now for a half pitch roof, we have the length of hip *JF* and the common rafter *AF* and the length of the jack rafters; *At* equals the length of jack to stand over the seat *et; Ar* to stand over *dr, &c.*

Bevels. The bevel at *8* gives the down and foot cuts for the common and jacks rafters; the bevels at *9* and *10* give the down and foot cuts for the hip *FJ;* for the cut of jacks against the hip, prolong *dr* to equal its length *Ar*, as *dg*, join *Ag* for the bevel at *g.* For the cut of hip against the ridge plate at *11;* take any point on the seat *FB* of hip, say at the intersection of the jack from *i* at *u*, draw *uL* at right angles to *FB;* from *u* and parallel to the base line *AB*, draw a line to intersect the hip as *u3;* make *uG* equal *J3*, join *LG* for the bevel as shown.

This completes the drawing for a pair of rafters, two hips and the length of 6 jack rafters and the cuts for the same for a ½ pitch roof; the bevel as shown for the cut of hip against the ridge plate is applied before backing.

For a ¼ pitch the principle is the same: let *EG* be ¼ the span *AB*, join *AG* and *GB;* the intersection with the seat of jacks gives the length of jack on the common rafter *AG* as at *z* and *s; As* is the length of the jack to stand over its seat *et*, and so of all the rest respectively. For the length and cuts of hip, join *GJ;* for the cut of hip against the ridge plate, from *k* draw *k2*, make *u5* equal *J2*, join *5L* for the bevel at *5;* for the cut of jack against the hip prolong the seat of jack *et* to equal its increased length *As* as *eh*, join *Ah* for the bevel as shown.

For a ⅔ pitch this system is the same. Let *EH* equal ⅔ the span *AB*, join *AH* and *BH* for a pair of common rafters and their cuts; join *HJ* for the length and cuts of hip rafter; for the length of the jacks prolong their seats to insert the common rafter at *x* and *y;* then *Ay* is the length of jack to stand over its seat *et*, and so of all the rest; for the cut of jack against the hip, prolong the seat *Bu* to equal its increased length *Ap*, as *bf*, join *Af* for the bevel required at *f.* For the miter of hip against the ridge plate, prolong *iu* to *u*, draw *u4* parallel to *AB;* make *u7* equal *J4*, join *7 L* for the bevel as shown.

This is the most simple method to line off a square hip, less lines and room is required by this system; if the hip be backed less lines may be used, the bevels shown at *f, g* and *h*, for the jacks will also give the miter cut for their respective hips against the ridge-plate if applied on the plane of backing. PLATE 49 shows the most practical method to obtain the different bevels, also the backing.

The young man should first study how to draw the lines on the board for a hip and valley roof, then from the drawing thus made to a #4" scale, proceed to frame the roof. For a square hip it is very easy to apply the square for all the principal cuts, but for a hip or valley that accommodates two pitches it is more difficult, a drawing then is necessary, and if the student first learns to draw off the roof, he afterwards will be better qualified to find his way out when framing one more complicated, even with the steel square.

Fig 9. [Scale ⅛ =1] *Shows the end of a building finished with octagonal corners.*

The octagon is carried up to the comb of main roof instead of a gable; one side of the octagon to admit windows is shown increased in width, the cornice is to project the same at the eaves and to be raking; unless the workman has had some experience in the framing of such a roof he may be taken unawares.

Let *AB, BC, CD, DE* and *EF*. Fig. 9, indicate the outside measurements of walls and *GH, HJ, JK, KL* and *LM* the projection for the ends of rafters to receive the cornice. Now from the points *H, J, K* and *L* draw lines to the centre *O* for the seat lines of hips, also space off and draw the seat of jack rafters as may be desired.

Let it be observed that the seat of hips does not intersect the angle of walls at the points *BCD* and *E*, but cuts to one side, this cannot be avoided in a roof with two pitches and a raking cornice, for the look-outs for a cornice having the same projection all around and of different pitches, the points of hips and other rafters must be on the same level, therefore we must draw their seats from the utmost projection. If the cornice was a level one then the seat of hips may be drawn from the points *BCD* and *E*.

Now *AF* equals the span of building and *OG, OM* and *Of,* show the seat of common rafters and they are equal from the centre *O;* but the seats *OK, On* are longer, therefore we have two pitches; the planes *OML, OGH* and *OJK* have the same pitch; but the planes *OHJ* and *OKL* have a flatter pitch; their length, pitch and location of the wall plates must be determined by drawing them in elevation.

Fig. 10. *Shows in elevation the pitch and length of the different rafters, also the location of the wall plates, all on the pitching plane.*

Draw the base line *XX ;* from *b* erect the perpendicular *bo* equal to the rise of roof; make *ba* equal *OA* Fig. 9; draw *oa* prolonged to intersect the horizontal projection of rafter at *c;* from *c* and parallel to *XX* draw *cm* indefinate; now the points of all the rafters must terminate at this line *cm* as shown. At *a* is shown the wall plate; next set off the width of look-out required for the cornice and draw the back of rafter intersecting *bo* at *v.* then *vo* is the heighth above the plate on line with the wall at *a* for all the rafters.

Make *bd* equal *Ot* on plan Fig. 9; draw *od* prolonged to intersect the line *mc* at *q;* from *v* and parallel to *oq* draw the back of hip rafter, the common and hip rafter are now the same plumb heighth on the plates *a* and *d*, at the wall line. Make *ln* equal *OK* Fig. 9, join *on;* thus establishing the flatter pitch for the planes *OKL* and *OHJ* on plan Fig. 9. Make *lp* equal *Os* Fig. 9; from *p* erect the perpendicular intersecting *on*, at *s* draw *SK*, thus establishing the position of the wall plates for the flatter pitch relative to the wall plates for the steeper pitch; observe the plate at *s* drops down below that at *a* about *"*1½, this will require the plates *BC* and *DE* Fig. 9 to be framed *"*1½ lower than those for *AB, CD* and *EF*, as the difference in this case is so little another way would be to notch out at *s* 1½ *"* more on all the jacks and construct all the plates to the same level if the look-outs would not be too much weakened, this the workman would be governed by his judgement. Make *lm* equal the seat *OL* Fig. 9, join *om* intersecting *ab* prolonged at *r;* from *v* draw the back of common rafter paralell to *so* and also the back of hip rafter parallel to *om*, thus establishing their proper heighth above the plates at the wall line.

Next, draw the length of jacks from plan to elevation as shown the length of jacks *de, ab* and *gh* on plan Fig. 9, are shown in elevation as *CG. CE* and *nt.* The jack *de* on plan, scales [3' 10½+ 1', 7½=5', 6] in elevation 5' 6"; the jack *ab* on plan, scales [1' 3"+1' 7½' =3' 10½"] in elevation 3', 10½"; the rafter at *f* on plan buts the end of ridge plate and scales [6' 3" plus 1' 7½" equals 7', 10½'] in elevation 7', 10½" for the total length to the long points; the length of jacks for the planes *OJK* and *OLM* are the same as for the plane *OGH*. The length of jack *gh* on plan scales [2'. 7½"+1, 6½=4', 2] in elevation 4', 2" for its total length; the jacks at *n* and *k* on plan miter between two hips, and scale [6', 7 +1, 6½=8', 1½"] to the long point 8', 1½ in elevation; the common rafter GO miters to the hip OH and scales [6′, 7½″+1′, 7½″=8′, 2″] in elevation 8′ 2″. The two hips OL and OH miter to the ridge plate and scale [7, 3″+1′, 9½=9′, 0″½] for their length 9′, 0½′; the hips OJ and OK on plan, miter against the ridge and adjacent hips as shown and scales [7′, 0″+ 1′, 9½′=8′, 9½″] for their length in elevation 8′, 9½″. Observe the lower end of hip is cut to the bevel at i and the length is measured square from the point at q; make all measurements on the back of rafters by first lining off for the projection of cornice to the line of wall, then the exact length from wall to the point of rafters; use a ternplate shown at Fig. 7 to line off all look-outs and cuts for the different rafters.

Observe at t on plan the seat of hip intersects the line of wall to one side of the angle C; now in mitering the planceer the centre of hip will be the centre of miter, this will look bad, as the miter should run from angle J to angle C; to accomplish this two methods may be adopted, either to cut the look-outs for the planes OGH, OJK and OML by dropping as shown by the dotted lines at c and q Fig 10 and thus make the pitch for the planceer agree with the lesser pitch os; or to make the pitch of planceer for the lesser pitch os agree with the greater pitch oa by reducing the look-outs at S as shown by the dotted line, this reduction will only be for the three jacks on each side for the odd pitch, the hips and all other rafters will remain straight; the better way then will be to make the underside of look-outs for the lesser pitch agree with those of the greater pitch in this case; this will allow the raking planceer to miter from angle to angle.

Bevels. The bevels at a and f give the foot and down cut for all the common and jack rafters for the steep pitch; the bevels shown at u and s, give the foot and plumb cuts for the lesser pitch; the bevels at d and o give the foot and down cuts for all the hips. *For the cut of hip at the lower end to agree with the square ends of the jacks.* From b and perpendicular to the back of rafter oc draw hb, draw hi paralell to XX, join bi for the bevel shown at i; this bevel gives the cut on side of hips for the planes OGH, OML and OJK; for the opposite side of hips on the planes OHJ and OKL Fig. 9; from K and perpendicular to the back of rafter so draw wk; draw wy parallel to XX, join yk for the bevel required.

For the mitre cut of hips HO and LO against the ridge-plate. Apply the bevel shown at 6 to the sole cut of hip as shown for Plate 49, this bevel will also give the cut on top of the hip at the lower end for one side, for the opposite side on the lesser pitch the bevel at J applied in the same way will give the cut.

For the cut of jacks against the hips. On plan Fig. 9 prolong ab to equal its increaseed length In elevation as ac, join c to the side of rafter at y; the bevel at c gives the miter cut for all the jacks on the planes OGH, OJK and OML, the bevel in the angle at y gives the cut for the sheathing and edge cut of corona, also the cut of the two hips HO and LO against the ridge plate, also for the back of hips at the lower end for the above planes if applied after backing.

The same bevels may be found from the sole cut of common rafter by applying the bevel at 3, also the miter cut for the hips OK and OJ at their upper ends by applying the bevels shown at 4 and 5 Fig. 9 For the cut of jacks against the hips on the planes OHJ and OKL; prolong the seat of jack gh to equal nt in elevation, as gi join iv, the bevel at i gives the cut, the bevel at v gives the cut of sheathing also the edge cut of corona and the cut on the back of hips at the lower end if applied after backing.

To find the bevel to miter the planceer. If the planceer was to miter so as to agree with the hips as drawn, then the bevels shown at H and K would give the miter cut for their respective pitches, and the bevels shown at z and j would give the cut on the edge; also for the edge cut of sheathing.

But the look-outs being all cut to agree with the regular pitch oa; then from E Fig. 9, and perpendicular to KL draw Ex prolonged to

equal cut Fig. 10, as at *r*, join *rL*, the bevel at *L* gives the miter cut
for the planceer ; *for the cut on the edge of planceer.*   At Fig. *B*
draw the right angle *spm*, let *sn* be the inclination of the look-out
on its under side, and *sm* equal the pitch of the miter over the seat
EL on plan Fig. 9; from *p* and perpendicular to *sn*, draw *pt*
from *t* and parallel to *pm* draw *tr*, with *P* for a centre and *pr* for a
radius draw arc to intersect *sn* at *f*, join *fp* for the bevel required.
*For the cut of corona or outer fascia on the eaves GH, ML and
JK Fig. 9.*   Return to Fig. 10, with *b* for a centre and *bi* for a
radius draw arc to intersect *ru* at *j*, join *jb* for the bevel required.
For the bevel on the eaves *HJ* and *KL* Fig. 9; at Fig. 10 take *k* for a
centre and *ky* for a radius draw arc to intersect the back of rafter *rn*
at *z* for the bevel required.   These two bevels also give the edge cut
of sheathing on their respective planes, also in case purlines are used
they give the side cut against the hip rafters.

Figs. 11 and 12.   [Scale ⅛″=1′]   *Shows the plan and elevation of a spire on an octagon base and how to obtain the lengths and
cuts of timbers.*

Fig 11.   *Shows one half the plan.*   Draw the rectangle *A BGH.*
for one half the plan, bisect *AB* at *L*; with *G* for a center and the
diagonal *GL* for a radius, draw the arc from *L* to *E*; make *HF, GC,
GD,* equal *HE*; join *EF* and *CD* for one half the octagon base.   Join
LC LD, LE and *LF*, for the seat of the hips; *a, a,* shows twisted
irons bolted to the girts and hips for binders at the several bays.

Fig. 12.   *Shows the length and cuts of the hips, girts and struts
in elevation and development*

Let *AB* indicate a base line, draw *LJ* perpendicular to *AB*, make
LD and *LE* equal *KD* and *KE* on plan Fig. 11; also make *LA* and
LB, equal *LA* and *LB* on plan Fig. 11.   Make *LC,* equal *LC* on
plan.   Now determine the height of spire as *LI,* join *IB* and *IA,*
for the inclination of the side, join *IC* for the inclination of the hip;
yy shows the girts.

To find the development of one side of the spire ; make *LJ*
equal *AI* join *JD* and *JE,* parallel to *JD* and *JE,* draw the face
of backing; make *Lzz,* equal *Ayy,* for the spacing of the girts.   Now
draw the struts as shown, this gives all the miters or face cuts for
the struts and girts for the different bays; the bevel shown at *D* gives
all the miter cuts for the girts; the bevels at *3* and *4,* give the miter
cuts for the struts in the first bay; the bevels shown at *5* and *6,* gives
the miter cuts for the struts of the second bay; those for the upper
bay are shown in the proper place.   The bevels at *u, t* and *r* give the
cuts at the crossing of the struts.

Now for the side cut of the girts and struts against the hips ; draw
the dotted lines *sq, po* and *mn* at the center of the struts and to
intersect the sides *JD, JE,* and also the perpendicular *JL,* at the
points *u, t* and *r.*   Make *Ab, Ac* and *Ab* equal *Lu, Lt* and *Lr*;
from *b, c* and *d,* draw perpendiculars to *AI* intersecting *LJ* at *a, e*
and *f.*   *Now for the side cut of girts against the hip;* from *b,* and
parallel to *AB* draw *bh,* join *ah* prolonged; with *a* for a center and
ah for a radius draw arc to intersect the inclination *AI* at *i,* join *ai*
for the bevel required.   If the girts are to be gained into the hips,
the bevel at *h* gives the cut on the hip.   *For the side cut of the
struts against the hips.*   At *u,* and perpendicular to *mn* draw *ug,*
equal to *ba* join *gm,* also *gn*; the bevels at *m* and *n* give the side
cut for all the struts of the first bay; for the second bay, from *t,* and
perpendicular to *po,* draw *tj* equal to *ce,* join *jp* and *jo* for the
bevels at *p* and *o* required for the side cuts of all the struts for the
second bay; for the third bay, from *r,* and perpendicular to *sq,* draw
rk equal in length to *df,* join *ks* and *kq,* the bevels at *s* and *q* give the
side cuts for all the struts of the third bay.   The bevel shown at *B
2,* give the foot and down cuts for the sides, if required, and the
bevels shown at *c* and *8* give the foot and down cuts for the hips; the
bevel shown at *D* also give the miter cut of sheathing, and the bevel
shown at *i* gives the cut on the edge.   This system of bevels for the